P9-AGF-764

"TERRIFIC, EERILY IMPRESSIVE, OMINOUS . . . KING REALLY GETS TO YOU WITH HIS SNARLING, MURDEROUS MONSTER ON WHEELS."
—*The New York Times*

"KING'S BEST NOVEL YET! Leave it to Stephen King to craftily conjure a wholly satisfying novel . . . the most frightening and compelling in recent memory. . . . Like *Carrie*, it captures the kinetic energy and cultural wasteland of teenage milieu. . . . Like *The Shining*, it displays psychological tensions and supernatural phenomena that jolt characters and readers alike."—*Los Angeles News*

"WHAT'S BETTER THAN A GOOD SPOOKY SCARE? Stephen King is expert at this dark art. . . . The superbly macabre *Christine* is truly memorable . . . it will frighten millions."
—*St. Louis Post Dispatch*

"FOR HORROR FANS, A PRIZE IN THE KING TRADITION!"—*Library Journal*

(Please turn page for more rave reviews of Stephen King's latest, greatest triumph . . .)

"PLENTY OF GORE ... A STORY THAT RACES ALONG IN HIGH GEAR."
—*Newsweek*

"GREAT STUFF. ... Read Stephen King's new chiller, and you'll never trust a 1958 Plymouth Fury again. ... Stephen King scares the pants off us, but he does it with such style that we can't be mad at him."—*Southwest Magazine*

"Like the movie director Steven Spielberg, King is a master of infusing life into inanimate objects or non–human forms."
—*New York Times Book Review*

"A BRILLIANT CONJURING UP OF TERRORS ... the kind of story that could make you afraid to walk in front of your own car."
—*Milwaukee Journal*

"SCARY, SATISFYINGLY INTRICATE."
—*People*

"HORROR WITH IMMENSE APPEAL ... KING HAS NEVER BEEN MORE READABLE."—*Kirkus Reviews*

"A MUST READ FOR KING FANS!"
—*Newsday*

"DAZZLINGLY WELL-WRITTEN!"
—*Indianapolis Star*

"A RIVETING EXPLORATION OF POSSESSION, THE SUPERNATURAL, AND TERROR . . . King's horrific visions, the growing terror of this small town, dance ghoulishly in the shadows of blinking headlights. . . . Once again, King has created a world all too familiar with a nightmare."—*Associated Press*

"Hell hath no fury like a Fury scorned . . . readable and fast-paced, readers will love it."
—*Detroit News*

"Stephen King's mastery in conjuring up an aura of mystery and suspense will keep you glued to the pages."—*King Features Syndicate*

"NO-HOLDS-BARRED HORROR . . . ACHINGLY REAL!"—*Cleveland Plain Dealer*

"Stephen King, the master of modern horror, takes the reader for a fast ride of ghoulish fun."
—*Atlanta Constitution*

"TERRIFYING . . . KING IS A TERRIFIC STORYTELLER!"—*San Francisco Chronicle*

"KING'S FINEST NOVEL TO DATE in which poignantly drawn teenagers become seduced by both the facts of life and the macabre fantasies of death."—*Houston Chronicle*

SIGNET Titles by Stephen King You'll Want to Read

(0451)

10	☐	**CHRISTINE.**	(128370—$4.50)*
9	☐	**DIFFERENT SEASONS.**	(124340—$3.95)*
8	☐	**CUJO.**	(117298—$3.95)*
1	☐	**CARRIE.**	(119630—$2.95)
6	☐	**THE DEAD ZONE.**	(119614—$3.95)
7	☐	**FIRESTARTER.**	(099648—$3.95)
4	☐	**NIGHT SHIFT.**	(099311—$3.50)
2	☐	**SALEM'S LOT.**	(125452—$3.95)*
3	☐	**THE SHINING.**	(125444—$3.95)*
5	☐	**THE STAND.**	(127897—$4.50)*

*Price slightly higher in Canada

Buy them at your local bookstore or use this convenient coupon for ordering.

THE NEW AMERICAN LIBRARY, INC.,
P.O. Box 999, Bergenfield, New Jersey 07621

Please send me the books I have checked above. I am enclosing $_____
(please add $1.00 to this order to cover postage and handling). Send check
or money order—no cash or C.O.D.'s. Prices and numbers are subject to change
without notice.

Name_____

Address_____

City _____ State _____ Zip Code _____
Allow 4-6 weeks for delivery.
This offer is subject to withdrawal without notice.

CHRISTINE

STEPHEN KING

A SIGNET BOOK

NEW AMERICAN LIBRARY

PUBLISHER'S NOTE

This novel is a work of fiction. Names, characters, places, and incidents either are the product of the author's imagination or are used fictitiously, and any resemblance to actual persons, living or dead, events, or locales is entirely coincidental.

NAL BOOKS ARE AVAILABLE AT QUANTITY DISCOUNTS WHEN USED TO PROMOTE PRODUCTS OR SERVICES. FOR INFORMATION PLEASE WRITE TO PREMIUM MARKETING DIVISION, THE NEW AMERICAN LIBRARY, INC., 1633 BROADWAY, NEW YORK, NEW YORK 10019.

Copyright © 1983 by Stephen King

All rights reserved. For information address
The New American Library, Inc.

A hardcover edition of this book was published by
The Viking Press, 40 West 23rd Street,
New York, New York 10010.
The hardcover edition was published simultaneously in
Canada by Penguin Books Canada Limited.

A special limited first edition of 1000 numbered and signed copies
of this book has been published by Donald M. Grant, Publisher,
Rhode Island.

All of the song lyrics which appear in these pages are separately
copyrighted, and all rights in such lyrics are reserved to such copyright proprietors. If there are any questions about song titles,
copyright proprietors, and/or copyright dates, please submit such
questions in writing and The Viking Press will promptly forward
the same to the appropriate copyright proprietor for response.

SIGNET TRADEMARK REG. U.S. PAT. OFF. AND FOREIGN COUNTRIES
REGISTERED TRADEMARK—MARCA REGISTRADA
HECHO EN CHICAGO, U.S.A.

SIGNET, SIGNET CLASSIC, MENTOR, PLUME, MERIDIAN AND NAL
BOOKS are published by The New American Library, Inc.,
1633 Broadway, New York, New York 10019

First Signet Printing, December, 1983

3   4   5   6   7   8   9

PRINTED IN THE UNITED STATES OF AMERICA

PERMISSIONS

SOMETHIN' ELSE by Eddie Cochran. © 1959 by Unart Music Corporation. Used by permission. All rights reserved.

YAKETY-YAK by Jerry Leiber and Mike Stoller. © 1958 by Tiger Music, Inc. Copyright assigned to Chappell & Co., Inc., Quintet Music, Inc. and Bienstock Publishing Co. All rights controlled by Chappell & Co., Inc. (Intersong Music, Publisher).

HOT ROD LINCOLN by Charles Ryan and W. S. Stevenson. © copyright 1960 by Acuff-Rose Songs. Used by permission of the publisher. All rights reserved.

THIS CAR OF MINE by Brian Wilson and Mike Love. © 1964 Irving Music Co., Inc. (BMI). All rights reserved. International copyright secured. Used by permission.

SURF CITY by Jan Berry and Brian Wilson. Copyright © 1963 by Screen Gems-EMI Music Inc. Used by permission. All rights reserved.

PARTY TOWN by Glenn Frey and Jack Tempchin. © 1982 by Red Cloud Music and Night River Publishing. All rights reserved.

ROAD RUNNER by Ellas McDaniel. Copyright © 1960 by Arc Music Corporation. Used by permission.

NO PARTICULAR PLACE TO GO by Chuck Berry. © 1964, 1965 by Arc Music Corp. Used by permission.

MERCURY BLUES by K. C. Douglas. Copyright © 1970 by B-Flat Music Company and Tradition Music Company. All rights reserved. Used by permission.

CADILLAC WALK by Moon Martin. © 1977 Bug Music/Rockslam Music (BMI). Administered worldwide by Bug Music. All rights reserved. Used by permission.

DRIVE MY CAR by John Lennon and Paul McCartney. © 1965 Northern Songs Limited. All rights for the U.S.A., Mexico and the Philippines controlled by Maclen Music, Inc. c/o ATV Music Corp. Used by permission. All rights reserved.

CADILLAC RANCH by Bruce Springsteen. © 1980 Bruce Springsteen. Used by permission. All rights reserved.

ROADRUNNER by Jonathan Richman. © 1975 Modern Love Songs. Used by permission. All rights reserved.

MAYBELLINE by Chuck Berry, Russ Fratto, and Allan Freed. Arc Music Corp. Used by permission. All rights reserved.

LESS THAN ZERO by Elvis Costello. Copyright © 1977 by Visions Music Inc. Used by permission. All rights reserved.

DEACON BLUES words and music by Walter Becker and Donald Fagen. © copyright 1977 by Duchess Music Corporation, New York, N.Y. Rights administered by MCA Music, a division of MCA Inc. Used by permission. All rights reserved.

LITTLE DEUCE COUPE lyrics by Roger Christian, music by Brian Wilson. © 1963 Irving Music Co., Inc. (BMI). All rights reserved. International copyright secured. Used by permission.

MY MUSTANG FORD by Chuck Berry. © 1966 Isalee Music Corp. Used by permission. All rights reserved.

MERCEDES-BENZ by Janis Joplin. © Strong Arm Music. Used by permission.

SHUT DOWN by Brian Wilson and Roger Christian. © 1963 Irving Music Co., Inc. (BMI). All rights reserved. International copyright secured. Used by permission.

NO MONEY DOWN by Chuck Berry. © 1956 by Arc Music Corp. Used by permission.

SHE'S IN LOVE WITH MY CAR by Jude Cole and Moon Martin. © 1982 Collision Music/Rockslam Music (BMI). Administered worldwide by Bug Music. All rights reserved. Used by permission.

RIDING IN MY CAR by Woody Guthrie. TRO - © copyright 1954 and renewed 1982 by Folkways Music Publishers, Inc. Used by permission.

RACING IN THE STREETS by Bruce Springsteen. © 1978 by Bruce Springsteen. Used by permission. All rights reserved.

TRANSFUSION by Paul Barrett. © Paul Barrett Music Company. Used by permission.

BUICK '59 by Dootsie Williams. © by Dootsie Williams. Used by permission. All rights reserved.

THE MAGIC BUS by Peter Townshend. © 1967 and 1969 by Fabulous Music Ltd., London, England. Used by permission of Essex Music, Inc. New York. All rights reserved.

YOU CAN'T CATCH ME by Chuck Berry. © 1956 by Big Seven Music Corp. Used by permission of the copyright owner. All rights reserved.

WHO DO YOU LOVE? by Ellas McDaniel. © 1956-1963 by Arc Music Corp. Used by permission.

"409" by Gary Usher and Brian Wilson. © 1962 Irving Music Co., Inc. (BMI). All rights reserved. International copyright secured. Used by permission

RIDE ON, JOSEPHINE by Ellas McDaniel. © 1960 by Arc Music Corp. Used by permission. All rights reserved.

BRAND NEW CADILLAC by Vince Taylor. Copyright © 1959 Belinda (london) Ltd. Published in the U.S.A. by Unichappel Music Inc. International Copyright secured. Used by permission. All rights reserved.

MEXICAN BLACKBIRD by Billy Gibbons, Dusty Hill and Frank Beard. © 1975, 1977 Hamstein Music Company. Used by permission. All rights reserved.

I CAN'T SLEEP by P. Staines. © 1979 Carlin Music Corporation. Carbert Music Inc. Used by permission. All rights reserved.

RIDING IN THE MOONLIGHT by Chester Brunett and Jules Taub. © 1951 (renewed) by Arc Music Corp. Used by permission.

MY CUSTOM MACHINE, lyrics and music by Brian Wilson. © 1964 Irving Music Co., Inc. (BMI). All rights reserved. International copyright secured. Used by permission.

MARY LOU by Jessie Young and Sam Ling. © 1959 by Big Seven Music Corp. Used by permission of the copyright owner. All rights reserved.

RAMROD by Bruce Springsteen. © 1980 Bruce Springsteen. Used by permission. All rights reserved.

FROM A BUICK 6 by Bob Dylan. © 1965 Warner Bros. Inc. All rights reserved. Used by permission.

A YOUNG MAN IS GONE by Bobby Troup. © 1963 and 1975. Fred Raphael Music, Inc. International copyright secured. Used by permission. All rights reserved.

TEEN ANGEL by Jean Surrey. © copyright 1960 by Acuff-Rose Publishing Inc. Used by permission of the publisher. All rights reserved.

WRECK ON THE HIGHWAY. © 1980 Bruce Springsteen. Used by permission. All rights reserved.

RIDERS ON THE STORM by James Morrison, Robert Krieger, Ray Manzarek and John Densmore. © 1971 Door Music Co. Used by permission. All rights reserved.

DEAD MAN'S CURVE by Jan Berry, Roger Christian and Art Kornfeld. Copyright © 1963 by Screen Gems-EMI Music Inc. Used by permission. All rights reserved.

LAST KISS by Wayne Cochran. © 1964 Fort Knox Music Company. Used by permission. All rights reserved.

I KNOW A MAN by Robert Creeley. (A poem) © 1962 by Robert Creeley. Used by permission of Charles Scribner's Sons. All rights reserved.

AUTHOR'S NOTE

Lyrics quoted in this book are assigned to the singer (or singers, or group) most commonly associated with them. This may offend the purist, who feels that a song lyric belongs more to the writer than the singer. What you have done, the purist might argue, is akin to ascribing the works of Mark Twain to Hal Holbrook. I don't agree. In the world of popular song, it is as the Rolling Stones say: the singer, not the song. For those who want to know the names of the writers, they are here. And I thank them all—most particularly Chuck Berry, Bruce Springsteen, Brian Wilson . . . and Jan Berry, of Jan and Dean. He *did* come back from Deadman's Curve.

Getting the necessary legal permissions to use lyrics is hard work, and I'd like to thank some of the people who helped me remember the songs and then make sure it was okay to use them. They include: Dave Marsh, rock critic and rock historian; James Feury, a.k.a. "Mighty John Marshall," who rocks my little town on WACZ; his brother, Pat Feury, who throws oldies hops in Portland; Debbie Geller; Patricia Dunning; and Pete Batchelder. Thanks to all you guys, and may your old Coasters records never warp so bad you can't play 'em.

—S.K.

*This is for George Romero and
Chris Forrest Romero.*

And the Burg.

Contents

PART III: Christine—Teenage Death-Songs

CHRISTINE

Prologue

This is the story of a lover's triangle, I suppose you'd say
—Arnie Cunningham, Leigh Cabot, and, of course, Christine. But I want you to understand that Christine was there
first. She was Arnie's first love, and while I wouldn't presume
to say for sure (not from whatever heights of wisdom I've at-
tained in my twenty-two years, anyway), I think she was his
only true love. So I call what happened a tragedy.

Arnie and I grew up on the same block together, went to
Owen Andrews Grammar School and Darby Junior High together, then to Libertyville High together. I guess I was the
main reason Arnie didn't just get gobbled up in high school. I
was a big guy there—yeah, I know that doesn't mean don-
keyshit; five years after you've graduated you can't even
cadge a free beer on having been captain of the football and
baseball teams and an All-Conference swimmer—but because
I was, Arnie at least never got killed. He took a lot of abuse,
but he never got killed.

He was a loser, you know. Every high school has to have
at least two; it's like a national law. One male, one female.
Everyone's dumping ground. Having a bad day? Flunked a
big test? Had an argument with your folks and got grounded
for the weekend? No problem. Just find one of those poor
sad sacks that go scurrying around the halls like criminals before the home-room bell and walk it right to him. And sometimes they *do* get killed, in every important way except the
physical; sometimes they find something to hold onto and
they survive. Arnie had me. And then he had Christine.
Leigh came later.

I just wanted you to understand that.

Arnie was a natural out. He was out with the jocks because he was scrawny—five-ten and about a hundred and
forty pounds soaking wet in all his clothes plus a pair of
Desert Driver boots. He was out with the high school intellec-
tuals (a pretty "out" group themselves in a burg like Libertyville) because he had no specialty. Arnie was smart, but his

1

brains didn't go naturally to any one thing . . . unless it was automotive mechanics. He was great at that stuff. When it came to cars, the kid was some kind of a goofy born natural. But his parents, who both taught at the University in Horlicks, could not see their son, who had scored in the top five percent on his Stanford-Binet, taking the shop courses. He was lucky they let him take Auto Shop I, II, and III. He had to battle his butt off to get that. He was out with the druggies because he didn't do dope. He was out with the macho pegged-jeans-and-Lucky-Strikes group because he didn't do booze and if you hit him hard enough, he'd cry.

Oh yes, and he was out with the girls. His glandular machinery had gone totally bananas. I mean, Arnie was pimple city. He washed his face maybe five times a day, took maybe two dozen showers a week, and tried every cream and nostrum known to modern science. None of it did any good. Arnie's face looked like a loaded pizza, and he was going to have one of those pitted, poxy faces forever.

I liked him just the same. He had a quirky sense of humor and a mind that never stopped asking questions, playing games, and doing funky little calisthenics. It was Arnie who showed me how to make an ant farm when I was seven, and we spent just about one whole summer watching those little buggers, fascinated by their industry and their deadly seriousness. It was Arnie's suggestion when we were ten that we sneak out one night and put a load of dried horseapples from the Route 17 Stables under the gross plastic horse on the lawn of the Libertyville Motel just over the line in Monroeville. Arnie knew about chess first. He knew about poker first. He showed me how to maximize my Scrabble score. On rainy days, right up until the time I fell in love (well, sort of—she was a cheerleader with a fantastic body and I sure was in love with that, although when Arnie pointed out that her mind had all the depth and resonance of a Shaun Cassidy 45, I couldn't really tell him he was full of shit, because he wasn't), it was Arnie I thought of first, because Arnie knew how to maximize rainy days just like he knew how to maximize Scrabble scores. Maybe that's one of the ways you recognize really lonely people . . . they can always think of something neat to do on rainy days. You can always call them up. They're always home. Fucking *always*.

For my part, I taught him how to swim. I worked out with him and got him to eat his green vegetables so he could build up that scrawny bod a little. I got him a job on a road crew the year before our senior year at Libertyville High—and for that one we both battled our butts off with his parents, who saw themselves as great friends of the farm workers in California and the steel-workers in the Burg, but who were horrified at the idea of their gifted son (top five percent on his Stanford-Binet, remember) getting his wrists dirty and his neck red.

Then, near the end of that summer vacation, Arnie saw Christine for the first time and fell in love with her. I was with him that day—we were on our way home from work—and I would testify on the matter before the Throne of Almighty God if called upon to do so. Brother, he fell and he fell hard. It could have been funny if it hadn't been so sad, and if it hadn't gotten scary as quick as it did. It could have been funny if it hadn't been so bad.

How bad was it?

It was bad from the start. And it got worse in a hurry.

1
Dennis— Teenage Car— Songs

1 / First Views

Hey, looky there!
Across the street!
There's a car made just for me,
To own that car would be a luxury . . .
That car's fine-lookin, man,
That's somethin else.

—Eddie Cochran

"Oh my God!" my friend Arnie Cunningham cried out suddenly.

"What is it?" I asked. His eyes were bulging from behind his steel-rimmed glasses, he had plastered one hand over his face so that his palm was partially cupping his mouth, and his neck could have been on ball-bearings the way he was craning back over his shoulder.

"Stop the car, Dennis! Go back!"

"What are you—"

"Go back, I want to look at her again."

Suddenly I understood. "Oh, man, forget it," I said. "If you mean that . . . *thing* we just passed—"

"Go back!" He was almost screaming.

I went back, thinking that it was maybe one of Arnie's subtle little jokes. But it wasn't. He was gone, lock, stock, and barrel. Arnie had fallen in love.

She was a bad joke, and what Arnie saw in her that day I'll never know. The left side of her windshield was a snarled spiderweb of cracks. The right rear deck was bashed in, and an ugly nest of rust had grown in the paint-scraped valley. The back bumper was askew, the trunk-lid was ajar, and upholstery was bleeding out through several long tears in the seat covers, both front and back. It looked as if someone had worked on the upholstery with a knife. One tire was flat. The others were bald enough to show the canvas cording. Worst of all, there was a dark puddle of oil under the engine block.

Arnie had fallen in love with a 1958 Plymouth Fury, one of the long ones with the big fins. There was an old and sun-

7

faded FOR SALE sign propped on the right side of the wind-shield—the side that was not cracked.

"Look at her lines, Dennis!" Arnie whispered. He was run-ning around the car like a man possessed. His sweaty hair flew and flopped. He tried the back door on the passenger side, and it came open with a scream.

"Arnie, you're having me on, aren't you?" I said. "It's sun-stroke, right? Tell me it's sunstroke. I'll take you home and put you under the frigging air conditioner and we'll forget all about this, okay?" But I said it without much hope. He knew how to joke, but there was no joke on his face then. Instead, there was a kind of goofy madness I didn't like much.

He didn't even bother to reply. A hot, stuffy billow of air, redolent of age, oil, and advanced decomposition, puffed out of the open door. Arnie didn't seem to notice that, either. He got in and sat down on the ripped and faded back seat. Once, twenty years before, it had been red. Now it was a faded wash pink.

I reached in and pulled up a little puff of upholstery, looked at it, and blew it away. "Looks like the Russian army marched over it on their way to Berlin," I said.

He finally noticed I was still there. "Yeah . . . yeah. But she could be fixed up. She could . . . she could be tough. A moving unit, Dennis. A beauty. A real—"

"Here! Here! What you two kids up to?"

It was an old guy who looked as if he was enjoying—more or less—his seventieth summer. Probably less. This particular dude struck me as the sort of man who enjoyed very little. His hair was long and scraggy, what little there was left of it. He had a good case of psoriasis going on the bald part of his skull.

He was wearing green old man's pants and low-topped Keds. No shirt; instead there was something cinched around his waist that looked like a lady's corset. When he got closer I saw it was a back brace. From the look of it I would say, just offhand, that he had changed it last somewhere around the time Lyndon Johnson died.

"What you kids up to?" His voice was shrill and strident.

"Sir, is this your car?" Arnie asked him. Not much ques-tion that it was. The Plymouth was parked on the lawn of the postwar tract house from which the old man had issued. The lawn was horrible, but it looked positively great with that Plymouth in the foreground for perspective.

"What if it is?" The old guy demanded.

"I"—Arnie had to swallow—"I want to buy it."

The old dude's eyes gleamed. The angry look on his face was replaced by a furtive gleam in the eye and a certain hungry sneer around the lips. Then a large resplendent shit-eating grin appeared. That was the moment, I think—then, just at that moment—when I felt something cold and blue inside me. There was a moment—just then—when I felt like slugging Arnie and dragging him away. Something came into the old man's eyes. Not just the gleam; it was something *behind* the gleam.

"Well, you should have said so," the old guy told Arnie. He stuck out his hand and Arnie took it. "LeBay's the name. Roland D. LeBay. U.S. Army, retired."

"Arnie Cunningham."

The old sport pumped his hand and sort of waved at me. I was out of the play; he had his sucker. Arnie might as well have handed LeBay his wallet.

"How much?" Arnie asked. And then he plunged ahead. "Whatever you want for her, it's not enough."

I groaned inside instead of sighing. His checkbook had just joined his wallet.

For a moment LeBay's grin faltered a little, and his eyes narrowed down suspiciously. I think he was evaluating the possibility that he was being put on. He studied Arnie's open, longing face for signs of guile, and then asked the murderously perfect question:

"Son, have you ever owned a car before?"

"He owns a Mustang Mach II," I said quickly. "His folks bought it for him. It's got a Hurst shifter, a supercharger, and it can boil the road in first gear. It—"

"No," Arnie said quietly. "I just got my driver's license this spring."

LeBay tipped me a brief but crafty gaze and then swung his full attention back to his prime target. He put both hands in the small of his back and stretched. I caught a sour whiff of sweat.

"Got a back problem in the Army," he said. "Full disability. Doctors could never put it right. Anyone ever asks you what's wrong with the world, boys, you tell em it's three things: Doctors, commies, and nigger radicals. Of the three, commies is the worst, closely followed by doctors. And if they want to know who told you, tell em Roland D. LeBay. Yessir."

He touched the old, scuffed hood of the Plymouth with a kind of bemused love.

"This here is the best car I ever owned. Bought her in September 1957. Back then, that's when you got your new model year, in September. All summer long they'd show you pictures of cars under hoods and cars under tarps until you were fair dyin t'know what they looked like underneath. Not like now." His voice dripped contempt for the debased times he had lived to see. "Brand-new, she was. Had the smell of a brand-new car, and that's about the finest smell in the world."

He considered.

"Except maybe for pussy."

I looked at Arnie, nibbling the insides of my cheeks madly to keep from braying laughter all over everything. Arnie looked back at me, astounded. The old man appeared to notice neither of us; he was off on his own planet.

"I was in khaki for thirty-four years," LeBay told us, still touching the hood of the car. "Went in at sixteen in 1923. I et dust in Texas and seen crabs as big as lobsters in some o them Nogales whoredens. I saw men with their guts comin out their ears during Big Two. In France I saw that. Their guts was comin out their *ears*. You believe that, son?"

"Yessir," Arnie said. I don't think he'd heard a word LeBay said. He was shifting from foot to foot as if he had to go to the bathroom bad. "About the car, though—"

"You go to the University?" LeBay barked suddenly. "Up there at Horlicks?"

"Nosir, I go to Libertyville High."

"Good," LeBay said grimly. "Steer clear of colleges. They're full of niggerlovers that want to give away the Panama Canal. 'Think-tanks,' they call em. 'Asshole-tanks,' say I."

He gazed fondly at the car sitting on its flat tire, its paintjob mellowing rustily in the late afternoon sunlight.

"Hurt my back in the spring of '57," he said. "Army was going to rack and ruin even then. I got out just in time. I came on back to Libertyville. Looked over the rolling iron. I took my time. Then I walked into Norman Cobb's Plymouth dealership—where the bowling alley is now on outer Main Street—and I ordered this here car. I said you get it in red and white, next year's model. Red as a fire-engine on the inside. And they did it. When I got her, she had a total of six miles on the odometer. Yessir."

He spat.

I glanced over Arnie's shoulder at the odometer. The glass was cloudy, but I could read the damage all the same: 97,-432. And six-tenths. Jesus wept.

"If you love the car so much, why are you selling it?" I asked.

He turned a milky, rather frightening gaze on me. "Are you cracking wise on me, son?"

I didn't answer, but I didn't drop my gaze either.

After a few moments of eye-to-eye duelling (which Arnie totally ignored; he was running a slow and loving hand over one of the back fins), he said, "Can't drive anymore. Back's gotten too bad. Eyes are going the same way."

Suddenly I got it—or thought I did. If he had given us the correct dates, he was seventy-one. And at seventy, this state makes you start taking compulsory eye exams every year before they'll renew your driver's license. LeBay had either failed his eye exam or was afraid of failing. Either way, it came to the same thing. Rather than submit to that indignity, he had put the Plymouth up. And after that, the car had gotten old fast.

"How much do you want for it?" Arnie asked again. Oh, he just couldn't wait to be slaughtered.

LeBay turned his face up to the sky, appearing to consider it for rain. Then he looked down at Arnie again and gave him a large, kindly smile that was far too much like the previous shit-eating grin for me.

"I've been asking three hundred," he said. "But you seem a likely enough lad. I'll make it two-fifty for you."

"Oh my *Christ*," I said.

But he knew who his sucker was, and he knew exactly how to drive the wedge in between us. In the words of my grandfather, he hadn't fallen off a haytruck yesterday.

"Okay," he said brusquely. "If that's how you want it. I got my four-thirty story to watch. *Edge of Night*. Never miss it if I can help it. Nice chinning with you boys. So long."

Arnie threw me such a smoking look of pain and anger that I backed off a step. He went after the old man and took his elbow. They talked. I couldn't hear it all, but I could see more than enough. The old man's pride was wounded. Arnie was earnest and apologetic. The old man just hoped Arnie understood that he couldn't stand to see the car that had brought him through safe to his golden years insulted. Arnie agreed. Little by little, the old man allowed himself to be led back. And again I felt something consciously dreadful about him . . . it was as if a cold November wind could think. I can't put it any better than that.

"If he says one more word, I wash my hands of the whole thing," LeBay said, and cocked a horny, callused thumb at me.

"He won't, he won't," Arnie said hastily. "Three hundred, did you say?"

"Yes, I believe that was—"

"Two-fifty was the quoted price," I said loudly.

Arnie looked stricken, afraid the old man would walk away again, but LeBay was taking no chances. The fish was almost out of the pond now.

"Two-fifty would do it, I guess," LeBay allowed. He glanced my way again, and I saw that we had an understanding—he didn't like me and I didn't like him.

To my ever-increasing horror, Arnie pulled his wallet out and began thumbing through it. There was silence among the three of us. LeBay looked on. I looked away at a little kid who was trying to kill himself on a puke-green skateboard. Somewhere a dog barked. Two girls who looked like eighth- or ninth-graders went past, giggling and holding clutches of library books to their blooming chests. I had only one hope left for getting Arnie out of this; it was the day before pay-day. Given time, even twenty-four hours, this wild fever might pass. Arnie was beginning to remind me of Toad, of Toad Hall.

When I looked back, Arnie and LeBay were looking at two fives and six ones—all that had been in his wallet, apparently.

"How about a check?" Arnie asked.

LeBay offered Arnie a dry smile and said nothing.

"It's a good check," Arnie protested. It would be, too. We had been working all summer for Carson Brothers on the I-376 extension, the one which natives of the Pittsburgh area firmly believe will never be really finished. Arnie sometimes declared that Penn-DOT had begun taking bids on the I-376 work shortly after the Civil War ended. Not that either of us had any right to complain; a lot of kids were either working for slave wages that summer or not working at all. We were making good money, even clocking some overtime. Brad Jeffries, the job foreman, had been frankly dubious about taking a kid like Arnie on, but had finally allowed that he could use a flagman; the girl he had been planning to hire had gotten herself pregnant and had run off to get married. So Arnie had started off flagging in June but had gotten into the harder

work little by little, running mostly on guts and determination. It was the first real job he'd ever had, and he didn't
want to screw it up. Brad was reasonably impressed, and the
summer sun had even helped Arnie's erupting complexion a
little. Maybe it was the ultraviolet.

"I'm sure it's a good check, son," Lebay said, "but I gotta
make a cash deal. You understand."

I didn't know if Arnie understood, but I did. It would be
too easy to stop payment on a local check if this rustbucket
Plymouth threw a rod or blew a piston on the way home.

"You can call the bank," Arnie said, starting to sound desperate.

"Nope," LeBay said, scratching his armpit above the sca-
brous brace. "It's going on five-thirty. Bank's long since
closed."

"A deposit, then," Arnie said, and held out the sixteen dollars. He looked positively wild. It may be that you're having
trouble believing a kid who was almost old enough to vote
could have gotten himself so worked up over an anonymous
old clunk in the space of fifteen minutes. I was having some
trouble believing it myself. Only Roland D. LeBay seemed
not to be having trouble with it, and I supposed it was because at his age he had seen everything. It was only later that
I came to believe that his odd sureness might come from
other sources. Either way, if any milk of human kindness had
ever run in his veins, it had curdled to sour cream long ago.

"I'd have to have at least ten percent down," LeBay said.
The fish was out of the water; in a moment it would be
netted. "If I had ten percent, I'd hold her for twenty-four
hours."

"Dennis," Arnie said. "Can you loan me nine bucks until
tomorrow?"

I had twelve in my own wallet, and no particular place to
go. Day after day of spreading sand and digging trenches for
culverts had done wonders when it came to getting ready for
football practice, but I had no social life at all. Lately I
hadn't even been assaulting the ramparts of my cheerleader
girlfriend's body in the style to which she had become accustomed. I was rich but lonely.

"Come on over here and let's see," I said.

LeBay's brow darkened, but he could see he was stuck with
my input, like it or not. His frizzy white hair blew back and
forth in the mild breeze. He kept one hand possessively on
the Plymouth's hood.

Arnie and I walked back toward where my car, a '75 Duster, was parked at the curb. I put an arm around Arnie's shoulders. For some reason I remembered the two of us up in his room on a rainy fall day when we were both no more than six years old—cartoons flickering on an ancient black-and-white TV as we colored with old Crayolas from a dented coffee can. The image made me feel sad and a little scared. I have days, you know, when it seems to me that six is an optimum age, and that's why it only lasts about 7.2 seconds in real time.

"Have you got it, Dennis? I'll get it back to you tomorrow afternoon."

"Yeah, I've got it," I said. "But what in God's name are you doing, Arnie? That old fart has got total disability, for Christ's sake. He doesn't need the money and you're not a charitable institution."

"I don't get it. What are you talking about?"

"He's screwing you. He's screwing you for the simple pleasure of it. If he took that car to Darnell's, he couldn't get fifty dollars for parts. It's a piece of shit."

"No. No, it isn't." Without the bad complexion, my friend Arnie would have looked completely ordinary. But God gives everyone at least one good feature, I think, and with Arnie it was his eyes. Behind the glasses that usually obscured them they were a fine and intelligent gray, the color of clouds on an overcast autumn day. They could be almost uncomfortably sharp and probing when something was going on that he was interested in, but now they were distant and dreaming. "It's not a piece of shit at all."

That was when I really began to understand it was more than just Arnie suddenly deciding he wanted a car. He had never even expressed an interest in owning one before; he was content to ride with me and chip in for gas or to pedal his three-speed. And it wasn't as if he needed a car so he could step out; to the best of my knowledge Arnie had never had a date in his life. This was something different. It was love, or something like it.

I said, "At least get him to start it for you, Arnie. And get the hood up. There's a puddle of oil underneath. I think the block might be cracked. I really think—"

"Can you loan me the nine?" His eyes were fixed on mine.

I gave up. I took out my wallet and gave him the nine dollars.

"Thanks, Dennis," he said.

"Your funeral, man."

He took no notice. He put my nine with his sixteen and went back to where LeBay stood by the car. He handed the money over and LeBay counted it carefully, wetting his thumb.

"I'll only hold it for twenty-four hours, you understand," LeBay said.

"Yessir, that'll be fine," Arnie said.

"I'll just go in the house and write you out a receipt," he said. "What did you say your name was, soldier?"

Arnie smiled a little. "Cunningham. Arnold Cunningham."

LeBay grunted and walked across his unhealthy lawn to his back door. The outer door was one of those funky aluminum combination doors with a scrolled letter in the center—a big L in this case.

The door slammed behind him.

"The guy's weird, Arnie. The guy is really fucking w—"

But Arnie wasn't there. He was sitting behind the wheel of the car. That same sappy expression was on his face.

I went around to the front and found the hood release. I pulled it, and the hood went up with a rusty scream that made me think of the sound effects you hear on some of those haunted-house records. Flecks of metal sifted down. The battery was an old Allstate, and the terminals were so glooped up with green corrosion that you couldn't tell which was positive and which was negative. I pulled the air cleaner and looked glumly into a four-barrel carb as black as a mineshaft.

I lowered the hood and went back to where Arnie was sitting, running his hand along the edge of the dashboard over the speedometer, which was calibrated up to an utterly absurd 120 miles per hour. Had cars ever really gone that fast?

"Arnie, I think the engine block's cracked. I really do. This car is lunch, my friend. It's just total lunch. If you want wheels, we can find you something a lot better than this for two-fifty. I mean it. A *lot* better."

"It's twenty years old," he said. "Do you realize a car is officially an antique when it's twenty years old?"

"Yeah," I said. "The junkyard behind Darnell's is full of official antiques, you know what I mean?"

"Dennis—"

The door banged. LeBay was coming back. It was just as well; further discussion would have been meaningless. I may not be the world's most sensitive human being, but when the signals are strong enough, I can pick them up. This was something Arnie felt he had to have, and I wasn't going to talk him out it. I didn't think anyone was going to talk him out of it.

LeBay handed him the receipt with a flourish. Written on a plain sheet of notepaper in an old man's spidery and slightly trembling script was: *Received from Arnold Cunningham, $25.00 as a 24-hr. deposit on 1958 Plymouth, Christine.* And below that he had signed his name.

"What's this Christine?" I asked, thinking I might have misread it or he might have misspelled it.

His lips tightened and his shoulders went up a little, as if he expected to be laughed at . . . or as if he were daring me to laugh at him. "Christine," he said, "is what I always called her."

"Christine," Arnie said. "I like it. Don't you, Dennis?"

Now he was talking about naming the damned thing. It was all getting to be a bit much.

"What do you think, Dennis, do you like it?"

"No," I said. "If you've got to name it, Arnie, why don't you name it Trouble?"

He looked hurt at that, but I was beyond caring. I went back to my car to wait for him, wishing I had taken a different route home.

2 / The First Argument

Just tell your hoodlum friends outside,
You ain't got time to take a ride!
(Yakety-yak!)
Don't talk back!

> —The Coasters

I drove Arnie to his house and went in with him to have a piece of cake and a glass of milk before going home. It was a decision I repented very quickly.

Arnie lived on Laurel Street, which is in a quiet residential neighborhood on the west side of Libertyville. As far as that goes, most of Libertyville is quiet and residential. It isn't ritzy, like the neighboring suburb of Fox Chapel (where most of the homes are estates like the ones you used to see every week on *Columbo*), but it isn't like Monroeville, either, with its miles of malls, discount tire warehouses, and dirty book emporiums. There isn't any heavy industry; it's mostly a bed-room community for the nearby University. Not ritzy, but sort of *brainy*, at least.

Arnie had been quiet and contemplative all the way home; I tried to draw him out, but he wouldn't be drawn. I asked him what he was going to do with the car. "Fix it up," he said absently, and lapsed back into silence.

Well, he had the ability; I wasn't questioning that. He was good with tools, he could listen, he could isolate. His hands were sensitive and quick with machinery; it was only when he was around other people, particularly girls, that they got clumsy and restless, wanting to crack knuckles or jam them-selves in his pockets, or, worst of all, wander up to his face and run over the scorched-earth landscape of his cheeks and chin and forehead, drawing attention to it.

He could fix the car up, but the money he had earned that summer was earmarked for college. He had never owned a car before, and I didn't think he had any idea of the sinister way that old cars can suck money. They suck it the way a vampire is supposed to suck blood. He could avoid labor costs in most cases by doing the work himself, but the parts alone would half-buck him to death before he was through.

I said some of these things to him, but they just rolled off. His eyes were still distant, dreaming. I could not have told you what he was thinking.

Both Michael and Regina Cunningham were at home—she was working one of an endless series of goofy jigsaw puzzles (this one was about six thousand different cogs and gears on a plain white background; it would have driven me out of my skull in about fifteen minutes), and he was playing his re-corder in the living room.

It didn't take long for me to start wishing I had skipped the cake and milk. Arnie told them what he had done, showed them the receipt, and they both promptly went through the roof.

You have to understand that Michael and Regina were University people to the core. They were into doing good, and to them that meant being into protest. They had protest-ed in favor of integration in the early 60s, had moved on to Viet Nam, and when that gave out there was Nixon, questions of racial balance in the schools (they could quote you chapter and verse on the Alan Bakke case until you fell asleep), police brutality, and parental brutality. Then there was the talk—all the talk. They were almost as much into talking as they were into protesting. They were ready to take part in an all-night bull-session on the space program or a teach-in on the ERA or a seminar on possible alternatives to fossil fuels at the drop of an opinion. They had done time on God alone knew how many "hotlines"—rape hotlines, drug hotlines, hotlines where runaway kids could talk to a friend, and good old DIAL HELP, where people thinking about suicide could call up and listen to a sympathetic voice say don't do it, buddy, you have a social commitment to Spaceship Earth. Twenty or thirty years of University teaching and you're prepared to run your gums the way Pavlov's dogs were prepared to salivate when the bell rang. I guess you can even get to like it.

Regina (they insisted I call them by their first names) was forty-five and handsome in a rather cold, semi-aristocratic way—that is, she managed to look aristocratic even when she was wearing bluejeans, which was most of the time. Her field was English, but of course when you teach at the college level, that's never enough; it's like saying "America" when someone asks you where you're from. She had it refined and calibrated like a blip on a radar screen. She specialized in the earlier English poets and had done her thesis on Robert Herrick.

Michael was in the history biz. He looked as mournful and melancholy as the music he played on his recorder, although mournful and melancholy were not ordinarily a part of his makeup. Sometimes he made me think of what Ringo Starr was supposed to have said when the Beatles first came to America and some reporter at a press conference asked him if he was really as sad as he looked. "No," Ringo replied, "it's just me face." Michael was like that. Also, his thin face and the thick glasses he wore combined to make him look a little like a caricature professor in an unfriendly editorial cartoon. His hair was receding and he wore a small, fuzzy goatee.

"Hi, Arnie," Regina said as we came in. "Hello, Dennis." It was just about the last cheerful thing she said to either of us that afternoon.

We said hi and got our cake and milk. We sat in the breakfast nook. Dinner was cooking in the oven, and I'm sorry to say so, but the aroma was fairly rank. Regina and Michael had been flirting with vegetarianism for some time, and tonight it smelled as if Regina had a good old kelp quiche or something on the way. I hoped they wouldn't invite me to stay.

The recorder music stopped, and Michael wandered out into the kitchen. He was wearing bluejean cutoffs and looking as if his best friend had just died.

"You're late, boys," he said. "Anything going down?" He opened the refrigerator and began to root around in it. Maybe the kelp quiche didn't smell so wonderful to him either.

"I bought a car," Arnie said, cutting himself another piece of cake.

"You did what?" his mother cried at once from the other room. She got up too quickly and there was a thud as her thighs connected solidly with the edge of the cardtable she did her jigsaws on. The thud was followed by the rapid patter of pieces falling to the floor. That was when I started to wish I had just gone home.

Michael Cunningham had turned from the refrigerator to stare at his son, holding a Granny Smith apple in one hand and a carton of plain yogurt in the other.

"You're kidding," he said, and for some absurd reason I noticed for the first time that his goatee—which he had worn since 1970 or so—was showing quite a bit of gray. "Arnie, you're kidding, right? Say you're kidding."

Regina came in, looking tall and semi-aristocratic and pretty damn mad. She took one close look at Arnie's face and *knew* he wasn't kidding. "You can't buy a car," she said. "What in the world are you talking about? You're only seventeen years old."

Arnie looked slowly from his father by the fridge to his mother in the doorway leading to the living room. There was a stubborn, hard expression on his face that I couldn't remember ever having seen there before. If he looked that way more often around school, I thought, the machine-shop kids wouldn't be so apt to push him around.

"Actually, you're wrong," he said. "I can buy it with no trouble at all. I couldn't finance it, but buying it for cash presents no problems. Of course, *registering* a car at seventeen is something else entirely. For that I need your permission."

They were looking at him with surprise, uneasiness, and—I

saw this last and felt a sinking sensation in my belly—rising anger. For all their liberal thinking and their commitment to the farm workers and abused wives and unwed mothers and all the rest, they pretty much managed Arnie. And Arnie let himself be managed.

"I don't think there's any call to talk to your mother that way," Michael said. He put back the yogurt, held onto the Granny Smith, and slowly closed the fridge door. "You're too young to have a car."

"Dennis has one," Arnie said promptly.

"Say! Wow! Look how late it's getting!" I said. "I ought to be getting home! I ought to be getting home right away! I—"

"What Dennis's parents choose to do and what your own choose to do are different things," Regina Cunningham said. I had never heard her voice so cold. Never. "And you had no right to do such a thing without consulting your father and me about—"

"*Consult* you!" Arnie roared suddenly. He spilled his milk. There were big veins standing out on his neck in cords.

Regina took a step backward, her jaw dropping. I would be willing to bet she had never been roared at by her ugly-duckling son in her entire life. Michael looked just as flabbergasted. They were getting a taste of what I had already felt—for inexplicable reasons of his own, Arnie had finally happened on something he really wanted. And God help anyone who got in his way.

"*Consult* you! I've consulted you on every damn thing I've ever done! Everything was a committee meeting, and if it was something I didn't want to do, I got outvoted two to one! But this is no goddam committee meeting. I bought a car and that's . . . *it!*"

"It most certainly is not *it,*" Regina said. Her lips had thinned down, and oddly (or perhaps not) she had stopped looking just semi-aristocratic; now she looked like the Queen of England or someplace, jeans and all. Michael was out of it for the time being. He looked every bit as bewildered and unhappy as I felt, and I knew an instant of sharp pity for the man. He couldn't even go home to dinner to get away from it; he *was* home. Here was a raw power-struggle between the old guard and the young guard, and it was going to be decided the way those things almost always are, with a monstrous overkill of bitterness and acrimony. Regina was apparently ready for that even if Michael wasn't. But I wanted no part of it. I got up and headed for the door.

"You let him do this?" Regina asked. She looked at me haughtily, as if we'd never laughed together or baked pies together or gone on family camp-outs together. "Dennis, I'm surprised at you."

That stung me. I had always liked Arnie's mom well enough, but I had never completely trusted her, at least not since something that had happened when I was eight years old or so.

Arnie and I had ridden our bikes downtown to take in a Saturday afternoon movie. On the way back, Arnie had fallen off his bike while swerving to avoid a dog and had jobbed his leg pretty good. I rode him home double on my bike, and Regina took him to the emergency room, where a doctor put in half a dozen stitches. And then, for some reason, after it was all over and it was clear that Arnie was going to be perfectly fine, Regina turned on me and gave me the rough side of her tongue. She read me out like a top sergeant. When she finished, I was shaking all over and nearly crying—what the hell, I was only eight, and there had been a lot of blood. I can't remember chapter and verse of that bawling-out, but the overall feeling it left me with was disturbing. As best I remember, she started out by accusing me of not watching him closely enough—as if Arnie were much younger instead of almost exactly my own age—and ended up saying (or seeming to say) that it should have been me.

This sounded like the same thing all over again—*Dennis, you weren't watching him closely enough*—and I got angry myself. My wariness of Regina was probably only part of it, and to be completely honest, probably only the small part. When you're a kid (and after all, what is seventeen but the outermost limit of kidhood?), you tend to be on the side of other kids. You know with a strong and unerring instinct that if you don't bulldoze down a few fences and knock some gates flat, your folks—out of the best of intentions—would be happy to keep you in the kid corral forever.

I got angry, but I held onto it as well as I could.

"I didn't *let* him do anything," I said. "He wanted it, he bought it." Earlier I might have told them that he had done no more than lay down a deposit, but I wasn't going to do that now. Now I had my back up. "I tried to talk him out of it, in fact."

"I doubt if you tried very hard," Regina shot back. She might as well have come out and said *Don't bullshit me, Dennis, I know you were in it together*. There was a flush on her high cheekbones, and her eyes were throwing off sparks. She was trying to make me feel eight again, and not doing too bad a job. But I fought it.

"You know, if you got all the facts, you'd see this isn't much to get hot under the collar about. He bought it for two hundred and fifty dollars, and—"

"Two hundred and fifty dollars!" Michael broke in. "What kind of car can you get for two hundred and fifty dollars?" His previous uncomfortable disassociation—if that's what it had been, and not just simple shock at the sound of his quiet son's voice raised in protest—was gone. It was the price of the car that had gotten to him. And he looked at his son with an open contempt that sickened me a little. I'd like to have kids myself someday, and if I do, I hope I can leave that particular expression out of my repertoire.

I kept telling myself to just stay cool, that it wasn't my affair or my fight, nothing to get hot under the collar about . . . but the cake I had eaten was sitting in the center of my stomach in a large sticky glob and my skin felt too hot. The Cunninghams had been my second family since I was a little kid, and I could feel all the distressing physical symptoms of a family quarrel inside myself.

"You can learn a lot about cars when you're fixing up an old one," I said. I suddenly sounded like a loony imitation of LeBay to myself. "And it'll take a lot of work before it's even street-legal." (If it ever is, I thought.) "You could look at it as a . . . a hobby . . ."

"I look upon it as madness," Regina said.

Suddenly I just wanted to get out. I suppose that if the emotional vibrations in the room hadn't been getting so heavy, I might have found it funny. I had somehow gotten into the position of defending Arnie's car when I thought the whole thing was preposterous to begin with.

"Whatever you say," I muttered. "Just leave me out of it. I'm going home."

"Good," Regina snapped.

"That's it," Arnie said tonelessly. He stood up. "I'm getting the fuck out of here."

Regina gasped, and Michael blinked as if he had been slapped.

"*What* did you say?" Regina managed. "What did you—"

"I don't get what you're so upset about," Arnie told them in an eerie, controlled voice, "but I'm not going to stick around and listen to a lot of craziness from either of you.

"You wanted me in the college courses, I'm there." He looked at his mother. "You wanted me in the chess club instead of the school band; okay, I'm there too. I've managed to get through seventeen years without embarrassing you in front of the bridge club or landing in jail."

They were staring at him, wide-eyed, as if one of the kitchen walls had suddenly grown lips and started to talk.

Arnie looked at them, his eyes odd and white and dangerous. "I'm telling you, I'm going to have this. This one thing."

"Arnie, the insurance—" Michael began.

"Stop it!" Regina shouted. She didn't want to start talking about the specific problems because that was the first step on the road to possible acceptance; she simply wanted to crush the rebellion under her heel, quickly and completely. There are moments when adults disgust you in ways they would never understand; I believe that, you know. I had one of those moments then, and it only made me feel worse. When Regina shouted at her husband, I saw her as both vulgar and scared, and because I loved her, I had never wanted to see her either way.

Still I remained in the doorway, wanting to leave but unhealthily fascinated by what was going on—the first full-scale argument in the Cunningham family that I had ever seen, maybe the first ever. And it surely was a wowser, at least ten on the Richter scale.

"Dennis, you'd better leave while we thrash this out," Regina said grimly.

"Yes," I said. "But don't you see, you're making a mountain out of a molehill. This car—Regina . . . Michael—if you could see it . . . it probably goes from zero to thirty in twenty minutes, if it moves at all—"

"Dennis! *Go!*"

I went.

As I was getting into my Duster, Arnie came out the back door, apparently meaning to make good on his threat to leave. His folks came after him, now looking worried as well as pissed off. I could understand a little bit how they felt. It had been as sudden as a cyclone touching down from a clear blue sky.

I keyed the engine and backed out into the quiet street. A lot had surely happened since the two of us had punched out at four o'clock, two hours ago. Then I had been hungry enough to eat almost anything (kelp quiche excepted). Now my stomach was so roiled I felt as if I would barf up anything I swallowed.

When I left, the three of them were standing in the driveway in front of their two-car garage (Michael's Porsche and Regina's Volvo wagon were snuggled up inside—*they got their cars,* I remember thinking, a little meanly; *what do they care*), still arguing.

That's it, I thought, now feeling a little sad as well as upset. *They'll beat him down and LeBay will have his twentyfive dollars and that '58 Plymouth will sit there for another thousand years or so.* They had done similar things to him before. Because he was a loser. Even his parents knew it. He was intelligent, and when you got past the shy and wary exterior, he was humorous and thoughtful and . . . sweet, I guess, is the word I'm fumbling around for.

Sweet, but a loser.

His folks knew it as well as the machine-shop white-soxers who yelled at him in the halls and thumb-rubbed his glasses.

They knew he was a loser and they would beat him down.

That's what I thought. But that time I was wrong.

3 / The Morning After

My poppa said "Son,
You're gonna drive me to drink
If you don't quit drivin that
Hot-rod Lincoln."

— Charlie Ryan

I cruised by Arnie's house the next morning at 6:30 A.M. and just parked at the curb, not wanting to go in even though his mother and father would still be in bed—there had been too many bad vibes flying around in that kitchen the evening before for me to feel comfortable about the usual doughnut and coffee before work.

Arnie didn't come out for almost five minutes, and I started to wonder if maybe he hadn't made good on his threat to just take off. Then the back door opened and he came down the driveway, his lunch bucket banging against one leg.

He got in, slammed the door, and said, "Drive on, Jeeves." This was one of Arnie's standard witticisms when he was in a good humor.

I drove on, looked at him cautiously, almost decided to say something, and then decided I better wait for him to start . . . if he had anything to say at all.

For a long time it seemed that he didn't. We drove most of the way to work with no conversation between us at all, nothing but the sound of WMDY, the local rock-and-soul station. Arnie beat time absently against his leg.

At last he said, "I'm sorry you had to be in on that last night, man."

"That's okay, Arnie."

"Has it ever occurred to you," he said abruptly, "that parents are nothing but overgrown kids until their children drag them into adulthood? Usually kicking and screaming?"

I shook my head.

"Tell you what I think," he said. We were coming up on the construction site now; the Carson Brothers trailer was only two rises over. The traffic this early was light and somnolent. The sky was a sweet peach color. "I think that part of being a parent is trying to kill your kids."

"That sounds very rational," I said. "Mine are always trying to kill me. Last night it was my mother sneaking in with a pillow and putting it over my face. Night before it was Dad chasing my sister and me around with a screwdriver." I was kidding, but I wondered what Michael and Regina might think if they could hear this rap.

"I know it sounds a little crazy at first," Arnie said, unperturbed, "but there are lots of things that sound nuts until you really consider them. Penis envy. Oedipal conflicts. The Shroud of Turin."

"Sounds like horseshit to me," I said. "You had a fight with your folks, that's all."

"I really believe it, though," Arnie said pensively. "Not that they know what they're doing; I don't believe that at all. And do you know why?"

"Do tell," I said.

"Because as soon as you have a kid, you know for sure that you're going to die. When you have a kid, you see your own gravestone."

"You know what, Arnie?"

"What?"

"I think that's fucking gruesome," I said, and we both burst out laughing.

"I don't mean it that way," he said.

We pulled into the parking lot and I turned off the engine. We sat there for a moment or two.

"I told them I'd opt out of the college courses," he said. "Told them I'd sign up for V.T. right across the board."

V.T. was vocational training. The same sort of thing the reform-school boys get, except of course they don't go home at night. They have what you might call a compulsory live-in program.

"Arnie," I began, unsure of just how to go on. The way this thing had blown up out of nothing still freaked me out. "Arnie, you're still a minor. They have to sign your program—"

"Sure, of course," Arnie said. He smiled at me humorlessly, and in that cold dawn light he looked at once older and much, much younger . . . like a cynical baby, somehow. "They have the power to cancel my entire program for another year, if they want to, and substitute their own. They could sign me up for Home Ec and World of Fashion, if they wanted to. The law says they can do it. But no law says they can make me pass what they pick."

That brought it home to me—the distance he had gone, I mean. How could that old clunker of a car have come to mean so much to him so damned *fast?* In the following days that question kept coming at me in different ways, the way I've always imagined a fresh grief would. When Arnie told Michael and Regina he meant to have it, he sure hadn't been kidding. He had gone right to that place where their expectations for him lived the most strongly, and he had done it with a ruthless expediency that surprised me. I'm not sure that lesser tactics would have worked against Regina, but that Arnie had actually been able to do it surprised me. In fact, it surprised the shit out of me. What it boiled down to was if Arnie spent his senior year in V.T., college went out the window. And to Michael and Regina, that was an impossibility.

"So they just . . . gave up?" It was close to punch-in time, but I couldn't let this go until I knew everything.

"Not just like that, no. I told them I'd find garage space for it and that I wouldn't try to have it inspected or registered until I had their approval."

"Do you think you're going to get that?"

He flashed me a grim smile that was somehow both confident and scary. It was the smile of a bulldozer operator lowering the blade of a D-9 Cat in front of a particularly difficult stump.

"I'll get it," he said. "When I'm ready, I'll get it."

And you know what? I believed he would.

4 / Arnie Gets Married

I remember the day
When I chose her over all those other
* junkers,*
Thought I could tell
Under the coat of rust she was gold,
No clunker . . .

—The Beach Boys

We could have had two hours of overtime that Friday evening, but we declined it. We picked up our checks in the office and drove down to the Libertyville branch of Pittsburgh Savings and Loan and cashed them. I dumped most of mine into my savings account, put fifty into my checking account (just having one of those made me feel disquietingly adult—the feeling, I suppose, wears off), and held onto twenty in cash.

Arnie drew all of his in cash.

"Here," he said, holding out a ten-spot.

"No," I said. "You hang onto it, man. You'll need every penny of it before you're through with that clunk."

"Take it," he said. "I pay my debts, Dennis."

"Keep it. Really."

"Take it." He held the money out inexorably.

I took it. But I made him take out the dollar he had coming back. *He* didn't want to do that.

Driving across town to LeBay's tract house, Arnie got more jittery, playing the radio too loud, beating boogie riffs first on his thighs and then on the dashboard. Foreigner came on, singing "Dirty White Boy."

"Story of my life, Arnie my man," I said, and he laughed too loud and too long.

He was acting like a man waiting for his wife to have a baby. At last I guessed he was scared LeBay had sold the car out from under him.

"Arnie," I said, "stay cool. It'll be there."

"I'm cool, I'm cool," he said, and offered me a large, glowing, false smile. His complexion that day was the worst I ever saw it, and I wondered (not for the first time, or the last) what it must be like to be Arnie Cunningham, trapped behind that oozing face from second to second and minute to minute and . . .

"Well, just stop sweating. You act like you're going to make lemonade in your pants before we get there."

"I'm not," he said, and beat another quick, nervous riff on the dashboard just to show me how nervous he wasn't. "Dirty White Boy" by Foreigner gave way to "Jukebox Heroes" by Foreigner. It was Friday afternoon, and the Block Party Weekend had started on FM-104. When I look back on that year, my senior year, it seems to me that I could measure it out in blocks of rock . . . and an escalating, dreamlike sense of terror.

"What exactly is it?" I asked. "What is it about this car?"

He sat looking out at Libertyville Avenue without saying anything for a long time, and then he turned off the radio with a quick snap, cutting off Foreigner in mid-flight.

"I don't know exactly," he said. "Maybe it's because for the first time since I was eleven and started getting pimples, I've seen something even uglier than I am. Is that what you want me to say? Does that let you put it in a neat little category?"

"Hey, Arnie, come on," I said. "This is Dennis here, remember me?"

"I remember," he said. "And we're still friends, right?"

"Sure, last time I checked. But what has that got to do with—"

"And that means we don't have to lie to each other, or at least I think that's what it's supposed to mean. So I got to tell you, maybe it's not all jive. I know what I am. I'm ugly. I don't make friends easily. I . . . alienate people somehow. I don't mean to do it, but somehow I do. You know?"

I nodded with some reluctance. As he said, we were friends, and that meant keeping the bullshit to a bare minimum.

He nodded back, matter-of-factly. "Other people—" he said, and then added carefully, "you, for instance, Dennis— don't always understand what that means. It changes how you look at the world when you're ugly and people laugh at you. It makes it hard to keep your sense of humor. It plugs up your sinuses. Sometimes it makes it a little hard to stay sane."

"Well, I can dig that. But—"

"No," he said quietly. "You can't dig it. You might think you can, but you can't. Not really. But you like me, Dennis—"

"I love you, man," I said. "You know that."

"Maybe you do," he said. "And I appreciate it. If you do, you know it's because there's something else—something underneath the zits and my stupid face—"

"Your face isn't stupid, Arnie," I said. "Queer-looking, maybe, but not stupid."

"Fuck you," he said, smiling.

"And de cayuse you rode in on, Range Rider."

"Anyway, that car's like that. There's something underneath. Something else. Something better. I see it, that's all."

"Do you?"

"Yeah, Dennis," he said quietly. "I do."

I turned onto Main Street. We were getting close to Le-Bay's now. And suddenly I had a truly nasty idea. Suppose Arnie's father had gotten one of his friends or students to beat his feet over to LeBay's house and buy that car out from under his son? A touch Machiavellian, you might say, but Michael Cunningham's mind was more than a little devious. His specialty was military history.

"I saw that car—and I felt such an *attraction* to it . . . I can't explain it very well even to myself. But . . ."

He trailed off, those gray eyes looking dreamily ahead.

"But I saw I could make her better," he said.

"Fix it up, you mean?"

"Yeah . . . well, no. That's too impersonal. You fix tables, chairs, stuff like that. The lawnmower when it won't start. And ordinary cars."

Maybe he saw my eyebrows go up. He laughed, anyway— a little defensive laugh.

"Yeah, I know how that sounds," he said. "I don't even like to say it, because I know how it sounds. But you're a friend, Dennis. And that means a minimum of bullshit. I don't think she's any ordinary car. I don't know why I think that . . . but I do."

I opened my mouth to say something I might later have regretted, something about trying to keep things in perspective or maybe even about avoiding obsessive behavior. But just then we swung around the corner and onto LeBay's street.

Arnie pulled air into his lungs in a harsh, hurt gasp.

There was a rectangle of grass on LeBay's lawn that was even yellower, balder, and uglier than the rest of his lawn. Near one end of that patch there was a diseased-looking oil-spill that had sunk into the ground and killed everything that had once grown there. That rectangular piece of ground was so fucking gross I almost believe that if you looked at it for too long you'd go blind.

It was where the 1958 Plymouth had been standing on yesterday.

The ground was still there but the Plymouth was gone.

"Arnie," I said as I swung my car in to the curb, "take it easy. Don't go off half-cocked, for Christ's sake."

He paid not a bit of attention. I doubt if he had even heard me. His face had gone pale. The blemishes covering it stood out in purplish, glaring relief. He had the passenger door of my Duster open and was lunging out of the car even before it had stopped moving.

"Arnie—"

"It's my father," he said in anger and dismay. "I smell that bastard all *over* this."

And he was gone, running across the lawn to LeBay's door.

I got out and hurried after him, thinking that this crazy shit was never going to end. I could hardly believe I had just heard Arnie Cunningham call Michael a bastard.

Arnie was raising his fist to hammer on the door when it opened. There stood Roland D. LeBay himself. Today he was wearing a shirt over his back brace. He looked at Arnie's furious face with a benignly avaricious smile.

"Hello, son," he said.

"Where is she?" Arnie raged. "We had a deal! Dammit, we had a deal! I've got a receipt!"

"Simmer down," LeBay said. He saw me, standing on the bottom step with my hands shoved down in my pockets. "What's wrong with your friend, son?"

"The car's gone," I said. "That's what's wrong with him."

"Who bought it?" Arnie shouted. I'd never seen him so

mad. If he had had a gun right then, I believe he would have put it to LeBay's temple. I was fascinated in spite of myself. It was as if a rabbit had suddenly turned carnivore. God help me, I even wondered fleetingly if he might not have a brain tumor.

"Who bought it?" LeBay repeated mildly. "Why nobody has yet, son. But you got a lien on her. I backed her into the garage, that's all. I put on the spare and changed the oil." He preened and then offered us both an absurdly magnanimous smile.

"You're a real sport," I said.

Arnie stared at him uncertainly, then turned his head creakily to look at the closed door of the modest one-car garage that was attached to the house by a breezeway. The breezeway, like everything else around LeBay's place, had seen better days.

"Besides, I didn't want to leave her out once you'd laid some money down on her," he said. "I've had some trouble with one or two of the folks on this street. One night some kid threw a rock at my car. Oh yeah, I got some neighbors straight out of the old A.B."

"What's that?" I asked.

"The Asshole Brigade, son."

He swept the far side of the street with a baleful sniper's glance, taking in the neat, gas-thrifty commuters' cars now home from work, the children playing tag and jumprope, the people sitting out on their porches and having drinks in the first of the evening cool.

"I'd like to know who it was threw that rock," he said softly. "Yessir, I'd surely like to know who it was."

Arnie cleared his throat. "I'm sorry I gave you a hard time."

"Don't worry," LeBay said briskly. "Like to see a fellow stand up for what's his . . . or what's almost his. You bring the money, kid?"

"Yes, I have it."

"Well, come on in the house. You and your friend both. I'll sign her over to you, and we'll have a glass of beer to celebrate."

"No thanks," I said. "I'll stay out here, if that's okay."

"Suit yourself, son," LeBay said . . . and winked. To this day I have no idea exactly what that wink was supposed to mean. They went in, and the door banged shut behind them. The fish had been netted and was about to be cleaned.

Feeling depressed, I walked through the breezeway to the garage and tried the door. It ran up easily and exhaled the same odors I had smelled when I opened the Plymouth's door yesterday—oil, old upholstery, the accumulated heat of a long summer.

Rakes and a few old garden implements were ranked along one wall. On the other was a very old hose, a bicycle pump, and an ancient golf-bag filled with rusty clubs. In the center, nose outward, sat Arnie's car, Christine, looking a mile long in this day and age when even Cadillacs looked squeezed together and boxy. The spiderweb snarl of cracks at the side of the windshield caught the light and turned it to a dull quicksilver. Some kid with a rock, as LeBay had said—or maybe a little accident coming home from the VFW hall after a night of drinking boilermakers and telling stories about the Battle of the Bulge or Pork Chop Hill. The good old days, when a man could see Europe, the Pacific, and the mysterious East from behind the sight of a bazooka. Who knew . . . and what did it matter? Either way, it was not going to be easy, finding a replacement for a big wrap windshield like that.

Or cheap.

Oh, Arnie, I thought. *Man, you are getting in so deep.*

The flat LeBay had taken off rested against the wall. I got down on my hands and knees and peered under the car. A fresh oil-stain was starting to form there, black against the brownish ghost of an older, wider stain that had sunk into the concrete over a period of years. It did nothing to alleviate my depression. The block was cracked for sure.

I walked around to the driver's side, and as I grasped the handle, I saw a wastecan at the far corner of the garage. A large plastic bottle was poking out of the top. The letters SAPPH were visible over the rim.

I groaned. Oh, he had changed the oil, all right. Big of him. He had run out the old—whatever was left of it—and had run in a few quarts of Sapphire Motor Oil. This is the stuff you can get for $3.50 per recycled five-gallon jug at the Mammoth Mart. Roland D. LeBay was a real prince, all right. Roland D. LeBay was all heart.

I opened the car door and slid in behind the wheel. Now the smell in the garage didn't seem quite so heavy, or so freighted with feelings of disuse and defeat. The car's wheel was wide and red—a confident wheel. I looked at that amazing speedometer again, that speedometer which was calibrated not to 70 or 80 but all the way up to 120 miles an hour. No kilometers in little red numbers underneath; when this babe had rolled off the assembly line, the idea of going metric had yet to occur to anyone in Washington. No big red 55 on the speedometer, either. Back then, gas went for 29.9 a gallon, maybe less if a price-war happened to be going on in your town. The Arab oil-embargoes and the double-nickel speed limit had still been fifteen years away.

The good old days, I thought, and had to smile a little. I fumbled down to the left side of the seat and found the little button console that would move the seat back and forth and up and down (if it still worked, that was). More power to you, to coin a crappy little pun. There was factory air (that *certainly* wouldn't work), and cruise control, and a big push-button radio with lots of chrome—AM only, of course. In 1958, FM was mostly a blank wasteland.

I put my hands on the wheel and something happened.

Even now, after much thought, I'm not sure exactly what it was. A vision, maybe—but if it was, it sure wasn't any big deal. It was just that for a moment the torn upholstery seemed to be gone. The seat covers were whole and smelling pleasantly of vinyl . . . or maybe that smell was real leather. The worn places were gone from the steering wheel; the chrome winked pleasantly in the summer evening light falling through the garage door.

Let's go for a ride, big guy, Christine seemed to whisper in the hot summer silence of LeBay's garage. *Let's cruise.*

And for just a moment it seemed that *everything* changed. That ugly snarl of cracks in the windshield was gone—or seemed to be. The little swatch of LeBay's lawn that I could see was not yellowed, balding, and crabgrassy but a dark, rich, newly cut green. The sidewalk beyond it was freshly cemented, not a crack in sight. I saw (or thought I did, or dreamed I did) a '57 Cadillac motor by out front. That GM high-stepper was a dark minty green, not a speck of rust on her, big gangster whitewall tires, and hubcaps as deeply reflective as mirrors. A Cadillac the size of a boat, and why not? Gas was almost as cheap as tap-water.

Let's go for a ride, big guy . . . let's cruise.

Sure, why not? I could pull out and turn toward downtown, toward the old high school that was still standing—it wouldn't burn down for another six years, not until 1964—and I could turn on the radio and catch Chuck Berry singing "Maybelline" or the Everlys doing "Wake Up Little

Susie" or maybe Robin Luke wailing "Susie Darling." And then I'd . . .

And then I got out of that car just about as fast as I could. The door opened with a rusty, hellish screech, and I cracked my elbow good on one of the garage walls. I pushed the door shut (I didn't really even want to touch it, to tell you the truth) and then just stood there looking at the Plymouth which, barring a miracle, would soon be my friend Arnie's. I rubbed my bruised crazybone. My heart was beating too fast.

Nothing. No new chrome, no new upholstery. On the other hand, plenty of dents and rust, one headlamp missing (I hadn't noticed that the day before), the radio aerial crazily askew. And that dusty, dirty smell of age.

I decided right then that I didn't like my friend Arnie's car.

I walked out of the garage, glancing back constantly over my shoulder—I don't know why, but I didn't like it behind my back. I know how stupid that must sound, but it was how I felt. And there it sat with its dented, rusty grille, nothing sinister or even strange, just a very old Plymouth automobile with an inspection sticker that had gone invalid on June 1, 1976—a long time ago.

Arnie and LeBay were coming out of the house. Arnie had a white slip of paper in his hand—his bill of sale, I assumed. LeBay's hands were empty; he had already made the money disappear.

"Hope you enjoy her," LeBay was saying, and for some reason I thought of a very old pimp huckstering a very young boy. I felt a surge of real disgust for him—him with his psoriasis of the skull and his sweaty back brace. "I think you will. In time."

His slightly rheumy eyes found mine, held there for a second, and then slipped back to Arnie.

"In time," he repeated.

"Yessir, I'm sure I will," Arnie said absently. He moved toward the garage like a sleepwalker and stood looking at his car.

"Keys are in her," LeBay said. "I'll have to have you take her along. You understand that, don't you?"

"Will she start?"

"Started for me yesterday evenin," LeBay said, but his eyes shifted away toward the horizon. And then, in the tone of one who has washed his hands of the whole thing: "Your friend here will have a set of jumpers in his trunk, I reckon."

Well, as a matter of fact I *did* have a set of jumper cables in my trunk, but I didn't much like LeBay guessing it. I didn't like him guessing it because . . . I sighed a little. Because I didn't want to be involved in Arnie's future relationship with the old clunker he had bought, but I could see myself getting dragged in, step by step.

Arnie had dropped out of the conversation completely. He walked into the garage and got into the car. The evening sun was slanting strongly in now, and I saw the little puff of dust that went up when Arnie sat down and I automatically brushed at the seat of my own pants. For a moment he just sat there behind the wheel, hands gripping it loosely, and I felt a return of my unease. It was, in a way, as if the car had swallowed him. I told myself to stop it, that there was no damn reason for me to be acting like a goosey seventh-grade schoolgirl.

Then Arnie bent forward a little. The engine began to turn over. I turned and shot LeBay an angry, accusatory glance, but he was studying the sky again, as if for rain.

It wasn't going to start; no way it was going to start. My Duster was in pretty good shape, but the two I'd owned before it were clunkers (*modified* clunkers; neither was in the same class as Christine); and I'd become very familiar with that sound on cold winter mornings, that slow and tired cranking that meant the battery was scraping the bottom of the barrel.

Rurr-rurr-rurr . . . rurr . . . rurrr . . . . . . rurrr . . . . . . rurr—

"Don't bother, Arnie," I said. "It's not going to fire up."

He didn't even raise his head. He turned the key off and then turned it on again. The motor cranked with painful, dragging slowness.

I walked over to LeBay. "You couldn't even leave it running long enough to build up a charge, could you?" I asked.

LeBay glanced at me from his yellowing, rheumy eyes, said nothing, and then began checking the sky for rain again.

"Or maybe it never started at all. Maybe you just got a couple of friends to come over and help you push it into the garage. If an old shit like you has any friends."

He looked down at me. "Son," he said. "You don't know everything. You ain't even dry behind the ears yet. When you've slogged your way through a couple of wars, like I have—"

I said deliberately: "Fuck your couple of wars," and walked toward the garage where Arnie was still trying to start his car. Might as well try to drink the Atlantic dry with a straw or ride a hot-air balloon to Mars, I thought.

Rurr . . . . rurr . . . . rurr.

Pretty soon the last ohm and erg would be sucked out of that old corroded Sears battery, and then there would be nothing but that most dismal of all automotive sounds, most commonly heard on rainy back roads and deserted highways: the dull, sterile click of the solenoid, followed by an awful sound like a death-rattle.

I opened the driver's side door. "I'll get my cables," I said.

He looked up. "I think she'll start for me," he said.

I felt my lips stretch in a large, unconvincing grin. "Well, I'll get them, just in case."

"Sure, if you want," he said absently, and then in a voice almost too low to hear he said, "Come on, Christine. What do you say?"

In the same instant, that voice awoke in my head and spoke again—*Let's go for a ride, big guy . . . let's cruise*—and I shuddered.

He turned the key again. What I expected was that dull solenoid click and death-rattle. What I heard was the slow crank of the engine suddenly speeding up. The engine caught, ran briefly, then quit. Arnie turned the key again. The engine cranked over faster. There was a backfire that sounded as loud as a cherry-bomb in the closed space of the garage. I jumped. Arnie didn't. He was lost in his own world.

At this point I would have cursed it a couple of times, just to help it along: *Come on, you whore* is always a good one; *Let's go, cocksucker* has its merits, and sometimes just a good, hearty *shit-FIRE!* will turn the trick. Most guys I know would do the same; I think it's just one of the things you pick up from your father.

What your mother leaves you is mostly good hard-headed practical advice—if you cut your toenails twice a month you won't get so many holes in your socks; put that down, you don't know where it's been; eat your carrots, they're good for you—but it's from your father that you get the magic, the talismans, the words of power. If the car won't start, curse it . . . and be sure you curse it female. If you went seven generations back, you'd probably find one of your forebears cursing the goddam bitch of a donkey that stopped in the middle of the tollbridge somewhere in Sussex or Prague.

But Arnie didn't swear at it. He murmured under his breath, "Come on, doll, what do you say?"

He turned the key. The engine kicked twice, backfired again, and then started up. It sounded horrible, as if maybe four of the eight pistons had taken the day off, but he had it running. I could hardly believe it, but I didn't want to stand around and discuss it with him. The garage was rapidly filling up with blue smoke and fumes. I went outside.

"That turned out all right, after all, didn't it?" LeBay said. "And you don't have to risk your own precious battery." He spat.

I couldn't think of anything to say. To tell you the truth, I felt a little embarrassed.

The car came slowly out of the garage, looking so absurdly long that it made you want to laugh or cry or do something. I couldn't believe how long it looked. It was like an optical illusion. And Arnie looked very small behind the wheel.

He rolled down the window and beckoned me over. We had to raise our voices to make ourselves heard clearly—that was another thing about Arnie's girl Christine; she had an extremely loud and rumbling voice. She was going to have to be Midasized in a hurry. If there was anything left of the exhaust system to attach a muffler to, that was, besides a lot of rusty lace. Since Arnie sat down behind the wheel, the little accountant in the automobile section of my brain had totted up expenses of about six hundred dollars—not including the cracked windshield. God knew how much that might cost to replace.

"I'm taking her down to Darnell's!" Arnie yelled. "His ad in the paper says I can park it in one of the back bays for twenty dollars a week!"

"Arnie, twenty a week for one of those back bays is too much!" I bellowed back.

Here was more robbery of the young and innocent. Darnell's Garage sat next door to a four-acre automobile wasteland that went by the falsely cheerful name of Darnell's Used Auto Parts. I had been there a few times, once to buy a starter for my Duster, once to get a rebuilt carb for the Mercury which had been my first car. Will Darnell was a great fat pig of a man who drank a lot and smoked long rank cigars, although he was reputed to have a bad asthmatic condition. He professed to hate almost every car-owning teenager in Libertyville . . . but that didn't keep him from catering to them and rooking them.

"I know," Arnie yelled over the bellowing engine. "But it's only for a week or two, until I find a cheaper place. I can't take it home like this, Dennis, my dad and mom would have a shit fit!"

That was certainly true. I opened my mouth to say something else—maybe to beg him again to stop this madness before it got completely out of control. Then I shut my mouth again. The deal was done. Besides, I didn't want to compete with that bellowing muffler anymore, or stand there pulling a lot of evil fried-carbon exhaust into my lungs.

"All right," I said. "I'll follow you."

"Good deal," he said, grinning. "I'm going by Walnut Street and Basin Drive. I want to stay off the main roads."

"Okay."

"Thanks, Dennis."

He dropped the hydramatic transmission into D again, and the Plymouth lurched forward two feet and then almost stalled. Arnie goosed the accelerator a little and Christine broke dirty wind. The Plymouth crept down LeBay's driveway to the street. When he pushed the brake, only one of the taillights flashed. My mental automotive accountant relentlessly rang up another five dollars.

He hauled the wheel to the left and pulled out into the street. The remains of the muffler scraped rustily at the lowest point of the driveway. Arnie gave it more gas, and the car roared like a refugee from the demo derby at Philly Plains. Across the street, people leaned forward on their porches or came to their doors to see what was going on.

Bellowing and snarling, Christine rolled up the street at about ten miles an hour, sending out great stinking clouds of blue oilsmoke that hung and then slowly raftered in the mellow August evening.

At the stop sign forty yards up, it stalled. A kid rode past the hulk on his Raleigh, and his impudent, brassy shout drifted back to me: "Put it in a trash-masher, mister!"

Arnie's closed fist popped out of the window. His middle finger went up as he flipped the kid the bird. Another first. I had never seen Arnie flip anyone the bird in my life.

The starter whined, the motor sputtered and caught. This time there was a whole rattling series of backfires. It was as if someone had just opened up with a machine-gun on Laurel Drive, Libertyville, U.S.A. I groaned.

Someone would call the cops pretty soon, reporting a public nuisance, and they would grab Arnie for driving an unregistered, uninspected vehicle—and probably for the nuisance charge as well. That would not exactly ease the situation at home.

There was one final echoing bang—it rolled down the street like the explosion of a mortar shell—and then the Plymouth turned left on Martin Street, which brought you to Walnut about a mile up. The westering sun turned its battered red body briefly to gold as it moved out of sight. I saw that Arnie had his elbow cocked out the window.

I turned to LeBay, mad all over again, ready to give him some more hell. I tell you I felt sick inside my heart. But what I saw stopped me cold.

Roland D. LeBay was crying.

It was horrible and it was grotesque and most of all it was pitiable. When I was nine, we had a cat named Captain Beefheart, and he got hit by a UPS truck. We took him to the vet's—my mom had to drive slow because she was crying and it was hard for her to see—and I sat in the back with Captain Beefheart. He was in a box, and I kept telling him the vet would save him, it was going to be okay, but even a little nine-year-old dumbhead like me could see it was never going to be all right for Captain Beefheart again, because some of his guts were out and there was blood coming out of his asshole and there was shit in the box and on his fur and he was dying. I tried to pet him and he bit my hand, right in the sensitive webbing between the thumb and the first finger. The pain was bad; that terrible feeling of pity was worse. I had not felt anything like that since then. Not that I was complaining, you understand; I don't think people should have feelings like that often. You have a lot of feelings like that, and I guess they take you away to the funny-farm to make baskets.

LeBay was standing on his balding lawn not far from the place where that big patch of oil had defoliated everything, and he had this great big old man's snotrag out and his head was down and he was wiping his eyes with it. The tears gleamed greasily on his cheeks, more like sweat than real tears. His adam's apple went up and down.

I turned my head so I wouldn't have to look at him cry and happened to stare straight into his one-car garage. Before, it had seemed really full—the stuff along the walls, of course, but most of all that huge old car with its double headlights and its wraparound windshield and its acre of hood. Now the stuff along the walls only served to accentuate the garage's essential emptiness. It gaped like a toothless mouth.

That was almost as bad as LeBay. But when I looked back, the old bastard had gotten himself under control—well, mostly. He had stopped leaking at the eyes and he had stuffed the snotrag into the back pocket of his patented old man's pants. But his face was still bleak. Very bleak.

"Well, that's that," he said hoarsely. "I'm shut of her, sonny."

"Mr. LeBay," I said. "I only wish my friend could make the same statement. If you knew the trouble he was in over that rustbucket with his folks—"

"Get out of here," he said. "You sound like a goddam sheep. Just baa, baa, baa, that's all I hear comin out'n your hole. I think your friend there knows more than you do. Go and see if he needs a hand."

I started down the lawn to my car. I didn't want to hang around LeBay a moment longer.

"Nothin but baa, baa, baa!" he yelled shrewishly after me, making me think of that old song by the Youngbloods—*I am a one-note man, I play it all I can.* "You don't know half as much as you think you do!"

I got into my car and drove away. I glanced back once as I made the turn onto Martin Street and saw him standing there on his lawn, the sunlight gleaming on his bald head.

As things turned out, he was right.

I didn't know half as much as I thought I did.

5 / How We Got to Darnell's

I got a '34 wagon and we call it a woody,
You know she's not very cherry,
She's an oldy but a goody . . .

                                   —Jan and Dean

I drove down Martin to Walnut and turned right, toward
Basin Drive. It didn't take long to catch up with Arnie. He
was pulled into the curb, and Christine's trunk-lid was up. An
automobile jack so old that it almost looked as if it might
once have been used for changing wheels on Conestoga wag-
ons was leaning against the crooked back bumper. The right
rear tire was flat.

I pulled in behind him and had no more than gotten out
when a young woman waddled down toward us from her
house, skirting a pretty good collection of plastic-fantastic
that was planted on her lawn (two pink flamingos, four or
five little stone ducks in a line behind a big stone mother
duck, and a really good plastic wishing well with plastic flowers planted in the plastic bucket). She was in dire need of
Weight Watchers.

"You can't leave that junk here," she said around a mouthful of chewing gum. "You can't leave that junk parked in
front of our house, I just hope you know that."

"Ma'am," Arnie said. "I had a flat tire, is all. I'll get it out
of here just as soon as—"

"You can't leave it there and I hope you know that," she
said with a maddening kind of circularity. "My husband'll be
home pretty soon. He don't want no junk car in front of the
house."

"It's not junk," Arnie said, and something in his tone made
her back up a step.

"You don't want to take that tone of voice to me, sonny,"
this overweight be-bop queen said haughtily. "It don't take
much to get my husband mad."

"Look," Arnie began in that same dangerous flat voice he had used when Michael and Regina began ganging up on him. I grabbed his shoulder hard. More hassle we didn't need.

"Thanks, ma'am," I said. "We'll get it taken care of right away. We're going to take care of it so quick you'll think you hallucinated this car."

"You better," she said, and then hooked a thumb at my Duster. "And *your* car is parked in front of my driveway."

I backed my Duster up. She watched and then joggled back up to her house, where a little boy and a little girl were crammed into the doorway. They were pretty porky, too. Each of them was eating a nice nourishing Devil Dog.

"Wassa matta, Ma?" the little boy asked. "Wassa matta that man's car, Ma? Wassa matta?"

"Shut up," the be-bop queen said, and hauled both kids back inside. I always like to see enlightened parents like that; it gives me hope for the future.

I walked back to Arnie.

"Well," I said, dragging out the only witticism I could think of, "it's only flat on the bottom, Arnie. Right?"

He smiled wanly. "I got a slight problem, Dennis," he said.

I knew what his problem was; he had no spare.

Arnie dragged out his wallet again—it hurt me to see him do it—and looked inside. "I got to get a new tire," he said.

"Yeah, I guess you do. A retread—"

"No retreads. I don't want to start out that way."

I didn't say anything, but I glanced back toward my Duster. I had two retreads on it and I thought they were just fine.

"How much do you think a new Goodyear or Firestone would cost, Dennis?"

I shrugged and consulted the little automotive accountant, who guessed that Arnie could probably get a new no-frills blackwall for around thirty-five dollars.

He pulled out two twenties and handed them to me. "If it's more—with the tax and everything—I'll pay you back."

I looked at him sadly. "Arnie, how much of your week's pay you got left?"

His eyes narrowed and shifted away from mine. "Enough," he said.

I decided to try one more time—you must remember that I was only seventeen and still under the impression that people could be shown where their best interest lay. "You couldn't get into a nickel poker game," I said. "You plugged just about the whole fucking wad into that car. Dragging out your wallet is going to become a very familiar action to you, Arnie. Please, man. Think it over."

His eyes went flinty. It was an expression I had not seen before on his face, and although you'll probably think I was the most naive teenager in America, I couldn't really remember having seen it on *any* face before. I felt a mixture of surprise and dismay—I felt the way I might have felt if I suddenly discovered I was trying to have a rational conversation with a fellow who just happened to be a lunatic. I have seen the expression since, though; I imagine you have too. Total shutdown. It's the expression a man gets on his face when you tell him the woman he loves is whoring around behind his back.

"Don't get going on that, Dennis," he said.

I threw my hands up in exasperation. "All right! All right!"

"And you don't have to go after the damn tire, either, if you don't want to." That flinty, obdurate, and—so help me, it's true—stupidly stubborn expression was still on his face. "I'll find a way."

I started to reply, and I might have said something pretty hot, but then I happened to glance to my left. The two porky little kids were there at the edge of their lawn. They were astride identical Big Wheels, their fingers smeared with chocolate. They were watching us solemnly.

"No big deal, man," I said. "I'll get the tire."

"Only if you want to, Dennis," he said. "I know it's getting late."

"It's cool," I said.

"Mister?" the little boy said, licking chocolate off his fingers.

"What?" Arnie asked.

"My mother says that car is poopy."

"That's right," the little girl chimed. "Poopy-kaka."

"Poopy-kaka," Arnie said. "Why, that's very perceptive, isn't it, kids? Is your mother a philosopher?"

"No," the little boy said. "She's a Capricorn. I'm a Libra. My sister is a—"

"I'll be back quick as I can," I said awkwardly.

"Sure."

"Stay cool."

"Don't worry, I'm not going to punch anybody."

I trotted to my car. As I slipped behind the wheel I heard the little girl ask Arnie loudly, "Why is your face all messy like that, mister?"

I drove a mile and a half down to JFK Drive, which—according to my mother, who grew up in Libertyville—used to be at the center of one of the town's most desirable neighborhoods back around the time Kennedy was killed in Dallas. Maybe renaming Barnswallow Drive for the slain President had been bad luck, because since the early sixties, the neighborhood around the street had degenerated into an exurban strip. There was a drive-in movie, a McDonald's, a Burger King, an Arby's, and the Big Twenty Lanes. There were also eight or ten service stations, since JFK Drive leads to the Pennsylvania Turnpike.

Getting Arnie's tire should have gone lickety-split, but the first two stations I came to were those self-service jobbies that don't even sell oil; there's just gas and a marginally retarded girl in a booth made of bullet-proof glass who sits in front of a computer console reading a *National Enquirer* and chewing a wad of Bubblicious Gum big enough to choke a Missouri mule.

The third one was a Texaco having a tire sale. I was able to buy Arnie a blackwall that would fit his Plymouth (I could not bring myself then to call her Christine or even think of her—*it*—by that name) for just twenty-eight-fifty plus tax, but there was only one guy working there, and he had to put the new tire on Arnie's wheel-rim and pump gas at the same time. The operation stretched out over forty-five minutes. I offered to pump gas for the guy while he did it, but he said the boss would shoot him if he heard of it.

By the time I had the mounted tire back in my trunk and had paid the guy two bucks for the job, the early evening light had become the fading purple of late evening. The shadow of each bush was long and velvety, and as I cruised slowly back up the street I saw the day's last light streaming almost horizontally through the trash-littered space between the Arby's and the bowling alley. That light, so much flooding gold, was nearly terrible in its strange, unexpected beauty.

I was surprised by a choking panic that climbed up in my throat like dry fire. It was the first time a feeling like that came over me that year—that long, strange year—but not the last. Yet it's hard for me to explain, or even define. It had something to do with realizing that it was August 11, 1978, that I was going to be a senior in high school next month, and that when school started again it meant the end of a long, quiet phase of my life. I was getting ready to be a grown-up, and I saw that somehow—saw it for sure, for the first time in that lovely but somehow ancient spill of golden light flooding down the alleyway between a bowling alley and a roast beef joint. And I think I understood then that what really scares people about growing up is that you stop trying on the life-mask and start trying on another one. If being a kid is about learning how to live, then being a grown-up is about learning how to die.

The feeling passed, but in its wake I felt shaken and melancholy. Neither state was much like my usual self.

When I turned back onto Basin Drive I was feeling suddenly removed from Arnie's problems and trying to cope with my own—thoughts of growing up had led naturally to such gigantic (at least they seemed gigantic to me) and rather unpleasant ideas as college and living away from home and trying to make the football team at State with sixty other qualified people competing for my position instead of only ten or twelve. So maybe you're saying, Big deal, Dennis, I got some news for you: one billion Red Chinese don't give a shit if you make the first squad as a college freshman. Fair enough. I'm just trying to say that those things seemed really real to me for the first time . . . and really frightening. Your mind takes you on trips like that sometimes—and if you don't want to go, it takes you anyway.

Seeing that the be-bop queen's husband had indeed arrived home, and that he and Arnie were standing almost nose to nose, apparently ready to start mixing it up at any second, didn't help my mood at all.

The two little kids still sat solemnly astride their Big Wheels, their eyes shifting back and forth from Arnie to Daddy and back again to Arnie like spectators at some apocalyptic tennis match where the ref would cheerfully shoot the loser. They seemed to be waiting for the moment of combustion when Daddy would flatten my skinny friend and do the Cool Jerk all the way up and down his broken body.

I pulled over quickly and got out, almost running over to them.

"I'm done talkin atcha face!" Dads bellowed. "I'm telling you I want it out and I want it out right now!" He had a big flattened nose full of burst veins. His cheeks were flushed to the color of new brick, and above his gray twill workshirt, corded veins stood out on his neck.

"I'm not going to drive it on the rim," Arnie said. "I told you that. You wouldn't do it if it was yours."

"I'll drive *you* on the rim, Pizza-Face," Daddy said, apparently intent on showing his children how big people solve their problems in the Real World. "You ain't parking your cruddy hotrod in front of my house. Don't you aggravate me, kiddo, or you're gonna get hurt."

"Nobody's going to get hurt," I said. "Come on, mister. Give us a break."

Arnie's eyes shifted gratefully to me, and I saw how scared he had been—how scared he still was. Always an out, he knew there was something about him, God knew what, that made a certain type of guy want to pound the living shit out of him. He must have been pretty well convinced it was going to happen again—but this time he wasn't backing down.

The man's eyes shifted to me. "Another one," he said, as if marveling that there could be so many assholes in the world. "You want me to take you both on? Is that what you want? Believe me, I can do it."

Yes, I knew the type. Ten years younger and he would have been one of the guys at school who thought it was terribly amusing to slam Arnie's books out of his arms when he was on his way to class or to throw him into the shower with all his clothes on after phys ed. They never change, those guys. They just get older and develop lung cancer from smoking too many Luckies or step out with a brain embolism at fifty-three or so.

"We don't want to take you on," I said. "He had a flat tire, for God's sake! Didn't you ever have a flat?"

"Ralph, I want them out of here!" The porky wife was standing on the porch. Her voice was high and excited. This was better than the *Phil Donahue Show*. Other neighbors had come out to watch developments, and I thought again with great weariness that if someone had not called the cops already, someone soon would.

"I never had a flat and left some old piece of junk sitting in front of someone's house for three hours," Ralph said loudly. His lips were pulled back and I could see spit shining on his teeth in the light of the setting sun.

"It's been an hour," I said quietly, "if that."

"Don't give me any of your smartmouth, kid," Ralph said. "I ain't interested. I ain't like you guys. I work for a living. I come home tired, I ain't got time to argue. I want it out and I want it out *now*."

"I've got a spare right in my trunk," I said. "If we could just put it on—"

"And if you had any common decency—" Arnie began hotly.

That almost did it. If there was one thing our buddy Ralph wasn't going to have impugned in front of his kids, it was his common decency. He swung on Arnie. I don't know how it would have ended—with Arnie in jail, maybe, his precious car impounded—but somehow I was able to get my own hand up and catch Ralph's hand by the wrist. The two of them coming together made a flat smacking sound in the dusk.

The porky little girl burst into whiny tears.

The porky little boy sat astride his Big Wheel with his lower jaw hanging almost to his chest.

Arnie, who had always scuttered past the smoking area at school like a hunted thing, never even flinched. He actually seemed to *want* it to happen.

Ralph whirled on me, his eyes bulging with fury.

"All right, you little shit," he said. "You first."

I held onto his hand, straining. "Come on, man," I said in a low voice. "The tire's in my trunk. Give us five minutes to change it and get out of your face. Please."

Little by little the pressure of holding his hand back slacked off. He glanced at his kids, the little girl snivelling, the little boy wide-eyed, and that seemed to decide him.

"Five minutes," he agreed. He looked at Arnie. "You're just goddam lucky I ain't calling the police on you. That thing's uninspected and it ain't got no tags, either."

I waited for Arnie to say something else inflammatory and send the game into extra innings, but maybe he hadn't forgotten everything he knew about discretion.

"Thank you," he said. "I'm sorry if I got hot under the collar."

Ralph grunted and tucked his shirt back into his pants with savage little jabs. He looked over at his kids again. "Get in the house!" he roared. "What you doing out here? You want me to put a bang-shang-a-lang on you?"

Oh God, what an onomatopoeic family, I thought. For Christ's sake don't put a bang-shang-a-lang on them, Pops—they might make poopy-kaka in their pants.

The kids fled to their mother, leaving their Big Wheels behind.

"Five minutes," he repeated, looking at us balefully. And later tonight, when he was hoisting a few with the boys, he would be able to tell them how he had done his part to hold the line against the drugs-and-sex generation. Yessir, boys, I told em to get that fucking junk away from my house before I put a bang-shang-a-lang on them. And you want to believe they moved like their feet was on fire and their asses were catching. And then he would light up a Lucky. Or a Camel.

We put Arnie's jack under the bumper. Arnie hadn't pumped the lever more than three times when the jack snapped in two. It made a dusty sound when it went, and rust puffed up. Arnie looked at me, his eyes at once humble and stricken.

"Never mind," I said. "We'll use mine."

It was twilight now, starting to get dark. My heart was still beating too fast and my mouth was sour from the confrontation with the Big Cheese of 119 Basin Drive.

"I'm sorry, Dennis," he said in a low voice. "I won't get you involved with any of this again."

"Forget it. Let's just get the tire on."

We used my jack to get the Plymouth up (for several horrible seconds I thought the rear bumper was just going to rip off in a screech of decaying metal) and pulled the dead tire. We got the new one on, tightened the lug-nuts some, and then let it down. It was a great relief to have the car standing on the street again; the way that rotted bumper bent up under the jack had scared me.

"There," Arnie said, clapping the ancient, dented hubcap back on over the lug-nuts.

I stood looking at the Plymouth, and the feeling I'd had in LeBay's garage suddenly recurred. It was looking at the fresh new Firestone on the rear right that did it. The blackwall still had one of the manufacturer's stickers on it and the bright yellow chalk-marks from the gas-jockey's hurried wheel-balancing.

I shivered a little—but to convey the sudden weirdness I felt would be impossible. It was as if I had seen a snake that was almost ready to shed its old skin, that some of that old skin had already flaked away, revealing the glistening newness underneath. . . .

Ralph was standing on his porch, glowering down at us. In one hand he was holding a drippy hamburger sandwich on Wonder Bread. His other hand was fisted around a can of Iron City.

"Handsome, ain't he?" I muttered to Arnie as I slung his busted jack into the Plymouth's trunk.

"A regular Robert Deadford," Arnie muttered back, and that was it—we both got the giggles, the way you sometimes will at the end of a long and tense situation.

Arnie threw the flat into the trunk on top of the jack and then got snorting and holding his hands over his mouth. He looked like a kid who just got caught raiding the jam-jar. Thinking that made me break up all the way.

"What are you two punks laughing at?" Ralph roared. He came to the steps of his porch. "Huh? You want to try laughing on the other sides of your faces for a while? I can show you how, believe me!"

"Get out of here *quick*," I said to Arnie, and bolted back to my Duster. Nothing could stop the laughter now; it just came rolling out. I fell into the front seat and keyed the engine, whinnying with laughter. In front of me, Arnie's Plymouth started up with a bellowing roar and a huge stinking cloud of blue exhaust. Even over it, I could hear his high, helpless laughter, a sound that was close to hysteria.

Ralph came charging across his lawn, still holding his drippy burger and his beer.

"*What are you laughing at, you punks? Huh?*"

"*You, you nerd!*" Arnie shouted triumphantly, and pulled out with a rattling fusillade of backfires. I tromped the gas pedal of my own car and had to swerve to avoid Ralph, who was now apparently intent on murder. I was still laughing, but it wasn't good laughter anymore, if it ever had been—it was a shrill, breathless sound, almost like screaming.

"*I'll kill you, punk!*" Ralph roared.

I goosed the accelerator again, and this time I almost tailgated Arnie.

I flipped Ralph the old El Birdo. "*Jam it!*" I yelled.

Then he was behind us. He tried to catch up; for a few seconds he came pounding along the sidewalk, and then he stopped, breathing hard and snarling.

"What a crazy day," I said aloud, a little frightened by the shaky, teary quality of my own voice. That sour taste was back in my mouth. "What a crazy fucking day."

Darnell's Garage on Hampton Street was a long building with rusty corrugated-tin sides and a rusty corrugated-tin roof. Out front was a grease-caked sign which read: SAVE

MONEY! YOUR KNOW-HOW, OUR TOOLS! Below that was another sign in smaller type, reading *Garage Space Rented by the Week, Month, or Year*.

The automobile junkyard was behind Darnell's. It was a block-long space enclosed in five-foot-high strips of the same corrugated tin, Will Darnell's apathetic nod toward the Town Zoning Board. Not that there was any way the Board was going to bring Will Darnell to heel, and not just because two of the three Zoning Board members were his friends. In Libertyville, Will Darnell knew just about everyone who counted. He was one of those fellows you find in almost any large town or small city, moving quietly behind any number of scenes.

I had heard that he was mixed up in the lively drug traffic at Libertyville High and Darby Junior High, and I had also heard that he was on a nodding acquaintance with the big-time crooks in Pittsburgh and Philly. I didn't believe that stuff—at least, I didn't *think* I did—but I knew that if you wanted firecrackers or cherry-bombs or bottle-rockets for the Fourth of July, Will Darnell would sell them to you. I had also heard, from my father, that Will had been indicted twelve years before, when I was but a lad of five, as one of the kingpins in a stolen-car ring that stretched from our part of the world east to New York City and all the way up to Bangor, Maine. Eventually the charges were dropped. But my dad also said he was pretty sure that Will Darnell might be up to his ears in other shenanigans; anything from truck hijacking to fake antiques.

A good place to stay away from, Dennis, my father had said. This had been a year ago, not long after I got my first clunker and had invested twenty dollars in renting one of Darnell's Do-It-Yourself Garage bays to try and replace the carburetor, an experiment that had ended in dismal failure.

A good place to stay away from—and here I was, pulling in through the main gates behind my friend Arnie after dark, nothing left of the day but a tinge of furnace red to the horizon. My headlights picked out enough discarded auto parts, wreckage, and general all-around dreck to make me feel more depressed and tired than ever. I realized I hadn't called home, and that my mother and father would probably be wondering just where the hell I was.

Arnie drove up to a big garage door with a sign beside it reading HONK FOR ENTRY. There was a feeble light spilling out through a grime-coated window beside the door—somebody was at home—and I barely restrained an impulse to lean out of my window and tell Arnie to drive his car over to my house for the night. I had a vision of us stumbling onto Will Darnell and his cronies inventorying hijacked color TVs or repainting stolen Cadillacs. The Hardy Boys come to Libertyville.

Arnie just sat there, not honking, not doing anything, and I was about to get out and ask him what was what when he came back to where I was parked. Even in the last of the failing light, he looked deeply embarrassed.

"Would you mind honking your horn for me, Dennis?" he said humbly. "Christine's doesn't seem to work."

"Sure."

"Thanks."

I beeped my horn twice, and after a pause the big garage door went rattling up. Will Darnell himself was standing there, his belly pushing out over his belt. He waved Arnie inside impatiently.

I turned my car around, parked it facing out, and went inside myself.

The interior was huge, vaultlike, and terribly silent at the end of the day. There were as many as five dozen slant-parking stalls, each equipped with its own bolted-down toolbox for do-it-yourselfers who had ailing cars but no tools. The ceiling overhead was high, and crossed with naked, gantrylike beams.

Signs were plastered everywhere: ALL TOOLS MUST BE INSPECTED BEFORE YOU LEAVE and MAKE APPOINTMENT FOR LIFT-TIME IN ADVANCE and MOTOR MANUALS ON FIRST-COME FIRST-SERVE BASIS and NO PROFANITY OR SWEARING WILL BE TOLERATED. Dozens of others; everywhere you turned, one seemed to jump right out at you. A big sign-man was Will Darnell.

"Stall twenty! Stall twenty!" Darnell yelled at Arnie in his irritable, wheezy voice. "Get it over there and shut it off before we all choke!"

"We all" seemed to be a group of men at an oversized cardtable in the far corner. Poker-chips, cards, and bottles of beer were scattered across the table. They were looking at Arnie's new acquisition with varying expressions of disgust and amusement.

Arnie drove across to stall twenty, parked it, and shut it off. Blue exhaust drifted in the huge, cavernous space.

Darnell turned to me. He was wearing a sail-like white shirt and brown khaki pants. Great rolls of fat bulged out his neck and hung in dewlaps from below his chin.

"Kiddo," he said in that same wheezing voice, "if you sold him that piece of shit, you ought to be ashamed of yourself."

"I didn't sell it to him." For some absurd reason I felt I had to justify myself before this fat slob in a way I wouldn't have done before my own father. "I tried to talk him out of it."

"You should have talked harder." He walked across to where Arnie was getting out of his car. He slammed the door; rust flaked down from the rocker panel on that side in a fine red shower.

Asthma or no asthma, Darnell walked with the graceful, almost feminine movements of a man who has been fat for a long time and sees a long future of fathood ahead of him. And he was yelling at Arnie before Arnie even got turned around, asthma or not. I guess you could say he was a man who hadn't let his infirmities get him down.

Like the kids in the smoking area at school, like Ralph on Basin Drive, like Buddy Repperton (we'll be talking about him all too soon, I'm afraid), he had taken an instant dislike to Arnie—it was a case of hate at first sight.

"Okay, that's the last time you run that mechanical asshole in here without the exhaust hose!" he yelled. "I catch you doin it, you're out, you understand?"

"Yes." Arnie looked small and tired and whipped. Whatever wild energy had carried him this far was gone now. It broke my heart a little to see him looking that way. "I—"

Darnell didn't let him get any further. "You want an exhaust hose, that's two-fifty an hour if you reserve in advance. And I'm telling you something else right now, and you want to take it to heart, my young friend. I don't take any shit from you kids. I don't have to. This place is for working guys that got to keep their cars running so they can put bread on the table, not for rich college kids who want to go out dragging on the Orange Belt. I don't allow no smoking in here. If you want a butt, you go outside in the junkyard."

"I don't sm—"

"Don't interrupt me, son. Don't interrupt me and don't get smart," Darnell said. Now he was standing in front of Arnie. Being both taller and wider, he blotted my friend out entirely.

I began to get angry again. I could actually feel my body

moan in protest at the yo-yo string my emotions had been on ever since we pulled up to LeBay's house and saw that the damned car wasn't on the lawn anymore.

Kids are a downtrodden class; after a few years you learn to do your own version of an Uncle Tom routine on kid-haters like Will Darnell. *Yessir, nosir, okay, you bet.* But, Jesus, he was laying it on thick.

I suddenly grabbed Darnell's arm. "Sir?"

He swung around on me. I find that the more I dislike adults, the more apt I am to call them Sir.

"What?"

"Those men over there are smoking. You better tell them to stop." I pointed to the guys at the poker table. They had dealt out a fresh hand. Smoke hung over the table in a blue haze.

Darnell looked at them, then back at me. His face was very solemn. "You trying to help your buddy right out of here, Junior?"

"No," I said. "Sir."

"Then shut your pie-hole."

He turned back to Arnie and put his meaty hands on his wide, well-padded hips.

"I know a creep when I see one," he said, "and I think I'm lookin at one right now. You're on probation, kid. You screw around with me just one time and it don't matter how much you paid up in front, I'll put you out on your ass."

Dull fury went up from my stomach to my head and made it throb. Inside I begged Arnie to tell this fat fuck to bore it and stroke it and then drive it straight up his old tan track just as fast and far as it would go. Of course then Darnell's poker buddies would get into it and we'd both probably end this enchanting evening at the emergency room of Liber-tyville Community Hospital getting our heads stitched up . . . but it would almost be worth it.

Arnie, I begged inside, *tell him to shove it and let's get out of here. Stand up to him, Arnie. Don't let him pull this shit on you. Don't be a loser, Arnie—if you can stand up to your mother, you can stand up to this happy asshole. Just this once, don't be a loser.*

Arnie stood silent for a long time, his head down, and then he said, "Yessir." The word was so low it was nearly inaudi-ble. It sounded as if he was choking on it.

"What did you say?"

Arnie looked up. His face was deadly pale. His eyes were swimming with tears. I couldn't look at that. It hurt me too bad to look at that. I turned away. The poker players had suspended their game to watch developments over at stall twenty.

"I said, 'Yessir,'" Arnie said in a trembling voice. It was as if he had just signed his name to some terrible confession. I looked at the car again, the '58 Plymouth, sitting in here when it should have been out back in the junkyard with the rest of Darnell's rotten plugs, and I hated it all over again for what it was doing to Arnie.

"Arright, get out of here," Darnell said. "We're closed."

Arnie stumbled away blindly. He would have walked right into a stack of old bald tires if I hadn't grabbed his arm and steered him away. Darnell went back the other way to the poker table. When he got there he said something to the others in his wheezy voice. They all roared laughter.

"I'm all right, Dennis," Arnie said, as if I had asked him. His teeth were locked together and his chest was heaving in quick, shallow breaths. "I'm all right, let go of me, I'm all right, I'm okay."

I let go of his arm. We walked across to the door and Darnell hollered at us, "And you ain't going to bring your hoodlum friends in here, or you're out!"

One of the others chimed, "And leave your dope at home!"

Arnie cringed. He was my friend, but I hated him when he cringed that way.

We escaped into the cool darkness. The door rattled down behind us. And that's how we got Christine to Darnell's Garage. Some great time, huh?

6 / Outside

I got me a car and I got me some gas,
Told everybody they could kiss my
    ass . . .

                      —Glenn Frey

We got into my car and I drove out of the yard. Somehow it had gotten around to past nine o'clock. How the time flies when you're having fun. A half-moon stood out in the sky. That and the orange lights in the acres of parking lot at the Monroeville Mall took care of any wishing stars there might have been.

We drove the first two or three blocks in utter silence, and then Arnie suddenly burst into a fury of weeping. I had thought he might cry, but the force of this frightened me. I pulled over immediately.

"Arnie—"

I gave up right there. He was going to do it until it was done. The tears and the sobs came in a shrill, bitter flood, and they came without restraint—Arnie had used up his quota of restraint for the day. At first it seemed to be nothing but reaction; I felt the same sort of thing myself, only mine had gone to my head, making it ache like a rotted tooth, and to my stomach, which was sickly clenched up.

So, yeah, at first I thought it was nothing but a reaction sort of thing, a spontaneous release, and maybe at first it was. But after a minute or two, I realized it was a lot more than that; it went a lot deeper than that And I began to get words out of the sounds he was making: just a few at first, then strings of them.

"*I'll get them!*" he shouted thickly through the sobs. "*I'll get those fucking sons of bitches I'll get them Dennis I'll make them sorry I'll make those fuckers eat it . . . EAT IT . . . EAT IT!*"

"Stop it," I said, scared. "Arnie, quit it."

But he wouldn't quit it. He began to slam his fists down on

55

the padded dashboard of my Duster, hard enough to make marks.

"I'll get them, you see if I don't!"

In the dim glow of the moon and a nearby streetlight, his face looked ravaged and haglike. He was like a stranger to me then. He was off walking in whatever cold places of the universe a fun-loving God reserves for people like him. I didn't know him. I didn't want to know him. I could only sit there helplessly and hope that the Arnie I did know would come back. After a while, he did.

The hysterical words disappeared into sobs again. The hate was gone and he was only crying. It was a deep, bawling, bewildered sound.

I sat there behind the wheel of my car, not sure what I should do, wishing I was someplace else, anyplace else, trying on shoes at Thom McAn's, filling out a credit application in a discount store, standing in front of a pay toilet stall with diarrhea and no dime. Anyplace, man. It didn't have to be Monte Carlo. Mostly I sat there wishing I was older. Wishing we were both older.

But that was a copout job. I knew what to do. Reluctantly, not wanting to, I slid across the seat and put my arms around him and held him. I could feel his face, hot and fevered, mashed against my chest. We sat that way for maybe five minutes, and then I drove him to his house and dropped him off. After that I went home myself. Neither of us talked about it later, me holding him like that. No one came along the sidewalk and saw us parked at the curb. I suppose if someone had, we would have looked like a couple of queers. I sat there and held him and loved him the best I could and wondered how come it had to be that I was Arnie Cunningham's only friend, because right then, believe me, I didn't want to be his friend.

Yet somehow—I realized it then, if only dimly—maybe Christine was going to be his friend now, too. I wasn't sure if I liked that either, although we had been through the same shit-factory on her behalf that long crazy day.

When we rolled up to the curb in front of his house I said, "You going to be all right, man?"

He managed a smile. "Yeah, I'll be okay." He looked at me sadly. "You know, you ought to find some other favorite charity. Heart Fund. Cancer Society. Something."

"Ahh, get out of here."

"You know what I mean."

"If you mean you're a wet end, you're not telling me anything I didn't know."

The front porch light came on, and both Michael and Regina came flying out, probably to see if it was us or the State Police come to inform them that their only chick and child had been run over on the highway.

"Arnold?" Regina called shrilly.

"Bug out, Dennis," Arnie said, grinning a little more honestly now. "This shit you don't need." He got out of the car and said dutifully, "Hi, Mom. Hi, Dad."

"Where have you been?" Michael asked. "You had your mother badly frightened, young man!"

Arnie was right. I could do without the reunion scene. I glanced back in the rearview mirror just briefly and saw him standing there, looking solitary and vulnerable—and then the two of them enfolded him and began shepherding him back to the $60,000 nest, no doubt turning the full force of all their latest parenting trips on him—Parent Effectiveness Training, est, who knows what else. They were so perfectly rational about it, that was the thing. They had played such a large part in what he was, and they were just too motherfucking (and fatherfucking) rational to see it.

I turned the radio on to FM-104, where the Block Party Weekend was continuing, and got Bob Seger and the Silver Bullet Band singing "Still the Same." The serendipity was just a little too hideously perfect, and I dialled away to the Phillies game.

The Phillies were losing. That was all right. That was par for the course.

7 / Bad Dreams

I'm a roadrunner, honey,
And you can't catch me.
Yes, I'm a roadrunner, honey,
And you can't keep up with me.
Come on over here and race,
Baby, baby, you'll see.
Move over, honey! Stand back!
I'm gonna put some dirt in your eye!
—Bo Diddley

When I got home, my dad and my sister were sitting in the kitchen eating brown-sugar sandwiches. I started feeling hungry right away and realized I'd never gotten any supper.

"Where you been, Boss?" Elaine asked, hardly looking up from her *16* or *Creem* or *Tiger Beat* or whatever it was. She had been calling me Boss ever since I discovered Bruce Springsteen the year before and became a fanatic. It was supposed to get under my skin.

At fourteen Elaine was beginning to leave her childhood behind and to turn into the full-fledged American beauty that she eventually became—tall, dark-haired, and blue-eyed. But in that late summer of 1978 she was the total teenaged crowd animal. She had begun with Donny and Marie at nine, then had gotten all moony for John Travolta at eleven (I made the mistake of calling him John Revolta one day and she scratched me so badly that I almost needed a stitch in my cheek—I supposed I deserved it, sort of). At twelve she was gone for Shaun. Then it was Andy Gibb. Just lately she had developed more ominous tastes: heavy-metal rockers like Deep Purple and a new group, Styx.

"I was helping Arnie get his car squared away," I said, as much to my father as to Ellie. More, really.

"That creep." Ellie sighed and turned the page of her magazine.

I felt a sudden and amazingly strong urge to rip the magazine out of her hands, tear it in two, and throw the pieces in

58

her face. That went further toward showing me exactly how stressful the day had been than anything else could have done. Elaine doesn't really think Arnie's a creep; she just takes every possible opportunity to get under my skin. But maybe I had heard Arnie called a creep too often over the last few hours. His tears were still drying on the front of my shirt, for Christ's sake, and maybe I felt a little bit creepy myself.

"What's Kiss doing these days, dear?" I asked her sweetly. "Written any love-letters to Erik Estrada lately? 'Oh, Erik, I'd die for you, I go into a total cardiac arrest every time I think of your thick, greasy lips squelching down on mine . . .' "

"You're an animal," she said coldly. "Just an animal, that's all you are."

"And I don't know any better."

"That's right." She picked up her magazine and her brown-sugar sandwich and flounced away into the living room.

"Don't you get that stuff on the floor, Ellie," Dad warned her, spoiling her exit a bit.

I went to the fridge and rummaged out some bologna and a tomato that didn't look as if it was working. There was also half a package of processed cheese, but wild overindulgence in that shit as a grade-schooler had apparently destroyed my craving for it. I settled for a quart of milk to go with my sandwich and opened a can of Campbell's Chunky Beef.

"Did he get it?" Dad asked me. My dad is a tax-consultant for H&R Block. He also does freelance tax work. In the old days he used to be a full-time accountant for the biggest architectural firm in Pittsburgh, but then he had a heart attack and got out. He's a good man.

"Yeah, he got it."

"Still look as bad to you as it did?"

"Worse. Where's Mom?"

"Her class," he said.

His eyes met mine, and we both almost got the giggles. We immediately looked away in separate directions, ashamed of ourselves—but even being honestly ashamed didn't seem to help much. My mom is forty-three and works as a dental hygienist. For a long time she didn't work at her trade, but after Dad had his heart attack, she went back.

Four years ago she decided she was an unsung writer. She began to produce poems about flowers and stories about sweet old men in the October of their years. Every now and then she would get grittily realistic and do a story about a young girl who was tempted "to take a chance" and then decided it would be immeasurably better if she Saved It for the Marriage Bed. This summer she had signed up for a directed writing course at Horlicks—where Michael and Regina Cunningham taught, you will remember—and was putting all her themes and stories in a book she called Sketches of Love and Beauty.

Now you could be saying to yourself (and more power to you if you are) that there is nothing funny about a woman who has managed to hold a job and also to raise her family deciding to try something new, to expand her horizons a little. And of course you'd be right. Also you could be saying to yourself that my father and I had every reason to be ashamed of ourselves, that we were nothing more than a couple of male sexist pigs oinking it up in our kitchen, and again you'd be perfectly right. I won't argue either point, although I will say that if you had been subjected to frequent oral readings from Sketches of Love and Beauty, as Dad and I—and also Elaine—had been, you might understand the source of the giggles a little better.

Well, she was and is a great mom, and I guess she is also a great wife for my father—at least I never heard him complain, and he's never stayed out all night drinking—and all I can say in our defense is that we never laughed to her face, either of us. That's pretty poor, I know, but at least it's better than nothing. Neither of us would have hurt her like that for the world.

I put a hand over my mouth and tried to squeeze the giggles off. Dad appeared to be momentarily choking on his bread and brown sugar. I don't know what he was thinking of, but what had lodged in my mind was a fairly recent essay titled "Did Jesus Have a Dog?"

On top of the rest of the day, it was nearly too much.

I went to the cabinets over the sink and got a glass for my milk, and when I looked back, my father had himself under control again. That helped me do likewise.

"You looked sort of glum when you came in," he said. "Is everything all right with Arnie, Dennis?"

"Arnie's cool," I said, dumping the soup into a saucepan and throwing it on the stove. "He just bought a car, and that's a mess, but Arnie's all right." Of course Arnie wasn't all right, but there are some things you can't bring yourself to tell your dad, no matter how well he's succeeding at the great American job of dadhood.

"Sometimes people can't see things until they see them for themselves," he said.

"Well," I said, "I hope he sees it soon. He's got the car at Darnell's for twenty a week because his folks didn't want him to park it at home."

"Twenty a week? For just a stall? Or a stall and tools?"

"Just a stall."

"That's highway robbery."

"Yeah," I said, noticing that my father didn't follow up that judgement with an offer that Arnie could park it at our place.

"You want to play a game of cribbage?"

"I guess so," I said

"Cheer up, Dennis. You can't make other people's mistakes for them."

"Yeah, really."

We played three or four games of cribbage, and he beat me every time—he almost always does, unless he's very tired or has had a couple of drinks. That's okay with me, though. The times that I do beat him mean more. We played cribbage, and after a while my mother came in, her color high and her eyes glowing, looking too young to be my mom, her book of stories and sketches clasped to her breasts. She kissed my father—not her usual brush, but a real kiss that made me feel all of a sudden like I should be someplace else.

She asked me the same stuff about Arnie and his car, which was fast becoming the biggest topic of conversation around the house since my mother's brother, Sid, went into bankruptcy and asked my dad for a loan. I went through the same song-and-dance. Then I went upstairs to bed. My ass was dragging, and it looked to me as if my mom and dad had business of their own to attend to . . . although that was a topic I never went into all that deeply in my mind, as I'm sure you'll understand.

Elaine was in on her bed, listening to the latest K-Tel comglomeration of hits. I asked her to turn it down because I was going to bed. She stuck out her tongue at me. No way I allow that kind of thing. I went in and tickled her until she said she was going to puke. I said go ahead and puke, it's your bed, and tickled her some more. Then she put on her "please don't kid me Dennis because this is something *terribly* important" expression and got all solemn and asked me if it

was really true you could light farts. One of her girlfriends,
Carolyn Shambliss, said it was, but Carolyn lied about almost *everything*

I told her to ask Milton Dodd, her dorky-looking
boyfriend Then Elaine really did get mad and tried to hit me
and asked me why do you always have to be so *awful*, Dennis? So I told her yes, it was true you could light farts, and
advised her not to try it, and then I gave her a hug (which I
rarely did anymore—it made me uncomfortable since she
started to get boobs, and so did the tickling, to tell the truth)
and then I went to bed.

And undressing. I thought, The day didn't end so bad, after all There are people around here who think I'm a human
being, and they think Arnie is, as well. I'll get him to come
over tomorrow or Sunday and we'll just hang out, watch the
Phillies on TV, maybe, or play some dumb board-game,
Careers or Life or maybe that old standby, Clue, and get rid
of the weirdness. Get feeling decent again.

So I went to bed with everything straight in my mind, and
I should have gone right to sleep, but I didn't. Because it
wasn't straight, and I knew it. Things get started, and sometimes you don't know what the hell they are.

Engines. That's something else about being a teenager.
There are all these engines, and somehow you end up with
the ignition keys to some of them and you start them up but
you don't know what the fuck they are or what they're supposed to do. There are clues, but that's all. The drug thing is
like that, and the booze thing, and the sex thing, and sometimes other stuff too—a summer job that generates a new interest, a trip, a course in school. Engines. They give you the
keys and some clues and they say, Start it up, see what it will
do, and sometimes what it does is pull you along into a life
that's really good and fulfilling, and sometimes what it does is
pull you right down the highway to hell and leave you all
mangled and bleeding by the roadside.

Engines.

Big ones. Like the 382s they used to put in those old cars.
Like Christine

I lay there in the dark, twisting and turning until the sheet
was pulled out and all balled up and messy, and I thought
about LeBay saying, *Her name is Christine.* And somehow,
Arnie had picked up on that. When we were little kids we had
had scooters and then bikes, and I named mine but Arnie
never named his—he said names were for dogs and cats and

guppies. But that was then and this was now. Now he was calling that Plymouth Christine, and, what was somehow worse, it was always "her" and "she" instead of "it."

I didn't like it, and I didn't know why.

And even my own father had spoken of it as if, instead of buying an old junker, Arnie had gotten married. But it wasn't like that. Not at all. Was it?

Stop the car, Dennis. Go back. . . . I want to look at her again.

Simple as that.

No consideration at all, and that wasn't like Arnie, who usually thought things out so carefully—his life had made him all too painfully aware of what happened to guys like him when they went off half-cocked and did something (gasp!) on impulse. But this time he had been like a man who meets a showgirl, indulges in a whirlwind courtship, and ends up with a hangover and a new wife on Monday morning.

It had been . . . well . . . like love at first sight.

Never mind, I thought. We'll start over again. Tomorrow we'll start over. We'll get some perspective on this.

And so finally I went to sleep. And dreamed.

The whining spin of a starter in darkness.

Silence.

The starter, whining again.

The engine fired, missed, then caught.

An engine running in darkness.

Then headlights came on, high beams, old-fashioned twin beams, spearing me like a bug on glass.

I was standing in the open doorway of Roland D. LeBay's garage, and Christine sat inside—a new Christine with not a dent or a speck of rust on her. The clean, unblemished windshield darkened to a polarized blue strip at the top. From the radio came the hard rhythmic sounds of Dale Hawkins doing "Susie-Q"—a voice from a dead age, full of somehow frightening vitality.

The motor muttering words of power through dual glass-pack mufflers. And somehow I knew there was a Hurst shifter inside, and Feully headers; the Quaker State oil had just been changed—it was a clean amber color, automotive lifeblood.

The wipers suddenly start up, and that's strange because there's no one behind the wheel, the car is empty.

—Come on, big guy. Let's go for a ride. Let's cruise.

I shake my head. I don't want to get in there. I'm scared to get in there. I don't want to cruise. And suddenly the engine begins to rev and fall off, rev and fall off; it's a hungry sound, frightening, and each time the engine revs Christine seems to lunge forward a bit, like a mean dog on a weak leash . . . and I want to move . . . but my feet seem nailed to the cracked pavement of the driveway.

—Last chance, big guy.

And before I can answer—or even think of an answer— there is the terrible scream of rubber kissing off concrete and Christine lunges out at me, her grille snarling like an open mouth full of chrome teeth, her headlights glaring—

I screamed myself awake in the dead darkness of two in the morning, the sound of my own voice scaring me, the hurried, running thud of bare feet coming down the hall scaring me even worse. I had double handfuls of sheet in both hands. I'd pulled the sheet right out; it was all wadded up in the middle of the bed. My body was sweat-slippery.

Down the hall, Ellie cried out "What was that?" in her own terror.

My light flooded on and there was my mom in a shorty nightgown that showed more than she would have allowed except in the direst of emergencies, and right behind her, my dad, belting his bathrobe closed over nothing at all.

"Honey, what is it?" my mom asked me. Her eyes were wide and scared. I couldn't remember the last time she had called me "honey" like that—when I was fourteen? twelve? ten, maybe? I don't know.

"Dennis?" Dad asked.

Then Elaine was standing behind and between them, shivering.

"Go back to bed," I said. "It was a dream, that's all. Nothing."

"Wow," Elaine said, shocked into respect by the hour and the occasion. "Must have been a real horror-movie. What was it, Dennis?"

"I dreamed that you married Milton Dodd and then came to live with me," I said.

"Don't tease your sister," Mom said. "What was it, Dennis?"

"I don't remember," I said.

I was suddenly aware that the sheet was a mess, and there

was a dark tuft of pubic hair poking out. I rearranged things in a hurry, with guilty thoughts of masturbation, wet dreams, God knows what else shooting through my head. Total dislocation. For the first spinning moment or two, I hadn't even been sure if I was big or little—there was only that dark, terrifying, and overmastering image of the car lunging forward a little each time the engine revved, dropping back, lunging forward again, the hood vibrating over the engine-bucket, the grille like steel teeth—

Last chance, big guy.

Then my mother's hand, cool and dry, was on my forehead, hunting fever.

"It's all right, Mom," I said. "It was nothing. Just a nightmare."

"But you don't remember—"

"No. It's gone now."

"I was scared," she said, and then uttered a shaky little laugh. "I guess you don't know what scared is until one of your kids screams in the dark."

"Ugh, gross, don't talk about it," Elaine said.

"Go back to bed, little one," Dad said, and gave her butt a light swat.

She went, not looking totally happy about it. Maybe once she was over her own initial fright, she was hoping I'd break down and have hysterics. That would have given her a real scoop with the training bra set down at the rec program in the morning.

"You really okay?" my mother asked. "Dennis? Hon?"

That word again, bringing back memories of knees scraped falling out of my red wagon; her face, lingering over my bed as it had while I lay in the feverish throes of all those childhood illnesses—mumps, measles, a bout of scarletina. Making me feel absurdly like crying. I had nine inches and seventy pounds on her.

"Sure," I said.

"All right," she said. "Leave the light on. Sometimes it helps."

And with a final doubtful look at my dad, she went out. I had something to be bemused about—the idea that my mother had ever had a nightmare. One of those things that never occur to you, I guess. Whatever her nightmares were, none of them had ever found their way into *Sketches of Love and Beauty.*

My dad sat down on the bed. "You really don't remember what it was about?"

I shook my head.

"Must have been bad, to make you yell like that, Dennis." His eyes were on mine, gravely asking if there was something he should know.

I almost told him—the car, it was Arnie's goddam car, Christine the Rust Queen, twenty years old, ugly fucking thing. I almost told him. But then somehow it choked in my throat, almost as if to speak would have been to betray my friend. Good old Arnie, whom a fun-loving God had decided to swat with the ugly-stick.

"All right," he said, and kissed my cheek. I could feel his beard, those stiff little bristles that only come out at night, I could smell his sweat and feel his love. I hugged him hard, and he hugged me back.

Then they were all gone, and I lay there with the bedtable lamp burning, afraid to go back to sleep. I got a book and lay back down, knowing that my folks were lying awake downstairs in their room, wondering if I was in some kind of a mess, or if I had gotten someone else—the cheerleader with the fantastic body, maybe—in some kind of a mess.

I decided sleep was an impossibility. I would read until daylight and catch a nap tomorrow afternoon, maybe, during the dull part of the ballgame. And thinking that, I fell asleep and woke up in the morning with the book lying unopened on the floor beside the bed.

8 / First Changes

If I had money I will tell you
*   what I'd do,*
I would go downtown and buy
*   a Mercury or two,*
I would buy me a Mercury,
And cruise up and down this road.
                    —The Steve Miller Band

I thought Arnie would turn up that Saturday, so I hung around the house—mowed the lawn, cleaned up the garage, even washed all three cars. My mother watched all this industry with some amazement and commented over a lunch of hotdogs and green salad that maybe I should have nightmares more often.

I didn't want to phone Arnie's house, not after all the unpleasantness I had seen there lately, but when the pre-game show came on and he still hadn't shown, I took my courage in my hands and called. Regina answered, and although she was doing a good facsimile of nothing-has-changed, I thought I detected a new coolness in her voice. It made me feel sad. Her only son had been seduced by a baggy old whore named Christine, and old buddy Dennis must have been an accomplice. Maybe he had even pimped the deal. Arnie wasn't home, she said. He was at Darnell's Garage. He had been there since nine that morning.

"Oh," I said lamely. "Oh, wow. I didn't know that." It sounded like a lie. Even more, it *felt* like a lie.

"No?" Regina said in that new cool way. "Goodbye, Dennis."

The phone was dead in my hand. I looked at it awhile and then hung up.

Dad was parked in front of the TV in his gross purple Bermudas and his Jesus-shoes, a six-pack of Stroh's crashed down in the cooler beside him. The Phillies were having a good day, belting the almighty hell out of Atlanta. My mom had gone out to visit one of her classmates (I think they read

67

each other their sketches and poems and got exalted together). Elaine had gone over to her friend Della's house.
Our place was quiet; outside, the sun played tag with a few
benign white clouds. Dad gave me a beer, which he does only
when he's feeling extraordinarily mellow.

But Saturday still felt flat. I kept thinking of Arnie, not
watching the Phillies or soaking up the rays, not even
mowing the grass over at his house and getting his feet green.
Arnie in the oily shadows of Will Darnell's Do-It-Yourself
Garage, playing games with that silent, rusting hulk while
men shouted and tools clanged on the cement with that
piercing white-metal sound, the machine-gun drill of pneumatic guns loosening old bolts, Will Darnell's wheezy voice
and asthmatic cough—

And goddammit, was I *jealous?* Was that what it was?

When the seventh inning came along I got up and started
to go out.

"Where you going?" my dad asked.

Yeah, just where was I going? Down there? To watch him,
cluck over him, listen to Will Darnell get on his case? Heading for another dose of misery? Fuck it. Arnie was a big boy
now.

"Noplace," I said. I found a Twinkie tucked carefully
away in the back of the breadbox and took it with a certain
doleful glee, knowing how pissed Elaine was going to be
when she shlepped out during one of the commercials on *Saturday Night Live* and found it gone. "Noplace at all."

I came back into the living room and sat down and cadged
another beer off my dad and ate Elaine's Twinkie and even
lapped the cardboard it had been on. We watched Philly finish the job of ruining Atlanta ("They roont em, Denny," I
could hear my grandfather, now five years dead, saying in his
cackly old man's voice, "they roont em good!") and didn't
think about Arnie Cunningham at all.

Hardly at all.

He came over on his tacky old three-speed the next afternoon while Elaine and I were playing croquet on the back
lawn. Elaine kept accusing me of cheating. She was on one of
her rips. Elaine always went on "rips" when she was "getting
her period." Elaine was very proud of her period. She had
been having one regularly all of fourteen months.

"Hey," Arnie said, ambling around the corner of the

house, "it's either the Creature from the Black Lagoon and the Bride of Frankenstein or Dennis and Ellie."

"What do you say, man?" I asked. "Grab a mallet."

"I'm not playing," Elaine said, throwing her mallet down. "He cheats even worse than you do. *Men!*"

As she stalked off, Arnie said in a trembling affected voice. "That's the first time she ever called me a man, Dennis."

He fell to his knees, a look of exalted adoration on his face. I started laughing. He could do it good when he wanted to, Arnie could. That was one of the reasons I liked him as well as I did. And it was a kind of secret thing, you know. I don't think anyone really saw that wit except me. I once heard about some millionaire who had a stolen Rembrandt in his basement where no one but him could see it. I could understand that guy. I don't mean that Arnie was a Rembrandt, or even a world-class wit, but I could understand the attraction of knowing about something good . . . something that was good but still a secret.

We goofed around the croquet course for a while, not really playing, just whopping the Jesus out of each other's balls. Finally one went through the hedge into the Blackfords' yard, and after I crawled through to get it, neither of us wanted to play anymore. We sat down in the lawn chairs. Pretty soon our cat, Screaming Jay Hawkins, Captain Beefheart's replacement, came creeping out from under the porch, probably hoping to find some cute little chipmunk to murder slowly and nastily. His amber-green eyes glinted in the afternoon light, which was overcast and muted.

"Thought you'd be over for the game yesterday," I said. "It was a good one."

"I was at Darnell's," he said. "Heard it on the radio, though." His voice went up three octaves and he did a very good imitation of my granddad. "They roont em! They roont em, Denny!"

I laughed and nodded. There was something about him that day—perhaps it was only the light, which was bright enough but still somehow gloomy and spare—something that looked different. He looked tired, for one thing—there were circles under his eyes—but at the same time his complexion seemed a trifle better than it had been lately. He had been drinking a lot of Cokes on the job, knowing he shouldn't, of course, but unable to help succumbing to temptation from time to time. His skin problems tended to go in cycles, as most teenagers' do, depending on their moods—except in Arnie's case, the cycles were usually from bad to worse and back to bad again.

Or maybe it was just the light.

"What'd you do on it?" I asked.

"Not much. Changed the oil. Looked the block over. It's not cracked, Dennis, that's one thing. LeBay or somebody left the drain-plug out somewhere along the line, that's all. A lot of the old oil had leaked out. I was lucky not to fry a piston driving it Friday night."

"How'd you get lift-time? I thought you had to reserve that in advance."

His eyes shifted away from mine. "No problem there," he said, but there was deception in his voice. "I ran a couple of errands for Mr. Darnell."

I opened my mouth to ask what errands, and then I decided I didn't want to hear. Probably the "couple of errands" boiled down to no more than running around the corner to Schirmer's Luncheonette and bringing back coffee-and for the regulars or crating up various used auto parts for later sale, but I didn't want to be involved in the Christine end of Arnie's life, and that included how he was getting along (or not getting along) down at Darnell's Garage.

And there was something else—a feeling of letting go. I either couldn't define that feeling very well back then or didn't want to. Now I guess I'd say it's the way you feel when a friend of yours falls in love and marries a right high-riding, dyed-in-the-wool bitch. You don't like the bitch and in ninety-nine cases out of a hundred the bitch doesn't like you, so you just close the door on that room of your friendship. When the thing is done, you either let go of the subject . . . or you find your friend letting go of you, usually with the bitch's enthusiastic approval.

"Let's go to the movies," Arnie said restlessly.

"What's on?"

"Well, there's one of those gross Kung-fu movies down at the State Twin, how does that sound? *Heee-yah!*" He pretended to administer a savage karate kick to Screaming Jay Hawkins, and Screaming Jay took off like a shot.

"Sounds pretty good. Bruce Lee?"

"Nah, some other guy."

"What's it called?"

"I don't know. Fists of Danger. Flying Hands of Death. Or maybe it was Genitals of Fury, I don't know. What do you say? We can come back and tell the gross parts to Ellie and make her puke."

"All right," I said. "If we can still get in for a buck each."

"Yeah, we can until three."

"Let's go."

We went. It turned out to be a Chuck Norris movie, not bad at all. And on Monday we went back to building the Interstate extension. I forgot about my dream. Gradually I realized that I wasn't seeing as much of Arnie as I used to; again, it was the way you seem to fall out of touch with a guy who has just gotten married. Besides, my thing with the cheerleader began to heat up around then. My thing was heating up, all right—more than one night I brought her home from the submarine races at the drive-in with my balls throbbing so badly I could barely walk.

Arnie, meanwhile, was spending most of his evenings at Darnell's.

9 / Buddy Repperton

And I know, no matter what the cost,
Oooooh, that dual exhaust
Makes my motor cry,
My baby's got the Cadillac Walk.
                                        —Moon Martin

Our last full week of work before school started was the week before Labor Day. When I pulled up to Arnie's house to pick him up that morning, he came out with a great big blue-black shiner around one eye and an ugly scrape upside his face.

"What happened to you?"

"I don't want to talk about it," he said sullenly. "I had to talk to my parents about it until I thought I was gonna croak." He tossed his lunch pail in back and lapsed into a grim silence that lasted all the way to work. Some of the other guys ribbed him about his shiner, but Arnie just shrugged it off.

I didn't say anything about it on the way home, just played

the radio and kept myself to myself. And I might not have heard the story at all if I hadn't been waylaid by this greasy Irish wop named Gino just before we turned off Main Street.

Back then Gino was always waylaying me—he could reach right through a closed car window and do it. Gino's Fine Italian Pizza is on the corner of Main and Basin Drive, and every time I saw that sign with the pizza going up in the air and all the i's dotted with shamrocks (it flashed off and on at night, how funky can you get, am I right?), I'd feel the waylaying start again. And tonight my mother would be in class, which meant a pick-up supper at home. The prospect didn't fill me with joy. Neither my dad nor I was much of a cook, and Ellie would burn water.

"Let's get a pizza," I said, pulling into Gino's parking lot. "What do you say? A big greasy one that smells like armpits."

"Jesus, Dennis, that's gross!"

"*Clean* armpits," I amended. "Come on."

"Nah, I'm pretty low on cash," Arnie said listlessly.

"I'll buy. You can even have those horrible fucking anchovies on your half. What do you say?"

"Dennis, I really don't—"

"And a Pepsi," I said.

"Pepsi racks my complexion. You know that."

"Yeah, I know. A great *big* Pepsi, Arnie."

His gray eyes gleamed for the first time that day. "A great *big* Pepsi," he echoed. "Think of that. You're mean, Dennis. Really."

"Two, if you want," I said. It was mean, all right—like offering Hershey bars to the circus fat lady.

"Two." he said, clutching my shoulder. "Two Pepsis, Dennis!" He began to flop around in the seat, clawing at his throat and screaming, "Two! Quick! Two! Quick!"

I was laughing so hard I almost drove into the cinderblock wall, and as we got out of the car, I thought, Why shouldn't he have a couple of sodas? He sure must have been steering clear of them lately. The slight improvement in his complexion I'd noticed on that overcast Sunday two weeks ago was definite now. He still had plenty of bumps and craters, but not so many of them were—pardon me, but I must say it—oozing. He looked better in other ways too. A summer of road-ganging had left him deeply tanned and in better shape than he'd ever been in his life. So I thought he deserved his Pepsi. To the victor goes the spoils.

Gino's is run by a wonderful Italian fellow named Pat Donahue. He has a sticker on his cash register which reads IRISH MAFIA, he serves green beer on St. Patrick's Day (on March 17 you can't even get near Gino's, and one of the cuts on the jukebox is Rosemary Clooney singing "When Irish Eyes Are Smiling"), and affects a black derby hat, which he usually wears tipped far back on his head.

The juke is an old Wurlitzer bubbler, a holdover from the late forties, and all the records—not just Rosemary Clooney—are on the Prehistoric label. It may be the last jukebox in America where you get three plays for a quarter. On the infrequent occasions when I smoke a little dope, it's Gino's I fantasize about—just walking in there and ordering three loaded pizzas, a quart of Pepsi, and six or seven of Pat Donahue's home-made fudge brownies. Then I imagine just sitting down and scarfing everything up while a steady stream of Beach Boys and Rolling Stones hits pours out of that juke.

We went in, ordered up, and sat there watching the three pizza cooks fling the dough into the air and catch it. They were trading such pungent Italian witticisms as, "I seenya at the Shriners' dance last night, Howie, who was that skag your brother was wit?" "Oh, *her?* That was your sister."

I mean, like, how Old World can you get?

People came in and went out, a lot of them kids from school. Before long I'd be seeing them in the halls again, and I felt a recurrence of that fierce nostalgia-in-advance and that sense of fright In my head I could hear the home-room bell going off, but somehow its long bray sounded like an alarm: *Here we go again, Dennis, last time, after this year you got to learn how to be a grown-up.* I could hear locker doors crashing closed, could hear the steady *ka-chonk, ka-chonk, ka-chonk* of linemen hitting the tackling dummies, could hear Marty Bellerman yelling exuberantly, "My ass and your face, Pedersen! Remember that! My ass and your face! It's easier to tell the fuckin Bobbsey Twins apart!" The dry smell of chalk dust in the classrooms in the Math Wing. The sound of the typewriters from the big secretarial classrooms on the second floor. Mr. Meecham, the principal, giving the announcements at the end of the day in his dry, fussy voice. Lunch outdoors on the bleachers in good weather. A new crop of freshmen looking dorky and lost. And at the end of it all, you march down the aisle in this big purple bathrobe, and that's it. High school's over. You are released on an unsuspecting world.

"Dennis, do you know Buddy Repperton?" Arnie asked, pulling me out of my reverie. Our pizza had come.

"Buddy who?"

"Repperton."

The name was familiar. I worked on my side of the pizza and tried to put a face with it. After a while, it came. I had had a run-in with him when I was one of the dorky little freshmen. It happened at a mixer dance. The band was taking a break and I was waiting in the cold-drink line to get a soda. Repperton gave me a shove and told me freshmen had to wait until all the upperclassmen got drinks. He had been a sophomore then, a big, hulking, mean sophomore. He had a lantern jaw, a thick clot of greasy black hair, and little eyes set too close together. But those eyes were not entirely stupid; an unpleasant intelligence lurked in them. He was one of those guys who spend their high school time majoring in Smoking Area

I had advanced the heretical opinion that class seniority didn't mean anything in the refreshment line. Repperton invited me to come outside with him. By then the cold-drink line had broken up and rearranged itself into one of those cautious but eager little circles that so often presage a scuffle. One of the chaperones came along and broke it up. Repperton promised he would get me, but he never did. And that had been my only contact with him, except for seeing his name every now and then on the detention list that circulated to the home rooms at the end of the day. It seemed to me that he'd been dismissed from school a couple of times, too, and when that happened it was usually a pretty good sign that the guy wasn't in the Young Christian League.

I told Arnie about my one experience with Repperton, and he nodded wearily. He touched the shiner, which was now turning a gruesome lemon color. "He was the one."

"Repperton messed up your face?"

"Yeah."

Arnie told me he knew Repperton from the auto-shop courses. One of the ironies of Arnie's rather hunted and certainly unhappy school life was that his interests and abilities took him into direct contact with the sort of people who feel it is their appointed duty to kick the stuffing out of the Arnie Cunninghams of this world.

When Arnie was a sophomore and taking a course called Engine Fundamentals (which used to be plain old Auto Shop I before the school got a whole bunch of vocational training

money from the Federal government), a kid named Roger
Gilman beat the living shit out of him. That's pretty fucking
vulgar, I know, but there's just no fancy, elegant way to put
it. Gilman just beat the living shit out of Arnie. The beating
was bad enough to keep Arnie out of school for a couple of
days, and Gilman got a one-week vacation, courtesy of the
management. Gilman was now in prison on a hijacking
charge. Buddy Repperton had been part of Roger Gilman's
circle of friends and had more or less inherited leadership of
Gilman's group.

For Arnie, going to class in the shop area was like visiting
a demilitarized zone. Then, if he got back alive after period
seven, he'd run all the way to the other end of the school
with his chessboard and men under his arm for a chess club
meeting or a game.

I remember going to a city chess tourney in Squirrel Hill
one day the year before and seeing something which, to me,
symbolized my friend's schizo school life. There he was,
hunched gravely over his board in the thick, carved silence
which is mostly what you hear at such affairs. After a long,
thoughtful pause, he moved a rook with a hand into which
grease and motor-oil had been so deeply grimed that not even
Boraxo would take it all out.

Of course not all the shoppies were out to get him; there
were plenty of good kids down that way, but a lot of them
were either into their own tight circles of friends or permanently stoned. The ones in the tight little cliques were usually from the poorer section of Libertyville (and don't ever
let anyone tell you high school students aren't tracked according to what part of town they come from; they are),
very serious and so quiet you might make the mistake of dismissing them as stupid. Most of them looked like leftovers
from 1968 with their long hair tied back in ponytails and
their jeans and their tie-dyed T-shirts, but in 1978 none of
these guys wanted to overthrow the government; they wanted
to grow up to be Mr. Goodwrench.

And shop is still the final stopping place for the misfits and
hardasses who aren't so much attending school as they are
being incarcerated there. And now that Arnie brought up
Repperton's name, I could think of several guys who circled
him like a planetary system. Most of them were twenty and
still struggling to get out of school. Don Vandenberg, Sandy
Galton, Moochie Welch. Moochie's real name was Peter, but

the kids all called him Moochie because you always saw him outside of the rock concerts in Pittsburgh, spare-changing.

Buddy Repperton had come by a two-year-old blue Camaro that had been rolled over a couple of times out on Route 46 near Squantic Hills State Park—he picked it up from one of Darnell's poker buddies, Arnie said. The engine was okay, but the body had really taken chong from the tong in the rollover. Repperton brought it into Darnell's about a week after Arnie brought Christine in, although Buddy had been hanging around even before then.

For the first couple of days, Repperton hadn't appeared to notice Arnie at all, and Arnie, of course, was just as happy not to be noticed. Repperton was on good terms with Darnell, though. He seemed to have no trouble obtaining high-demand tools that were usually only available on a reserve basis.

Then Repperton had started getting on Arnie's case. He'd walk by on his way back from the Coke machine or the bathroom and knock a boxful of balljoint wrench attachments that Arnie was using all over the floor in Arnie's stall. Or if Arnie had a coffee on his shelf, Repperton would manage to hit it with his elbow and spill it. Then he'd bugle "Well ex-cuuuuuse . . . ME!" like Steve Martin, with this big shit-eating grin on his face. Darnell would holler over for Arnie to pick up those attachments before one of them went down through a drain in the floor or something.

Soon Repperton was swerving out of his way to give Arnie a whistling clap on the back, accompanied by a bellowed "How ya doin, Cuntface?"

Arnie bore these opening salvos with the stoicism of a guy who has seen it all before, been through it all before. He was probably hoping for one of two things—either that the harassment would reach a constant level of annoyance and stop there, or that Buddy Repperton would find some other victim and move on. There was a third possibility as well, one almost too good to hope for—it was always possible that Buddy would get righteously busted for something and just disappear from the scene, like his old buddy Roger Gilman.

It had come to blows on the Saturday afternoon just past. Arnie was doing a grease-job on his car, mostly because he hadn't yet accumulated sufficient funds to do any of the hundred other things the car cried out for. Repperton came by, whistling cheerfully, a Coke and a bag of peanuts in one hand, a jackhandle in the other. And as he passed stall twenty, he whipped the jackhandle out sidearm and broke one of Christine's headlights.

"Smashed it to shit," Arnie told me over our pizza.

"Oh, jeez, lookit what I did!" Buddy Repperton had said, an exaggerated expression of tragedy on his face. "Well ex-cuuuuuu—"

But that was all he got out. The attack on Christine managed what the attacks on Arnie himself hadn't been able to do—it provoked him into retaliation. He came around the side of the Plymouth, hands balled into fists, and struck out blindly. In a book or a movie, he probably would have socked Repperton right on the old knockout button and put him on the floor for a ten-count.

Things rarely work out that way in real life. Arnie didn't get anywhere near Repperton's chin. Instead he hit Repperton's hand, knocked the bag of peanuts on the floor, and spilled Coca-Cola all over Repperton's face and shirt.

"All right, you fucking little prick!" Repperton cried. He looked almost comically stunned. "There goes your ass!" He came for Arnie with the jackhandle.

Several of the other men ran over then, and one of them told Repperton to drop the jackhandle and fight fair. Repperton threw it away and waded in.

"Darnell never tried to put a stop to it?" I asked Arnie.

"He wasn't there, Dennis. He disappeared fifteen minutes or half an hour before it started. It's like he *knew* it was going to happen." Arnie said that Repperton had done most of the damage right away. The black eye was first; the scrape on his face (made by the class ring Repperton had purchased during one of his many sophomore years) came directly afterward. "Plus assorted other bruises," he said.

"What other bruises?"

We were sitting in one of the back booths. Arnie glanced around to make sure no one was looking at us and then raised his T-shirt. I hissed in breath at what I saw. A terrific sunset of bruises—yellow, red, purple, brown—covered Arnie's chest and stomach. They were just starting to fade. How he had been able to come to work after getting mashed around like that I couldn't begin to understand.

"Man, are you sure he didn't spring any of your ribs?" I asked. I was really horrified. The shiner and the scrape looked tame next to this shit. I had seen high school scuffles, of course, had even been in a few, but I was looking at the results of a serious beating for the first time in my life.

"Pretty sure," he said levelly. "I was lucky."

"I guess you were."

Arnie didn't say a lot more, but a kid I knew named Randy Turner was there, and he filled me in on what had happened in more detail after school had started again. He said that Arnie might have gotten hurt a lot worse, but he came back at Buddy a lot harder and a lot madder than Buddy had expected.

In fact, Randy said, Arnie went after Buddy Repperton as if the devil had blown a charge of red pepper up his ass. His arms were windmilling, his fists were everywhere. He was yelling, cursing, spraying spittle. I tried to picture it and couldn't—the picture I kept coming up with instead was Arnie slamming his fists down on my dashboard hard enough to make dents, screaming that he would make them eat it.

He drove Repperton halfway across the garage, bloodied his nose (more by good luck than good aim), and got one to Repperton's throat that made him start to cough and gag and generally lose interest in busting Arnie Cunningham's ass.

Buddy turned away, holding his throat and trying to puke, and Arnie drove one of his steel-toed workboots into Repperton's jeans-clad butt, knocking him flat on his belly and forearms. Repperton was still gagging and holding his throat with one hand, his nose was bleeding like mad, and (again, according to Randy Turner) Arnie was apparently gearing up to kick the son of a bitch to death when Will Darnell magically reappeared, hollering in his wheezy voice to cut the shit over there, cut the shit, cut the *shit*.

"Arnie thought that fight was going to happen," I told Randy. "He thought it was a put-up job."

Randy shrugged. "Maybe. Could be. It sure was funny, the way Darnell showed up when Repperton really started to lose."

About seven guys grabbed Arnie and dragged him away. At first he fought them like a wildman, screaming for them to let him go, screaming that if Repperton didn't pay for the broken headlight he'd kill him. Then he subsided, bewildered and hardly aware how it had happend that Repperton was down and he was still on his feet.

Repperton finally got up, his white T-shirt smeared with dirt and grease, his nose still bubbling blood. He made a lunge for Arnie. Randy said it looked like a pretty half-hearted lunge, mostly for form's sake. Some of the other guys got hold of him and led him away. Darnell came over to Arnie and told him to hand in his toolbox key and get out.

"Jesus, Arnie! Why didn't you call me Saturday afternoon?"

He sighed. "I was too depressed."

We finished our pizza, and I bought Arnie a third Pepsi. That stuff's murder on your complexion, but it's great for depression.

"I don't know if he meant get out just for Saturday or from then on," Arnie said to me on our way home. "What do you think, Dennis? You think he kicked me out for good?"

"He asked for your toolbox key, you said."

"Yeah. Yeah, he did. I never got kicked out of *anyplace* before." He looked like he was going to cry.

"That place bites the root anyway. Will Darnell's an asshole."

"I guess it would be stupid to try and keep it there anymore anyway," he said. "Even if Darnell lets me come back, Repperton's there. I'd fight him again—"

I started to hum the theme from *Rocky*.

"Yeah, fuck you and the cayuse you rode in on, Range Rider," he said, smiling a little. "I really *would* fight him. But Repperton might take after her with that jackhandle again when I wasn't there. I don't think Darnell would stop him if he did."

I didn't answer, and maybe Arnie thought that meant I agreed with him, but I didn't. I didn't think his old rustbucket Plymouth Fury was the main target. And if Repperton felt that he couldn't accomplish the demolition of the main target by himself, he would simply get by with a little help from his friends—Don Vandenberg, Moochie Welch, *et al.* Get on your motorhuckle boots, boys, we got plenty good stompin tonight.

It occurred to me that they could kill him. Not just kill him but really, honest-to-Christ *kill* him. Guys like that sometimes did. Things just went a little too far and some kid wound up dead. You read about it in the paper sometimes.

"—keep her?"

"Huh?" I hadn't followed that. Up ahead, Arnie's house was in view.

"I asked if you had any ideas about where I could keep her."

The car, the car, the car, that's all he could talk about. He was starting to sound like a broken record. And, worse, it was always her, her, her. He was bright enough to see his growing obsession with her—*it*, damn it, *it*—but he wasn't picking it up. He wasn't picking it up at all.

"Arnie," I said. "My man. You've got more important things to worry about than where to keep the car. I want to know where you're going to keep *you*."

"Huh? What are you talking about?"

"I'm asking you what you're going to do if Buddy and Buddy's buddies decide they want to put you in traction."

His face suddenly grew wise—it grew wise so suddenly that it was frightening to watch. It was wise and helpless and enduring. It was a face I recognized from the news when I was only eight or nine or so, the face of all those soldiers in black pajamas who had kicked the living shit out of the best-equipped and best-supported army in the world.

"Dennis," he said, "I'll do what I can."

10 / LeBay Passes

*I've Got No Car And It's Breaking My Heart
But I've Found A Driver And That's A Start ...*
—Lennon and McCartney

The movie version of *Grease* had just opened, and I took the cheerleader out to see it that night. I thought it was dumb. The cheerleader loved it. I sat there, watching those totally unreal teenagers dance and sing (if I want *realistic* teenagers—well, more or less—I'll catch *The Blackboard Jungle* sometime on a revival), and my mind just drifted away. And suddenly I had a brainstorm, the way you sometimes will when you're not thinking about anything in particular.

I excused myself and went into the lobby to use the payphone. I called Arnie's house, dialling quick and sure. I'd had his number memorized since I was eight or so. It could have waited until the movie was over, but it just seemed like such a damned good idea.

Arnie himself answered. "Hello?"

"Arnie, it's Dennis."

"Oh, Dennis."

His voice was so odd and flat that I got a little scared. "Arnie? Are you all right?"

"Huh? Sure. I thought you were taking Roseanne to the movies."

"That's where I'm calling from."

"It must not be that exciting," Arnie said. His voice was still flat—flat and dreary.

"Roseanne thinks it's great."

I thought that would get a laugh out of him, but there was only a patient, waiting silence.

"Listen," I said, "I thought of the answer."

"Answer?"

"Sure," I said. "LeBay. LeBay's the answer."

"Le—" he said in a strange, high voice . . . and then there was more silence. I was starting to get more than a little scared. I'd never known him to be quite this way.

"Sure," I babbled. "LeBay. LeBay's got a garage, and I got the idea that he'd eat a dead-rat sandwich if the profit margin looked high enough. If you were to approach him on the basis of, say, sixteen or seventeen bucks a week—"

"Very funny, Dennis." His voice was cold and hateful.

"Arnie, what—"

He hung up.

I stood there, looking at the phone, wondering what the hell it was about. Some new move from his parents? Or had he maybe gone back to Darnell's and found some new damage to his car? Or—

A sudden intuition—almost a certainty—struck me. I put the telephone back in its cradle and walked over to the concession stand and asked if they had today's paper. The candy-and-popcorn girl finally fished it out and then stood there snapping her gum while I thumbed to the back, where they print the obituaries. I guess she wanted to make sure I wasn't going to perform some weird perversion on it, or maybe eat it.

There was nothing at all—or so I thought at first. Then I turned the page and saw the headline. LIBERTYVILLE VETERAN DIES AT 71. There was a picture of Roland D. LeBay in his Army uniform, looking twenty years younger and considerably more bright-eyed than he had on the occasions Arnie and I had seen him. The obit was brief. LeBay had died suddenly on Saturday afternoon. He was survived by a brother,

George, and a sister, Marcia. Funeral services were scheduled for Tuesday at two.

Suddenly.

In the obits, it's always "after a long illness," "after a short illness," or "suddenly." Suddenly can mean anything from a brain embolism to electrocuting yourself in the bathtub. I remembered something I had done to Ellie when she was hardly more than a baby—three, maybe. I scared the bejesus out of her with a Jack-in-the-box. There was the little handle going around in big brother Dennis's hand, making music. Not bad. Kind of fun. And then—*ka-BONZO!* Out comes this guy with a grinning face and an ugly hooked nose, almost hitting her in the eye. Ellie went off bawling to find her mother and I sat there, looking glumly at Jack as he nodded back and forth, knowing I was probably going to get hollered at, knowing that I probably *deserved* to get hollered at—I had known it was going to scare her, coming out of the music like that, all at once, with an ugly bang.

Coming out so suddenly.

I gave the paper back and stood there, looking blankly at the posters advertising NEXT ATTRACTION and COMING SOON.

Saturday afternoon.

Suddenly.

Funny how things sometimes worked out. My brainstorm had been that maybe Arnie could take Christine back where she had come from; maybe he could pay LeBay for space. Now it turned out that LeBay was dead. He had died, as a matter of fact, on the same day that Arnie had gotten into it with Buddy Repperton—the same day Buddy had smashed Christine's headlight.

All at once I had an irrational picture of Buddy Repperton swinging that jackhandle—*and at the exact same moment,* LeBay's eye gushes blood, he keels over, and suddenly, very suddenly . . .

Cut the shit, Dennis, I lectured. *Just cut the—*

And then, somewhere deep in my mind, somewhere near the center, a voice whispered *Come on, big guy, let's cruise*—and then fell still.

The girl behind the counter popped her gum and said, "You're missing the end of the picture. Ending's the best part."

"Yeah, thanks."

I started back toward the door of the theater and then detoured to the drinking fountain. My throat was very dry.

Before I'd finished getting my drink, the doors opened and people came streaming out. Beyond and above their bobbing heads, I could see the credit-roll. Then Roseanne came out, looking around for me. She caught many appreciative glances and fielded them cleanly in that dreamy, composed way of hers.

"Den-Den," she said, taking my arm. Being called Den-Den isn't the worst thing in the world—having your eyes put out with a hot poker or having a leg amputated with a chain-saw is probably worse—but I've never really dug it all that much. "Where were you? You missed the ending. Ending's—"

"—the best part," I finished with her. "Sorry. I just had this call of nature. It came on very suddenly."

"I'll tell you all about it if you take me up to the Embankment for a while," she said, pressing my arm against the soft sideswell of her breast. "If you want to talk, that is."

"Did it have a happy ending?"

She smiled up at me, her eyes wide and sweet and a little dazed, as they always were. She held my arm even more tightly against her breast.

"Very happy," she said. "I like happy endings, don't you, Den-Den?"

"Love them," I said. I should maybe have been thinking about the promise of her breast, but instead I found myself thinking about Arnie.

That night I had a dream again, only in this one Christine was old—no, not just old; she was ancient, a terrible hulk of a car, something you'd expect to see in a Tarot deck: instead of the Hanged Man, the Death Car. Something you could almost believe was as old as the pyramids. The engine roared and missed and jetted filthy blue oil-smoke.

It wasn't empty. Roland D. LeBay was lolling behind the wheel. His eyes were open but they were glazed and dead. Each time the engine revved and Christine's rust-eaten body vibrated, he flopped like a ragdoll. His peeling skull nodded back and forth.

Then the tires screamed their terrible scream, the Plymouth lunged out of the garage at me, and as it did the rust melted away, the old, bleary glass clarified, the chrome winked with savage newness, and the old, balding tires suddenly bloomed into plump new Wide Ovals, each tread seemingly as deep as the Grand Canyon.

It screamed at me, headlights glaring white circles of hate, and as I raised my hands in a stupid, useless, warding-off gesture, I thought, *God, its unending fury—*

I woke up.

I didn't scream. That night I kept the scream in my throat. Just barely.

I sat up in my bed, a cold puddle of moonlight caught in a lapful of sheet, and I thought, *Died suddenly.*

That night I didn't get back to sleep so quickly.

11 / The Funeral

Eldorado fins, whitewalls and skirts,
Rides just like a little bit of heaven here on earth,
Well buddy when I die throw my body in the back
And drive me to the junkyard in my Cadillac.
                                        —Bruce Springsteen

Brad Jeffries, our road-crew foreman, was in his mid-forties, balding, stocky, permanently sunburned. He liked to holler a lot—particularly when we were behind schedule—but was a decent enough man. I went to see him during our coffee break to find out if Arnie had asked for part or all of the afternoon off.

"He asked for two hours so he could go to a buryin," Brad said. He took off his steel-rimmed glasses and massaged the red spots they had left on the sides of his nose. "Now don't *you* ask—I'm losing you both at the end of the week anyway, and all the jerk-offs are staying."

"Brad, I have to ask."

"Why? Who is this guy? Cunningham said he sold him a car, that's all. Christ, I didn't think anyone went to a used car salesman's funeral, except for his family."

"It wasn't a used car salesman, it was just a guy. Arnie's having some problems about this, Brad. I feel like I ought to go with him."

Brad sighed.

"Okay. Okay, okay, okay. You can have one to three, just

like him. *If* you'll agree to work through your lunch hour and
stay on till six Thursday night."

"Sure. Thanks, Brad."

"I'll punch you out just like regular," Brad said. "And if
anybody at Penn-DOT in Pittsburgh finds out about this, my
ass is going to be grass."

"They won't."

"Gonna be sorry to lose you guys," he said. He picked up
the paper and shook it out to the sports. Coming from Brad,
that was high praise.

"It's been a good summer for us, too."

"I'm glad you feel that way, Dennis. Now get out of here
and let me read the paper."

I did.

At one o'clock I caught a ride up to the main construction
shed on a grader. Arnie was inside, hanging up his yellow
hardhat and putting on a clean shirt. He looked at me,
startled.

"Dennis! What are you doing here?"

"Getting ready to go to a funeral," I said. "Same as you."

"No," he said immediately, and it was more that word
than anything else—the Saturdays he was no longer there, the
coolness of Michael and Regina over the phone, the way he
had been when I called him from the movies—that made me
realize how much he had shut me out of his life, and how it
had happened in just the same way LeBay had died. Suddenly.

"Yes," I said. "Arnie, I dream about the guy. You hear me
talking to you? I *dream* about him. I'm going. We can go
separately or together, but I'm going."

"You weren't joking, were you?"

"Huh?"

"When you called me on the phone from that theater. You
really didn't know he was dead."

"Jesus Christ! You think I'd joke about something like
that?"

"No," he said, but not right away. He didn't say no until
he'd thought it over carefully. He saw the possibility of all
hands being turned against him now. Will Darnell had done
that to him, and Buddy Repperton, and I suppose his mother
and father too. But it wasn't just them, or even principally
them, because none of them was the first cause. It was the
car.

"You dream about him."

"Yes."

He stood there with his clean shirt in his hands, musing over that.

"The paper said Libertyville Heights Cemetery," I said finally. "You going to take the bus or ride with me?"

"I'll ride with you."

"Good deal."

We stood on a hill above the graveside service, neither daring nor wanting to go down and join the handful of mourners. There were less than a dozen of them all told, half of them old guys in uniforms that looked old and carefully preserved—you could almost smell the mothballs. LeBay's casket was on runners over the grave. There was a flat on it. The preacher's words drifted up to us on a hot late-August breeze: man is like the grass which grows and then is cut down, man is like a flower which blooms in the spring and fades in the summer, man is in love, and loves what passes.

When the service ended, the flag was removed and a man who looked to be in his sixties threw a handful of earth onto the coffin. Little particles trickled off and fell into the hole beneath. The obit had said he was survived by a brother and a sister. This had to be the brother; the resemblance wasn't overwhelming, but it was there. The sister evidently hadn't made it; there was no one but the boys down there around that hole in the ground.

Two of the American Legion types folded the flag into a cocked hat, and one of them handed it to LeBay's brother. The preacher asked the Lord to bless them and keep them, to make His face shine upon them, to lift them up and give them peace. They started to drift away. I looked around for Arnie and Arnie wasn't beside me anymore. He had gone a little distance away. He was standing under a tree. There were tears on his cheeks.

"You okay, Arnie?" I asked. It occurred to me that I sure as hell hadn't seen any tears down there, and if Roland D. LeBay had known that Arnie Cunningham was going to be the only person to shed a tear for him at his small-time graveside ceremonies in one of western Pennsylvania's lesser-known boneyards, he might have knocked fifty bucks off the price of his shitty car. After all, Arnie still would have been paying a hundred and fifty more than it was worth.

He skidded the heels of his hands up the sides of his face

in a gesture that was nearly savage. "Fine," he said hoarsely. "Come on."

"Sure."

I thought he meant it was time to go, but he didn't start back toward where I'd parked my Duster; he started down the hill instead. I started to ask him where he was going and then shut my mouth. I knew well enough; he wanted to talk to LeBay's brother.

The brother was standing with two of the Legionnaire types, talking quietly, the flag under his arm. He was dressed in the suit of a man who is approaching retirement on a questionable income; it was a blue pinstripe with a slightly shiny seat. His tie was wrinkled at the bottom, and his white shirt had a yellowish tinge at the collar.

He glanced around at us.

"Pardon me," Arnie said, "but you're Mr. LeBay's brother, aren't you?"

"Yes, I am." He looked at Arnie questioningly and, I thought, a little warily.

Arnie put out his hand. "My name is Arnold Cunningham. I knew your brother slightly. I bought a car from him a short while ago."

When Arnie put his hand out, LeBay had automatically reached for it—with American men, the only gesture which may be more ingrained than the handshake response is checking your fly to make sure it's zipped after you come out of a public restroom. But when Arnie went on to say he had bought a car from LeBay, the hand hesitated on its course. For a moment I thought the man was not going to shake after all, that he would pull back and just leave Arnie's hand floating out there in the ozone.

But he didn't do that . . . at least, not quite. He gave Arnie's hand a single token squeeze and then dropped it.

"Christine," he said in a dry voice. Yes, the family resemblance was there—in the way the brow shelved over the eyes, the set of the jaw, the light blue eyes. But this man's face was softer, almost kind; I did not think he was ever going to have the lean and vulpine aspect that had been Roland D. LeBay's. "The last note I got from Rollie said he'd sold her."

Good Christ, he was using that damned female pronoun, too. And *Rollie!* It was hard to imagine LeBay, with his peeling skull and his pestiferous back brace, as anyone's Rollie. But his brother had spoken the nickname in that same dry voice. There was no love in that voice, at least none that I could hear.

LeBay went on: "My brother didn't write often, but he had a tendency to gloat, Mr. Cunningham. I wish there was a gentler word for it, but I don't believe there is. In his note, Rollie spoke of you as a 'sucker' and said he had given you what he called 'a royal screwing.'"

My mouth dropped open. I turned to Arnie, half-expecting another outburst of rage. But his face hadn't changed at all.

"A royal screwing," he said mildly, "is always in the eye of the beholder. Don't you think so, Mr. LeBay?"

LeBay laughed . . . a little reluctantly, I thought.

"This is my friend. He was with me the day I bought the car."

I was introduced and shook George LeBay's hand.

The soldiers had drifted away. The three of us, LeBay, Arnie, and I, were left eyeing one another uncomfortably. LeBay shifted his brother's flag from one hand to the other.

"Can I do something for you, Mr. Cunningham?" LeBay asked at last.

Arnie cleared his throat. "I was wondering about the garage," he said finally. "You see, I'm working on the car, trying to get her street-legal again. My folks don't want it at my house, and I was wondering—"

"No."

"—if maybe I could rent the garage—"

"No, out of the question, it's really—"

"I'd pay you twenty dollars a week," Arnie said. "Twenty-five, if you wanted." I winced. He was like a kid who has stumbled into quicksand and decides to cheer himself up by eating a few arsenic-laced brownies.

"—impossible." LeBay was looking more and more distressed.

"Just the garage," Arnie said, his calm starting to crack. "Just the garage where it originally *was*."

"It can't be done," LeBay said. "I listed the house with Century 21, Libertyville Realty, and Pittsburgh Homes just this morning. They'll be showing the house—"

"Yes, sure, in time, but until—"

"—and it wouldn't do to have you tinkering around. You see, don't you?" He bent toward Arnie a little. "Please don't misunderstand me. I have nothing against teenagers in general—if I did, I'd probably be in a lunatic asylum now, because I've taught high school in Paradise Falls, Ohio, for almost forty years—and you seem to be a very intelligent, well-spoken example of the genus adolescent. But all I want to do here in Libertyville is sell the house and split whatever proceeds there may be with my sister in Denver. I want to be shut of the house, Mr. Cunningham, and I want to be shut of my brother's life."

"I see," Arnie said. "Would it make any difference if I promised to look after the place? Mow the grass? Repaint the trim? Make little repairs? I can be handy that way."

"He really is good at stuff like that," I chipped in. It wouldn't hurt, I thought, for Arnie to remember later that I had been on his side . . . even if I wasn't.

"I've already hired a fellow to keep an eye on the place and do a little maintenance," he said. It sounded plausible, but I knew, suddenly and surely, that it was a lie. And I think Arnie knew it, too.

"All right. I'm sorry about your brother. He seemed like a . . . a very strong-willed man." As he said it, I found myself remembering turning around and seeing LeBay with large, greasy tears on his cheeks. *Well, that's that. I'm shut of her, sonny.*

"Strong-willed?" LeBay smiled cynically. "Oh, yes. He was a strong-willed son of a bitch." He appeared not to notice Arnie's shocked expression. "Excuse me, gentlemen. I'm afraid the sun has upset my stomach a little."

He started to walk away. We stood not far from the grave and watched him go. All at once he stopped, and Arnie's face brightened; he thought LeBay had suddenly changed his mind. For a moment LeBay just stood there on the grass, his head bent in the posture of a man thinking hard. Then he turned back to us.

"My advice to you is to forget the car," he said to Arnie. "Sell her. If no one will buy her whole, sell her for parts. If no one will buy her for parts, junk her. Do it quickly and completely. Do it the way you would quit a bad habit. I think you will be happier."

He stood there, looking at Arnie, waiting for Arnie to say something, but Arnie made no reply. He only held LeBay's gaze with his own. His eyes had gone that peculiar slaty color they got when his mind was made up and his feet were planted. LeBay read the look and nodded. He looked unhappy and a little ill.

"Gentlemen, good day."

Arnie sighed. "I guess that's that." He eyed LeBay's re-treating back with some resentment.

"Yeah," I said, hoping I sounded more unhappy than I felt. It was the dream. I didn't like the idea of Christine back in that garage. It was too much like my dream.

We started back toward my car, neither of us speaking. Le-Bay nagged at me. Both LeBays nagged at me. I came to a sudden, impulsive decision—God only knows how much different things might have been if I hadn't followed the impulse.

"Hey, man," I said, "I gotta take a whiz. Give me a minute or two, okay?"

"Sure," he said, hardly looking up. He walked on, hands in his pockets and eyes on the ground.

I walked off to the left, where a small, discreet sign and an even smaller arrow pointed the way toward the restrooms. But when I was over the first rise and out of Arnie's view, I cut to the right and started to sprint toward the parking lot. I caught George LeBay slowly folding himself behind the wheel of an extremely tiny Chevette with a Hertz sticker on the windshield.

"Mr. LeBay!" I puffed. "Mr. LeBay?" He looked up curiously. "Pardon me," I said. "Sorry to bother you again."

"That's all right," he said, "but I'm afraid what I said to your friend still stands. I can't let him garage the car there."

"Good," I said.

His bushy eyebrows went up.

"The car," I said. "That Fury. I don't like it."

He went on looking at me, not talking.

"I don't think it's been good for him. Maybe part of it's being . . . I don't know . . ."

"Jealous?" he asked me quietly. "Time he used to spend with you he now spends with her?"

"Well, yeah, right," I said. "He's been my friend for a long time. But I—I don't think that's all of it."

"No?"

"No." I looked around to see if Arnie was in sight, and while I wasn't looking at him, I was finally able to come out with it. "Why did you tell him to junk it and forget it? Why did you say it was like a bad habit?"

He said nothing, and I was afraid he had nothing to say—at least, not to me. And then, almost too softly to hear, he asked, "Son, are you sure this is your business?"

"I don't know." Suddenly it seemed very important to meet

his eyes. "But I care about Arnie, you know. I don't want to see him get hurt. This car has already gotten him in trouble. I don't want to see it get any worse."

"Come by my motel this evening. It's just off the Western Avenue exit from 376. Can you find that?"

"I hotpatched the sides of the ramp," I said, and held out my hands. "Still got the blisters."

I smiled, but he didn't smile back. "Rainbow Motel. There are two at the foot of that exit. Mine is the cheap one."

"Thanks," I said awkwardly. "Listen, really, th—"

"It may not be your business, or mine, or anyone's," Le-Bay said in his soft, schoolteacherish voice, so different from (but somehow so eerily similar to) his late brother's wild croak.

(*and that's about the finest smell in the world . . . except maybe for pussy*)

"But I can tell you this much right now. My brother was not a good man. I believe the only thing he ever truly loved in his whole life was that Plymouth Fury your friend has purchased. So the business may be between them and them alone, no matter what you tell me, or I tell you."

He smiled at me. It wasn't a pleasant smile, and in that instant I seemed to see Roland D. LeBay looking out through his eyes, and I shivered.

"Son, you're probably too young to look for wisdom in anyone's words but your own, but I'll tell you this: love is the enemy." He nodded at me slowly. "Yes. The poets continually and sometimes willfully mistake love. Love is the old slaughterer. Love is not blind. Love is a cannibal with extremely acute vision. Love is insectile; it is always hungry."

"What does it eat?" I asked, not aware I was going to ask anything at all. Every part of me but my mouth thought the entire conversation insane.

"Friendship," George LeBay said. "It eats friendship. If I were you, Dennis, I would now prepare for the worst."

He closed the door of the Chevette with a soft *chuck!* and started up its sewing-machine engine. He drove away, leaving me to stand there on the edge of the blacktop. I suddenly remembered that Arnie should see me coming from the direction of the comfort stations, so I headed that way as fast as I could.

As I went it occurred to me that the gravediggers or sextons or eternal engineers or whatever they were calling themselves these days would now be lowering LeBay's coffin into the earth. The dirt George LeBay had thrown at the end of the ceremony would be splattered across the top like a conquering hand. I tried to dismiss the image, but another image, even worse, came in its place: Roland D. LeBay inside the silk-lined casket, dressed in his best suit and his best underwear—*sans* smelly, yellowing back brace, of course.

LeBay was in the ground. LeBay was in his coffin, his hands crossed on his chest . . . and why was I so sure that a large, shit-eating grin was on his face?

12 / Some Family History

Can't you hear it out in Needham?
Route 128 down by the powerlines . . .
It's so cold here in the dark,
It's so exciting in the dark . . .
        —Jonathan Richmond and the
            Modern Lovers

The Rainbow Motel was pretty bad, all right. It was one level high, the parking-lot paving was cracked, two of the letters in the neon sign were out. It was exactly the sort of place you'd expect to find an elderly English teacher. I know how depressing that sounds, but it's true. And tomorrow he would turn in his Hertz car at the airport and fly home to Paradise Falls, Ohio.

The Rainbow Motel looked like a geriatric ward. There were old parties sitting outside their rooms in the lawn-chairs the management supplied for that purpose, their bony knees crossed, their white socks pulled up over their hairy shins. The men all looked like aging alpinists, skinny and tough. Most of the women were blooming with the soft fat of post-fifty and no hope. Since then I've noticed that there are motels which seem filled up with nothing but people over fifty—it's like they hear about these places on some Oldies but Goodies Hotline. Bring Your Hysterectomy and Enlarged Prostate to the Not-So-Scenic Rainbow Motel. No Cable TV but We Do Have Magic Fingers, Just a Quarter a Shot. I saw no young people outside the units, and off to one side the rusty playground equipment stood empty, the swings casting long still shadows on the ground. Overhead, a neon rainbow arced over the sign. It buzzed like a swarm of flies caught in a bottle.

LeBay was sitting outside Unit 14 with a glass in his hand. I went over and shook hands with him.

"Would you like a soft drink?" he asked. "There's a machine in the office that dispenses them."

"No, thanks," I said. I got one of the lawn-chairs from in front of an empty unit and sat down beside him.

"Then let me tell you what I can," he said in his soft, cultured voice. "I am eleven years younger than Rollie, and I am still a man who is learning to be old."

I shifted awkwardly in my chair and said nothing.

"There were four of us," he said. "Rollie was the oldest, I the youngest. Our brother Drew died in France in 1944. He and Rollie were both career Army. We grew up here, in Libertyville. Only Libertyville was much, much smaller then, you know, only a village. Small enough to have the ins and the outs. We were the outs. Poor folks. Shiftless. Wrong side of the tracks. Pick your cliché."

He chuckled softly in the dusk and poured more 7-Up into his glass.

"I really remember only one constant thing about Rollie's childhood—after all, he was in the fifth grade when I was born—but I remember that one thing very well."

"What was it?"

"His anger," LeBay said. "Rollie was always angry. He was angry that he had to go to school in castoff clothes, he was angry that our father was a drunkard who could not hold a steady job in any of the steel mills, he was angry that our mother could not make our father stop drinking. He was angry at the three smaller children—Drew, Marcia, and myself—who made the poverty insurmountable."

He held his arm out to me and pushed up the sleeve of his shirt to show me the withered, corded tendons of his old man's arm which lay just below the surface of the shiny, stretched skin. A scar skidded down from his elbow toward his wrist, where it finally petered out.

"That was a present from Rollie," he said. "I got it when I was three and he was fourteen. I was playing with a few painted blocks of wood that were supposed to be cars and trucks on the front walk when he slammed out on his way to school. I was in his way, I suppose. He pushed me, went on to the sidewalk, and then he came back and threw me. I landed with my arm stuck on one of the pickets of the fence that went around the bunch of weeds and sunflowers that my mother insisted on calling 'the garden.' I bled enough to scare all of them into tears—all of them except Rollie, who just kept shouting, 'You stay out of my way from now on, you goddam snotnose, stay out of my way, you hear?"

I looked at the old scar, fascinated, realizing that it looked like a skid because that small, chubby three-year-old's arm had grown over the course of years into the skinny, shiny old man's arm I was now looking at. A wound that had been an ugly gouge spilling blood everywhere in the year 1921 had slowly elongated into this silvery progression of marks like ladder-rungs. The wound had closed, but the scar had . . . spread.

A terrible, hopeless shudder twisted through me. I thought of Arnie slamming his fists down on the dashboard of my car, Arnie crying hoarsely that he would make them eat it, eat it, eat it.

George LeBay was looking at me. I don't know what he saw on my face, but he slowly rolled his sleeve back down, and when he buttoned it securely over that scar, it was as if he had drawn the curtain on an almost unbearable past.

He sipped more 7-Up.

"My father came home that evening—he had been on one of the toots that he called 'hunting up a job'—and when he heard what Rollie had done, he whaled the tar out of him. But Rollie would not recant. He cried, but he would not recant." LeBay smiled a little. "At the end my mother was terrified, screaming for my father to stop before he killed him. The tears were rolling down Rollie's face, and still he would not recant. 'He was in my way,' Rollie said through his tears. 'And if he gets in my way again I'll do it again, and you can't stop me, you damned old tosspot.' Then my father struck him in the face and made his nose bleed and Rollie fell on the floor with the blood squirting through his fingers. My mother was screaming, Marcia was crying, Drew was cringing in one corner, and I was bawling my head off, holding my bandaged arm. And Rollie went right on saying, 'I'd do it again, you tosspot-tosspot-damned-old-tosspot!' "

Above us, the stars had begun to come out. An old woman left a unit down the way, took a battered suitcase out of a Ford, and carried it back into her unit. Somewhere a radio was playing. It was not tuned to the rock sounds of FM-104.

"His unending fury is what I remember best," LeBay repeated softly. "At school, he fought with anyone who made fun of his clothes or the way his hair was cut—he would fight anyone he even *suspected* of making fun. He was suspended again and again. Finally he left and joined the Army.

"It wasn't a good time to be in the Army, the twenties. There was no dignity, no promotion, no flying flags and banners. There was no nobility. He went from base to base, first in the South and then in the Southwest. We got a letter every three months or so. He was still angry. He was angry at what he called 'the shitters.' Everything was the fault of 'the shitters.' The shitters wouldn't give him the promotion he deserved, the shitters had cancelled a furlough, the shitters couldn't find their own behinds with both hands and a flashlight. On at least two occasions, the shitters put him in the stockade.

"The Army held onto him because he was an excellent mechanic—he could keep the old and decrepit vehicles which were all Congress would allow the Army in some sort of running condition."

Uneasily, I found myself thinking of Arnie again—Arnie who was so clever with his hands.

LeBay leaned forward. "But that talent was just another wellspring for his anger, young man. And it was an anger that never ended until he bought that car that your friend now owns."

"What do you mean?"

LeBay chuckled dryly. "He fixed Army convoy trucks, Army staff cars, Army weapons-supply vehicles. He fixed bulldozers and kept staff cars running with spit and baling-wire. And once, when a visiting Congressman came to visit Fort Arnold in west Texas and had car trouble, he was ordered by his commanding officer, who was desperate to make a good impression, to fix the Congressman's prized Bentley. Oh, yes, we got a four-page letter from that particular 'shitter'—a four-page rant of Rollie's anger and vitriol. It was a wonder the words didn't smoke on the page.

"All those vehicles . . . but Rollie never owned a car himself until after World War II. Even then the only thing he was able to afford was an old Chevrolet that ran poorly and was eaten up with rust. In the twenties and thirties there was never money enough, and during the war years he was too busy trying to stay alive.

"He was in the motor pool for all those years, and he fixed

thousands of vehicles for the shitters and never had one that was all his. It was Libertyville all over again. Even the old Chevrolet couldn't assuage that, or the old Hudson Hornet he bought used the year after he got married."

"Married?"

"Didn't tell you that, did he?" LeBay said. "He would have been happy to go on and on about his Army experiences—his war experiences and his endless confrontations with the shitters—for as long as you and your friend could listen without falling alseep . . . and him with his hand in your pocket feeling for your wallet the whole time. But he wouldn't have bothered to tell you about Veronica or Rita."

"Who were they?"

"Veronica was his wife," LeBay said. "They were married in 1951, shortly before Rollie went to Korea. He could have stayed Stateside, you know. He was married, his wife was pregnant, he himself was approaching middle age. But he chose to go."

LeBay looked reflectively at the dead playground equipment.

"It was bigamy, you know. By 1951 he was forty-four, and he was married already. He was married to the Army. And to the shitters."

He fell silent again. His silence had a morbid quality. "Are you all right?" I asked finally.

"Yes," he said. "Just thinking. Thinking ill of the dead." He looked at me calmly—except for his eyes; they were dark and wounded. "You know, all of this hurts me, young man . . . what did you say your name was? I don't want to sit here and sing these old sad songs to someone I can't call by his first name. Was it Donald?"

"Dennis," I said. "Look, Mr. LeBay—"

"It hurts more than I would have suspected," he went on. "But now that it's begun, let's finish it, shall we? I only met Veronica twice. She was from West Virginia. Near Wheeling. She was what we then called shirt-tail southern, and she was not terribly bright. Rollie was able to dominate her and take her for granted, which was what he seemed to want. But she loved him, I think—at least until the rotten business with Rita. As for Rollie, I don't think he really married a woman at all. He married a kind of . . . of wailing wall.

"The letters that he sent us . . . well, you must remember that he left school very early. The letters, illiterate as they were, represented a tremendous effort for my brother. They were his suspension bridge, his novel, his symphony, his great effort. I don't think he wrote them to get rid of the poison in his heart. I think he wrote them to spread it around.

"Once he had Veronica, the letters stopped. He had his set of eternal ears, and he didn't have to bother with us anymore. I suppose he wrote letters to her during the two years he was in Korea. I only got one during that period, and I believe Marcia got two. There was no pleasure over the birth of his daughter in early 1952, only a surly complaint that there was another mouth to feed at home and the shitters took a little more out of him."

"Did he never advance in rank?" I asked. The year before I had seen part of a long TV show, one of those novels for television called *Once an Eagle*. I had seen the paperback book in the drugstore the next day and had picked it up, hoping for a good war story. As it turned out, I got both war and peace, and some new ideas about the armed services. One of them was that the old promotion train really gets rolling along in times of war. It was hard for me to understand how LeBay could have gone into the service in the early twenties, slogged through two wars, and still have been running junk when Ike became President.

LeBay laughed. "He was like Prewitt in *From Here to Eternity*. He would advance, and then he would be busted back down for something—insubordination or impertinence or drunkenness. I told you he had spent time in the stockade? One of those times was for pissing in the punchbowl at the Officers Club at Fort Dix before a party. He only did ten days for that offense, because I believe they must have looked into their own hearts and believed it was nothing more than a drunken joke, such as some of the officers themselves had probably played as fraternity boys—they didn't, they *couldn't*, have any idea of the hate and deadly loathing that lay behind that gesture. But I imagine that by then Veronica could have told them."

I glanced at my watch. It was quarter past nine. LeBay had been talking for nearly an hour.

"My brother came home from Korea in 1953 to meet his daughter for the first time. I understand he looked her over for a minute or two, then handed her back to his wife, and went out to tinker on his old Chevrolet for the rest of the day . . . getting bored, Dennis?"

"No," I said truthfully.

"All through those years, the one thing that Rollie really

wanted was a brand-new car. Not a Cadillac or a Lincoln; he didn't want to join the upper class, the officers, the shitters. He wanted a new Plymouth or maybe a Ford or a Dodge.

"Veronica wrote now and then, and she said that they spent most of their Sundays going around to car dealerships wherever Rollie was currently stationed. She and the baby would sit in the old Hornet Rollie had then, and Veronica would read little storybooks to Rita while Rollie walked around dusty lot after dusty lot with salesman after salesman, talking about compression and horsepower and hemi heads and gear ratios . . . I think, sometimes, of the little girl growing up to the background sound of those plastic pennants whipping in the hot wind of half a dozen Army tank-towns, and I don't know whether to laugh or cry."

My thoughts turned back to Arnie again.

"Was he obsessed, would you say?"

"Yes. I would say he was obsessed. He began to give Veronica money to put away. Other than his failure to get promoted past Master Sergeant at any point in his career, my brother had a problem with drink. He wasn't an alcoholic, but he went on periodic binges every six or eight months. What money he had would be gone when the binge was over. He was never sure where he spent it.

"Veronica was supposed to put a stop to that. It was one of the things he married her for. When the binges started, Rollie would come to her for the money. He threatened her with a knife once; held it to her throat. I got this from my sister, who sometimes talked to Veronica on the telephone. Veronica would not give him the money, which at that time, in 1955, totaled about eight hundred dollars. 'Remember the car, honey,' she told him, with the point of his knife on her throat. 'You'll never get that new car if'n you booze the money away.'"

"She must have loved him," I said.

"Well, maybe she did. But please don't make the romantic assumption that her love changed Rollie in any way. Water can wear away stone, but only over hundreds of years. People are mortal."

He seemed to debate saying something else along that line and then to decide against it. The lapse struck me as peculiar.

"But he never put a mark on either of them," he said. "And you must remember that he was drunk on the occasion when he held the knife to her throat. There is a great outcry about drugs in the schools now, and I don't oppose that outcry because I think it's obscene to think of children fifteen and sixteen years old reeling around full of dope, but I still believe alcohol is the most vulgar, dangerous drug ever invented—and it is legal.

"When my brother finally left the Army in 1957, Veronica had put away a little over twelve hundred dollars. Adding to it was a substantial disability pension for his back injury—he fought the shitters for it and won, he said.

"So the money was finally there. They got the house you and your friend visited, but before the house was even considered, of course, the car came. The car was always paramount. The visits to the car dealerships reached a fever pitch. And at last he settled upon Christine. I got a long letter about her. She was a 1958 Fury sport coupe, and he gave me all the facts and figures in his letter. I don't remember them, but I bet your friend could cite her vital statistics chapter and verse."

"Her measurements," I said.

LeBay smiled humorlessly. "Her measurements, yes. I do remember that he wrote her sticker price was just a tad under $3000, but he 'jewed em down,' as he put it, to $2100 with the trade-in. He ordered her, paid ten percent down, and when she came, he paid the balance in cash—ten- and twenty-dollar bills.

"The next year, Rita, who was then six, choked to death."

I jumped in my chair and almost knocked it over. His soft, teacherish voice had a lulling quality, and I was tired; I had been half-asleep. That last had been like a dash of cold water in my face.

"Yes, that's right," he said to my questioning, startled glance. "They had been out 'motorvating' for the day. That was what replaced the car-hunting expeditions. 'Motorvating.' That was his word for it. He got that from one of those rock and roll songs he was always listening to. Every Sunday the three of them would go out 'motorvating.' There were litter-bags in the front and the back. The little girl was forbidden to drop anything on the floor. She was forbidden to make any messes. She knew that lesson well. She . . ."

He fell into that peculiar, thinking silence again and then came back on a new tack.

"Rollie kept the ashtrays clean. Always. He was a heavy smoker, but he'd poke his cigarette out the wing window instead of tapping it into the ashtray, and when he was done with a cigarette, he'd snuff it and toss it out the window. If he had someone with him who did use the ashtray, he'd dump the ashtray and then wipe it out with a paper towel when the drive was over. He washed her twice a week and Simonized her twice a year. He serviced her himself, buying time at a local garage."

I wondered if it had been Darnell's.

"On that particular Sunday, they stopped at a roadside stand for hamburgers on the way home—there were no McDonald's in those days, you know, just roadside stands. And what happened was . . . simple enough, I suppose . . ."

That silence again, as if he wondered just how much he should tell me, or how to separate what he knew from his speculations.

"She choked to death on a piece of meat," he said finally. "When she started to gag and put her hands to her throat, Rollie pulled over, dragged her out of the car, and thudded her on the back, trying to bring it up. Of course now they have a method—the Heimlich Maneuver—that works rather well in situations like that. A young girl, a student teacher, actually, saved a boy who was choking in the cafeteria at my school just last year by employing the Heimlich Maneuver. But in those days . . .

"My niece died by the side of the road. I imagine it was a filthy, frightening way to die."

His voice had resumed that sleepy schoolroom cadence, but I no longer felt sleepy. Not at all.

"He tried to save her. I believe that. And I try to believe that it was only ill luck that she died. He had been in a ruthless business for a long time, and I don't believe he loved his daughter very deeply, if at all. But sometimes, in mortal matters, a lack of love can be a saving grace. Sometimes ruthlessness is what is required."

"But not this time," I said.

"In the end he turned her over and held her by her ankles. He punched her in the belly, hoping to make her vomit. I believe he would have tried to do a tracheotomy on her with his pocket-knife if he had even the slightest idea of how to go about it. But of course he did not. She died.

"Marcia and her husband and family came to the funeral. So did I. It was our last family reunion. I remember thinking, He will have traded the car, of course. In an odd way, I was a little disappointed. It had figured so largely in Veronica's letters and the few which Rollie wrote that I felt it was almost a member of their family. But he hadn't. They pulled up to the Libertyville Methodist Church in it, and it was polished . . . and shining . . . and hateful. It was *hateful*." He turned to look at me. "Do you believe that, Dennis?"

I had to swallow before I could answer. "Yes," I said. "I believe it."

LeBay nodded grimly. "Veronica was sitting in the passenger seat like a wax dummy. Whatever she had been—whatever there was inside her—was gone. Rollie had had the car, she had had the daughter. She didn't just grieve. She died."

I sat there and tried to imagine it—tried to imagine what I would have done if it had been me. My daughter starts to choke and strangle in the back seat of my car and then dies by the side of the road. Would I trade the car away? Why? It wasn't the *car* that killed her; it was whatever she strangled on, the bit of hamburger and bun that had blocked her windpipe. So why trade the car? Other than the small fact that I wouldn't even be able to look at it, wouldn't even be able to think of it, without horror and sorrow. Would I trade it? Man, does a bear shit in the woods?

"Did you ask him about it?"

"I asked him, all right. Marcia was with me. It was after the service. Veronica's brother had come up from Glory, West Virginia, and he took her back to the house after the graveside ceremony—she was in a kind of walking swoon, anyway.

"We got him alone, Marcia and I. That was the real reunion. I asked him if he intended to trade the car. It was parked directly behind the hearse that had brought his daughter to the cemetery—the same cemetery where Rollie himself was buried today, you know. It was red and white—Chrysler never offered the 1958 Plymouth Fury in those colors; Rollie had gotten it custom-painted. We were standing about fifty feet away from it, and I had the strangest feeling . . . the strangest *urge* . . . to move yet farther away, as if it could hear us."

"What did you say?"

"I asked him if he was going to trade the car. That hard, mulish look came onto his face, that look I remembered so well from my early childhood. It was the look that had been on his face when he threw me onto the picket fence. The look that was on his face when he kept calling my father a tosspot, even after my father made his nose bleed. He said, 'I'd be crazy to trade her, George, she's only a year old and she's only got 11,000 miles on her. You know you never get your money out of a trade until a car's three years old.'

"I said, 'If this is a matter of money to you, Rollie, some-one stole what was left of your heart and replaced it with a piece of stone. Do you want your wife looking at it every day? *Riding* in it? Good God, man!'

"That look never changed. Not until he looked at the car, sitting there in the sunlight . . . sitting there behind the hearse. That was the only time his face softened. I remember wondering if he'd ever looked at Rita that way. I don't sup-pose he ever did. I don't think it was in him."

He fell silent for a moment and then went on.

"Marcia told him all the same things. She was always afraid of Rollie, but that day she was more mad than afraid—she had gotten Veronica's letters, remember, and she knew how much Veronica loved her little girl. She told him that when someone dies, you burn the mattress they slept on, you give their clothes to the Salvation Army, whatever, you put finish to the life any way you can so that the living can get on with their business. She told him that his wife was never going to be able to get on with her business as long as the car where her daughter died was still in the garage.

"Rollie asked her in that ugly, sarcastic way he had if she wanted him to douse his car with gasoline and touch a match to her just because his daughter had choked to death. My sis-ter started to cry and told him she thought that was a fine idea. Finally I took her by the arm and led her away. There was no talking to Rollie, then or ever. The car was his, and he could talk on and on about keeping a car three years be-fore you trade it, he could talk about mileage until he was blue in the face, but the simple fact was, he was going to keep her because he wanted to keep her.

"Marcia and her family went back to Denver on a Grey-hound, and so far as I know, she never saw Rollie again or even wrote him a note. She didn't come to Veronica's fu-neral."

His wife. First the kid, and then the wife. I knew, some-how, that it had been just like that. Bang-bang. A kind of numbness crept up my legs to the pit of my stomach.

"She died six months later. In January of 1959."

"But nothing to do with the car," I said. "Nothing to do with the car, right?"

"It had everything to do with the car," he said softly.

I don't want to hear it, I thought. But of course I would hear it. Because my friend owned that car now, and because it had become something that had grown out of all proportion to what it should have been in his life.

"After Rita died, Veronica went into a depression. She simply never came out of it. She had made some friends in Libertyville, and they tried to help her . . . help her find her way again. I guess one would say. But she was not able to find her way. Not at all.

"Otherwise, things were fine. For the first time in my brother's life, there was plenty of money. He had his Army pension, his disability pension, and he had gotten a job as a night watchman at the tire factory over on the west side of town. I drove over there after the funeral, but it's gone."

"It went broke twelve years ago," I said. "I was just a kid. There's a Chinese fast-food place there now."

"They were paying off the mortgage at the rate of two payments a month. And, of course, they had no little girl to take care of any longer. But for Veronica, there was never any light or impulse toward recovery.

"She went about committing suicide quite cold-bloodedly, from all that I have been able to find out. If there were textbooks for aspiring suicides, her own might be included as an example to emulate. She went down to the Western Auto store here in town—the same one where I got my first bicycle many, many years ago—and bought twenty feet of rubber hose. She fitted one end over Christine's exhaust pipe and put the other end in one of the back windows. She had never gotten a driver's license, but she knew how to start a car. That was really all she needed to know."

I pursed my lips, wet them with my tongue, and heard my voice, little more than a rusty croak. "I think I'll get that soda now."

"Perhaps you'd be good enough to get me another," he said. "It will keep me awake—they always do—but I suspect I'd be awake most of tonight anyway."

I suspected I would be, too. I went to get the sodas in the motel office, and on my way back I stopped halfway across the parking lot. He was only a deeper shadow in front of his motel unit, his white socks glimmering like small ghosts. I thought, *Maybe the car is cursed. Maybe that's what it is. It sounds like a ghost story, all right. There's a signpost up ahead . . . next stop, the Twilight Zone!*

But that was ridiculous, wasn't it?

Of course it was. I went on walking again. Cars didn't carry curses any more than people carried them; that was horror-movie stuff, sort of amusing for a Saturday night at the drive-in, but very, very far from the day-to-day facts that make up reality.

I gave him his can of soda and heard the rest of his story, which could be summed up in one line: He lived unhappily ever after. The one and only Roland D. LeBay had kept his small tract house, and he had kept his 1958 Plymouth. In 1965 he had hung up his night watchman's cap and his check-in clock. And somewhere around that same time he had stopped his painstaking efforts to keep Christine looking and running like new—he had let her run down the way a man might let a watch run down.

"You mean it just sat out there?" I asked. "Since 1965? For thirteen years?"

"No, he put it in the garage, of course," LeBay said. "The neighbors would never have stood for a car just mouldering away out on someone's lawn. In the country, maybe, but not in Suburbia, U.S.A."

"But it was out there when we—"

"Yes, I know. He put it out on the lawn with a FOR SALE sign in the window. I asked about that. I was curious, and so I asked. At the Legion. Most of them had lost touch with Rollie, but one of them said he thought he'd seen the car out there on the lawn for the first time this May."

I started to say something and then fell silent. A terrible idea had come to me, and that idea was simply this: *It was too convenient.* Much too convenient. Christine had sat in that dark garage for years—four, eight, a dozen, more. Then—a few months before Arnie and I came along and Arnie saw it—Roland LeBay had suddenly hauled it out and stuck a FOR SALE sign on it.

Later on—much later—I checked back through issues of the Pittsburgh papers and the Libertyville paper, the *Keystone*. He had never advertised the Fury, at least not in the papers, where you usually hawk a car that you want to sell. He just put it out on his suburban street—not even a thoroughfare—and waited for a buyer to come along.

I did not completely realize the rest of the thought then—not in any logical, intellectual way, at least—but I had enough of it to feel a recurrence of that cold, blue feeling of fright. It was as if he knew a buyer would be coming. If not in May, then in June. Or July. Or August. Sometime soon.

No, I didn't get this idea logically or rationally. What came instead was a wholly visceral image: a Venus Flytrap at the edge of a swamp, its green jaws wide open, waiting for an insect to land.

The *right* insect.

"I remember thinking he must have given it up because he didn't want to take a chance of flunking the driver's exam," I said finally. "After you get so old, they make you take one every year or two. The renewal stops being automatic."

George LeBay nodded. "That sounds like Rollie," he said. "But . . ."

"But what?"

"I remember reading somewhere—and I can't remember who said it, or wrote it, for the life of me—that there are 'times' in human existence. That when it came to be 'steam-engine time,' a dozen men invented steam engines. Maybe only one man got the patent, or the credit in the history books, but all at once there they were, all those people working on that one idea. How do you explain it? Just that it's steam-engine time."

LeBay took a drink of his soda and looked up at the sky.

"Comes the Civil War and all at once it's 'ironclad time.' Then it's 'machine-gun time.' Next thing you know it's 'electricity time' and 'wireless time' and finally it's 'atom-bomb time.' As if those ideas all come not from individuals but from some great wave of intelligence that always keeps flowing . . . some wave of intelligence that is outside of humanity."

He looked at me.

"That idea scares me if I think about it too much, Dennis. There seems to be something . . . well, decidedly unchristian about it."

"And for your brother there was 'sell Christine time'?"

"Perhaps. Ecclesiastes says there's a season for everything—a time to sow, a time to reap, a time for war, a time for peace, a time to put away the sling, and a time to gather stones together. A negative for every positive. So if there was 'Christine time' in Rollie's life, there might have come a time for him to put Christine away, as well.

"If so, he would have known it. He was an animal, and animals listen very well to their instincts.

"Or maybe he finally just tired of it," LeBay finished.

I nodded that that might be it, mostly because I was anxious to be gone, not because that explained it to my complete satisfaction. George LeBay hadn't seen that car on the day Arnie had yelled at me to go back. I had seen it, though. The '58 hadn't looked like a car that had been resting peacefully in a garage. It had been dirty and dented, the windshield cracked, one bumper mostly torn away. It had looked like a corpse that had been disinterred and left to decay in the sun.

I thought of Veronica LeBay and shivered.

As if reading my thoughts—part of them, anyway—LeBay said, "I know very little about how my brother may have lived or felt during the last years of his life, but I'm quite sure of one thing, Dennis. When he felt, in 1965 or whenever it was, that it was time to put the car away, he put it away. And when he felt it was time to put it up for sale, he put it up for sale."

He paused.

"And I don't think I have anything else to tell you . . . except that I really believe your friend would be happier if he got rid of that car. I looked at him closely, your friend. He didn't look like a particularly happy young man at the present. Am I wrong about that?"

I considered his question carefully. No, happiness wasn't exactly Arnie's thing, and never had been. But until the thing had begun with the Plymouth, he had seemed at least content . . . as if he had reached a *modus vivendi* with life. Not a completely happy one, but at least a workable one.

"No," I said. "You're not wrong."

"I don't believe my brother's car will make him happy. If anything, just the opposite." And as if he had read my thoughts of a few minutes before, he went on: "I don't believe in curses, you know. Not in ghosts or anything precisely supernatural. But I do believe that emotions and events have a certain . . . lingering resonance. It may be that emotions can even communicate themselves in certain circumstances, if the circumstances are peculiar enough . . . the way a carton of milk will take the flavor of certain strongly spiced foods if it's left open in the refrigerator. Or perhaps that's only a ridiculous fancy on my part. Possibly it's just that I would feel better knowing the car my niece choked in and my sister-in-law killed herself in had been pressed down into a cube of meaningless metal. Perhaps all I feel is a sense of outraged propriety."

"Mr. LeBay, you said you'd hired someone to take care of your brother's house until it was sold. Was that true?"

He shifted a little in his chair. "No, it wasn't. I lied on impulse. I didn't like the thought of that car back in that garage . . . as if it had found its way home. If there are emotions and feelings that still live on, they would be there, as well as in the car herself." And very quickly he corrected himself: "*It*self."

Not long after, I said my goodbyes and followed my headlights home through the dark, thinking over everything LeBay had told me. I wondered if it would make any difference to Arnie if I told him one person had had a mortal accident in his car and another had actually died in it. I pretty well knew that it wouldn't; in his own way, Arnie could be every bit as stubborn as Roland LeBay himself. The lovely little scene over the car with his parents had shown that quite conclusively. The fact that he went on taking auto-shop courses down there in the Libertyville High version of the DMZ showed the same thing.

I thought of LeBay saying, *I didn't like the thought of that car back in that garage . . . as if it had found its way home.*

He had also said that his brother took the car someplace to work on it. And the only do-it-yourself garage in Libertyville now was Will Darnell's. Of course, there might have been another back in the 50s, but I didn't believe it. In my heart what I believed was that Arnie had been working on Christine in a place where she had been worked on before.

Had been. That was the operant phrase. Because of the fight with Buddy Repperton, Arnie was afraid to leave it there any longer. So maybe that avenue to Christine's past was blocked off as well.

And, of course, there were no curses. Even LeBay's idea about lingering emotions was pretty farfetched. I doubted if he really believed it himself. He had shown me an old scar, and he had used the word vengeance. And that was probably a lot closer to the truth than any phony supernatural bullshit. Of course.

No; I was seventeen years old, bound for college in another year, and I didn't believe in such things as curses and emotions that linger and grow rancid, the spilled milk of dreams. I would not have granted you the power of the past to reach out horrid dead hands toward the living.

But I'm a little older now.

13 / Later That Evening

As I was motorvating over the hill
I saw Maybelline in a Coupe de Ville.
Cadillac rollin down the open road,
But nothin outrun my V8 Ford . . .
                    —Chuck Berry

My mother and Elaine had gone to bed, but my dad was
up, watching the eleven o'clock news on TV. "Where you
been, Dennis?" he asked.

"Bowling," I said, the lie coming naturally and instinctively
to my lips. I didn't want my father to know any of this.
Peculiar as it was, it really wasn't peculiar enough to be more
than moderately interesting. Or so I rationalized.

"Arnie called," he said. "Asked me to have you call back
if you got in before eleven-thirty or so."

I glanced at my watch. It was only eleven-twenty. But
hadn't I had enough of Arnie and Arnie's problems for one
day?

"Well?"

"Well what?"

"Are you going to call him?"

I sighed. "Yeah, I guess I will."

I went into the kitchen, slapped together a cold chicken
sandwich, poured myself a glass of Hawaiian Punch—gross
stuff, but I love it—and dialled Arnie's house. He picked up
the phone himself on the second ring. He sounded happy and
excited.

"Dennis! Where you been?"

"Bowling." I said.

"Listen, I went down to Darnell's tonight, you know?
And—this is great, Dennis—he gave Repperton the boot!
Repperton's gone and I can stay!"

That sensation of unformed dread in my belly again. I put
my sandwich down. Suddenly I didn't want it anymore.

"Arnie, do you think taking it back there is really such a
good idea?"

108

"What do you mean? Repperton's gone. That doesn't sound like a good idea to *you?*"

I thought about Darnell ordering Arnie to turn off his car before it polluted his cruddy garage, Darnell telling Arnie he didn't take any shit from kids like him. I thought about the shamefaced way Arnie had cut his eyes away from mine when he told me he had gotten lift-time to change his oil by doing "a couple of errands." I had an idea that Darnell might find it amusing to turn Arnie into his pet gofer. It would amuse the shit out of his other regulars and his poker buddies. Arnie goes out for coffee, Arnie goes out for doughnuts, Arnie changes the toilet paper rolls in the crapper and loads up the Nibroc dispenser with paper towels. *Hey, Will, who's the four-eyes swamping out the toilet in there? . . . Him? Name's Cunningham. His folks teach up at the college. He's taking a shithouse postgrad course down here.* And they would laugh. Arnie would become the local joke down at Darnell's Garage on Hampton Street.

I thought about those things, but I didn't say them. I figured Arnie could make up his own mind about whether he was treading water or shit. This couldn't go on forever—Arnie was just too smart Or so I hoped. He was ugly, but he wasn't dumb

"Repperton being gone sounds like a fine idea," I said. "It was just that I thought Darnell's was sort of a temporary measure I mean, twenty a week, Arnie, that's pretty stiff on top of the tools fees and the lift fees and all that happy crappy."

"That's why I thought renting Mr. LeBay's garage would be so great," Arnie said "I figured that even at twenty-five a week I'd be better off."

"Well, there you go If you put an ad in the paper for garage space, I bet you'd—"

"No, no, let me finish," Arnie said. He was still excited. "When I went down there this afternoon Darnell took me aside right away. Said he was sorry about the ragging I had to take from Repperton. He said he misjudged me."

"He said that?" I guess I believed it, but I didn't trust it.

"Yeah He asked me how I'd like to work for him part-time Ten, maybe twenty hours a week during school. Putting stuff away, lubing the lifts, that kind of thing. And I can have the space for ten a week, tools fees and lift fees at half. How does that sound?"

I thought it sounded too fucking good to be true.

"Watch your ass, Arnie."

"What?"

"My dad says he's a crook."

"I haven't seen any sign of it. I think that's all just talk, Dennis. He's a loudmouth, but I think that's all."

"I'm just telling you to stay loose, that's all." I switched the phone to my other ear and drank some Hawaiian Punch. "Keep your eyes open and move away quick if anything starts to look heavy."

"Are you talking about anything specific?"

I thought of the vague stories about drugs, the more specific ones about hot cars.

"No," I said. "I just don't trust him."

"Well . . ." he said doubtfully, trailing away, and then came back to the original subject: Christine. With him it always got back to Christine. "But it's a break, a real break for me, Dennis, if it works out. Christine . . . she's really hurting. I've been able to do some things with her, but for everything I do it looks like there's four more. Some of it I don't even know how to do, but I'm going to learn."

"Yeah," I said, and took a bite out of my sandwich. After my conversation with George LeBay, my enthusiasm for the subject of Arnie's best girl Christine had passed zero and entered the negative regions.

"She needs a front-end alignment—hell, she needs a new front end—and new brake shoes . . . a ring-job . . . I may try to re-grind the pistons . . . but I can't do any of that stuff with my fifty-four-buck Craftsman toolkit. You see what I mean, Dennis?"

He sounded like he was pleading for my approval. With a sinking in my stomach, I suddenly remembered a guy we had gone to school with. Freddy Darlington, his name had been. Freddy was no ball of fire, but he was an okay kid with a good sense of humor. Then he met some slut from Penn Hills—and I mean a real slut, one more than happy to stoop for the troops, bang for the gang, pick your pejorative. She had a mean, stupid face that reminded me of the back end of a Mack truck and she never stopped chewing gum. The stink of Juicy Fruit hung around her in a constant cloud. She got pregnant at about the same time Freddy got hung up on her. I always sort of figured he got hung up on her because she was the first girl to let him go all the way. So what happens is he drops out of school, gets a job in a warehouse, the princess has the baby, and he shows up with her at a party after the Junior Prom last December, wanting everything to seem the same when nothing is the same; she is looking at all of us guys with those dead, contemptuous eyes, her jaws are going up and down like the jaws of a cow working over a particularly tasty cud, and all of us have heard the news; she's back at the bowling alley, she's back at the Libertyville Rec, she's back at Gino's, she's back out cruising while Freddy is working, she's back hard at work, banging for the gang and stooping for the troops. I know they say that a stiff dick has no conscience, but I tell you now that some cunts have teeth, and when I looked at Freddy, looking ten years older than he should have, I felt like I wanted to cry. And when he talked about her, he did it in that same pleading tone I had heard in Arnie's voice just now—*You really like her, guys, don't you? She's all right, isn't she, guys? I didn't fuck up too bad, did I guys? I mean, this is probably just a bad dream and I'll wake up pretty soon, right? Right? Right?*

"Sure," I said into the telephone. That whole stupid, ugly Freddy Darlington business had gone through my mind in maybe two seconds. "I see what you mean, Arnie."

"Good," he said, relieved.

"Just watch out for your ass. And that goes double when you get back to school. Keep away from Buddy Repperton."

"Yeah. You bet."

"Arnie—"

"What?"

I paused. I wanted to ask him if Darnell had said anything about Christine being in his shop before, if he recognized her. Even more, I wanted to tell him what had happened to Mrs. LeBay and to her small daughter, Rita. But I couldn't. He would know right away where I had gotten the information. And in his touchy state over the damn car, he would be apt to think I had gone behind his back—and in a way I had. But to tell him I had might well mean the end of our friendship.

I had had enough of Christine, but I still cared for Arnie. Which meant that door had to be closed for good. No more creeping around and asking questions. No more lectures.

"Nothing," I said. "I was just going to say that I guess you found a home for your rustbucket. Congratulations."

"Dennis, are you eating something?"

"Yeah, a chicken sandwich. Why?"

"You're chewing in my ear. It really sounds gross."

I began to smack as loudly as I could. Arnie made puking

sounds. We both got laughing, and it was good—it was like the old days before he married that dumb fucking car.

"You're an asshole, Dennis."

"That's right. I learned it from you."

"Get bent," he said, and hung up.

I finished my sandwich and my Hawaiian Punch, rinsed the plate and the glass, and went back into the living room, ready to shower and go to bed. I was beat.

Sometime during our phone conversation I had heard the TV go off and had assumed that my father had gone upstairs. But he hadn't. He was sitting in his recliner chair with his shirt open. I noticed with some unease how gray the hair on his chest was getting, and the way the reading lamp beside him shone through the hair on his head and showed his pink scalp. Getting thinner up there. My father was no kid. I realized with greater unease that in five years, by the time I would theoretically finish college, he would be fifty and balding—a stereotype accountant. Fifty in five years if he didn't just drop dead of another heart attack. The first one had not been bad—no myocardial scarring, he had told me on the one occasion I had asked. But he did not try to tell me that a second heart attack wasn't likely. I knew it was, my mom knew it was, and he did too. Only Ellie still thought he was invulnerable—but hadn't I seen a question in her eyes once or twice? I thought maybe I had.

Died suddenly.

I felt the hairs on my scalp stir. *Suddenly.* Straightening up at his desk, clutching his chest. *Suddenly.* Dropping his racket on the tennis court. You didn't want to think those thoughts about your father, but sometimes they come. God knows they do.

"I couldn't help overhearing some of that," he said.

"Yeah?" Warily.

"Has Arnie Cunningham got his foot in a bucket of something warm and brown, Dennis?"

"I . . . I don't know for sure," I said slowly. Because, after all, what did I have? Vapors, that was all.

"You want to talk about it?"

"Not right now, Dad, if it's okay."

"It's fine," he said. "But if it . . . as you said on the phone, if it gets heavy, will you for God's sake tell me what's happening?"

"Yes."

"Okay." I started for the stairs and was almost there when he stopped me by saying, "I ran Will Darnell's accounts and did his income-tax returns for almost fifteen years, you know."

I turned back to him, really surprised.

"No. I didn't know that."

My father smiled. It was a smile I had never seen before, one I would guess my mother had seen only a few times, my sis maybe not at all. You might have thought it was a sleepy sort of smile at first, but if you looked more closely you would have seen it was not sleepy at all—it was cynical and hard and totally aware.

"Can you keep your mouth shut about something, Dennis?"

"Yes," I said. "I think so."

"Don't just think so."

"Yes. I can."

"Better. I did his figures up until 1975, and then he got Bill Upshaw over in Monroeville."

My father looked at me closely.

"I won't say that Bill Upshaw is a crook, but I will say that his scruples are thin enough to read a newspaper through. And last year he bought himself a $300,000 English Tudor in Sewickley. Damn the interest rates, full speed ahead."

He gestured at our own home with a small sweep of his right arm and then let it drop back into his own lap. He and my mother had bought it the year before I was born for $62,000—it was now worth maybe $150,000—and they had only recently gotten their paper back from the bank. We had a little party in the back yard late last summer; Dad lit the barbecue, put the pink slip on the long fork, and each of us got a chance at holding it over the coals until it was gone.

"No English Tudor here, huh, Denny?" he said.

"It's fine," I said. I came back and sat down on the couch.

"Darnell and I parted amicably enough," my father went on, "not that I ever cared very much for him in a personal way. I thought he was a wretch."

I nodded a little, because I liked that; it expressed my gut feelings about Will Darnell better than any profanity could.

"But there's all the difference in the world between a personal relationship and a business relationship. You learn that very quickly in this business, or you give it up and start selling Fuller Brushes door-to-door. Our business relationship was good, as far as it went . . . but it didn't go far enough. That was why I finally called it quits."

"I don't get you."

"Cash kept showing up," he said. "Large amounts of cash with no clear ancestry. At Darnell's direction I invested in two corporations—Pennsylvania Solar Heating and New York Ticketing—that sounded like two of the dummiest dummy corporations I've ever heard of. Finally I went to see him, because I wanted all my cards on the table. I told him that my professional opinion was that, if he got audited either by the IRS or by the Commonwealth of Pennsylvania tax boys, he was apt to have a great deal of explaining to do, and that before long I was going to know too much to be an asset to him."

"What did he say?"

"He began to dance," my father said, still wearing that sleepy, cynical smile. "In my business, you start to get familiar with the steps of the dance by the time you're thirty-eight or so . . . if you're good at your business, that is. And I'm not all that bad. The dance starts off with the guy asking you if you're happy with your work, if it's paying you enough. If you say you like the work but you sure could be doing better, the guy encourages you to talk about whatever you're carrying on your back: your house, your car, your kids' college education—maybe you've got a wife with a taste for clothes a little fancier than she can by rights afford . . . see?"

"Sounding you out?"

"It's more like feeling you up," he said, and then laughed. "But yeah. The dance is every bit as mannered as a minuet. There are all sorts of phrases and pauses and steps. After the guy finds out what sort of financial burdens you'd like to get rid of, he starts asking you what sort of things you'd like to have. A Cadillac, a summer place in the Catskills or the Poconos, maybe a boat."

I gave a little start at that, because I knew my dad wanted a boat about as badly as he wanted anything these days; a couple of times I had gone with him on sunny summer afternoons to marinas along King George Lake and Lake Passeeonkee. He'd price out the smaller yachts and I'd see the wistful look in his eyes. Now I understood it. They were out of his reach. Maybe if his life had taken a different turn—if he didn't have kids to think about putting through college, for instance—they wouldn't have been.

"And you said no?" I asked him.

He shrugged. "I made it clear pretty early on that I didn't want to dance. For one thing, it would have meant getting more involved with him on a personal level, and, as I said, I thought he was a skunk. For another thing, these guys are all fundamentally stupid about numbers—which is why so many of them have gone up on tax convictions. They think you can hide illegal income. They're sure of it." He laughed. "They've all got this mystic idea that you can wash money like you wash clothes, when all you can really do is juggle it until something falls down and smashes all over your head."

"Those were the reasons?"

"Two out of three." He looked in my eyes. "I'm no fucking crook, Dennis."

There was a moment of electric communication between us—even now, four years later, I get goosebumps thinking of it, although I'm by no means sure that I can get it across to you. It wasn't that he treated me like an equal for the first time that night; it wasn't even that he was showing me the wistful knight-errant still hiding inside the button-down man scrambling for a living in a dirty, hustling world. I think it was sensing him as a *reality*, a person who had existed long before I ever came onstage, a person who had eaten his share of mud. In that moment I think I could have imagined him making love to my mother, both of them sweaty and working hard to make it, and not have been embarrassed.

Then he dropped his eyes, grinned a defensive grin, and did his husky Nixon-voice, which he was very good at: "You people deserve to know if your father is a crook. Well, I am not a crook, I could have taken the money, but that . . . *harrum!* . . . that would have been wrong."

I laughed too loud, a release of tension—I felt the moment passing, and although part of me didn't want it to pass, part of me did; it was too intense. I think maybe he felt that, too.

"Shhh, you'll wake your mother and she'll give us both the devil for being up this late."

"Yeah, sorry. Dad, do you know what he's into? Darnell?"

"I didn't know then; I didn't want to know, because then I'd be a part of it. I had my ideas, and I've heard a few things. Stolen cars, I imagine—not that he'd run them through that garage on Hampton Street; he's not a completely stupid man, and only an idiot shits where he eats. Maybe hijacking as well."

"Guns and stuff?" I asked, sounding a little hoarse.

"Nothing so romantic. If I had to guess, I'd guess cigarettes, mostly—cigarettes and booze, the two old standbys. Contraband like fireworks. Maybe a shipment of microwave ovens or color TVs every once in a while, if the risk looked low. Enough to keep him busy lo these many years."

He looked at me soberly.

"He's played the odds good, but he's also been lucky for a long time, Dennis. Oh, maybe he hasn't really needed luck here in town—if it was just Libertyville, I guess he could go on forever, or at least until he dropped dead of a heart attack—but the state tax boys are sand sharks and the feds are Great Whites. He's been lucky, but one of these days they're going to fall on him like the Great Wall of China."

"Have you . . . have you heard things?"

"Not a whisper. Nor am I apt to. But I like Arnie Cunningham a great deal, and I know you've been worried about this car thing."

"Yeah. He's . . . he's not acting healthy about it, Dad. Everything's the car, the car, the car."

"People who have not had a great deal tend to do that," he said. "Sometimes it's a car, sometimes it's a girl, sometimes it's a career or a musical instrument or an unhealthy obsession with some famous person. I went to college with a tall, ugly fellow we all called Stork. With Stork it was his model train set . . . he'd been hooked on model trains ever since the third grade, and his set was pretty damn near the eighth wonder of the world. He flunked out of Brown the second semester of his freshman year. His grades were going to hell, and what it came down to was a choice between college and his Lionels. Stork picked the trains."

"What happened to him?"

"He killed himself in 1961," my father said, and stood up. "My point is just that good people can sometimes get blinded, and it's not always their fault. Probably Darnell will forget all about him—he'll just be another guy tinkering around under his car on a crawlie-gator. But if Darnell tries to use him, you be his eyes, Dennis. Don't let him get pulled into the dance."

"All right. I'll try. But there may not be that much I can do."

"Yeah. How well I know it. Want to go up?"

"Sure."

We went up, and tired as I was, I lay awake a long time. It had been an eventful day. Outside, a night wind tapped a branch softly against the side of the house, and far away, downtown, I heard some kid's rod peeling rubber—it made a sound in the night like a hysterical woman's desperate laughter.

14 / Christine and Darnell

He said he heard about a couple
living in the U.S.A.,
He said they traded in their baby
for a Chevrolet:
Let's talk about the future now,
We've put the past away . . .
—Elvis Costello

Between working on the construction project days and working on Christine nights, Arnie hadn't been seeing much of his folks. Relations there had been getting pretty strained and abrasive. The Cunningham house, which had always been pleasant and low-key in the past, was now an armed camp. It is a state of affairs a lot of people can remember from their teenage years, I guess; too many, maybe. The kid is egotistical enough to think he or she is the first person in the world to discover some particular thing (usually it's a girl, but it doesn't have to be), and the parents are too scared and stupid and possessive to want to let go of the halter. Sins on both sides. Sometimes it gets painful and outrageous—no war is as dirty and bitter as a civil war. And it was particularly painful in Arnie's case because the split had come so late, and his folks had gotten much too used to having their own way. It wouldn't be unfair to say that they had blueprinted his life.

So when Michael and Regina proposed a four-day weekend at their lakeshore cottage in upstate New York before school started again, Arnie said yes even though he badly wanted those last four days to work on Christine. More and more often at work he had told me how he was going to "show them"; he was going to turn Christine into a real street-rod and "show them all." He had already planned to restore the car to its original bright red and ivory after the bodywork was done.

But he went off with them, determined to yassuh and tug his forelock for the whole four days and have a good time with his folks—or a reasonable facsimile. I got over the evening before they left and was relieved to find they had both absolved me of blame in the affair of Arnie's car (which they still hadn't even seen). They had apparently decided it was a private obsession. That was fine by me.

Regina was busy packing. Arnie and Michael and I got their Oldtown canoe on top of their Scout and tied it down. When it was done, Michael suggested to his son—with the air of a powerful king conferring an almost unbelievable favor on two of his favorite subjects—that Arnie go in and get a few beers.

Arnie, affecting both the expression and the tones of amazed gratitude, said that would be super. As he left, he dropped a wink my way.

Michael leaned against the Scout and lit a cigarette.

"Is he going to get tired of this car business, Denny?"

"I don't know," I said.

"You want to do me a favor?"

"Sure, if I can," I said cautiously. I was pretty sure he was going to ask me to go to Arnie, act the Dutch uncle part, and try to "talk him out of it."

But instead he said, "If you get a chance, go down to Darnell's while we're gone and see what sort of progress he's making. I'm interested."

"Why is that?" I asked, thinking immediately it was a pretty damn rude question—but by then it was already out.

"Because I want him to succeed," he said simply, and glanced at me. "Oh, Regina's still dead set against it. If he has a car, that means he's growing up, that means . . . all sorts of things," he finished lamely. "But I'm not so down on it. You couldn't characterize me as dead set against it anyway, at least not anymore. Oh, he caught me by surprise at first . . . I had visions of some dead dog sitting out in front of our house until Arnie went off to college—that or him choking to death on the exhaust some night."

The thought of Veronica LeBay jumped into my head, all unbidden.

"But now . . ." He shrugged, glanced at the door between

the garage and the kitchen, dropped his cigarette, and scuffed it out. "He's obviously committed. He's got his sense of self-respect on the line. I'd like to see him at least get it running."

Maybe he saw something in my face; when he went on he sounded defensive.

"I haven't quite forgotten everything about being young," he said. "I know a car is important to a kid Arnie's age. Regina can't see that quite so clearly. She always got picked up. She was never faced with the problems of being the picker-upper. I remember that a car is important . . . if a kid's ever going to have any dates."

So that's where he thought it was at. He saw Christine as a means to an end rather than as the end itself. I wondered what he'd think if I told him that I didn't think Arnie had ever looked any further than getting the Fury running and legal. I wondered if that would make him more or less uneasy.

The thump of the kitchen door closing.

"Would you go take a look?"

"I guess so," I said. "If you want."

"Thanks."

Arnie came back with the beers. "What's the thanks for?" he asked Michael. His voice was light and humorous, but his eyes flicked between us carefully. I noticed again that his complexion was really clearing, and his face seemed to have strengthened. For the first time, the two thoughts *Arnie* and *dates* didn't seem mutually exclusive. It occurred to me that his face was almost handsome—not in any jut-jawed lifeguard king-of-the-prom way, but in an interesting, thoughtful way. He would never be Roseanne's type, but . . .

"For helping with the canoe," Michael said casually.

"Oh."

We drank our beers. I went home. The next day the happy threesome went off together to New York, presumably to rediscover the family unity that had been lost over the latter third of the summer.

The day before they were due back, I took a ride down to Darnell's Garage—as much to satisfy my own curiosity as Michael Cunningham's.

The garage, standing in front of the block-long lot of junked cars, looked just as attractive in daylight as it had on the evening we had brought Christine—it had all the charm of a dead gopher.

I pulled into a vacant slot in front of the speed shop that

Darnell also ran—well stocked with such items as Feully heads, Hurst shifters, and Ram-jett superchargers (for all those working men who had to keep their old cars running so they could continue to put bread on the table, no doubt), not to mention a wide selection of huge mutant tires and a variety of spinner hubcaps. Looking through the window of Darnell's speed shop was like looking into a crazy automotive Disneyland.

I got out and walked back across the tarmac toward the garage and the clanging sound of tools, shouts, the machine-gun blast of pneumatic wrenches. A sleazy-looking guy in a cracked leather jacket was dorking around with an old BSA bike by one of the garage bays, either removing the bike's manifold or putting it back on. There was a stutter of road-rash down his left cheek. The back of his jacket displayed a skull wearing a Green Beret and the charming motto KILL EM ALL AND LET GOD SORT EM OUT.

He looked up at me with bloodshot and lunatic Rasputin eyes, then looked back at what he was doing. He had a surgical array of tools spread out beside him, each one die-stamped with the words DARNELL'S GARAGE.

Inside, the world was full of the echoey, evocative bang of tools and the sound of men working on cars and hollering profanity at the rolling iron they were working on. Always the profanity, and always female in gender: come offa there, you bitch, come loose, you cunt, come on over here, Rick, and help me get this twat off.

I looked around for Darnell and didn't see him any place. No one took any particular notice of me, so I walked over to stall twenty where Christine sat, now pointing nose-out, just like I had every right in the world to be there. In the stall to the right, two fat guys in bowling league shirts were putting a camper cap on the back of a pickup truck that had seen better days. The stall on the other side was deserted.

As I approached Christine, I felt that chill coming back. There was no reason for it, but I seemed helpless to stop it—and without even thinking, I moved a bit to the left, toward the empty stall. I didn't want to be in front of her.

My first thought was that Arnie's complexion had improved in tandem with Christine's. My second thought was that he was making his improvements in a strangely haphazard way . . . and Arnie was usually so methodical.

The twisted, broken antenna had been replaced with a straight new one that glimmered under the fluorescent bars.

Half the Fury's front grille had been replaced; the other half was still flecked and pitted with rust. And there was something else . . .

I walked along her right flank to the rear bumper, frowning.

Well, it was on the other side, that's all, I thought.

So I walked around to the other side, and it wasn't there, either.

I stood by the back wall, still frowning, trying to remember. I was pretty sure that when we first saw her standing on LeBay's lawn, with a FOR SALE sign propped against her windshield, there had been a good-sized rusty dent on one side or the other, near the rear end—the sort of deep dent that my grandfather always called a "hoss-kick." We'd be driving along the turnpike and we'd go by a car with a big dent in it somewhere and Grampy would say, "Hey, Denny, take a look there! Hoss kicked that one!" My grandfather was the sort of guy who had a downhome phrase for everything.

I started to think I must have imagined it, and then gave my head a little shake. That was sloppy thinking. It had been there; I remembered it clearly. Just because it wasn't here now didn't mean it hadn't been then. Arnie had obviously knocked it out, and had done a damn good piece of bodywork covering it up.

Except . . .

There was no *sign* that he had done anything. There was no primer paint, no gray body fill, no flaked paint. Just Christine's dull red and dirty white.

But it had *been there*, goddammit! A deep dimple filled with a snarl of rust, on one side or the other.

But it sure was gone now.

I stood there in the clatter and thud of tools and machinery and felt very alone and suddenly very scared. It was all wrong, it was all crazy. He had replaced the radio antenna when the tailpipe was practically dragging on the ground. He had replaced one half of the grille but not the other. He had talked to me about doing a front-end job, but inside he had replaced the ripped and dusty back seat cover with a bright red new one. The front seat cover was still a dusty wreck with a spring peeking through on the passenger side.

I didn't like it at all. It was crazy and it wasn't like Arnie.

Something came to me, a trace of memory, and without

even thinking about it, I stood back and looked at the entire car—not just one thing here and one thing there, but everything. And I had it; it clicked into place, and the chill came back.

That night when we had brought it here. The flat tire. The replacement. I had looked at that new tire on that old car and thought it was as if a little bit of the old car had been scratched away and that the new car—fresh, resplendent, just off the assembly line in a year when Ike had been President and Batista had still been in charge of Cuba—was peeking through.

What I was seeing now was like that . . . only instead of just a single new tire, there were all sorts of things—the aerial, a wink of new chrome from the grille, one taillight that was a bright deep red, that new seat cover in the back.

In its turn, that brought back something else from childhood. Arnie and I had gone to Vacation Bible School together for two weeks each summer, and every day the teacher would tell a Bible story and leave it unfinished. Then she would give each kid a blank sheet of "magic paper." And if you scraped the edge of a coin or the side of your pencil over it, a picture would gradually emerge out of the white—the dove bringing the olive branch back to Noah, the walls of Jericho tumbling down, good miracle stuff like that. It used to fascinate both of us, seeing the pictures gradually emerge. At first just lines floating in the void . . . and then the lines would connect with other lines . . . they would take on coherence . . . take on *meaning* . . .

I looked at Arnie's Christine with growing horror, trying to shake the feeling that in her I was seeing something terribly similar to those magic miracle pictures.

I wanted to look under the hood.

Suddenly it seemed very important that I look under the hood.

I went around to the front (I didn't like to stand in front of it—no good reason why not, I just didn't) and fumbled around for the hood release. I couldn't get it. Then I realized that it was probably inside.

I started to go around, and then I saw something else, something that scared me shitless. I could have been wrong about the hoss-kick, I suppose. I knew I wasn't, but at least *technically* . . .

But this was something else entirely.

The web of cracks in the windshield was smaller.

I was *positive* it was smaller.

My mind raced back to that day a month ago when I had wandered into LeBay's garage to look at the car while Arnie went into the house with the old man to do the deal. The entire left side of the windshield had been a spider's web of cracks radiating out from one central, zigzagging fault that had probably been caused by a flying stone.

Now the spider's web seemed smaller, simpler—you could see into the car from that side, and you hadn't been able to before, I was sure of that (*just a trick of the light, that's all,* my mind whispered).

Yet I *had* to be wrong—because it was impossible. Simply impossible. You could replace a windshield; that was no problem if you had the money. But to make a webbing of cracks *shrink*—

I laughed a little. It was a shaky sound, and one of the guys working on the camper cap looked up at me curiously and said something to his buddy. It was a shaky sound, but maybe better than no sound at all. Of *course* it was the light, and nothing more. I had seen the car for the first time with the westering sun shining fully on the flawed windshield, and I had seen it the second time in the shadows of LeBay's garage. Now I was seeing it under these high-set fluorescent tubes. Three different kinds of light, and all it added up to was an optical illusion.

Still, I wanted to look under the hood. More than ever.

I went around to the driver's side door and gave it a yank. The door didn't open. It was locked. Of course it was; all four of the door-lock buttons were down. Arnie wouldn't be apt to leave it unlocked in here, so anybody could get inside and poke around. Maybe Repperton was gone, but genus *Creepus* was weed-common. I laughed again—silly old Dennis—but this time it sounded even more shrill and shaky. I was starting to feel spaced-out, the way I sometimes felt the morning after I smoked a little too much pot.

Locking the Fury's doors was a very natural thing to do, all right. Except that, when I walked around the car the first time, I thought I had noticed the door-lock buttons had all been up.

I stepped slowly backward again, looking at the car. It sat there, still little more than rusting hulk. I was not thinking any one thing specific—I am quite sure of that—except maybe it was as if it knew that I wanted to get inside and pull the hood release.

And because it didn't want me to do that, it had locked its own doors?

That was really a very humorous idea. So humorous that I had another laugh (several people were glancing at me now, the way that folks always glance at people who laugh for no apparent reason when they are by themselves).

A big hand fell on my shoulder and turned me around. It was Darnell, with a dead stub of cigar stuck in the side of his mouth. The end of it was wet and pretty gross-looking. He was wearing small half-specs, and the eyes behind them were coldly speculative.

"What are you doing, kiddo?" he asked. "This ain't your property."

The guys with the camper cap were watching us avidly. One of them nudged the other and whispered something.

"It belongs to a friend of mine," I said. "I brought it in with him. Maybe you remember me. I was the one with the large skin-tumor on the end of my nose and the—"

"I don't give a shit if you wheeled it in on a skateboard," he said. "It ain't your property. Take your bad jokes and get lost, kid. Blow."

My father was right—he was a wretch. And I would have been more than happy to blow; I could think of at least six thousand places I'd rather be on this second-to-last day of my summer vacation. Even the Black Hole of Calcutta would have been an improvement. Not a big one, maybe, yet an improvement, all the same. But the car bothered me. A lot of little things, all adding up to a big itch that needed to be scratched. *Be his eyes*, my father had said, and that sounded good. The problem was I couldn't believe what I was seeing.

"My name is Dennis Guilder," I said. "My dad used to do your books, didn't he?"

He looked at me for a long time with no expression at all in his cold little pig eyes, and I was suddenly sure he was going to tell me he didn't give a fuck who my father was, that I'd better blow and let these working men go about the business of fixing their cars so they could go on putting bread on their tables. Et cetera.

Then he smiled—but the smile didn't touch his eyes at all. "You're Kenny Guilder's boy?"

"Yes, that's right."

He patted the hood of Arnie's car with one pale, fat hand—there were two rings on it, and one of them looked like a real diamond. Still, what does a kid like me know?

"I guess you're straight enough, then. If you're Kenny's kid." There was a second when I thought he was going to ask for some identification.

The two guys next to us had gone back to work on their camper, apparently having decided nothing interesting was going to transpire.

"Come on into the office and let's have a talk," he said, then turned away and moved across the floor without even a glance backward. That I would comply was taken for granted. He moved like a ship under full sail, his white shirt billowing, the girth of his hips and backside amazing, improbable. Very fat people always affect me that way, with a feeling of distinct improbability, as if I were looking at a very good optical illusion—but then, I come from a long line of skinny people. For my family I'm a heavyweight.

He paused here and there on his way back to his office, which had a glass wall looking out onto the garage. He reminded me a little bit of Moloch, the god we read about in my Origins of Literature class—he was the one who was supposed to be able to see everywhere with his one red eye. Darnell bawled at one guy to get the hose on his tailpipe before he threw him out; yelled something to another guy about how "Nicky's back was acting up on him again" (this inspired a fuming, ferocious burst of laughter from both of them); hollered at another guy to pick up those fucking Pepsi-Cola cans, was he born in a dump? Apparently Will Darnell didn't know anything about what my mother always called "a normal tone of voice."

After a moment's hesitation, I followed him. Curiosity killed the cat, I suppose.

His office was done in Early American Carburetor—it was every scuzzy garage office from coast to coast in a country that runs on rubber and amber gold. There was a greasy calendar with a pin-up of a blond goddess in short-shorts and an open blouse climbing over a fence in the country. There were unreadable plaques from half a dozen companies which sold auto parts. Stacks of ledgers. An ancient adding machine. There was a photograph, God save us, of Will Darnell wearing a Shriner's fez and mounted on a miniature motorcycle that looked about to collapse under his bulk. And there was the smell of long-departed cigars and sweat.

Darnell sat down in a swivel chair with wooden arms. The cushion wheezed beneath him. It sounded tired but resigned.

He leaned back. He took a match from the hollow head of a ceramic Negro jockey. He struck it on a strip of sandpaper that ran along the edge of his desk and fired up the wet stub of cigar. He coughed long and hard, his big, loose chest heaving up and down. Directly behind him, tacked to the wall, was a picture of Garfield the Cat. "Want a trip to Loose-Tooth City?" Garfield was inquiring over one cocked paw. It seemed to sum up Will Darnell, Wretch in Residence, perfectly.

"Want a Pepsi, kid?"

"No, thank you," I said, and sat down in the straight chair opposite him.

He looked at me—that cold look of appraisal again—and then nodded. "How's your dad, Dennis? His ticker still okay?"

"He's fine. When I told him Arnie had his car here, he remembered you right off. He says Bill Upshaw's doing your figures now."

"Yeah. Good man. Good man. Not as good as your dad, but good."

I nodded. A silence fell between us, and I began to feel uneasy. Will Darnell didn't look uneasy; he didn't look anything at all. That cold look of appraisal never changed.

"Did your buddy send you to find out if Repperton was really gone?" he asked me, so suddenly that I jumped.

"No," I said. "Not at all."

"Well, you tell him he is," Darnell went on, ignoring what I'd just said. "Little wiseass. I tell em when they run their junk in here: get along or get out. He was working for me, doing a little of this and a little of that, and I guess he thought he had the gold key to the crapper or something. Little wiseass *punk*."

He started coughing again, and it was a long time before he stopped. It was a sick sound. I was beginning to feel claustrophobic in the office, even with the window looking out on the garage.

"Arnie's a good boy," Darnell said presently, still measuring me with his eyes. Even while he was coughing, that expression hadn't changed. "He's picked up the slack real good."

Doing what? I wanted to ask, and just didn't dare.

Darnell told me anyway. Cold glance aside, he was apparently feeling expansive. "Sweeps the floor, takes the crap out of the garage bays at the end of the day, keeps the tools inventoried, along with Jimmy Sykes. Have to be careful with tools around here, Dennis. They got a way of walkin away when your back's turned." He laughed, and the laugh turned into a wheeze. "Got him started strippin parts out back, as well. He's got good hands. Good hands and bad taste in cars. I ain't seen such a dog as that '58 in years."

"Well, I guess he sees it as a hobby," I said.

"Sure," Darnell said expansively. "Sure he does. Just as long as he doesn't want to ramrod around with it like that punk, that Repperton. But not much chance of that for a while, huh?"

"I guess not. It looks pretty wasted."

"What the fuck is he doing to it?" Darnell asked. He leaned forward suddenly, his big shoulders going up all the way to his hairline. His brows pulled in, and his eyes disappeared except for small twin gleams. "What the fuck is he up to? I been in this business all my life, and I *never* seen anyone go at fixing a car up the crazy-ass way he is. Is it a joke? A game?"

"I'm not getting you," I said, although I was—I was getting him perfectly.

"Then I'll draw you a pitcher," Darnell said. "He brings it in, and at first he's doing all the things I'd expect him to do. What the fuck, he ain't got money falling out of his asshole, right? If he did, he wouldn't be here. He changes the oil. He changes the filter. Grease-job, lube, I see one day he's got two new Firestones for the front to go with the two on the back."

Two on the back? I wondered, and then decided he'd just bought three new tires to go with the original new one I'd gotten the night we were bringing it over here.

"Then I come in one day and see he's replaced the windshield wipers," Darnell continued. "Not so strange, except that the car's not going to be going anywhere—rain *or* shine—for a long time. Then it's a new antenna for the radio, and I think, He's gonna listen to the radio while he's working on it and drain his battery. Now he's got one new seat cover and half a grille. So what is it? A game?"

"I don't know," I said. "Did he buy the replacement parts from you?"

"No," Darnell said, sounding aggravated. "I don't know where he gets them. That grille—there isn't a spot of rust on it. He must have ordered it from somewhere. Custom

Chrysler in New Jersey or someplace like that. But where's the other half? Up his ass? I never even *heard* of a grille that came in two pieces."

"I don't know. Honest."

He jammed the cigar out. "Don't tell me you're not curious, though. I saw the way you was lookin at that car."

I shrugged. "Arnie doesn't talk about it much," I said.

"No, I bet he doesn't. He's a close-mouthed sonofabitch. He's a fighter, though. That Repperton pushed the wrong button when he started in on Cunningham. If he works out okay this fall, I might find a steady job for him this winter. Jimmy Sykes is a good boy, but he ain't much in the brains department." His eyes measured me. "Think he's a pretty good worker, Dennis?"

"He's okay."

"I got a lot of irons in the fire," he said. "Lot of irons. I rent out flatbeds to guys that need to haul their stockers up to Philadelphia City. I haul away the junkers after races. I can always use help. Good, trustworthy help."

I began to have a horrid suspicion that I was being asked to dance. I got up hurriedly, almost knocking over the straight chair. "I really ought to get going," I said. "And . . . Mr. Darnell . . . I'd appreciate it if you didn't mention to Arnie that I was here. He's . . . a little touchy about the car. To tell you the truth, his father was curious about how he was coming along."

"Took a little shit on the home front, did he?" Darnell's right eye closed shrewdly in something that was not quite a wink. "Folks ate a few pounds of Ex-Lax and then stood over him with their legs spread, did they?"

"Yeah, well, you know."

"You bet I know." He was up in one smooth motion and clapped me on the back hard enough to stagger me on my feet. Wheezy respiration and cough or not, he was strong.

"Wouldn't mention it," he said, walking me toward the door. His hand was still on my shoulder, and that also made me feel nervous—and a little disgusted.

"I tell you something else that bothers me," he said. "I must see a hundred thousand cars a year in this place—well, not that many, but you know what I mean—and I got an eye for em. You know, I could swear I've seen that one before. When it wasn't such a dog. Where did he get it?"

"From a man named Roland LeBay," I said, thinking of

LeBay's brother telling me that LeBay did all the maintenance himself at some do-it-yourself garage. "He's dead now."

Darnell stopped cold. "LeBay? *Rollie* LeBay?"

"Yes, that's right."

"Army? Retired?"

"Yes."

"Holy Christ, sure! He brought it in here just as regular as clockwork for six, maybe eight years, then he stopped coming. A long time ago. What a bastard that man was. If you poured boiling water down that whoremaster's throat, he would have peed ice cubes. He couldn't get along with a living soul." He gripped my shoulder harder. "Does your friend Cunningham know LeBay's wife committed suicide in that car?"

"What?" I said, acting surprised—I didn't want him to know I'd been interested enough to talk to LeBay's brother after the funeral. I was afraid Darnell might repeat the information to Arnie—complete with his source.

Darnell told me the whole story. First the daughter, then the mother.

"No," I said when he was done. "I'm pretty sure Arnie doesn't know that. Are you going to tell him?"

The eyes, appraising again. "Are you?"

"No," I said. "I don't see any reason to."

"Then neither do I." He opened the door, and the greasy air of the garage smelled almost sweet after the cigar smoke in the office. "That sonofabitch LeBay, I'll be damned. I hope he's doing right-face-left-face and to-the-rear-harch down in hell." His mouth turned down viciously for just a moment, and then he glanced over at where Christine sat in stall twenty with her old, rusting paint and that new radio antenna and half a grille. "*That* bitch back again," he said, and then he glanced at me. "Well, they say bad pennies always turn up, huh?"

"Yes," I said. "I guess they do."

"So long, kid," he said, sticking a fresh cigar in his mouth. "Say hi to your dad for me."

"I will."

"And tell Cunningham to keep an eye out for that punk Repperton. I got an idea he might be the sort who'd hold a grudge."

"Me too," I said.

I walked out of the garage, pausing once to glance back—but looking in from the glare, Christine was little more than a shadow among shadows. *Bad pennies always turn up*, Darnell said. It was a phrase that followed me home.

15 / Football Woes

Learn to work the saxophone,
I play just what I feel,
Drink Scotch whiskey
All night long,
And die behind the wheel . . .
                                        —Steely Dan

School started, and nothing much happened for a week or two. Arnie didn't find out I'd been down to the garage, and I was glad. I don't think he would have taken kindly to the news. Darnell kept his mouth shut as he had promised (probably for his own reasons). I called Michael one afternoon after school when I knew Arnie would be down at the garage. I told him Arnie had done some stuff to the car, but it was nowhere near street-legal. I told him my impression was that Arnie was mostly farting around. Michael greeted this news with a mixture of relief and surprise, and that ended it . . . for a while.

Arnie himself flickered in and out of my view, like something you see from the corner of your eye. He was around the halls, and we had three classes together, and he sometimes came over after school or on weekends. There were times when it really seemed as if nothing had changed. But he was at Darnell's a lot more than he was at my house, and on Friday nights he went out to Philly Plains—the stock-car track—with Darnell's half-bright handyman, Jimmy Sykes. They ran out sportsters and charger-class racers, mostly Camaros and Mustangs with their glass knocked out and roll bars installed. They took them out on Darnell's flatbed and came back with fresh junk for the automobile graveyard.

It was around that time that Arnie hurt his back. It wasn't a serious injury—or so he claimed—but my mother noticed that something was wrong with him almost right away. He came over one Sunday to watch the Phillies, who were pounding down the homestretch to moderate glory that year, and happened to get up during the third inning to pour us each a glass of orange juice. My mother was sitting on the couch with my father, reading a book. She glanced up when Arnie came back in and said, "You're limping, Arnie."

I thought I saw a surprising, unexpected expression on Arnie's face for a second or two—a furtive, almost guilty look. I could have been wrong. If it *was* there, it was gone a second later.

"I guess I strained my back out at the Plains last night," he said, giving me my orange juice. "Jimmy Sykes stalled out the last of the clunks we were loading just when it was almost up on the bed of the truck. I could see it rolling back down and then the two of us goofing around for another two hours, trying to get it started again. So I gave it a shove. Guess I shouldn't have."

It seemed like an elaborate explanation for a simple little limp, but I could have been wrong about that too.

"You have to be more careful of your back," my mother said severely. "The Lord—"

"Mom, could we watch the game now?" I asked.

"—only gives you one," she finished.

"Yes, Mrs. Guilder," Arnie said dutifully.

Elaine wandered in. "Is there any more juice, or did you two coneheads drink it all?"

"Come on, give me a break!" I yelled. There had been some sort of disputed play at second and I had missed the whole thing.

"Don't shout at your sister, Dennis," my father muttered from the depths of *The Hobbyist* magazine he was reading.

"There's a lot left, Ellie," Arnie told her.

"Sometimes, Arnie," Elaine told him, "you strike me as almost human." She flounced out to the kitchen.

"Almost human, Dennis!" Arnie whispered to me, apparently on the verge of grateful tears. "Did you hear that? Almost *hyooooman*."

And perhaps it is also only retrospection—or imagination—that makes me think his humor was forced, unreal, only a facade. False memory or true one, the subject of his back passed off, although that limp came and went all through the fall.

I was pretty busy myself. The cheerleader and I had broken it off, but I could usually find someone to step out with on Saturday nights . . . if I wasn't too tired from the constant football practice.

Coach Puffer wasn't a wretch like Will Darnell, but he was no rose; like half the smalltown high school coaches in America, he had patterned his coaching techniques on those of the late Vince Lombardi, whose chief scripture was that winning wasn't everything, it was the *only* thing. You'd be surprised how many people who should know better believe that half-baked horseshit.

A summer of working for Carson Brothers had left me in rugged shape and I think I could have cruised through the season—if it had been a winning season. But by the time Arnie and I had the ugly confrontation near the smoking area behind the shop with Buddy Repperton—and I think that was during the third week of classes—it was pretty clear we weren't going to have a winning season. That made Coach Puffer extremely hard to live with, because in his ten years at LHS, he had *never* had a losing season. That was the year Coach Puffer had to learn a bitter humility. It was a hard lesson for him . . . and it wasn't so easy for us, either.

Our first game, away against the Luneburg Tigers, was September ninth. Now, Luneburg is just that—a burg. It's a little piss-ant rural high school at the extreme west of our district, and over my years at Libertyville, the usual battle cry after Luneburg's bumbling defense had allowed yet another touchdown was: *TELL-US-HOW-IT-FEELS-TO-HAVE-COWSHIT-ON-YOUR-HEELS!* Followed by a big, sarcastic cheer: *RAAAAYYYYYY, LUUUUNEBURG!*

It had been over twenty years since Luneburg beat a Libertyville team, but that year they rose up and smote us righteously. I was playing left end, and by halftime I was morally sure that I was going to have cleat-mark scars all over my back for the rest of my life. By then the score was 17–3. It ended up 30–10. The Luneburg fans were delirious; they tore down the goalposts as if it had been the Regional Championship game and carried their players off the field on their shoulders.

Our fans, who had come up in buses specially laid on, sat huddled on the visitors' bleachers in the blaring early September heat, looking blank. In the dressing room, Coach Puffer, looking stunned and pallid, suggested we get down on our knees and pray for guidance in the weeks to come. I knew then that the hurting had not ended but was just beginning.

We got down on our knees, aching, bruised, and battered, wanting nothing but to get into the shower and start washing that loser smell off ourselves, and listened as Coach Puffer explained the situation to God in a ten-minute peroration that ended with a promise that we would do our part if He would do His.

The next week, we practiced three hours a day (instead of the customary ninety minutes to two hours) under the broiling sun. I tumbled into bed nights and dreamed of his bellowing voice: *"Hit that sucker! Hit! Hit!"* I ran windsprints until I began to feel that my legs were going to undergo spontaneous decomposition (at the same instant my lungs burst into flames, probably). Lenny Barongg, one of our tailbacks, had a mild sunstroke and was mercifully—for him, at least—excused for the rest of the week.

So I saw Arnie, and he came over and took dinner with my folks and Ellie and me on Thursday or Friday nights, he checked out a ballgame or two with us on Sunday afternoons, but beyond that I lost sight of him almost completely. I was too busy hauling my aches and pains to class, to practice, then home to my room to do my assignments

Going back to my football woes—I think the worst thing was the way people looked at me, and Lenny, and the rest of the team, in the hallways. Now, that "school spirit" business is mostly a lot of bullshit made up by school administrators who remember having a helluva time at the Saturday-afternoon gridiron contests of their youth but have conveniently forgotten that a lot of it resulted from being drunk, horny, or both. If you had held a rally in favor of legalizing marijuana, you would have seen some school spirit. But about football, basketball, and track, most of the student body didn't give a shit. They were too busy trying to get into college or someone's pants or trouble. Business as usual.

All the same, you get used to being a winner—you start to take it for granted. Libertyville had been fielding killer football teams for a long time; the last time the school had had a losing record—at least, before my senior year—was twelve years before, in 1966. So in the week after the loss to Luneburg, while there was no weeping and gnashing of teeth, there were hurt, puzzled looks in the hall and some booing at the regular Friday afternoon rally at the end of period seven. The boos made Coach Puffer turn nearly purple, and he invited those "poor sports and fair-weather friends" to turn out Saturday afternoon to watch the comeback of the century.

I don't know if the poor sports and fair-weather friends turned out or not, but I was there. We were at home, and our opponents were the Ridge Rock Bears. Now Ridge Rock is a mining town, and while the kids going to Ridge Rock High are hicks, they are not soft hicks. They are mean, ugly, tough hicks. The year before, Libertyville's football team had barely edged them out for the regional title, and one of the local sports commentators had said it wasn't because Libertyville had a better team but because it had more warm bodies to draw on. Coach Puffer had hit the ceiling over that too, I can tell you.

This, however, was the Bears' year. They steamrollered us. Fred Dann went out of the game with a concussion in the first period. In the second period, Norman Aleppo got a ride to the Libertyville Community Hospital with a broken arm. And in the last period, the Bears scored three consecutive touchdowns, two on punt returns. The final score was 40–6. All false modesty aside, I'll tell you that I scored the six. But I won't put realism aside with the modesty: I was lucky.

So . . . another week of hell on the practice field. Another week of Coach yelling *Hit that sucker*. One day we practiced for nearly four hours, and when Lenny suggested to Coach that it might be nice to have some time left for doing homework, I thought—just for an instant—that Puffer was going to belt him one. He had taken to jingling his keys constantly from hand to hand, reminding me of Captain Queeg in *The Caine Mutiny*. I believe that how you lose is a much better index to character than how you win. Puffer, who had never been 0–2 in his coaching career, reacted with baffled, pointless fury, like a caged tiger being teased by cruel children.

The next Friday afternoon—that would have been September 22—the usual rally during the last fifteen minutes of period seven was cancelled. I didn't know any of the players who minded; standing up there and being introduced by twelve prancing cheerleaders for the umpty-umpth time was sort of a bore. It was an ominous sign, all the same. That night we were invited back to the gym by Coach Puffer, where we went to the movies for two hours, watching our humiliation by the Tigers and the Bears in the game films. Perhaps this was supposed to fire us up, but it only depressed me.

That night, before our second home game of the year, I

had a peculiar dream. It was not exactly a nightmare, not like the one where I woke the house screaming, certainly, but it was . . . uncomfortable. We were playing the Philadelphia City Dragons, and a strong wind was blowing. The sounds of the cheers, the blaring, distorted voice of Chubby McCarthy from the loudspeaker as he announced downs and yards, even the sounds of players hitting other players, all sounded weird and echoey in that constant, flat wind.

The faces in the stands seemed yellow and oddly shadowed, like the faces of Chinese masks. The cheerleaders danced and capered like jerky automatons. The sky was a queer gray, running with clouds. We were being badly beaten. Coach Puffer was yelling in plays, but no one could hear him. The Dragons were running away from us. The ball was always theirs. Lenny Barongg looked as if he was playing with terrible pain; his mouth was drawn down in a trembling bow like a mask of tragedy.

I was hit, knocked down, run over. I lay on the playing field, far behind the line of scrimmage, writhing, trying to get my breath back. I looked up and there, parked in the middle of the track field, behind the visitors' bleachers, was Christine. Once more she was sparkling and brand-new, as if she had rolled out of the showroom only an hour before.

Arnie was sitting on the roof, crosslegged like Buddha, looking at me expressionlessly. He hollered something at me, but the steady howl of the wind almost buried it. It sounded as if he said: *Don't worry, Dennis. We'll take care of everything. So don't worry. All is cool.*

Take care of what? I wondered as I lay there on the dream playing field (which my dreaming self had, for some reason, converted into Astro-Turf), struggling for breath with my jock digging cruelly into the fork of my thighs just below my testicles. *Take care of what?*

Of what?

No answer. Only the baleful shine of Christine's yellow headlamps and Arnie sitting serenely crosslegged on her roof in that steady, rushing wind.

The next day we got out there and did battle for good old Libertyville High again. It wasn't as bad as it had been in my dream—that Saturday no one got hurt, and for a brief while in the third quarter it even looked as though we might have a chance—but then the Philadelphia City quarterback got lucky with a couple of long passes—when things start to go wrong, *everything* goes wrong—and we lost again.

After the game, Coach Puffer just sat there on the bench. He wouldn't look at any of us. There were eleven games left on our schedule, but he was already a beaten man.

16 / Enter Leigh, Exit Buddy

I'm not braggin, babe, so don't put me down,
But I've got the fastest set of wheels in town,
When someone comes up to me he don't even try
Cause if she had a set of wings, man,
*   I know she could fly,*
She's my little deuce coupe,
You don't know what I got . . .

—The Beach Boys

It was, I am quite sure, the Tuesday after our loss to the Philadelphia City Dragons that things began moving again. That would have been the twenty-sixth of September.

Arnie and I had three classes together, and one of them was Topics in American History, a block course, period four. The first nine weeks were being taught by Mr. Thompson, the head of the department. The subject of that first nine weeks was Two Hundred Years of Boom and Bust. Arnie called it a boing-boing-going-going class, because it was right before lunch and everybody's stomach seemed to be doing something interesting.

When the class was over that day, a girl came over to Arnie and asked him if he had the English assignment. He did. He dug it out of his notebook carefully, and while he did, this girl watched him seriously with her dark blue eyes, never taking them off his face. Her hair was a darkish blond, the color of fresh honey—not the strained stuff, but honey the way it first comes from the comb—and held back with a wide blue band that matched her eyes. Looking at her, my stomach did a happy little flip-flop. As she copied the assignment down, Arnie looked at her.

That wasn't the first time I had seen Leigh Cabot, of course; she had transferred from a town in Massachusetts to Libertyville three weeks ago, so she had been around. Somebody had told me her father worked for 3M, the people who make Scotch tape.

It wasn't even the first time I had noticed her, because Leigh Cabot was, to put it with perfect simplicity, a beautiful girl. In a work of fiction, I've noticed that writers always invent a flaw here or a flaw there in the women and girls they make up, maybe because they think real beauty is a stereotype or because they think a flaw or two makes the lady more realistic. So she'll be beautiful except her lower lip is too long, or in spite of the fact that her nose is a little too sharp, or maybe she's flat-chested. It's always something.

But Leigh Cabot was just beautiful, with no qualifications. Her skin was fair and perfect, usually with a touch of perfectly natural color. She stood about five feet eight, tall for a girl but not too tall, and her figure was lovely—firm, high breasts, a small waist that looked as if you could almost put your hands around it (anyway, you longed to try), nice hips, good legs. Beautiful face, sexy, smooth figure—artistically dull, I suppose, without a too-long lower lip or a sharp nose or a wrong bump or bulge anywhere (not even an endearing crooked tooth—she must have had a great orthodontist, too), but she sure didn't *feel* dull when you were looking at her.

A few guys had tried to date her and had been pleasantly turned down. It was assumed she was probably carrying a torch for some guy back in Andover or Braintree or wherever it was she had come from, and that she'd probably come around in time. Two of the classes I had with Arnie I also had with Leigh, and I had only been biding my time before making my own move.

Now, watching them steal glances at each other as Arnie found the assignment and she wrote it carefully down, I wondered if I was going to have a chance to make my move. Then I had to grin at myself. Arnie Cunningham, Ole Pizza-Face himself, and Leigh Cabot. That was totally ridiculous. That was—

Then the interior smile sort of dried up. I noticed for the third time—the definitive time—that Arnie's complexion was taking care of itself with almost stunning rapidity. The blemishes were gone. Some of them had left those small, pitted scars along his cheeks, true, but if a guy's face is a strong one, those pits don't seem to matter as much; in a crazy sort of way, they can even add character.

Leigh and Arnie studied each other surreptitiously and I studied Arnie surreptitiously, wondering exactly when and how this miracle had taken place. The sunlight slanted strongly through the windows of Mr. Thompson's room, delineating the lines of my friend's face clearly. He looked . . . older. As if he had beaten the blemishes and the acne not only by regular washing or the application of some special cream but by somehow turning the clock ahead about three years. He was wearing his hair differently, too—it was shorter, and the sideburns he had affected ever since he could grow them (that was since about eighteen months ago) were gone.

I thought back to that overcast afternoon when we had gone to see the Chuck Norris Kung-fu picture. That was the first time I had noticed an improvement, I decided. Right around the time he had bought the car. Maybe that was it. Teenagers of the world, rejoice. Solve painful acne problems forever. Buy an old car and it will—

The interior grin, which had been surfacing once more, suddenly went sour.

Buy an old car and it will what? Change your head, your way of thinking, and thus change your metabolism? Liberate the real you? I seemed to hear Stukey James, our old high school math teacher, whispering his oft-repeated refrain in my own head: *If we follow this line of reasoning to the bitter end, ladies and gentlemen, where does it take us?*

Where indeed?

"Thank you, Arnie," Leigh said in her soft, clear voice. She had folded the assignment into her notebook.

"Sure," he said.

Their eyes met then—they were looking at each other instead of just sneaking glances at each other—and even I could feel the spark jump.

"See you period six," she said, and walked away, hips undulating gently under a green knitted skirt, hair swinging against the back of her sweater.

"What have you got with her period six?" I asked. I had a study hall that period—and one proctored by the formidable Miss Raypach, whom all the kids called Miss Rat-Pack . . . but never to her face, you can believe that.

"Calculus," he said in this dreamy, syrupy voice that was

so unlike his usual one that I got giggling. He looked around at me, brows drawing together. "What are you laughing at, Dennis?"

"Cal-Q-lussss," I said. I rolled my eyes and flapped my hands and laughed harder.

He made as if to punch me. "You better watch it, Guilder," he said.

"Off my case, potato-face."

"They put you on varsity and look what happens to the fucking football team."

Mr. Hodder, who teaches freshmen the finer points of grammar (and also how to jerk off, some wits said) happened to be passing by just then, and he frowned impressively at Arnie. "Watch your language in the halls," he said, and passed onward, a briefcase in one hand and a hamburger from the hot-lunch line in the other.

Arnie had gone beet-red; he always does when a teacher speaks to him (it was such an automatic reaction that when we were in grammar school he would end up getting punished for things he hadn't done just because he *looked* guilty). It probably says something about the way Michael and Regina brought him up—I'm okay, you're okay, I'm a person, you're a person, we all respect each other to the hilt, and whenever anybody does anything wrong, you're going to get what amounts to an allergic guilt reaction. All part of growing up liberal in America, I guess.

"Watch your language, Cunningham," I said. "You in a *heap* o trouble."

Then he got laughing too. We walked down the echoing, banging hallway together. People rushed here and there or leaned up against their lockers, eating. You weren't supposed to eat in the hallways, but lots of people did.

"Did you bring your lunch?" I asked.

"Yeah, brown-bagging it."

"Go get it. Let's eat out on the bleachers."

"Aren't you sick of that football field by now?" Arnie asked. "If you'd spent much more time on your belly last Saturday, I think one of the custodians would have planted you."

"I don't mind. We're playing away this week. And I want to get out of here."

"All right, meet you out there."

He walked away, and I went to my locker to get my lunch. I had four sandwiches, for starters. Since Coach Puffer had started his marathon practice sessions, it seemed as if I was always hungry.

I walked down the hall, thinking about Leigh Cabot and how it would pretty much stand everyone on their ear if they started going out together. High school society is very conservative, you know. No big lecture, but it is. The girls all wear the latest nutty fashions, the boys sometimes wear their hair most of the way down to their assholes, everyone is smoking a little dope or sniffing a little coke—but all of that is just the outward patina, the defense you put up while you try and figure out exactly what's happening with your life. It's like a mirror—what you use to reflect sunlight back into the eyes of teachers and parents, hoping to confuse them before they can confuse you even more than you already are. At heart, most high school kids are about as funky as a bunch of Republican bankers at a church social. There are girls who might have every album Black Sabbath ever made, but if Ozzy Osbourne went to their school and asked one of them for a date, that girl (and all of her friends) would laugh herself into a hemorrhage at the very idea.

With his acne and pimples gone, Arnie looked okay—in fact, he looked more than okay. But there wasn't a girl who had gone to school with him when his face was at its running worst that would go out with him, I guessed. They didn't really see him the way he was now; they saw a memory of him. But Leigh was different. Because she was a transfer, she had no idea of how really gross Arnie had looked his first three years at LHS. Of course she would if she got last year's *Libertonian* and took a look at the picture of the chess club, but oddly enough, that same Republican tendency would almost surely make her disregard it. *What's now is forever*—ask any Republican banker and he'll tell you that's just the way the world ought to run.

High school kids and Republican bankers . . . when you're little you take it for granted that everything changes constantly. When you're a grown-up, you take it for granted that things are going to change no matter how much you try to maintain the status quo (even Republican bankers know that—they may not like it, but they know it). It's only when you're a teenager that you talk about change constantly and believe in your heart that it never really happens.

I went outside with my gigantic bag lunch in one hand and angled across the parking lot toward the shop building. It is a long, barnlike structure with corrugated metal sides painted blue—not very different in design from Will Darnell's garage, but much neater. It houses the wood shop, the auto shop, and the graphic arts department. Supposedly the smoking area is around at the rear, but on nice days during the lunch break, there are usually shoppies lined up along both sides of the building with their motorcycle boots or their pointy-toed Cuban shitkickers cocked up against the building, smoking and talking to their girlfriends. Or feeling them up.

Today there was nobody at all along the right side of the building, and that should have told me something was up, but it didn't. I was lost in my own amusing thoughts about Arnie and Leigh and the psychology of the Modern American High School Student.

The real smoking area—the "designated" smoking area—is in a small cul-de-sac behind the auto shop. And beyond the shops, fifty or sixty yards away, is the football field, dominated with the big electric scoreboard with GO GET THEM TERRIERS emblazoned across the top.

There was a group of people just beyond the smoking area, twenty or thirty of them in a tight little circle. That pattern usually means a fight or what Arnie likes to call a "pushy-pushy"—two guys who aren't really mad enough to fight sort of shoving each other around and whacking each other on the shoulders and trying to protect their macho reputations.

I glanced that way, but with no real interest. I didn't want to watch a fight; I wanted to eat my lunch and find out if anything was going on between Arnie and Leigh Cabot. If there was a little something happening there, it might take his mind off his obsession with Christine. One thing for sure: Leigh Cabot didn't have any rust on her rocker panels.

Then some girl screamed and someone else yelled, "Hey, no! Put that away, man!" That sounded very much ungood. I changed direction to see what was going on.

I pushed my way through the crowd and saw Arnie in the circle, standing with his hands held out a little in front of him at chest level. He looked pale and scared, but not quite panicked. A little distance to his left was a lunch-sack, squashed flat. There was a large sneakerprint in the middle of it. Standing opposite him, in jeans and a white Hanes T-shirt that clung to every ripple and bulge on his chest, was Buddy Repperton. He had a switchblade knife in his right hand and he was moving it slowly back and forth in front of his face like a magician making mystic passes.

He was tall and broad-shouldered. His hair was long and

black. He wore it tied back in a ponytail with a hank of rawhide. His face was heavy and stupid and mean-looking. He was smiling just a little. What I felt was an unmanning mixture of dismay and cold fear. He didn't look *just* stupid and mean; he looked crazy.

"Told you I was gonna getcha, man," he said softly to Arnie. He tilted the knife and jabbed softly at the air with it in Arnie's direction. Arnie flinched back a little. The switchblade had an ivory handle with a little chrome button to flick out the blade set into it. The blade itself looked to be about eight inches long—it wasn't a knife at all, it was a fucking bayonet.

"Hey, Buddy, brand 'im!" Don Vandenberg yelled happily, and I felt my mouth go dry.

I looked around at the kid next to me, some nerdy freshman I didn't know. He looked absolutely hypnotized, all eyes. "Hey," I said, and when he didn't look around I slammed my elbow into his side. *"Hey!"*

He jumped and looked around at me in terror.

"Go get Mr. Casey. He eats his lunch in the wood-shop office. Go get him right now."

Repperton glanced at me, then glanced at Arnie. "Come on, Cunningham," he said. "What do you say, you want to go for it?"

"Put down the knife and I will, you shitter," Arnie said. His voice was perfectly calm. Shitter, where had I heard that word before? From George LeBay, hadn't it been? Sure. It had been his brother's word.

It apparently wasn't a word Repperton cared for. He flushed and stepped closer to Arnie. Arnie circled away. I thought something was going to happen pretty quick—maybe one of those things that call for stitches and leave a scar.

"You go get Casey *now,"* I told the nerdy-looking freshman, and he went. But I thought everything would probably go down before Mr. Casey got back . . . unless I could maybe slow things down a little.

"Put down the knife, Repperton," I said.

His glance came over my way again. "What do you know," he said. "It's Cuntface's friend. You want to make me put it down?"

"You've got a knife and he doesn't," I said. "In my book that makes you a fucking chicken-shit."

The flush deepened. Now his concentration was broken. He looked at Arnie, then over at me. Arnie flashed me a glance of pure gratitude—and moved a little closer to Repperton. I didn't like that.

"Put it down," someone yelled at Repperton. And then someone else: "Put it *down!*" They started to chant: "Put it *down,* put it *down,* put it *down!*"

Repperton didn't like it. He didn't mind being the center of attention, but this was the wrong sort of attention. His glance began to flicker around nervously, first at Arnie, then at me, then at the others. A hank of hair fell across his forehead, and he tossed it back.

When he looked my way again, I made a move as if to go for him. The knife swivelled in my direction, and Arnie moved—he moved faster than I would have believed. He brought the side of his right hand down in a half-assed but effective karate chop. He hit Repperton's wrist hard and knocked the knife out of his hand. It clattered onto the butt-littered hottop. Repperton bent and grabbed for it. Arnie timed it with a deadly accuracy and when Repperton's hand came all the way to the asphalt, Arnie stamped on it. Hard. Repperton screamed.

Don Vandenberg moved in then, quickly, hauled Arnie off, and threw him to the ground. Hardly aware that I was going to do it, I stepped into the ring and kicked Vandenberg in the ass just as hard as I could—I brought my foot up rather than pistoning it out; I kicked him as if I were punting a football.

Vandenberg, a tall, thin guy who was either nineteen or twenty at that time, began to scream and dance around holding his butt. He forgot all about helping his Buddy; he ceased to be a factor in things. To me it's amazing that I didn't paralyze him. I never kicked anyone or anything harder; and my friend, it sho did feel fine.

Just then an arm locked itself around my windpipe and there was a hand between my legs. I realized what was going to happen just a second too late to wholly prevent it. My balls were given a good, firm squeeze that sent sick pain bellowing and raving up from my crotch and into my stomach and down into my legs, unmanning them so that when the arm around my windpipe let go, I simply collapsed in a puddle on the smoking-area tarmac.

"How did you like that, dickface?" a squarish guy with bad teeth asked me. He was wearing small and rather delicate wire-frame glasses that looked absurd on his wide, blocky face. This was Moochie Welch, another of Buddy's friends.

Suddenly the circle of watchers began to melt away and I

heard a man's voice yelling, "Break it up! Break it up *right now!* You kids take a walk! Take a walk, dammit!"

It was Mr. Casey. Finally, Mr. Casey.

Buddy Repperton snatched his switchblade off the pavement. He retracted the blade and shoved the knife into the hip pocket of his jeans in one quick motion. His hand was scraped and bleeding, and it looked as if it was going to swell. The miserable sonofabitch, I hoped it would swell until it looked like one of those gloves Donald Duck wears in the funnypages.

Moochie Welch backed away from me, glanced toward the sound of Mr. Casey's voice, and touched the corner of his mouth delicately with his thumb. "Later, dickface," he said.

Don Vandenberg was dancing more slowly now, but he was still rubbing the affected part. Tears of pain were spilling down his face.

Then Arnie was beside me, getting an arm around me, helping me up. There was a lot of dirt smeared across his shirt from where Vandenberg had thrown him down. There were cigarette butts squashed into the knees of his jeans.

"You okay, Dennis? What'd he do to you?"

"Gave my balls a little squeeze. I'll be all right."

At least I hoped I would be. If you're a man and you've slammed your nuts a good one at some point (and what man has not), you know. If you're a woman, you don't—can't. The initial agony is only the start; it fades, to be replaced by a dull, throbbing feeling of pressure that coils in the pit of the stomach. And what that feeling says is *Hi, there! Good to be here, just sitting around in the pit of your stomach and making you feel like you're going to simultaneously blow lunch and shit your pants! I guess I'll just hang around for a while, okay? How does half an hour or so sound? Great!* Getting your nuts squeezed is not one of life's great thrills.

Mr. Casey shoved his way through the loosening knot of spectators and took in the situation. He wasn't a big guy like Coach Puffer; he didn't even look particularly rugged. He was of medium height and age, and going bald. Big horn-rimmed glasses set squarely on his face. He favored plain white shirts—no tie—and he was wearing one of them now. He wasn't a big guy, but Mr. Casey got respect. Nobody fucked around with him, because he wasn't afraid of kids deep down the way so many teachers are. The kids knew it, too. Buddy and Don and Moochie knew it; it was in the sullen way they dropped their eyes and shuffled their feet.

"Get lost," Mr. Casey said briskly to the few remaining spectators. They started to drift away. Moochie Welch decided to try and drift with them. "Not you, Peter," Mr. Casey said.

"Aw, Mr. Casey, I ain't been doing nothing," Moochie said.

"Me neither," Don said. "How come you always pick on us?"

Mr. Casey came over to where I was still leaning on Arnie for support. "Are you all right, Dennis?"

I was finally beginning to get over it—I wouldn't have been if one of my thighs hadn't partially blocked Welch's hand. I nodded.

Mr. Casey walked back to where Buddy Repperton, Moochie Welch, and Don Vandenberg stood in a shuffling, angry line. Don hadn't been joking; he had been speaking for all of them. They really did feel picked on.

"This is cute, isn't it?" Mr. Casey said finally. "Three on two. That the way you like to do things, Buddy? Those odds don't seem stacked enough for you."

Buddy looked up, threw Casey a smoldering, ugly glance, and then dropped his eyes again. "They started it. Those guys."

"That's not true—" Arnie began.

"Shut up, Cuntface," Buddy said. He started to add something, but before he could get it out, Mr. Casey grabbed him and threw him up against the back wall of the shop. There was a tin sign there which read SMOKING HERE ONLY. Mr. Casey began to slam Buddy Repperton against that sign, and every time he did it, the sign jangled, like dramatic punctuation. He handled Repperton the way you or I might have handled a great big ragdoll. I guess he had muscles somewhere, all right.

"You want to shut your big mouth," he said, and slammed Buddy against the sign. "You want to *shut* your mouth or *clean up* your mouth. Because I don't have to listen to that stuff coming from *you*, Buddy."

He let go of Repperton's shirt. It had pulled out of his jeans, showing his white, untanned belly. He looked back at Arnie. "What were you saying?"

"I came past the smoking area on my way out to the bleachers to eat my lunch," Arnie said. "Repperton was smoking with his friends there. He came over and knocked my lunchbag out of my hand and then stepped on it. He squashed it." He seemed about to say something more, struggled with it, and swallowed it again. "That started the fight."

But I wasn't going to leave it at that. I'm no stoolie or tattletale, not under ordinary circumstances, but Repperton had apparently decided that more than a good beating was required to avenge himself for getting kicked out of Darnell's. He could have punched a hole in Arnie's intestines, maybe killed him.

"Mr. Casey," I said.

He looked at me. Behind him, Buddy Repperton's green eyes flashed at me balefully—a warning. *Keep your mouth shut, this is between us.* Even a year before, some twisted sense of pride might have forced me to go along him and play the game, but not now.

"What is it, Dennis?"

"He's had it in for Arnie since the summer. He's got a knife, and he looked like he was planning to stick it in."

Arnie was looking at me, his gray eyes opaque and unreadable. I thought about him calling Repperton a shitter—LeBay's word—and felt a prickle of goosebumps on my back.

"You fucking liar!" Repperton cried dramatically. "I ain't got no knife!"

Casey looked at him without saying anything. Vandenberg and Welch looked extremely uncomfortable now—scared. Their possible punishment for this little scuffle had progressed beyond detention, which they were used to, and suspension, which they had experienced, toward the outer limits of expulsion.

I only had to say one more word. I thought about it. I almost didn't. But it had been Arnie, and Arnie was my friend, and inside where it mattered, I didn't just *think* he had meant to stick Arnie with that blade; I *knew* it. I said the word.

"It's a switchblade."

Now Repperton's eyes did not just flash; they blazed, promising hellfire, damnation, and a long period of traction. "That's bullshit, Mr. Casey," he said hoarsely. "He's lying. I swear to God."

Mr. Casey still said nothing. He looked slowly at Arnie.

"Cunningham," he said. "Did Repperton here pull a knife on you?"

Arnie wouldn't answer at first. Then in a low voice that was little more than a sigh, he said, "Yeah."

Now Repperton's blazing glance was for both of us.

Casey turned to Moochie Welch and Don Vandenberg. All at once I could see that his method of handling this had changed; he had begun to move slowly and carefully, as if testing the footing beneath carefully each time he moved a step forward. Mr. Casey had already grasped the consequences.

"Was there a knife involved?" he asked them.

Moochie and Vandenberg looked at their feet and would not answer. That was answer enough.

"Turn out your pockets, Buddy," Mr. Casey said.

"Fuck I will!" Buddy said. His voice went shrill. "You can't make me!"

"If you mean I don't have the authority, you're wrong," Mr. Casey said. "If you mean I can't turn your pockets out for myself if I decide to try it, that's also wrong. But—"

"Yeah, try it, try it," Buddy shouted at him. "I'll knock you through that wall, you little bald fuck!"

My stomach was rolling helplessly. I hated stuff like this, ugly confrontation scenes, and this was the worst one I'd ever been a part of.

But Mr. Casey had things under control, and he never deviated from his course.

"But I'm not going to do it," he finished. "You're going to turn out your pockets yourself."

"Fat fucking chance," Buddy said. He was standing against the back wall of the shop so that the bulge in his hip pocket wouldn't show. His shirttail hung in two wrinkled flaps over the crotch of his jeans. His eyes darted here and there like the eyes of an animal brought to bay.

Mr. Casey glanced at Moochie and Don Vandenberg. "You two boys go up to the office and stay there until I come up," he said. "Don't go anywhere else; you've got enough trouble without that."

They walked away slowly, close together, as if for protection. Moochie threw one glance back. In the main building, the bell went off. People started to stream back inside, some of them giving us curious glances. We had missed lunch. It didn't matter. I wasn't hungry anymore.

Mr. Casey turned his attention back to Buddy.

"You're on school grounds right now," he said. "You should thank God you are, because if you do have a knife, Buddy, and if you pulled it, that's assault with a deadly weapon. They send you to prison for that."

"Prove it, prove it!" Buddy shouted. His cheeks were flaming, his breath coming in quick, nervous little gasps.

"If you don't turn out your pockets right now, I'm going to write a dismissal slip on you. Then I'm going to call the cops, and the minute you step outside the main gate, they'll grab you. You see the bind you're in?" He looked grimly at Buddy. "We keep our own house here," he said. "But if I have to write you a dismissal, Buddy, your ass belongs to them. Of course if you have no knife, you're okay. But if you do and they find it . . ."

There was a moment of silence. The four of us stood in tableau. I didn't think he was going to do it; he would take his dismissal and try to ditch the knife somewhere quickly. Then he must have realized that the cops would hunt for it and probably find it, because he pulled the knife out of his back pocket and threw it down on the tarmac. It landed on the go-button. The blade popped out and winked wickedly in the afternoon sunlight, eight inches of chromed steel.

Arnie looked at it and wiped his mouth with the heel of his hand.

"Go up to the office, Buddy," Mr. Casey said quietly. "Wait until I get up there."

"Screw the office!" Buddy cried. His voice was thin and hysterical with anger. Hair had fallen across his forehead again, and he flipped it back. "I'm getting out of this fucking pigsty."

"Yes, all right, fine," Mr. Casey said, with no more inflection or excitement in his voice than he would have shown if Buddy had offered him a cup of coffee. I knew then that Buddy was all finished at Libertyville High. No detention or three-day vacation; his parents would be receiving the stiff blue expulsion form in the mail—the form would explain why their son was being expelled and would inform them of their rights and legal options in the matter.

Buddy looked at Arnie and me—and he smiled. "I'll fix you," he said. "I'll get even. You'll wish you were never fucking born." He kicked the knife away, spinning and flashing. It came to rest on the edge of the hottop, and Buddy walked off, the cleats on the heels of his motorcycle boots clicking and scraping.

Mr. Casey looked at us; his face was sad and tired. "I'm sorry," he said.

"That's okay," Arnie replied.

"Do you boys want dismissal slips? I'll write them for you if you feel you'd like to go home for the rest of the day."

I glanced at Arnie, who was brushing off his shirt. He shook his head.

"No, that's okay," I said.

"All right. Just late slips then."

We went into Mr. Casey's room and he wrote us late slips for our next class, which happened to be one we shared together—Advanced Physics. Coming into the physics lab, a lot of people looked at us curiously, and there was some whispering behind hands.

The afternoon absence slip circulated at the end of period six. I checked it and saw the names Repperton, Vandenberg, and Welch, each with a (D) after his name. I thought that Arnie and I would be called to the office at the end of school to tell Ms. Lothrop, the discipline officer, what had happened. But we weren't.

I looked for Arnie after school, thinking we'd ride home together and talk it over a little, but I was wrong about that too. He'd already left for Darnell's Garage to work on Christine.

17 / Christine on the Street Again

I got a 1966 cherry-red Mustang Ford
She got a 380 horsepower overload,
You know she's way too powerful
To be crawling on these Interstate roads.
                                        —Chuck Berry

I didn't get a chance to really talk to Arnie until after the football game the following Saturday. And that was also the first time since the day he had bought her that Christine was out on the street.

The team went up to Hidden Hills, about sixteen miles away, on the quietest school-activity bus ride I've ever been on. We might have been going to the guillotine instead of to a football game. Even the fact that their record, 1–2, was only slightly better than ours, didn't cheer anybody up much. Coach Puffer sat in the seat behind the bus driver, pale and silent, as if he might be suffering from a hangover.

Usually a trip to an away game was a combination caravan and circus. A second bus, loaded up with the cheerleaders, the band, and all the LHS kids who had signed up as "rooters" ("rooters," dear God! if we hadn't all been through high school, who the hell would believe it?), trundled along behind the team bus. Behind the two buses would be a line of fifteen or twenty cars, most of them full of teenagers, most with THUMP EM TERRIERS bumper stickers—beeping, flashing their lights, all that stuff you probably remember from your own high school days.

But on this trip there was only the cheerleader/band bus (and that wasn't even full—in a winning year if you didn't sign up for the second bus by Tuesday, you were out of luck) and three or four cars behind that. The fair-weather friends had already bailed out. And I was sitting on the team bus next to Lenny Barongg, glumly wondering if I was going to get knocked out of my jock that afternoon, totally unaware that one of the few cars behind the bus was Christine.

I saw it when we got out of the bus in the Hidden Hills High School parking lot. Their band was already out on the field, and the thud from the big drum came clearly, oddly magnified under the lowering, cloudy sky. It was going to be the first really good Saturday for football, cool, overcast, and fallish.

Seeing Christine parked beside the band bus was surprise enough, but when Arnie got out on one side and Leigh Cabot got out on the other, I was downright stunned—and more than a little jealous. She was wearing a clinging pair of brown woollen slacks and a white cableknit pullover, her blond hair spilling gorgeously over her shoulders.

"Arnie," I said. "Hey, man!"

"Hi, Dennis," he said a little shyly.

I was aware that some of the players getting off the bus were also doing double-takes; here was Pizza-Face Cunningham with the gorgeous transfer from Massachusetts. How in God's name did *that* happen?

"How are you?"

"Good," he said. "Do you know Leigh Cabot?"

"From class," I said. "Hi, Leigh."

"Hi, Dennis. Are you going to win today?"

I lowered my voice to a hoarse whisper. "It's all been fixed. Bet your ass off."

Arnie blushed a little at that, but Leigh cupped her hand to her mouth and giggled.

"We're going to try, but I don't know," I said.

"We'll root you on to victory," Arnie said. "I can see it in tomorrow's paper now—Guilder Becomes Airborne, Breaks Conference TD Record."

"Guilder Taken to Hospital with Fractured Skull, that's more likely," I said. "How many kids came up? Ten? Fifteen?"

"More room on the bleachers for those of us that did," Leigh said. She took Arnie's arm—surprising and pleasing him, I think. Already I liked her. She could have been a bitch or mentally fast asleep—it seems to me that a lot of really beautiful girls are one or the other—but she was neither.

"How's the rolling iron?" I asked, and walked over to the car.

"Not too bad." He followed me over, trying not to grin too widely.

The work had progressed, and now there was enough done on the Fury so that it didn't look quite so crazy and helter-skelter. The other half of the old, rusted front grille had been replaced, and the nest of cracks in the windshield was totally gone.

"You replaced the windshield," I said.

Arnie nodded.

"And the hood."

The hood was clean; brand-spanking new, in sharp contrast to the rust-flecked sides. It was a deep fire-engine red. Sharp-looking. Arnie touched it possessively, and the touch turned into a caress.

"Yeah. I put that on myself."

Something about that jagged on me. He had done it *all* himself, hadn't he?

"You said you were going to turn it into a showpiece," I said. "I think I'm starting to believe you." I walked around to the driver's side. The upholstery on the insides of the doors and floor was still dirty and scuffed up, but now the front seat cover had been replaced as well as the back one.

"It's going to be beautiful," Leigh said, but there was a flat note in her voice—it wasn't as naturally bright and effervescent as it had been when we were talking about the game—and that made me glance at her. A glance was all it took. She didn't like Christine. I realized it just like that, completely and absolutely, as if I had plucked one of her brainwaves out of the air. She would try to like the car because she liked Arnie. But . . . she wasn't ever going to *really* like it.

"So you got it street-legal," I said.

"Well . . ." Arnie looked uncomfortable. "It isn't. Quite."

"What do you mean?"

"The horn doesn't work, and sometimes the taillights go out when I step on the brake. It's a dead short somewhere, I think, but so far I haven't been able to chase it out."

I glanced at the new windshield—there was a new inspection sticker on it. Arnie followed my glance and managed to look both embarrassed and a bit truculent at the same time. "Will gave me my sticker. He knows it's ninety percent there." *And besides,* I thought, *you had this hot date, right?*

"It's not dangerous, is it?" Leigh asked, addressing the question somewhere between Arnie and me. Her brow had creased slightly—I think maybe she sensed a sudden cold current between Arnie and me.

"No," I said. "I don't think so. When you ride with Arnie you're riding with the original Old Creeping Jesus anyway."

That broke the odd little pocket of tension that had built up. From the playing field there was a discordant shriek of brass, and then the band instructor's voice, carrying to us, thin but perfectly clear under the low sky: *"Again, please! This is Rodgers and Hammerstein, not rock and ro-ool! Again, please!"*

The three of us looked at each other. Arnie and I started to laugh, and after a moment Leigh joined in. Looking at her, I felt that momentary jealousy again. I wanted nothing but the best for my friend Arnie, but she was really something—seventeen going on eighteen, gorgeous, perfect, healthy, alive to everything in her world. Roseanne was beautiful in her way, but Leigh made Roseanne look like a tree-sloth taking a nap.

Was that when I started to want her? When I started to want my best friend's girl? Yeah, I suppose it was. But I swear to you, I never would have put a move on her if things had happened differently. I just don't think they were meant to happen differently. Or maybe I just have to feel that way.

"We better go, Arnie, or we won't get a good seat in the visitors' bleachers," Leigh said with ladylike sarcasm.

Arnie smiled. She was still holding his arm lightly, and he

looked rather bowled over by it all. Why not? If it had been me, having my first experience with a live girl, and one as pretty as Leigh, I would have been three-quarters to being in love with her already. I wished him nothing but well with her. I guess I want you to believe that, even if you don't believe anything else I have to tell you from here on out. If anyone deserved a little happiness, it was Arnie.

The rest of the team had gone into the visitors' dressing rooms at the back of the gymnasium of the school, and now Coach Puffer poked his head out.

"Do you think you could favor us with your presence, Mr. Guilder?" he called. "I know it's a lot to ask, and I hope you'll forgive me if you had something more important to do, but if you don't, would you get your tail down into this locker room?"

I muttered to Arnie and Leigh, "This is Rodgers and Hammerstein, not rock and ro-ool," and trotted toward the building.

I walked toward the dressing rooms—Coach had popped back inside—and Arnie and Leigh started across to the bleachers. Halfway to the doors I stopped and went back to Christine. Late to suit up or not, I approached her in a circle; that absurd prejudice against walking in front of the car still held.

On the rear end I saw a Pennsylvania dealer plate held on with a spring. I flipped it down and saw a Dymo tape stuck to the back side: THIS PLATE PROPERTY OF DARNELL'S GARAGE, LIBERTYVILLE, PA.

I let the plate snap back and stood up, frowning. Darnell had given him a sticker while his car was still a ways from being street-legal; Darnell had loaned him a dealer plate so he could use the car to bring Leigh to the game. Also, he had stopped being "Darnell" to Arnie; today he had called him "Will." Interesting, but not very comforting.

I wondered if Arnie was dumb enough to think that the Will Darnells of this world ever did favors out of the goodness of their hearts. I hoped he wasn't, but I wasn't sure. I wasn't sure of much about Arnie anymore. He had changed a lot in the last few weeks.

We surprised the hell out of ourselves and won the game—as it turned out, that was one of only two we won that whole season . . . not that I was with the team when the season ended.

We had no right to win; we went out on the field feeling like losers, and we lost the toss. The Hillmen (dumb name for a team, but what's so bright about being known as the Terriers when you get right down to it?) went forty yards on their first two plays, going through our defensive line like cheese through a goose. Then, on the third play—their third first-and-ten in a row—their quarterback coughed up the ball. Gary Tardiff grabbed it up and rambled sixty yards for the score, a great big grin on his face.

The Hillmen and their coach went bananas protesting that the ball had been dead at the line of scrimmage, but the officials disagreed and we led 6-0. From my place on the bench I was able to look across at the visitors' bleachers and could see that the few Libertyville fans there were going crazy. I guess they had a right to; it was the first time we'd led in a game all season. Arnie and Leigh were waving Terriers pennants. I waved at them. Leigh saw me, waved back, then elbowed Arnie. He waved back too. They looked as if they were getting pretty chummy up there, which made me grin.

As for the game, we never looked back after that first flukey score. We had that mystic thing, momentum, on our side—maybe for the only time that year. I didn't break the Conference touchdown record as Arnie had predicted, but I scored three times, one of them on a ninety-yard runback, the longest I ever made. At halftime it was 17-0, and Coach was a new man. He saw a complete turnaround ahead of us, the greatest comeback in the history of the Conference. Of course that turned out to be a fool's dream, but he surely was excited that day, and I felt good for him, as I had for Arnie and Leigh, getting to know each other so profitably and easily.

The second half was not so good; our defense resumed the mostly prone posture it had assumed in our first three games, but it was still never really close. We won 27-18.

Coach had taken me out halfway through the fourth quarter to put in Brian McNally, who would be replacing me next year—actually even earlier than that, as it turned out. I showered and changed up, then came back out just as the two-minute warning went off.

The parking lot was full of cars but empty of people. Wild cheering came from the field as the Hillmen fans urged their team to do the impossible in the last two minutes of play. From this distance it all seemed as unimportant as it undoubtedly was.

I walked over toward Christine.

There she sat with her rust-flecked sides and her new hood and her tailfins that seemed a thousand miles long. A dinosaur from the dark ditty-bop days of the 50s when all the oil millionaires were from Texas and the Yankee dollar was kicking the shit out of the Japanese yen instead of the other way around. Back in the days when Carl Perkins was singing about pink pedal pushers and Johnny Horton was singing about dancing all night on a honky-tonk hardwood floor and the biggest teen idol in the country was Edd "Kookie" Byrnes.

I touched Christine. I tried to caress it as Arnie had done; to like it for Arnie's sake as Leigh had done. Surely if anyone should be able to make himself like it, it should be me. Leigh had only known Arnie a month. I had known him my whole life.

I slipped my hand along the rusty surface and I thought of George Lebay, and Veronica and Rita LeBay, and somewhere along the line the hand that was supposed to be caressing closed into a fist and I suddenly slammed it down on Christine's flank as hard as I could—plenty hard enough to hurt my hand and make myself utter a defensive little laugh and wonder what the hell I thought I was doing.

The sound of rust sifting down onto the hottop in small flakes.

The sound of a bass drum from the football field, like a giant's heartbeat.

The sound of my own heartbeat.

I tried the front door.

It was locked.

I licked my lips and realized I was scared.

It was almost as if—this was very funny, this was hilarious—it was almost as if this car didn't like me, as if it suspected me of wanting to come between it and Arnie, and that the reason I didn't want to walk in front of it was because—

I laughed again and then remembered my dream and stopped laughing. This was too much like it for comfort. It wasn't Chubby McCarthy blaring over the PA, of course, not in Hidden Hills, but the rest of it brought on a dreamy, unpleasant sense of *déjà vu*—the sound of the cheers, the sound of padded body contact, the wind hissing through the trees that looked like cutouts under an overcast sky.

The engine would gun. The car would lurch forward, drop

back, lurch forward, drop back. And then the tires would scream as it roared right at me——

I shook the thought off. It was time to stop pandering to myself with all of this crazy shit. It was time—and over-time—to get my imagination under control. This was a car, not a she but an it, not really Christine at all but only a 1958 Plymouth Fury that had rolled off an assembly line in Detroit along with about four hundred thousand others.

It worked . . . at least temporarily. Just to demonstrate how little afraid of it I was, I got down on my knees and looked under it. What I saw there was even crazier than the haphazard way the car was being rebuilt on top. There were three new Pleasurizer shocks, but the fourth was a dark, oil-caked ruin that looked as if it had been on there forever. The tailpipe was so new it was still silvery, but the muffler looked at least middle-aged and the header pipe was in very bad shape. Looking at the header, thinking about exhaust fumes that could leak into the car from it, made me flash on Ver-nonica LeBay again. Because exhaust fumes can kill. They——

"Dennis, what are you doing?"

I guess I was still more uneasy than I thought, because I was up from my knees like a shot with my heart beating in my throat. It was Arnie. He looked cold and angry.

Because I was looking at his car? Why should that make him mad? Good question. But it had, that was obvious.

"I was looking over your mean machine," I said, trying to sound casual. "Where's Leigh?"

"She had to go to the Ladies'," he said, dismissing her. His gray eyes never left my face. "Dennis, you're the best friend I've got, the best friend I've ever had. You might have saved me a trip to the hospital the other day when Repperton pulled that knife, and I know it. But don't you go behind my back, Dennis. Don't you ever do that."

From the playing field there was a tremendous cheer—the Hillmen had just made the final score of the game, with less than thirty seconds to play.

"Arnie, I don't know what the hell you're talking about," I said, but I felt guilty. I felt guilty the way I had felt being in-troduced to Leigh, sizing her up, wanting her a little—wanting the girl he so obviously wanted himself. But . . . going behind his back? Was that what I had been doing?

I suppose he could have seen it that way. I had known that his irrational—interest, obsession, put it however you like—his irrational *thing* about the car was the locked room in the house of our friendship, the place I could not go without inviting all sorts of trouble. And if he hadn't caught me trying to jimmy the door, he had at least come upon me trying to peek through a keyhole.

"I think you know *exactly* what I'm talking about," he said, and I saw with a tired sort of dismay that he was not just a little mad; he was furious. "You and my father and mother are all spying on me 'for my own good,' that's the way it is, isn't it? They sent you down to Darnell's Garage to snoop around, didn't they?"

"Hey, Arnie, wait just a—"

"Boy, did you think I wouldn't find out? I didn't say anything then—because we're friends. But I don't know, Dennis. There has to be a line, and I think I'm drawing it. Why don't you just leave my car alone and stop butting in where you don't belong?"

"First of all," I said, "it wasn't your father *and* your mother. Your father got me alone and asked me if I'd take a look at what you were doing with the car. I said sure I would, I was curious myself. Your dad has always been okay to me. What was I supposed to say?"

"You were supposed to say no."

"You don't get it. He's on your side. Your mother still hopes it doesn't come to anything—that was the idea I got—but Michael really hopes you get it running. He said so."

"Sure, that's the way he'd come on to you." He was almost sneering. "Really all he's interested in is making sure I'm still hobbled. That's what they're both interested in. They don't want me to grow up because then they'd have to face getting old."

"That's too hard, man."

"Maybe you think so. Maybe coming from a halfway-normal family makes you soft in the head, Dennis. They offered me a new car for high school graduation, did you know that? All I had to do was give up Christine, make all A's, and agree to go to Horlicks . . . where they could keep me in direct view for another four years."

I didn't know what to say. That was pretty crass, all right.

"So just butt out of it, Dennis. That's all I'm saying. We'll both be better off."

"I didn't tell him anything, anyhow," I said. "Just that you were doing a few things here and there. He seemed sort of relieved."

"Yeah, I'll bet."

"I didn't have any idea it was as close to street-legal as it is. But it isn't all the way yet. I looked underneath, and that header pipe's a mess. I hope you're driving with your windows open."

"Don't tell me how to drive it! I know more about what makes cars run than you ever will!"

That was when I started to get pissed off at him. I didn't like it—I didn't want to have an argument with Arnie, especially not now, when Leigh would be joining him in another moment—but I could feel somebody upstairs in the brain-room starting to pull those red switches, one by one.

"That's probably true," I said, controlling my voice. "But I'm not sure how much you know about people. Will Darnell gave you an improper sticker—if you got picked up he could lose his state inspection certificate. He gave you a dealer plate. Why did he do those things, Arnie?"

For the first time Arnie seemed defensive. "I told you. He knows I'm doing the work."

"Don't be a numbskull. That guy wouldn't give a crippled crab a crutch unless there was something in it for him, and you know it."

"Dennis, will you leave it alone, for God's sake?"

"Man," I said, stepping toward him. "I don't give a fuck if you have a car. I just don't want you in a bind over it. Sincerely."

He looked at me uncertainly.

"I mean, what are we yelling at each other about? Because I looked underneath your car to see how the exhaust pipe was hanging?"

But that hadn't been all I was doing. Some . . . but not quite all. And I think we both knew it.

On the playing field, the final gun went off with a flat bang. A slight drizzle had started to come down, and it was getting cold. We turned toward the sound of the gun and saw Leigh coming toward us, carrying her pennant and Arnie's. She waved. We waved back.

"Dennis, I can take care of myself," he said.

"Okay," I said simply. "I hope you can." Suddenly I wanted to ask him how deep he was in with Darnell. And that was a question I couldn't ask; that would bring on an even more bitter argument. Things would be said that could maybe never be repaired.

"I can," he repeated. He touched his car, and the hard look in his eyes softened.

I felt a mixture of relief and dismay—the relief because we weren't going to have a fight after all; we had both managed to avoid saying anything completely irreparable. But it also seemed to me that it wasn't just one room of our friendship that had been closed off; it was a whole damn wing. He had rejected what I'd had to say with complete totality and had made the conditions for continuing the friendship pretty clear: everything will be okay as long as you do it my way.

Which was also his parents' attitude, if only he could have seen it. But then, I suppose he had to learn it somewhere.

Leigh came up, drops of rain gleaming in her hair. Her color was high, her eyes sparkling with good health and good excitement. She exuded a naive and untested sexuality that made me feel a little light-headed. Not that I was the main object of her attention; Arnie was.

"How did it end?" Arnie asked.

"Twenty-seven to eighteen," she said, and then added gleefully, "We *destroyed* them. Where were you two?"

"Just talking cars," I said, and Arnie shot me an amused glance—at least his sense of humor hadn't disappeared with his common sense. And I thought there was some cause for hope in the way he looked at her. He was falling for her, head over heels. The tumble was slow right now, but it would almost surely speed up if things went right. I was really curious about how it had happened, the two of them getting together. Arnie's complexion had cleared up and he looked pretty good, but in a rather bookish, bespectacled sort of way. He wasn't the sort of guy you'd have expected Leigh Cabot to want to be with; you'd expect her to be hanging from the arm of the American high school version of Apollo.

People were streaming back across the field now, our players and theirs, our fans and theirs.

"Just talking cars," Leigh repeated, mocking softly. She turned her face up to Arnie's and smiled. He smiled back, a sappy, dopey smile that did my heart a world of good. I could tell, just looking at him, that whenever Leigh smiled at him that way, Christine was the farthest thing from his mind; she was demoted back to her proper place as an *it*, a means of transportation.

I liked that just fine.

18 / On the Bleachers

O Lord, won't you buy me a Mercedes-Benz?
My friends all drive Porsches,
I must make amends . . .

—Janis Joplin

I saw Arnie and Leigh in the halls a lot over the first two
weeks in October, first leaning against his locker or hers, talking before the home-room bell; then holding hands; then going out after school with their arms around each other. It had
happened. In high school parlance, they were "going together." I thought it was more than that. I thought they were
in love.

I hadn't seen Christine since the day we beat Hidden Hills.
She had apparently gone back to Darnell's for more work—
maybe that was part of the agreement Arnie had struck with
Darnell when Darnell issued the dealer plate and the illegal
sticker that day. I didn't see the Fury, but I saw a lot of
Leigh and Arnie . . . and heard a lot about them. They were
a hot item of school gossip. Girls wanted to know what she
saw in him, for heaven's sake; boys, always more practical
and prosaic, only wanted to know if my runt friend had managed to get into her pants. I didn't care about either of those
things, but I did wonder from time to time what Regina and
Michael thought of their son's extreme case of first love.

One Monday in mid-October, Arnie and I ate our lunch
together on the bleachers by the football field, as we had
been planning to do on the day Buddy Repperton had pulled
the knife—Repperton had indeed been expelled for that.
Moochie and Don had gotten three-day vacations. They were
currently being pretty good boys. And, in the not-so-sweet
meanwhile, the football team had been run over twice more.
Our record was now 1–5, and Coach Puffer had lapsed back
into morose silence.

My lunchbag wasn't as full as it had been on the day of
Repperton and the knife; the only virtue I could see of being
1–5 was that we were now so far behind the Bears of Ridge

160

Rock (they were 5-0-1) that it would be impossible for us to do anything in the Conference unless their team bus went over a cliff.

We sat in the mellow October sunshine—the time for the little spooks in their bedsheets and rubber masks and Woolworth's Darth Vader costumes wasn't far off—munching and not saying too much. Arnie had a devilled egg and swapped it for one of my cold meatloaf sandwiches. Parents know very little about the secret lives of their children, I guess. Every Monday since first grade, Regina Cunningham had put a devilled egg in Arnie's lunchbag, and every day after we had a meatloaf dinner (which was usually Sunday suppers), I had a cold meatloaf sandwich in mine. Now I have always hated cold meatloaf and Arnie has always hated devilled eggs, although I never saw him turn one down done any other way. And I've often wondered what our mothers would think if they knew how few of the hundreds of devilled eggs and dozens of cold meatloaf sandwiches that went into our respective lunch-sacks had actually been eaten by him for whom each was intended.

I got down to my cookies and Arnie got down to his fig-bars. He glanced over at me to make sure I was watching and then crammed all six fig-bars into his mouth at once and crunched down on them. His cheeks puffed out grotesquely.

"Oh, Jesus, what a gross-out!" I cried.

"Ung-ung-gooth-ung," Arnie replied.

I started to poke my fingers at his sides, where he's always been extremely ticklish, screaming, "Side-noogies! Look out, Arnie, I got side-noogies onya!"

Arnie started to laugh, spraying out little wads of munched-up fig-bars. I know how obnoxious that must sound, but it was really funny.

"Quit it, Dennith!" Arnie said, his mouth still full of fig-bars.

"What was that? I can't understand you, you fucking barbarian." I kept poking my fingers at him, giving him what we used to call "side-noogies" when we were little kids (for some reason now lost in the sands of time), and he kept wiggling and twisting and laughing.

He swallowed mightily, then belched.

"You're so fucking gross, Cunningham," I said.

"I know." He seemed really pleased by it. Probably was; so far as I know, he'd never pulled the six-fig-bars-at-once trick in front of anyone else. If he had done it in front of his

parents, I figure Regina would have had a kitty and Michael possibly a brain-hemorrhage.

"What's the most you ever did?" I asked him.

"I did twelve once," he said. "But I thought I was going to choke."

I snorted laughter. "Have you done it for Leigh yet?"

"I'm holding it back for the prom," he said. "I'll give her a few side-noogies too." We got laughing over that, and I realized how much I missed Arnie sometimes—I had football, student council, a new girlfriend who would (I hoped) consent to give me a hand-job before the drive-in season ended. I had little hope of getting her to do more than that; she was a little too enchanted with herself. Still, it was fun trying.

Even with all of that going on, I had missed Arnie. First there had been Christine, now there was Leigh and Christine. In that order, I hoped.

"Where is she today?" I asked.

"Sick," he said. "She got her period, and I guess it really hurts."

I raised a set of mental eyebrows. If she was discussing her female problems with him, they were getting chummy indeed.

"How did you happen to ask her to the football game that day?" I asked. "The day we played Hidden Hills?"

He laughed. "The only football game I've been to since my sophomore year. We brought you luck, Dennis."

"You just called her up and asked her to go?"

"I almost didn't. That was the first date I ever had." He glanced over at me shyly. "I don't think I slept more than two hours the night before. After I called her up and she said she'd go with me, I was scared to death I'd make an asshole of myself, or that Buddy Repperton would show up and want to fight, or something else would happen."

"You seemed to have everything under control."

"Did I?" He looked pleased. "Well, that's good. But I was scared. She'd talk to me in the halls, you know—ask me about assignments and stuff like that. She joined the chess club even though she wasn't very good . . . but she's getting better. I'm teaching her."

I'll bet you are, you dog, I thought, but didn't quite dare say it—I still remembered the way he had blown up at me the same day at Hidden Hills. Besides, I wanted to hear this. I was pretty curious; captivating a girl as stunning as Leigh Cabot had been a real coup.

"So after a while I started to think maybe she was inter-

ested in me," Arnie went on. "It probably took a lot longer for the penny to drop for me than it would for some other guys—guys like you, Dennis."

"Sure, I'm a smoothie," I said. "What James Brown used to call 'a sex machine.' "

"No, you're no sex machine, but you know about girls," he said seriously. "You understand them. I was always just scared of them. Never knew what to say. Still don't, I guess. Leigh's different.

"I was afraid to ask her out." He seemed to consider this. "I mean, she's a beautiful girl, really beautiful. Don't you think so, Dennis?"

"Yes. As far as I can tell, she's the prettiest girl in school."

He smiled, pleased. "I think so, too . . . but I thought, maybe it's only because I love her that I think that way."

I looked at my friend, hoping he wasn't going to get into more trouble than he could handle. At that point, of course, I had no idea what trouble meant.

"Anyway, I heard these guys talking one day in chem lab—Lenny Barongg and Ned Stroughman—and Ned was telling Lenny that he'd asked her out and she'd said no, but in a nice way . . . like maybe if he asked her again she might try it out. And I had this picture of her going steady with Ned by spring, and I started to feel really jealous. It's ridiculous. I mean, she told him no and I'm feeling jealous, you dig what I'm saying?"

I smiled and nodded. Out on the field the cheerleaders were trying out some new routines. I didn't think they would help our team very much, but it was pleasant to watch them. Their shadows puddled at their heels on the green grass in the bright noontime.

"The other thing that got me was that Ned didn't sound pissed off or . . . or ashamed . . . or rejected, or anything like that. He tried for a date and got turned down, that was all. I decided I could do that, too. Still, when I called her up on the phone I was sweating all over. Man, that was bad. I kept imagining her laughing at me and saying something like, *'Me go out with you, you little creep? You must be dreaming! I'm not that hard up yet!'* "

"Yeah," I said. "I can't figure out why she didn't."

He poked me in the stomach. "Gut-noogies, Dennis! Make you puke!"

"Never mind," I said. "Tell me the rest."

He shrugged. "Not much else to tell. Her mother answered

the phone when I called and said she'd get her. I heard the phone go clunking down on the table, and I almost hung up." Arnie held up two fingers a quarter of an inch apart. "I came this close to hanging up. No shit."

"I know the feeling," I said, and I did—you worry about the laughter, you imagine the contempt to some degree or other, no matter if you're a football player or some pimply little four-eyed runt—but I don't think I could understand the *degree* to which Arnie must have felt it. What he had done had taken monumental courage. It's a small thing, a date, but in our society there are all sorts of charged forces swirling behind that simple concept—I mean, there are kids who go all the way through high school and *never* get up enough courage to ask a girl for a date. Never *once*, in all four years. And that isn't just one or two kids, it's lots of them. And there are lots of sad girls who never get asked. It's a shitty way to run things, when you stop to think about it. A lot of people get hurt. I could dimly imagine the naked terror Arnie must have felt, waiting for Leigh to come to the phone; the sense of dread amazement at the idea that he was not planning to ask just any girl out but *the prettiest girl in school.*

"She answered," Arnie went on. "She said 'Hello?' and, man, I couldn't say anything. I tried and nothing came out but this little whistle of air. So she said 'Hello, who is this?' like it might be some kind of practical joke, you know, and I thought, This is ridiculous. If I can talk to her in the hall, I should be able to talk to her on the goddam phone, all she can say is no, I mean she can't *shoot* me or anything if I ask her for a date. So I said hi, this is Arnie Cunningham, and she said hi, and blah-blah-blahdy-blah, bullshit-bullshit-bullshit, and then I realized I didn't even know where the hell I wanted to ask her to go, and we're running out of things to say, pretty soon she's going to hang up. So I asked her the first thing I could think of, would she want to go to the football game on Saturday. She said she'd love to go, right off like that, like she had just been waiting for me to ask her, you know?"

"Probably she was."

"Yeah, maybe," Arnie considered this, bemused.

The bell rang, signifying five minutes to period five. Arnie and I got up. The cheerleaders trotted off the field, their little skirts flipping saucily.

We climbed down the bleachers, tossed our lunchbags in one of the trash barrels painted with the school colors—

orange and black, talk about Halloween—and walked toward the school.

Arnie was still smiling, recalling the way it had worked itself out, that first time with Leigh. "Asking her to the game was sheer desperation."

"Thanks a lot," I said. "That's what I get for playing my heart out every Saturday afternoon, huh?"

"You know what I mean. Then, after she said she'd go with me, I had this really horrible thought and called you— remember?"

Suddenly I did. He had called to ask me if that game was at home or away and had seemed absurdly crushed when I told him it was at Hidden Hills.

"So there I was, I've got a date with the prettiest girl in school, I'm crazy about her, and it turns out to be an away game and my car's in Will's garage."

"You could have taken the bus."

"I know that now, but I didn't then. The bus always used to be full up a week before the game. I didn't know so many people would stop coming to the games if the team started losing."

"Don't remind me," I said.

"So I went to Will. I knew Christine could do it, but no way she was street-legal. I mean, I was desperate."

How desperate? I wondered coldly and suddenly.

"And he came through for me. Said he understood how important it was, and if . . ." Arnie paused; seemed to consider. "And that's the story of the big date," he finished gracelessly.

And if . . .

But that wasn't my business.

Be his eyes, my father had said.

But I pushed that away too.

We were walking past the smoking area now, deserted except for three guys and two girls, hurriedly finishing a joint. They had it in a makeshift matchbook roachclip, and the evocative odor of pot, so similar to the aroma of slowly burning autumn leaves, slipped into my nostrils.

"Seen Buddy Repperton around?" I asked.

"No," he said. "And don't want to. You?"

I had seen him once, hanging out at Vandenberg's Happy Gas, an extra-barrel service station out on Route 22 in Monroeville. Don Vandenberg's dad owned it, and the place had been on the ragged edge of going bust ever since the Arab oil embargo in '73. Buddy hadn't seen me; I was just cruising by.

"Not to talk to."

"You mean he can talk?" Arnie said with a scorn that wasn't like him. "What a shitter."

I started. That word again. I thought about it, told myself what the fuck, and asked him where he had gotten that particular term.

He looked at me thoughtfully. The second bell rang suddenly, braying out from the side of the building. We were going to be late to class, but right then I didn't care at all.

"You remember that day I bought the car?" he said. "Not the day I put the deposit on it, but the day I actually bought it?"

"Sure."

"I went in with LeBay while you stayed outside. He had this tiny kitchen with a red-checked tablecloth on the table. We sat down and he offered me a beer. I figured I better take it. I really wanted the car, and I didn't want to, you know, offend him somehow. So we each had a beer and he got off on this long, rambling . . . what would you call it? Rant, I guess. This rant about how all the shitters were against him. It was his word. Dennis. The shitters. He said it was the shitters that were making him sell his car."

"What did he mean?"

"I guess he meant that he was too old to drive, but he wouldn't put it that way. It was all their fault. The shitters. The shitters wanted him to take a driver's road-test every two years and an eye exam every year. It was the eye exam that bothered him. And he said they didn't like him on the street—no one did. So someone threw a stone at the car.

"I understand all that. But I don't understand why . . ." Arnie paused in the doorway, oblivious of the fact that we were late for class. His hands were shoved into the back pockets of his jeans and he was frowning. "I don't understand why he let Christine go to rack and ruin like that, Dennis. Like she was when I bought her. Mostly he talked about her like he really loved her—I know you thought it was just part of his sales-pitch but it wasn't—and then near the end, when he was counting the money, he sort of growled, 'That shitting car, I'll be fucked if I know why you want it, boy. It's the ace of spades.' And I said something like I thought I could fix it up really nice. And he said, 'All that and more. If the shitters will let you.' "

We went inside. Mr. Leheureux, the French teacher, was

going someplace fast, his bald head gleaming under the fluorescent lights. "You boys are late," he said in a harried voice that reminded me of the white rabbit in *Alice in Wonderland*. We hurried up until he was out of sight and then we slowed down again.

Arnie said, "When Buddy Repperton got after me like that, I was really scared." He lowered his voice, smiling but serious. "I almost pissed my pants, if you want to know the truth. Anyway, I guess I used LeBay's word without even thinking about it. In Repperton's case it fits, wouldn't you say?"

"Yes."

"I gotta go," Arnie said. "Calculus, then Auto Shop III. I think I've learned the whole course on Christine the last two months anyway."

He hurried off and I just stood there in the hall for a minute, watching him go. I had a study hall with Miss Rat-Pack period six on Mondays, and I thought I could slip in the back unnoticed . . . I had done it before. Besides, seniors get away with murder, as I was rapidly learning.

I stood there, trying to shake a feeling of fright that would never be so amorphous or un-concrete again. Something was wrong, something was out of place, out of joint. There was a chill, and not all the bright October sunshine spilling through all the high school windows in the world would dispel it. Things were as they always had been, but they were getting ready to change—I felt it.

I stood there trying to get myself in gear, trying to tell myself that the chill was no more than my fears about my own future, and that was the change coming that I was uneasy about. Maybe that was part of it. But it wasn't all. *That shitting car, I'll be fucked if I know why you want it, boy. It's the ace of spades,* I saw Mr. Leheureux coming back from the office, and I started moving.

I think that everybody has a backhoe in his or her head, and at moments of stress or trouble you can fire it up and simply push everything into a great big slit-trench in the floor of your conscious mind. Get rid of it. Bury it. Except that that slit-trench goes down into the subconscious, and sometimes, in dreams, the bodies stir and walk. I dreamed of Christine again that night, Arnie behind the wheel this time, the decomposing corpse of Roland D. LeBay lolling obscenely in the shotgun seat as the car roared out of the garage at me, pinning me with the savage circles of its headlights.

I woke up with my pillow crammed against my mouth to stifle the screams.

19 / The Accident

Tach it up, tach it up,
Buddy, gonna shut you down.
                    —The Beach Boys

That was the last time I talked to Arnie—really talked to him—until Thanksgiving, because the following Saturday was the day I got hurt. That was the day we played the Ridge Rock Bears again, and this time we lost by the truly spectacular score of 46-3. I wasn't around at the end of the game, however. About seven minutes into the third quarter I got into the open, took a pass, and was setting myself to run when I was hit simultaneously by three Bears defensive linemen. There was an instant of terrible pain—a bright flare, as if I had been caught on ground zero of a nuclear blast. Then there was a lot of darkness.

Things stayed dark for a fairly long time, although it didn't seem long to me. I was unconscious for about fifty hours, and when I woke up late on the afternoon of Monday the twenty-third of October, I was in Libertyville Community Hospital. My dad and mom were there. So was Ellie, looking pale and strained. There were dark brown circles under her eyes, and I was absurdly touched; she had found it in her heart to cry for me in spite of all the Twinkies and Yodels I had hooked out of the breadbox after she went to bed, in spite of the time, when she was twelve, that I had given her a little bag of Vigoro after she had spent about a week looking at herself sideways in the mirror with her tightest T-shirt on so she could see if her boobs were getting any bigger (she had burst into tears and my mother had been super-pissed at me for almost two weeks), in spite of all the teasing and the shitty little I'm-one-up-on-you sibling games.

Arnie wasn't there when I woke up, but he joined my

family shortly; he and Leigh had been down in the waiting room. That evening my aunt and uncle from Albany showed up, and the rest of that week was a steady parade of family and friends—the entire football team showed up, including Coach Puffer, who looked as if he had aged about twenty years. I guess he had found out there were worse things than a losing season. Coach was the one who broke the news to me that I was never going to play football again, and I don't know what he expected—for me to bust out crying or maybe have hysterics, from the drawn, tense look on his face. But I didn't have much of a reaction at all, inwardly or outwardly. I was just glad to be alive and to know I would walk again, eventually.

If I had been hit just once, I probably could have bounced right up and gone back for more. But the human body was never meant to get creamed from three different angles at the same time. Both of my legs were broken, the left in two places. My right arm had whipped around behind me when I went down, and I had sustained a nasty greenstick fracture of the forearm. But all of that was really only the icing on the cake. I had also gotten a fractured skull and sustained what the doctor in charge of my case kept calling "a lower spinal accident," which seemed to mean that I had come within about a centimeter of being paralyzed from the waist down for the rest of my life.

I got a lot of visitors, a lot of flowers, a lot of cards. All of it was, in some ways, very enjoyable—like being alive to help celebrate your own wake.

But I also got a lot of pain and a lot of nights when I couldn't sleep; I got an arm suspended over my body by weights and pulleys, likewise a leg (they both seemed to itch all the time under the casts), and a temporary cast—what is called a "presser cast"—around my lower back. Also, of course, I got the prospect of a long hospital stay and endless trips in a wheelchair to that chamber of horrors so innocently labelled the Therapy Wing.

Oh, and one other thing—I got a lot of time.

I read the paper; I asked questions of my visitors; and on more than a few occasions, as things went on and my suspicions began to get out of hand, I asked myself if I might not be losing my mind.

I was in the hospital until Christmas, and by the time I got home, my suspicions had almost taken their final shape. I was finding it more and more difficult to deny that monstrous shape, and I knew damned well I wasn't losing my mind. In some ways it would have been better—more comforting—if I could have believed that. By then I was badly frightened, and more than half in love with my best friend's girl, as well.

Time to think . . . too much time.

Time to call myself a hundred names for what I was thinking about Leigh. Time to look up at the ceiling of my room and wish I had never heard of Arnie Cunningham . . . or Leigh Cabot . . . or of Christine.

tep, and I know ... and I ... 't ... 'e always for the ... it
entire ways it would have been ... rist—more comforting—if I

2 ✍

Arnie—
Teenage Love-
Songs

20 / The Second Argument

The Dealer came to me and said,
"Trade in your Fo'd,
And I'll put you in a car that'll
Eat up the road!
Just tell me what you want and
Sign that line,
I'll have it brought down to you
In an hour's time."
I'm gonna get me a car
And I'll be headed on down the road;
Then I won't have to worry about
That broken-down, ragged Ford.
                                    —Chuck Berry

Arnie Cunningham's 1958 Plymouth became street-legal on the afternoon of November 1, 1978. He finished the process, which had really begun the night he and Dennis Guilder changed that first flat tire, by paying an excise tax fee of $8.50, a municipal road tax of $2.00 (which also enabled him to park free at the meters in the downtown area), and a license-plate fee of $15.00. He was issued Pennsylvania plate HY-6241-J at the Motor Vehicle Bureau in Monroeville.

He drove back from the MVB in a car Will Darnell had loaned him and rolled out of Darnell's Do-It-Yourself Garage behind the wheel of Christine. He drove her home.

His father and mother arrived together from Horlicks University an hour or so later. The fight started almost at once.

"Did you see it?" Arnie asked, speaking to them both but perhaps a little more to his father. "I registered it just this afternoon."

He was proud; he had reason to be. Christine had just been washed and waxed, and she gleamed in the late afternoon autumn sunlight. There was still a lot of rust on her, but she looked a thousand times better than she had on the day Arnie

173

bought her. The rocker panels, like the hood and the back deck, were brand new. The interior was spick and span and neat as a pin. The glass and the chrome gleamed.

"Yes, I—" Michael began.

"Of course we saw it," Regina snapped. She was making a drink, spinning a swizzle-stick in a Waterford glass in furious counter-clockwise circles. "We almost ran into it. I don't want it parked here. The place looks like a used-car lot."

"Mom!" Arnie said, stunned and hurt. He looked to Michael, but Michael had left to make a drink of his own—perhaps he had decided he was going to need it.

"Well it does," Regina Cunningham said. Her face was a trifle paler than usual; the rouge on her cheeks stood out almost like clown-color. She knocked back half of her gin and tonic at a swallow, grimacing the way people grimace at the taste of bad medicine. "Take it back where you had it. I don't want it here and I won't have it here, Arnie. That's final."

"Take it back?" Arnie said, now angry as well as hurt. "That's great, isn't it? It's costing me twenty bucks a week there!"

"It's costing you a lot more than that," Regina said. She drained her drink and set the glass down. She turned to look at him. "I took a look at your bankbook the other day—"

"You did *what?*" Arnie's eyes widened.

She flushed a little but did not drop her eyes. Michael came back and stood in the doorway, looking unhappily from his wife to his son.

"I wanted to know how much you'd been spending on that damned car," she said. "Is that so unnatural? You have to go to college next year. So far as I know, they're not giving away free college educations in Pennsylvania."

"So you just went into my room and hunted around until you found my bankbook?" Arnie said. His gray eyes were hard with anger. "Maybe you were hunting for pot, too. Or girlie books. Or maybe come-stains on the sheets."

Regina's mouth dropped open. She had perhaps expected hurt and anger from him, but not this utter, no-holds-barred fury.

"Arnie!" Michael roared.

"Well, why not?" Arnie shouted back. "I thought that was *my* business! God knows you spent enough time telling me how it was my responsibility, the both of you!"

Regina said, "I'm very disappointed that you feel that way, Arnold. Disappointed and hurt. You're behaving like—"

"Don't tell me how I'm behaving! How do you think I feel? I work my ass off getting the car street-legal—over two and a half months I worked on it—and when I bring it home, the first thing you say is get it out of the driveway. How am I supposed to feel? Happy?"

"That's no reason to take that tone to your mother," Michael said. In spite of the words, the tone was one of awkward conciliation. "Or to use that sort of language."

Regina held her glass out to her husband. "Make me another drink. There's a fresh bottle of gin in the pantry."

"Dad, stay here," Arnie said. "Please. Let's get this over."

Michael Cunningham looked at his wife; his son; at his wife again. He saw flint in both places. He retreated to the kitchen clutching his wife's glass.

Regina turned grimly back to her son. The wedge had been in the door since late last summer; she had perhaps recognized this as her last chance to kick it back out again.

"This July you had almost four thousand dollars in the bank," she said. "About three-quarters of all the money you've made since ninth grade, plus interest—"

"Oh, you've really been keeping track, haven't you?" Arnie said. He sat down suddenly, gazing at his mother. His tone was one of disgusted surprise. "Mom—why didn't you just take the damn money and put it in an account under your own name?"

"Because," she said, "until recently, you seemed to understand what the money was for. In the last couple of months it's all been car-car-car and more recently girl-girl-girl. It's as if you've gone insane on both subjects."

"Well, thanks. I can always use a nice, unprejudiced opinion on the way I'm conducting my life."

"This July you had almost four thousand dollars. For your *education*, Arnie. For your *education*. Now you have just over twenty-eight hundred. You can go on about snooping all you want—and I admit it hurts a little—but that's a fact. You've gone through twelve hundred dollars in two months. Maybe that's why I don't want to look at that car. You ought to be able to understand that. To me it looks like—"

"Listen—"

"—like a big dollar bill flying away."

"Can I tell you a couple of things?"

"No, I don't think so, Arnie," she said with finality. "I really don't think so."

Michael had come back with her glass, half full of gin. He added tonic at the bar and handed it to her. Regina drank, making that bitter grimace of distaste again. Arnie sat in the chair near the TV, looking at her thoughtfully.

"You teach college?" he said. "You teach college and that's your attitude? 'I have spoken. The rest of you can just shut up.' Great. I pity your students."

"You watch it, Arnie," she said, pointing a finger at him. "Just watch it."

"Can I tell you a couple of things or not?"

"Go ahead. But it won't make any difference."

Michael cleared his throat. "Reg, I think Arnie's right, that's hardly a constructive atti—"

She turned on him like a cat. "Not one word from you, either!"

Michael flinched back.

"The first thing is this," Arnie said. "If you gave my savings passbook more than a cursory look—and I'm sure you did—you must have noticed that my total savings went down to an all-time low of twenty-two hundred dollars the first week of September. I had to buy a whole new front-end kit for Christine."

"You speak as if you're proud of it," she said angrily.

"I am." He met her eyes levelly. "I put that front-end kit in myself, with no help from anybody. And I did a really good job. You wouldn't"—here his voice seemed to falter momentarily, and then firmed again—"you wouldn't be able to tell it from the original. But my point is, the total savings is back up six hundred dollars from then. Because Will Darnell liked my work and took me on. If I can add six hundred dollars to my savings account every two months—and I might do better if he puts me on the run over to Albany where he buys his used cars—there'll be forty-six hundred dollars in my account by the time school ends. And if I work there full-time next summer, I'll be starting college with nearly seven thousand dollars. And you can lay it all at the door of that car you hate so much."

"That won't do you any good if you can't get into a good school," she countered, shifting her ground deftly as she had in so many department committee meetings when someone dared to question one of her opinions . . . which was not often. She did not concede the point; she simply passed on to something else. "Your grades have slipped."

"Not enough to matter," Arnie said.

"What do you mean, 'not enough to matter'? You got a deficient in Calculus! We got the red-card just a week ago!" Red-cards, sometimes known as flunk-cards by the student body, were issued halfway through each marking period to students who had posted a 75-average grade or lower during the first five weeks of the quarter.

"That was based on a single examination," Arnie said calmly. "Mr. Fenderson is famous for giving so few exams in the first half of a quarter that you can bring home a red-card with an F on it because you didn't understand one basic concept, and end up with an A for the whole marking period. All of which I would have told you, if you'd asked. You didn't. Also, that's only the third red-card I've gotten since I started high school. My overall average is still 93, and you know how good that is—"

"It'll go lower!" she said shrilly, and stepped toward him. "It's this goddam obsession with the car! You've got a girlfriend; I think that's fine, wonderful, super! But this car thing is insane! Even Dennis says—"

Arnie was up, and up fast, so close to her that she took a step backward, surprised out of her anger, at least momentarily, by his. "You leave Dennis out of this," he said in a deadly soft voice. "This is between us."

"All right," she said, shifting ground once more. "The simple fact is that your grades are going to go down. I know it, and your father knows it, and that mathematics red-card is an indication of it."

Arnie smiled confidently, and Regina looked wary.

"Good," he said. "I tell you what. Let me keep the car here until the marking period ends. If I've got any grade lower than a C, I'll sell it to Darnell. He'll buy it; he knows he could get a grand for it in the shape it's in now. The value's not going to do anything but go up."

Arnie considered.

"I'll go you one better. If I'm not on the semester honor roll, I'll also get rid of it. That means I'm betting my car I'll get a B in Calculus not just for the quarter but for the whole semester. What do you say?"

"No," Regina said immediately. She shot a warning look at her husband—*Stay out of this.* Michael, who had opened his mouth, closed it with a snap.

"Why not?" Arnie asked with deceptive softness.

"Because it's a trick, and you know it's a trick!" Regina shouted at him, her fury suddenly total and uncontained. "And I'm not going to stand here any longer chewing this rag and listening to a lot of insolence from you! I—I changed your dirty diapers! I said get it out of here, drive it if you have to, but don't leave it where I have to look at it! That's it! The end!"

"How do you feel, Dad?" Arnie asked, shifting his gaze.

Michael opened his mouth again to speak.

"He feels as I do," Regina said.

Arnie looked back at her. Their eyes, the same shade of gray, met.

"It doesn't matter what I say, does it?"

"I think this has gone quite far e—"

She began to turn away, her mouth still hard and determined, her eyes oddly confused. Arnie caught her arm just above the elbow.

"It doesn't, does it? Because when you've made up your mind about something, you don't see, you don't hear, you don't *think*."

"Arnie, stop it!" Michael shouted at him.

Arnie looked at her and Regina looked back at him. Their eyes were frozen, locked.

"I'll tell you why you don't want to look at it," he said in that same soft voice. "It isn't the money, because the car's let me connect with a job that I'm good at and will end up making me money. You know that. It isn't my grades, either. They're no worse than they ever were. You know that, too. It's because you can't stand not to have me under your thumb, the way your department is, the way *he* is"—he jerked a thumb at Michael, who managed to look angry and guilty and miserable all at the same time—"the way I always was."

Now Arnie's face was flushed, his hands clenched into fists at his sides.

"All that liberal bullshit about how the family decided things together, discussed things together, worked things out together. But the fact is, *you* were always the one who picked out my school-clothes, my school-shoes, who I was supposed to play with and who I couldn't, *you* decided where we were going on vacation, *you* told him when to trade cars and what to trade for. Well, this is one thing you can't run, and you fucking hate it, don't you?"

She slapped his face. The sound was like a pistol-shot in the living room. Outside, dusk had fallen and cars cruised by, indistinct, their headlights like yellow eyes. Christine sat in the Cunninghams' asphalted driveway as she had once sat on Roland D. LeBay's lawn, but looking considerably better now than she had then—she looked cool and above all this ugly, undignified family bickering. She had, perhaps, come up in the world.

Abruptly, shockingly, Regina Cunningham began to cry. This was a phenomenon, akin to rain in the desert, that Arnie had seen only four or five times in his entire life—and on none of the other occasions had he been the cause of the tears.

Her tears were frightening, he told Dennis later, by virtue of the simple fact that they were there. That was enough, but there was more—the tears made her look old in a single terrifying stroke, as if she had made a quantum leap from forty-five to sixty in a space of seconds. The hard gray shine in her gaze turned blurry and weak, and suddenly the tears were spilling down her cheeks, cutting through her makeup.

She fumbled on the mantelpiece for her drink, jogged the glass instead with the tips of her fingers. It fell onto the hearth and shattered. A kind of incredulous silence held among the three of them, and amazement that things had come this far.

And somehow, even through the weakness of the tears, she managed to say, "I won't have it in our garage or in this driveway, Arnold."

He answered coldly, "I wouldn't have it here, Mother."

He walked to the doorway, turned back, and looked at them both. "Thanks. For being so understanding. Thanks a lot, both of you."

He left.

21 / Arnie and Michael

Ever since you've been gone
I walk around with sunglasses on
But I know I will be just fine
As long as I can make my jet black
*   Caddy shine.*

—Moon Martin

Michael caught Arnie in the driveway, headed for Christine. He put a hand on Arnie's shoulder. Arnie shook it off and went on digging for his car-keys.

"Arnie. Please."

Arnie turned around fast. For a moment he seemed on the verge of making that evening's blackness total by striking his father. Then some of the tenseness in his body subsided and he leaned back against the car, touching it with his left hand, stroking it, seeming to draw strength from it.

"All right," he said. "What do you want?"

Michael opened his mouth and then seemed unsure how to proceed. An expression of helplessness—it would have been funny if it hadn't been so grimly awful—spread over his face. He seemed to have aged, to have gone gray and haggard around the edges.

"Arnie," he said, seeming to force the words out against some great weight of opposing inertia, "Arnie, I'm so sorry."

"Yeah," Arnie said, and turned away again, opening the driver's side door. A pleasant smell of well-cared-for car drifted out. "I could see that from the way you stood up for me."

"Please," he said. "This is hard for me. Harder than you know."

Something in his voice made Arnie turn back. His father's eyes were desperate and unhappy.

"I didn't say I wanted to stand up for you," Michael said. "I see her side as well, you know. I see the way you pushed her, determined to have your own way at any cost—"

180

Arnie uttered a harsh laugh. "Just like her, in other words."

"Your mother is going through the change of life," Michael said quietly. "It's been extremely difficult for her."

Arnie blinked at him, at first not even sure what he had heard. It was as if his father had suddenly said something to him in igpay atinlay; it seemed to have no more relevance to what they were talking about than baseball scores.

"W-What?"

"The change. She's frightened, and she's drinking too much, and sometimes she's in physical pain. Not often," he said, seeing the alarmed look on Arnie's face, "and she's been to the doctor, and the change is all it is. But she's in an emotional uproar. You're her only child, and the way she is now, all she can see is that she wants things to be right for you, no matter what the cost."

"She wants things her way. And that isn't anything new. She's *always* wanted things her way."

"That she thinks the right thing for you is whatever she thinks the right thing is goes without saying," Michael said. "But what makes you think you are so different? Or better? You were after her ass in there, and she knew it. So did I."

"She started it—"

"No, you started it when you brought the car home. You knew how she felt. And she's right about another thing. You've changed. From that first day you came home with Dennis and said you'd bought a car; that's when it started. Do you think that hasn't upset her? Or me? To have your kid start exhibiting personality traits you didn't even know existed?"

"Hey, Dad, come on! That's a little—"

"We never see you, you're always working on your car or out with Leigh."

"You're starting to sound just like her."

Michael suddenly grinned—but it was a sad grin. "You're wrong about that. Just as wrong as you can be. *She* sounds like her, and *you* sound like her, but *I* just sound like the guy in charge of some dumb UN peacekeeping force that's about to get its collective ass shot off."

Arnie slumped a little; his hand found the car again and began caressing, caressing.

"All right," he said. "I guess I see what you mean. I don't know why you want to let her push you around like that, but okay."

The sad, humiliated grin remained, a little like the grin of a dog that has chased a woodchuck a long piece on a hot summer day. "Maybe some things get to be a way of life. And maybe there are compensations that you can't understand and I can't explain. Like . . . well, I love her, you know."

Arnie shrugged. "So . . . what now?"

"Can we go for a ride?"

Arnie looked surprised, then pleased. "Sure. Hop in. Any place in particular?"

"The airport."

Arnie's eyebrows went up. "The airport? Why?"

"I'll tell you as we go."

"What about Regina?"

"Your mother's gone to bed," Michael said quietly, and Arnie had the good grace to flush a little himself.

Arnie drove firmly and well. Christine's new sealed-beam headlights cut the early dark in a clean, deep tunnel of light. He passed the Guilders' house, then turned left onto Elm Street at the stop sign and started out toward JFK Drive. I-376 took them to I-278 and then out toward the airport. Traffic was light. The engine muttered softly through new pipes. The dashboard instrument panel glowed a mystic green.

Arnie turned on the radio and found WDIL, the AM station from Pittsburgh that plays only oldies. Gene Chandler was chanting "The Duke of Earl."

"This thing runs like a dream," Michael Cunningham said. He sounded awed.

"Thanks," Arnie said, smiling.

Michael inhaled deeply. "It smells *new*."

"A lot of it is. These seat covers set me back eighty bucks. Part of the money Regina was bitching about. I went to the library and got a lot of books and tried to copy everything the best I could. But it hasn't been as easy as people might think."

"Why not?"

"Well, for one thing, the '58 Plymouth Fury wasn't anybody's idea of a classic car, so no one wrote much about it, even in the car retrospective volumes—*American Car, American Classics, Cars of the 1950s*, things like that. The '58 Pontiac was a classic, only the second year Pontiac made the

Bonneville model; and the '58 T-Bird with the rabbit-ear fins, that was the last really great Thunderbird, I think; and—"

"I had no idea you knew so much about old cars," Michael said. "How long have you been harboring this interest, Arnie?"

He shrugged vaguely. "Anyway, the other problem was just that LeBay himself customized the original Detroit rolling stock—Plymouth didn't offer a Fury in red and white, for one thing—and I've been trying to restore the car more the way he had it than the way Detroit meant it to be. So I've just been sort of flying by the seat of my pants."

"Why do you want to restore it the way LeBay had it?"

That vague shrug again. "I don't know. It just seems like the right thing to do."

"Well, I think you're doing a hell of a job."

"Thank you."

His father leaned toward him, looking at the instrument panel.

"What are you looking at?" Arnie asked, a little sharply.

"I'll be damned," Michael said. "I've never seen *that* before."

"What?" Arnie glanced down. "Oh. The odometer."

"It's running backward, isn't it?"

The odometer was indeed running backward; at that time, on the evening of November 1, it read 79,500 and some-odd miles. As Michael watched, the tenths-of-a-mile indicator rolled from .2 to .1 to 0. As it went back to .9, the actual miles slipped back by one.

Michael laughed. "That's one thing you missed, son."

Arnie smiled—a small smile. "That's right," he said. "Will says there's a wire crossed in there someplace. I don't think I'll fool with it. It's sort of neat, having an odometer that runs backward."

"Is it accurate?"

"Huh?"

"Well, if you go from our house to Station Square, would it subtract five miles from the total?"

"Oh," Arnie said. "I get you. No, it's not accurate at all. Turns back two or three miles for every actual mile travelled. Sometimes more. Sooner or later the speedometer cable will break, and when I replace that, it'll take care of itself."

Michael, who had had a speedometer cable or two break on him in his time, glanced at the needle for the characteristic jitter that indicated trouble there. But the needle hung dead still just above forty. The speedometer seemed fine; it was only the odometer that had gotten funky. And did Arnie really believe that the speedometer and odometer ran off the same cables? Surely not.

He laughed and said, "That's weird, son."

"Why the airport?" Arnie asked.

"I'm going to treat you to a thirty-day parking stub," Michael said. "Five dollars. Cheaper than Darnell's garage. And you can get your car out whenever you want it. The airport's a regular stop on the bus run. End of the line, in fact."

"Holy Christ, that's the craziest thing I ever heard!" Arnie shouted. He pulled into the turnaround drive of a darkened dry cleaner's shop. "I'm to take the bus twenty miles out to the airport to get my car when I need it? It's like something out of *Catch-22!* No! No way!"

He was about to say something more, when he was suddenly grabbed by the neck.

"You listen," Michael said. "I'm your father, so you listen to me. Your mother was right, Arnie. You've gotten unreasonable—more than unreasonable—in the last couple of months. You've gotten downright peculiar."

"Let go of me," Arnie said, struggling in his father's grip.

Michael didn't let go, but he loosened up. "I'll put it in perspective for you," he said. "Yes, the airport is a long way to come, but the same quarter that would take you to Darnell's will take you out here. There are parking garages closer in, but there are more incidents of theft and vandalism in the city. The airport is, by contrast, quite safe."

"No public parking lot is safe."

"Second, it's cheaper than a downtown garage and *much* cheaper than Darnell's."

"That's not the point, and you know it!"

"Maybe you're right," Michael said. "But you're missing something too, Arnie. You're missing the *real* point."

"Well suppose you tell me what the *real* point is."

"All right. I will." Michael paused for a moment, looking steadily at his son. When he spoke his voice was low and even, almost as musical as his recorder. "Along with any sense of what is reasonable, you seem to have totally lost your sense of perspective. You're almost eighteen, in your last year at public school. I think you've made up your mind not to go to Horlicks; I've seen the college brochures you've brought home—"

"No, I'm not going to Horlicks," Arnie said. He sounded a

little calmer now. "Not after all of this. You have no idea how badly I want to get away. Or maybe you do."

"Yes. I do. And maybe that's best. Better than this constant abrasion between you and your mother. All I ask is that you not tell her yet; wait until you have to submit the application papers."

Arnie shrugged, promising nothing either way.

"You'll be taking your car to school, that is if it's still running—"

"It'll be running."

"—and *if* it's a school that allows freshmen to have cars on campus."

Arnie turned toward his father, surprised out of his smouldering anger—surprised and uneasy. This was a possibility he had never considered.

"I won't go to a school that says I can't have my wheels," he said. His tone was one of patient instruction, the sort of voice an instructor with a class of mentally retarded children might use.

"You see?" Michael asked. "She's right. Basing your choice of a college on the school's policy concerning freshmen and cars is totally irrational. You've gotten obsessed with this car."

"I wouldn't expect you to understand."

Michael pressed his lips together for a moment.

"Anyway, what's running out to the airport on the bus to pick up your car, if you want to take Leigh out? It's an inconvenience, granted, but not really a major one. It means you won't use it unless you have to, for one thing, and you'll save gas money. Your mother can have her little victory; she won't have to look at it." Michael paused and then smiled his sad grin again. "She doesn't see it as money flying away, both of us know that. She sees it as your first decisive step away from her . . . from us. I guess she . . . oh, shit, I don't know."

He stopped, looking at his son. Arnie looked back thoughtfully.

"Take it to college with you; even if you choose a campus that doesn't allow freshmen to have cars on campus, there are ways to get around—"

"Like parking it at the airport?"

"Yes. Like that. When you come home for weekends, Regina will be so glad to see you she'll never mention the car. Hell, she'll probably get out there in the driveway and help you wash it and Turtlewax it just so she can find out what you're doing. Ten months. Then it'll be over. We can have peace in the family again. Go on, Arnie. Drive."

Arnie pulled out of the dry cleaner's and back into traffic.

"Is this thing insured?" Michael asked abruptly.

Arnie laughed. "Are you kidding? If you don't have liability insurance in this state and you get in an accident, the cops kill you. Without liability, it'd be your fault even if the other car fell out of the sky and landed on top of you. It's one of the ways the shitters keep kids off the roads in Pennsylvania."

Michael thought of telling Arnie that a disproportionate number of fatal accidents in Pennsylvania—41 percent—involved teenage drivers (Regina had read the statistic to him as part of a Sunday supplement article, rolling that figure out in slow, apocalyptic tones: "For-ty-one per-cent!" shortly after Arnie bought his car), and decided it wasn't anything Arnie would want to hear . . . not in his present mood.

"Just liability?"

They were passing under a reflecting sign which read LEFT LANE FOR AIRPORT. Arnie put on his blinker and changed lanes. Michael seemed to relax a little.

"You can't get collision insurance until you're twenty-one. I mean that; those shitting insurance companies are all as rich as Croesus, but they won't cover you unless the odds are stacked *outrageously* in their favor." There was a bitter, somehow weakly peevish note in Arnie's voice that Michael had never heard before, and although he said nothing, he was startled and a little dismayed by his son's choice of words— he had assumed Arnie used that sort of language with his peers (or so he later told Dennis Guilder, apparently totally unaware of the fact that, up until his senior year, Arnie had really had no peers except for Guilder), but he had never used it in front of Regina and himself.

"Your driving record and whether or not you had driver ed don't have anything to do with it," Arnie went on. "The reason you can't get collision is because their fucking actuarial tables *say* you can't get collision. You can get it at twenty-one only if you're willing to spend a fortune—usually the premiums end up being more than the car books for until you're twenty-three or so, unless you're married. Oh, the shitters have got it all figured out. They know how to walk it right to you, all right."

Up ahead the airport lights glowed, runways outlined in mystic parallels of blue light. "If anyone ever asks me what the lowest form of human life is, I'll tell them it's an insurance agent."

"You've made quite a study of it," Michael commented. He didn't quite dare to say anything else; Arnie seemed only waiting to fly into a fresh rage.

"I went around to five different companies. In spite of what Mom said, I'm not anxious to throw my money away."

"And straight liability was the best you could do?"

"Yeah, that's right. Six hundred and fifty dollars a year."

Michael whistled.

"That's right," Arnie agreed.

Another twinkling sign, advising that the two left-hand lanes were for parking, the right lanes for departures. At the entrance to the parking lot, the way split again. To the right was an automated gate where you took a ticket for short-term parking. To the left was the glass booth where the parking-lot attendant sat, watching a small black-and-white TV and smoking a cigarette.

Arnie sighed. "Maybe you're right. Maybe this is the best solution all the way around."

"Of course it is," Michael said, relieved. Arnie sounded more like his old self now, and that hard light had died out of his eyes at last. "Ten months, that's all."

"Sure."

He drove up to the booth, and the attendant, a young guy in a black-and-orange high school sweater with the Libertyville logo on the pockets, pushed back the glass partition and leaned out. "Help ya?"

"I'd like a thirty-day ticket," Arnie said, digging for his wallet.

Michael put his hand over Arnie's. "This one's my treat," he said.

Arnie pushed his hand away gently but firmly and took his wallet out. "It's my car," he said. "I'll pay my own way."

"I only wanted—" Michael began.

"I know," Arnie said. "But I mean it."

Michael sighed. "I know you do. You and your mother. Everything will be fine if you do it my way."

Arnie's lips tightened momentarily, and then he smiled. "Well . . . yeah," he said.

They looked at each other and both burst out laughing.

At the instant that they did, Christine stalled. Up until then the engine had been ticking over with unobtrusive perfection. Now it just quit; the oil and amp idiot lights came on.

Michael raised his eyebrows. "Say what?"

"I don't know," Arnie answered, frowning. "It never did that before."

He turned the key, and the engine started at once.

"Nothing, I guess," Michael said.

"I'll want to check the timing later in the week," Arnie muttered. He gunned the engine and listened carefully. And in that instant, Michael thought that Arnie didn't look like his son at all. He looked like someone else, someone much older and harder. He felt a brief but extremely nasty lance of fear in his chest.

"Hey, do you want this ticket or are you just gonna sit there all night talkin about your timing?" the parking-lot attendant asked. He looked vaguely familiar to Arnie, the way people do when you've seen them moving around in the corridors at school but don't have anything else to do with them.

"Oh yeah. Sorry." Arnie passed him a five-dollar bill, and the attendant gave him a time-ticket.

"Back of the lot," the attendant said. "Be sure to revalidate it five days before the end of the month if you want the same space again."

"Right."

Arnie drove to the back of the lot, Christine's shadow growing and shrinking as they passed under the hooded sodium-arc lights. He found a vacant space and backed Christine in. As he turned off the key, he grimaced and put a hand to his lower back.

"That still bothering you?" Michael asked.

"Only a little," Arnie said. "I was almost over it, and it came back on me yesterday. I must have lifted something wrong. Don't forget to lock your door."

They got out and locked up. Once out of the car, Michael felt better—he felt closer to his son, and, maybe just as important, he felt less that he had played the impotent fool with his jingling cap of bells in the argument that had taken place earlier. Once out of the car, he felt as if he might have salvaged something—maybe a lot—out of the night.

"Let's see how fast that bus really is," Arnie said, and they began to walk across the parking lot toward the terminal, companionably close together.

Michael had formed an opinion of Christine on the ride out to the airport. He was impressed with the job of restoration Arnie had done, but he disliked the car itself—disliked it intensely. He supposed it was ridiculous to hold such feelings about an inanimate object, but the dislike was there all the same, big and unmistakable, like a lump in the throat.

The source of the dislike was impossible to isolate. It had caused bitter trouble in the family, and he supposed that was the real reason . . . but it wasn't all. He hadn't liked the way Arnie *seemed* when he was behind the wheel: somehow arrogant and petulant at the same time, like a weak king. The impotent way he had railed about the insurance . . . his use of that ugly and striking word "shitters" . . . even the way the car had stalled when they laughed together.

And it had a smell. You didn't notice it right away, but it was there. Not the smell of new seat covers, that was quite pleasant; this was an undersmell, bitter, almost (but not quite) secret. It was an old smell. *Well,* Michael told himself, *the car is old, why in God's name do you expect it to smell new?* And that made undeniable sense. In spite of the really fantastic job Arnie had done of restoring it, the Fury was twenty years old. That bitter, mouldy smell might be coming from old carpeting in the trunk, or old matting under the new floormats; perhaps it was coming from the original padding under the bright new seat covers. Just a smell of age.

And yet that undersmell, low and vaguely sickening, bothered him. It seemed to come and go in waves, sometimes very noticeable, at other times completely undetectable. It seemed to have no specific source. At its worst, it smelled like the rotting corpse of some small animal—a cat, a woodchuck, maybe a squirrel—that had gotten into the trunk or maybe crawled up into the frame and then died there.

Michael was proud of what his son had accomplished . . . and very glad to get out of his son's car.

22 / Sandy

First I walked past the Stop and Shop,
Then I drove past the Stop and Shop.
I liked that much better when I drove
     past the Stop and Shop,
'Cause I had the radio on.
                    —Jonathan Richmond and the
                       Modern Lovers

The parking-lot attendant that night—every night from six until ten, as a matter of fact—was a young man named Sandy Galton, the only one of Buddy Repperton's close circle of hoodlum friends who had not been in the smoking area on the day Repperton had been expelled from school. Arnie didn't recognize him, but Galton recognized Arnie.

Buddy Repperton, out of school and with no interest in initiating the procedures that might have gotten him readmitted at the beginning of the spring semester in January, had gone to work at the gas station run by Don Vandenberg's father. In the few weeks he had been there, he had already begun a number of fairly typical scams—shortchanging gas customers who looked as if they might be in too big a hurry to count the bills he gave back to them, running the retread game (which consists of charging the customer for a new tire and then actually putting on a retread and pocketing the fifteen- to sixty-dollar difference), running the similar used-parts game, plus selling inspection stickers to kids from the high school and nearby Horlicks—kids desperate to keep their death-traps on the road.

The station was open twenty-four hours a day, and Buddy worked the late shift, from 9 P.M. to 5 A.M. Around eleven o'clock, Moochie Welch and Sandy Galton were apt to drop by in Sandy's old dented Mustang; Richie Trelawney might come by in his Firebird; and Don, of course, was in and out all the time—when he wasn't goofing off at school. By midnight on any given week night there might be six or eight guys sitting around in the office, drinking beer out of dirty teacups, passing around a bottle of Buddy's Texas Driver, doing a joint or maybe a little hash, farting, telling dirty jokes, swapping lies about how much pussy they were getting, and maybe helping Buddy fiddle around with whatever was up on the lift.

During one of these late-night gatherings in early November, Sandy happened to mention that Arnie Cunningham was parking his machine in the long-term lot out at the airport. He had, in fact, bought a thirty-day ticket.

Buddy, whose usual demeanor during these late-night bull-sessions was one of sullen withdrawal, tipped his cheap contour-plastic chair abruptly back down on all four legs and put his bottle of Driver down on the windshield-wiper cabinet with a bang.

"What did you say?" he asked. "Cunningham? Ole Cunt-face?"

"Yeah," Sandy said, surprised and a little uneasy. "That's him."

"You sure? The guy that got me kicked out of school?"

Sandy looked at him with mounting alarm. "Yeah. Why?"

"And he's got a thirty-day ticket, which means he's parked in the long-term lot?"

"Yeah. Maybe his folks didn't want him to have it at . . ."

Sandy trailed off. Buddy Repperton had begun to smile. It was not a pleasant sight, that smile, and not only because the teeth it revealed were already going rotten. It was as if, somewhere, some terrible machinery had just whined into life and was beginning to cycle up and up to full running speed.

Buddy looked around from Sandy to Don to Moochie Welch to Richie Trelawney. They looked back at him, interested and a little scared.

"Cuntface," he said in a soft, marvelling voice. "Ole Cunt-face got his machine street-legal and his funky folks have got him parking it out at the airport."

He laughed.

Moochie and Don exchanged a glance that was somehow both uneasy and eager.

Buddy leaned toward them, elbows on the knees of his jeans.

"Listen," he said.

23 / Arnie and Leigh

Ridin along in my automobile,
My baby beside me at the wheel,
I stole a kiss at the turn of a mile,
My curiosity running wild—
Cruisin and playin the radio,
With no particular place to go.
                    —Chuck Berry

WDIL was on the car radio and Dion was singing "Runaround Sue" in his tough, streetwise voice, but neither of them was listening.

His hand had slipped up under the T-shirt she was wearing and had found the soft glory of her breasts, capped with nipples that were tight and hard with excitement. Her breath came in short, steep gasps. And for the first time her hand had gone where he wanted it, where he *needed* it, into his lap, where it pressed and turned and moved, without experience but with enough desire to make up for the lack.

He kissed her and her mouth opened wide, her tongue was there, and the kiss was like inhaling the clean aroma/taste of a rain forest. He could feel excitement and arousal coming off her like a glow.

He leaned toward her, *strained* toward her, all of him, and for a moment he could feel her respond with a pure, clean passion.

Then she was gone.

Arnie sat there, dazed and stupefied, a little to the right of the steering wheel, as Christine's dome-light came on. It was brief; the passenger door clunked solidly shut and the light clicked off again.

He sat a moment longer, not sure what had happened, momentarily not even sure of where he was. His body was in a complete stew—a helter-skelter array of emotions and erratic physical reactions that were half wonderful and half terrible. His glands hurt; his penis was hard iron; his balls throbbed dully. He could feel adrenaline whipping rapidly through his bloodstream, up and down and all around.

He made a fist and brought it down on his leg, hard. Then he slid across the seat, opened the door, and went after her.

Leigh was standing on the very edge of the Embankment, looking down into the darkness. Within a bright rectangle in the middle of that darkness, Sylvester Stallone strode across the night in the costume of a young labor leader from the 1930s. Again Arnie had that feeling of living in some marvellous dream that might at any moment skew off into nightmare . . . perhaps it had already begun to happen.

She was too close to the edge—he took her arm and pulled her gently backward. The ground up here was dry and crumbly. There was no fence or guardrail. If the earth at the edge let go, Leigh would be gone; she would land somewhere in the suburban development loosely scattered around the Liberty Hill Drive-In.

The Embankment had been the local lovers' lane since time out of mind. It was at the end of Stanson Road, a long, meandering stretch of two-lane blacktop that first curved out of town and then hooked back toward it, dead-ending on Libertyville Heights, where there had once been a farm.

It was November 4, and the rain that had begun earlier that Saturday night had turned to a light sleet. They had the Embankment and the free (if silent) view of the drive-in to themselves. He got her back into the car—she came willingly enough—thinking it was sleet on her cheeks. It was only inside, by the ghostly green glow of the dashboard lights, that he saw for sure she was crying.

"What's the matter?" he asked. "What's wrong?"

She shook her head and cried harder.

"Did I . . . was it something you didn't want to do?" He swallowed and made himself say it. "Touch me like that?"

She shook her head again, but he wasn't sure what that meant. Arnie held her, clumsy and worried. And in the back of his mind he was thinking about the sleet, the trip back down, and the fact that he had no snow tires on Christine as yet.

"I never did that for any boy," she said against his shoulder. "That's the first time I ever touched . . . you know. I did it because I wanted to. Because I wanted to, that's all."

"Then what is it?"

"I can't . . . here." The words came out slowly and painfully, one at a time, with an almost awful reluctance.

"The Embankment?" Arnie said, gazing around, thinking stupidly that maybe she thought he had really brought them up here so they could watch $F \bullet I \bullet S \bullet T$ free.

"In this car!" she shouted at him suddenly. "I can't make love to you in this car!"

"Huh?" He stared at her, thunderstruck. "What are you talking about? Why not?"

"Because . . . because . . . I don't know!" She struggled to say something else and then burst into fresh tears. Arnie held her again until she quieted.

"It's just that I don't know which you love more," Leigh said when she was able.

"That's . . ." Arnie paused, shook his head, smiled. "Leigh, that's crazy."

"Is it?" she asked, searching his face. "Which of us do you spend more time with? Me . . . or her?"

"You mean Christine?" He looked around him, smiling that puzzled smile that she could find either lovely and lovable or horridly hateful—sometimes both at once.

"Yes," she said tonelessly. "I do." She looked down at her hands, lying lifelessly on her blue woollen slacks. "I suppose it's stupid."

"I spend a lot more time with you," Arnie said. He shook his head. "This is crazy. Or maybe it's normal—maybe it just seems crazy to me because I never had a girl before." He reached out and touched the fall of her hair where it spilled over one shoulder of her open coat. The T-shirt beneath read GIVE ME LIBERTYVILLE OR GIVE ME DEATH, and her nipples poked at the thin cotton cloth in a sexy way that made Arnie feel a little delirious.

"I thought girls were supposed to be jealous of other girls. Not cars."

Leigh laughed shortly. "You're right. It must be because you've never had a girl before. Cars *are* girls. Didn't you know that?"

"Oh, come on—"

"Then why don't you call this Christopher?" And she suddenly slammed her open palm down on the seat, hard. Arnie winced.

"Come on, Leigh. Don't."

"Don't like me slapping your girl?" she asked with sudden and unexpected venom. Then she saw the hurt look in his eyes. "Arnie, I'm sorry."

"Are you?" he asked, looking at her expressionlessly.

"Seems like nobody likes my car these days—you, my dad and mom, even Dennis. I worked my ass off on it, and it means zero to everybody."

"It means something to me," she said softly. "The *effort* it took."

"Yeah," he said morosely. The passion, the heat, had fled. He felt cold and a little sick to his stomach. "Look, we better get going. I don't have any snow tires. Your folks'd think it was cute, us going bowling and then getting racked up on Stanson Road."

She giggled. "They don't know where Stanson Road ends up."

He cocked an eyebrow at her, some of his good humor returning. "That's what *you* think," he said.

He drove back down toward town slowly, and Christine managed the twisting, steeply descending road with easy surefootedness. The sprinkle of earth-stars that was Libertyville and Monroeville grew larger and drew closer together and then ceased to have any pattern at all. Leigh watched this a little sadly, feeling that the best part of a potentially wonderful evening had somehow slipped away. She felt irritated, chafed, out of sorts with herself—unfulfilled, she supposed. There was a dull ache in her breasts. She didn't know if she had meant to let him go what was euphemistically known as "all the way" or not, but after things had reached a certain point, nothing had gone as she had hoped . . . all because she had to open her big fat mouth.

Her body was in a mess, and her thoughts were the same way. Again and again on the mostly silent drive back down she opened her mouth to try to clarify how she felt . . . and then closed it again, afraid of being misunderstood, because she didn't understand how she felt herself.

She didn't feel jealous of Christine . . . and yet she did. About that Arnie hadn't told the truth. She had a good idea of how much time he spent tinkering on the car, but was that so wrong? He was good with his hands, he liked to work on it, and it ran like a watch . . . except for that funny little glitch with the odometer numbers running backward.

Cars are *girls*, she had said. She hadn't been thinking of what she was saying; it had just popped out of her mouth. And it certainly wasn't always true; she didn't think of their family sedan as having any particular gender; it was just a Ford.

But—

Forget it, get rid of all the hocus-pocus and phony stuff. The truth was much more brutal and even crazier, wasn't it? She couldn't make love to him, couldn't touch him in that intimate way, much less think about bringing him to a climax that way (or the other, the real way—she had turned that over and over in her mind as she lay in her narrow bed, feeling a new and nearly amazing excitement steal over her), in the car.

Not in the car.

Because the really crazy part was that she felt Christine was *watching* them. That she was jealous, disapproving, maybe hating. Because there were times (like tonight, as Arnie skated the Plymouth so smoothly and delicately across the building scales of sleet) when she felt that the two of them—Arnie and Christine—were welded together in a disturbing parody of the act of love. Because Leigh did not feel that she *rode* in Christine; when she got in to go somewhere with Arnie she felt *swallowed* in Christine. And the act of kissing him, making love to him, seemed a perversion worse than voyeurism or exhibitionism—it was like making love inside the body of her rival.

The really crazy part of it was that she hated Christine.

Hated her and feared her. She had developed a vague dislike of walking in front of the new grille, or closely behind the trunk; she had vague thoughts of the emergency brake letting go or the gearshift popping out of park and into neutral for some reason. Thoughts she had never had about the family sedan.

But mostly it was not wanting to do anything in the car ... or even go anywhere in the car, if she could help it. Arnie seemed somehow different in the car, a person she didn't really know. She loved the feel of his hands on her body— her breasts, her thighs (she had not yet allowed him to touch the center of her, but she wanted his hands there; she thought if he touched her there she would probably just melt). His touch always brought a coppery taste of excitement to her mouth, a feeling that every sense was alive and deliciously attuned. But in the car that feeling seemed blunted ... maybe because in the car Arnie always seemed less honestly passionate and somehow more lecherous.

She opened her mouth again as they turned onto her street, wanting to explain some of this, and again nothing would come. Why should it? There was really nothing to explain—it was all vapors. Nothing but vague humors. Well . . . there was one thing. But she couldn't tell him that; it would hurt him too badly. She didn't want to hurt him because she thought she was beginning to love him.

But it was there.

The smell—a rotten, thick smell under the aromas of new seat covers and the cleaning fluid he had used on the floormats. It was there, faint but terribly unpleasant. Almost stomach-turning.

As if, at some time, something had crawled into the car and died there.

He kissed her good night on her doorstep, the sleet shining silver in the cone of yellow light thrown by the carriage lamp at the foot of the porch steps. It shone in her dark blond hair like jewels. He would have liked to have really kissed her, but the fact that her parents might be watching from the living room—probably were, in fact—forced him to kiss her almost formally, as you might kiss a dear cousin.

"I'm sorry," she said. "I was silly."

"No," Arnie said, obviously meaning yes.

"It's just that"—and her mind supplied her with something that was a curious hybrid of the truth and a lie—"that it doesn't seem right in the car. *Any* car. I want us to be together, but not parked in the dark at the end of a dead-end road. Do you understand?"

"Yes," he said. Up at the Embankment, in the car, he had felt a little angry with her . . . well, to be honest, he had been pretty goddam pissed off. But now, standing here on her stoop, he thought he could understand—and marvel that he could want to deny her anything or cross her will in any way. "I know exactly what you mean."

She hugged him, her arms locked around his neck. Her coat was still open, and he could feel the soft, maddening weight of her breasts.

"I love you," she said for the first time, and then slipped inside to leave him standing there on the porch momentarily, agreeably stunned, and much warmer than he should have been in the ticking, pattering sleet of late autumn.

The idea that the Cabots might find it peculiar if he stood on their front stoop much longer in the sleet at last percolated down into his bemused brain. Arnie went back down the walk through the tick and patter, snapping his fingers and grinning. He was riding the roller-coaster now, the one that's the best ride, the one they really only let you take once.

Near the place where the concrete path joined the sidewalk, he stopped, the smile fading off his face. Christine stood at the curb, drops of melted sleet pearling her glass, smearing the red idiot lights from the dash inside, and he wondered passingly what the source of that particular bit of slang was—*idiot lights;* it was an unpleasant term. Then that was wiped out by the more important consideration. He had left Christine running, and she had stalled. This was the second time.

"Wet wires," he muttered under his breath. "That's all." It couldn't be plugs; he had put in a whole new set just the day before yesterday, at Will's. Eight new Champion and—

Which of us do you spend more time with? Me . . . or her?

The smile returned, but this time it was uneasy. Well, he spent more time around cars in *general*—of course. That came of working for Will. But it was ridiculous to think that . . .

You lied to her. That's the truth, isn't it?

No, he answered himself uneasily. *No, I don't think you could say I really* lied *to her . . .*

No? Then just what do you call it?

For the first and only time since he had taken her to the football game at Hidden Hills, he had told her a big fat lie. Because the truth was, he spent more time with Christine, and he hated having her parked in the thirty-day section of the airport parking lot, out in the wind and rain, soon to be snow—

He had lied to her.

He spent more time with Christine.

And that was—

Was—

"Wrong," he croaked, and the word was almost lost in the slick, mysterious sound of the falling sleet.

He stood on the walk, looking at his stalled car, marvellously resurrected time traveller from the era of Buddy Holly and Khrushchev and Laika the Space Dog, and suddenly he hated it. It had done something to him, he wasn't sure what. Something.

The idiot lights, blurred into football-shaped red eyes by the moisture on the window, seemed to mock him and reproach him at the same time.

He opened the driver's side door, slipped behind the wheel, and pulled the door shut again. He closed his eyes. Peace flowed over him and things seemed to come back together. He had lied to her, yes, but it was a little lie. A mostly unimportant lie. No—a *completely* unimportant lie.

He reached out without opening his eyes and touched the leather rectangle the keys were attached to—old and scuffed, the initials R.D.L. burned into it. He had seen no need to get a new keyring, or a piece of leather with his own initials on it.

But there was something peculiar about the leather tab the keys were attached to, wasn't there? Yes. Quite peculiar indeed.

When he had counted out the cash on LeBay's kitchen table and LeBay had skittered the keys across the red-and-white-checked oilcloth to him, the rectangle of leather had been scuffed and nicked and darkened by age, the initials almost obliterated by time and the constant friction of rubbing against the change in the old man's pocket and the material of the pocket itself.

Now the initials stood out fresh and clear again. They had been renewed.

But, like the lie, that was really unimportant. Sitting inside the metal shell of Christine's body, he felt very strongly that that was true.

He *knew* it. Quite unimportant, all of it.

He turned the key. The starter whined, but for a long time the engine wouldn't catch. Wet wires. Of course that was what it was.

"Please," he whispered. "It's all right, don't worry, everything is the same."

The engine fired, missed. The starter whined on and on. Sleet ticked coldly on the glass. It was safe in here; it was dry and warm. If the engine would start.

"Come on," Arnie whispered. "Come on, Christine. Come on, hon."

The engine fired again, caught. The idiot lights flickered and went out. The GEN light pulsed weakly again as the motor stuttered, then went out for good as the beat of the engine smoothed out into a clean hum.

The heater blew warm air gently around his legs, negating the winter chill outside.

It seemed to him that there were things Leigh could not understand, things she could never understand. Because she hadn't been around. The pimples. The cries of *Hey Pizza-Face!* The wanting to speak, the wanting to reach out to other people, and the inability. The impotence. It seemed to him that she couldn't understand the simple fact that, had it not been for Christine, he never would have had the courage to call her on the phone even if she had gone around with I WANT TO DATE ARNIE CUNNINGHAM tattooed on her forehead. She couldn't understand that he sometimes felt thirty years older than his age—no! more like fifty!—and not a boy at all but some terribly hurt veteran back from an undeclared war.

He caressed the steering wheel. The green cats' eyes on the dash instruments glowed back at him comfortingly.

"Okay," he said. Almost sighed.

He dropped the gearshift into big D and flicked on the radio. Dee Dee Sharp singing "Mashed Potato Time"; mystic nonsense on the radio waves coming out of the dark.

He pulled out, planning to head for the airport, where he would park his car and catch the bus that ran back to town on the hour. And he did that, but not in time to take the 11:00 P.M. bus as he intended. He took the midnight bus instead, and it was not until he was in bed that night, recalling Leigh's warm kisses instead of the way Christine wouldn't fire up, that it occurred to him that somewhere that evening, after leaving the Cabot house and before arriving at the airport, he had lost an hour. It was so obvious that he felt like a man who has turned the house upside down looking for a vital bit of correspondence, only to discover that he has been holding it in his other hand all along. Obvious . . . and a little scary.

Where had he been?

He had a blurry memory of drawing away from the curb in front of Leigh's and then just . . .

. . . just cruising.

Yeah. Cruising. That was all. No big deal.

Cruising through the thickening sleet, cruising empty streets that were plated with the stuff, cruising without snow tires (and yet Christine, incredibly surefooted, never missed her way or skidded around a corner, Christine seemed to find the safe and secure way as if by magic, the ride as solid as it would have been if the car had been on trolley-tracks), cruising with the radio on, spilling out a constant stream of oldies that seemed to consist solely of girls' names: Peggy Sue, Carol, Barbara-Ann, Susie Darlin'.

It seemed to him that at some point he had gotten a little frightened and had punched one of the chrome buttons on the converter he'd installed, but instead of FM-104 and the Block Party Weekend he got WDIL all over again, only now the disc jockey sounded crazily like Alan Freed, and the voice that followed was that of Screamin' Jay Hawkins, hoarse and chanting: *"I put a spell on youuu . . . because you're miiiiiine . . ."*

And then at last there had been the airport with its foul-weather lights pulsing sequentially like a visible heartbeat. Whatever had been on the radio faded to a meaningless jumble of static and he had turned it off. Getting out of the car he had felt a sweaty, incomprehensible sort of relief.

Now he lay in bed, needing to sleep but unable. The sleet had thickened and curdled into fat white splats of snow.

It wasn't right.

Something had been started, something was wrong. He couldn't even lie to himself and say that he didn't know about it. The car—Christine—several people had commented on how beautifully he had restored her. He had driven it to school and the kids from auto shop were all over it; they were underneath it on crawlers to look at the new exhaust system, the new shocks, the bodywork. They were waist-deep in the engine compartment, checking out the belts and the radiator, which was miraculously free of the corrosion and the green gunk that is the residue of years of antifreeze, checking out the generator and the tight, gleaming pistons socketed in their valves. Even the air cleaner was new, with the numbers 318 painted across the top, raked backward to indicate speed.

Yes, he had become something of a hero to his fellow shoppies, and he had taken all the comments and the compliments with just the right deprecatory grin. But even then, hadn't the confusion been there, somewhere deep inside? Sure.

Because he couldn't remember what he had done to Christine and what he hadn't.

The time spent working on her at Darnell's was nothing but a blur now, like his ride out to the airport earlier this evening had been. He could remember starting the bodywork on the dented rear end, but he couldn't remember finishing it. He could remember painting the hood—covering the windshield and mudguards with masking tape and donning the white mask in the paint-shop out back—but exactly when he had replaced the springs he couldn't remember. Nor could he remember where he had gotten them. All he could remember for sure was sitting behind the wheel for long periods, stupefied with happiness . . . feeling the way he had felt when Leigh whispered "I love you" before slipping in her front door. Sitting there after most of the guys who worked on their cars at Darnell's had gone home to get their suppers. Sitting there and sometimes turning on the radio to listen to the oldies on WDIL.

Maybe the windshield was the worst.

He hadn't bought a new windshield for Christine, he was sure of that. His bankbook would be dented a lot more than it was if he'd bought one of those fancy wrap jobs. And wouldn't he have a receipt? He had even hunted for such a receipt once in the desk-file marked CAR STUFF that he kept in his room. But he hadn't found one, and the truth was, he had hunted rather half-heartedly.

Dennis had said something—that the snarl of cracks had looked smaller, less serious. Then, that day at Hidden Hills, it had just been . . . well, gone. The windshield had been clear and unflawed.

But *when* had it happened? *How* had it happened?

He didn't know.

He finally fell asleep and dreamed unpleasantly, twisting the covers into a ball as the scud of clouds blew away and the autumnal stars shone coldly down.

24 / Seen in the Night

Take you for a ride in my car-car,
Take you for a ride in my car-car.
Take you for a ride,
Take you for a ride,
Take you for a ride in my car-car.
                    —Woody Guthrie

It was a dream—she was sure, almost until the very end, that it must be a dream.

In the dream she awoke from a dream of Arnie, making love to Arnie not in the car but in a very cool blue room that was unfurnished except for a deep blue shag rug and a scatter of throw-pillows covered in a lighter blue satin . . . she awoke from this dream to her room in the small hours of Sunday morning.

She could hear a car outside. She went to the window and looked out and down.

Christine was standing at the curb. She was running—Leigh could see exhaust raftering up from the straight-pipes—but was empty. In the dream she thought that Arnie must be at the door, although there was no knock as yet. She ought to go down, and quickly. If her father woke up and found Arnie here at four in the morning, he would be furious.

But she didn't move. She looked down at the car and thought how much she hated it—and feared it.

And it hated her, too.

Rivals, she thought, and the thought—in this dream—was not grim and hotly jealous but rather despairing and afraid. There it sat at the curb, there it was—there *she* was—parked outside her house in the dead trench of morning, waiting for her. Waiting for Leigh. *Come on down, honey. Come on. We'll cruise, and we'll talk about who needs him more, who cares for him more, and who will be better for him in the long run. Come on . . . you're not scared, are you?*

She was terrified.

It's not fair, she's older, she knows the tricks, she'll beguile him—

"Get out," Leigh whispered fiercely in the dream, and rapped softly on the glass with her knuckles. The glass felt cold to her touch; she could see the small, crescent-shaped marks her knuckles left in the frost. It was amazing how real some dreams could be.

But it *had* to be a dream. It had to be because the car heard her. The words were no more than out of her mouth when the wipers suddenly started up, flicking wet snow off the windshield in somehow contemptuous swipes. And then it—or she—drew smoothly away from the curb and was gone up the street—

With no one driving it.

She was sure of that . . . as sure as one can be of anything in a dream. The passenger window had been dusted with snow but was not opaque with it. She had been able to see inside, and there was no one behind the wheel. So of course it had to be a dream.

She drifted back to her bed (into which she had never brought a lover; like Arnie, she had never had a lover at all) thinking of a Christmas quite long ago—twelve, maybe even fourteen years ago. Surely she could have been no more than four at the time. She and her mother had been in one of the big department stores in Boston, Filene's, maybe . . .

She put her head down on her pillow and fell asleep (in her dream) with her eyes open, looking at the faint gleam of early light in the window, and then—in dreams anything could happen—she saw the Filene's toy department on the other side of the window: tinsel, glitter, lights.

They were looking for something for Bruce, Mother and Dad's only nephew. Somewhere a department-store Santa Claus was ho-ho-ho-ing into a PA system, and the amplified sound was not jolly but somehow ominous, the laughter of a maniac who had come in the night not with presents but with a meat cleaver.

She had held out her hand toward one of the displays, had pointed and told her mother that she wanted Santa Claus to bring her *that*.

No, honey, Santa can't bring you that. That's a boy-toy.
But I want it!
Santa will bring you a nice doll, maybe even a Barbie—
Want that—!

Only boy elves make those, Lee-Lee my love-love. For boys. The nice girl elves make nice dolls—

I don't want a DOLL! I don't want a BARBIE! I . . . want . . . THAT!

If you're going to throw a tantrum, I'll have to take you home, Leigh. I mean it, now.

So she had submitted, and Christmas had brought her not only Malibu Barbie but also Malibu Ken, and she had enjoyed them (she supposed), but still she remembered the red Remco racing car on its green surface of painted hills, running without a cord along a painted road so perfect that there were even tiny metal guardrails—a road whose essential illusion was given away only by its pointless circularity. Ah, but it ran fast, that car, and was it bright red magic in her eye and her mind? It was. And the car's essential illusion was also magic. That illusion was somehow so captivating that it stole her heart. The illusion, of course, was that the car was driving itself. She knew that a store employee was really controlling it from a booth to the right, pushing buttons on a square wireless device. Her mother told her that was how it was happening, and so it must be so, but her eyes denied it.

Her heart denied it.

She stood fascinated, her small gloved hands on the rail of the display area, watching it race around and around, moving fast, driving itself, until her mother pulled her gently away.

And over everything, seeming to cause the very tinsel strung along the ceiling to vibrate, the ominous laughter of the department-store Santa.

Leigh slept more deeply, dreams and memories slowly fading, and outside daylight came creeping in like cold milk, illuminating a street that was Sunday-morning empty and Sunday-morning silent. The season's first fall of snow was unmarred except for the tire tracks that swerved to the curb in front of the Cabot house and then moved smoothly away again, toward the intersection at the end of this suburban block.

She didn't rise until nearly ten o'clock (her mother, who didn't believe in slugabeds, finally called for her to come down and have breakfast before lunch), and by then the day had already warmed up to nearly sixty degrees—in western Pennsylvania, early November is apt to be every bit as capricious as early April. So by ten o'clock the snow had melted. And the tracks were gone.

25 / Buddy Visits the Airport

We shut 'em up and then we shut 'em down.
—Bruce Springsteen

One night some ten days later, as cardboard turkeys and construction-paper cornucopias were beginning to appear in grammar school windows, a blue Camaro, so radically jacked in the back that its nose seemed almost to scrape the road, slid into the long-term parking lane at the airport.

Sandy Galton looked out from his glass booth nervously. From the driver's side of the Chevrolet the happy smiling face of Buddy Repperton tilted up toward him. Buddy's face was scrubbed with a week-old beard and his eyes held a maniacal glitter that was more cocaine than Thanksgiving cheer—he and the boys had scored a pretty good gram that evening. All in all, Buddy looked quite a bit like a depraved Clint Eastwood.

"How are they hanging, Sandy?" Buddy asked.

Dutiful laughter from the Camaro greeted this sally. Don Vandenberg, Moochie Welch, and Richie Trelawney were with Buddy, and between the gram of coke and the six bottles of Texas Driver Buddy had procured for the occasion, they were feeling pretty much reet and compleet. They had come to do a little dirty boogie on Arnie Cunningham's Plymouth

"Listen, if you guys get caught, I'm gonna lose my job," Sandy said nervously. He was the only one cold sober, and he was regretting ever having mentioned that Cunningham was parking his heap here. The thought that he might go to jail as well had fortunately not occurred to him.

"If you or any of your Mission Imfuckingpossible force are caught, the Secretary will disavow you ever fuckin lived," Moochie said from the back seat, and there was more laughter.

Sandy looked around for other cars—witnesses—but there

were no planes due for more than an hour and the parking lot was as deserted as the mountains of the moon. The weather had turned very cold, and a wind as keen as a fresh razor-blade whined across the runways and taxi-ways and hooted miserably between the ranks of empty cars. Above and to his left, the Apco sign banged restlessly back and forth.

"You can laugh, you retard," Sandy said. "I never saw you, that's all. If you get caught, I'll say I was takin a crap."

"Jesus, what a baby," Buddy said. He looked sorrowful. "I never thought you were such a baby, Sandy. Honest."

"Arf! Arf!" Richie barked, and there was more laughter. "Roll over and play dead for Daddy Warbucks, Sandy!"

Sandy flushed. "I don't care," he said. "Just be careful."

"We will, man," Buddy said sincerely. He had saved back a seventh bottle of Texas Driver and a pretty decent toot of nose-candy. Now he handed both up to Sandy. "Here. Enjoy yourself."

Sandy grinned in spite of himself. "Okay," he said, and added, just so they'd know he was no sad sack: "Do a good job."

Buddy's smile hardened, became metallic. The light went out of his eyes; they became dull and dead and frightening. "Oh, we will," he said. "We will."

The Camaro drifted into the parking lot. For a while Sandy could follow its progress toward the back by the moving taillights, and then Buddy doused them. The sound of the motor, burbling through twin glasspack mufflers, came back for a few moments on the wind, and then that sound was gone, too.

Sandy dumped the coke out on the counter by his portable TV and tooted it with a rolled-up dollar bill. Then he got into the Texas Driver. He knew that being discovered drunk on the job would also get him canned, but he didn't much care. Being drunk was better than being cat-jumpy and always staring around for one of the two gray Airport Security cars.

The wind was blowing toward him, and he could hear— too much, he could hear.

A tinkle of breaking glass, muffled laughter, a loud metallic *thonk.*

More breaking glass.

A pause.

Low voices drifting to him on the cold wind. He was unable to pick up the individual words; they were distorted.

Suddenly there was a perfect fusillade of blows; Sandy winced at the sound. More breaking glass in the dark, and a tinkle of metal falling on the pavement—chrome or something, he supposed. He found himself wishing Buddy had brought more coke. Coke was sort of cheery stuff, and he sure could use some cheering up right about now. It sounded as if some pretty bad stuff was going on down at the far end of that parking lot.

And then a louder voice, urgent and commanding, Buddy's for sure:

"Do it there!"

A mutter of protest.

Buddy again: "Never mind that! On the dashboard, I said!"

Another mutter.

Buddy: "I don't *give* a shit!"

And for some reason this produced a stifle of laughter.

Sweaty now in spite of the knifing cold, Sandy suddenly slid his glass window shut and snapped on the TV. He drank deeply, grimacing at the heavy taste of the mixed fruit juice and cheap wine. He didn't care for it, but Texas Driver was what *they* all drank when they weren't drinking Iron City beer, and what was he supposed to do? Make out he was better than them, or something? That would get him fried, sooner or later. Buddy didn't like wimps.

He drank, and began to feel a little better—or at least a little drunker. When one of the Airport Security cars *did* pass, he hardly even flinched. The cop raised a hand to Sandy. Sandy raised a hand right back, just as cool as you could want.

About fifteen minutes after it had cruised toward the back of the lot, the blue Camaro reappeared, this time in the exit lane. Buddy sat cool and relaxed behind the wheel, a three-quarters-empty bottle of Driver propped in his crotch. He was smiling, and Sandy noted uneasily how bloodshot and weird his eyes looked. That wasn't just wine, and it wasn't just coke, either. Buddy Repperton was no one to fuck with; Cunningham would find that out, if nothing else.

"All taken care of, my good man," Buddy said.

"Good," Sandy said, and tried a smile. It felt a little sick. He had no feelings about Cunningham one way or another, and he was not a particularly imaginative person, but he could make a good guess about how Cunningham was going to feel when he saw what had come of all his careful work restoring that red and white Plymouth. Still, it was Buddy's business, not his.

"Good," he said again.

"Keep your jock on, man,'" Richie said, and giggled.

"Sure," Sandy said. He was glad they were going. Maybe he wouldn't hang around Vandenberg's Happy Gas so much after this. Maybe after this he didn't want to. This was heavy shit. Too heavy, maybe. And maybe he would pick up a couple of night courses, too. He'd have to give this job up, but maybe that wouldn't be so bad, either—it was a pretty dull fucking job.

Buddy was still looking at him, smiling that hard, gonzo smile, and Sandy took a big drink of Texas Driver. He nearly gagged. For an instant he had an image of puking down into Buddy's upturned face, and his unease became terror.

"If the cops get in on it," Buddy said, "you don't know nothing, you didn't see nothing. Like you said, you had to go in and take a crap around nine-thirty."

"Sure, Buddy."

"We all wore our wittle mittens. We didn't leave any prints.".

"Sure."

"Stay cool, Sandy," Buddy said softly.

"Yeah, okay."

The Camaro began to roll again. Sandy raised the gate with the manual button. The car headed toward the airport exit road at a sedate pace.

Someone called "Arf! Arf!" The sound drifted back to Sandy against the wind.

Troubled, he sat down to watch TV.

Shortly before the rush of customers who had come in on the ten-forty from Cleveland began to arrive, he poured the rest of the Driver out of the window and onto the ground. He didn't want it anymore.

26 / Christine Laid Low

Transfusion, transfusion,
Oh I'm never-never-never gonna speed again,
Pass the blood to me, Bud.

—"Nervous" Norvus

The next day Arnie and Leigh rode out to the airport together after school to pick up Christine. They were planning
on a trip to Pittsburgh to do some early Christmas shopping,
and they were looking forward to doing it together—it
seemed somehow terribly adult.

Arnie was in a fine mood on the bus, making up fanciful
little vignettes about their fellow passengers and making her
laugh in spite of her period, which was usually depressing
and almost always painful. The fat lady in the man's work-
shoes was a lapsed nun, he said. The kid in the cowboy hat
was a hustler. And on and on. She got into the spirit of the
thing but was not as good at it as he. It was amazing, the
way he had come out of his shell . . . the way he had
bloomed. That was really the only word for it. She felt the
smug, pleased satisfaction of a prospector who has suspected
the presence of gold by certain signs and has been proved
correct. She loved him, and she had been right to love him.

They got off the bus at the terminal stop together and
walked across the access road to the parking lot hand in
hand.

"This isn't bad," Leigh said. It was the first time she had
come out with him to pick up Christine. "Twenty-five
minutes from school."

"Yeah, it's okay," Arnie said. "It keeps peace in the
family, that's the important thing. I'm telling you, when my
mom got home that night and saw Christine in the driveway,
she went totally bullshit."

Leigh laughed, and the wind flipped her hair out behind
her. The temperature had moderated from last night's bitter
mid-teens, but it was still chilly. She was glad. Without a certain chill in the air, it didn't feel like Christmas shopping.

210

Bad enough the decorations in Pittsburgh wouldn't be up yet. But it wasn't bad; it was good. And suddenly she was glad about everything, most of all glad to be alive. And in love.

She had thought about it, the way she loved him. She had had crushes before, and once, in Massachusetts, she had thought she *might* be in love, but about this boy there was simply no question. He troubled her sometimes—his interest in the car seemed almost obsessive—but even her occasional unease played a part in her feelings, which were richer than anything she had ever known. And part of it, she admitted to herself, was of course selfish—she had, in weeks only, begun to make him over . . . to *complete* him.

They cut between the cars, headed for the thirty-day section of the parking lot. Overhead, a USAir jet was coming in on its final approach, the thunder of its engines rolling away in great flat waves of sound. Arnie was saying something, but the plane obliterated his voice altogether after the first few words—something about Thanksgiving dinner—and she turned to look at his face, secretly amused by his silently moving mouth.

Then, quite suddenly, his mouth stopped moving. He stopped walking. His eyes opened wider . . . and then seemed to bulge. His mouth began to *twist*, and the hand holding Leigh's suddenly clamped down ruthlessly, grinding her fingerbones painfully together.

"Arnie—"

The jet-roar was fading, but he seemed not to have heard. His hand clamped tighter. His mouth had slammed shut now, and it was knotted into an awful grimace of surprise and terror. She thought, *He's having a heart attack . . . stroke . . . something.*

"Arnie, what's wrong?" she cried. "Arnie . . . *ooowwwhoww, that hurts!*"

For one unbearable moment the pressure on the hand he had been holding so lightly and lovingly just before increased until it seemed that the bones would actually splinter and break. The high color in his cheeks was gone, and his skin was as leaden as a slate headstone.

He said one word—"Christine!"—and suddenly let go of her. He ran, thumping his leg against the bumper of a Cadillac, spinning away, almost falling, catching himself, and running forward again.

She realized at last it was something about the car—the

car, the car, always it was the goddam car—and a bitter anger rose in her that was both total and despairing. For the first time she wondered if it would be possible to love him; if Arnie would allow it.

Her anger was quenched the instant she really looked . . . and saw.

Arnie ran to what remained of his car, hands out, and stopped so abruptly in front of it that the gesture seemed almost to be a horrified warding-off; the classic movie pose of the hit-and-run victim an instant before the lethal collision.

He stood that way for a moment, as if to stop the car, or the whole world. Then he lowered his arms. His adam's apple lurched up and down twice as he struggled to swallow something back—a moan, a cry—and then his throat seemed to lock solid, every muscle standing out, each cord standing out, even the blood-vessels standing out in perfect relief. It was the throat of a man trying to lift a piano.

Leigh walked slowly toward him. Her hand still throbbed, and tomorrow it would be swollen and virtually useless, but for now she had forgotten it. Her heart went out to him and seemed to find him; she felt his sorrow and shared it—or it seemed to her that she did. It was only later that she realized how much Arnie shut her out that day—how much of his suffering he elected to do alone, and how much of his hate he hid away.

"Arnie, who did it?" she asked, her voice breaking with grief for him. No, she had not liked the car, but to see it reduced to this made her understand fully what Arnie's commitment had been, and she could hate it no longer—or so she thought.

Arnie made no answer. He stood looking at Christine, his eyes burning, his head slightly down.

The windshield had been smashed through in two places; handfuls of safety glass fragments were strewn across the slashed seat covers like trumpery diamonds. Half of the front bumper had been pried off and now dragged on the pavement, near a snarl of black wires like octopus tentacles. Three of the four side windows had also been broken. Holes had been punched through the sides of the body at waist-level in ragged, wavering lines. It looked as if some sharp, heavy instrument—maybe the pry-end of a tire iron—had been used. The passenger door hung open, and she saw that all the dashboard glass had been broken. Tufts and wads of stuffing were everywhere. The speedometer needle lay on the driver's side floormat.

Arnie walked slowly around his car, noting all of this. Leigh spoke to him twice. He didn't answer either time. Now the leaden color of his face was broken by two hectic, burning spots of flush riding high up on his cheekbones. He picked up the octopus-thing that had been lying on the pavement and she saw it was a distributor cap—her father had pointed that out to her once when he had been tinkering with their car.

He looked at it for a moment, as if examining an exotic zoological specimen, and then threw it down. Broken glass gritted under their heels. She spoke to him again. He didn't answer, and now, as well as a terrible pity for him, she began to feel afraid, too. She told Dennis Guilder later that it seemed—at least at the time—perfectly possible that he might have lost his mind.

He booted a piece of chrome trim out of his way. It struck the cyclone fence at the back of the lot with a little tinkling sound. The taillights had been smashed, more trumpery gems, this time rubies, this time on the pavement instead of the seat.

"Arnie—" she tried again.

He stopped. He was looking in through the hole in the driver's side window. A terrible low sound began to come from his chest, a jungle sound. She looked over his shoulder, saw, and suddenly felt a crazy need to laugh and scream and faint all at the same time. On the dashboard . . . she hadn't noticed at first; in the midst of the general destruction she hadn't noticed what was on the dashboard. And she wondered, with vomit suddenly rising in her throat, who could be so low, so completely low, as to do such a thing, to . . .

"Shitters!" Arnie cried, and his voice was not his own. It was high and shrill and cracked with fury.

Leigh turned around and threw up, holding blindly onto the car next to Christine, seeing small white dots in front of her eyes that expanded like puffed rice. Dimly she thought of the county fair—every year they'd haul an old junk car up onto a plank platform and lean a sledgehammer against it and you got three swings for a quarter. The idea was to demolish the car. But not . . . not to . . .

"You goddam *shitters!*" Arnie screamed. "I'll get you! I'll get you if it's the last thing I do! If it's the last motherfucking thing *I ever do!*"

Leigh threw up again and for one terrible moment found herself wishing that she had never ever met Arnie Cunningham.

27 / Arnie and Regina

Would you like to go riding
In my Buick '59?
I said, would you like to go riding
In my Buick '59?
It's got two carburetors
And a supercharger up the side.
                              —The Medallions

He let himself into the house that night at quarter of twelve. The clothes he had been wearing with the shopping trip to Pittsburgh in mind were grease- and sweat-stained. His hands were more deeply grimed, and a shallow cut cork-screwed across the back of the left like a brand. His face looked haggard and stunned. There were dark circles under his eyes.

His mother sat at the table, a game of solitaire laid out in front of her. She had been waiting for him to come home and dreading it deeply at the same time. Leigh had called and told her what had happened. The girl, who had impressed Regina as being quite a nice girl (if perhaps not quite good enough for her son), sounded as if she had been crying.

Regina, alarmed, had hung up as quickly as she could and had dialled Darnell's Garage. Leigh had told her Arnie had called for a tow-truck from there and had ridden in with the driver. He had put her in a taxi, over her protests. The phone had rung twice and then a wheezy yet gravelly voice had said, "Yuh. Darnell's."

She had hung up, realizing it would be a mistake to talk to him there—and it looked as if she and Mike had already made enough mistakes about Arnie and his car. She would wait until he came home. Say what she had to say looking him in the face.

She said it now. "Arnie, I'm sorry."

It would have been better if Mike could be here, too. But he was in Kansas City, attending a symposium on trade and the beginnings of free enterprise in the Middle Ages. He wouldn't be back until Sunday, unless this brought him home early. She thought it might. She realized—not without some rue—that she might just be awakening to the full seriousness of this situation.

"Sorry," Arnie echoed in a flat, accentless voice.

"Yes, I—that is, *we*—" She couldn't go on. There was something terrible in the deadwood of his expression. His eyes were blanks. She could only look at him and shake her head, her eyes brimming, the hateful taste of tears in her nose and throat. She hated to cry. Strong-willed, one of two girls in a Catholic family that consisted of her blue-collar construction-worker father, her washed-out mother, and seven brothers, hellbent on college in spite of her father's belief that the only things girls learned there was how to stop being virgins and how to throw over the church, she had shed her fair share of tears and more. And if her own family thought she was hard sometimes, it was because they didn't understand that when you went through hell you came out baked by the fire. And when you had to burn to have your own way, you always wanted to have it.

"You know something?" Arnie asked.

She shook her head, still feeling the hot, slithery burn of the tears under her lids.

"You'd make me laugh, if I wasn't so tired I could hardly stand up. You could have been out there swinging the tire irons and the hammers along with the guys that did it. You're probably happier about it than they are."

"Arnie, that's not fair!"

"It *is* fair!" he roared at her, his eyes suddenly blazing with a horrible fire. For the first time in her life she was afraid of her son. "Your idea to get it out of the driveway! His idea to put it in the airport lot! Who do you think is to blame here? Just who do you think? Do you think it would have happened if it had been here? Huh?"

He took a step toward her, fists clenched at his sides, and she had all she could do to keep from flinching backward.

"Arnie, can't we even talk about this?" she asked. "Like two rational human beings?"

"One of them took a shit on the dashboard of my car," he said coldly. "How's that for rational, Mom?"

She had honestly believed she had the tears under control, but this news—news of such a stupid, irrational fury—brought them back. She cried. She cried in grief for what her son had seen. She lowered her head and cried in bewilderment and pain and fear.

All her life as a mother she had felt secretly superior to the women around her who had children older than Arnie. When he was one, those other mothers had shaken their heads dolefully and told her to wait until he was five—that was when the trouble started, that was when they were old enough to say "shit" in front of their grandmothers and play with matches when left alone. But Arnold, as good as gold at one, had still been as good as gold at five. Then the other mothers had rolled their eyes and said wait until he's ten; and then it had been fifteen, that was when it really got sticky, what with the dope and the rock concerts and girls that would do anything and—God forbid—stealing hubcaps and those . . . well, diseases.

And through it all she had continued to smile inside because it was all working out according to plan, it was all working out the way she felt her own childhood should have. Her son had warm, supportive parents who cared about him, who would give him anything (within reason), who would gladly send him to the college of his choice (as long as it was a good one), thereby finishing the game/business/vocation of Parenting with a flourish. If you had suggested that Arnie had few friends and was often bullyragged by the others, she would have starchily pointed out that *she* had gone to a parochial school in a tough neighborhood where girls' cotton panties were sometimes torn off for a joke and then set on fire with Zippo lighters engraved with the crucified body of Jesus. And if you had suggested that her own attitudes toward child-rearing differed only in terms of material goals from the attitudes of her hated father, she would have been furious and pointed out her good son as her final vindication.

But now her good son stood before her, pale, exhausted, and greased to the elbows, seeming to thrum with the same sort of barely chained anger that had been his grandfather's trademark, even *looking* like him. Everything seemed to have fallen into a shambles.

"Arnie, we'll talk about what's to be done in the morning,"

she said, trying to pull herself together and beat back the tears. "We'll talk about it in the morning."

"Not unless you get up real early," he said, seeming to lose interest. "I'm going upstairs and catch about four hours, and then I'm going down to the garage again."

"What for?"

He uttered a crazy laugh and flapped his arms under the kitchen's fluorescent bars as if he would fly. "What do you think for? I got a lot of work to do! More work than you'd believe!"

"No—you have school tomorrow . . . I . . . I forbid it, Arnie, I absolutely—"

He turned to look at her, study her, and she flinched again. This was like some grinding nightmare that was just going to go on and on.

"I'll get to school," he said. "I'll take some fresh clothes in a pack and I'll even shower so I don't smell offensive to anyone in homeroom. Then, after school's out, I'll go back down to Darnell's. There's a lot of work to be done, but I can do it . . . I know I can . . . it's going to eat up a lot of my savings, though. Plus, I'll have to keep on top of the stuff I'm doing for Will."

"Your homework . . . your studies!"

"Oh. Those." He smiled the dead, mechanical smile of a clockwork figure. "They'll suffer, of course. Can't kid you about that. I can't promise you a ninety-three average anymore, either. But I'll get by. I can make C's. Maybe some B's."

"No! You've got college to think about!"

He came back to the table, limping again, quite badly. He planted his hands on the table before her and leaned slowly down. She thought: *A stranger . . . my son is a stranger to me. Is this really my fault? Is it? Because I only wanted what was best for him? Can that be? Please, God, make this a nightmare I'll wake up from with tears on my cheeks because it was so real.*

"Right now," he said softly, holding her gaze, "the only things I care about are Christine and Leigh and staying on the good side of Will Darnell so I can get her fixed up as good as new. I don't give a shit about college. And if you don't get off my case, I'll drop out of high school. That ought to shut you up if nothing else will."

"You can't," she said, meeting his gaze. "You understand that, Arnold. Maybe I deserve your . . . your cruelty . . .

but I'll fight this self-destructive streak of yours with everything I have. So don't you talk about dropping out of school."

"But I'll really do it," he answered. "I don't want you to even kid yourself into thinking I won't. I'll be eighteen in February, and I'll do it on my own then if you don't stay out of this from now on. Do you understand me?"

"Go to bed," she said tearfully. "Go to bed, you're breaking my heart."

"Am I?" Shockingly, he laughed. "Hurts, doesn't it? I know."

He left then, walking slowly, the limp pulling his body slightly to the left. Shortly she heard the heavy, tired clump of his shoes on the stairs—also a sound terribly reminiscent of her childhood, when she had thought to herself, *The ogre's going to bed.*

She burst into a fresh spasm of weeping, got up clumsily, and went out the back door to do her crying in private. She held herself—thin comfort, but better than none—and looked up at a horned moon that was quadrupled through the film of her tears. Everything had changed, and it had happened with the speed of a cyclone. Her son hated her; she had seen it in his face—it wasn't a tantrum, a temporary pique, a passing squall of adolescence. He *hated* her, and this wasn't the way it was supposed to go with her good boy, not at all.

Not at *all.*

She stood on the stoop and cried until the tears began to run their course and the sobs became occasional hitchings and gasps. The cold gnawed her bare ankles above her mules and bit more bluntly through her housecoat. She went inside and upstairs. She stood outside Arnie's room indecisively for almost a minute before going in.

He had fallen asleep on the coverlet of his bed. His pants were still on. He seemed more unconscious than asleep, and his face looked horribly old. A trick of the light, coming from the hall and falling into the room from over her shoulder, made it seem for a moment to her that his hair was thinning, that his sleep-gaping mouth was without teeth. A small squeal of horror strained itself through the hand clapped to her mouth and she hurried toward him.

Her shadow, which had been on the bed, moved with her and she saw it was only Arnie, the impression of age no more than the light and her own exhausted confusion.

She looked at his clock-radio and saw that it was set for

4:30 A.M. She thought of turning the alarm off; she even stretched her hand out to do it. Ultimately she found she couldn't.

Instead she went down to her bedroom, sat down at the phone table, and picked up the handset. She held it for a moment, debating. If she called Mike in the middle of the night, he would think that . . .

That something terrible had happened?

She giggled. Well, *hadn't* it? It surely had. And it was still happening.

She dialled the number of the Ramada Inn in Kansas City where her husband was staying, vaguely aware that she was, for the first time since she had left the grim and grimy three-story house in Rocksburg for college twenty-seven years before, calling for help.

28 / Leigh Makes a Visit

I don't want to cause no fuss,
But can I buy your magic bus?
I don't care how much I pay,
I'm gonna drive that bus to my bay-by.
I want it . . . I want it . . . I want it . . .
(You can't have it . . .)

—The Who

She got through most of the story okay, sitting in one of the two visitors' chairs with her knees pressed firmly together and her ankles crossed, neatly dressed in a multicolored wool sweater and a brown corduroy skirt. It was not until the end that she began to cry, and she couldn't find a handkerchief. Dennis Guilder handed her the box of tissues from the table beside the bed.

"Take it easy, Leigh," he said.

"I cuh-cuh-can't! He hasn't been to see me . . . and in school he just seems so tired . . . and you s-said he hasn't been here—"

"He'll come if he needs me," Dennis said.

"You're full of muh-macho b-bull-sh-sh-shit!" she said, and

then looked comically stunned at what she had said. The tears had cut tracks in the light makeup she was wearing. She and Dennis looked at each other for a moment, and then they laughed. But it was brief laughter, and not really that good.

"Has Motormouth seen him?" Dennis asked.

"Who?"

"Motormouth. That's what Lenny Barongg calls Mr. Vickers. The guidance counsellor."

"Oh! Yes, I think he has. He was called to the guidance office the day before yesterday—Monday. But he didn't say anything. And I didn't dare ask him anything. He won't talk. He's gotten so strange."

Dennis nodded. Although he didn't think Leigh realized it—she was deep in her own trouble and confusion—he felt a sense of impotence and a deepening fear for Arnie. From the reports that had filtered into his room over the last few days, Arnie sounded on the verge of a nervous breakdown; Leigh's report was only the most recent and the most graphic. He had never wanted to be *out* as badly as he did now. Of course, he could call Vickers and ask him if there was anything he could do. And he could call Arnie . . . except, from what Leigh had said, Arnie was now always at school, at Darnell's, or sleeping. His father had come home early from some sort of convention and there had been another fight, Leigh had told him. Although Arnie had not come right out and said so, Leigh told Dennis she believed that he had come very close to simply leaving home.

Dennis didn't want to talk to Arnie at Darnell's.

"What can I do?" she asked him. "What would you do, in my place?"

"Wait," Dennis said. "I don't know what else you can do."

"But that's hardest," she answered in a voice so low it was almost inaudible. Her hands were clenching and unclenching on the Kleenex, shredding it, dotting her brown skirt with speckles of lint. "My folks want me to stop seeing him—to drop him. They're afraid . . . that Repperton and those other boys will do something else."

"You're pretty sure it was Buddy and his friends, huh?"

"Yes. Everybody is. Mr. Cunningham called the police even though Arnie told him not to. He said he'd settle the score in his own way, and that scared them both. It scares me, too. The police picked up Buddy Repperton, and one of

his friends, the one they call Moochie . . . do you know who
I mean?"

"Yes."

"And the boy who works nights at the airport parking lot,
they picked him up, too. Galton, his name is—"

"Sandy."

"They thought he must have been in on it, that maybe he
let them in."

"He runs with them, all right," Dennis said, "but he's not
quite as degenerate as the rest of them. I'll say this, Leigh—if
Arnie didn't talk to you, someone sure did."

"First Mrs. Cunningham and then his father. I don't think
either of them knew the other one had talked to me.
They're . . ."

"Upset," Dennis suggested.

She shook her head. "It's more than that," she said. "They
both look like they were just . . . just mugged, or something.
I can't really feel sorry for *her*—all she wants is her own
way, I think—but I could cry for Mr. Cunningham. He just
seems so . . . so . . ." She trailed off and then began again.
"When I got there yesterday afternoon after school, Mrs.
Cunningham—she asked me to call her Regina, but I just
can't seem to do it—"

Dennis grinned.

"Can you do it?" Leigh asked.

"Well, yeah—but I've had a lot more practice."

She smiled, the first good one of her visit. "Maybe that
would make a difference. Anyway, when I went over, she was
there but Mr. Cunningham was still at school . . . the University, I mean."

"Yeah."

"She took the whole week off—what there is of it. She said
she couldn't go back, even for the three days before Thanksgiving."

"How does she look?"

"She looks shattered," Leigh said, and reached for a fresh
Kleenex. She began shredding the edges. "She looks ten years
older than when I first met her a month ago."

"And him? Michael?"

"Older, but tougher," Leigh said hesitantly. "As if this had
somehow . . . somehow gotten him into gear."

Dennis was silent. He had known Michael Cunningham for
thirteen years and had never seen him in gear, so he wouldn't
know. Regina had always been the one in gear; Michael

trailed along in her wake and made the drinks at the parties (mostly faculty parties) the Cunninghams hosted. He played his recorder, he looked melancholy . . . but by no stretch of the imagination could Dennis say he had ever seen the man "in gear."

The final triumph, Dennis's father had said once, standing at the window and watching Regina lead Arnie by the hand down the Guilders' walk to where Michael waited behind the wheel of the car. Arnie and Dennis had been perhaps seven then. *Momism supreme. I wonder if she'll make the poor slob wait in the car when Arnie gets married. Or maybe she can—*

Dennis's mother had frowned at her husband and shushed him by cutting her eyes at Dennis in a little-pitchers-have-big-ears gesture. He never forgot the gesture or what his father had said—at seven he hadn't understood all of it, but even at seven he knew perfectly well what a "poor slob" was. And even at seven he vaguely understood why his father might think Michael Cunningham was one. He had felt sad for Michael Cunningham . . . and that feeling had held, off and on, right up to the present.

"He came in around the time she was finishing *her* story," Leigh went on. "They asked me to stay for supper—Arnie has been eating down at Darnell's—but I told them I really had to get back. So Mr. Cunningham offered me a ride, and I got his side on the way home."

"Are they on different sides?"

"Not exactly, but . . . Mr. Cunningham was the one who went to see the police, for instance. Arnie didn't want to, and Mrs. Cunningham—Regina—couldn't bring herself to do it."

Dennis asked cautiously, "He's really trying to put Humpty back together again, huh?"

"Yes," she whispered, and then burst out shrilly: "But that's not all! He's in deep with that guy Darnell, I know he is! Yesterday in period three study hall he told me he was going to drop a new front end into her—into his car—this afternoon and this evening, and I said won't that be awfully expensive Arnie, and he said not to worry about it because his credit was good—"

"Slow down."

She was crying again. "His credit was good because he and someone named Jimmy Sykes were going to do some errands for Will Friday and Saturday. That's what he said. And . . . I don't think the errands he does for that sonofabitch are legal!"

"What did he tell the police when they came to ask about Christine?"

"He told them about finding it . . . that way. They asked him if he had any ideas who might have done it, and Arnie said no. They asked him if it wasn't true that he had gotten into a fight with Buddy Repperton, that Repperton had pulled a knife and had been expelled for it. Arnie said that Repperton had knocked his bag lunch out of his hand and stepped on it, then Mr. Casey came over from the shop and broke it up. They asked him if Repperton hadn't said he would get him for it, and Arnie said he might have said something like that, but talk was cheap."

Dennis was silent, looking out his window at a dull November sky, considering this. He found it ominous. If Leigh had the interview with the police right, then Arnie hadn't told a single lie . . . but he had edited things to make what had happened in the smoking area sound like your ordinary pushy-pushy.

Dennis found that extremely ominous.

"Do you know what Arnie might be doing for that man Darnell?" Leigh asked.

"No," Dennis answered, but he had some ideas. A little internal tape recorder started up, and he heard his father saying, *I've heard a few things . . . stolen cars . . . cigarettes and booze . . . contraband like fireworks. . . . He's been lucky for a long time, Dennis.*

He looked at Leigh's face, too pale, her makeup cut open by her tears. She was hanging on, hanging onto Arnie as best she could. Maybe she was learning something about being tough that she wouldn't have learned otherwise, with her looks, for another ten years. But that didn't make it any easier, and it didn't necessarily make it right. It occurred to him suddenly, almost randomly, that he had first noticed the improvement in Arnie's face more than a month before Arnie and Leigh clicked . . . but after Arnie and Christine had clicked.

"I'll talk to him," he promised.

"Good," she said. She stood up. "I—I don't want things to be like they were before, Dennis. I know that nothing ever is. But I still love him, and . . . and I just wish you'd tell him that."

"Yeah, okay."

They were both embarrassed, and neither of them could say anything for a long, long moment. Dennis was thinking that this would be the point, in a c & w song, where the Best Friend steps in. And a sneaking, mean (and randy) part of him wouldn't be averse to that. Not at all. He was still powerfully attracted to her, more attracted than he had been to any girl in a long time. Maybe ever. Let Arnie run bottle-rockets and cherry-bombs over to Burlington and fuck around with his car. He and Leigh could get to know each other better in the meantime. A little aid and comfort. You know how it is.

And he had a feeling at just that awkward moment, after her profession of love for Arnie, that he could do it; she was vulnerable. She was maybe learning how to be tough, but it's not a school anyone goes to willingly. He could say something—the right something, maybe only *Come here*—and she would come, sit on the edge of the bed, they would talk some more, maybe about pleasanter things, and maybe he would kiss her. Her mouth was lovely and full, sensual, made to kiss and be kissed. Once for comfort. Twice out of friendship. And three times pays for all. Yes, he felt with an instinct that had so far been quite reliable that it could be done.

But he didn't say any of the things that could have started those things happening, and neither did Leigh. Arnie was between them, and almost surely always would be. Arnie and his lady. If it hadn't been so ludicrously ghastly, he could have laughed.

"When are they letting you out?" she asked.

"On an unsuspecting public?" he asked, and began to giggle. After a moment she joined him in his laughter.

"Yes, something like that," Leigh said, and then snickered again. "Sorry."

"Don't be," Dennis said. "People have been laughing at me all my life. I'm used to it. They say I'm stuck here until January, but I'm going to fool them. I'm going home for Christmas. I'm working my buns off down in the torture chamber."

"Torture chamber?"

"Physical therapy. My back's looking good. The other bones are knitting busily—the itch is terrible sometimes. I'm gobbling rosehips by the bushel basket. Dr. Arroway says that's nothing but a folk-tale. But Coach Puffer swears by them, and he checks the bottle every time he comes to visit."

"Does he come often? The Coach?"

"Yeah, he does. Now he's got me half-believing that stuff about rosehips making your broken bones knit faster." Dennis paused. "Of course, I'm not going to be playing any more football, not ever. I'm going to be on crutches for a while, and then, with luck, I'll graduate to a cane. Cheerful old Dr. Arroway tells me I'm going to limp for maybe a couple of years. Or maybe I'll always limp."

"I'm so sorry," she said in a low voice. "I'm sorry it had to happen to a nice guy like you, Dennis, but part of it's selfish. I just wonder if all the rest of this, all this horrible stuff with Arnie, if it would have happened if you'd been up and around."

"That's right," Dennis said, rolling his eyes dramatically, "blame it on me."

But she didn't smile. "I've started to worry about his sanity, did you know that? That's the one thing I haven't told my folks or his folks. But I think his mother . . . that she might . . . I don't know what he said to her that night, after we found the car all smashed up, but . . . I think they must have really put their claws into each other."

Dennis nodded.

"But it's all so . . . so mad! His parents offered to buy him a good used car to replace Christine, and he said no. Then Mr. Cunningham told me, on the ride home, that he offered to buy Arnie a new car . . . to cash in some bonds he's held ever since 1955. Arnie said no, he couldn't just take a present like that. And Mr. Cunningham said he could understand that, and it didn't have to be a present, that Arnie could pay him back, that he'd even take interest if that was what Arnie wanted. . . . Dennis, do you see what I'm saying?"

"Yeah," Dennis said. "It can't be just any car. It's got to be *that* car. Christine."

"But to me that seems obsessive. He's found one object and fixed on it. Isn't that what an obsession is? I'm scared, and sometimes I feel hateful . . . but it's not him I'm scared of. It's not him I hate. It's that frig—no, it's that *fucking* car. That bitch Christine."

High color bloomed in her cheeks. Her eyes narrowed. The corners of her mouth turned down. Her face was suddenly no longer beautiful, not even pretty; the light on it was pitiless, changing it into something that was ugly but all the same striking, compelling. Dennis realized for the first time why they called it the monster, the green-eyed monster.

"I'll tell you what I wish would happen," Leigh said. "I wish somebody would take his precious fucking Christine out back some night by mistake, out where they put the junks from Philly Plains." Her eyes sparkled venomously. "And the next day I wish that crane with the big round magnet would come and pick it up and put it in the crusher and I wish someone would push the button and what would come out would be a little cube of metal about three by three by three. Then this would be over, wouldn't it?"

Dennis didn't answer, and after a moment he could almost see the monster turn around and wrap its scaly tail around itself and steal out of her face. Her shoulders sagged.

"Guess that sounds pretty horrible, doesn't it? Like saying I wish those hoods had finished the job."

"I understand how you feel."

"Do you?" she challenged.

Dennis thought of Arnie's look as he had pounded his fists on the dashboard. The kind of maniacal light that came into his eyes when he was around her. He thought of sitting behind the wheel in LeBay's garage, and the kind of vision that had come over him.

Last of all, he thought of his dream: headlights bearing down on him in the high womanscream of burning rubber.

"Yes," he said. "I think I do."

They looked at each other in the hospital room.

29 / Thanksgiving

Two-three hours passed us by,
Altitude dropped to 505,
Fuel consumption way too thin,
Let's get home before we run out of gas.
Now you can't catch me—
No, baby, you can't catch me—
'Cause if you get too close,
I'm gone like a cooool breeze.

—Chuck Berry

At the hospital they served Thanksgiving dinner in shifts from eleven in the morning until one in the afternoon. Dennis got his at quarter past twelve: three careful slices of white turkey breast, one careful ladleful of brown gravy, a scoop of instant mashed potatoes the exact size and shape of a baseball (lacking only the red stitches, he thought with sour amusement), a like scoop of frozen squash that was an arrogant fluorescent orange, and a small plastic container of cranberry jelly. For dessert there was ice cream. Resting on the corner of his tray was a small blue card.

Wise to the ways of the hospital by now—once you have been treated for the first set of bedsores to crop up on your ass, Dennis had discovered, you're wiser to the ways of the hospital than you ever wanted to be—he asked the candy-striper who came to take away his tray what the yellow and red cards got for their Thanksgiving dinner. It turned out that the yellow cards got two pieces of turkey, no gravy, potato, no squash, and Jell-O for dessert. The red cards got one slice of white meat, pureed, and potato. Fed to them, in most cases.

Dennis found it all pretty depressing. It was only too easy to imagine his mother bringing a great big crackling capon to the dining-room table around four in the afternoon, his father sharpening his carving knife, his sister, flushed with importance and excitement, a red velvet ribbon in her hair, pouring each of them a glass of good red wine. It was also easy to imagine the good smells, the laughter as they sat down.

Easy to imagine . . . but probably a mistake.

It was, in fact, the most depressing Thanksgiving of his life. He drifted off into an unaccustomed early afternoon nap (no Physical Therapy because of the holiday) and dreamed an unsettling dream in which several candy-stripers walked through the IC ward and slapped turkey decals onto the life-support machinery and IV drips.

His mother, father, and sister had come over to visit for an hour in the morning, and for the first time he had sensed in Ellie an anxiousness to be gone. They had been invited over to the Callisons' for a light Thanksgiving brunch, and Lou Callison, one of the three Callison boys, was fourteen and "cute." Her racked-up brother had become boring. They hadn't discovered a rare and tragic form of cancer breeding in his bones. He wasn't going to be paralyzed for the rest of his life. There was no movie-of-the-week in him.

They had called him from the Callisons' around twelve-thirty and his father sounded a bit drunk—Dennis guessed he was maybe on his second bloody Mary and was maybe getting some disapproving looks from Mom. Dennis himself had just been finishing up his dietician-approved blue-carded Thanksgiving dinner—the only such dinner he had ever been able to finish in fifteen minutes—and he did a good job of sounding cheerful, not wanting to spoil their good time. Ellie came on the wire briefly, sounding giggly and rather screamy. Maybe it was talking to Ellie that had tired him out enough to need a nap.

He had fallen asleep (and had his unsettling dream) around two o'clock. The hospital was unusually quiet today, running on a skeleton staff. The usual babble of TVs and transistor radios from the other rooms was muted. The candy-striper who took his tray smiled brightly and said she hoped he had enjoyed his "special dinner." Dennis assured her that he had. After all, it was Thanksgiving for her, too.

And so he dreamed, and the dream broke up and became a darker sleep, and when he woke up it was nearly five o'clock and Arnie Cunningham was sitting in the hard plastic contour chair where his girl had sat only the day before.

Dennis was not at all surprised to see him there; he simply assumed that it was a new dream.

"Hi, Arnie," he said. "How's it hanging?"

"Hanging good," Arnie said, "but you look like you're still asleep, Dennis. Want some head-noogies? That'll wake you up."

There was a brown bag on his lap, and Dennis's sleepy mind thought: *Got his lunch after all. Maybe Repperton didn't squash it as bad as we thought.* He tried to sit up in the bed, hurt his back, and used the control panel to get into what was almost a sitting position. The motor whined. "Jesus, it's really you!"

"Were you expecting Ghidrah, the Three-Headed Monster?" Arnie asked amiably.

"I was sleeping. I guess I thought I still was." Dennis rubbed his forehead hard, as if to get rid of the sleep behind it. "Happy Thanksgiving, Arnie."

"You bet," Arnie said. "Same to you. Did they feed you turkey with all the trimmings?"

Dennis laughed. "I got something that looked like those play-dinners that came with Ellie's Happy-Time Cafeteria when she was about seven. Remember?"

Arnie put his cupped hands to his mouth and made ralphing noises. "I remember. What a gross-out."

"I'm really glad you came," Dennis said, and for a moment he was perilously close to tears. Maybe he hadn't realized just how depressed he had been. He redoubled his determination to be home by Christmas. If he was here on Christmas Day, he'd probably commit suicide.

"Your folks didn't come?"

"Sure they did," Dennis said, "and they'll be back again tonight—Mom and Dad will be, anyway—but it's not the same. You know."

"Yeah. Well, I brought some stuff. Told the lady downstairs I had your bathrobe." Arnie giggled a little.

"What *is* that?" Dennis asked, nodding at the bag. It wasn't just a lunchbag, he saw; it was a shopping bag.

"Aw, I raided the fridge after we et the bird," Arnie said. "My mom and dad went around visiting their friends from the University—they do that every year on Thanksgiving afternoon. They won't even be back until around eight."

As he talked, he took things out of the bag. Dennis watched, amazed. Two pewter candle-holders. Two candles. Arnie slammed the candles into the holders, lit them with a matchbook advertising Darnell's Garage, and turned off the overhead light. Then four sandwiches, clumsily wrapped in waxed paper.

"The way I recall it," Arnie said, "you always said that scarfing up a couple of turkey sandwiches around eleven-thirty Thursday night was better than Thanksgiving dinner, anyway. Because the pressure was off."

"Yeah," Dennis said. "Sandwiches in front of the TV. Carson or some old movie. But, honest to God, Arnie, you didn't have to—"

"Ah, shit, I haven't even been around to see you in almost three weeks. Good thing for me you were sleeping when I came in or you probably would have shot me." He tapped Dennis's two sandwiches. "Your favorite, I think. White meat and mayo on Wonder Bread."

Dennis got giggling at that, then laughing, then roaring. Arnie could see it hurt his back, but he couldn't stop. Wonder Bread had been one of Arnie and Dennis's great common secrets as children. Both of their mothers had been very serious about the subject of bread; Regina bought Diet-Thin loaves, with an occasional side-trip into the Land of Stone-Ground Rye. Dennis's mother favored Roman Meal and pumpernickel loaves. Arnie and Dennis ate what was given them—but both were secret Wonder Bread freaks, and on more than one occasion they had pooled their money and instead of buying sweets they had gotten a loaf of Wonder and a jar of French's Mustard. They would then slink out into

Arnie's garage (or Dennis's tree-house, sadly demolished in a windstorm almost nine years before) and gobble mustard sandwiches and read Richie Rich comic books until the whole loaf was gone.

Arnie joined him in his laughter, and for Dennis that was the best part of Thanksgiving.

Dennis had been between roommates for almost ten days, and so had the semi-private room to himself. Arnie closed the door and produced a six-pack of Busch beer from the brown bag.

"Wonders will never cease," Dennis said, and had to laugh again at the unintentional pun.

"No," Arnie said, "I don't think they ever will." He toasted Dennis over the candles with a bottle of beer. *"Prosit."*

"Live forever," Dennis responded. They drank.

After they had finished the thick turkey sandwiches, Arnie produced two plastic Tupperware pie-wedges from his apparently bottomless bag and pried off the lids. Two pieces of home-made apple pie rested within.

"No, man, I can't," Dennis said. "I'll bust."

"Eat," Arnie commanded.

"I really can't," Dennis said, taking the Tupperware container and a fresh plastic fork. He finished the slice of pie in four huge bites and then belched. He upended the remainder of his second beer and belched again. "In Portugal, that's a compliment to the cook," he said. His head was buzzing pleasantly from the beer.

"Whatever you say," Arnie responded with a grin. He got up, turned on the overhead fluorescent, and snuffed the candles. Outside a steady rain had begun to beat against the windows; it looked and sounded cold. And for Dennis, some of the warm spirit of friendship and real Thanksgiving seemed to go out with the candles.

"I'm gonna hate you tomorrow," Dennis said. "I'll probably have to sit on that john in there for an hour. And it hurts my back."

"You remember the time Elaine got the farts?" Arnie asked, and they both laughed. "We teased her until your mother gave us holy old hell."

"They didn't smell, but they sure were loud," Dennis said, smiling.

"Like gunshots," Arnie agreed, and they both laughed a little—but it was a sad sort of laughter, if there is such a

thing. A lot of water under the bridge. The thought that Ellie's attack of the farts had happened seven years ago was
somehow more unsettling than it was amusing. There was a
breath of mortality in the realization that seven years could
steal past with such smooth and unobtrusive ease.

Conversation lapsed a little, both of them lost in their own
thoughts.

At last Dennis said, "Leigh came by yesterday. Told me
about Christine. I'm sorry, man. Bummer."

Arnie looked up, and his expression of thoughtful melancholy was lost in a cheerful smile that Dennis didn't really
believe.

"Yeah," he said. "It was crude. But I went way overboard
about it."

"Anyone would," Dennis said, aware that he had become
suddenly watchful, hating it but unable to help it. The friendship part was over; it had been here, warming the room and
filling it, and now it had simply slipped away like the ephem-
eral, delicate thing it was. Now they were just dancing.
Arnie's cheerful eyes were also opaque and—he would have
sworn to it—watchful.

"Sure. I gave my mother a hard time. Leigh too, I guess. It
was just the shock of seeing all that work . . . all that work
down the tubes." He shook his head. "Bad news."

"Are you going to be able to do anything with it?"

Arnie brightened immediately—really brightened this time,
Dennis felt. "Sure! I already have. You wouldn't believe it,
Dennis, if you'd seen the way it looked in that parking lot.
They made them tough in those days, not like now when all
the stuff that looks like metal is really just shiny plastic. That
car is nothing but a damn tank. The glass was the worst part.
And the tires, of course. They slashed the tires."

"What about the engine?"

"Never got at it," Arnie said promptly, and that was the
first lie. They had been at it, all right. When Arnie and Leigh
had gotten to Christine that afternoon, the distributor cap
had been lying on the pavement. Leigh had recognized it and
had told Dennis about it. What else had they done under the
hood, Dennis wondered. The radiator? If someone was going
to use a tire iron to punch holes in the bodywork, might they
not be apt to use the same tool to spring the radiator in a few
places? What about the plugs? The voltage regulator? The
carburetor?

Arnie, why are you lying to me?

"So what are you doing with it now?" Dennis asked.

"Spending money on it, what else?" Arnie said, and laughed his almost-genuine laugh. Dennis might even have accepted it as genuine if he hadn't heard the real article once or twice over the Thanksgiving supper Arnie had brought. "New tires, new glass. Got some bodywork to do, and then it will be as good as new."

As good as new. But Leigh had said that they had found something that was little more than a smashed hulk, a carny three-swings-for-a-quarter derelict.

Why are you lying?

For a cold moment he found himself wondering if maybe Arnie hadn't gone a little crazy—but no, that wasn't the impression he gave. The feeling Dennis got from him was one of . . . furtiveness. Craftiness. Then, for the first time, the crazy thought came to him, the thought that maybe Arnie was only half-lying, trying to lay a groundwork of plausibility for . . . for what? A case of spontaneous regeneration? That was pretty crazy, wasn't it?

Wasn't it?

It was indeed, Dennis thought, unless you had happened to see a mass of cracks in a windshield seem to *shrink* between one viewing and the next.

Just a trick of the light. That's what you thought then, and you were right.

But a trick of the light didn't explain the haphazard way Arnie had gone about rebuilding Christine, the hopscotch of old and new parts. It didn't explain that weird feeling Dennis had gotten sitting behind the wheel of Christine in LeBay's garage, or the sense, after the new tire had been put on en route to Darnell's, that he was looking at an old-car picture with a new-car picture directly underlying it, and that a hole had been cut out of the old-car picture at the spot where one of the old-car tires had been.

And nothing explained Arnie's lie now . . . or the narrow, thoughtful way he was watching Dennis to see if his lie was going to be accepted. So he smiled . . . a big, easy, relieved grin. "Well, that's great," he said.

Arnie's narrow, evaluating expression held for a moment longer; then he smiled an aw-shucks grin and shrugged. "Luck," he said. "When I think of the things they could have done—sugar in the gas tank, molasses in the carb—they were stupid. Lucky for me."

"Repperton and his merry crew?" Dennis asked quietly.

The suspicious look, so dark and unlike Arnie, appeared again and then sank from sight. Arnie looked grim now. Grim and morose. He seemed to speak, then sighed instead. "Yeah," he said. "Who else?"

"But you didn't report it."

"My dad did."

"That's what Leigh said."

"What else did she tell you?" Arnie asked sharply.

"Nothing, and I didn't ask," Dennis said, holding his hand out. "Your business, Arnie. Peace."

"Sure." He laughed a little and then passed a hand over his face. "I'm still not over it. Fuck. I don't think I'm ever going to be over it, Dennis. Coming into that parking lot with Leigh, feeling like I was on top of the world, and seeing—"

"Won't they just do it again if you fix her up again?"

Arnie's face went dead-cold, set. "They won't do it again," he said. His gray eyes were like March ice, and Dennis found himself suddenly very glad he wasn't Buddy Repperton.

"What do you mean?"

"I'll be parking it at home, that's what I mean," he said, and once more his face broke into that large, cheerful, unnatural grin. "What did you think I meant?"

"Nothing," Dennis said. The image of ice remained. Now it was a feeling of thin ice, creaking uneasily under his feet. Beneath that, black, cold water. "But I don't know, Arnie. You seem awful sure that Buddy wants to let this go."

"I'm hoping he'll see it as a standoff," Arnie said quietly. "We got him expelled from school—"

"He got *himself* expelled!" Dennis said hotly. "He pulled a knife—hell, it wasn't even a knife, it was a goddam pigsticker!"

"I'm just telling it the way he'll see it," Arnie said, then held out his hand and laughed. "Peace."

"Yeah, okay."

"We got him expelled—or more accurately, I did—and he and his buddies beat hell out of Christine. Evens. The end."

"Yeah, if he sees it that way."

"I think he will," Arnie said. "The cops questioned him and Moochie Welch and Richie Trelawney. Scared them. And almost got Sandy Galton to confess, I guess." Arnie's lip curled. "Fucking crybaby."

This was so unlike Arnie—the old Arnie—that Dennis sat up in bed without thinking and then winced at the pain in his back and lay down again quickly. "Jesus, man, you sound like you want him to stonewall it!"

"I don't care what he or any of those shitters do," Arnie said, and then, in a strangely offhand voice he added, "It doesn't matter anymore anyhow."

Dennis said, "Arnie, are you all right?"

And for a moment a look of desperate sadness passed over Arnie's face—more than sadness. He looked harried and haunted. It was the face, Dennis thought later (it is so easy to see these things later; too much later) of someone so bewildered and entangled and weary of struggling that he hardly knows anymore what it is he is doing.

Then that expression, like that other look of dark suspicion, was gone.

"Sure," he said. "I'm great. Except that you're not the only one with a hurt back. You remember when I strained it at Philly Plains?"

Dennis nodded.

"Check this out." He stood up and pulled his shirt out of his pants. Something seemed to dance in his eyes. Something flipping and turning at a black depth.

He lifted his shirt. It wasn't old-fashioned like LeBay's; it was cleaner, too—a neat, seemingly unbroken band of Lycra about twelve inches across. But, Dennis thought, a brace was a brace. It was too close to LeBay for comfort.

"I put another hurt on it getting Christine back to Will's," Arnie said. "I don't even remember how I did it, that's how upset I was. Hooking her up to the wrecker, I guess, but I don't know for sure. At first it wasn't too bad, then it got worse. Dr. Mascia prescribed—Dennis, are you okay?"

With what felt like a fantastic effort, Dennis kept his voice even. He moved his features around into an expression which felt at least faintly like pleasant interest . . . and still there was that something dancing in Arnie's eyes, dancing and dancing.

"You'll shake it off," Dennis said.

"Sure, I imagine," Arnie said, tucking his shirt back in around the back brace. "I'm just supposed to watch what I lift so I don't do it again."

He smiled at Dennis.

"If there was still a draft, it would keep me out of the Army," he said.

Once again Dennis restrained himself from any movement

that could have been interpreted as surprise, but he put his arms under the bed's top sheet. At the sight of that back brace, so like LeBay's, they had broken out in gooseflesh.

Arnie's eyes—like black water under thin gray March ice. Black water and glee dancing far down within them like the twisting, decomposing body of a drowned man.

"Listen," Arnie said briskly. "I gotta move. Hope you didn't think I could hang around a lousy place like this all night."

"That's you, always in demand," Dennis said. "Seriously, man, thanks. You cheered up a grim day."

For one strange instant, he thought Arnie was going to weep. That dancing thing down deep in his eyes was gone and his friend was there—really there. Then Arnie smiled sincerely. "Just remember one thing, Dennis: nobody misses you. Nobody at all."

"Eat me raw through a Flavor Straw," Dennis said solemnly.

Arnie gave him the finger.

The formalities were now complete; Arnie could leave. He gathered up his brown shopping bag, considerably deflated, candle-holders and empty beer bottles clinking inside.

Dennis had a sudden inspiration. He rapped his knuckles on his leg cast. "Sign this, Arnie, would you?"

"I already did, didn't I?"

"Yeah, but it wore off. Sign it again?"

Arnie shrugged. "If you've got a pen."

Dennis gave him one from the drawer of the night-table. Grinning, Arnie bent over the cast, which was hoisted to an angle over the bed with a series of weights and pulleys, found white space in the intaglio of names and mottoes, and scribbled:

For Dennis Guilder, The Worlds Biggest Dork

Arnie Cunningham

He patted the cast when he was done and handed the pen back to Dennis. "Okay?"

"Yeah," Dennis said. "Thanks. Stay loose, Arnie."

"You know it. Happy Thanksgiving."

"Same to you."

Arnie left. Later on, Dennis's mother and father came in; Ellie, apparently exhausted by the day's hilarity, had gone home to bed. On their way home, the Guilders commented to each other on how withdrawn Dennis had seemed.

"He was in a blue study, all right," Guilder said. "Holidays in the hospital aren't any fun."

As for Dennis himself, he spent a long and thoughtful time that evening examining two signatures. Arnie had indeed signed his cast, but at a time when both of Dennis's legs had been in full-leg casts. That first time, he had signed the cast on the right leg, which had been up in the air when Arnie came in. Tonight he had signed the left.

Dennis buzzed for a nurse and used all his charm persuading her to lower his left leg so he could compare the two signatures, side by side. The cast on his right leg had been cut down, and would come off altogether in a week or ten days. Arnie's signature had not rubbed off—that had been one of *Dennis's* lies—but it had very nearly been cut off.

Arnie had not written a message on the right leg, only his signature. With some effort (and some pain), Dennis and the nurse were able to maneuver his legs close enough together so he could study the two signatures side by side. In a voice so dry and cracked he was hardly able to recognize it as his own, he asked the nurse, "Do they look the same to you?"

"No," the nurse said. "I've heard of forging checks, but never casts. Is it a joke?"

"Sure," Dennis said, feeling an icy coldness rise from his stomach to his chest. "It's a joke." He looked at the signatures; he looked at them side by side and felt that rising coldness steal all through him, lowering his body temperature, making the hairs on the back of his neck stir and stiffen:

Arnie Cunningham   *Arnie Cunningham*

They were nothing alike.

Late that Thanksgiving night, a cold wind rose, first gusting, then blowing steadily. The clear eye of the moon stared down from a black sky. The last brown and withered leaves of autumn were ripped from the trees and then harried through the gutters. They made a sound like rolling bones.

Winter had come to Libertyville.

30 / Moochie Welch

The night was dark, the sky was blue,
and down the alley an ice-wagon flew.
Door banged open,
Somebody screamed,
You oughtta heard just what I seen.
                        —Bo Diddley

The Thursday after Thanksgiving was the last day of November, the night that Jackson Browne played the Pittsburgh Civic Center to a sellout crowd. Moochie Welch went up with Richie Trelawney and Nickey Billingham but got separated from them even before the show began. He was spare-changing, and whether it was because the impending Browne concert had created some extremely mellow vibes or because he was becoming something of an endearing fixture (Moochie, a romantic, liked to believe the latter), he had had a remarkably good night. He had collected nearly thirty dollars' worth of "spare change." It was distributed among all his pockets; Moochie jingled like a piggy bank. Thumbing home had been remarkably easy too, with all the traffic leaving the Civic Center. The concert ended at eleven-forty, and he was back in Libertyville shortly after one-fifteen.

His last ride was with a young guy who was headed back to Prestonville on Route 63. The guy dropped him at the 376 ramp on JFK Drive. Moochie decided to walk up to Vandenberg's Happy Gas and see Buddy. Buddy had a car, which meant that Moochie, who lived far out on Kingsfield Pike, wouldn't have to walk home. It was hard work, hitching rides, once you got out in the boonies—and the Kingsfield

Pike was Boondocks City. It meant he wouldn't be home until well past dawn, but in cold weather a sure ride was not to be sneezed at. And Buddy might have a bottle.

He had walked a quarter of a mile from the 376 exit ramp in the deep single-number cold, his cleated heels clicking on the deserted sidewalk, his shadow waxing and waning under the eerie orange streetlamps, and had still perhaps a mile to go when he saw the car parked at the curb up ahead. Exhaust curled out of its twin pipes and hung in the perfectly still air, clouding it, before drifting lazily away in stacked layers. The grille, bright chrome highlighted with pricks of orange light, looked at him like a grinning idiot mouth. Moochie recognized the car. It was a two-tone Plymouth. In the light of the maximum-illumination streetlamps the two tones seemed to be ivory and dried blood. It was Christine.

Moochie stopped, and a stupid sort of wonder flooded through him—it was not fear, at least not at that moment. It couldn't be Christine, that was impossible—they had punched a dozen holes in the radiator of Cuntface's car, they had dumped a nearly full bottle of Texas Driver into the carb, and Buddy had produced a five-pound sack of Domino sugar, which he had funnelled into the gas tank through Moochie's cupped hands. And all of that was just for starters. Buddy had demonstrated a kind of furious invention when it came to destroying Cuntface's car; it had left Moochie feeling both delighted and uneasy. All in all, that car should not have moved under its own power for six months, if ever. So this could not be Christine. It was some other '58 Fury.

Except it was Christine. He knew it.

Moochie stood there on the deserted early-morning sidewalk, his numb ears poking out from beneath his long hair, his breath pluming frostily on the air.

The car sat at the curb facing him, engine growling softly. It was impossible to tell who, if anyone, was behind the wheel; it was parked directly beneath one of the streetlights, and the orange globe burned across the glass of the unmarred windshield like a waterproof jack-o'-lantern seen deep down in dark water.

Moochie began to be afraid.

He slicked his tongue over dry lips and looked around. To his left was JFK Drive, six lanes wide and looking like a dry riverbed at this empty hour of the morning. To his right was a photography shop, orange letters outlined in red spelling KODAK across its window.

He looked back at the car. It just sat there, idling.

He opened his mouth to speak and produced no sound. He tried again and got a croak. "Hey. Cunningham."

The car sat, seeming to brood. Exhaust curled up. The engine rumbled, idling fat on high-test gas.

"That you, Cunningham?"

He took one more step. A cleat scraped on cement. His heart was thudding in his neck. He looked around at the street again; surely another car would come, JFK Drive couldn't be totally deserted even at one-twenty-five in the morning, could it? But there were no cars, only the flat orange glare of the streetlights.

Moochie cleared his throat.

"You ain't mad, are you?"

Christine's duals suddenly came on, pinning him in harsh white light. The Fury ripped toward him, peeling out, the tires screaming black slashes of rubber onto the pavement. It came with such sudden power that the rear end seemed to squat, like the haunches of a dog preparing to spring—a dog or a she-wolf. The onside wheels jumped up on the pavement and it ran at Moochie that way, offside wheels down, onside wheels up over the curb, canted at an angle. The undercarriage scraped and shrieked and shot off a swirling flicker of sparks.

Moochie screamed and tried to sidestep. The edge of Christine's bumper barely flicked his left calf and took a chunk of meat. Warm wetness coursed down his leg and puddled in his shoe. The warmth of his own blood made him realize in a confused way just how cold the night was.

He thudded hip-first into the doorway of the photo shop, barely missing the plate-glass window. A foot to the left and he would have crashed right through, landing in a litter of Nikons and Polaroid One-Steps.

He could hear the car's engine, suddenly revving up. That horrible, unearthly shrieking of the undercarriage on the cement again. Moochie turned around, panting harshly. Christine was reversing back up the gutter, and as it passed him, he saw. He saw.

There was no one behind the wheel.

Panic began to pound in his head. Moochie took to his heels. He ran out into JFK Drive, sprinting for the far side. There was an alley over there between a market and a dry-cleaning place. Too narrow for the car. If he could get in there—

Change jingled madly in his pants pockets and in the five or six pockets of his Army-surplus duffel coat. Quarters, nickels, dimes. A jingling silver carillon. He pumped his knees almost to his chin. His cleated engineer boots drummed the pavement. His shadow chased him.

The car somewhere behind him revved again, fell off, revved again, fell off, and then the motor began to shriek. The tires wailed, and Christine shot at Moochie Welch's back, crossing the lanes of JFK Drive at right angles. Moochie screamed and could not hear himself scream because the car was still peeling rubber, the car was still shrieking like an insanely angry, murderous woman, and that shriek filled the world.

His shadow was no longer chasing him. It was leading him and getting longer. In the window of the dry-cleaning shop he saw great yellow eyes blossom.

It wasn't even close.

At the very last moment Moochie tried to jig left, but Christine jigged with him as if she had read his final desperate thought. The Plymouth hit him squarely, still accelerating, breaking Moochie Welch's back and knocking him spang out of his engineer's boots. He was thrown forty feet into the brick siding of the little market, again narrowly missing a plunge through a plate-glass window.

The force of his strike was hard enough to cause him to rebound into the street again, leaving a splash of blood on the brick like an inkblot. A picture of it would appear the next day on the front page of the Libertyville *Keystone*.

Christine reversed, screeched to a skidding, sliding stop, and roared forward again. Moochie lay near the curbing, trying to get up. He couldn't get up. Nothing seemed to work. All the signals were scrambled.

Bright white light washed over him.

"No," he whispered through a mouthful of broken teeth. "N—"

The car roared forward and over him. Change flew everywhere. Moochie was pulled and rolled first one way and then the other as Christine reversed into the street again. She stood there, engine revving and falling off to a rich idle, then revving again. She stood there as if thinking.

Then she came at him again. She hit him, jumped the curb, skidded around, and then reversed again, thumping back down.

She screamed forward.

And back.

And forward.

Her headlights glared. Her exhaust pipes jetted hot blue smoke.

The thing in the street no longer looked like a human being; it looked like a scattered bundle of rags.

The car reversed a final time, skidded around in a half-circle, and accelerated, roaring over the bleeding bundle in the street again and going down the Drive, the blast of its engine, still winding up to full rev, racketing off the walls of the sleeping buildings—but not entirely sleeping now; lights were beginning to flick on, people who lived over their stores were going to their windows to see what all the racket had been about, and if there had been an accident.

One of Christine's headlights had been shattered. Another flickered unsteadily off and on, bleared with a thin wash of Moochie's blood. The grille had been bent inward, and the dents in it approximated the shape and size of Moochie's torso with all the gruesome perfection of a deathmask. Blood was splashed across the hood in fans that spread out as windspeed increased. The exhaust had taken on a heavy, blatting sound; one of Christine's two mufflers had been destroyed.

Inside, on the instrument panel, the odometer continued to run backward, as if Christine were somehow slipping back into time, leaving not only the scene of the hit-and-run behind but the actual *fact* of the hit-and-run.

The muffler was the first thing.

Suddenly that heavy, blatting sound diminished and smoothed out.

The fans of blood on the hood began to run toward the front of the car again in spite of the wind—as if a movie film had been reversed.

The flickering headlight suddenly shone steadily, and a tenth of a mile later the deadlight became a headlight again. With an unimportant tinkling sound—no more than the sound of a small boy's boot breaking the thin scum of ice on a mudpuddle—the glass reassembled itself from nowhere.

There was a hollow *punk! punk! punk!* sound from the front end, the sound of denting metal, the sound you sometimes get when you squeeze a beer-can. But instead of denting, Christine's grille was popping back out—a bodyshop veteran with fifty years' experience in putting fender-benders right could not have done it more neatly.

Christine turned onto Hampton Street even before the first of those awakened by the screaming of her tires had reached Moochie's remains. The blood was gone. It had reached the front of the hood and disappeared. The scratches were gone. As she rolled quietly toward the garage door with its HONK FOR ENTRY sign, there was one final *punk!* as the last dimple—this one in the left front bumper, the spot where Christine had struck Moochie's calf—popped back out.

Christine looked like new.

The car stopped in front of the large garage door in the middle of the darkened, silent building. There was a small plastic box clipped to the driver's side sun-visor. This was a little doodad Will Darnell had given Arnie when Arnie began to run cigarettes and booze over into New York State for him—it was, perhaps, Darnell's version of a gold key to the crapper.

In the still air the door-opener hummed briefly, and the garage door rattled obediently up. Another circuit was made by the rising door, and a few interior lights came on, burning weakly.

The headlight knob on the dashboard suddenly went in, and Christine's duals went out. She rolled inside and whispered across the oil-stained concrete to stall twenty. Behind her, the overhead door, which had been set on a thirty-second timer, rolled back down. The light circuit was broken, and the garage was dark again.

In Christine's ignition switch, the keys dangling down suddenly turned to the left. The engine died. The leather patch with the initials R.D.L. branded into it swung back and forth in decreasing arcs . . . and was finally still.

Christine sat in the dark, and the only sound in Darnell's Do-It-Yourself Garage was the slow tick of her cooling engine.

31 / The Day After

I got a '69 Chevy with a 396,
Feully heads and a Hurst on the floor,
She's waiting tonight
Down in the parking-lot
Outside the 7-11 store . . .
                    —Bruce Springsteen

Arnie Cunningham did not go to school the next day. He said he thought he might be coming down with the flu. But that evening he told his parents that he felt enough improved to go down to Darnell's and do some work on Christine.

Regina protested—although she did not come right out and say so, she thought Arnie looked like death warmed over. His face was now entirely free of acne and blemishes, but there was a trade-off: it was much too pale, and there were dark circles under his eyes, as if he hadn't been sleeping. In addition, he was still limping. She wondered uneasily if her son could be using some sort of drug, if perhaps he had hurt his back worse than he had let on and had started taking pills so he could go on working on the goddamned car. Then she dismissed the thought. Obsessed as he might be with the car, Arnie would not be that stupid.

"I'm really fine, Mom," he said.

"You don't look fine. And you hardly touched your supper."

"I'll get some chow later on."

"How's your back? You're not lifting a lot of heavy stuff down there, are you?"

"No, Mom." This was a lie. And his back had hurt terribly all day long. This was the worst it had been since the original injury at Philly Plains (*oh, was that where it started?* his mind whispered, *oh really? are you sure?*). He had taken the brace off for a while, and his back had throbbed fit to kill him. He had put it on again after only fifteen minutes, cinching it tighter than ever. Now his back really was a little

243

better. And he knew why. He was going to her. That was why.

Regina looked at him, worried and at a loss. For the first time in her life she simply did not know how to proceed. Arnie was beyond her control now. Knowing it brought on a horrible feeling of despair that sometimes crept up on her and filled her brain with an awful, empty, rotten coldness. At these times a depression so total she could barely credit it would steal through her, making her wonder exactly what it was she had lived her life for—so her son could fall in love with a girl and a car all in the same terrible fall? Was that it? So she could see exactly how hateful to him she had become when she looked in his gray eyes? Was that it? And it really didn't have anything to do with the girl at all, did it? No. In her mind, it always came back to the car. Her rest had become broken and uneasy, and for the first time since her miscarriage nearly twenty years before, she had found herself considering making an appointment with Dr. Mascia to see if he would give her some pill for the stress and the depression and the attendant insomnia. She thought about Arnie on her long sleepless nights, and about mistakes that could never be rectified; she thought about how time had a way of swinging the balance of power on its axis, and how old age had a way of sometimes looking through a dressing-table mirror like the hand of a corpse poking through eroded earth.

"Will you be back early?" she asked, knowing this was the last breastwork of the truly powerless parent, hating it, unable—now—to change it.

"Sure," he said, but she didn't much trust the way he said it.

"Arnie, I wish you'd stay home. You really don't look good at all."

"I'll be fine," he said. "Got to be. I have to run some auto parts over to Jamesburg for Will tomorrow."

"Not if you're sick," she said. "That's nearly a hundred and fifty miles."

"Don't worry." He kissed her cheek—the passionless kiss-on-the-cheek of cocktail-party acquaintances.

He was opening the kitchen door to go out when Regina asked, "Did you know the boy who was run down last night on Kennedy Drive?"

He turned back to look at her, his face expressionless. "What?"

"The paper said he went to Libertyville."

"Oh, the hit-and-run . . . that's what you're talking about."

"Yes."

"I had a class with him when I was a freshman," Arnie said. "I think. No, I really didn't know him, Mom."

"Oh." She nodded, pleased. "That's good. The paper said there were residues of drugs in his system. You'd never take drugs, would you, Arnie?"

Arnie smiled gently at her pallid, watchful face. "No, Mom," he said.

"And if your back started to hurt you—I mean, if it *really* started to hurt you—you'd go see Dr. Mascia about it, wouldn't you? You wouldn't buy anything from a . . . a drug-pusher, would you?"

"No, Mom," he repeated, and went out.

There had been more snow. Another thaw had melted most of it, but this time it had not disappeared completely; it had only withdrawn into the shadows, where it formed a white rime under hedges, the bases of trees, the overhang of the garage. But in spite of the snow around the edges—or maybe because of it—their lawn looked oddly green as Arnie stepped out into the twilight, and his father looked like a strange refugee from summer as he raked the last of the autumn leaves.

Arnie raised his hand briefly to his father and made as if to go past without speaking. Michael called him over. Arnie went reluctantly. He didn't want to be late for his bus.

His father had also aged in the storms that had blown up over Christine, although other things had undoubtedly played a part. He had made a bid for the chairmanship of the History Department at Horlicks late in the summer and had been rebuffed quite soundly. And during his annual October checkup, the doctor had pointed out an incipient phlebitis problem—phlebitis, which had nearly killed Nixon; phlebitis, an old folks' problem. As that late fall moved toward another gray western-Pennsylvania winter, Michael Cunningham looked gloomier than ever.

"Hi, Dad. Listen, I've got to hurry if I'm going to catch—"

Michael looked up from the little pile of frozen brown leaves he had managed to get together; the sunset caught the planes of his face and appeared to make them bleed. Arnie stepped back involuntarily, a little shocked. His father's face was haggard.

"Arnold," he said, "where were you last night?"

"What—?" Arnie gaped, then closed his mouth slowly. "Why, here. Here, Dad. You know that."

"All night?"

"Of course. I went to bed at ten o'clock. I was bushed. Why?"

"Because I had a call from the police today," Michael said. "About that boy who was run over on JFK Drive last night."

"Moochie Welch," Arnie said. He looked at his father with calm eyes that were deeply circled and socketed for all their calmness. If the son had been shocked by the father's appearance, the father was also dully shocked by his son's—to Michael, the boy's eyesockets looked nearly like a skull's vacant orbs in the failing light.

"The last name was Welch, yes."

"They would be in touch. I suppose. Mom doesn't know—that he might have been one of the guys that trashed Christine?"

"Not from me."

"I didn't tell her either. I'd be glad if she didn't find that out," Arnie said.

"She may find it out eventually," Michael said. "In fact, she almost certainly will. She's an extremely intelligent woman, in case you've never noticed. But she won't find it out from me."

Arnie nodded, then smiled humorlessly. " 'Where were you last night?' Your trust is touching, Dad."

Michael flushed, but his eyes didn't drop. "Maybe if you'd been standing outside yourself these last couple of months," he said, "you'd understand why I asked."

"What the hell does that mean?"

"You know damn well. It hardly even bears discussing anymore. We just go around and around the same old mulberry bush. Your entire life is jittering apart and you stand there and ask me what I'm talking about."

Arnie laughed. It was a hard, contemptuous sound. Michael seemed to shrivel a little before it. "Mom asked me if I was on drugs. Maybe you want to check that one out, too." Arnie made as if to push up the sleeves of his warmup jacket. "Want to check for needle-tracks?"

"I don't need to ask if you're on drugs," Michael said. "You're only on one I know of, and that's enough. It's that goddam car."

Arnie turned as if to go, and Michael pulled him back.

"Get your hand off my arm."

*Scenes on the following pages are from
John Carpenter's CHRISTINE, a Richard Kobritz Production,
released by Columbia Pictures.*

Car for sale—a dilapidated 1958 Plymouth Fury.

Arnie Cunningham (Keith Gordon), right, looks over the car
with his high-school buddy, Dennis Guilder (John Stockwell).

At school, Arnie is viewed with contempt by the Auto Shop
teacher (David Spielberg, front right) and three shop bullies
(from left, William Ostrander, Steven Tash and
Malcolm Danare).

The ugly group taunts Arnie by stealing his lunch.

Arnie is treated shabbily by Will Darnell (Robert Prosky), owner of a car repair shop.

While the car, Christine, is becoming almost miraculously restored, Arnie wins himself a new girl friend, Leigh Cabot (Alexandra Paul).

Arnie takes Leigh in Christine to a drive-in movie.

Some strange force seems to be choking Leigh to death.

The punks strike back and wreck Christine.

Arnie surveys the dreadful damage done to his car.

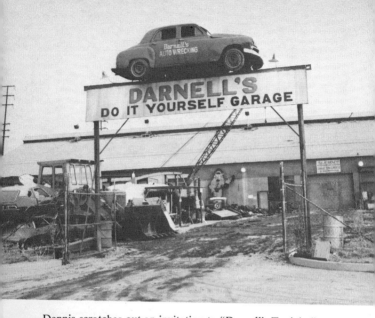

Dennis scratches out an invitation to "Darnell's Tonight."

Michael dropped his hand. "I wanted you to be aware," he said. "I no more think you'd kill someone than I think you could walk across the Symonds' swimming pool. But the police are going to question you, Arnie, and people can look surprised when the police turn up suddenly. To them, surprise can look like guilt."

"All of this because some drunk ran over that shitter Welch?"

"It wasn't like that," Michael said. "I got that much out of this fellow Junkins who called me up on the phone. Whoever killed the Welch boy ran him down and then backed over him and ran over him again and backed up *again* and—"

"Stop it," Arnie said. He suddenly looked sick and frightened, and Michael had much the same feeling Dennis had had on Thanksgiving evening: that in this tired unhappiness the real Arnie was suddenly close to the surface, perhaps reachable.

"It was . . . incredibly brutal," Michael said. "That's what Junkins said. You see, it doesn't look like an accident at all. It looks like murder."

"Murder," Arnie said, dazed. "No, I never—"

"What?" Michael asked sharply. He grabbed Arnie's jacket again. "What did you say?"

Arnie looked at his father. His face was masklike again. "I never thought it could be that," he said. "That's all I was going to say."

"I just wanted you to know," he said. "They'll be looking for someone with a motive, no matter how thin. They know what happened to your car, and that the Welch boy might have been involved, or that you might *think* he was involved. Junkins may be around to talk to you."

"I don't have anything to hide."

"No, of course not," Michael said. "You'll miss your bus."

"Yeah," Arnie said. "Gotta go." But he stayed a moment longer, looking at his father.

Michael suddenly found himself thinking of Arnie's ninth birthday. He and his son had gone to the little zoo in Philly Plains, had eaten lunch out, and had finished the day by playing eighteen holes at the indoor miniature golf course on outer Basin Drive. That place had burned down in 1975. Regina had not been able to come; she had been flat on her back with bronchitis. The two of them had had a fine time. For Michael, that had been his son's best birthday, the one that symbolized for him above all others his son's sweet and uneventful American boyhood. They had gone to the zoo and come back and nothing much had happened except that they had had a great time—Michael and his son, who had been and who still was so dear to him.

He wet his lips and said, "Sell her, Arnie, why don't you? When she's completely restored, sell her away. You could get a lot of money. A couple—three thousand, maybe."

Again that frightened, tired look seemed to sweep over Arnie's face, but Michael couldn't tell for sure. The sunset had faded to a bitter orange line on the western horizon, and the little yard was dark. Then the look—if it had been there at all—went away.

"No, I couldn't do that, Dad," Arnie said gently, as if speaking to a child. "I couldn't do that now. I've put too much into her. Way too much." And then he was gone, cutting across the yard to the sidewalk, joining the other shadows, and there was only the sound of his footfalls coming back, soon lost.

Put too much into her? Have you? Exactly what, Arnie? What have you put into her?

Michael looked down at the leaves, then around at his yard. Beneath the hedge and under the overhang of the garage, cold snow glimmered in the coming dark, livid and stubbornly waiting for reinforcements. Waiting for winter.

32 / Regina and Michael

She's real fine, my 409,
My four-speed, dual-quad, Positraction 409.
                              —The Beach Boys

Regina was tired—she tired more easily these days, it seemed—and they went to bed together around nine, long before Arnie came in. They made love that was dutiful and joyless (lately they made love a lot, it was almost always dutiful and joyless, and Michael had begun having the unpleasant feeling that his wife was using his penis as a sleeping pill), and as they lay in their twin beds after, Michael asked casually: "How did you sleep last night?"

"Quite well," Regina said candidly, and Michael knew she was lying. Good.

"I came up around eleven and Arnie seemed restless," Michael said, still keeping his voice casual. He was deeply uneasy now—there had been something in Arnie's face tonight, something he hadn't been able to read because of the damned shadows. It was probably nothing, nothing at all, but it glowed in his mind like a baleful neon sign that simply would not shut off. Had his son looked guilty and scared? Or had it just been the light? Unless he could resolve that, sleep would be a long time coming tonight—and it might not come at all.

"I got up around one," Regina said, and then hurried to add, "just to use the bathroom. I checked in on him." She laughed a little wistfully. "Old habits die hard, don't they?"

"Yes," Michael said. "I guess they do."

"He was sleeping deeply then. I wish I could get him to wear pajamas in cold weather."

"He was in his skivvies?"

"Yes."

He settled back, immeasurably relieved and more than a little ashamed of himself as well. But it was better to know . . . for sure. It was all very well for him to tell Arnie that he knew the boy could no more commit a murder than he could walk on water. But the mind, that perverse monkey—the mind can conceive of anything and seems to take a perverse delight in doing so. Just maybe, Michael thought, lacing his hands behind his head and looking up at the dark ceiling, just maybe that's the peculiar damnation of the living. In the mind a wife can rut, laughing, with a best friend, a best friend can cast plots against you and plan backstabbings, a son can commit murder by auto.

Better to be ashamed and put the monkey to sleep.

Arnie had been here at one o'clock. It was unlikely Regina was mistaken about the time because of the digital clock-radio on their bureau—it told the time in numbers that were big and blue and unmistakable. His son had been here at one o'clock, and the Welch boy had been run down three miles away twenty-five minutes later. Impossible to believe that Arnie could have dressed, gone out (without Regina, who had surely been lying wakeful, hearing him), gone down to Darnell's, gotten Christine, and driven out to where Moochie Welch had been killed. Physically impossible.

Not that he had ever believed it to begin with.

The mind-monkey was satisfied. Michael rolled over on his right side, slept, and dreamed that he and his nine-year-old son were playing miniature golf on an endless series of small Astro-Turfed greens where windmills turned and tiny water-hazards lay in wait . . . and he dreamed that they were alone, all alone in the world, because his son's mother had died in childbirth—very sad; people still remarked on how inconsolable Michael had been—but when they went home, he and his son, the house would be theirs alone, they would eat spaghetti right from the pot like a couple of bachelor slobs, and when the dishes were washed they would sit at a kitchen table hidden beneath spread newspapers and build model cars with harmless plastic engines.

In his sleep, Michael Cunningham smiled. Beside him, in the other bed, Regina did not. She lay awake and waited for the sound of the door that would tell her that her son had come in from the world outside.

When she heard the door open and close . . . when she heard his step on the stairs . . . then she would be able to sleep.

Maybe.

33 / Junkins

I think you better slow down and drive
*   with me, baby . . .*
You say what?
Hush up and mind my own bidness?
But Baby, you are my bidness!
You gooood bidness, baby,
And I love good bidness!
What kind of car am I drivin?
I'm drive a '48 Cadillac
With Thunderbird wings,
I tell you, baby, she's a movin thing,
Ride on, Josephine, ride on . . .
*   —Ellas McDaniel*

Junkins turned up at Darnell's around eight-forty-five that evening. Arnie had just finished with Christine for the night. He had replaced the radio antenna that Repperton's gang had snapped off with a new one, and for the last fifteen minutes or so he had been sitting behind the wheel, listening to WDIL's Friday Night Cavalcade of Gold.

He had meant to do no more than turn the radio on and dial across once, making sure that he had hooked up the antenna plug properly and that there was no static. But he had run onto WDIL's strong signal and had sat there, looking straight through the windshield, his gray eyes musing and far away, as Bobby Fuller sang "I Fought the Law," as Frankie Lymon and the Teenagers sang "Why Do Fools Fall in Love?," as Eddie Cochran sang "C'mon, Everybody," and Buddy Holly sang "Rave On." There were no commercials on WDIL Friday nights, and no deejays. Just the sounds. Gone from the charts but not from our hearts. Every now and then a soothing female voice would break in and tell him what he already knew—that he was listening to WDIL-Pittsburgh, the sound of Blue Suede Radio.

Arnie sat dreaming behind the wheel, the red idiot lights glowing on the dash, tapping his fingers lightly. The antenna was fine. Yes. He had done a good job. It was like Will said; he had a light touch. Look at Christine; Christine proved it. She had been a hunk of junk sitting on LeBay's lawn and he had brought her back; then she had been a hunk of junk sitting in the long-term lot out at the airport and he had brought her back again. He had . . .

> Rave on . . . rave on and tell me . . .
> Tell me . . . not to be lonely. . . .

He had what?

Replaced the antenna, yes. And he had popped some of the dents, he could remember that. But he hadn't ordered any glass (although it was all replaced), he hadn't ordered any new seat covers (but they were all replaced, too), and he had only looked closely under the hood once before slamming it back down in horror at the damage they had done to Christine's mill.

But now the radiator was whole, the engine block clean and glowing, the pistons moving free and clear. And it purred like a cat.

But there had been dreams.

He had dreamed of LeBay behind the wheel of Christine, LeBay dressed in an Army uniform that was spotted and splotched with blue-gray patches of graveyard mould. Le-Bay's flesh had sloughed and run. White, gleaming bone poked through in places. The sockets where LeBay's eyes had once been were empty and dark (but something was squirming in there, ah, yes, something). And then Christine's headlights had come on and someone had been pinned there, pinned like a bug on a white square of cardboard. Someone familiar.

Moochie Welch?

Maybe. But as Christine suddenly rocketed forward, tires screaming, it had seemed to Arnie that the terrified face out there on the street ran like tallow, changing even as the Plymouth bore down on it: now it was Repperton's face, now Sandy Galton's, now it was Will Darnell's heavy moon face.

Whoever was out there had jumped aside, but LeBay had thrown Christine into reserve, working the shift lever with black rotting fingers—a wedding ring hung on one, as loose as a hoop thrown over the branch of a dead tree—and then he threw it back into drive as the figure raced for the far side of the street. And as Christine bore down again, the head had turned, throwing a terrified glance backward, and Arnie had seen the face of his mother . . . the face of Dennis Guilder . . . Leigh's face, all eyes under a floating cloud of dark-blond hair . . . and finally his own face, the twisted mouth forming the words *No! No! No!*

Overriding everything, even the heavy thunder of the exhaust (something underneath had been damaged for sure), was LeBay's rotting, triumphant voice, coming from a decayed larynx, passing lips that were already shrivelled away from the teeth and tattooed with a delicate spidering of dark green mould, LeBay's triumphant, shrieking voice:

Here you go, you shitter! See how you like it!

There had been the heavy, mortal thud of Christine's bumper striking flesh, the gleam of a pair of spectacles rising in the night air, turning over and over, and then Arnie had awakened in his room, curled into a trembling ball and clutching his pillow. It had been quarter of two in the morning, and his first feeling had been a great and terrible relief, relief that he was still alive. He was alive, LeBay was dead, and Christine was safe. The only three things in the world that mattered.

Oh but Arnie, how did you hurt your back?

Some voice inside, sly and insinuating—asking a question he was afraid to answer.

I hurt it at Philly Plains, he had told everyone. *One of the junkers started to slip back down the ramp of Will's flatbed and I pushed it back up—didn't think about it; I just did it. Strained something really bad.* So he had said. And one of the junkers *had* started to slip, and he *had* pushed it back up, but that hadn't been how he hurt his back, had it? No.

That night after he and Leigh had found Christine smashed to hell in the parking lot, sitting on four slashed tires . . . that night at Darnell's, after everyone was gone . . . he had tuned the radio in Will's office to the oldies on WDIL . . . Will trusted him now, why not? He was running cigarettes across the state line into New York, he was running fireworks all the way over to Burlington, and twice he had run something wrapped in flat brown-paper packages into Wheeling, where a young guy in an old Dodge Challenger traded him another, slightly larger, brown-paper package for it. Arnie thought maybe he was trading cocaine for money, but he didn't want to know for sure.

He drove a boat on these trips, Will's private car, a 1966 Imperial as black as midnight in Persia. It was whisper-quiet, and the trunk had a false bottom. If you kept to the speed limit, it was no problem. Why should it be? The important thing was that he now had the keys to the garage. He could come in after everyone else was gone. Like he had that night. And he had turned on WDIL . . . and he had . . . he had . . .

Hurt his back somehow.

What had he been doing to hurt his back?

A strange phrase came to him in answer, floating up from his subconscious: *It's just a funny little glitch.*

Did he really want to know? He didn't. In fact, there were times when he didn't want the car at all. There were times when he felt he would be better off just . . . well, junking it. Not that he ever would, or could. It was just that, sometimes (in the sweaty, shaking aftermath of that dream last night, for instance), he felt that if he got rid of it, he would be . . . happier.

The radio suddenly spat an almost feline burst of static.

"Don't worry," Arnie whispered. He ran his hand slowly over the dashboard, loving the feel of it. Yes, the car frightened him sometimes. And he supposed his father was right; it had changed his life to some degree. But he could no more junk it than he could commit suicide.

The static cleared. The Marvelettes were singing "Please Mr. Postman."

And then a voice said in his ear, "Arnold Cunningham?"

He jumped and snapped off the radio. He turned around. A small, dapper little man was leaning in Christine's window. His eyes were a dark brown, and his color was high—from the cold outside, Arnie guessed.

"Yes?"

"Rudolph Junkins. State Police, Detective Division." Junkins stuck his hand in through the open window.

Arnie looked at it for a moment. So his father had been right.

He grinned his most charming grin, took the hand, shook it firmly, and said, "Don't shoot, copper, I'll throw out my guns."

Junkins returned Arnie's grin, but Arnie noticed that the grin did no more than touch his eyes, which were exploring the car in a quick, thorough fashion that Arnie didn't like. Not at all.

"Whoo! I got the feeling from the local police that the guys who worked over your rolling iron had really tattooed it. It sure doesn't look like it."

Arnie shrugged and got out of the car. Friday nights were slow at the garage; Will himself rarely came in, and he wasn't in tonight. Across the way, in stall ten, a fellow named Gabbs was putting a new muffler on his old Valiant, and down at the far end of the garage there was the periodic burr of an air wrench as some fellow put on his snow tires. Otherwise, he and Junkins had the place to themselves.

"It wasn't anywhere near as bad as it looked," Arnie said. He thought that this smiling, dapper little man might be extremely clever. As if it was a natural outgrowth of the thought, he rested his hand easily on Christine's roof and immediately felt better. He could cope with this man, clever or not. After all, what was there to worry about? "There was no structural damage."

"Oh? I understood they punched holes in the body with some sharp instrument," Junkins said, looking closely at Christine's flank. "I'll be damned if I can see the fill. You must be a bodywork genius, Arnie. The way my wife drives, maybe I ought to put you on retainer." He smiled disarmingly, but his eyes went on running back and forth over the car. They would dart momentarily to Arnie's face and then go back to the car again. Arnie liked it less and less.

"I'm good but not God," Arnie said. "You can see the bodywork if you really look for it." He pointed at a minute ripple in Christine's back deck. "And there." He pointed at another. "I was lucky enough to find some original Plymouth body parts up in Ruggles. I replaced the entire back door on this side. You see the way the paint doesn't quite match?" He knocked his knuckles on the door.

"Nope," Junkins said. "I might be able to tell with a microscope, Arnie, but it looks like a perfect match to me."

He also knocked his knuckles on the door. Arnie frowned.

"Hell of a job," Junkins said. He walked slowly around to the front of the car. "*Hell* of a job, Arnie. You're to be congratulated."

"Thanks." He watched as Junkins, in the guise of the sincere admirer, used his sharp brown eyes to look for suspicious dents, flaked paint, maybe a spot of blood or a snarl of matted hair. Looking for signs of Moochie Welch. Arnie was suddenly sure that was just what the shitter was doing. "What exactly can I do for you, Detective Junkins?"

Junkins laughed. "Man, that's formal! I can't take that! Make it Rudy, okay?"

"Sure," Arnie said, smiling. "What can I do for you, Rudy?"

"You know, it's funny," Junkins said, squatting to look at the driver's side headlights. He tapped one of them reflectively with his knuckles and then, with seeming absent-mindedness, he ran his forefinger along the headlight's semicircular metal hood. His overcoat pooled on the oil-stained cement floor for a moment; then he stood up. "We get reports on anything of this nature—the trashing of your car, I mean—"

"Oh, hey, they didn't really *trash* it," Arnie said. He was beginning to feel as if he was on a tightrope, and he touched Christine again. Her solidity, her *reality*, once more seemed to comfort him. "They tried, you know, but they didn't do a very good job."

"Okay. I guess I'm not up on the current terminology." Junkins laughed. "Anyway, when it came to my attention, what do you think I said? 'Where's the photographs?' That's what I said. I thought it was an oversight, you know. So I called the Libertyville P.D. and they said there *were* no photographs."

"No," Arnie said. "A kid my age can't get anything but liability insurance, you know that. Even the liability comes with a seven-hundred-dollar deductible. If I had damage insurance,

I would have taken plenty of pictures. But since I didn't, why would I? I sure wouldn't want them for my scrapbook."

"No, I guess not," Junkins said, and walked idly around to the rear of the car, eyes searching for broken glass, for scrapes, for guilt. "But you know what else I thought was funny? You didn't even report the crime!" He raised his dark questioning eyes to Arnie's, looked at him closely—and then smiled a phony, bewildered little smile. "Didn't even report it! 'Huh,' I said. 'Sonofabitch! Who reported it?' Guy's father, they tell me." Junkins shook his head. "I don't get that, Arnie, I don't mind telling you. A guy works his ass off restoring an old car until it's worth two, maybe five thousand dollars, then some guys come along and beat the hell out of it—"

"I told you—"

Rudy Junkins raised his hand and smiled disarmingly. For one weird second Arnie thought he was going to say "Peace," as Dennis sometimes did when things got heavy.

"Damaged it. Sorry."

"Sure," Arnie said.

"Anyhow, according to what your girlfriend said, one of the perpetrators . . . well, defecated on the dashboard. I would have thought you would have been mad as hell. I would have thought you would have reported it."

Now the smile faded altogether and Junkins looked at Arnie soberly, even sternly.

Arnie's cool gray eyes met Junkins's brown ones.

"Shit wipes off," he said finally. "You want to know something, Mr.—Rudy? You want me to tell you something?"

"Sure, son."

"When I was one and a half, I got hold of a fork and marked up an antique bureau that my mother had saved up for over a period of maybe five years. Saved up her pin money, that's what she said. I guess I racked the hell out of it in a very short time. Of course I don't remember it, but she says she just sat right down and bawled." Arnie smiled a little. "Up until this year, I couldn't feature my mother doing that. Now I think I can. Maybe I'm growing up a little, what do you think?"

Junkins lit a cigarette. "Am I missing the point, Arnie? Because I don't see it yet."

"She said that she would rather have had me in diapers until I was three than have had me do that. Because, she said, shit wipes off." Arnie smiled. "You flush it away and it's gone."

"The way Moochie Welch is gone?" Junkins asked.

"I know nothing about that."

"No?"

"No."

"Scout's honor?" Junkins asked. The question was humorous but the eyes were not; they probed at Arnie, looking for the smallest break, a crucial flicker.

Down the aisle, the fellow who had been putting on his winter snows dropped a tool on the concrete. It clanged musically and the fellow chanted, almost chorally, "Oh shit on you, you whore."

Junkins and Arnie both glanced that way briefly, and the moment was broken.

"Sure, Scout's honor," Arnie said. "Look, I suppose you have to do this, it's your job—"

"Sure it's my job," Junkins agreed softly. "The boy was run over three times each way. He was meat. They scraped him up with a shovel."

"Come on," Arnie said sickly. His stomach did a lazy barrel roll.

"Why? Isn't that what you're supposed to do with shit? Scrape it up with a shovel?"

"*I had nothing to do with it!*" Arnie cried, and the man across the way, who had been tinkering with his muffler, looked up, startled.

Arnie lowered his voice.

"I'm sorry. I just wish you'd leave me alone. You know damn well I didn't have anything to do with it. You just went over the whole car. If Christine had hit that Welch kid that many times and that hard, it would be all busted up. I know that much just from watching TV. And when I was taking Auto Shop I two years ago, Mr. Smolnack said that the two best ways he knew to totally destroy a car's front end was to either hit a deer or a person. He was joking a little, but he wasn't kidding . . . if you know what I mean." Arnie swallowed and heard a click in his throat, which was very dry.

"Sure," Junkins said. "Your car looks all right. But you don't, kid. You look like a sleepwalker. You look absolutely fucked over. Pardon my French." He flicked his cigarette away. "You know something, Arnie?"

"What?"

"I think you're lying faster than a horse can trot." He slapped Christine's hood. "Or maybe I should say faster than a Plymouth can run."

Arnie looked at him, his hand on the outside mirror on the passenger side. He said nothing.

"I don't think you're lying about killing the Welch boy. But I think you're lying about what they did to your car; your girl said they mashed the crap out of it, and she's a hell of a lot more convincing than you are. She cried while she told me. She said there was broken glass everywhere. . . . Where did you buy replacement glass, by the way?"

"McConnell's," Arnie said promptly. "In the Burg."

"Still got the receipt?"

"Tossed it out."

"But they'll remember you. Big order like that."

"They might," Arnie said, "but I wouldn't count on it, Rudy. They're the biggest auto-glass specialists west of New York and east of Chicago. That covers a lot of ground. They do yea business, and a lot of it's old cars."

"Still, they'll have the paperwork."

"I paid cash."

"But your name will be on the invoice."

"No," Arnie said, and smiled a wintry smile. "Darnell's Do-It-Yourself Garage. That way I got a ten percent discount."

"You got it all covered, don't you?"

"Lieutenant Junkins—"

"You're lying about the glass too, although I'll be goddamned if I know why."

"You'd think Christ was lying on Calvary, that's what I think," Arnie said angrily. "Since when is it a crime to buy replacement glass if someone busts up your windows? Or pay cash? Or get a discount?"

"Since never," Junkins said.

"Then leave me be."

"More important, I think you're lying about not knowing anything about what happened to the Welch boy. You know something. I want to know what."

"I don't know anything," Arnie said.

"What about—"

"I don't have anything more to say to you," Arnie said. "I'm sorry."

"All right," Junkins said, giving up so quickly that Arnie was immediately suspicious. He rummaged around in the sportcoat he was wearing under his topcoat and took out his wallet. Arnie saw that Junkins was carrying a gun in a shoulder holster and suspected Junkins had wanted him to see it.

He produced a card and gave it to Arnie. "I can be reached at either of those numbers. If you want to talk about anything. Anything at all."

Arnie put the card in his breast pocket.

Junkins took one more leisurely stroll around Christine. "Hell of a restoration job," he repeated. He looked squarely at Arnie. "Why didn't you report it?"

Arnie let out a low shuddering sigh. "Because I thought that would be the end," he said. "I thought they'd let off."

"Yeah," Junkins said. "I thought that might be it. Good night, son."

"Good night."

Junkins started away, turned, came back. "Think it over," he said. "You really do look like hell, you know what I mean? You have a nice girl there. She's worried about you, and she feels bad about what happened to your car. Your dad's worried about you, too. I could get that even over the phone. Think it over and then give me a call, son. You'll sleep better."

Arnie felt something trembling behind his lips, something small and tearful, something that hurt. Junkins's brown eyes were kind. He opened his mouth—God alone knew what might have spilled out—and then a monstrous jab of pain walloped him in the back, making him straighten suddenly. It also had the effect of a slap on a hysteric. He felt calmer, clear-headed again.

"Good night," he repeated. "Good night, Rudy."

Junkins looked at him a moment longer, troubled, and then left.

Arnie began to shake all over. The trembling started in his hands and spread up his forearms to his elbows, and then it was suddenly everywhere. He grabbed blindly for the door-handle, found it at last, and slipped into Christine, into the comforting smells of car and fresh upholstery. He turned the key to ACC, the idiot lights glowed, and he felt for the radio dial.

As he did so his eyes fell on the swinging leather tab with R.D.L. branded into it and his dream recurred with sudden terrible force: the rotting corpse sitting where he was sitting now; the empty eyesockets staring out through the windshield; the fingerbones gripping the wheel; the empty grin of the skull's teeth as Christine bore down on Moochie Welch while the radio, tuned to WDIL, played "Last Kiss" by J. Frank Wilson and the Cavaliers.

He suddenly felt sick—puking-sick. Nausea fluttered sickeningly in his stomach and in the back of his throat. Arnie scrambled out of the car and ran for the head, his footfalls hammering crazily in his ears. He just made it. Everything came up; he vomited again and again until there was nothing left but sour spit. Lights danced in front of his eyes. His ears rang and the muscles in his gut throbbed tiredly.

He looked at his pale, harried face in the spotty mirror, at the dark circles under his eyes and the lank spill of hair across his forehead. Junkins was right. He looked like hell.

But his pimples were all gone.

He laughed crazily. He wouldn't give Christine up, no matter what. That was the one thing he wouldn't do. He—

And suddenly he had to do it again, only there was nothing left to come up: only ripping, clenching dry-heaves and that electric taste of spit in his mouth again.

He had to talk to Leigh. Quite suddenly he had to talk to Leigh.

He let himself into Will's office, where the only sound was the thump of the time clock bolted on the wall turning up fresh minutes. He dialled the Cabots' number from memory but miscued twice because his fingers were trembling so badly.

Leigh herself answered, her voice sounding sleepy.

"Arnie?"

"I have to talk to you, Leigh. I have to see you."

"Arnie, it's almost ten o'clock. I just got out of the shower and into bed . . . I was almost asleep. . . ."

"Please," he said, and shut his eyes.

"Tomorrow," she said. "It can't be tonight, my folks wouldn't let me out so late—"

"It's only ten. And it's Friday."

"They really don't want me to see so much of you, Arnie. They liked you at first, and my dad still does . . . but they both think you've gotten a little spooky." There was a long, long pause at Leigh's end. "I think you have, too," she said finally.

"Does that mean you don't want to see me anymore?" he asked dully. His stomach hurt, his back hurt, everything hurt.

"No." Now the faintest reproach crept into her voice. "I was kind of getting the idea that *you* didn't want to see *me* . . . not at school, and nights you're always down there at the garage. Working on your car."

"That's all done," he said. And then, with a monstrous effort: "It's the car I want to—*oww, goddammit!*" He grabbed at his back, where there had been another huge bolt of pain, and got only a handful of back brace.

"Arnie?" She was alarmed. "Are you all right?"

"Yeah. I had a twinge in my back."

"What were you going to say?"

"Tomorrow," he said. "We'll drive over to Baskin-Robbins and have an ice cream and maybe do some Christmas shopping and have some supper and I'll have you home by seven. And I won't be weird. I promise."

She laughed a little, and Arnie felt a great, sweeping relief. It was like balm. "You dummy."

"Does that mean okay?"

"Yes, it means okay." Leigh paused and then said softly, "I said my parents didn't want me to see so much of you. I didn't say I wanted that."

"Thanks," he said, struggling to keep his voice steady. "Thanks for that."

"What do you want to talk to me about?"

Christine. I want to talk to you about her—and about my dreams. And about why I look like hell. And why I always want to listen to WDIL now, and about what I did that night after everyone was gone . . . the night I hurt my back. Oh Leigh I want—

Another slash of pain up his back like cat's claws.

"I think we just talked about it," he said.

"Oh." A slight, warm pause. "Good."

"Leigh?"

"Umm."

"There'll be more time now. I promise. All the time you want." And thought: *Because now, with Dennis in the hospital, you're all that's left, all that's left between me . . . me and . . .*

"That's good," Leigh said.

"I love you."

"Goodbye, Arnie."

Say it back! he wanted to shout suddenly. *Say it back, I need you to say it back!*

But there was only the click of the phone in his ear.

He sat behind Will's desk for a long time, head lowered, getting hold of himself. She didn't need to say it back every time he said it to her, did she? He didn't need reassurance that badly, did he? Did he?

Arnie got up and went to the door. She was coming out with him tomorrow, that was the important thing. They would do the Christmas shopping they had been planning on the day those shitters trashed Christine; they would walk and talk, they would have a good time. She would say she loved him.

"She'll say it," he whispered, standing in the doorway, but halfway down the left-hand side of the garage Christine sat like a mute and stupid denial, her grille poking forward as if hunting something.

And the voice whispered out of his lower consciousness, the dark questioning voice: *How did you hurt your back? How did you hurt your back? How did you hurt your back, Arnie?*

It was a question he shrank from. He was afraid of the answer.

34 / Leigh and Christine

My baby drove up in a brand-new Cadillac,
She said, "Hey, come here, Daddy,
I ain't never comin back!"
Baby, baby, won't you hear my plea?
Come on, sugar, come on back to me!
She said, "Balls to you, big daddy,
I ain't never comin back!"

—The Clash

It was a gray day, threatening snow, but Arnie was right on both counts—they had a good time and he wasn't weird. Mrs. Cabot had been at home when Arnie got there, and her initial reception was cool. But it was a long time—perhaps twenty minutes—before Leigh came downstairs, wearing a caramel-colored sweater that clung lovingly to her breasts and a new pair of cranberry-colored slacks that clung lovingly to her hips. This inexplicable lateness in a girl who was almost always perfectly on time might have been on purpose. Arnie asked her later and Leigh denied it with an innocence that was perhaps just a little too wide-eyed, but in any case it served its purpose.

Arnie could be charming when he had to be, and he went to work on Mrs. Cabot with a will. Before Leigh finally came bouncing downstairs, twisting her hair into a ponytail, Mrs. Cabot had thawed. She had gotten Arnie a Pepsi-Cola and was listening raptly as he regaled her with tales of the chess club.

"It's the only *civilized* extra-curricular activity I've ever heard of," she told Leigh, and smiled approvingly at Arnie.

"*BORRRRR-ing*," Leigh trumpeted. She put an arm around Arnie's waist and smacked him loudly on the cheek.

"Leigh *Cabot!*"

"Sorry, Mums, but he looks cute in lipstick, doesn't he? Wait a minute, Arnie, I've got a Kleenex. Don't *claw* at it."

She dug in her purse for a tissue. Arnie looked at Mrs. Cabot and rolled his eyes. Natalie Cabot put a hand to her mouth and giggled. The *rapprochement* between her and Arnie was complete.

Arnie and Leigh went to Baskin-Robbins, where an initial awkwardness, left over from the phone conversation of the night before, finally melted away. Arnie had had a vague fear that Christine would not run well, or that Leigh would find something nasty to say about her; she had never liked riding in his car. Both were needless worries. Christine ran like a fine Swiss watch, and the only things Leigh had to say about her rang of pleasure and amazement.

"I never would have believed it," she said as they drove out of the ice-cream parlor's small parking lot and joined the flow of traffic headed toward the Monroeville Mall. "You must have worked like a dog."

"It wasn't as bad as it probably looked to you," Arnie said. "Mind some music?"

"No, of course not."

Arnie turned on the radio—The Silhouettes were kip-kip-ping and boom-booming through "Get a Job."

Leigh made a face. "DIL, yuck. Can I change it?"

"Be my guest."

Leigh switched it to a Pittsburgh rock station and got Billy Joel. "You may be right," Billy admitted cheerfully, "I may be crazy." This was followed by Billy telling his girl Virginia that Catholic girls started much too late—it was the Block Party Weekend. *Now*, Arnie thought. *Now she'll start to hitch*

. . . *back off* . . . *something.* But Christine only went rolling along.

The mall was thronged with hectic but mostly goodnatured shoppers; the last frantic and sometimes ugly Christmas rush was better than two weeks off. The Yuletide spirit was still new enough to be novel, and it was possible to look at the tinsel strung through the wide mall hallways without feeling sour and Ebenezer Scroogey. The steady ringing of the Salvation Army Santas' bells had not yet become a guilty annoyance; they still chanted good tidings and good will rather than the monotonous, metallic chant of *The poor have no Christmas the poor have no Christmas the poor have no Christmas* that Arnie always seemed to hear as the day grew closer and both the shopgirls and the Salvation Army Santas grew more harried and hollow-eyed.

They held hands until the parcels grew too many for that, and then Arnie complained goodnaturedly about how she was turning him into her beast of burden. As they were going down to the lower level and B. Dalton, where Arnie wanted to look for a book on toy-making for Dennis Guilder's old man, Leigh noticed that it had begun to snow. They stood for a moment at the window of the glassed-in stairwell, looking out like children. Arnie took her hand and Leigh looked at him, smiling. He could smell her skin, clean and a bit soapy; he could smell the fragrance of her hair. He moved his head forward a bit; she moved hers a bit toward him. They kissed lightly and she squeezed his hand. Later, after the bookstore, they stood above the rink in the center of the mall, watching the skaters as they dipped and pirouetted and swooped to the sound of Christmas carols.

It was a very good day right up until the moment that Leigh Cabot almost died.

She almost surely would have died, if not for the hitch-hiker. They had been on their way back then, and an early December twilight had long since turned to snowy dark. Christine, surefooted as usual, purred easily through the four inches of fresh light powder.

Arnie had made a reservation for an early dinner at the British Lion Steak House, Libertyville's only really good restaurant, but the time had gotten away from them and they had agreed on a quick to-go meal from the McDonald's on JFK Drive. Leigh had promised her mother she would be in by eight-thirty because the Cabots were "having friends in," and it had been quarter of eight when they left the mall.

"Just as well," Arnie said. "I'm damn near broke anyway."

The headlights picked out the hitchhiker standing at the intersection of Route 17 and JFK Drive, still five miles outside of Libertyville. His black hair was shoulder-length, speckled with snow, and there was a duffel-bag between his feet.

As they approached him, the hitchhiker held up a sign painted with Day-Glo letters. It read: LIBERTYVILLE, PA. As they drew closer, he flipped it over. The other side read: NON-PSYCHO COLLEGE STUDENT.

Leigh burst out laughing. "Let's give him a ride, Arnie."

Arnie said, "When they go out of their way to advertise their non-psychotic status, that's when you got to look out. But okay." He pulled over. That evening he would have tried to catch the moon in a bushel basket if Leigh had asked him to give it a shot.

Christine rolled smoothly to the verge of the road, tires barely slipping. But as they stopped, static blared across the radio, which had been playing some hard rock tune, and when the static cleared, there was the Big Bopper, singing "Chantilly Lace."

"What happened to the Block Party Weekend?" Leigh asked as the hitchhiker ran toward them.

"I don't know," Arnie said, but he knew. It had happened before. Sometimes all that Christine's radio would pick up was WDIL. It didn't matter what buttons you pushed or how much you fooled with the FM converter under the dashboard; it was WDIL or nothing.

He suddenly felt that stopping for the hitchhiker had been a mistake.

But it was too late for second thoughts now; the fellow had opened one of Christine's rear doors, tossed his duffel-bag onto the floor, and slipped in after it. A blast of cold air and a swirl of snow came in with him.

"Ah, man, thanks." He sighed. "My fingers and toes all took off for Miami Beach about twenty minutes ago. They must have gone somewhere, anyway, cause I sure can't feel em anymore."

"Thank my lady," Arnie said shortly.

"Thank you, ma'am," the hitchhiker said, tipping an invisible hat gallantly.

"Don't mention it," Leigh said, and smiled. "Merry Christmas."

"Same to you," the hitchhiker said, "although you'd never know there was such a thing if you'd been standing out there trying to hook a ride tonight. People just breeze by and then they're gone. *Voom.*" He looked around appreciatively. "Nice car, man. Hell of a nice car."

"Thanks," Arnie said.

"You restore it yourself?"

"Yeah."

Leigh was looking at Arnie, puzzled. His earlier expansive mood had been replaced by a curtness that was not like his usual self at all. On the radio, the Big Bopper finished and Richie Valens came on, doing "La Bamba."

The hitchhiker shook his head and laughed. "First the Big Bopper, then Richie Valens. Must be death night on the radio. Good old WDIL."

"What do you mean?" Leigh asked.

Arnie snapped the radio off. "They died in a plane crash. With Buddy Holly."

"Oh," Leigh said in a small voice.

Perhaps the hitchhiker also sensed the change in Arnie's mood; he fell silent and meditative in the back seat. Outside, the snow began to fall faster and harder. The first good storm of the season had come in.

At length, the golden arches twinkled up out of the snow.

"Do you want me to go in, Arnie?" Leigh asked. Arnie had gone nearly as quiet as stone, turning aside her bright attempts at conversation with mere grunts.

"I will," he said, and pulled in. "What do you want?"

"Just a hamburger and french fries, please." She had intended to go the whole hog—Big Mac, shake, even the cookies—but her appetite seemed to have shrunk away to nothing.

Arnie parked. In the yellow light flaring from the squat brick building's undersides, his face looked jaundiced and somehow diseased. He turned around, arm trailing over the seat. "Can I grab you something?"

"No thanks," the hitchhiker said. "Folks'll be waiting supper. Can't disappoint my mom. She kills the fatted calf every time I come h—"

The chunk of door cut off his final word. Arnie had gotten out and was headed briskly across to the IN door, his boots kicking up little puffs of new snow.

"Is he always that cheery?" the hitchhiker asked. "Or does he get sorta taciturn sometimes?"

"He's very sweet," Leigh said firmly. She was suddenly nervous. Arnie had turned off the engine and taken the keys, and she was left alone with this stranger in the back seat. She could see him in the rearview mirror, and suddenly his long black hair, tangled by the wind, his scruff of beard, and his dark eyes made him seem Manson-like and wild.

"Where do you go to school?" she asked. Her fingers were plucking at her slacks, and she made them stop.

"Pitt," the hitchhiker said, and no more. His eyes met hers in the mirror, and Leigh dropped hers hastily to her lap. Cranberry-red slacks. She had worn them because Arnie had once told her he liked them—probably because they were the tightest pair she owned, even tighter than her Levi's. She suddenly wished she had worn something else, something that could be considered provocative by no stretch of the imagination: a grain-sack, maybe. She tried to smile—it was a funny thought, all right, a grain-sack, get it, ha-ha-ho-ho, wotta knee-slapper—but no smile came. There was no way she could keep from admitting it to herself: Arnie had left her alone with this stranger (as punishment? it had been her idea to pick him up), and now she was scared.

"Bad vibes," the hitchhiker said suddenly, making her actually catch her breath. His words were flat and final. She could see Arnie through the plate-glass window, standing fifth or sixth in line. He wouldn't get up to the counter for a while. She found herself imagining the hitchhiker suddenly clamping his gloved hands around her throat. Of course she could reach the horn-ring—but would the horn sound? She found herself doubting it for no sane reason at all. She found herself thinking she could hit the horn ninety-nine times and it would honk satisfyingly. But if, on the hundredth, she was being strangled by this hitchhiker on whose behalf she had interceded, the horn wouldn't blow. Because . . . because Christine didn't like her. In fact, she believed that Christine hated her guts. It was as simple as that. Crazy but simple.

"P-Pardon me?" She glanced back in the rearview mirror and was immeasurably relieved to see that the hitchhiker wasn't looking at her at all; he was glancing around the car. He touched the seat cover with his palm, then lightly brushed the roof upholstery with the tips of his fingers.

"Bad vibes," he said, and shook his head. "This car, I don't know why, but I get bad vibes."

"Do you?" she asked, hoping her voice sounded neutral.

"Yeah. I got stuck in an elevator once when I was a little kid. Ever since then I get attacks of claustrophobia. I never had one in a car before, but boy, I got one now. In the worst way. I think you could light a kitchen match on my tongue, that's how dry my mouth is."

He laughed a short, embarrassed laugh.

"If I wasn't already so late, I'd just get out and walk. No offense to you or your guy's car," he added hastily, and when Leigh looked back into the mirror his eyes did not seem wild at all, only nervous. Apparently he wasn't kidding about the claustrophobia, and he no longer looked like Charlie Manson to her at all. Leigh wondered how she could have been so stupid . . . except she knew how, and why. She knew perfectly well.

It was the car. All day long she had felt perfectly okay riding in Christine, but now her former nervousness and dislike were back. She had merely projected her feelings onto the hitchhiker because . . . well, because you could be scared and nervous about some guy you just picked up off the road, but it was insane to be scared by a car, an inanimate construct of steel and glass and plastic and chrome. That wasn't just a little eccentric, it was *insane*.

"You don't smell anything, do you?" he asked abruptly.

"Smell anything?"

"A bad smell."

"No, not at all." Her fingers were plucking at the bottom of her sweater now, pulling off wisps of angora. Her heart was knocking unpleasantly in her chest. "It must be part of your claustrophobia whatzis."

"I guess so."

But she *could* smell it. Under the good new smells of leather and upholstery there was a faint odor: something like gone-over eggs. Just a whiff . . . a lingering whiff.

"Mind if I crank the window down a little?"

"If you want," Leigh said, and found it took some effort to keep her voice steady and casual. Suddenly her mind's eye showed her the picture that had been in the paper yesterday morning, a picture of Moochie Welch probably culled from the yearbook. The caption beneath read: *Peter Welch, victim of fatal hit-and-run incident that police feel may have been murder.*

The hitchhiker unrolled his window three inches and crisp cold air came in, driving that smell away. Inside McD's, Arnie had reached the counter and was giving his order. Looking at him, Leigh experienced such an odd swirl of love and fear that she felt nauseated by the mixture—for the sec-

ond or third time lately she found herself wishing that she had
fixed on Dennis first, Dennis who seemed so safe and sensi-
ble . . .

She turned her thoughts away from that.

"Just tell me if it gets cold on you," the hitchhiker said
apologetically. "I'm weird, I know it." He sighed. "Sometimes
I think I never should have given up drugs, you know?"

Leigh smiled.

Arnie came out with a white bag, skidded a little in the
snow, and then got behind the wheel.

"Cold like an icebox in here," he grunted.

"Sorry, man," the hitchhiker said from the back, and rolled
the window up again. Leigh waited to see if that smell would
come back, but now she could smell nothing but leather,
upholstery, and the faint aroma of Arnie's aftershave.

"Here you go, Leigh." He gave her a burger, fries, and a
small Coke. He had gotten himself a Big Mac.

"Want to thank you again for the ride, man," the hitchhiker said. "You can just drop me off at the corner of JFK
and Center, if that's cool."

"Fine," Arnie said shortly, and pulled out. The snow was
coming down even more heavily now, and the wind had begun to whoop. For the first time Leigh felt Christine skid a
bit as she felt for a grip on the wide street, which was now
almost deserted. They were less than fifteen minutes from
home.

With the smell gone, Leigh discovered that her appetite
had come back. She wolfed half of her hamburger, drank
some Coke, and stifled a burp with the back of her hand. The
corner of Center and JFK, marked with a war memorial,
came up on the left, and Arnie pulled over, pumping the
brakes lightly so Christine wouldn't slide.

"Have a nice weekend," Arnie said. He sounded more like
his usual self now. Maybe all he needed was some food,
Leigh thought, amused.

"Same goes to both of you," the hitchhiker said. "And
have a merry Christmas."

"You too," Leigh said. She took another bite of her hamburger, chewed, swallowed . . . and felt it lodge halfway
down her throat. Suddenly she couldn't breathe.

The hitchhiker was getting out. The noise of the door
opening was very loud. The sound of the latch clicking
sounded like the thud of tumblers falling in a bank-vault.
The sound of the wind was like a factory whistle.

(*this is stupid I know but I can't Arnie I can't breathe*)

I'm choking! she tried to say, and what came out was a faint, fuzzy sound that she was sure the whine of the wind must have covered. She clawed at her throat and it felt swollen and throbbing in her hand. She tried to scream. No breath to scream, no breath

(*Arnie I can't*)

at all, and she could *feel* it in there, a warm lump of burger and bun. She tried to cough it up and it wouldn't come. The dashboard lights, bright green, circular

(*cat like the eyes of a cat dear God I can't BREATHE*)

watching her—

(*God I can't BREATHE can't BREATHE can't*)

Her chest began to pound for air. Again she tried to cough up the lump of half-chewed burger and bun in her throat, but it wouldn't come. Now the sound of the wind was bigger than the world, bigger than any sound she had ever heard before, and Arnie was finally turning away from the hitchhiker to look at her; he was turning in slow motion, his eyes widening almost comically, and even his voice seemed too loud, like thunder, the voice of Zeus speaking to some poor mortal from behind a massy skystack of thunderclouds:

"LEIGH . . . ARE YOU . . . WHAT THE HELL? . . . SHE'S CHOKING! OH MY GOD SHE'S—"

He reached for her in slow motion, and then he drew his hands back, immobilized by panic.

(*Oh help me help me for God's sake do something I'm dying oh my dear God I'm choking to death on a McDonald's hamburger Arnie why don't you HELP ME?*)

and of course she knew why, he drew back because Christine didn't *want* her to have any help, this was Christine's way of getting rid of her, Christine's way of getting rid of the other woman, the competition, and now the dashboard instruments really *were* eyes, great round unemotional eyes watching her choke to death, eyes she could see only through a growing jitter of black dots, dots that burst and spread as

(*mamma oh my dear this I'm dying and SHE SEES ME SHE IS ALIVE ALIVE ALIVE OH MAMMA MY GOD CHRISTINE IS ALIVE*)

Arnie reached for her again. Now she had begun to thrash on the seat, her chest heaving spasmodically as she clawed at her throat. Her eyes were bulging. Her lips had begun to turn blue. Arnie was pounding her ineffectually on the back and yelling something. He grabbed her shoulder, apparently meaning to pull her out of the car, and then he suddenly winced and straightened, his hands going involuntarily to the small of his back.

Leigh twitched and thrashed. The blockage in her throat felt huge and hot and throbbing. She tried again to cough it up, more weakly this time. The lump didn't budge. Now the whistle of the wind was beginning to fade, everything was beginning to fade, but her need for air didn't seem so awful. Maybe she was dying, but suddenly it didn't seem so bad. Nothing was so bad, except for those green eyes staring at her from the instrument panel. They weren't unemotional anymore. Now they were blazing with hate and triumph.

(*o my God I am heartily sorry for having offended Thee I am for offending this is my act my act of of*)

Arnie had reached across from the driver's side. Now Leigh's door was suddenly jerked open and she spilled sideways into a brutal, cutting cold. The air partially revived her, made her struggle for breath seem important again, but the obstruction wouldn't move . . . it just wouldn't move.

From far away, Arnie's voice thundering sternly, the voice of Zeus: *"WHAT ARE YOU DOING? GET YOUR HANDS OFF HER!"*

Arms around her. Strong arms. The wind on her face. Snow swirling in her eyes.

(*o my God hear me a sinner this is my act of contrition I am heartily sorry for having offended OH! OWWW! what are you DOING my ribs hurts what what are you*)
and suddenly there were arms around her, crushing, and a pair of hard hands were clasped together in a knot just below her breasts, in the hollow of her solar plexus. And suddenly one thumb popped up, the thumb of a hitchhiker signalling for a ride, only the thumb drove painfully into her breastbone. At the same time the grip of the arms tightened brutally. She felt caught

(*Ohhhhhhh you're breaking my RIBS*)
in a gigantic bearhug. Her whole diaphragm seemed to heave, and something flew out of her mouth with the force of a projectile. It landed in the snow: a wet chunk of bun and meat.

"Let her *go!*" Arnie was shouting as he slipped and slid around Christine's rear deck to where the hitchhiker held Leigh's limp body like a life-sized marionette. "Let her go, you're killing her!"

Leigh began to breathe in great, tearing gasps. Her throat

and lungs seemed to burn in rivers of fire with each gulp of the cold, wonderful air. She was dimly aware that she was sobbing.

The brutal bearhug relaxed and the hands let her go. "Are you okay, girl? Are you all—"

Then Arnie was reaching past her, grabbing for the hitchhiker. He turned toward Arnie, his long black hair flying in the wind, and Arnie hit him in the mouth. The hitchhiker flailed backward, boots slipping in the snow, and landed on his back. Fresh snow as fine and dry as confectioners' sugar puffed up around him.

Arnie advanced, fists held up, eyes slitted.

She took another convulsive breath—oh, it hurt, it was like being stabbed with knives—and screamed: *"What are you doing, Arnie? Stop it!"*

He turned toward her, dazed. "Huh? Leigh?"

"He saved my life, what are you hitting him for?"

The effort was too much and the black dots began to spiral up before her eyes again. She could have leaned against the car, but she didn't want to go near it, didn't want to touch it. The dashboard instruments. Something had happened to the dashboard instruments. Something

(*eyes they turned into eyes*)

she didn't want to think about.

She staggered to a lamppost instead and hung onto it like a drunk, head down, panting. A soft, tentative arm went around her waist. "Leigh . . . honey, are you all right?"

She turned her head slightly and saw his miserable, scared face. She burst into tears.

The hitchhiker approached them carefully, wiping his bloody mouth on the sleeve of his jacket.

"Thank you," Leigh said between harsh, swift breaths. The pain was ebbing a trifle now, and the hard, cold wind was soothing on her hot face. "I was choking. I think . . . I think I would have died if you hadn't . . ."

Too much. The black dots again, all sounds fading into an eerie wind-tunnel again. She put her head down and waited for it to pass.

"It's the Heimlich Maneuver," the hitchhiker said. "They make you learn it when you go to work in the cafeteria. At school. Make you practice on a rubber dummy. Daisy Mae, they call her. And you do it, but you don't have any idea if it'll—you know—work on a real person or not." His voice was shaky, jumping in pitch from low to high and back to low again like the voice of a kid entering puberty. His voice seemed to want to laugh or cry—something—and even in the uncertain light and heavily falling snow, Leigh could see how pallid his face was. "I never thought I'd actually have to use it. Works pretty good. Did you see that fucking piece of meat fly?" The hitchhiker wiped his mouth and looked blankly at the thin froth of blood on the palm of his hand.

"I'm sorry I hit you," Arnie said. He sounded close to tears. "I was just . . . I was . . ."

"Sure, man, I know." He clapped Arnie on the shoulder. "No harm, no foul. Girl, are you all right?"

"Yes," Leigh said. Her breath was coming evenly now. Her heart was slowing down. Only her legs were bad; they were so much helpless rubber. *My God*, she thought. *I could be dead now. If we hadn't picked that guy up, and we almost didn't—*

It occurred to her that she was lucky to be alive. This cliché struck her forcibly with a stupid, undeniable power that made her feel faint. She began to cry harder. When Arnie led her back toward the car, she came with him, her head on his shoulder.

"Well," the hitchhiker said uncertainly, "I'll be off."

"Wait," Leigh said. "What's your name? You saved my life, I'd like to know your name."

"Barry Gottfried," the hitchhiker said. "At your service." Again he swept off an imaginary hat.

"Leigh Cabot," she said. "This is Arnie Cunningham. Thank you again."

"For sure," Arnie added, but Leigh heard no real thanks in his voice—only that shakiness. He handed her into the car and suddenly the smell assaulted her, attacked her: nothing mild this time, much more than just a whiff underneath. It was the smell of rot and decomposition, high and noxious. She felt a mad fright invade her brain and she thought: *It is the smell of her fury—*

The world slipped sideways in front of her. She leaned out of the car and threw up.

Then everything there went gray for a little while.

"Are you sure you're all right?" Arnie asked her for what seemed to be the hundredth time. It would also have to be for one of the last, Leigh realized with some relief. She felt very, very tired. There was a dull, throbbing pain in her chest and another one at her temples.

"I'm fine now."

"Good. Good."

He moved irresolutely, as if wanting to go but not sure it would be right yet; perhaps not until he had asked his seemingly eternal question at least once more. They were standing in front of the Cabot house. Oblongs of yellow light spilled from the windows and lay smoothly on the fresh and unmarked snow. Christine stood at the curb, idling, showing parking lights.

"You scared me when you fainted like that," Arnie said.

"I didn't faint . . . I only got fogged in for a few minutes."

"Well, you scared me. I love you, you know."

She looked at him gravely. "Do you?"

"Of course I do! Leigh, you know I do!"

She drew in a deep breath. She was tired, but it had to be said, and said right now. Because if she didn't say it now, what had happened would seem completely ridiculous by morninglight—or maybe more than ridiculous; by morninglight the idea would likely seem mad. A smell that came and went like the "mouldering stench" in a Gothic horror story? Dashboard instruments that turned into eyes? And most of all the insane feeling that the car had actually tried to kill her?

By tomorrow, even the fact that she had almost choked to death would be nothing but a vague ache in her chest and the conviction that it had been nothing, really, not a close call at all.

Except it was all true, and Arnie knew it was—yes, some part of him did—and it had to be said now.

"Yes, I think you do love me," she said slowly. She looked at him steadily. "But I won't go anywhere with you again in that car. And if you really love me, you'll get rid of it."

The expression of shock on his face was so large and so sudden that she might have struck him in the face.

"What—what are you talking about, Leigh?"

Was it shock that had caused that slapped expression? Or was some of it guilt?

"You heard what I said. I don't think you'll get rid of it—I don't know if you even can anymore—but if you want to go someplace with me, Arnie, we go on the bus. Or thumb a ride. Or fly. But I'm never going to ride in your car again. It's a death-trap."

There. She had said it; it was out.

Now the shock on his face was turning to anger—the blind, obdurate sort of anger she had seen on his face so frequently lately. Not just over the big things, but over the little ones as well—a woman going through a traffic light on the yellow, a cop who held up traffic just before it was their turn to go—but it came to her now with all the force of a revelation that his anger, corrosive and so unlike the rest of Arnie's personality, was always associated with the car. With Christine.

" 'If you love me you'll get rid of it,' " he repeated. "You know who you sound like?"

"No, Arnie."

"My mother, that's who you sound like."

"I'm sorry." She would not allow herself to be drawn; neither would she defend herself with words or end it by just going into the house. She might have been able to if she didn't feel anything for him, but she did. Her original impressions—that behind the quiet shyness Arnie Cunningham was good and decent and kind (and maybe sexy as well)—had not changed much. It was the car, that was all. That was the change. It was like watching a strong mind slowly give way under the influence of some evil, corroding, addictive drug.

Arnie ran his hands through his snow-dusted hair, a characteristic gesture of bewilderment and anger. "You had a bad choking spell in the car, okay, I can understand that you don't feel great about it. But it was the *hamburger*, Leigh, that's all. Or maybe not even that. Maybe you were trying to talk while you were chewing or inhaled at just the wrong second or something. You might as well blame Ronald McDonald. People choke on their food every now and then, that's all. Sometimes they die. You didn't. Thank God for that. But to blame my car—!"

Yes, it all sounded perfectly plausible. And *was*. Except that something was going on behind Arnie's gray eyes. A frantic something that was not precisely a lie, but . . . rationalization! A willful turning away from the truth?

"Arnie," she said, "I'm tired and my chest hurts and I've got a headache and I think I've only got the strength to say this once. Will you listen?"

"If it's about Christine, you're wasting your breath," he said, and that stubborn, mulish look was on his face again. "It's crazy to blame her and you know it is."

"Yes, I know it's crazy, and I know I'm wasting my breath," Leigh said. "But I'm asking you to listen."

"I'll listen."

She took a deep breath, ignoring the pull in her chest. She looked at Christine, idling a plume of white vapor into the thickly falling snow, then looked hastily away. Now it was the parking lights that looked like eyes: the yellow eyes of a lynx.

"When I choked . . . when I was choking . . . the instrument panel . . . the lights on it changed. They *changed*. They were . . . no, I won't go that far, but they *looked* like eyes."

He laughed, a short bark in the cold air. In the house a curtain was pulled aside, someone looked out, and then the curtain dropped back again.

"If that hitchhiker . . . that Gottfried fellow . . . if he hadn't been there, I would have died, Arnie. I would have *died*." She searched his eyes with her own and pushed ahead. *Once*, she told herself. *I only have to say this once.* "You told me that you worked in the cafeteria at LHS your first three years. I've seen the Heimlich Maneuver poster on the door to the kitchen. You must have seen it too. But you didn't try that on me, Arnie. You were getting ready to clap me on the back. That doesn't work. I had a job in a restaurant back in Massachusetts, and the first thing they teach you, even before they teach you the Heimlich Maneuver, is that *clapping a choking victim on the back doesn't work.*"

"What are you saying?" he asked in a thin, out-of-breath voice.

She didn't answer; only looked at him. He met her gaze for only a moment, and then his eyes—angry, confused, almost haunted—shifted away.

"Leigh, people forget things. You're right, I should have used it. But if you had the course, you know you can use it on yourself." Arnie laced his hands together into a fist with one thumb sticking up and pressed against his diaphragm to demonstrate. "It's just that in the heat of the moment, people forget—"

"Yes, they do. And you seem to forget a lot of things in that car. Like how to be Arnie Cunningham."

Arnie was shaking his head. "You need time to think this over, Leigh. You need—"

"That is just what I don't need!" she said with a fierceness she wouldn't have believed she still had left in her. "I never had a supernatural experience in my life—I never even be-

lieved in stuff like that—but now I wonder just what's going on and what's happening to you. They looked like *eyes*, Arnie. And later . . . afterward . . . there was a smell. A horrible, rotten smell."

He recoiled.

"You know what I'm talking about."

"No. I don't have the slightest idea."

"You just jumped as if the devil had twisted your ear."

"You're imagining things," Arnie said hotly. "A lot of things."

"That smell was *there*. And there are other things as well. Sometimes your radio won't get anything but that oldies station—"

Another flicker in his eyes, and a slight twitch at the left corner of his mouth.

"And sometimes when we're making out it just stalls, as if it didn't like it. *As if the car didn't like it, Arnie*."

"You're upset," he said with ominous flatness.

"Yes, I *am* upset," she said, beginning to cry. "Aren't *you*?" The tears trickled slowly down her cheeks. *I think this is the end of it for us, Arnie—I loved you, but I think it's over. I really think it is, and that makes me feel so sad, and so sorry.* "Your relationship with your parents has turned into a . . . an armed camp, you're running God knows what into New York and Vermont for that fat pig Will Darnell, and that car . . . that car . . ."

She could not say anything more. Her voice dissolved. She dropped her packages and bent blindly to pick them up. Exhausted and weeping, she succeeded in doing little more than stirring them around. He bent to help her and she pushed at him roughly. "Leave them alone! I'll get them!"

He stood up, his face pale and set. His expression was one of wooden fury, but his eyes . . . oh, to Leigh his eyes seemed lost.

"All right," he said, and now his voice roughened with his own tears. "Good. Join up with the rest of them if you want. You just saddle up and ride right along with all those other shitters. Who gives a tin shit?" He drew in a shivering breath, and a single hurt sob escaped him before he could clap a gloved hand brutally over his mouth.

He began to walk backward toward the car; he reached out blindly behind himself for the Plymouth and Christine was there. "Just as long as you know you're crazy. Right out of your mind! So go on and play your games! I don't need you! I don't need *any* of you!"

His voice rose to a thin scream, in devilish harmony with the wind:

"I don't need you so fuck off!"

He rushed around to the driver's side, his feet slid, and he grabbed for Christine. She was there and he didn't fall. He got in, the engine revved, the headlights came on in a huge white glare, and the Fury pulled out, rear tires spinning up a fog of snow.

Now the tears came fast and hard as she stood watching the taillights fade to round red periods and wink out as the car went around the corner. Her packages lay scattered at her feet.

And then, suddenly, her mother was there, absurdly clothed in an open raincoat, green rubber boots, and her blue flannel nightgown.

"Honey, what's wrong?"

"Nothing," Leigh sobbed.

I almost choked to death, I smelled something that might have come from a freshly opened tomb, and I think . . . yes, I think that somehow that car is alive . . . more alive every day. I think it's like some kind of horrible vampire, only it's taking Arnie's mind to feed itself. His mind and his spirit.

"Nothing, nothing's wrong, I had a fight with Arnie, that's all. Help me pick up my things, would you?"

They picked up Leigh's parcels and went in. The door shut behind them and the night belonged to the wind and to the swiftly falling snow. By morning there would be better than eight inches.

Arnie cruised until sometime after midnight, and later had no memory of it. The snow had filled the streets; they were deserted and ghostly. It was not a night for the great American motor-car. Nevertheless, Christine moved through the deepening storm with surefooted ease, even without snow tires. Now and then the prehistoric shape of a snowplow loomed and was gone.

The radio played. It was WDIL all the way across the dial. The news came on. Eisenhower had predicted, at the AFL/CIO convention, a future of labor and management marching harmoniously into the future together. Dave Beck had denied that the Teamsters Union was a front for the rackets. Rock 'n roller Eddie Cochran had been killed in a car crash while en route to London's Heathrow Airport; three hours of emergency surgery had failed to save his life. The Russians were rattling their ICBMs. WDIL played the oldies all week long, but on the weekends they got really dedicated. Fifties newscasts wow. That was

(*never heard anything like that before*)

a really neat idea. That was

(*totally insane*)

pretty neat.

The weather promised more snow.

Then music again: Bobby Darin singing "Splish-Splash," Ernie K-Doe singing "Mother-in-Law," the Kalin twins singing "When." The wipers beat time.

He looked to his right, and Roland D. LeBay was riding shotgun.

Roland D. LeBay sat there in his green pants and a faded shirt of Army twill, looking out of dark eyesockets. A beetle sat, preening, within one.

You have to make them pay, Roland D. LeBay said. *You have to make the shitters pay, Cunningham. Every last fucking one of them.*

"Yes," Arnie whispered. Christine hummed through the night, cutting the snow with fresh, sure tracks. "Yes, that's a fact." And the wipers nodded back and forth.

35 / Now This Brief Interlude

Drive that old Chrysler to Mexico, boy.
—Z. Z. Top

At Libertyville High, Coach Puffer had given way to Coach Jones, and football had given way to basketball. But nothing really changed: the LHS cagers didn't do much better than the LHS gridiron warriors—the only bright spot was Lenny Barongg, a three-sport man whose major one was basketball. Lenny stubbornly went about having the great year he needed to have if he was going to get the athletic scholarship to Marquette that he lusted after.

Sandy Galton suddenly blew town. One day he was there, the next he was gone. His mother, a forty-five-year-old wino who didn't look a day over sixty, did not seem terribly concerned. Neither did his younger brother, who pushed more dope than any other kid in Gornick Junior High. A romantic rumor that he had cut out for Mexico made the rounds at Libertyville High. Another, less romantic, rumor also made the rounds: that Buddy Repperton had been on Sandy about something and he felt it would be safer to make himself scarce.

The Christmas break approached and the school's atmosphere grew restless and rather thundery, as it always did before a long vacation. The student body's overall grade average took its customary pre-Christmas dip. Book reports were turned in late and often bore a suspicious resemblance to jacket copy (after all, how many sophomore English students are apt to call *The Catcher in the Rye* "this burning classic of postwar adolescence"?). Class projects were left half done or undone, the percentage of detention periods given for kissing and petting in the halls skyrocketed, and busts for marijuana went way up as the Libertyville High School students indulged in a little pre-Christmas cheer. So a good many of the students were up; teacher absenteeism was up; in the hallways and home-rooms, Christmas decorations were up.

Leigh Cabot was not up. She flunked an exam for the first time in her high school career and got a D on an executive typing drill. She could not seem to study; she found her mind wandering back, again and again, to Christine—to the green dashboard instruments that had become hateful, gloating cat's-eyes, watching her choke to death.

But for most, the last week of school before the Christmas break was a mellow period when offenses which would have earned detention slips at other times of the year were excused, when hard-hearted teachers would sometimes actually throw a scale on an exam where everyone had done badly, when girls who had been bitter enemies made it up, and when boys who had scuffled repeatedly over real or imagined insults did the same. Perhaps more indicative of the mellow season than anything else was the fact that Miss Rat-Pack, the gorgon of Room 23 study hall, was seen to smile . . . not just once, but several times.

In the hospital, Dennis Guilder was moderately up—he had swapped his bedfast traction casts for walking casts. Physical therapy was no longer the torture it had been. He swung through corridors that had been strung with tinsel and decorated with first-, second-, and third-grade Christmas pictures, his crutches thump-thumping along, sometimes in time to the carols spilling merrily from the overhead speakers.

It was a *caesura*, a lull, an interlude, a period of quiet. During his seemingly endless walks up and down the hospital corridors, Dennis reflected that things could be worse—much, much worse.

Before too long, they were.

36 / Buddy and Christine

Well it's out there in the distance
And it's creeping up on me
I ain't got no resistance
Ain't nothing gonna set me free.
Even a man with one eye could see
Something bad is gonna happen to me . . .
                    —The Inmates

On Tuesday, December 12, the Terriers lost to the Buccaneers 54–48 in the Libertyville High gym. Most of the fans went out into the still black cold of the night not too disappointed: every sportswriter in the Pittsburgh area had predicted another loss for the Terriers. The result could hardly be called an upset. And there was Lenny Barongg for the Terriers fans to be proud of: he scored a mind-boggling 34 points all by himself, setting a new school record.

Buddy Repperton, however, *was* disappointed.

Because he was, Richie Trelawney was also at great pains to be disappointed. So was Bobby Stanton in the back seat.

In the few months since he had been ushered out of LHS, Buddy seemed to have aged. Part of it was the beard. He looked less like Clint Eastwood and more like some hard-drinking young actor's version of Captain Ahab. Buddy had been doing a lot of drinking these last few weeks. He had been having dreams so terrible he could barely remember them. He awoke sweaty and trembling, feeling he had barely esaped some awful doom that ran dark and quiet.

The booze cut them off, though. Cut them right off at the fucking knees. Goddam right. Working nights and sleeping days, that's all it was.

He unrolled the window of his scuffed and dented Camaro, scooping in frigid air, and tossed out an empty bottle. He reached back over his shoulder and said, "Another Molotov cocktail, mess-sewer."

"Right on, Buddy," Bobby Stanton said respectfully, and slapped another bottle of Texas Driver into Buddy's hand. Buddy had treated them to a case of the stuff—enough to paralyze the entire Egyptian Navy, he said—after the game.

He spun off the cap, steering momentarily with his elbows, and then gulped down half the bottle. He handed it to Richie and uttered a long, froggy belch. The Camaro's headlights cut Route 46, running northeast as straight as a string through rural Pennsylvania. Snow-covered fields lay dreaming on either side of the road, twinkling in a billion points of light that mimed the stars in the black winter sky. He was headed—in a sort of casual, half-drunk way—for Squantic Hills. Another destination might take his fancy in the meantime, but if not, the Hills were a fine and private place to get high in peace.

Richie passed the bottle back to Bobby again, who drank big even though he hated the taste of Texas Driver. He supposed that when he got a little drunker, he wouldn't mind the taste at all. He might be hung over and puking tomorrow, but tomorrow was a thousand years away. Bobby was still excited just to be with them; he was only a freshman, and Buddy Repperton, with his near-mythic reputation for bigness and badness, was a figure he viewed with mixed fear and awe.

"Fucking clowns," Buddy said morosely. "What a bunch of fucking clowns. You call that a basketball game?"

"All a bunch of retards," Richie agreed. "Except for Barongg. Thirty-four points, not too tacky."

"I hate that fucking spade," Buddy said, giving Richie a long, measuring, drunken look. "You taking up for that jungle bunny?"

"No way, Buddy," Richie said promptly.

"Better not. I'll Barongg him."

"Which do you want first?" Bobby asked abruptly from the back seat. "The good news or the bad news?"

"Bad news first," Buddy said. He was into his third bottle of Driver now and feeling no pain—only an aggrieved anger. He had forgotten—at least for the moment—that he had been expelled; he was concentrating only on the fact that the old school team, that bunch of fucking retard assholes, had let him down. "Always bad news first." The Camaro rolled northeast at sixty-five over two-lane tar that was like a swipe of black paint across a hilly white floor. The land had begun to rise slightly as they approached Squantic Hills.

"Well, the bad news is that a million Martians just landed in New York," Bobby said. "Now you wanna hear the good news?"

"There is no good news," Buddy said in a low, morose, grieving voice. Richie would have liked to tell the kid you didn't try to cheer Buddy up when he was in a mood like this; that only made it worse. The thing to do was to let it run its course.

Buddy had been this way ever since Moochie Welch, that little four-eyed panhandling dork, got run down by some psycho on JFK Drive.

"The good news is that they eat niggers and piss gasoline," Bobby said, and roared with laughter. He laughed for quite a while before he realized he was laughing alone. Then he shut up quickly. He glanced up and saw Buddy's bloodshot eyes looking at him over the uppermost tendrils of his beard, and that red, ferrety gaze floating in the rearview mirror gave him an unpleasant thrill of fear. It occurred to Bobby Stanton that he might have shut up a minute or two too late.

Behind them, distant, perhaps as much as three miles back, headlights twinkled like insignificant yellow sparks in the night.

"You think that's funny?" Buddy asked. "You tell a fucking racist joke like that and you think it's *funny?* You're a fucking bigot, you know that?"

Bobby's mouth dropped open. "But you said—"

"I said I didn't like *Barongg.* In general I think spades are as good as white people."

Buddy considered.

"Well, almost as good."

"But—"

"You want to watch out or you'll be walking home," Buddy snarled. "With a rupture. Then you can write I HATE NIGGERS all over your fuckin truss."

"Oh," Bobby said in a small, scared voice. He felt as if he

had reached up to turn on a light and had got a whopper of an electric shock. "Sorry."

"Give me that bottle and shut your head."

Bobby handed the Driver up front with alacrity. His hand was shaking.

Buddy killed the bottle. They passed a sign which read SQUANTIC HILLS STATE PARK 3 MI. The lake at the center of the state park was a popular beach area in the summertime, but the park was closed from November to April. The road which wound through the park to Squantic Lake was kept plowed for periodic National Guard maneuvers and winter Explorer Scouts camping trips, however, and Buddy had discovered a side entrance which went around the main gate and then joined the park road. Buddy liked to go into the silent, wintry state park and cruise and drink.

Behind them, the distant twin sparks had grown to circles—dual headlights about a mile back.

"Hand me up another Molotov cocktail, you fucking racist pig."

Bobby handed up a fresh bottle of Driver, remaining prudently silent.

Buddy drank deeply, belched, and then handed the bottle across to Richie.

"No thanks, man."

"You drink it, or you may find yourself getting an enema with it."

"Sure, okay," Richie said, wishing mightily that he had stayed home tonight. He drank.

The Camaro sped along, its headlights cutting the night.

Buddy glanced into the rearview and saw the other car. It was now coming up fast. He glanced at his speedometer and saw he was doing sixty-five. The car behind them had to be doing close to seventy. Buddy felt something—a curious kind of doubling back to the dreams he could not quite remember. A cold finger seemed to press lightly against his heart.

Ahead, the road branched in two, Route 46 continuing east toward New Stanton, the other road bearing north toward Squantic Hills State Park. A large orange sign advised: CLOSED WINTER MONTHS.

Barely slowing, Buddy dragged left and shot up the hill. The approach road to the park was not so well-plowed, and overarching trees had kept the warm afternoon sun from melting off the snowpack. The Camaro slid a little before grabbing the road again. In the back seat, Bobby Stanton made a low, uneasy sound.

Buddy looked up in the rearview, expecting to see the other car shoot by along 46—after all, there was nothing up this road but a dead end as far as most drivers were concerned—but instead it took the turn even faster than Buddy had and pounded along after them, now less than a quarter of a mile behind. Its headlights were four glowing white circles that washed the Camaro's interior.

Bobby and Richie turned around to look.

"What the fuck?" Richie muttered.

But Buddy knew. Suddenly he knew. It was the car that had run down Moochie. Oh yes it was. The psycho who had greased Moochie was behind the wheel of that car, and now he was after Buddy.

He stepped down on the go, and the Camaro started to fly. The speedometer needle crept up to seventy and then gradually heeled over toward eighty. Trees blurred past, dark sketches in the night. The lights behind them did not fall back; the truth was that they were still gaining. The duals had merged into two great white eyes.

"Man, you want to slow down," Richie said. He grabbed for his seatbelt, actively scared now. "If we roll at this speed—"

Buddy didn't answer. He hunched over the wheel, alternating glances at the road ahead with glances shot into the rearview mirror, where those lights grew and grew.

"The road curves up ahead," Bobby said hoarsely. And as the curve approached, guardrail reflectors flickering chrome in the Camaro's headlights, he screamed it: *"Buddy! It curves! It curves!"*

Buddy changed down to second gear and the Camaro's engine bellowed in protest. The tachometer needle hit 6,000 rpm, danced briefly at redline-7,000, and then dropped back into a more normal range. Backfires blatted through the Camaro's straight-pipes like machine-gun fire. Buddy pulled the wheel over, and the car floated into the sharp bend. The rear wheels skimmed over hard-packed snow. At the last possible instant he shifted back up, tramped on the accelerator pedal, and let his body sway freely as the Camaro's left rear end slammed into the snowbank, digging a coffin-sized divot and then bouncing off. The Camaro slewed the other way. He went with it, then goosed the accelerator again. For one moment he thought it would not respond, that the skid would continue and they would simply barrel sideways up the road at seventy-five until they hit a bare patch and flipped over.

But the Camaro straightened out

"Holy Jesus Buddy slow down!" Richie wailed.

Buddy hung over the wheel, grinning through his beard, bloodshot eyes bulging. The bottle of Driver was clamped between his legs. *There! There, you crazy murdering sonofabitch. Let's see you do that without rolling it over!*

A moment later the headlights reappeared, closer than ever. Buddy's grin faltered and faded. For the first time he felt a sickish, unmanning tingle running up his legs toward his crotch. Fear—real fear—stole into him.

Bobby had been looking behind as the car chasing them rounded the bend, and now he turned around, his face slack and cheesy. "It dint even skid," he said. "But that's impossible! That's—"

"Buddy, who is it?" Richie asked.

He reached out to touch Buddy's elbow, and his hand was flung away with such force that his knuckles cracked on the glass of his window.

"You don't want to touch me," Buddy whispered. The road unrolled straight in front of him, not black tar now but white snow, packed and treacherous. The Camaro was rolling over this greasy surface at better than ninety miles an hour, only its roof and the orange Ping-Pong ball jammed on the top of its radio aerial visible between chest-high embankments. "You don't want to touch me, Richie. Not going this fast."

"Is it—" Richie's voice cracked and he couldn't go on.

Buddy spared him a glance, and at the sight of the fear in Buddy's small red eyes, Richie's own terror came up in his throat like hot, smooth oil.

"Yeah," Buddy said. "I think it is."

No houses up here; they were already on state land. Nothing up here but the high snow embankments and the dark interlacing of trees.

"It's gonna bump us!" Bobby screeched from the back seat. His voice was as high as an old woman's. Between his feet the remaining bottles of Texas Driver chattered wildly in their carton. "Buddy! It's gonna bump us!"

The car behind them had come to within five feet of the Camaro's back bumper; its high beams flooded the car with light bright enough to read fine print. It slipped forward even closer. A moment later there was a thud.

The Camaro shifted its stance on the road as the car behind them fell back a trifle; to Buddy it was as if they were suddenly floating, and he knew they were a hair's breadth from going into a wild, looping skid, the front end and the rear briskly swapping places until they hit something and rolled.

A droplet of sweat, warm and stinging as a tear, ran into his eye.

Gradually, the Camaro straightened out again.

When he felt that he had control, Buddy let his right foot smoothly depress the accelerator all the way. If it was Cunningham in that old rustbucket '58—ah, and hadn't that been part of the dreams he could barely remember?—the Camaro would shut him down.

The engine was now screaming. The tach needle was again on the edge of the red line at 7,000 rpm. The speedometer had passed the one hundred post, and the snowbanks streamed past them on either side in ghastly silence. The road ahead looked like a point-of-view shot in a film that had been insanely speeded up.

"Oh dear God," Bobby babbled, "oh dear God please don't let me get killed oh dear God oh holy shit—"

He wasn't there the night we trashed Cuntface's car, Buddy thought. *He doesn't know what's going on. Poor busted-luck sonofawhore.* He did not really feel sorry for Bobby, but if he could have been sorry for anyone, it would have been for the little shit-for-brains freshman. On his right, Richie Trelawney sat bolt upright and as pallid as a gravestone, his eyes eating up his face. Richie knew the score, all right.

The car whispered toward them, headlights swelling in the rearview mirror.

He can't be gaining! Buddy's mind screamed. *He can't be!* But the car behind them was indeed gaining, and Buddy sensed it was boring in for the kill. His mind ran like a rat in a cage, looking for a way out, and there was none. The slot in the left snowbank that marked the little side road he usually used to bypass the gate and get into the state park had already flashed by. He was running out of time, room, and options.

There was another soft bump, and again the Camaro slewed—this time at something over a hundred and ten miles an hour. *No hope, man,* Buddy thought fatalistically. He took his hands off the wheel altogether and grabbed his seatbelt. For the first time in his life, he snapped it shut across his waist.

At the same time, Bobby Stanton in the back seat screamed in a shrill ecstasy of fear: *"The gate, man! Oh Jesus Buddy it's the gaaaaayyyy—"*

The Camaro had breasted a final steep hill. The far side sloped down to a place where the road branched in two, becoming the ingress and egress from the state park. Between the two ways stood a small gatehouse on a concrete island—in the summertime, a lady sat in there on a camp chair and took a buck from each car that entered the park.

Now the gatehouse was flooded with ghastly light as the two cars raced toward it, the Camaro heeling steadily to port as the skid worsened.

"Fuck you, Cuntface!" Buddy screamed. *"Fuck you and the horse you rode in on!"* He yanked the wheel all the way round, twirling it with the death-knob that held one bobbing red die in alcohol.

Bobby screamed again. Richie Trelawney clapped his hands over his face, his last thought on earth a constant repetition of *Watch out for broken glass watch out for broken glass watch out for broken glass*—

The Camaro swapped ends, and now the headlights of the car following blared directly into them, and Buddy began to scream because it was Cuntface's car, all right, that grille was impossible to mistake, it seemed at least a mile wide, *only there was no one behind the wheel. The car was totally empty.*

In the last two seconds before impact, Christine's headlights shifted away to what was now Buddy's left. The Fury shot into the ingress roadway as neatly and exactly as a bullet shoots down a rifle barrel. It snapped off the wooden barrier and sent it flying end over end into the black night, round yellow reflectors flashing.

Buddy Repperton's Camaro rammed ass-backwards into the concrete island where the gatehouse stood. The eight-inch concrete lip peeled off everything bolted to the lower deck, leaving the twisted wreckage of the straight-pipes and the mufflers sitting on the snow like some weird sculpture. The Camaro's rear end was first accordioned and then demolished. Bobby Stanton was demolished along with it. Buddy was dimly aware of something hitting his back like a bucket of warm water. It was Bobby Stanton's blood.

The Camaro flipped into the air end for end, a mangled projectile in a squall of flying splinters and shattered boards, one headlight still glaring maniacally. It did a complete three-sixty and came down with a glass-jangling thud and rolled over. The firewall ruptured and the engine slid backward at an angle, crushing Richie Trelawney from the waist down. There was a coughing explosion of fire from the ruptured gas tank as the Camaro came to rest.

Buddy Repperton was alive. He had been cut in several places by flying glass—one ear had been clipped off with surgical neatness, leaving a red hole on the left side of his head—and his leg had been broken, but he was alive. His seatbelt had saved him. He thumbed the catch and it let go. The crackle of fire was like someone crumpling paper. He could feel the baking heat.

He tried to open the door, but the door was crimped shut.

Panting hoarsely, he threw himself through the empty space where the windshield had been—

—and there was Christine.

She stood forty yards away, facing him at the end of a long, slewing skidmark. The rumble of her engine was like the slow panting of some gigantic animal.

Buddy licked his lips. Something in his left side pulled and jabbed with every breath. Something busted in there too. Ribs.

Christine's engine gunned and fell off; gunned and fell off. Faintly, like something from a lunatic's nightmare, he could hear Elvis Presley singing "Jailhouse Rock."

Orange-pink points of light on the snow. The rumbling whoosh of fire. It was going to blow. It was—

It *did* blow. The Camaro's gas tank went with a hard thudding noise. Buddy felt a rude hand shove him in the back, and he flew through the air and landed in the snow on his hurt side. His jacket was flaming. He grunted and rolled in the snow, putting himself out. Then he tried to get to his knees. Behind him, the Camaro was a blazing pyre in the night.

Christine's engine, revving and falling off, revving and falling off, now more quickly, more urgently.

Buddy finally managed to get to his hands and knees. He peered at Cunningham's Plymouth through the sweaty tangles of hair hanging in his eyes. The hood had been crimped up when the Plymouth blasted through the barrier arm, and the radiator was dripping a mixture of water and antifreeze that steamed on the snow like fresh animal spoor.

Buddy licked his lips again. They felt as dry as lizard skin. His back felt warm, as if he had gotten a moderately bad sunburn; he could smell smoking cloth, but in the extremity of his shock he was unaware that both his parka and the two shirts beneath had been burned away.

"Listen," he said, hardly aware he was speaking. "Listen, hey—"

Christine's engine screamed and she came at him, rear end flirting back and forth as her tires spun through the sugary snow. The crimped hood was like a mouth in a frozen snarl.

Buddy waited on his hands and knees, resisting the overpowering urge to leap and scramble away at once, resisting—as much as he could—the wild panic that was ripping away his self-control. No one in the car. A more imaginative person would already have gone mad, perhaps.

At the last possible second he rolled to the left, screaming as the splintered ends of the broken bone in his leg ground together. He felt something bullet past him inches away, there was warm, foul-smelling exhaust in his face for a moment, and then the snow was red as Christine's taillights flashed.

She wheeled, skidding, and came back at him.

"No!" Buddy screamed. Pain lanced at his chest. "No! No! N—"

He leaped, blind reflexes taking over, and this time the bullet was closer, clipping leather off one shoe and turning his left foot instantly numb. He turned crazily on his hands and knees, like a small child playing I Witness at a birthday party. Blood from his mouth now mixed with the snot running freely from his nose; one of his broken ribs had nicked a lung. Blood ran down his cheek from the hole in his head where his ear had been. Frosty air jetted from his nose. His breath came in whistling sobs.

Christine paused.

White vapor drifted from her tailpipe; her engine throbbed and purred. The windshield was a black blank. Behind Buddy, the remains of the Camaro shot greasy flames at the sky. A razor-sharp wind fluttered and fanned them. Bobby Stanton sat in the inferno of the back seat, his head cocked, a grin locked onto his blackening face.

Playing with me, Buddy thought. *Playing with me, that's what it's doing. Like a cat with a mouse.*

"Please," he croaked. The headlights were blinding, turning the blood dripping down his cheek and from the sides of his mouth to an insectile black. "Please . . . I . . . I'll tell him I'm sorry . . . I'll crawl to him on my fucking hands and knees if that's what you want . . . only please . . . pl—"

The engine screamed. Christine leaped at him like old

doom from a dark age. Buddy howled and lunged aside again, and this time the bumper struck his shin and broke his other leg and threw him toward the embankment at the side of the park road. He hit and sprawled like a loose bag of grain.

Christine wheeled back toward him, but Buddy had seen a chance, one thin chance. He began to scramble wildly up the embankment, digging into the snow with bare hands from which the feeling had already departed, digging with his feet, ignoring the tremendous clouts of pain from his shattered legs. Now his breath came in little screams as the headlights grew brighter and the engine louder; every clod of snow threw its own jagged black shadow and he could feel it, he could feel it behind him like some horrible man-eating tiger—

There was a crunch and jangle of metal, and Buddy cried out as one of his feet was driven into the snow by Christine's bumper. He yanked it out of the snow, leaving his shoe wedged deep.

Laughing, gibbering, crying, Buddy gained the top of the bank thrown up by some National Guard Motor Pool plow days ago, tottered on the edge of balance there, pinwheeled his arms, and barely kept from rolling back down.

He turned to face Christine. The Plymouth had reversed across the road and now came forward again, rear tires spinning, digging at the snow. It crashed into the bank a foot below where Buddy was perched, making him sway and sending down a minor avalanche of snow. The hit crimped her hood in further, but Buddy was not touched. She reversed again through a mist of churned-up snow, engine now seeming to howl with frustrated anger.

Buddy screamed in triumph and shook his middle finger at her. "*Fuck you! Fuck you! Fuck you!*" A spray of mixed blood and spittle flew from his lips. With each gasping breath, the pain seemed to sink deeper into his left side, numbing and paralyzing.

Christine roared forward and slammed into the embankment again.

This time a large section of the bank, loosened in the car's first charge, came sliding down, burying Christine's wrinkled, snarling snout, and Buddy almost came down with it. He saved himself only by skittering backward rapidly, sliding on his butt and pulling himself with hands that were clawed into the snow like bloody grappling hooks, His legs were in agony now, and he flopped over on his side, gasping like a beached fish.

Christine came again.

"Get outta *here!*" Buddy cried. "Get outta *here*, you crazy *WHORE!*"

She slammed into the embankment again, and this time enough snow fell to douse her hood to the windshield. The wipers came on and began to arc back and forth, flicking melting snow away.

She reversed again, and Buddy saw that one more hit would send him cascading down onto Christine's hood with the snow. He let himself fall over backward and went rolling down the far side of the embankment, screaming each time his broken ribs bumped the ground. He came to rest in loose powder, staring up at the black sky, the cold stars. His teeth began to click helplessly together. Shudders raced through his body.

Christine didn't come again, but he could hear the soft mutter of her engine. Not coming, but waiting.

He glanced at the snowbank bulking against the sky. Beyond it, the glow of the burning Camaro had begun to wane a bit. How long had it been since the crash? He didn't know. Would anyone see the fire and come to rescue him? He didn't know that either.

Buddy became aware of two things simultaneously: that blood was flowing from his mouth—flowing at a frightening rate—and that he was very cold. He would freeze to death if someone didn't come.

Frightened all over again, he struggled and thrashed his way into a sitting position. He was trying to decide if he could worm his way back up and watch the car—it was worse, not being able to see it—when he glanced up at the embankment again. His breath snagged and stopped.

A man was standing there.

Only it wasn't a man at all; it was a corpse. A rotting corpse in green pants. It was shirtless, but a back brace splotched with gray mould was cinched around its blackening torso. White bone gleamed through the skin stretched across its face.

"That's it for you, you shitter," this starlit apparition whispered.

The last of Buddy's control broke and he began to scream hysterically, his eyes bulging, his long hair seeming to puff into a grotesque helmet around his bloody, soot-smudged face as the root of each strand stiffened and stood on end. Blood poured from his mouth in freshets and drenched the collar of his parka; he tried to skid backward, hooking into the snow with his hands again and sliding his buttocks as the thing came toward him. It had no eyes. Its eyes were gone, eaten out of its face by God knew what squirming things. *And he could smell it, oh God he could smell it and the smell was like rotting tomatoes, the smell was death.*

The corpse of Roland D. LeBay held out its decayed hands to Buddy Repperton and grinned.

Buddy screamed. Buddy howled. And suddenly he stiffened, his lips forming an O of perfect finality, puckered as if he wished to kiss the horror shambling toward him. His hands scratched and scrabbled at the left side of his shredded parka above his heart, which had finally been punctured by the jagged stub of a splintered rib. He fell backward, feet kicking grooves in the snow, his final breath slipping out in a long white jet from his slack mouth . . . like auto exhaust.

On the embankment, the thing he had seen flickered and was gone. There were no tracks.

From the far side, Christine's engine cranked up into an exhaust-crackling bellow of triumph that struck the frowning, snow-covered uplands of Squantic Hills and then echoed back.

On the far verge of Squantic Lake, some ten miles away as the crow flies, a young man who had gone out for a cross-country ski by starlight heard the sound and suddenly stopped, his hands on his poles and his head cocked.

Abruptly the skin on his back prickled into bumps, as if a goose had just walked over his grave, and although he knew it was only a car somewhere on the other side—sound carried a long way up here on still winter nights—his first thought was that something prehistoric had awakened and had tracked its prey to earth: a great wolf, or perhaps a saber-toothed tiger.

The sound was not repeated and he went on his way.

37 / Darnell Cogitates

Baby, lemme ride in your automobile,
Hey, babe, lemme ride in your automobile!
Tell me, sweet baby,
Tell me: Just how do you feel?

—Chester Burnett

Will Darnell was at the garage until after midnight on the night Buddy Repperton and his friends met Christine in Squantic Hills. His emphysema had been particularly bad that day. When it got bad, he was afraid to lie down, although he was ordinarily a perfect bear for sleep.

The doctor told him it was not at all likely that he would choke to death in his sleep, but as he grew older and the emphysema slowly tightened its grip on his lungs, he feared it more and more. The fact that his fear was irrational didn't change it in the least. Although he hadn't been inside a church of any faith since he had been twelve years old—forty-nine years ago now!—he had been morbidly interested in the circumstances surrounding the death of Pope John Paul I ten weeks before. John Paul had died in bed and had been found there in the morning. Already stiffening, probably. That was the part that haunted Will: *already stiffening, probably.*

He pulled into the garage at half-past nine, driving his 1966 Chrysler Imperial—the last car he intended to ever own. At about the same time Buddy Repperton was noticing the twin sparks of distant headlights in his rearview mirror.

Will was worth better than two million dollars, but money didn't give him much pleasure anymore, if indeed it ever had. The money didn't even seem completely real anymore. Nothing did, except the emphysema. That was hideously real, and Will welcomed anything that took his mind off it.

The problem of Arnie Cunningham, now—*that* had taken his mind off his emphysema. He supposed that was why he had let Cunningham hang around the place when all of his strongest instincts told him to get the kid out of the garage, he was in some way dangerous. Something was going on with Cunningham and his rebuilt '58. Something very peculiar.

The kid wasn't in tonight; he and the entire LHS chess club were in Philadelphia for three days at the Northern States Fall Tourney. Cunningham had laughed about that; he was much changed from the pimply, big-eyed kid that Buddy Repperton had jumped on, the kid Will had immediately (and erroneously) dismissed as a crybaby jellyfish and maybe a goddam queer in the bargain.

For one thing, he had grown cynical.

He had told Will in the office yesterday afternoon over cigars (the boy had developed a taste for those as well; Will doubted if his parents knew) that he had missed so many chess club meetings that according to the by-laws, he was no longer a member. Slawson, the faculty advisor, knew it but was conveniently overlooking it until after the Northern States Tourney.

"I've missed more meetings than anyone, but I also happen to play better than anyone else, and the shitter knows—" Arnie winced and shoved both hands into the small of his back for a moment.

"You ought to get a doctor to look at that," Will remarked.

Arnie winked, suddenly looking much older than nearly eighteen. "I don't need anything but a good Christian fuck to stretch the vertebrae."

"So you're going to Philly?" Will had been disappointed, even though Cunningham had the off-time coming; it meant he would have to put Jimmy Sykes in charge for the next couple of nights, and Jimmy didn't know his ass from ice cream.

"Sure. I'm not about to turn down three days of bright lights," Arnie said. He saw Will's sour face and had grinned. "Don't worry, man. This close to Christmas, all your regulars are buying toys for the kiddies instead of spark plugs and carburetor kits. This place will be dead until next year, and you know it."

That was certainly true enough, but he hadn't needed a snotnose kid to point it out for him.

"You want to go to Albany for me after you get back?" Will had asked.

Arnie looked at him carefully. "When?"

"This weekend."

"Saturday?"

"Yes."

"What's the deal?"

"You take my Chrysler to Albany, that's the fucking deal. Henry Buck has fourteen clean used cars he wants to get rid of. He *says* they're clean. You go look at them. I'll give you a blank check. If they look good, you make the deal. If they look hot, tell him to take a flying fuck at a rolling doughnut."

"And what do I take with me?"

Will had looked at him for a long time. "Getting scared, Cunningham?"

"No." Arnie crushed his cigar out half-smoked. He looked at Will defensively. "Maybe I just feel the odds getting a little longer each time I do it. Is it coke?"

"I'll get Jimmy to do it," Will said brusquely.

"Just tell me what it is."

"Two hundred cartons of Winstons."

"All right."

"You sure? Just like that?"

Arnie had laughed. "It'll be a break from chess."

Will parked the Chrysler in the stall closest to his office, the one with MR. DARNELL   DO NOT BLOCK! painted inside the lines. He got out and slammed the door, puffing, laboring for breath. The emphysema was sitting on his chest, and tonight it seemed to have brought its brother. No, he just wasn't going to lie down, no matter what that asshole doctor said.

Jimmy Sykes was apathetically wielding the big push broom. Jimmy was tall and gangling, twenty-five years old. His light mental retardation made him look perhaps eight years younger. He had started combing his hair back in a fifties-style ducktail, in imitation of Cunningham, whom Jimmy almost worshipped. Except for the low *whssht, whssht* of the broom's bristles on the oil-stained concrete, the place was silent. And empty.

"Place is really jumpin tonight, Jimmy, huh?" Will wheezed.

Jimmy looked around. "No, sir, Mr. Darnell, nobody been in since Mr. Hatch came and got his Fairlane, an that was half an hour ago."

"Just joking," Will said, wishing again that Cunningham were here. You couldn't talk to Jimmy except on a perfectly literal Dick-and-Jane level. Still, maybe he would invite him in for a cup of coffee with a slug of Courvoisier tipped in for good measure. Make it a threesome. Him, Jimmy, and the emphysema. Or maybe, since the emphysema had brought its brother tonight, you'd have to call it a foursome. "What do you say about—"

He broke off suddenly, noticing that stall twenty was empty. Christine was gone.

"Arnie came in?" he said.

"Arnie?" Jimmy repeated, blinking stupidly.

"Arnie, Arnie Cunningham," Will said impatiently. "How many Arnies do you know? His car's gone."

Jimmy looked around at stall twenty and frowned. "Oh. Yeah."

Will smiled. "Hotshot got knocked out of his hotshot chess tournament, huh?"

"Oh, did he?" Jimmy asked. "Jeez, that's too bad, huh?"

Will restrained an urge to grab Jimmy and give him a shake and a wallop. He would not get angry; that only made it harder to breathe, and he would end up having to shoot his lungs full of the horrible-tasting stuff from his aspirator. "Well, what did he say, Jimmy? What did he say when you saw him?" But Will knew suddenly and surely that Jimmy hadn't seen Arnie.

Jimmy finally understood what Will was driving at. "Oh, I didn't *see* him. Just saw Christine go out the door, you know. Boy, that's some pretty car, ain't it? He fixed it up like magic."

"Yes," Will said. "Like magic." It was a word that had occurred to him in connection with Christine before. He suddenly changed his mind about inviting Jimmy in for coffee and brandy. Still looking at stall twenty, he said, "You can go home now, Jimmy."

"Aw, jeez, Mr. Darnell, you said I could have six hours tonight. That ain't over until ten."

"I'll punch you out at ten."

Jimmy's muddy eyes brightened at this unexpected, almost unheard-of largesse. "Really?"

"Yeah, really, really. Make like a tree and leave, Jimmy, okay?"

"Sure," Jimmy said, thinking that for the first time in the five or six years he had worked for Will (he had trouble remembering which it was, although his mother kept track of it, the same as she kept track of all his tax papers), the old grouch had gotten the Christmas spirit. Just like in that movie about the three ghosts. Summoning up his own Christmas spirit, Jimmy cried: "That's a big ten-four, good buddy!"

Will winced and lumbered into his office. He turned on the Mr. Coffee and sat down behind his desk, watching as Jimmy put away his broom, turned out most of the overhead fluorescents, and got his heavy coat.

Will leaned back and thought.

It was, after all, his brains that had kept him alive all these years, alive and one step ahead; he had never been handsome, he had been fat all of his adult life, and his health had always been terrible. A childhood bout of scarletina one spring had been followed by a mild case of polio; he had been left with a right arm that operated at only about seventy percent capacity. As a young man he had endured a plague of boils. When Will was forty-three his doctor had discovered a large, spongy growth under one arm. It had turned out to be non-malignant, but the removal surgery had kept him on his back most of one summer, and as a result he had developed bedsores. A year later he had almost died of double pneumonia. Now it was incipient diabetes and emphysema. But his brains had always been fine and dandy, and his brains kept him one step ahead.

So he leaned back and thought about Arnie. He supposed one of the things that had favorably impressed him about Cunningham after he had stood up to Repperton that day was a certain similarity to the long-ago teenaged Will Darnell. Of course, Cunningham wasn't sickly, but he had been pimply, disliked, a loner. Those things had all been true of the young Will Darnell.

Cunningham had brains, too.

Brains and that car. That strange car.

"Good night, Mr. Darnell," Jimmy called. He stood by the door for a moment and then added uncertainly, "Merry Christmas."

Will raised his hand in a wave. Jimmy left. Will heaved his bulk out of his chair, got the bottle of Courvoisier out of the filing cabinet, and set it down next to the Mr. Coffee. Then he sat down again. A rough chronology was ticking through his mind.

August: Cunningham brings in an old wreck of a '58 Plymouth and parks it in stall twenty. It looks familiar, and it should. It's Rollie LeBay's Plymouth. And Arnie doesn't know it—he has no need to know it—but once upon a time Rollie LeBay also made an occasional run to Albany or Burlington or Portsmouth for Will Darnell . . . only in those dim dead days, Will had a '54 Cadillac. Different transport cars, same false-bottom trunk with hidden compartment for fireworks, cigarettes, booze, and pot. In those days Will had never heard of cocaine. He supposed no one but jazz musicians in New York had.

Late August: Repperton and Cunningham get into it, and Darnell kicks Repperton out. He's tired of Repperton, the constant braggadocio, the cock-of-the-walk manner. He's hurting custom, and while he'll make all the runs into New York and New England that Will wants, he's careless, and carelessness is dangerous. He has a tendency to exceed the double-nickel speed limit, he's gotten speeding tickets. All it would take is one nosy cop to put them all in court. Darnell isn't afraid of going to jail—not in Libertyville—but it would look bad. There was a time when he didn't care much how things looked, but he's older now.

Will got up, poured coffee, and tipped in a capful of brandy. He paused, thought it over, and tipped in a second capful. He sat down, took a cigar out of his breast pocket, looked at it, and lit it. Fuck you, emphysema. Take this.

Fragrant smoke rising around him, good hot coffee laced with brandy before him, Darnell stared out into his shadowy, silent garage and thought some more.

September: The kid asks him to jump an inspection sticker and loan him a dealer plate so he can take his girl to a football game. Darnell does it—hell, there was a day when he used to *sell* an inspection sticker for seven dollars and never even look at the car it was going on. Besides, the kid's car is looking good. A little rough, maybe, and it's still more than a little noisy, but all in all, pretty damn good. He's doing a real job of restoration.

And that's pretty damn strange, isn't it, when you consider that *no one has ever seen him really work on it*.

Oh, little things, sure. Replacing bulbs in the parking lights. Changing tires. The kid is no dummy about cars: Will sat right in this chair one day and watched him replace the upholstery in the back seat. But no one has seen him working on the car's exhaust system, which was totally shot when he wheeled the '58 in here for the first time late last summer.

And no one has seen him doing any bodywork, either, although the Fury's bod, which had an advanced case of cancer when the kid brought it in, now looks cherry.

Darnell knew what Jimmy Sykes thought, because he had asked him once. Jimmy thought Arnie did the serious work at night, after everyone was gone.

"That's one hell of a lot of night work," Darnell said aloud, and felt a sudden chill that not even the brandy-laced coffee could dispel. A lot of night work, yeah. It must have been. Because what the kid seemed to be doing days was listening to the greaser music on WDIL. That, and a lot of aimless fooling around.

"I guess he does the big stuff at night," Jimmy had said, with all the guileless faith of a child explaining how Santa Claus gets down the chimney or how the tooth fairy put the quarter under his pillow. Will didn't believe in either Santa Claus or the tooth fairy, and he didn't believe that Arnie had restored Christine at night, either.

Two other facts rolled around uneasily in his mind like pool balls looking for a pocket in which to come to rest.

He knew that Cunningham had been driving the car around out back a lot before it was street-legal, that was one thing. Just cruising slowly up and down the narrow lanes between the thousands of junked cars in the block-long back lot. Driving at five miles an hour, around and around after dark, after everyone had gone home, circling the big crane with the round electromagnet and the great box of the car-crusher. Cruising. The one time Darnell asked him about it, Arnie had told him he was checking out a shimmy in the front end. But the kid couldn't lie for shit. No one ever checked out a shimmy at five miles an hour.

That was what Cunningham did after everyone else went home. That had been his night work. Cruising out back, threading his way in and out of the junkers, headlights flickering unsteadily in their rust-eaten sockets.

Then there was the Plymouth's odometer. It ran backward. Cunningham had pointed that out to him with a sly little smile. It ran backward at an extremely fast rate. He told Will that he figured the odometer turned back five miles or so for every actual mile travelled. Will had been frankly amazed. He had heard of setting odometers back in the used-car business, and he had done a good bit of it himself (along with stuffing transmissions full of sawdust to stifle their death whines and pouring boxes of oatmeal into terminally ill radiators to temporarily plug their leaks), but he had never seen one that ran backward spontaneously. He would have thought it impossible. Arnie had just smiled a funny little smile and called it a glitch.

It was a glitch, all right, Will thought. One hell of a glitch.

The two thoughts clicked lazily off each other and rolled in different directions.

Boy, that's some pretty car, isn't it? He fixed it up like magic.

Will didn't believe in Santa Claus or the tooth fairy, but he was perfectly willing to acknowledge that there were strange things in the world. A practical man recognized that and put it to use if he could. A friend of Will's who lived in Los Angeles claimed he had seen the ghost of his wife before the big quake of '67, and Will had no particular reason to doubt the claim (although he would have doubted it completely if the friend had had anything to gain). Quent Youngerman, another friend, had claimed to have seen his father, long dead, standing at the foot of his hospital bed after Quent, a steelworker, had taken a terrible fall from the fourth floor of a building under construction down on Wood Street.

Will had heard such stories off and on all his life, as most people undoubtedly did. And as most thinking people probably did, he put them in a kind of open file, neither believing nor disbelieving, unless the teller was an obvious crank. He put them in that open file because no one knew where people came from when they were born and no one knew where people went when they died, and not all the Unitarian ministers and born-again Jesus-shouters and Popes and Scientologists in the world could convince Will otherwise. Just because some people went crazy on the subject didn't mean they knew anything. He put stuff like that in that open file because nothing really inexplicable had ever happened to him.

Except maybe something like that was happening now.

November: Repperton and his good buddies beat the living shit out of Cunningham's car at the airport. When it comes in on the tow-truck, it looks like the Green Giant shat all over it. Darnell looks at it and thinks, *It's never gonna run again. That's all; it's never gonna run another foot.* At the end of the month the Welch kid gets killed on JFK Drive.

December: A State Police detective comes sucking around. Junkins. He comes sucking around one day and talks to Cunningham, then he comes sucking around on a day when Cunningham isn't here and wants to know how come the kid is lying about how much damage Repperton and his dogturd friends (of whom the late and unlamented Peter "Moochie" Welch was one) did to Cunningham's Plymouth. *Why you talking to me?* Darnell asks him, wheezing and coughing through a cloud of cigar smoke. *Talk to him, it's his fucking Plymouth, not mine. I just run this place so working joes can keep their cars running and keep putting food on the table for their families.*

Junkins listens patiently to this rap. He knows Will Darnell is doing a hell of a lot more than just running a do-it-yourself garage and a junkyard, but Darnell *knows* he knows, so that's okay.

Junkins lights a cigarette and says, *I'm talking to you because I already talked to the kid and he won't tell me. For a little while there I thought he wanted to tell me; I got the feeling he's scared green about something. Then he tightened up and wouldn't tell me squat.*

Darnell says, *If you think Arnie ran down that Welch kid, say so.*

Junkins says, *I don't. His parents say he was home asleep, and it doesn't feel like they're lying to cover up for him. But Welch was one of the guys that trashed his car, we're pretty sure of that, and I'm positive he's lying about how bad they trashed it and I don't know why and it's driving me crazy.*

Too bad, Darnell says with no sympathy at all.

Junkins asks, *How bad was it, Mr. Darnell? You tell me.*

And Darnell tells his first and only lie during the interview with Junkins: *I really didn't notice.*

He noticed, all right, and he knows why Arnie is lying about it, trying to minimize it, and this cop would know why too, if it wasn't so obvious he was walking all over it instead of seeing it. Cunningham is lying because the damage was *horrible,* the damage was much worse than this state gumshoe can imagine, those hoods didn't just beat up on Cunningham's '58, they *killed* it. Cunningham is lying because, although nobody saw him do much of anything during the week after the tow-truck brought Christine back to stall twenty, *the car was basically as good as new—even better than it had been before.*

Cunningham lied to the cop because the truth was incredible.

"Incredible," Darnell said out loud, and drank the rest of his coffee. He looked down at the telephone, reached for it, and then drew his hand back. He had a call to make, but it might be better to finish thinking this through first—have all his ducks in a row.

He himself was the only one (other than Cunningham himself) who could appreciate the incredibility of what had happened: the car's complete and total regeneration. Jimmy was too soft in the attic, and the other guys were in and out, not regular custom at all. Still, there had been comments about what a fantastic job Cunningham had done; a lot of the guys who had been doing repairs on their rolling iron during that week in November had used the word incredible, and several of them had looked uneasy. Johnny Pomberton, who bought and sold used trucks, had been trying to get an old dumpster he'd picked up in running shape that week. Johnny knew cars and trucks better than anyone else in Libertyville, maybe anyone else in all of Pennsylvania. He told Will frankly and flat-out that he couldn't believe it. *It's like voodoo,* Johnny Pomberton had said, and then uttered a laugh without much humor. Will only sat there looking politely interested, and after a second or two the old man shook his head and went away.

Sitting in his office and looking out at the garage, eerily silent in the slack time that came every year in the weeks before Christmas, Will thought (not for the first time) that most people would accept anything if they saw it happen right before their very eyes. In a very real sense there was no supernatural, no abnormal; what happened, happened, and that was the end.

Jimmy Sykes: *Like magic.*

Junkins: *He's lying about it, but I'll be goddamned if I know why.*

Will pulled open his desk drawer, denting his paunch, and found his note-minder book for 1978. He paged through it and found his own scrawled entry: *Cunningham. Chess tourney. Philly Sheraton Dec. 11–13.*

He called Directory Assistance, got the number of the hotel, and made the call. He was not too surprised to feel his heartbeat shifting into a higher gear as the phone rang and the desk clerk picked it up.

Like magic.

"Hello, Philadelphia Sheraton."

"Hello," Will said. "You have a chess tournament put up there, I th—"

"Northern States, yessir," the desk clerk broke in. He sounded quick and almost insufferably young.

"I'm calling from Libertyville, Pee-Ay," Will said. "I believe you have an LHS student named Arnold Cunningham registered. He's one of the chess tourney kids. I'd like to speak to him, if he's in."

"Just a moment, sir, I'll see."

Clunk. Will was put on hold. He cocked himself back in his swivel chair and sat that way for what seemed to be a very long time, although the red second-hand on the office clock only revolved once. *He won't be there, and if he is, I'll eat my—*

"Hello?"

The voice was young, warily curious, and unmistakably Cunningham's. Will Darnell felt a peculiar lift–drop in his belly, but none of it showed in his voice; he was much too old for that.

"Hi, Cunningham," he said. "Darnell."

"Will?"

"Yeah."

"What are you up to, Will?"

"How you doing, kid?"

"Won yesterday and drew today. Bullshit game. Couldn't seem to keep my mind on it. What's up?"

Yes, it was Cunningham—him without a doubt.

Will, who would no more call someone without a cover story than he would go out without his skivvies on, said smoothly, "You got a pencil, kiddo?"

"Sure."

"There's an outfit on North Broad Street, United Auto Parts. You think you could go by there and see what they've got for tires?"

"Retreads?" Arnie asked.

"First-lines."

"Sure, I can go by. I'm free tomorrow afternoon from noon until three."

"That'll be fine. You ask for Roy Mustungerra, and mention my name."

"Spell that."

Will spelled it.

"That's all?"

"Yeah . . . except I hope you get your ass whupped."

"Fat chance," Cunningham said, and laughed. Will told him goodbye and hung up.

It was Cunningham, no doubt about that. Cunningham was in Philadelphia tonight, and Philadelphia was almost three hundred miles away.

Who could he have given an extra set of keys to?

The Guilder kid.

Sure! Except the Guilder kid was in the hospital.

His girl.

But she didn't have a driver's license or even a permit. Arnie had said so.

Someone else.

There *was* no one else. Cunningham wasn't close to anyone else except for Will himself, and Will knew damned well Cunningham had never given him a dupe set of keys.

Like magic.

Shit.

Will leaned back in his chair again and lit another cigar. When it was going and the neatly clipped-off end was in his ashtray, he looked up at the raftering smoke and thought it over. Nothing came. Cunningham was in Philly and he had gone on the high school bus, but his car was gone. Jimmy Sykes had seen it pulling out, but Jimmy hadn't seen who was driving it. Now just what did all of that mean? What did it add up to?

Gradually, his mind turned into other channels. He thought of his own high school days, when he had had the lead part in the senior play. His part had been that of the minister who is driven to suicide by his lust for Sadie Thompson, the girl he has set out to save. He had brought down the house. His one moment of glory in a high school career that had been devoid of sporting or academic triumphs, and maybe the high point of his youth—his father had been a drunk, his mother a drudge, his one brother a deadbeat with his own moment of glory coming somewhere in Germany, his only applause the steady pounding of German 88s.

He thought of his one girlfriend, a pallid blonde named Wanda Haskins, whose white cheeks had been splattered with freckles which grew painfully profuse in the August sun. They almost surely would have been married—Wanda was one of four girls that Will Darnell had actually fucked (he excluded whores from his count). She was surely the only one he had ever loved (always assuming there was such a thing—and, like the supernatural events he had sometimes heard about but never witnessed, he could doubt its existence but not disprove it), but her father had been in the Army, and Wanda had been an Army brat. At the age of fifteen—perhaps only a year before the mystic shift in the balance of power from the hands of the old into those of the young—she and her family had moved to Wichita, and that had been the end of that.

There was a certain lipstick she had worn, and in that long-ago summer of 1934 it had tasted like fresh raspberries to a Will Darnell who was still quite slim and clear-eyed and ambitious and young. It had been a taste to make the left hand stray to the erect and enthusiastic root of the penis in the middle of the night . . . and even before Wanda Haskins consented, they had danced that sweet and special dance in Will Darnell's dreams. In his narrow child's bed that was too short for his growing legs, they had danced.

And, now thinking of this dance, Will ceased to think and began to dream and, ceasing to dream, began to dance again.

He awakened from a sleep that had never really deepened solidly some three hours later; he awoke to the sound of the big garage door rattling up and the inside light over the door—no fluorescent but a blaring 200-watt bulb—coming on.

Will tilted his chair back down in a hurry. His shoes hit the mat under his desk (BARDAHL written across it in raised rubber letters), and it was the shock of pins and needles in his feet more than anything else that brought him awake.

Christine moved slowly across the garage toward stall twenty and slipped in.

Will, hardly convinced even now that he was awake, watched her with a curious lack of excitement which perhaps only belongs to those summoned directly from their dreams. He sat upright behind his desk, hamlike arms planted on his dirty, doodled-upon blotter, and watched her.

The engine raced once, twice. The bright new exhaust pipe shot blue smoke.

Then the motor shut down.

Will sat there, not moving.

His door was shut, but there was an intercom, always on,

between the office and the long, barnlike garage area. It was the same intercom on which he had heard the beginnings of the Cunningham-Repperton title fight back in August. From the intercom's speaker he now heard the steady tick of metal as the engine cooled. He heard nothing else.

No one got out of Christine, because there was no one in her to get out.

He put stuff like that in an open file because nothing really inexplicable had ever happened to him . . . except maybe something like that was happening now.

He had seen her cross the cement to stall twenty, the automatic door rattling shut against the cold December night behind her. And experts, examining the case later, could say: *The witness had dozed and then fallen asleep, he admits that much, and that he was dreaming . . . what he claims to have seen was obviously nothing more or less than an extension of that dream, an outward stimulus causing a subjective range of spontaneous, dream-oriented imagery. . . .*

Yes, they could say that, just as Will could dream of dancing with fifteen-year-old Wanda Haskins . . . but the reality was a hard-headed man of sixty-one, a man who had long since jettisoned any last romantic notions.

And he had *seen* Cunningham's '58 glide across the garage empty, the steering wheel moving all by itself as the car slipped into her accustomed stall. He had *seen* the headlights go off, and he had heard the eight-cylinder engine as it died.

Now, feeling oddly boneless, Will Darnell got up, hesitated, went to the door of his office, hesitated again, and then opened it. He walked out and moved down the ranks of slant-parked cars to stall twenty. His footfalls echoed behind him and then died out in a mystery.

He stood beside the car with her rich two-tone body, red and white. The paintjob was deep and clear and perfect, unmarred by the smallest chip or the slightest touch of rust. The glass was clear and unbroken, not marked by so much as a nick caused by a random-flying pebble.

The only sound now was the slow drip of melting snow from the front and rear bumpers.

Will touched the hood. It was warm.

He tried the driver's side door, and it opened freely. The smell that issued forth was the warm smell of new leather, new plastic, new chrome—except that there seemed to be another, more unpleasant smell beneath it. An earthy smell.

Will breathed deep but could not place it. He thought briefly
of old turnips in his father's basement vegetable bin, and his
nose wrinkled.

He leaned in. There were no keys in the ignition. The
odometer read 52,107.8.

Suddenly, the empty ignition slot set into the dashboard
revolved, the black slit heeling over of its own accord past
ACC to START. The hot engine caught at once and rumbled
steadily, full of contented high-octane power.

Will's heart staggered in his chest. His breath caught. Gasping and whooping noisily for breath, he hurried back to his
office to find the spare aspirator in one of his desk drawers.
His breath, thin and impotent, sounded like winter wind under an entryway door. His face was the color of old candle-
wax. His fingers caught in the loose flesh of his throat and
pulled restlessly.

Christine's engine turned off again.

No sound now but the tick and click of cooling metal.

Will found his aspirator, plunged it deep into his throat,
depressed the trigger, and inhaled. Little by little, the feeling
that a wheelbarrowful of cinderblocks was sitting on his chest
dissipated. He sat down in the swivel chair and listened gratefully to the sane and expected creak of protest from its
springs. He covered his face momentarily with his fat hands.

Nothing really inexplicable . . . until now.

He had *seen* it.

*Nothing had been driving that car. It had come in empty,
smelling of something like rotting turnips.*

And even then, in spite of his dread, Will's mind began to
turn and he began wondering how he could put what he
knew to his own advantage.

38 / Breaking Connections

Well mister, I want a yellow convertible,
Four-door DeVille,
With a Continental spare and wire-chrome wheels.
I want power steering,
And power brakes;
I want a powerful motor with a jet offtake . . .
I want a shortwave radio,
I want TV and a phone,
You know I gotta talk to my baby
When I'm ridin along.

—Chuck Berry

The burned-out wreck of Buddy Repperton's Camaro was found late on Wednesday afternoon by a park ranger. An old lady who lived with her husband in the tiny town of Upper Squantic had called the ranger station on the lake side of the park. She was badly afflicted with arthritis, and sometimes she couldn't sleep. Last night she thought she had seen flames coming from near the park's south gate. At what time? She reckoned it to be around quarter past ten, because she had been watching the Tuesday Night Movie on CBS and it hadn't been but half over.

On Thursday, a news photo of the burned car appeared on the front page of the Libertyville *Keystone,* under a headline which read: THREE KILLED IN CAR CRASH AT SQUANTIC HILLS STATE PARK. A State Police source was quoted as saying "liquor was probably a factor"—an officially opaque way of saying that the shattered remains of over half a dozen bottles of a juice-and-wine combination sold under the trade name Texas Driver had been found in the wreckage.

The news struck particularly hard at Libertyville High School; the young always have the greatest difficulty accepting unpleasant intelligence of their own mortality. Perhaps the holiday season made it that much harder.

Arnie Cunningham found himself terribly depressed by the news. Depressed and frightened. First Moochie; now Buddy, Richie Trelawney, and Bobby Stanton. Bobby Stanton, a dip-shit little freshman Arnie had never even heard of—what had a dipshit little kid like that been doing with the likes of Buddy Repperton and Richie Trelawney anyway? Didn't he know that was like going into a den of tigers with nothing for protection but a squirt gun? He found it unaccountably hard to accept the grapevine version, which was simply that Buddy and his friends had gotten pretty well squiffed at the basket-ball game, had gone out cruising and drinking, and had come to a bad end.

He couldn't quite lose the feeling that he was somehow involved.

Leigh had stopped talking to him since the argument. Arnie didn't call her—partly out of pride, partly out of shame, partly out of a wish that she would call him first and things could go back to what they had been . . . before.

Before what? his mind whispered. *Well, before she almost choked to death in your car, for one thing. Before you tried to punch out the guy who saved her life.*

But she wanted him to sell Christine. And that was simply impossible . . . wasn't it? How could he do that after he had put so much time and effort and blood and—yes, it was true—even tears into it?

It was an old rap, and he didn't want to think about it. The final bell rang on that seemingly endless Thursday, and he went out to the student parking lot—almost ran out—and nearly dived into Christine.

He sat there behind the wheel and drew a long, shuddering breath, watching the first snowflakes of an afternoon flurry twist and skirl across the bright hood. He dug for his keys, pulled them out of his pocket, and started Christine up. The motor hummed confidently and he pulled out, tires rolling and crunching over the packed snow. He would have to put snow tires on eventually, he supposed, but the truth was, Christine didn't seem to need them. She had the best traction of any car he had ever driven.

He felt for the radio knob and turned on WDIL. Sheb Wooley was singing "The Purple People Eater." That raised a smile on his face at last.

Just being behind Christine's wheel, in control, made everything seem better. It made everything seem manageable.

Hearing about Repperton and Trelawney and the little shitter stepping out that way had been a terrible shock, naturally, and after the hard feelings of the late summer and this fall, it was probably natural enough for him to feel a little guilty. But the simple truth was, he had been in Philly. He hadn't had anything to do with it; it was impossible.

He had just been feeling low about things in general. Dennis was in the hospital. Leigh was behaving stupidly—as if his car had grown hands and jammed that piece of hamburger down her throat, for Christ's sake. And he had quit the chess club today.

Maybe the worst part of that had been the way Mr. Slawson, the faculty advisor, had accepted his decision without even trying to change his mind. Arnie had given him a lot of guff about how little time he had these days, and how he was simply going to have to cut back on some of his activities, and Mr. Slawson had simply nodded and said, *Okay, Arnie, we'll be right here in Room 30 if you change your mind.* Mr. Slawson had looked at him with his faded blue eyes that his thick glasses magnified to the size of repulsive boiled eggs, and there had been something in them—was it reproach?

Maybe it had been. But the guy hadn't even *tried* to persuade him to stay, that was the thing. He should have at least *tried,* because Arnie was the best the LHS chess club had to offer, and Slawson knew it. If he had tried, maybe Arnie would have changed his mind. The truth was, he did have a little more time now that Christine was . . . was . . .

What?

. . . well, fixed up again. If Mr. Slawson had said something like *Hey Arnie, don't be so rash, let's think this over, we could really use you . . .* if Mr. Slawson had said something like that, why, he might have reconsidered. But not Slawson. Just we'll be right here in Room 30 if you change your mind, and blah-blah and yak-yak, what a fucking shitter, just like the rest of them. It wasn't his fault that LHS had been knocked out in the semi-final round; he had won four games before that and would have won in the finals if he had gotten a chance. It was those two shitters Barry Qualson and Mike Hicks that had lost it for them; both of them played chess as if maybe they thought Ruy Lopez was some new kind of soft drink or something. . . .

He stripped the wrapper and the foil from a stick of gum,

folded the gum into his mouth, balled the wrapper, and flicked it into the litterbag hanging from Christine's ashtray with neat accuracy. "Right up the little tramp's ass," he muttered, and then grinned. It was a hard, spitless grin. Above it, his eyes moved restlessly from side to side, looking mistrustfully out at a world full of crazy drivers and stupid pedestrians and general idiocy.

Arnie cruised aimlessly around Libertyville, his thoughts continuing to run on in this softly paranoid and bitterly comforting fashion. The radio spilled out a steady flood of golden oldies, and today all of them seemed to be instrumentals— "Rebel Rouser," "Wild Weekend," "Telstar," Sandy Nelson's jungle-driven "Teen Beat," and "Rumble" by Linc Wray, the greatest of them all. His back nagged, but in a low key. The flurry intensified briefly to a dark gray cloud of snow. He popped on his headlights, and just as quickly the snow tapered off and the clouds broke, spilling through bars of remote and coldly beautiful late-afternoon winter sun.

He cruised.

He came out of his thoughts—which now were that Repperton had maybe come to a perfectly fitting end after all— and was shocked to realize that it was nearly quarter of six, and dark. Gino's Pizza was coming up on the left, the little green neon shamrocks shimmering in the dark. Arnie pulled over to the curb and got out. He started to cross the street, then realized he had left his keys in Christine's ignition.

He leaned in to get them . . . and suddenly the smell assaulted him, the smell Leigh had told him about, the smell he had denied.

It was here now, as if it had come out when he left the car—a high, rotten, meaty smell that made his eyes water and his throat close. He snatched the keys and stood back, trembling, looking at Christine with something like horror.

Arnie, there was a smell. A horrible, rotten smell . . . you know what I'm talking about.

No, I don't have the slightest idea . . . you're imagining things.

But if she was, so was he.

Arnie turned suddenly and ran across the street to Gino's as if the devil was on his tail.

Inside, he ordered a pizza he didn't really want, changed some quarters for dimes, and slipped into the telephone booth beside the juke. It was thumping some current tune Arnie had never heard before.

He called home first. His father answered, his voice oddly toneless—Arnie had never heard Michael's voice quite that way before, and his unease deepened. His father sounded like Mr. Slawson. This Thursday afternoon and evening were taking on the maroon tones of nightmare. Beyond the glass walls of the booth, strange faces drifted dreamily past, like untethered balloons on which someone had crudely drawn human faces. God at work with a Magic Marker.

Shitters, he thought disjointedly. *All a bunch of shitters.*

"Hello, Dad," he said uncertainly. "Look, I—uh, I kind of lost track of the time here. I'm sorry."

"That's all right," Michael said. His voice was almost a drone, and Arnie felt his unease deepen into something like fright. "Where are you, the garage?"

"No—uh, Gino's. Gino's Pizza. Dad, are you okay? You sound funny."

"I'm fine," Michael said. "Just scraped your dinner down the garbage disposal, your mother's upstairs crying again, and you're having a pizza. I'm fine. Enjoying your car, Arnie?"

Arnie's throat worked, but no sound came out.

"Dad," he managed finally, "I don't think that's very fair."

"I don't think I'm very interested anymore in what you think is fair and what you don't think is fair," Michael said. "You had some justification for your behavior at first, perhaps. But in the last month or so you've turned into someone I don't understand at all, and something is going on that I understand even less. Your mother doesn't understand it either, but she senses it, and it's hurting her very badly. I know she brought part of the hurt on herself, but I doubt if that changes the quality of the pain."

"Dad, I just lost track of the time!" Arnie cried. "Stop making such a big thing out of it!"

"Were you driving around?"

"Yes, but—"

"I notice that's when it usually happens," Michael said. "Will you be home tonight?"

"Yes, early," Arnie said. He wet his lips. "I just want to go by the garage, I have some information Will asked me to get while I was in Philly—"

"I'm not interested in that either, pardon me," Michael said. His voice was still polite, chillingly disconnected.

"Oh," Arnie said in a very small voice. He was very scared now, almost trembling.

"Arnie?"

"What?" Arnie nearly whispered.

"What *is* going on?"

"I don't know what you mean."

"Please. That detective came by to see me at my office. He was after Regina, as well. He upset her very badly. I don't think he meant to, but—"

"What was it this time?" Arnie asked fiercely. "That fucker, what was it this time? I'll—"

"You'll what?"

"Nothing." He swallowed something that tasted like a lump of dust. "What was it this time?"

"Repperton," his father said. "Repperton and those other two boys. What did you think it was? The geopolitical situation in Brazil?"

"What happened to Repperton was an *accident*," Arnie said. "Why did he want to talk to you and Mom about something that was an *accident*, for Christ's sake?"

"I don't know." Michael Cunningham paused. "Do you?"

"How would I?" Arnie yelled. "I was in Philadelphia, how would I know anything about it? I was playing chess, not . . . not . . . not anything else," he finished lamely.

"One more time," Michael Cunningham said. "Is something going on, Arnie?"

He thought of the smell, the high, rotting stink. Leigh choking, digging at her throat, turning blue. He had tried to thump her on the back because that's what you did when someone was choking, there was no such thing as a Heimlich Maneuver because it hadn't been invented yet, and besides, this was how it was supposed to end, only not in the car . . . beside the road . . . in his arms. . . .

He closed his eyes and the whole world seemed to tilt and swirl sickly.

"Arnie?"

"*There is nothing going on*," he said through clenched teeth and without opening his eyes. "Nothing but a lot of people who are on my case because I finally got something of my own and did it all by myself."

"All right," his father said, his lackluster voice once more terribly reminiscent of Mr. Slawson's. "If you want to talk about it, I'm here. I always have been, although I didn't always make that as clear as I should have. Be sure to kiss your mother when you come in, Arnie."

"Yeah, I will. Listen, Mi—"

Click.

He stood in the booth, listening stupidly to the sound of nothing at all. His father was gone. There wasn't even a dial tone because it was a dumb . . . fucking . . . phone booth.

He dug into his pocket and spread his change out on the little metal shelf where he could look at it. He picked up a dime, almost dropped it, and at last got it into the slot. He felt sick and overheated. He felt as if he had been very efficiently disowned.

He dialled Leigh's number from memory.

Mrs. Cabot picked the phone up and recognized his voice immediately. Her pleasant and rather sexy come-hither-thou-fascinating-stranger phone voice became instantly hard. Arnie had had his last chance with *her*, that voice said, and he had blown it.

"She doesn't want to talk to you and she doesn't want to see you," she said.

"Mrs. Cabot, please, if I could just—"

"I think you've done enough," Mrs. Cabot said coolly. "She came in crying the other night and she's been crying off and on ever since. She had some sort of a . . . an experience with you the last time you and she went out, and I only pray it wasn't what I thought it was. I—"

Arnie felt hysterical laughter bubbling up inside him. Leigh had almost choked to death on a hamburger, and her mother was afraid Arnie had tried to rape her.

"Mrs. Cabot, I have to talk to her."

"I'm afraid not."

He tried to think of something else to say, some way to get past the dragon at the gate. He felt a little like a Fuller Brush salesman trying to get in to see the lady of the house. His tongue wouldn't move. He would have made a lousy salesman. There was going to be that hard *click* and then smooth silence again.

Then he heard the telephone change hands. Mrs. Cabot said something in sharp protest, and Leigh said something back; it was too muffled for him to catch. Then Leigh's voice said, "Arnie?"

"Hi," he said. "Leigh, I just wanted to call and tell you how sorry I was about—"

"Yes," Leigh said. "I know you were, and I accept your apology, Arnie. But I won't—I can't go out with you anymore. Unless things change."

"Ask me something easy," he whispered.

"That's all I—" Her voice sharpened, moved slightly away from the telephone. "Mom, please stop hanging over me!" Her mother said something that sounded disgruntled, there was a pause, and then Leigh's voice again, low. "That's all I can say, Arnie. I know how crazy it sounds, but I still think your car tried to kill me the other night. I don't know how something like that could be, but no matter how I work it over in my mind, it comes out seeming that that was how it was. I *know* that's how it was. It's got you, doesn't it?"

"Leigh, if you'll pardon my French, that's pretty fucking stupid. It's a *car!* Can you spell that? C-A-R, *car!* There's nothing—"

"Yes," she said, and now her voice was wavering toward tears. "It's got you, *she's* got you, and I guess nobody can get you free except you."

His back suddenly awoke and began to throb, sending pain out in a sickish radiation that seemed to echo and amplify in his head.

"Isn't that the truth of it, Arnie?"

He didn't, couldn't, answer.

"Get rid of it," Leigh said. "Please. I read about that Repperton boy in the paper this morning, and—"

"What's that got to do with anything?" Arnie croaked. And for the second time: "That was an *accident.*"

"I don't know what it was. Maybe I don't *want* to know. But it isn't us I'm worried about anymore. It's *you*, Arnie. I'm scared for *you*. You ought to—no, you *have* to get rid of it."

Arnie whispered, "Just say you won't dump me, Leigh. Okay?"

Now she was even closer to crying—or perhaps she was already doing it. "Promise me, Arnie. You have to promise me and then you have to do it. Then we . . . we can see. Promise me you'll get rid of that car. It's all I want from you, nothing else."

He closed his eyes and saw Leigh walking home from school. And a block down, idling at the curb, was Christine. Waiting for her.

He opened his eyes quickly, as if he had seen a fiend in a dark room.

"I can't do that," he said.

"Then we don't have much to talk about, do we?"

"Yes! Yes, we do. We—"

"No. Goodbye, Arnie. I'll see you in school."

"Leigh, wait!"

Click. And dead smooth silence.

A moment of nearly total rage came over him. He had a sudden deadly impulse to swing the black phone receiver around and around his head like an Argentinian *bolas,* shattering the glass in this goddam torture-chamber of a telephone booth. They had run out on him, all of them. Rats deserting a sinking ship.

You have to be ready to help yourself before anyone else can help you.

Fuck that bullshit! They were rats deserting a sinking ship. Not one of them, from that shitter Slawson with his thick horn-rimmed glasses and his weird poached-egg eyes to his rotten shitting old man who was so fucking pussywhipped that he ought to just give that cunt he was married to a razor and invite her to cut it off to that cheap bitch in her fancy house with her legs crossed probably she'd been having her period and that's why she choked on the goddam hamburger and those shitters with their fancy goddam cars and the trunks full of golf-clubs those goddam officers I'd like to bend them over this here lathe I'd play some golf with them I could find the right hole to put those little white balls in you bet your ass but when I get out of here no one's going to tell me what to do it's gonna be my way my way mine mine mine mine mine MINE—

Arnie came back to himself suddenly, scared and wide-eyed, breathing hard. What had been happening to him? He had seemed like someone else there for a moment, someone on a crazed rant against humanity in general—

Not just someone. It was LeBay.

No! That's not true at all!

Leigh's voice: *Isn't that the truth of it, Arnie?*

Suddenly something very like a vision rose in his tired, confused mind. He was hearing a minister's voice: *Arnold, do you take this woman to be your loving—*

But it wasn't a church; it was a used-car lot with bright multicolored plastic pennants fluttering in a stiff breeze. Camp chairs had been set up. It was Will Darnell's lot, and Will was standing beside him in the best man's position.

There was no girl beside him. Christine was parked beside him, shining in a spring sun, even her whitewalls seeming to glow.

His father's voice: *Is there something going on?*

The preacher's voice: *Who giveth this woman to this man?*

Roland D. LeBay rose from one of the camp chairs like the prow of a skeletal ghost-ship from Hades. He was grinning—and for the first time Arnie saw who had been sitting around him: Buddy Repperton, Richie Trelawney, Moochie Welch. Richie Trelawney was black and charred, most of his hair burned off. Blood had poured down Buddy Repperton's chin and had caked his shirt like hideous vomit. But Moochie Welch was the worst; Moochie Welch had been ripped open like a laundry bag. They were smiling. All of them were smiling.

I do, Roland D. LeBay croaked. He grinned, and a tongue slimed with graveyard mould lolled from the stinking hole of his mouth. *I give her, and he's got the receipt to prove it. She's all his. The bitch is the ace of spades . . . and she's all his.*

Arnie became aware that he was moaning in the telephone booth, clutching the receiver against his chest. With a tremendous effort he pulled himself all the way out of the daze—vision, whatever it had been—and got hold of himself.

This time when he reached for the change on the ledge, he spilled half of it onto the floor. He plugged a dime into the slot and scrabbled through the telephone book until he found the hospital number. Dennis. Dennis would be there, Dennis always had been. Dennis wouldn't let him down. Dennis would help.

The switchboard girl answered, and Arnie said, "Room Two-forty, please."

The connection was made. The phone began to ring. It rang . . . and rang . . . and rang. Just as he was about to give up, a brisk female voice said, "Second floor, C Wing, who were you trying to reach?"

"Guilder," Arnie said. "Dennis Guilder."

"Mr. Guilder's in Physical Therapy right now," the female voice said. "You could reach him at eight o'clock."

Arnie thought of telling her it was important—very important—but suddenly he was overwhelmed with a need to get out of the phone booth. Claustrophobia was like a giant's hand pushing down on his chest. He could smell his own sweat. The smell was sour, bitter.

"Sir?"

"Yeah, okay, I'll call back," Arnie said. He broke the connection and nearly burst out of the booth, leaving his change scattered on the ledge and the floor. A few people turned around to look at him, mildly interested, and then turned back to their food again.

"Pizza's ready," the counterman said.

Arnie glanced up at the clock and saw he had been in the booth for almost twenty minutes. There was sweat all over his face. His armpits felt like a jungle. His legs were trembling—the muscles in his thighs felt as if they might simply give out and spill him onto the floor.

He paid for the pizza, nearly dropping his wallet as he tucked his three dollars in change back in.

"You okay?" the counterman asked. "You look a little white around the gills."

"I'm fine," Arnie said. Now he felt as if he might vomit. He snatched the pizza in its white box with the word GINO'S emblazoned across the top and fled into the cold sharp clarity of the night. The last of the clouds had blown away, and the stars twinkled like chipped diamonds. He stood on the sidewalk for a moment, looking first at the stars and then at Christine, parked across the street, waiting faithfully.

She would never argue or complain, Arnie thought. She would never demand. You could enter her anytime and rest on her plush upholstery, rest in her warmth. She would never deny. She—she—

She loved him.

Yes; he sensed that was true. Just as he sometimes sensed that LeBay would not have sold her to anyone else, not for two hundred and fifty, not for two thousand. She had been sitting there waiting for the right buyer. One who would . . .

One who would love her for herself alone, that voice inside whispered.

Yes. That was it; that was exactly it.

Arnie stood there with his pizza forgotten in his hands, white steam rising lazily from the grease-spotted box. He looked at Christine, and such a confusing whirl of emotions ran through him that there might have been a cyclone in his body, rearranging everything it did not simply destroy. Oh, he loved and loathed her, he hated her and cherished her, he needed her and needed to run from her, she was his and he was hers and

(I now pronounce you man and wife joined and sealed from this day forth for ever and ever, until death do you part)

But worst of all was the horror, the terrible numbing horror, the realization that ... that ...

(how did you hurt your back that night, Arnie? after Repperton—the late Clarence "Buddy" Repperton—and his buddies trashed her? how did you hurt your back so that now you have to wear this stinking brace all the time? how did you hurt your back?)

The answer rose—and Arnie began to run, trying to beat the realization, to get to Christine before he saw the whole thing plain and went mad.

He ran for Christine, running his tangled emotions and some terrible dawning realization a foot race; he ran to her the way a hype runs for his works when the shakes and the jitters get so bad he can no longer think of anything but relief; he ran the way that the damned run to their appointed doom; he ran as a bridegroom runs to the place where his bride stands waiting.

He ran because inside Christine none of these things mattered—not his mother, father, Leigh, Dennis, or what he had done to his back that night when everyone was gone, that night after he had taken his almost totally destroyed Plymouth from the airport and back to Darnell's, and after the place was empty he had put Christine's transmission in neutral and pushed her, pushed her until she began to roll on her flat tires, pushed her until she was out the door and he could hear the wind of November keening sharply around the wrecks and the abandoned hulks with their stellated glass and their ruptured gas tanks; he had pushed her until the sweat ran off him in rivers and his heart thudded like a runaway horse in his chest and his back cried out for mercy; he had pushed her, his body pumping as if in some hellish consummation; he had pushed her, and inside the odometer ran slowly backward, and some fifty feet beyond the door his back began to really throb, and he kept pushing, and then his back began to scream in protest, and he kept pushing, muscling it along on the flat, slashed tires, his hands going numb, his back screaming, screaming, screaming. And then—

He reached Christine and flung himself inside, shuddering

and panting. His pizza fell on the floor. He picked it up and set it on the seat, feeling calm slowly wash through him like a soothing balm. He touched the steering wheel, let his hands slip down it, tracing its delicious curve. He took one glove off and felt in his pocket for his keys. For LeBay's keys.

He could still remember what had happened that night, but it did not seem horrible now; now, sitting behind Christine's steering wheel, it seemed rather wonderful.

It had been a miracle.

He remembered how it had suddenly become easier to push the car because the tires were healing themselves magically, kneading themselves together without a scar and then inflating. The broken glass had begun to reassemble from nowhere, knitting itself upward with small, scratchy, crystalline sounds. The dents began to pop back out.

He simply pushed her until she was right enough to run, and then he had driven her, cruising between the rows until the odometer ran back past what Repperton and his friends had done. And then Christine was okay.

What could be so horrible about that?

"Nothing," a voice said.

He looked around. Roland D. LeBay was sitting on the passenger side of the car, wearing a black double-breasted suit, a white shirt, a blue tie. A row of medals hung askew on one lapel of his suit-coat—it was the outfit he had been buried in, Arnie knew that even though he had never actually seen it. Only LeBay looked younger and tougher. A man you'd not want to fool with.

"Start her up," LeBay said. "Get the heater going and let's motorvate."

"Sure," Arnie said, and turned the key. Christine pulled out, tires crunching on the packed snow. He had pushed her that night until almost all the damage had been repaired. No, not repaired—*negated*. Negated was the right word for what had happened. And then he had put her back in stall twenty, leaving the rest to do himself.

"Let's have us some music," the voice beside him said.

Arnie turned on the radio. Dion was singing "Donna the Prima Donna."

"You going to eat that pizza, or what?" The voice seemed to be changing somehow.

"Sure," Arnie said. "You want a piece?"

Leering: "I never say no to a piece of anything."

Arnie opened the pizza box with one hand and pulled a piece free. "Here you g—"

His eyes widened. The slice of pizza began to tremble, the long threads of cheese dangling down beginning to sway like the strands of a spiderweb broken by the wind.

It wasn't LeBay sitting there anymore.

It was *him.*

It was Arnie Cunningham at roughly age fifty, not as old as LeBay had been when he and Dennis first met him on that August day, not that old, but getting there, friends and neighbors, getting there. His older self was wearing a slightly yellowed T-shirt and dirty, oil-smeared bluejeans. The glasses were hornrims, taped at one bow. The hair was cut short and receding. The gray eyes were muddy and bloodshot. The mouth had taken all the tucks of sour loneliness. Because this—this thing, apparition, whatever it was—it was alone. He felt that.

Alone except for Christine.

This version of himself and Roland D. LeBay could have been son and father: the resemblance was that great.

"You going to drive? Or are you going to stare at me?" this thing asked, and it suddenly began to age before Arnie's stunned eyes. The iron-colored hair went white, the T-shirt rippled and thinned, the body beneath twisted with age. The wrinkles raced across the face and then sank in like lines of acid. The eyes sank into their sockets and the corneas yellowed. Now only the nose thrust forward, and it was the face of some ancient carrion-eater, but still *his* face, oh, yes, still his.

"See anything green?" this sept—no, this octogenarian Arnie Cunningham croaked, as its body twisted and writhed and withered on Christine's red seat. "See anything green? See anything green? See anything—" The voice cracked and rose and whined into a shrill, senile treble, and now the skin broke open in sores and surface tumors and behind the glasses milky cataracts covered both eyes like shades being pulled down. It was rotting before his very eyes and the smell of it was what he had smelled in Christine before, what Leigh had smelled, only it was worse now, it was the high, gassy, gagging smell of high-speed decay, the smell of his own death, and Arnie began to whine as Little Richard came on the radio singing "Tutti Frutti," and now the thing's hair was falling out in gossamer white drifts and its collarbones poked through the shiny, stretched skin above the T-shirt's sagging round collar, they poked through like grotesque white pencils. Its lips were shrivelling away from the final surviving teeth that leaned this way and that like tombstones, it was him, it was dead, and yet it lived—like Christine, it lived.

"*See anything green?*" it gibbered. "*See anything green?*"

Arnie began to scream.

39 / Junkins Again

The fenders were clickin the guard-rail posts,
The guys beside me were just as white as ghosts.
One says, "Slow down, I see spots,
The lines in the road just look like dots."

—Charlie Ryan

Arnie pulled into Darnell's Garage about an hour later. His rider—if there really *had* been a rider—was long gone. The smell was gone too; it had undoubtedly been just an illusion. If you hung around the shitters for long enough, Arnie reasoned, *everything* started to smell like shit. And that made them happy, of course.

Will was sitting behind his desk in his glassed-in office, eating a hoagie. He raised one drippy hand but didn't come out. Arnie blipped his horn and parked.

It had all been some kind of dream. Simple as that. Some crazy kind of dream. Calling home, calling Leigh, trying to call Dennis and having that nurse tell him Dennis was in Physical Therapy—it was like being denied three times before the cock crew, or something. He had freaked a little bit. Anyone would have freaked, after the shitstorm he's been through since August. It was all a question of perspective, after all, wasn't it? All his life he had been one thing to people, and now he was coming out of his shell, turning into a normal everyday person with normal everyday concerns. It was not at all surprising that people should resent this, because when someone changed

(for better or worse, for richer or poorer)

it was natural for people to get a little weird about it. It fucked up their perspective.

Leigh had spoken as if she thought he was crazy, and that was nothing but bullshit of the purest ray serene. He had been under strain, of course he had, but strain was a natural part of life. If Miss High-Box-Oh-So-Preppy Leigh Cabot thought otherwise, she was in for an abysmal fucking at the hands of that all-time champion rapist, Life. She'd probably end up taking Dexies to get out of first gear in the morning and Nembies or 'Ludes to come down at night.

Ah, but he wanted her—even now, thinking about her, he felt a great, unaccountable, unnameable desire sweep through him like cold wind, making him squeeze Christine's wheel fiercely in his hands. It was a hot wanting too great, too elemental, for naming. It was its own force.

But he was all right now. He felt he had . . . crossed the last bridge, or something.

He had come back to himself sitting in the middle of a narrow access road beyond the farthest parking-lot reaches of the Monroeville Mall—which meant he was roughly halfway to California. Getting out, looking behind the car, he had seen a hole smashed through a snowbank, and there was melting snow sprayed across Christine's hood. Apparently he had lost control, gone skating across the lot (which, even with the Christmas shopping season in full swing, was mercifully empty this far out), and had crashed through the bank. Damn lucky he hadn't been in an accident. *Damn* lucky.

He had sat there for a while, listening to the radio and looking through the windshield at the half-moon floating overhead. Bobby Helms had come on singing "Jingle Bell Rock," a Sound of the Season, as the deejays said, and he had smiled a little, feeling better. He couldn't remember what exactly it was that he had seen (or thought he had seen), and he didn't really want to. Whatever it had been, it was the first and last time. He was quite sure of that. People had gotten him imagining things. They'd probably be delighted if they knew . . . but he wasn't going to give them that satisfaction.

Things were going to be better all the way around. He would mend his fences at home—in fact, he could start tonight by watching some TV with his folks, just like in the old days. And he would win Leigh back. If she didn't like the car, no matter how weird her reasons were, fine. Maybe he would even buy another car sometime soon and tell her he had traded Christine in. He could keep Christine here, rent space. What she didn't know wouldn't hurt her. And Will. This was going to be his last run for Will, this coming weekend. That bullshit had gone just about far enough; he could feel it. Let Will think he was a chicken if that's what he wanted to think. A felony rap for interstate transport of unlicensed cigarettes and alcohol wouldn't look all that hot on his college application, would it? A *Federal* felony rap. No. Not too cool.

He laughed a little. He *did* feel better. Purged. On his way over to the garage he ate his pizza even though it was cold. He was ravenous. It had struck him a bit peculiar that one piece was gone—in fact, it made him a bit uneasy—but he dismissed it. He had probably eaten it during that strange blank period, or maybe even thrown it out the window. Whoo, that had been spooky. No more of that shit. And he laughed again, this time a little less shakily.

Now he got out of the car, slammed the door, and started toward Will's office to find out what he had for him to do this evening. It suddenly occurred to him that tomorrow was the last day of school before the Christmas vacation, and that put an extra spring in his step.

That was when the side door, the one beside the big carport door, opened and a man let himself in. It was Junkins. Again.

He saw Arnie looking at him and raised a hand. "Hi, Arnie."

Arnie glanced at Will. Through the glass, Will shrugged and went on eating his hoagie.

"Hello," Arnie said. "What can I do for you."

"Well, I don't know," Junkins said. He smiled, and then his eyes slid past Arnie to Christine, appraising, looking for damage. "Do you want to do something for me?"

"Not fucking likely," Arnie said. He could feel his head starting to throb with rage again.

Rudy Junkins smiled, apparently unoffended.

"I just dropped by. How you been?"

He stuck out his hand. Arnie only looked at it. Not embarrassed in the slightest, Junkins dropped his hand, walked around to Christine, and began examining her again. Arnie watched him, his lips pressed together so tightly they were white. He felt a fresh pulse of anger each time Junkins dropped one of his hands onto Christine.

"Look, maybe you ought to buy a season ticket or something," Arnie said. "Like to the Steelers games."

Junkins turned and looked at him questioningly.

"Never mind," Arnie said sullenly.

Junkins went on looking. "You know," he said, "it's a hell of a strange thing, what happened to Buddy Repperton and those other two boys, isn't it?"

Fuck it, Arnie thought. *I'm not going to fool around with this shitter.*

"I was in Philadelphia. Chess tourney."

"I know," Junkins said.

"*Jesus!* You're really checking me out!"

Junkins walked back to Arnie. There was no smile on his face now. "Yes, that's right," he said. "I'm checking you out. Three of the boys I believe were involved in vandalizing your car are now dead, along with a fourth boy who was apparently just along for the ride on Tuesday night. That's a pretty big coincidence. It's nine miles too big for me. You bet I'm checking you out."

Arnie stared at him, surprised out of his anger, uncertain. "I thought it was an accident . . . that they were liquored up and speeding and—"

"There was another car involved," Junkins said.

"How do you know that?"

"There were tracks in the snow, for one thing. Unfortunately, the wind had blurred them too much for us to be able to get a decent photo. But one of the barriers at the Squantic Hills State Park gate was broken, and we found traces of red paint on it. Buddy's Camaro wasn't red. It was blue."

He measured Arnie with his eyes.

"We also found traces of red paint embedded in Moochie Welch's skin, Arnie. Can you dig that? *Embedded.* Do you know how hard a car has to hit a guy to *embed* paint in his skin?"

"You ought to go out there and start counting red cars," Arnie said coldly. "You'll be up to twenty before you get to Basin Drive, I guarantee it."

"You bet," Junkins said. "But we sent our samples to the FBI lab in Washington, where they have samples of every shade of paint they ever used in Detroit. We got the results back today. Any idea what they were? Want to guess?"

Arnie's heart was thudding dully in his chest; there was a corresponding beat at his temples. "Since you're here, I'd guess it was Autumn Red. Christine's color."

"Give that man a Kewpie doll," Junkins said. He lit a cigarette and looked at Arnie through the smoke. He had abandoned any pretense of good humor; his gaze was stony.

Arnie clapped his hands to his head in an exaggerated gesture of exasperation. "Autumn Red, great. Christine's a custom job, but there were Fords from 1959 to 1963 painted Autumn Red, and Thunderbirds, and Chevrolet offered that shade from 1962 to 1964, and for a while in the mid-fifties you could get a Rambler painted Autumn Red. I've been working on my '58 for half a year now, I get the car books; you can't do work on an old car without the books, or you're screwed before you start. Autumn Red was a popular choice. I know it"—he looked at Junkins fixedly—"and you know it, too. Don't you?"

Junkins said nothing; he only went on looking at Arnie in that fixed, stony, unsettling way. Arnie had never been looked at in that way by anyone in his life, but he recognized the gaze. He supposed anyone would. It was a look of strong, frank suspicion. It scared him. A few months ago—even a few weeks ago—that was probably all it would have done. But now it made him furious as well.

"You're really reaching. Just what the hell have you got against me anyway, Mr. Junkins? Why are you on my ass?"

Junkins laughed and walked around in a large half-circle. The place was entirely empty except for the two of them out here and Will in his office, finishing his hoagie and licking olive oil off his hands and still watching them closely.

"What have I got against you?" he said. "How does first-degree murder sound to you, Arnie? Does that grab you with any force?"

Arnie grew very still.

"Don't worry," Junkins said, still walking. "No big tough cop scene. No menacing threats about going downtown—except in this case downtown would be Harrisburg. No Miranda card. Everything is still fine for our hero, Arnold Cunningham."

"I don't understand any of what you're—"

"*You . . . understand . . . PLENTY!*" Junkins roared at him. He had stopped next to a giant yellow hulk of a truck—another of Johnny Pomberton's dumpsters-in-the-making. He stared at Arnie. "Three of the kids who beat on your car are dead. Autumn Red paint samples were taken at both crime scenes, leading us to believe that the vehicle the perpetrator used in both cases was at least in part Autumn Red. And gee whiz! It just turns out that the car those kids trashed is mostly Autumn Red. And you stand there and push your glasses up on your nose and tell me you don't understand what I'm talking about."

"I was in Philadelphia when it happened," Arnie said quietly. "Don't you get that? Don't you get that at all?"

"Kiddo," Junkins said flipping his cigarette away, "that's the worst part of it. That's the part that really stinks."

"I wish you'd get out of here or put me under arrest or something. Because I'm supposed to punch in and do some work."

"For now," Junkins said, "talk is all I've got. The first time—when Welch got killed—you were supposed to be home in bed."

"Pretty thin, I know," Arnie said. "Believe me, if I'd known this shit was going to come down on my head, I would have hired a sick friend to sit up with me."

"Oh, no—that was *good*," Junkins said. "Your mother and father had no cause to doubt your tale. I could tell that from speaking to them. And alibis—the true ones—usually have more holes than a Salvation Army suit. It's when they start to look like suits of armor that I get nervous."

"Holy Jumping *Jesus!*" Arnie almost screamed. "It was a fucking *chess* meet! I've been in the chess club for *four years* now!"

"Until today," Junkins said, and Arnie grew still again. Junkins nodded. "Oh yeah, I talked to the club advisor. Herbert Slawson. He says that the first three years you never missed a meeting, even came to a couple with a low-grade case of the flu. You were his star player. Then, this year, you were spotty right from the start—"

"I had my car to work on . . . and I got a girl—"

"He said you missed the first three tourneys, and he was pretty surprised when your name turned up on the trip sheet for the Northern States meet. He thought you'd lost all your interest in the club."

"I told you—"

"Yes, you did. Too busy. Cars and girls, just what makes most kids too busy. But you regained your interest long enough to go to Philly—and then you dropped out. That strikes me as very odd."

"I can't see anything funny about it," Arnie said, but his

voice seemed distant, almost lost in the surf-roar of blood in his ears.

"Bullshit. It looks as if you knew it was coming down and set yourself up with an airtight alibi."

The roar in his head had even assumed the steady, wave-like beats of surf, each beat accompanied by a dull thrust of pain. He was getting a headache—why wouldn't this monstrous man with his prying brown eyes just go away? None of it was true, none of it. He hadn't set anything up, not an alibi, not anything. He had been as surprised as anyone else when he read in the paper what had happened. Of course he had been. There was nothing strange going on, unless it was this lunatic's paranoia, and

(how did you hurt your back anyway, Arnie? and by the way, do you see anything green? do you see)

he closed his eyes and for a moment the world seemed to lurch out of its orbit and he saw that green, grinning, rotting face floating before him, saying: *Start her up. Get the heater going and let's motorvate. And while we're at it, let's get the shitters that wrecked our car. Let's grease the little cock-knockers, kid, what do you say? Let's hit them so fucking hard the corpse-cutter down at city hospital will have to pull the paint-chips out of their carcasses with pliers. What do you say? Find some doowop music on the radio and let's cruise. Let's—*

He groped back behind him, touched Christine—her hard, cool, reassuring surface—and things dropped back into place again. He opened his eyes.

"There's only one other thing, really," Junkins said, "and it's very subjective. Nothing you could put on a report. You're different this time, Arnie. Harder, somehow. It's almost as if you've put on twenty years."

Arnie laughed, and was relieved to hear it sounded quite natural. "Mr. Junkins, you've got a screw loose."

Junkins didn't join him in his laughter. "Uh-huh. I know it. The whole thing is screwy—screwier than anything I've investigated in the ten years I've been a detective. Last time, I felt like I could reach you, Arnie. I felt you were . . . I don't know. Lost, unhappy, groping around, trying to get out. Now I don't feel that at all. I almost feel like I'm talking to a different person. Not a very nice one."

"I'm done talking to you," Arnie said abruptly, and began walking toward the office.

"I want to know what happened," Junkins called after him. "And I'm going to find out. Believe me."

"Do me a favor and stay away from here," Arnie said. "You're crazy."

He let himself into the office, closed the door behind him, and noticed his hands weren't shaking at all. The room was stuffy with the smells of cigar and olive oil and garlic. He crossed in front of Will without speaking, took his time-card out of the rack, and punched in: *ka-thud*. Then he looked through the glass window and saw Junkins standing there, looking at Christine. Will said nothing. Arnie could hear the noisy engine of the big man's respiration. A couple of minutes later Junkins left.

"Cop," Will said, and ripped out a long belch. It sounded like a chainsaw.

"Yeah."

"Repperton?"

"Yeah. He thinks I had something to do with it."

"Even though you were in Philly?"

Arnie shook his head. "He doesn't even seem to care about that."

He's a smart cop then, Will thought. *He knows the facts are wrong, and his intuition tells him there's something even wronger than that, so he's gotten further with it than most cops ever would, but he could spend a million years and not get all the way to the truth.* He thought of the empty car driving itself into stall twenty like some weird wind-up toy. The empty ignition slot turning over to START. The engine revving once, like a warning snarl, and then falling off.

And thinking of these things, Will did not trust himself to look Arnie in the face, even though his own experience in routine deceit was nearly lifelong.

"I don't want to send you to Albany if the cops are watching you."

"I don't care if you send me to Albany or not, but you don't have to worry about the heat. He's the only cop I've seen, and he's crazy. He's not interested in anything but two cases of hit-and-run."

Now Will's eyes did meet Arnie's: Arnie's gray and distant, Will's a faded no-color, the corneas a dim yellow; they were the eyes of an ancient tomcat who has seen a thousand mice turned inside out.

"He's interested in you," he said. "I'd better send Jimmy."

"You like the way Jimmy drives, do you?"

Will looked at Arnie for a moment and then sighed. "Okay," he said. "But if you see that cop, you back off. And if you get caught holding a bag, Cunningham, it's your bag. Do you understand that?"

"Yes," Arnie said. "Do you want me to do some work tonight, or what?"

"There's a '77 Buick in forty-nine. Pull the starter motor. Check the solenoid. If it seems okay, pull that too."

Arnie nodded and left. Will's thoughtful eyes drifted from his retreating back to Christine. He had no business sending him to Albany this weekend and he knew it. The kid knew it too, but he was going to push ahead anyway. He had said he'd go, and he was now going to by-God do it. And if anything happened, the kid would stand up. Will was sure of it. There was a time when he surely wouldn't have done, but that time was past now.

He had heard it all on the intercom.

Junkins had been right.

The kid was harder now.

Will began to look at the kid's '58 again. Arnie would be taking Will's Chrysler to New York. While he was gone, Will would watch Christine. He would watch Christine and see what happened.

40 / Arnie in Trouble

With Naugahyde bucket seats in front and back,
Everything's chrome, man, even my jack,
Step on the gas, she goes Waaaaahhhh—
I'll let you look,
But don't touch my custom machine.

　　　　　　　　　　　　　　　　　—The Beach Boys

Rudolph Junkins and Rick Mercer of the Pennsylvania State Police detective division sat drinking coffee the following afternoon in a glum little office with paint peeling from the walls. Outside, a depressing mixture of snow and sleet was falling.

"I'm pretty sure this is going to be the weekend," Junkins said. "That Chrysler has rolled every four or five weeks for the last eight months."

"Just understand that busting Darnell and whatever bee you've got in your bonnet about that kid are two different things."

"They're both the same thing to me," Junkins replied. "The kid knows something. If I get him rattled, I may find out what it is."

"You think he had an accomplice? Someone who used his car and killed those kids while he was at the chess tourney?"

Junkins shook his head. "No, goddammit. The kid has got exactly one good friend, and he's in the hospital. I don't know what I think, except that the car was involved . . . and he was involved too."

Junkins put his Styrofoam coffee cup down and pointed at the man on the other side of the desk.

"Once we get that place closed down, I want a six-pack of lab technicians to go over it from stem to stern, inside and out. I want it up on a lift, I want it checked for dents, bumps, repaint . . . and for blood. That's what I really want, Rick. Just one drop of blood."

"You don't like that kid, do you?" Rick asked.

Junkins uttered a bewildered little laugh. "You know, the first time I kind of did. I liked him and I felt sorry for him. I felt like maybe he was covering for somebody else who had something on him. But this time I didn't like him at all."

He considered.

"And I didn't like that car, either. The way he kept touching it every time I thought I had him on the ropes. It was spooky."

Rick said, "As long as you remember that Darnell is the guy I've got to bust. No one in Harrisburg has the slightest interest in your kid."

"I'll remember," Junkins said. He picked up his coffee again and looked at Rick grimly. "Because he's a means to the end. I'm going to nail the person who killed those kids if it's the last thing I ever do."

"It may not even go down this weekend," Rick said.

But it did.

Two plainclothes cops from Pennsylvania's State Felony Squad sat in the cab of a four-year-old Datsun pickup on the morning of Saturday, December 16, watching as Will Darnell's black Chrysler rolled out of the big door and into the street. A light drizzle was falling; it was not quite cold enough to be sleet. It was one of those misty days when it is impossible to tell where the lowering clouds end and the actual mist begins. The Chrysler was quite properly showing its parking lights. Arnie Cunningham was a safe driver.

One of the plainclothesmen lifted a walkie-talkie to his mouth and spoke into it. "He just came out in Darnell's car. You guys stay on your toes."

They followed the Chrysler to I-76. When they saw Arnie get on the eastbound ramp with its Harrisburg sign, they turned up the westbound ramp, toward Ohio, and reported. They would get off I-76 one exit down the line and return to their original position near Darnell's Garage.

"Okay," Junkins's voice came back, "let's make an omelette."

Twenty minutes later, as Arnie was cruising east at a sedate and legal 50, three cops with all the right paperwork in hand knocked on the door of William Upshaw, who lived in the very much upscale suburb of Sewickley. Upshaw answered the door in his bathrobe. From behind him came the cartoon squawks of Saturday-morning TV.

"Who is it, honey?" his wife called from the kitchen.

Upshaw looked at the papers, which were court orders, and felt that he might faint. One ordered that all of Upshaw's tax records relating to Will Darnell (an individual) and Will Darnell (a corporation) be impounded. These papers bore the signature of the Pennsylvania Attorney General and a Superior Court judge.

"Who is it, hon?" his wife asked again, and one of his kids came to look, all big eyes.

Upshaw tried to speak and could raise only a dusty croak. It had come. He had dreamed about it, and it had finally come. The house in Sewickley had not protected him from it; the woman he kept at a safe distance in King of Prussia had not protected him from it; it was here: he read it in the smooth faces of these cops in their off-the-rack Anderson-Little suits. Worst of all, one of them was Federal—Alcohol, Tobacco, and Firearms. He produced a second ID, proclaiming him an agent of something called the Federal Drug Control Task Force.

"Our information is that you keep an office in your home," the Federal cop said. He looked—what? Twenty-six? Thirty? Had he ever had to worry about what you were going to do when you had three kids and a wife who liked nice things maybe a little too much? Bill Upshaw didn't think so. When you had those things to think about, your face didn't stay that smooth. Your face only stayed that smooth when you could indulge in the luxury of grand thoughts—law and order, right and wrong, good guys and bad guys.

He opened his mouth to answer the Federal cop's question and produced only another dusty croak.

"Is this information correct?" the Federal cop asked patiently.

"Yes," Bill Upshaw croaked.

"And another office at 100 Frankstown Road in Monroeville?"

"Yes."

"Hon, who *is* it?" Amber asked, and came into the hallway. She saw the three men standing on the stoop and pulled the neck of her housecoat closed. The cartoons blared.

Upshaw thought suddenly, almost with relief, *It's the end of everything.*

The kid who had come out to see who had come to visit so early on a Saturday morning suddenly burst into tears and fled for the safety of the SuperFriends on channel 4.

When Rudy Junkins received the news that Upshaw had been served and that all the papers pertaining to Darnell, both at Upshaw's Sewickley home and his Monroeville office, had been impounded, he led half a dozen state cops in what he supposed would have been called a raid in the old days. Even during the holiday season the garage was moderately busy on Saturday (although it was by no means the bustling place it became on summer weekends), and when Junkins raised a battery-powered loudhailer to his lips and began to use it, perhaps two dozen heads whipped around. They would have conversation enough out of this to last them into the new year.

"*This is the Pennsylvania State Police!*" Junkins cried into the loudhailer. The words echoed and bounced. He found, even at this instant, that his eyes were drawn to the white-over-red Plymouth sitting empty in stall twenty. He had handled half a dozen murder weapons in his time, sometimes at the scene, more frequently in the witness box, but just looking at that car made him feel cold.

Gitney, the IRS man who had come along for this particular sleighride, was frowning at him to go on. *None of you know what this is about. None of you.* But he raised the loudhailer to his lips again.

"This place of business is closed! I repeat, this place of business is closed! You may take your vehicles if they are in running order—if not, please leave quickly and quietly! This place is closed!"

The loudhailer made an amplified *click* as he turned it off.

He looked toward the office and saw that Will Darnell was talking on the telephone, an unlit cigar jammed in his face. Jimmy Sykes was standing by the Coke machine, his simple face a picture of confused dismay—he didn't look much different from Bill Upshaw's kid at the moment before he burst into tears.

"Do you understand your rights as I have read them to you?" The cop in charge was Rick Mercer. Behind them, the garage was empty except for four uniformed cops, who were doing paperwork on the cars which had been impounded when the garage was closed.

"Yeah," Will said. His face was composed; the only sign of his upset was his deepening wheeze, the fast rise and fall of his big chest under his open-throated white shirt, the way he held his aspirator constantly in one hand.

"Do you have anything to say to us at this time?" Mercer asked.

"Not until my lawyer gets here."

"Your lawyer can meet us in Harrisburg," Junkins said.

Will glanced at Junkins contemptuously and said nothing. Outside, more uniformed police had finished affixing seals to every door and window of the garage except for the small side door. Until the state of impound ceased, all traffic would use that door.

"This is the craziest thing I ever heard of," Will Darnell said at last.

"It'll get crazier," Mercer said, smiling sincerely. "You're going away for a very long time, Will. Maybe someday they'll put you in charge of the prison motor pool."

"I know you," Will said, looking at him. "Your name is Mercer. I knew your father well. He was the crookedest cop that ever came out of King's County."

The blood fell out of Rick Mercer's face and he raised his hand.

"Stop it, Rick," Junkins said.

"Sure," Will said. "You guys have your fun. Make your jokes about the prison motor pool. I'll be back here doing business in two weeks. And if you don't know it, you're even stupider than you look."

He glanced around at them, his eyes intelligent, sardonic . . . and trapped. Abruptly he raised his aspirator to his mouth and breathed in deeply.

"Get this bag of shit out of here," Mercer said. He was still white.

"Are you all right?" Junkins asked. They were sitting in an unmarked state Ford half an hour later. The sun had decided to come out and shone blindingly on melting snow and wet streets. Darnell's Garage sat silent. Darnell's records—and Cunningham's street-rod Plymouth—were safely penned up inside.

"That crack he made about my father," Mercer said heavily. "My father shot himself, Rudy. Blew his head off. And I always thought . . . in college I read . . ." He shrugged. "Lots of cops eat the gun. Melvin Purvis did it, you know. He was the man who got Dillinger. But you wonder."

Mercer lit a cigarette and drew smoke downstairs in a long, shuddery breath.

"He didn't know anything," Junkins said.

"The *fuck* he didn't," Mercer said. He unrolled his window and threw the cigarette out. He unclipped the mike under the dash. "Home, this is Mobile Two."

"Ten-four, Mobile Two."

"What's happening with our carrier pigeon?"

"He's on Interstate Eighty-four, coming up on Port Jervis." Port Jervis was the crossover point between Pennsylvania and New York.

"New York is all ready?"

"Affirmative."

"You tell them again that I want him northeast of Middletown before they grab him, and his toll-ticket taken in evidence."

"Ten-four."

Mercer put the mike back and smiled thinly. "Once he crosses into New York, there's not a question in the world about it being Federal—but we've still got first dibs. Isn't that beautiful?"

Junkins didn't answer. There was nothing beautiful about it—from Darnell with his aspirator to Mercer's father eating his gun, there was nothing beautiful about it. Junkins was filled with a spooky feeling of inevitability, a feeling that the ugly things were not ending but only just beginning to happen. He felt halfway through a dark story that might prove too terrible to finish. Except he had to finish it now, didn't he? Yes.

The terrible feeling, the terrible image persisted: that the first time he had talked to Arnie Cunningham, he had been talking to a drowning man, and the second time he had talked to him the drowning had happened—and he was talking to a corpse.

The cloud cover over western New York was breaking, and Arnie's spirits began to rise. It always felt good to get away from Libertyville, away from . . . from everything. Not even the knowledge that he had contraband in the trunk could quench that feeling of lift. And at least it wasn't dope this time. Far in the back of his mind—hardly even acknowledged, but there—was the idle speculation about how things would be different and how his life would change if he just dumped the cigarettes and kept on going. If he just left the entire depressing mess behind.

But of course he wouldn't. Leaving Christine after he had put so much into her was of course impossible.

He turned up the radio and hummed along with something current. The sun, weakened by December but still trying to be bold, broke cover entirely and Arnie grinned.

He was still grinning when the New York State Police car pulled up beside him in the passing lane and paced him. The loudspeaker on top began to chant, *"This is for the Chrysler! Pull over, Chrysler! Pull over!"*

Arnie looked over, the grin fading from his lips. He stared into a pair of black sunglasses. Copglasses. The terror that seized him was deeper than he would have believed any emotion could be—and it wasn't for himself. His mouth went totally dry. His mind went into a blurring overdrive. He saw himself tramping the gas pedal and running for it, and perhaps he would have done it if he had been driving Christine . . . but he wasn't. He saw Will Darnell telling him that if he got caught holding a bag, it was *his* bag. Most of all he saw Junkins, Junkins with his sharp brown eyes, and knew this was Junkins's doing.

He wished Rudolph Junkins was dead.

"Pull over, Chrysler! I'm not talking to hear my own voice! Pull over right now!"

Can't say anything, Arnie thought incoherently as he veered over into the breakdown lane. His balls were crawling, his stomach churning madly. He could see his own eyes in the rearview, wall-eyed with fear behind his glasses—not for him, though. Not for him. Christine. He was afraid for Christine. What they might do to Christine.

His panic-stricken mind spun up a kaleidoscope of jumbled images. College application forms with the words REJECTED —CONVICTED FELON stamped across them. Prison bars, blued steel. A judge bending down from a high bench, his face white and accusing. Big bull queers in a prison yard looking for fresh meat. Christine riding the conveyor into the car-crusher in the junkyard behind the garage.

And then, as he stopped the Chrysler and put it in park, the State Police car pulling in behind him (and another, appearing like magic, pulling in ahead of him), a thought came from nowhere, full of cold comfort: *Christine can take care of herself.*

Another thought came as the cops got out and came toward him, one holding a search warrant in his hand. It also seemed to come from nowhere, but it reverberated in Roland D. LeBay's raspy, old man's tones:

And she'll take care of you, boy. All you got to do is go on believing in her and she'll take care of you.

Arnie opened the car door and got out a moment before one of the cops could open it.

"Arnold Richard Cunningham?" one of the cops asked.

"Yes, indeed," Arnie said calmly. "Was I speeding?"

"No, son," one of the others said. "But you are in a world of hurt, all the same."

The first cop stepped forward as formally as a career Army officer. "I have a duly executed document here permitting the search of this 1966 Chrysler Imperial in the name of the People of New York State and of the Commonwealth of Pennsylvania and of the United States of America. Further—"

"Well, that just about covers the motherfucking waterfront,

doesn't it?" Arnie said. His back flared dully, and he jammed his hands against it.

The cop's eyes widened slightly at the old voice coming out of this kid, but then he went on.

"Further, to seize any contraband found in the course of this search in the name of the People of New York State and of the Commonwealth of Pennsylvania and of the United States of America."

"Fine," Arnie said. None of it seemed real. Blue lights flashed a confusion. People passing in their cars turned to look, but he found he had no desire to turn from them, to hide his face, and that was something of a relief.

"Give me the keys, kid," one of the cops said.

"Why don't you just get them yourself, you shitter?" Arnie said.

"You're not helping yourself, kiddo," the cop said, but he looked startled and a little fearful all the same; for a moment the kid's voice had deepened and roughened and he had sounded forty years older and a pretty tough customer— nothing like the skinny kid he saw before him at all.

He leaned in, got the keys, and three of the cops immediately headed for the trunk. *They know,* Arnie thought, resigned. At least this had nothing to do with Junkins's obsession with Buddy Repperton and Moochie Welch and the others (at least not directly, he amended cautiously); this smelled like a well-planned and well-coordinated operation against Will's smuggling operations from Libertyville into New York and New England.

"Kid," one of the cops said, "would you like to answer some questions or make a statement? If you think you would, I'll read you the Miranda right now."

"No," Arnie said calmly. "I don't have anything to say."

"Things could go a lot easier with you."

"That's coercion," Arnie said, smiling a little. "Watch out or you'll put a big fat hole in your own case."

The cop flushed. "If you want to be an asshole, that's your lookout."

The Chrysler trunk was open. They had pulled out the spare tire, the jack, and several boxes of small parts—springs, nuts, bolts, and the like. One of the cops was almost entirely in the trunk; only his blue-gray-clad legs stuck out. For a moment Arnie hoped vaguely that they wouldn't find the under-compartment; then he dismissed the thought—it was just the childish part of him, the part he now wished burned away, because all that part of him did lately was hurt. They would find it. The quicker they found it, the quicker this nasty roadside scene would end.

As if some god had heard his wish and decided to grant it posthaste, the cop in the trunk called triumphantly. "Cigarettes!"

"All right," the cop who had read the warrant said. "Close it up." He turned to Arnie and read him the Miranda warning. "Do you understand your rights as I have read them to you?"

"Yes," Arnie said.

"Do you want to make a statement?"

"No."

"Get in the car, son. You're under arrest."

I'm under arrest, Arnie thought, and almost brayed laughter, the thought was so foolish. This was all a dream and he would wake up soon. *Under arrest*. Being hustled to a State Police cruiser. People looking at him—

Desperate, childish tears, hot salt, welled up in his throat and closed it.

His chest hitched—once, twice.

The cop who had read him his rights touched his shoulder and Arnie shrugged it off with a kind of desperation. He felt that if he could get deep down inside himself quickly enough, he would be okay—but sympathy might drive him mad.

"Don't touch me!"

"You do it the way you want to do it, son," the cop said, removing his hand. He opened the cruiser's rear door for Arnie and handed him in.

Do you cry in dreams? Of course you could—hadn't he read about people waking up from sad dreams with tears on their cheeks? But, dream or no dream, he wasn't going to cry.

Instead he would think of Christine. Not of his mother or father, not of Leigh or Will Darnell, not of Slawson—all the miserable shitters who had betrayed him.

He would think of Christine.

Arnie closed his eyes and leaned his pale, gaunt face forward into his hands and did just that. And as always, thinking about Christine made things better. After a while he was able to straighten up and look out at the passing scenery and think about his position.

Michael Cunningham put the telephone back into its cradle slowly—with infinite care—as if to do less might cause it to explode and spray his upstairs study with jagged black hooks of shrapnel.

He sat back in the swivel chair behind his desk, on which there sat his IBM Correcting Selectric II typewriter, an ashtray with the blue-and-gold legend HORLICKS UNIVERSITY barely legible across the dirty bottom, and the manuscript of his third book, a study of the ironclads *Monitor* and *Merrimac*. He had been halfway through a page when the telephone rang. Now he flipped the paper release on the right side of the typewriter and pulled the page bonelessly out from under the roller, observing its slight curve clinically. He put it down on top of the manuscript, which was now little more than a jungle of pencilled-in corrections.

Outside, a cold wind whined around the house. The morning's cloudy warmth had given way to a frigid, clear December evening. The earlier melt had frozen tight and his son was being held in Albany on charges of what amounted to smuggling: *no Mr. Cunningham it is not marijuana it is cigarettes, two hundred cartons of Winston cigarettes with no tax stamps.*

From downstairs he could hear the whir of Regina's sewing machine. He would have to get up now, go to the door and open it, go down the hall to the stairs, walk down the stairs, walk into the dining room, then into the plant-lined little room that had once been a laundry but which was now a sewing room, and stand there while Regina looked up at him (she would be wearing her half-glasses for the close work), and say "Regina, Arnie has been arrested by the New York State Police."

Michael attempted to begin this process by getting up from his desk chair, but the chair seemed to sense he was temporarily off-guard. It swivelled and rolled backward on its casters at the same moment, and Michael had to clutch the edge of his desk to keep from falling. He slipped heavily back into the chair, heart thudding with painful rapidity in his chest.

He was struck suddenly by such a complex wave of despair and sorrow that he groaned aloud and grabbed his forehead, squeezing his temples. The old thoughts swarmed back in, as predictable as summer mosquitoes and just as maddening. Six months ago, things had been okay. Now his son was sitting in a jail cell somewhere. What were the watershed moments? How could he, Michael, have changed things? What was the history of it, exactly? Where had the sickness started to creep in?

"Jesus—"

He squeezed harder, listening to the winter-whine outside the windows. He and Arnie had put the storms on just last month. That had been a good day, hadn't it? First Arnie holding the ladder and looking up, then him down and Arnie up there, him shouting for Arnie to be careful, the wind in his hair and dead brown leaves blowing over his shoes, their colors gone. Sure, it had been a good day. Even after that beastly car had come, seeming to overshadow everything in their son's life like a fatal disease, there had been some good days. Hadn't there?

"Jesus," he said again in a weak, teary voice that he despised.

Unbidden images rose behind his eyes. Colleagues looking at him sideways, maybe whispering in the faculty club. Discussions at cocktail parties in which his name bobbed uneasily up and down like a waterlogged body. Arnie wouldn't be eighteen for almost two months and he supposed that meant his name couldn't be printed in the paper, but everyone would still know. Word got around.

Suddenly, crazily, he saw Arnie at four, astride a red trike he and Regina had gotten at a rummage sale (Arnie at four had called them "Momma's rubbage sales"). The trike's red paint was flaked with scales of rust, the tires were bald, but Arnie had loved it; he would have taken that trike to bed with him, if he could. Michael closed his eyes and saw Arnie riding up and down the sidewalk, wearing his blue corduroy jumper, his hair flopping in his eyes, and then his mind's eye blinked or wavered or did something and the rusty rubbage-sale trike was Christine, her red paint scummed with rust, her windows milky-white with age.

He gritted his teeth together. Someone looking in might have thought he was smiling crazily. He waited until he had some kind of control, and then he got up and went downstairs to tell Regina what had happened. He would tell her and she would think of what they were going to do, just as she always had; she would steal the forward motion from him, taking whatever sorry balm that actually *doing* things had to give, and leave him with only sick sorrow and the knowledge that now his son was someone else.

41 / The Coming of the Storm

She took the keys to my Cadillac car,
Jumped in my kitty and drove her far.
                              —Bob Seger

The first of that winter's great northeast storms came to Libertyville on Christmas Eve, beating its way across the upper third of the U.S. on a wide and easily predictable storm track. The day began in bright thirty-degree sunshine, but morning deejays were already cheerfully predicting doom and gloom, urging those who had not finished their last-minute shopping to do so by mid-afternoon. Those planning trips to the old homestead for an old-fashioned Christmas were urged to rethink their plans if the trip could not be made in four to six hours.

"If you don't want to be spending Christmas Day in the breakdown lane of I-76 somewhere between Bedford and Carlisle, I'd leave early or not at all," the FM-104 jock advised his listening audience (a large part of which was too stoned to even consider going anyplace), and then resumed the Christmas Block Party with Springsteen's version of "Santa Claus Is Coming to Town."

By 11:00 A.M., when Dennis Guilder finally left Libertyville Community Hospital (as per hospital regulations, he was not allowed on his crutches until he was actually out of the building; until then he was pushed along in a wheelchair by Elaine), the sky had begun to scum over with clouds and there was an eerie fairy ring around the sun. Dennis crossed the parking lot carefully on his crutches, his mother and father bookending him nervously in spite of the fact that the lot had been scrupulously salted free of even the slightest trace of snow and ice. He paused by the family car, turning his face up slightly into the freshening breeze. Being outside was like a resurrection. He felt he could stand here for hours and not have enough of it.

By one o'clock that afternoon, the Cunningham family station wagon had reached the outskirts of Ligonier, ninety miles east of Libertyville. The sky had gone a smooth and pregnant slate-gray by this time, and the temperature had dropped six degrees.

It had been Arnie's idea that they not cancel the traditional Christmas Eve visit with Aunt Vicky and Uncle Steve, Regina's sister and her husband. The two families had created a casual, loosely rotating ritual over the years, with Vicky and Steve coming to their house some years, the Cunninghams going over to Ligonier on others. This year's trip had been arranged in early December. It had been cancelled after what Regina stubbornly called "Arnie's trouble," but at the beginning of last week, Arnie had begun restlessly agitating for the trip.

At last, after a long telephone conversation with her sister on Wednesday, Regina gave in to Arnie's wish—mostly because Vicky had seemed calm and understanding and most of all not very curious about what had happened. That was important to Regina—more important than she would perhaps ever be able to say. It seemed to her that in the eight days since Arnie had been arrested in New York, she had had to cope with a seemingly endless flood of rancid curiosity masquerading as sympathy. Talking to Vicky on the telephone, she had finally broken down and cried. It was the first and only time since Arnie had been arrested in New York that she had allowed herself that bitter luxury. Arnie had been in bed asleep. Michael, who was drinking much too much and passing it off as "the spirit of the season," had gone down to O'Malley's for a beer or two with Paul Strickland, another factory reject in the game of faculty politics. It would probably end up being six beers, or eight, or ten. And if she went upstairs to his study later on, she would find him sitting bolt upright behind his desk, looking out into the dark, his eyes dry but bloodshot. If she tried to speak with him, his conversation would be horribly confused and centered too much in the past. She supposed her husband might be having a very quiet mental breakdown. She would not allow herself the same luxury (for so, in her own hurt and angry state, she thought it), and every night her mind ticked and whirred with plans and schemes until three or four o'clock. All these thoughts and schemes were aimed at one end: "Getting us over this." The only two ways she would allow her mind to approach what had happened were deliberately vague. She thought about "Arnie's trouble" and "Getting us over this."

But, talking to Vicky on the phone a few days after her son's arrest, Regina's iron control had wavered briefly. She cried on Vicky's shoulder long-distance, and Vicky had been calmly comforting, making Regina hate herself for all the cheap shots she had taken at Vicky over the years. Vicky, whose only daughter had dropped out of junior college to get married and become a housewife, whose only son had been content with a vocational-technical school (none of that for *her* son! Regina had thought with a private exultation); Vicky whose husband sold, of all hilarious things, life insurance. And Vicky (hilariouser and hilariouser) sold Tupperware. But it was Vicky she had been able to cry to, it had been Vicky to whom she had been able to express at least part of her tortured sense of disappointment and terror and hurt; yes, and the terrible *embarrassment* of it, of knowing that people were talking and that people who had for years wanted to see her take a fall were now satisfied. It was Vicky, maybe it had always been Vicky, and Regina decided that if there was to be a Christmas at all for them this miserable year, it would be at Vicky and Steve's ordinary suburban ranchhouse in the amusingly middle-class suburb of Ligonier, where most people still owned American cars and called a trip to McDonald's "eating out."

Mike, of course, simply went along with her decision; she would have expected no more and brooked no less.

For Regina Cunningham the three days following the news that Arnie was "in trouble" had been an exercise in pure cold control, a hard lunge for survival. Her survival, the family's survival, Arnie's survival—he might not believe that, but Regina found she hadn't the time to care. Mike's pain had never entered her equations; the thought that they could comfort each other had never even crossed her mind as a speculation. She had calmly put the cover on her sewing machine after Mike came downstairs and gave her the news. She did that, and then she had gone to the phone and had gotten to work. The tears she would later shed while talking to her sister had then been a thousand years away. She had brushed past Michael as if he were a piece of furniture, and he had trailed uncertainly after her as he had done all of their married life.

She called Tom Sprague, their lawyer, who, hearing that

their problem was criminal, hastily referred her to a colleague, Jim Warberg. She called Warberg and got an answering service that would not reveal Warberg's home number. She sat by the phone for a moment, drumming her fingers lightly against her lips, and then called their family lawyer back. Sprague hadn't wanted to give her Warberg's home telephone number, but in the end he gave in. When Regina finally let him go, Sprague sounded dazed, almost shellshocked. Regina in full spate often caused such a reaction.

She called Warberg, who said he absolutely couldn't take the case. Regina had lowered her bulldozer blade again. Warberg ended up not only taking the case but agreeing to go immediately to Albany, where Arnie was being held, to see what could be done. Warberg, speaking in the weak, amazed voice of a man who has been filled full of Novocain and then run over by a tractor, protested that he knew a perfectly good man in Albany who could get the lay of the land. Regina was adamant. Warberg went by private plane and reported back four hours later.

Arnie, he said, was being held on an open charge. He would be extradited to Pennsylvania the following day. Pennsylvania and New York had coordinated the bust along with three Federal agencies: the Federal Drug Control Task Force, the IRS, and the Bureau of Alcohol, Tobacco, and Firearms. The main target was not Arnie, who was small beans, but Will Darnell—Darnell, and whomever Darnell was doing business with. Those guys, Warberg said, with their suspected ties to organized crime and disorganized drug smuggling in the new South, were the big beans.

"Holding someone on an open charge is illegal," Regina had snapped immediately, drawing on a deep backlog of TV crime-show fare.

Warberg, not exactly overjoyed to be where he was when he had planned on spending a quiet evening at home reading a book, rejoined crisply, "I'd be down on my knees thanking God that's what they're doing. They caught him with a trunkload of unstamped cigarettes, and if I push them on it, they'll be more than happy to charge him, Mrs. Cunningham. I advise you and your husband to get over here to Albany. Quickly."

"I thought you said he was going to be extradited tomorrow—"

"Oh, yes, that's all been arranged. If we've got to play

hardball with these guys, we ought to be glad the game's going to be played on our home court. Extradition isn't the problem here."

"What is?"

"These people want to play knock-over-the-dominoes. They want to knock your son over onto Will Darnell. Arnold is not talking. I want you two to get over here and persuade him that it's in his best interest to talk."

"Is it?" she had asked hesitantly.

"Hell, yes!" Warberg's voice crackled back. "These guys don't want to put your son in jail. He's a minor from a good family with no previous criminal record, not even a school record of disciplinary problems. He can get out of this without even facing a judge. But he's got to talk."

So they had gone to Albany, and Regina had been taken down a short, narrow hallway faced in white tile, lit with high-intensity bulbs sunken into small wells in the ceiling and covered with wire mesh. The place had smelled vaguely of Lysol and urine, and she kept trying to convince herself that her *son* was being held here, her *son*, but achieving that conviction was a hard go. It didn't seem possible that it could be true. The possibility that it was all a hallucination seemed much more likely.

Seeing Arnie had stripped away that possibility in a hurry. The protective jacket of shock was likewise stripped away, and she felt a cold, consuming fear. It was at this moment that she had first seized on the idea of "Getting us over this," the way a drowning person will seize a life preserver. It was Arnie, it was her son, not in a jail cell (that was the only thing she had been spared, but she was grateful for even small favors) but in a small square room whose only furnishings were two chairs and a table scarred with cigarette burns.

Arnie had looked at her steadily, and his face seemed horribly gaunt, skull-like. He had been to the barber only a week before, and had gotten a surprisingly short haircut (after years of wearing it long, in emulation of Dennis), and now the overhead light shone down cruelly through what was left, making him appear momentarily bald, as if they had shaved his head to loosen his lips.

"Arnie," she said, and went to him—halfway to him. He turned his head away from her, his lips pressing together, and she stopped. A lesser woman might have burst into tears then, but Regina was not a lesser woman. She let the coldness come back and have its way with her. The coldness was all that would help now.

Instead of embracing him—something he obviously didn't want—she sat down and told him what had to be done. He refused. She ordered him to talk to the police. He refused again. She reasoned with him. He refused. She harangued him. He refused. She pleaded with him. He refused. Finally she just sat there dully, a headache thudding at her temples, and asked him why. He refused to tell her.

"I thought you were smart!" she shouted finally. She was nearly mad with frustration—the thing she hated above all others was not getting her way when she absolutely wanted to have it, *needed* to have it; this had in fact never happened to her since she left home. Until now. It was infuriating to be so smoothly and seamlessly balked by this boy who had once drawn milk from her breasts. "I thought you were smart but you're stupid! You're . . . you're an asshole! They'll put you in jail! Do you want to go to jail for that man Darnell? Is that what you want? He'll laugh at you! He'll *laugh* at you!" Regina could imagine nothing worse, and her son's apparent lack of interest in whether or not he was laughed at infuriated her all the more.

She rose from her chair and pushed her hair away from her brow and eyes, the unconscious gesture of a person who is ready to fight. She was breathing rapidly, and her face was flushed. To Arnie, she looked both younger and much, much older than he had ever seen her.

"I'm not doing it for Darnell," he said quietly, "and I'm not going to jail."

"What are you, Oliver Wendell Holmes?" she rejoined fiercely, but her anger was in some measure overmastered by relief. At least he could say *something*. "They caught you in his car with the trunk loaded with cigarettes! Illegal cigarettes."

Mildly, Arnie said, "They weren't in the trunk. They were in a compartment under the trunk. A secret compartment. And it was Will's car. Will told me to take his car."

She looked at him.

"Are you saying you didn't know they were there?"

Arnie looked at her with an expression she simply couldn't accept, it was so foreign to his face—it was contempt. *Good as gold, my boy's as good as gold*, she thought crazily.

"I knew, and Will knew. But they have to prove it, don't they?"

She could only look at him, amazed.

"If they do drop it on me somehow," he said, "I'll get a suspended sentence."

"Arnie," she said at last, "you're not thinking straight. Maybe your father—"

"Yes," he interrupted. "I'm thinking straight. I don't know what you're doing, but I'm thinking very straight." And he looked at her, his gray eyes so horribly blank that she could no longer stand it and had to leave.

In the small green reception room she walked blindly past her husband, who had been sitting on a bench with Warberg. "You go in," she said. "You make him see reason." She went on without waiting for his reply, not stopping until she was outside and the cold December air was painting her hot cheeks.

Michael went in and had no better luck; he came out with nothing more than a dry throat and a face that looked ten years older than it had going in.

At the motel, Regina told Warberg what Arnie had said and asked him if there was any chance he might be right.

Warberg looked thoughtful. "Yes, that's a possible defense," he said. "But it would be a helluva lot more possible if Arnie was the first domino in line. He's not. There's a used-car dealer here in Albany named Henry Buck. He was the catcher. He's been arrested too."

"What has he said?" Michael asked.

"I have no way of knowing. But when I tried to speak to his lawyer, he declined to speak with me. I find that ominous. If Buck talks, he puts the onus on Arnie. I'll bet you my house and lot that Buck can testify your son knew that secret compartment was there, and that's bad."

Warberg looked at them closely.

"You see, what your boy said to you is really only half-smart, Mrs. Cunningham. I'll be talking to him tomorrow, before they move him back to Pennsylvania. What I hope to make him see is that there's a possibility this whole thing could come down on his head."

The first flakes of snow began to swirl out of the heavy sky as they turned onto Steve and Vicky's street. *Is it snowing in Libertyville yet?* Arnie wondered, and touched the keys on their leather tab in his pocket. Probably it was.

Christine was still in Darnell's Garage, impounded. That

was all right. At least she was out of the weather. He would pick her up again. In time.

The previous weekend was like a blurred bad dream. His parents, haranguing him in the little white room, had seemed to bear the disconnected faces of strangers; they were heads talking in a foreign language. The lawyer they had hired, Warley or Warmly or whatever, kept talking about something he called the domino theory, and about the need to get out of "the condemned building before the whole thing falls down on your head, boy—there are two states and three Federal agencies bringing up the wrecking balls."

But Arnie was more worried about Christine.

It seemed clearer and clearer to him that Roland D. LeBay was either with him or hovering someplace near—he was, perhaps, coalescing inside him. This idea did not frighten Arnie; it comforted him. But he had to be careful. Not of Junkins; he felt that Junkins had only suspicions, and that they all lay in wrong directions, radiating out from Christine rather than in toward her.

But Darnell . . . there could be problems with Will. Yes, real problems.

That first night in Albany, after his mother and father had gone back to their motel, Arnie had been conducted to a holding cell, where he had fallen asleep with surprising ease and speed. And he had had a dream—not quite a nightmare, but something that seemed terribly disquieting. He had awakened watchfully in the middle of the night, his body running with sweat.

He had dreamed that Christine had been reduced in scale to a tiny '58 Plymouth no longer than a man's hand. It was on a slotcar track surrounded by HO-scale scenery that was amazingly apt—here was a plastic street that could be Basin Drive, here was another that could be JFK Drive, where Moochie Welch had been killed. A Lego building that looked exactly like Libertyville High. Plastic houses, paper trees . . .

. . . and a gigantic, hulking Will Darnell was at the controls that dictated how fast or how slowly the tiny Fury ran through all of this. His breath wheezed in and out of his damaged lungs with a windstorm sound.

You don't want to open your mouth, kiddo, Will said. He loomed over this scale-model world like the Amazing Colossal Man. *You don't want to frig with me because I'm in control; I can do this—*

And slowly, Will began to turn the control knob over toward FAST.

No! Arnie tried to scream. *No, don't do that, please! I love her! Please, you'll kill her!*

On the track, the tiny Christine raced through the tiny Libertyville faster and faster, her rear end switching on the curves as she shimmied on the far edge of centrifugal force, that dish-shaped mystery. Now she was simply a blur of white-over-red, her engine a high, angry wasp-whine.

Please! Arnie screamed. *Pleeeeeaaaaase!*

At last, Will had begun to turn the control back, looking grimly pleased. The little car began to slow down.

If you start to get ideas, you just want to remember where your car is, kiddo. Keep your mouth shut and we'll both live to fight another day. I've been in tighter jams than this—

Arnie had reached out to grasp the little car, to rescue it from the track. The dream-Will had slapped his hand away.

Whose bag is it, kiddo?

Will, please—

Let me hear you say it.

It's my bag.

Just remember it, kiddo.

And Arnie had awakened with that in his ears. There had been no more sleep for him that night.

Was it so unlikely that Will would know . . . well, would know something about Christine? No. He saw a great deal from behind that window, but he knew how to keep his mouth shut—at least until the time was right to open it. He might know what Junkins did not, that Christine's regeneration in November was not just strange but totally impossible. He would know that a lot of the repairs had never been made, at least not by Arnie.

What else would he know?

With a creeping coldness that moved up his legs to the root of his guts, Arnie realized at last that Will could have been at the garage the night Repperton and the others had died. In fact, it was more than possible. It was *probable*. Jimmy Sykes was simple, and Will didn't like to trust him alone.

You don't want to open your mouth. You don't want to frig with me because I can do this. . . .

But even supposing Will knew, who would believe him? It was too late for self-delusion now, and Arnie could no longer put the unthinkable thought away from himself . . . he no longer even wanted to. Who would believe Will if Will decided to tell someone that Christine sometimes ran by herself? That she had been out on her own the night Moochie Welch was killed, and the night those other hoods were killed? Would the police believe that? They would laugh themselves into a hemorrhage. Junkins? Getting warmer, but Arnie didn't believe Junkins would be able to accept such a thing, even if he wanted to. Arnie had seen his eyes. So even if Will did know, what good would his knowledge do?

Then, with mounting horror, Arnie realized that it didn't matter. Will would be out on bail tomorrow or the next day, and then Christine would be his hostage. He could torch it—he had torched plenty of cars in his time, as Arnie knew from sitting in the office and listening to him yarn—and after she was torched, a burned hulk, helpless, there was the crusher out back. In goes the cindered hulk of Christine on the conveyor belt, out comes a smashed cube of metal.

The cops have sealed the place.

But that didn't cut any ice, either. Will Darnell was a very old fox, and he stayed prepared for any contingency. If Will wanted to get in and torch Christine, he would do it . . . although it was much more likely, Arnie thought, that he would hire an insurance specialist to do the job—a guy who would throw double handfuls of charcoal-lighter cubes into the car and then toss a match.

In his mind's eye Arnie could see the blossoming flames. He could smell charring upholstery.

He lay on the cell bunk, his mouth dry, his heart beating rapidly in his chest.

You don't want to open your mouth. You don't want to frig with me. . . .

Of course, if Will tried something and got careless—if his concentration lapsed for even a moment—Christine would get him. But somehow Arnie didn't think Will would get careless.

The next day he had been taken back to Pennsylvania, charged, then bailed for a nominal sum. There would be a preliminary hearing in January, and there was already talk of a grand jury. The bust was front-page material across the state, although Arnie was only identified as "a youth" whose name was "being withheld by state and Federal authorities due to his minor status."

Arnie's name was common enough knowledge in Libertyville, however. In spite of its new exurban sprawl of drive-ins, fast-food emporiums, and Bowl-a-Ramas, it was still a faculty town where a lot of people were living in other people's back pockets. These people, mostly associated with Horlicks University, knew who had been driving for Will Darnell and who had been arrested over the New York State line with a trunkful of contraband cigarettes. It was Regina's nightmare.

Arnie went home in the custody of his parents—bailed for a thousand dollars—after a brief detour to jail. It was all nothing but a big shitting game of Monopoly, really. His parents had come up with the Get Out of Jail Free card. As expected.

"What are you smiling about, Arnie?" Regina asked him. Michael was driving the wagon along at fast walking speed, looking through the swirls of snow for Steve and Vicky's ranchhouse.

"Was I smiling?"

"Yes," she said, and touched his hair.

"I don't really remember," he said remotely, and she took her hand away.

They had come home on Sunday and his parents had left him pretty much alone, either because they didn't know how to talk to him or because they were utterly disgusted with him . . . or perhaps it was a combination of the two. He didn't give a crap which, and that was the truth. He felt washed out, exhausted, a ghost of himself. His mother had gone to bed and slept all that afternoon, after taking the telephone off the hook. His father puttered aimlessly in his workroom, running his electric planer periodically and then shutting it off.

Arnie sat in the living room watching a football playoff doubleheader, not knowing who was playing, not caring, content to watch the players run around, first in bright warm California sunshine, later in a mixture of rain and sleet that turned the playing field to churned-up mud and erased the lines.

Around six o'clock he dozed off.

And dreamed.

He dreamed again that night and the next, in the bed

where he had slept since earliest childhood, the elm outside
casting its old familiar shadow (a skeleton each winter that
gained miraculous new flesh each May). These dreams were
not like the dream of the giant Will looming over the slotcar
track. He could not remember these dreams at all more than
a few moments after waking. Perhaps that was just as well. A
figure by the roadside; a fleshless finger tapping a decayed
palm in a lunatic parody of instruction; an uneasy sense of
freedom and . . . escape? Yes, escape. Nothing else except . . .

Yes, he escaped from these dreams and back into reality
with one repeating image: He was behind the wheel of Christine, driving slowly through a howling blizzard, snow so thick
that he could literally see no farther than the end of her
hood. The wind was not a scream; it was a lower, more sinister sound, a basso roar. Then the image had changed. The
snow wasn't snow any longer; it was tickertape. The roar of
the wind was the roar of a great crowd lining both sides of
Fifth Avenue. They were cheering him. They were cheering
Christine. They were cheering because he and Christine had
. . . had . . .

Escaped.

Each time this confused dream retreated, he thought,
*When this is over I'm getting out. Getting out for sure. Going
to drive to Mexico.* And Mexico, as he imagined its steady sun
and its rural quiet, seemed more real than the dreams.

Shortly after awakening from the last of these dreams, the
idea of spending Christmas with Aunt Vicky and Uncle
Steve, just like in the old days, had come to him. He awoke
with it, and it clanged in his head with a peculiar persistence.
The idea seemed to be an awfully good one, an all-important
one. To get out of Libertyville before . . .

Well, before Christmas. What else?

So he began talking to his mother and father about it,
coming down particularly hard on Regina. On Wednesday,
she abruptly gave in and agreed. He knew she had talked to
Vicky, and Vicky hadn't been inclined to lord it over her, so
it was all right.

Now, on Christmas Eve, he felt that *everything* would soon
be all right.

"There it is, Mike," Regina said, "and you're going to
drive right by it, just like you do every time we come here."

Michael grunted and turned into the driveway. "I saw it,"

he said in the perpetually defensive tone he always seemed to use around his wife. *He's a donkey*, Arnie thought. *She talks to him like a donkey, she rides him like a donkey, and he brays like a donkey.*

"You're smiling again," Regina said.

"I was just thinking about how much I love you both," Arnie said. His father looked at him, surprised and touched; there was a soft gleam in his mother's eyes that might have been tears.

They really believed it.

The shitters.

By three o'clock that Christmas Eve the snow was still only isolated flurries, although the flurries were beginning to blend into each other. The delay in the storm's arrival was not good news, the weather forecasters said. It had compacted itself and turned even more vicious. Predictions of possible accumulations had gone from a foot to a possible eighteen inches, with serious drifting in high winds.

Leigh Cabot sat in the living room of her house, across from a small natural Christmas tree that was already beginning to shed its needles (in her house she was the voice of traditionalism and for four years had successfully staved off her father's wish for a synthetic tree and her mother's wish to kick off the holiday season with a goose or a capon instead of the traditional Thanksgiving turkey). She was alone in the house. Her mother and father had gone over to the Stewarts' for Christmas Eve drinks; Mr. Stewart was her father's new boss, and they liked each other. This was a friendship Mrs. Cabot was eager to promote. In the last ten years they had moved six times, hopping all over the eastern seaboard, and of all the places they had been, her mom liked Libertyville the best. She wanted to stay here, and her husband's friendship with Mr. Stewart could go a long way toward ensuring that.

All alone and still a virgin, she thought. That was an utterly stupid thing to think, but all the same she got up suddenly, as if stung. She went into the kitchen, over-conscious of that Formica wonderland's little servo-sounds: electric clock, the oven where a ham was baking (*turn that off at five if they're not back*, she reminded herself), a cool clunk from the freezer as the Frigidaire's icemaker made another cube.

She opened the fridge, saw a six-pack of Coke sitting in there next to Daddy's beer, and thought: *Get thee behind me, Satan.* Then she grabbed a can anyway. Never mind what it did to her complexion. She wasn't going with anyone now. If she broke out, so what?

The empty house made her uneasy. It never had before; she had always felt pleased and absurdly competent when they left her alone—a holdover from childhood days, no doubt. The house had always seemed comforting to her. But now the sounds of the kitchen, of the rising wind outside, even the scuff of her slippers on the linoleum—those sounds seemed sinister, even frightening. If things had worked out differently, Arnie could have been here with her. Her folks, especially her mother, had liked him. At first. Now, of course, after what had happened, her mother would probably wash her mouth out with soap if she knew Leigh was even thinking of him. But she *did* think of him. Too much of the time. Wondering why he had changed. Wondering how he was taking the breakup. Wondering if he was okay.

The wind rose to a shriek and then fell off a little, reminding her—for no reason, of course—of a car's engine revving and then falling off.

Won't come back from Dead Man's Curve, her mind whispered strangely, and for no reason at all (of course) she went to the sink and poured her Coke down the drain and wondered if she was going to cry, or throw up, or what.

She realized with dawning surprise that she was in a state of low terror.

For no reason at all.

Of course.

At least her parents had left the car in the garage (cars, she had cars on the brain). She didn't like to think of her dad trying to drive home from the Stewarts' in this, half-soused from three or four martinis (except that he always called them martoonis, with typical adult kittenishness). It was only three blocks, and the two of them had left the house bundled up and giggling, looking like a couple of large children on their way to make a snowman. The walk home would sober them up. It would be good for them. It would be good for them if . . .

The wind rose again—gunning around the eaves and then falling off—and she suddenly saw her mother and father walking up the street through clouds of blowing snow, holding onto each other to keep from falling on their drunken, lovable asses, laughing. Daddy maybe goosing Mom through her snowpants. The way he sometimes goosed her when he got a buzz on was also something that had always irritated Leigh precisely because it seemed such a juvenile thing for a grown man to do. But of course she loved them both. Her love was a part of the irritation, and her occasional exasperation with them was very much a part of her love.

They were walking together through a snow as thick as heavy smoke and then two huge green eyes opened in the white behind them, seeming to float . . . eyes that looked terribly like the circles of the dashboard instruments she had seen as she was choking to death . . . and they were growing . . . stalking her helpless, laughing, squiffy parents.

She drew a harsh breath and went back into the living room. She approached the telephone, almost touched it, then veered away and went back to the window, looking out into the white and cupping her elbows in the palms of her hands.

What had she been about to do? Call them? Tell them she was alone in the house and had gotten to thinking about Arnie's old and somehow slinking car, his steel girlfriend Christine, and that she wanted them to come home because she was scared for them and herself? Was that what she was going to do?

Cute, Leigh. Cute.

The plowed blacktop of the street was disappearing under new snow, but slowly; it had only just begun to snow really hard, and the wind periodically tried to clear the street with strong gusts that sent membranes of powder twisting and rising to merge with the whitish-gray sky of the stormy afternoon like slowly twisting smoke-ghosts. . . .

Oh, but the terror was there, it was real, and something was going to happen. She knew it. She had been shocked to hear that Arnie had been arrested for smuggling, but that reaction had been nowhere as strong as the sick fear she had felt when she opened the paper on an earlier day and saw what had happened to Buddy Repperton and those other two boys, that day when her first crazy, terrible, and somehow certain thought had been: *Christine.*

And now the premonition of some new piece of black work hung heavily on her, and she couldn't get rid of it, it was crazy, Arnie had been in Philadelphia at a chess tourney, she had asked around that day, that was all there was to it and she would not think about this anymore she would turn on all the radios the TV fill the house up with sound not think about that car that smelled like the grave that car that had tried to kill her murder her—

"Oh damn," she whispered. "Can't you *quit?*"

Her arms, sculpted rigidly in gooseflesh.

Abruptly she went to the telephone again, found the phone book, and as Arnie had done on an evening some two weeks before, she called Libertyville Community Hospital. A pleasant-voiced receptionist told her that Mr. Guilder had been checked out that morning. Leigh thanked her and hung up.

She stood thoughtful in the empty living room, looking at the small tree, the presents, the manger in the corner. Then she looked up the Guilders' number in the phone book and dialled it.

"Leigh," Dennis said, happily pleased.

The phone in her hand felt cold. "Dennis, can I come over and talk to you?"

"Today?" he asked, surprised.

Confused thoughts tumbled through her mind. The ham in the oven. She had to turn the oven off at five. Her parents would be home. It was Christmas Eve. The snow. And . . . and she didn't think it would be safe to be out tonight. Out walking on the sidewalks, when anything might come looming out of the snow. Anything at all. Not tonight, that was the worst. She didn't think it would be safe to be out tonight.

"Leigh?"

"Not tonight," she said. "I'm house-sitting for my folks. They're at a cocktail party."

"Yeah, mine too," Dennis said, amused. "My sister and I are playing Parcheesi. She cheats."

Faintly: "I do not!"

At another time it might have been funny. It wasn't now. "After Christmas. Maybe on Tuesday. The twenty-sixth. Would that be all right?"

"Sure," he said. "Leigh, is it about Arnie?"

"No," she said, clutching the telephone so tightly that her hand felt numb. She had to struggle with her voice. "No— not Arnie. I want to talk to you about Christine."

42 / The Storm Breaks

Well she's a hot-steppin hemi with a four on the floor,
She's a Roadrunner engine in a '32 Ford,
Yeah, late at night when I'm dead on the line,
I swear I think of your pretty face when I let her wind.
Well look over yonder, see those city lights?
Come on, little darlin, go ramroddin tonight.
                                          —Bruce Springsteen

By five o'clock that evening the storm had blanketed Pennsylvania; it screamed across the state from border to border, its howling throat full of snow. There was no final Christmas Eve rush, and most of the weary and shell-shocked clerks and salespeople were grateful to Mother Nature in spite of the missed overtime. There would, they told each other over Christmas Eve drinks in front of freshly kindled fires, be plenty of that when returns started on Tuesday.

Mother Nature didn't seem all that motherly that evening as early dusk gave way to full dark and then to blizzardy night. She was a pagan, fearsome old witch that night, a harridan on the wind, and Christmas meant nothing to her; she ripped down Chamber of Commerce tinsel and sent it gusting high into the black sky, she blew the large nativity scene in front of the police station into a snowbank where the sheep, the goats, the Holy Mother and Child were not found until a late January thaw uncovered them. And as a final spit in the eye of the holiday season, she tipped over the forty-foot tree that had stood in front of the Libertyville Municipal Building and sent it through a big window and into the town Tax Assessor's office. A good place for it, many said later.

By seven o'clock the plows had begun to fall behind. A Trailways bus bulled its way up Main Street at quarter past seven, a short line of cars dogging its silvery rump like puppies behind their mother, and then the street was empty except for a few slant-parked cars that had already been buried to the bumpers by the passing plows. By morning, most of them would be buried entirely. At the intersection of Main

359

Street and Basin Drive, a stop-and-go light that directed no one at all twisted and danced from its power cable in the wind. There was a sudden electrical fizzing noise and the light went dark. Two or three passengers from the last city bus of the day were crossing the street at the time; they glanced up and then hurried on.

By eight o'clock, when Mr. and Mrs. Cabot finally arrived home (to Leigh's great but unspoken relief), the local radio stations were broadcasting a plea from the Pennsylvania State Police for everyone to stay off the roads.

By nine o'clock, as Michael, Regina, and Arnie Cunningham, equipped with hot rum punches (Uncle Steve's avowed Specialty of the Season), were gathering around the television with Uncle Steve and Aunt Vicky to watch Alastair Sim in *A Christmas Carol*, a forty-mile stretch of the Pennsylvania Turnpike had been closed by drifting snow. By midnight almost all of it would be closed.

By nine-thirty, when Christine's headlights suddenly came on in Will Darnell's deserted garage, cutting a bright arc through the interior blackness, Libertyville had totally shut down, except for the occasional cruising plows.

In the silent garage, Christine's engine gunned and fell off.

Gunned and fell off.

In the empty front seat, the gearshift lever dropped down into DRIVE.

Christine began to move.

The electric eye gadget clipped to the driver's sun-visor hummed briefly. Its low sound was lost in the howl of the wind. But the door heard; it rattled upward obediently on its tracks. Snow blew in and swirled gustily.

Christine passed outside, wraithlike in the snow. She turned right and moved down the street, her tires cutting through the deep snow cleanly and firmly, with no spin, skid, or hesitation.

A turnblinker came on—one amber, winking eye in the snow. She turned left, toward JFK Drive.

Don Vandenberg sat behind the desk inside the office of his father's gas station. Both his feet and his pecker were up. He was reading one of his father's fuckbooks, a deeply incisive and thought-provoking tome titled *Swap-Around Pammie*. Pammie had gotten it from just about everyone but the milkman and the dog, and the milkman was coming up the drive and the dog was lying at her feet when the bell dinged, signalling a customer.

Don looked up impatiently. He had called his father at six, four hours ago, and asked him if he shouldn't close the station down—there wouldn't be enough business tonight to pay for the electricity it took to light up the sign. His father, sitting home warm and toasty and safely shitfaced, had told him to keep it open until midnight. If there ever was a Scrooge, Don had thought resentfully as he slammed the phone back down, his old man was it.

The simple fact was, he didn't like being alone at night anymore. Once, and not so long ago at that, he would have had plenty of company. Buddy would have been here, and Buddy was a magnet, drawing the others with his booze, his occasional gram of coke, but most of all with the simple force of his personality. But now they were gone. All gone.

Except sometimes it seemed to Don that they weren't. Sometimes it seemed to him (when he was alone, as he was tonight) that he might look up and see them sitting there—Richie Trelawney on one side, Moochie Welch on the other, and Buddy between them with a bottle of Texas Driver in his hand and a joint cocked behind his ear. Horribly white, all three of them, like vampires, their eyes as glazed as the eyes of dead fish. And Buddy would hold out the bottle and whisper, *Catch yourself a drink, asshole—pretty soon you'll be dead, like us.*

These fantasies were sometimes real enough to leave him with his mouth dry and his hands shaking.

And the reason why wasn't lost on Don. They never should have trashed old Cuntface's car that night. Every single one of the guys in on that little prank had died horrible deaths. All of them, that was, except for him and Sandy Galton, and Sandy had gotten in that old, broken-down Mustang of his and taken off somewhere. On these long night sihfts, Don often thought he would like to do the same.

Outside, the customer beeped his horn.

Dom slammed the book down on the desk next to the greasy credit-card machine and struggled into his parka, peering out at the car and wondering who would be crazy enough to be out in a shitstorm like this one. In the blowing snow, it was impossible to tell anything about either the car or the customer; he could make out nothing for sure but the headlights and the shape of the body, which was too long for a new car.

Someday, he thought, drawing on his gloves and bidding a reluctant farewell to his hard-on, his father would put in self-service pumps and all this shit would end. If people were crazy enough to be out on a night like this, they should have to pump their own gas.

The door almost ripped itself out of his hand. He held onto it so it wouldn't slam back into the cinderblock side of the building and maybe shatter the glass; he almost went down on his ass for his pains. In spite of the steady hooting of the wind (which he had been trying not to hear), he had totally misjudged the force of the storm. The very depth of the snow—better than eight inches—helped to keep him on his feet. *That fucking car must be on snowshoes,* he thought resentfully. *Guy gives me a credit-card I'm gonna fuse his spine.*

He waded through the snow, approaching the first set of islands. The fuckstick had parked at the far set. Naturally. Don tried to glance up once, but the wind threw snow into his face in a stinging sheet and he lowered his head quickly, letting the top of the parka's hood take the brunt of it.

He crossed in front of the car, bathed for a moment in the bright but heatless glow of its dual headlights. He struggled and floundered around to the driver's side. The pump island's fluorescents made the car into a garish white-over-purple burgundy shade. His cheeks were already numb. *If this guy wants a dollar's worth and asks me to check the oil, I'm telling him to cram it,* he thought, and raised his head into the sting of the snow as the window went down.

"Can I h—" he began, and the *h*-sound of *help you* became a high, hissing, strengthless scream: *hhhhhhhhhaaaaa- aahhhh—*

Leaning out of the window, less than six inches from his own face, was a rotting corpse. Its eyes were wide, empty sockets, its mummified lips were drawn back from a few yellowed, leaning teeth. One hand lay whitely on the steering wheel. The other, clicking horridly, reached out to touch him.

Don floundered backward, his heart a runaway engine in his chest, his terror a monstrous hot rock in his throat. The dead thing beckoned him, grinning, and the car's engine suddenly screamed, piling up revs.

"Fill it up," the corpse whispered, and in spite of his shock and horror, Don saw it was wearing the tattered and moss- slimed remains of an Army uniform. *"Fill it up, you shitter."*

Skull-teeth grinned in the fluorescent light. Far back in that mouth a bit of gold twinkled.

"Catch yourself a drink, asshole," another voice whispered hoarsely, and Buddy Repperton leaned forward in the back seat, extending a bottle of Texas Driver toward Don. Worms spilled and squirmed through his grin. Beetles crawled in what remained of his hair. *"I think you must need one."*

Don shrieked, the sound bulleting up and out of him. He whirled away, running through the snow in great leaping cartoon steps; he shrieked again as the car's engine screamed V-8 power; he looked back over his shoulder and saw that it was Christine standing by the pumps, Arnie's Christine, now moving, churning snow up behind her rear tires, and the things he had seen were gone—that was even worse, somehow. The things were gone. The car was moving on its own.

He had turned toward the street, and now he climbed up over the snowbank thrown up by the passing plows and down the other side. Here the wind had swept the pavement clear of everything except an occasional blister of ice. Don skidded on one of these. His feet went out from under him. He landed on his back with a thump.

A moment later the street was flooded with white light. Don rolled over and looked up, eyes straining wildly in their sockets, in time to see the huge white circles of Christine's headlights as she slammed through the snowbank and bore down on him like a locomotive.

Like Gaul, all of Libertyville Heights was divided into three parts. The semicircle closest to town on the low shoal of hills that had been known as Liberty Lookout until the mid-nineteenth century (a Bicentennial Plaque on the corner of Rogers and Tacklin streets so reminded) was the town's only real poor section. It was an unhappy warren of apartments and wooden-frame buildings. Rope clotheslines spanned scruffy back yards which were, in more temperate seasons, littered with kids and Fisher-Price toys—in too many cases, both kids and toys had been badly battered. This neighborhood, once middle-class, had been growing tackier ever since the war jobs had dried up in 1945. The decline moved slowly at first, then began to gain speed in the 60s and early 70s. Now the worst yet had come, although nobody would come right out and say it, at least not in public, where he or she could be quoted. Now the blacks were moving in. It was said in private, in the better parts of town, over barbecues and drinks: The blacks, God help us, the blacks are discovering Libertyville. The area had even gained its own name—not Liberty Lookout but the Low Heights. It was a name many found chillingly ghetto-ish. The editor of the *Keystone* had been quietly informed by several of his biggest advertisers that to use that phrase in print, thus legitimizing it, would make them very unhappy. The editor, whose mother had raised no fools, never did so.

Heights Avenue split off from Basin Drive in Libertyville proper and then began to rise. It cut cleanly through the middle of the Low Heights and then left them behind. The road then climbed through a greenbelt and into a residential area. This section of town was known simply as the Heights. All this might seem confusing to you—Heights-this and Heights-that—but Libertyville residents knew what they were talking about. When you said the Low Heights, you meant poverty, genteel or otherwise. When you left off the adjective "Low," you meant poverty's direct opposite. Here were fine old homes, most of them set tastefully back from the road, some of the finest behind thick yew hedges. Libertyville's movers and shakers lived here—the newspaper publisher, four doctors, the rich and dotty granddaughter of the man who had invented the rapid-fire ejection system for automatic pistols. Most of the rest were lawyers.

Beyond this area of respectable small-town wealth, Heights Avenue passed through a wooded area that was really too thick to be called a greenbelt; the woods lined both sides of the road for more than three miles. At the highest point of the Heights, Stanson Road branched off to the left, dead-ending at the Embankment, overlooking the town and the Libertyville Drive-In.

On the other side of this low mountain (but also known as the Heights), was a fairly old middle-class neighborhood where houses forty and fifty years old were slowly mellowing. As this area began to thin out into countryside, Heights Avenue became County Road No. 2.

At ten-thirty on that Christmas Eve, a 1958 two-tone Plymouth moved up Heights Avenue, its lights cutting through the snow-choked, raving dark. Long-time natives of the Heights would have said that nothing—except maybe a four-wheel-drive—could have gotten up Heights Avenue that night, but Christine moved along at a steady thirty miles an hour, headlights probing, wipers moving rhythmically back and forth, totally empty within. Its fresh tracks were alone, and in places they were almost a foot deep. The steady wind filled them in quickly. Now and again her front bumper and hood would explode through the ridged back of a snowdrift, nosing the powder aside easily.

Christine passed the Stanson Road turnoff and the Embankment, where Arnie and Leigh had once trysted. She reached the top of Liberty Heights and headed down the far side, at first through black woods cut only by the white ribbon that marked the road, then past the suburban houses with their cozy living-room lights and, in some cases, their cheery trim of Christmas lights. In one of these houses, a young man who had just finished playing Santa and who was having a drink with his wife to celebrate, happened to glance out and see headlights passing by. He pointed it out to her.

"If that guy came over the Heights tonight," this young man said with a grin, "he must have had the devil riding shotgun."

"Never mind that," she said. "Now that the kids are taken care of, what do *I* get from Santa?"

He grinned. "We'll think of something."

Farther down the road, almost at the point where the Heights ceased being the Heights, Will Darnell sat in the living room of the simple two-story frame house he had owned for thirty years. He was wearing a bald and fading blue terrycloth robe over his pajama bottoms, his huge sack of stomach pushing out like a swollen moon. He was watching the final conversion of Ebenezer Scrooge to the side of Goodness and Generosity, but not really seeing it. His mind was once more sifting through the pieces of a puzzle that grew steadily more fascinating: Arnie, Welch, Repperton, Christine. Will had aged a decade in the week or so since the bust. He had told that cop Mercer that he would be back doing business at the same old stand in two weeks, but in his heart he wondered. It seemed that lately his throat was always slimy from the taste of that goddam aspirator.

Arnie, Welch, Repperton . . . Christine.

"Boy!" Scrooge hailed down from his window, a caricature of the Christmas Spirit in his nightgown and cap. "Is the prize turkey still in the butcher's window?"

"Wot?" the boy asked. "The one as big as I am?"

"Yes, yes," Scrooge answered, giggling wildly. It was as if the three spirits had, instead of saving him, driven him mad. "The one as big as you are!"

Arnie, Welch, Repperton . . . LeBay?

Sometimes he thought it was not the bust that had tired him out and made him feel so constantly beaten and afraid. That it was not even the fact that they had busted his pet accountant or that the Federal tax people were in on it and were obviously loaded for bear this time. The tax people weren't the reason that he had begun scanning the street before going out mornings; the State Attorney General's Office didn't have anything to do with the sudden glances he had begun throwing back over his shoulder when he was driving home nights from the garage.

He had gone over what he had seen that night—or what he thought he had seen—again and again, trying to convince himself that it was absolutely not real . . . or that it absolutely was. For the first time in years he found himself doubting his own senses. And as the event receded into the past, it became easier to believe he had fallen asleep and dreamed the whole thing.

He hadn't seen Arnie since the bust, or tried to call him on the telephone. At first he had thought to use his knowledge about Christine as a lever to keep Arnie's mouth shut if the kid weakened and took a notion to talk—God knew the kid could go a long way toward sending him to jail if he cooperated with the cops. It wasn't until after the police had landed everywhere that Will realized how much the kid knew, and he had had a few panicky moments of self-appraisal (something else that was upsetting because it was so foreign to his nature): had *all* of them known that much? Repperton, and all the hoody Repperton clones stretching back over the years? Could he actually have been so stupid?

No, he decided. It was only Cunningham. Because Cunningham was different. He seemed to understand things almost intuitively. He wasn't all brag and booze and bullshit. In a queer way, Will felt almost fatherly toward the boy—not that he would have hesitated to cut the kid loose if it started to look as if he was going to rock the boat. *And not that I'd hesitate now,* he assured himself.

On the TV, a scratchy black-and-white Scrooge was with the Cratchets. The film was almost over. The whole bunch of them looked like loonies, and that was the truth, but Scrooge was definitely the worst. The look of mad joy in his eye was not so different from the look in the eye of a man Will had known twenty years before, a fellow named Everett Dingle who had gone home from the garage one afternoon and murdered his entire family.

Will lit a cigar. Anything to take the taste of the aspirator out of his mouth, that rotten taste. Lately it seemed harder than ever to catch his breath. Damned cigars didn't help, but he was too old to change now.

The kid hadn't talked—at least not yet he hadn't. They had turned Henry Buck, Will's lawyer had told him; Henry, who was sixty-three and a grandfather, would have denied Christ three times if they had promised him a dismissal or even a suspended sentence in return. Old Henry Buck was sicking up everything he knew, which fortunately wasn't a great deal. He knew about the fireworks and cigarettes, but that had only been two rings of what had been, at one time, a six- or seven-ring circus encompassing booze, hot cars, discount firearms (including a few machine-guns sold to gun nuts and homicidal hunters who wanted to see if one "would really tear up a deer like I heard"), and stolen antiques from New England. And in the last couple of years, cocaine. That had been a mistake; he knew it now. Those Colombians down in Miami were as crazy as shithouse rats. Come to think of it, they *were* shithouse rats. Thank *Christ* they hadn't caught the kid holding a pound of coke.

Well, they were going to hurt him this time—how much or how little depended a great deal on that weird seventeen-year-old kid, and maybe on his weird car. Things were as delicately balanced as a house of cards, and Will hesitated to do or say anything, for fear he would change things for the worse. And there was always the possibility that Cunningham would laugh in his face and call him crazy.

Will got up, cigar clamped in his jaws, and shut off his television set. He should go to bed, but maybe he would have a brandy first. He was always tired now, but sleep came hard.

He turned toward the kitchen . . . and that was when the horn began to honk outside. The sound came over the howl of the wind in short, imperative blasts.

Will stopped cold in the kitchen doorway and belted his robe closed across his big stomach. His face was sharp and rapt and alive, suddenly the face of a much younger man. He stood there a moment longer.

Three more short, sharp honks.

He turned back, taking the cigar from his mouth, and walked slowly across the living room. An almost dreamlike sense of *déjà vu* washed over him like warm water. Mixed with it was a feeling of fatalism. He knew it was Christine out there even before he brushed the curtain back and looked out. She had come for him, as he supposed he knew she might.

The car stood at the head of his turnaround driveway, little more than a ghost in the membranes of blowing snow. Its brights shone out in widening cones that at last disappeared into the storm. For a moment it seemed to Will that someone was behind the wheel, but he blinked again and saw that the car was empty. As empty as it had been when it returned to the garage that night.

Whonk. Whonk. Whonk-whonk.

Almost as if it were talking.

Will's heart thudded heavily in his chest. He turned abruptly to the phone. The time had come to call Cunningham after all. Call him and tell him to bring his pet demon to heel.

He was halfway there when he heard the car's engine scream. The sound was like the shriek of a woman who scents treachery. A moment later there was a heavy crunch. Will went back to the window and was in time to see the car backing away from the high snowbank that fronted the end of his driveway. Its hood, sprayed with clods of snow, had crimped slightly. The engine revved again. The rear wheels spun in the powdery snow and then caught hold. The car leaped across the snowy road and struck the snowbank again. More snow exploded up and raftered away on the wind like cigar smoke blown in front of a fan.

Never do it, Will thought. *And even if you get into the driveway, what then? You think I'm going to come out and play?*

Wheezing more sharply than ever, he went back to the phone, looked up Cunningham's home number, and started to dial it. His fingers jittered, he misdialled, swore, hit the cutoff buttons, started again.

Outside, Christine's engine revved. A moment later there was a crunch as she hit the embankment for the third time. The wind wailed and snow struck the big picture window like dry sand. Will licked his lips and tried to breathe slowly. But his throat was closing up; he could feel it.

The phone began to ring on the other end. Three times. Four.

Christine's engine screamed. Then the heavy thud as she

hit the snowbank the passing plows had piled up at both ends of Will's semicircular driveway.

Six rings. Seven. Nobody home.

"Shit on it," Will whispered, and slammed the phone back down. His face was pale, his nostrils flared wide, like the nostrils of an animal scenting fire upwind. His cigar had gone out. He threw it on the carpet and groped to his bathrobe pocket as he hurried back to the window. His hand found the comforting shape of his aspirator, and his fingers curled around its pistol grip.

Headlights shone momentarily in his face, nearly blinding him, and Will raised his free hand to shield his eyes. Christine hit the snowbank again. Little by little she was bludgeoning her way through to the driveway. He watched her back up across the road and wished savagely for a plow to come along now and hit the damned thing broadside.

No plow came. Christine came again instead, engine howling, lights glaring across his snow-covered lawn. She struck the snowbank, pushing mounds of snow violently to either side. The front end canted up and for a moment Will thought she was going to come right over what was left of the frozen, hard-packed embankment. Then the rear wheels lost traction and spun frantically.

She backed up.

Will's throat felt as if its bore was down to a pinhole. His lungs strained for air. He took the aspirator out and used it. The police. He ought to call the police. They would come. Cunningham's '58 couldn't get him. He was safe in his house. He was—

Christine came again, accelerating across the road, and this time she hit the bank and came over it easily, front end at first tilting up, splashing the front of his house with light, then crashing back down. She was in the driveway. Yes, all right, but she could come no further, she . . . it . . .

Christine never slowed. Still accelerating, she crossed the semicircular driveway on a tangent, plowed through the shallower, looser snow of the side yard, and roared directly at the picture window where Will Darnell stood looking out.

He staggered backward, gasping hard, and tripped over his own easy chair.

Christine hit the house. The picture window exploded, letting in the shrieking wind. Glass flew in deadly arrows, each of them reflecting Christine's headlamps. Snow blew in and danced over the rug in erratic corkscrews. The headlights momentarily illuminated the room with the unnatural glare of a television studio, and then she withdrew, her front bumper dragging, her hood popped up, her grille smashed into a chrome-dripping grin full of fangs.

Will was on his hands and knees, gagging harshly for breath, his chest heaving. He was vaguely aware that, had he not tripped over his chair and fallen down, he probably would have been cut to ribbons by flying glass. His robe had come undone and flapped behind him as he got to his feet. The wind streaming in the window picked up the *TV Guide* from the little table by his chair, and the magazine flew across the room to the foot of the stairs, pages riffling. Will got the telephone in both hands and dialled 0.

Christine reversed along her own tracks through the snow. She went all the way back to the flattened snowbank at the entrance to the driveway. Then she came forward, accelerating rapidly, and as she came the hood immediately began to uncrimp, the grille to regenerate itself. She slammed into the side of the house below the picture window again. More glass flew; wood splintered and groaned and creaked. The big window's low ledge cracked in two, and for a moment Christine's windshield, now cracked and milky, seemed to peer in like a giant alien eye.

"Police," Will said to the operator. His voice was hardly there; it was all wheeze and whistle. His bathrobe flapped in the cold blizzard wind coming in through the shattered window. He saw that the wall below the window was nearly shattered. Broken chunks of lathing protruded like fractured bones. It couldn't get in, could it? *Could* it?

"I'm sorry, sir, you'll have to speak up," the operator said. "We seem to have a very bad connection."

Police, Will said, but this time it wasn't even a whisper; only a hiss of air. Dear God, he was strangling, he was choking; his chest was a locked bank vault. Where was his aspirator?

"Sir?" the operator asked doubtfully.

There it was, on the floor. Will dropped the telephone and scrabbled for it.

Christine came again, roaring across the lawn and striking the side of the house. This time the entire wall gave way in a shrapnel-burst of glass and lathing, and incredibly, nightmarishly, Christine's smashed and dented hood was in his living room, she was *in*, he could smell exhaust and hot engine.

Christine's underworks caught on something, and she reversed back out of the ragged hole with a screech of pulling boards, her front end a gored ruin dusted with snow and plaster. But she would come again in a few seconds, and this time she might—just might—

Will grabbed his respirator and ran blindly for the stairs.

He was only halfway up when the revving whine of her engine came again and he turned to watch, leaning on the railing more than grasping it.

The stairwell's height lent a certain nightmare perspective. He watched Christine come across the snow-covered lawn, saw her hood fly up so that now her front end resembled the mouth of a huge red and white alligator. Then it snapped off altogether as she struck the house again, this time doing better than forty. She ripped away the last of the window frame and sprayed more splintered boards across his living room. Her headlights bounced upward, glaring, and then she was *in,* she was *in his house,* leaving a huge torn hole in the wall behind her with an electrical cable hanging out onto the rug like a black severed artery. Little clouds of blown-in fiberglass insulation danced on the cold wind like milkweed puffs.

Will screamed and couldn't hear himself over the blatting roar of her engine. The Sears Muzzler Arnie had put on her—one of the few things he *really* put on her, Will thought crazily—had hung up on the sill of the house, along with most of the tailpipe.

The Fury roared across the living room, knocking Will's La-Z-Boy armchair onto its side, where it lay like a dead pony. The floor under Christine creaked uneasily and a part of Will's mind screamed: *Yes! Break! Break! Spill the goddam thing into the cellar! Let's see it climb out of there!* And this image was replaced with the image of a tiger in a pit that had been dug and then camouflaged by wily natives.

But the floor held—at least for the time being, it held.

Christine roared across the living room at him. Behind, she left a zig-zag pattern of snowy tire prints on the rug. She slammed into the stairs. Will was thrown back against the wall. His aspirator fell out of his hand and tumbled end over end all the way to the bottom.

Christine reversed across the room, floorboards groaning underneath. Her rear end stuck the Sony TV, and the picture tube imploded. She roared forward again and struck the side of the stairs again, shattering lath and gouging out plaster. Will could feel the entire structure grow wobbly under him.

There was an awful sensation of *lean*. For a moment Christine was directly beneath him; he could look down into the oily gut of her engine compartment, could feel the heat of her V-8 mill. She reversed again, and Will scrambled up the stairs, heaving for air, clawing at the fat sausage of his throat, eyes bulging.

He reached the top an instant before Christine hit the wall again, turning the center of the stairs into a jumbled wreck. A long splinter of wood fell into her engine. The fan chewed it up and spat out coarse-grained sawdust and smaller splinters. The entire house smelled of gas and exhaust. Will's ears rang with the heavy thunder of that merciless engine.

She backed up again. Now her tires had chewed ragged trenches in the carpet. *Down the hall*, Will thought. *Attic, Attic'll be safe. Yes, the at . . . oh God . . . oh God . . . oh my GOD—*

The final pain came with sharp, spiking suddenness. It was as if his heart had been punctured with an icicle. His left arm locked with pain. Still there was no breath; his chest heaved uselessly. He staggered backward. One foot danced out over nothingness, and then he fell back down the stairs in two great bone-snapping barrel rolls, legs flying over his head, arms waving, blue bathrobe sailing and flapping.

He landed in a heap at the bottom and Christine pounced upon him: struck him, reversed, struck him again, snapped off the heavy newel post at the foot of the stairs like a twig, reversed, struck him again.

From beneath the floor came the increasing mutter of supports splintering and bowing. Christine paused in the middle of the room for a moment, as if listening. Two of her tires were flat; a third had come half off the wheel. The left side of the car was punched inward, scraped clean of paint in great bald patches.

Suddenly her gearshift dropped into reverse. Her engine screamed, and she rocketed back across the room and out of the ragged hole in the side of Will Darnell's house, her rear end dropping down several inches and into the snow. The tires spun, found some purchase, and pulled her out. She backed limpingly toward the road, her engine chopping and missing now, blue smoke hazing the air around her, oil dripping and spraying.

At the road, she turned back toward Libertyville. The gearshift lever dropped into DRIVE, but at first the damaged transmission wouldn't catch; when it did she rolled slowly away from the house. Behind her, from Will's house, a broad bar of light shone out onto the churned-up snow in a shape that was not at all like the neat rectangle of light thrown by a window. The shape of the light on the snow was senseless and strange.

She moved slowly, lurching from side to side on her flats like a very old drunk making her way up an alley. Snow fell thickly, driven into slanting lines by the wind.

One of her headlights, shattered in her last destructive, trampling charge, flickered and came on.

One of the tires began to reinflate, then the other.

The clouds of stinking oil-smoke began to diminish.

The engine's chopping, uncertain note smoothed out.

The missing hood began to reappear, from the windshield end down, looking weirdly like a scarf or cardigan being knitted by invisible needles; the raw metal drew itself out of nothing, gleamed steel-gray, and then darkened to red as if filling with blood.

The cracks in the windshield began to run in reverse, leaving unflawed smoothness behind themselves.

The other headlights came on, one after the other; now she moved with swift surety through the stormy night, behind the cutting edge of her confident brights.

Her odometer spun smoothly backward.

Forty-five minutes later she sat in the darkness at the late Will Darnell's Do-It-Yourself Garage, in stall twenty. The wind howled and moaned in the ranks of the wrecks out back, rusting hulks that perhaps held their own ghosts and their own baleful memories as powdery snow skirled across the ripped and tattered seats, their balding floor carpets.

Her engine ticked slowly, cooling.

at were the wandered moments.
How could he, Michael, have changed things? What was the
worry of a memory? When had the sickness started to creep

He squinted harder, turning to the winter-whine outside.

3 ◦
Christine—
Teenage
Death—Songs

43 / Leigh Comes to Visit

James Dean in that Mercury '49,
Junior Johnson Bonner through the woods o' Caroline,
Even Burt Reynolds in that black Trans-Am,
All gonna meet down at the Cadillac Ranch.
—Bruce Springsteen

About fifteen minutes before Leigh was due, I got my crutches under me and worked my way to the chair closest the door, so she'd be sure to hear me when I hollered for her to come in. Then I picked up my copy of *Esquire* again and turned back to an article titled "The Next Vietnam," which was part of a school assignment. I still had no success reading it. I was nervous and scared, and part of it—a lot of it, I guess—was simple eagerness. I wanted to see her again.

The house was empty. Not too long after Leigh called that stormy Christmas Eve afternoon, I got my dad aside and asked him if he could maybe take Mom and Elaine someplace the afternoon of the twenty-sixth.

"Why not?" he agreed amiably enough.

"Thanks, Dad."

"Sure. But you owe me one, Dennis."

"Dad!"

He winked solemnly. "I'll scratch your back if you'll scratch mine."

"Nice guy," I said.

"A real prince," he agreed.

My dad, who is no slouch, asked me if it had to do with Arnie. "She's his girl, isn't she?"

"Well," I said, not sure just what the situation was, and uncomfortable for reasons of my own, "she has been. I don't know about now."

"Problems?"

"I didn't do such a hot job being his eyes, did I?"

"It's hard to see from a hospital bed, Dennis. I'll make sure your mother and Ellie are out Tuesday afternoon. Just be careful, okay?"

Since then, I've pondered exactly what he might have meant by that; he surely couldn't have been worried about me trying to jump Leigh's bones, with one upper leg still in plaster and a half-cast on my back. I think maybe he was just afraid that something had gotten terribly out of whack, with my old childhood friend suddenly a stranger, and a stranger who was out on bail at that.

I sure thought something was out of whack, and it scared the piss out of me. The *Keystone* doesn't publish on Christmas, but all three Pittsburgh network-TV affiliates and both the independent channels had the story of what had happened to Will Darnell, along with bizarre and frightening pictures of his house. The side facing the road had been demolished. It was the only word which fit. That side of the house looked as if some mad Nazi had driven a Panzer tank through it. The story had been headlined this morning—FOUL PLAY SUSPECTED IN BIZARRE DEATH OF SUSPECTED CRIME FIGURE. That was bad enough, even without another picture of Will Darnell's house with that big hole punched in the side. But you had to check page three to get the rest of it. The other item was smaller because Will Darnell had been a "suspected crime figure," and Don Vandenberg had only been a dipshit dropout gas-jockey.

SERVICE STATION ATTENDANT KILLED IN CHRISTMAS EVE HIT-AND-RUN, this headline read. A single column followed. The story ended with the Libertyville Chief of Police theorizing that the driver had probably been drunk or stoned. Neither he nor the *Keystone* made any attempt to connect the deaths, which had been separated by almost ten miles on the night of a screaming blizzard which had stopped all traffic in Ohio and western Pennsylvania. But I could make connections. I didn't want to, but I couldn't help it. And hadn't my father been looking at me strangely several times during the morning? Yes. Once or twice it had seemed he would say something—I had no idea what I would say if he did; Will Darnell's death, bizarre as it had been, was nowhere nearly as bizarre as my suspicions. Then he had closed his mouth without speaking. That, to be up front about it, was something of a relief.

The doorbell chimed at two past two.

"Come on in!" I yelled, getting up on my crutches again anyway.

The door opened and Leigh poked her head in. "Dennis?"

"Yeah. Come on in."

She did, looking very pretty in a bright red ski parka and dark blue pants. She pushed the parka's fur-edged hood back.

"Sit down," she said, unzipping her parka. "Go on, right now, that's an order. You look like a big dumb stork on those things."

"Keep it up," I said, sitting down again with an ungainly plop. When you're cast in plaster, it's never like in the movies; you never sit down like Cary Grant getting ready to have cocktails at the Ritz with Ingrid Bergman. It all happens at once, and if the cushion you land on doesn't give out a big loud raspberry, as if your sudden descent had scared you into cutting the cheese, you count yourself ahead of the game. This time I got lucky. "I'm such a sucker for flattery that I make myself sick."

"How are you, Dennis?"

"Mending," I said. "How about you?"

"I've been better," she said in a low voice, and bit at her lower lip. This can sometimes be a seductive gesture on a girl's part, but it wasn't this time.

"Hang up your coat and sit down yourself."

"Okay." Her eyes touched mine, and looking at them was a little much. I looked someplace else, thinking about Arnie.

She hung her coat up and came back into the living room slowly. "Your folks—?"

"I got my father to take everyone out," I said. "I thought maybe"—I shrugged—"we ought to talk just between ourselves."

She stood by the sofa, looking at me across the room. I was struck again by the simplicity of her good looks—her lovely girl's figure outlined in dark blue pants and a sweater of a lighter, powdery blue, an outfit that made me think about skiing. Her hair was tied in a loose pigtail and lay over her left shoulder. Her eyes were the color of her sweater, maybe a little darker. A cornfed American beauty, you would have said, except for the high cheekbones, which seemed a little arrogant, bespeaking some older, more exotic heritage. Maybe some fifteen or twenty generations back there was a Viking in the woodpile.

Or maybe that isn't what I was thinking at all.

She saw me looking at her too long and blushed. I looked away.

"Dennis, are you worried about him?"

"Worried? Scared might be a better word."

"What do you know about that car? What has he told you?"

"Not much," I said. "Look, would you like something to drink? There's some stuff in the fridge—" I felt for my crutches.

"Sit still," she said. "I would like something, but I'll get it. What about you?"

"I'll take a ginger ale, if there's one left."

She went into the kitchen and I watched her shadow on the wall, moving lightly, like a dancer. There was a momentary added weight in my stomach, almost like a sickness. There's a name for that sort of sickness. I think it's called falling in love with your best friend's girl.

"You've got an automatic ice-maker." Her voice floated back. "We've got one too. I love it."

"Sometimes it goes crazy and sprays ice-cubes all over the floor," I said. "It's like Jimmy Cagney in *White Heat*. 'Take that, you dirty rats.' It drives my mother crazy." I was babbling.

She laughed. Ice-cubes clinked in glasses. Shortly she came back with two glasses of ice and two cans of Canada Dry.

"Thanks," I said, taking mine.

"No, thank *you*," she said, and now her blue eyes were dark and sober. "Thanks for being around. If I had to deal with this alone, I think I'd . . . I don't know."

"Come on," I said. "It's not that bad."

"Isn't it? Do you know about Darnell?"

I nodded.

"And that other one? Don Vandenberg?"

So she had made the connection too.

I nodded again. "I saw it. Leigh, what is it about Christine that bothers you?"

For a long time I didn't know if she was going to answer. If she would be *able* to answer. I could see her struggling with it, looking down at her glass, held in both hands.

At last in a very low voice, she said, "I think she tried to kill me."

I don't know what I had expected, but it wasn't that. "What do you mean?"

She talked, first hesitantly, then more rapidly, until it was pouring out of her. It is a story you have already heard, so I won't repeat it here; suffice it to say that I tried to tell it pretty much as she told it to me. She hadn't been kidding about being scared. It was in the pallor of her face, the little hitches and gulps of her voice, the way her hands constantly caressed her upper arms, as if she was too cold in spite of the sweater, and the more she talked, the more scared I got.

She finished by telling me how, as consciousness dwindled, the dashboard lights had seemed to turn into watching eyes. She laughed nervously at this last, as if trying to take the curse off an obvious absurdity, but I didn't laugh back. I was remembering George LeBay's dry voice as we sat in cheap patio chairs in front of the Rainbow Motel, his voice telling me the story of Roland, Veronica, and Rita. I was remembering those things and my mind was making unspeakable connections. Lights were going on. I didn't like what they were revealing. My heart started to thud heavily in my chest, and I couldn't have joined her laughter if my life had depended on it.

She told me about the ultimatum she had given him—her or the car. She told me about Arnie's furious reaction. That had been the last time she went out with him.

"Then he got arrested," she said, "and I started to think . . . think about what had happened to Buddy Repperton and those other boys . . . and Moochie Welch. . . ."

"And now Vandenberg and Darnell."

"Yes. But that's not all." She drank from her glass of ginger ale and then poured in more. The edge of the can chattered briefly against the rim of the glass. "Christmas Eve, when I called you, my mom and dad went out for drinks at my dad's boss's house. And I started to get nervous. I was thinking about . . . oh, I don't know what I was thinking about."

"I think you do."

She put a hand to her forehead and rubbed it, as if she was getting a headache. "I suppose I do. I was thinking about that car being out. *Her.* Being out and getting them. But if she was out on Christmas Eve, I guess she had plenty to keep her busy without bothering my par—" She slammed her glass down, making me jump. "And why do I keep talking about that car as if it was a person?" she cried out. Tears had begun to spill down her cheeks. "Why do I keep doing that?"

On that night, I saw all too clearly what comforting her could lead to. Arnie was between us—and part of myself was, too. I had known him for a long time. A long good time.

But that was then; this was now.

I got my crutches under me, thumped my way across to

the couch, and plopped down beside her. The cushions sighed. It wasn't a raspberry, but it was close.

My mother keeps a box of Kleenex in the drawer of the little endtable. I pulled one out, looked at her, and pulled out a whole handful. I gave them to her and she thanked me. Then, not liking myself much, I put an arm around her and held her.

She stiffened for a moment . . . and then let me draw her against my shoulder. She was trembling. We just sat that way, both of us afraid of even the slightest movement, I think. Afraid we might explode. Or something. Across the room, the clock ticked importantly on the mantelpiece. Bright winterlight fell through the bow windows that give a three-way view of the street. The storm had blown itself out by noon on Christmas Day, and now the hard and cloudless blue sky seemed to deny that there even was such a thing as snow—but the dunelike drifts rolling across lawns all up and down the street like the backs of great buried beasts confirmed it.

"The smell," I said at last. "How sure are you about that?"

"It was *there!*" she said, drawing away from me and sitting up straight. I collected my arm again, with a mixed sensation of disappointment and relief. "It really was there . . . a rotten, horrible smell." She looked at me. "Why? Have you smelled it too?"

I shook my head. I never had. Not really.

"What do you know about that car, then?" she asked. "You know something. I can see it on your face."

It was my turn to think long and hard, and oddly what came into my mind was an image of nuclear fission from some science textbook. A cartoon. You don't expect to see cartoons in science books, but as someone once said to me, there are many devious twists and turns along the path of public education . . . in point of fact, that someone had been Arnie himself. The cartoon showed two hotrod atoms speeding toward each other and then slamming together. Presto! Instead of a lot of wreckage (and atom ambulances to take away the dead and wounded neutrons), critical mass, chain reaction, and one hell of a big bang.

Then I decided the memory of that cartoon really wasn't odd at all. Leigh had certain information I hadn't had before. The reverse was also true. In both cases a lot of it was guesswork, a lot of it was subjective feeling and circumstance . . . but enough of it was hard information to be really scary. I wondered briefly what the police would do if they knew what we did. I could guess: nothing. Could you bring a ghost to trial? Or a car?

"Dennis?"

"I'm thinking," I said. "Can't you smell the wood burning?"

"What do you know?" she asked again.

Collision. Critical mass. Chain reaction. Kaboom.

The thing was, I was thinking, if we put our information together, we would have to do something or tell someone. Take some action. We—

I remembered my dream: the car sitting there in LeBay's garage, the motor revving up and then falling off, revving up again, the headlights coming on, the shriek of tires.

I took her hand in both of mine. "Okay," I said. "Listen, Arnie: he bought Christine from a guy who is dead now. A guy named Roland D. LeBay. We saw her on his lawn one day when we were coming home from work, and—"

"You're doing it too," she said softly.

"What?"

"Calling it *she*."

I nodded, not letting go of her hands. "Yeah. I know. It's hard to stop. The thing is, Arnie wanted her—or it, or whatever that car is—from the first time he laid eyes on her. And I think now . . . I didn't then, but I do now . . . that LeBay wanted Arnie to have her just as badly; that he would have given her to him if it had come to that. It's like Arnie saw Christine and knew, and then LeBay saw Arnie and knew the same thing."

Leigh pulled her hands free of mine and began to rub her elbows restlessly again. "Arnie said he paid—"

"He paid, all right. And he's still paying. That is, if Arnie's left at all."

"I don't understand what you mean."

"I'll show you," I said, "in a few minutes. First, let me give you the background."

"All right."

"LeBay had a wife and daughter. This was back in the fifties. His daughter died beside the road. She choked to death. On a hamburger."

Leigh's face grew white, then whiter; for a moment she seemed as milky and translucent as clouded glass.

"Leigh!" I said sharply. "Are you all right?"

"Yes," she said with a chilling placidity. Her color didn't improve. Her mouth moved in a horrid grimace that was perhaps intended to be a reassuring smile. "I'm fine." She stood up. "Where is the bathroom, please?"

"There's one at the end of the hall," I said. "Leigh, you look awful."

"I'm going to vomit," she said in that same placid voice, and walked away. She moved jerkily now, like a puppet, all the dancer's grace I had seen in her shadow now gone. She walked out of the room slowly, but when she was out of sight the rhythm of her stride picked up; I heard the bathroom door thrown open, and then the sounds. I leaned back against the sofa and put my hands over my eyes.

When she came back she was still pale but had regained a touch of her color. She had washed her face and there were still a few drops of water on her cheeks.

"I'm sorry," I said.

"It's all right. It just . . . startled me." She smiled wanly. "I guess that's an understatement." She caught my eyes with hers. "Just tell me one thing, Dennis. What you said. Is it true? Really true?"

"Yeah," I said. "It's true. And there's more. But do you really want to hear any more?"

"No," she said. "But tell me anyway."

"We could drop it," I said, not really believing it.

Her grave, distressed eyes held mine. "It might be . . . safer . . . if we didn't," she said.

"His wife committed suicide shortly after their daughter died."

"The car . . ."

". . . was involved."

"How?"

"Leigh—"

"How?"

So I told her—not just about the little girl and her mother, but about LeBay himself, as his brother George had told me. His bottomless reservoir of anger. The kids who had made fun of his clothes and his bowl haircut. His escape into the Army, where everyone's clothes and haircuts were the same. The motor pool. The constant railing at the shitters, particularly those shitters who brought him their big expensive cars to be fixed at government expense. The Second World War. The brother, Drew, killed in France. The old Chevrolet. The old Hudson Hornet. And through it all, a steady and unchanging backbeat, the anger.

"That word," Leigh murmured.

"What word?"

"Shitters." She had to force herself to say it, her nose wrinkling in rueful and almost unconscious distaste. "*He* uses it. Arnie.*"

"I know."

We looked at each other, and her hands found mine again.

"You're cold," I said. Another bright remark from that font of wisdom, Dennis Guilder. I got a million of em.

"Yes. I feel like I'll never be warm again."

I wanted to put my arms around her and didn't. I was afraid to. Arnie was still too much mixed up in things. The most awful thing—and it *was* awful—was how it seemed more and more that he was dead . . . dead, or under some weird enchantment.

"Did his brother say anything else?"

"Nothing that seems to fit." But a memory rose like a bubble in still water and popped: *He was obsessed and he was angry, but he was not a monster,* George LeBay had told me. *At least . . . I don't* think *he was.* It had seemed that, lost in the past as he had been, he had been about to say something more . . . and then had realized where he was and that he was talking to a stranger. What had he been about to say?

All at once I had a really monstrous idea. I pushed it away. It went . . . but it was hard work, pushing that idea. Like pushing a piano. And I could still see its outlines in the shadows.

I became aware that Leigh was looking at me very closely, and I wondered how much of what I had been thinking showed on my face.

"Did you take Mr. LeBay's address?" she asked.

"No." I thought for a moment, and then remembered the funeral, which now seemed impossibly far back in time. "But I imagine the Libertyville American Legion Post has it. They buried LeBay and contacted the brother. Why?"

Leigh only shook her head and went to the window, where she stood looking out into the blinding day. *Shank of the year,* I thought randomly.

She turned back to me, and I was struck by her beauty again, calm and undemanding except for those high, arrogant cheekbones—the sort of cheekbones you might expect to see on a lady probably carrying a knife in her belt.

"You said you'd show me something," she said. "What was it?"

I nodded. There was no way to stop now. The chain reaction had started. There was no way to shut it down.

"Go upstairs," I said. "My room's the second door on the left. Look in the third drawer of my dresser. You'll have to dig under some of my undies, but they won't bite."

She smiled—only a little, but even a little was an improvement. "And what am I going to find? A Baggie of dope?"

"I gave that up last year," I said, smiling back. " 'Ludes this year. I finance my habit selling heroin down at the junior high."

"What is it? Really?"

"Arnie's autograph," I said, "immortalized on plaster."

"His autograph?"

I nodded. "In duplicate."

She found them, and five minutes later we were on the couch again, looking at two squares of plaster cast. They sat side by side on the glass-topped coffee table, slightly ragged on the sides, a little the worse for wear. Other names danced off into limbo on one of them. I had saved the casts, had even directed the nurse on where to cut them. Later I had cut out the two squares, one from the right leg, one from the left.

We looked at them silently:

Arnie Cunningham on the right;

Arnie Cunningham on the left.

Leigh looked at me, questioning and puzzled. "Those are pieces of your—"

"My casts, yeah."

"Is it . . . a joke, or something?"

"No joke. I watched him sign both of them." Now that it was out, there was a queer kind of loosening, of relief. It was good to be able to share this. It had been on my mind for a long time, itching and digging away.

"But they don't look anything alike."

"You're telling me," I said. "But Arnie isn't much like he used to be either. And it all goes back to that goddam car." I poked savagely at the square of plaster on the left. "That isn't his signature. I've known Arnie almost all my life. I've seen his homework papers, I've seen him send away for things, I've watched him endorse his paychecks, *and that is not his signature*. The one on the right, yes. This one, no. You want to do something for me tomorrow, Leigh?"

"What?"

I told her. She nodded slowly. "For us."

"Huh?"

"I'll do it for us. Because we have to do something, don't we?"

"Yes," I said. "I guess so. You mind a personal question?"

She shook her head, her remarkable blue eyes never leaving mine.

"How have you been sleeping lately?"

"Not so well," she said. "Bad dreams. How about you?"

"No. Not so good."

And then, because I couldn't help myself anymore, I put my hands on her shoulders and kissed her. There was a momentary hesitation, and I thought she was going to draw away . . . then her chin came up and she kissed me back, firmly and fully. Maybe it was sort of lucky at that, me being mostly immobilized

When the kiss was over she looked into my eyes, questioning.

"Against the dreams," I said, thinking it would come out stupid and phony-smooth, the way it looks on paper, but instead it sounded shaky and almost painfully honest.

"Against the dreams," she repeated gravely, as if it were a talisman, and this time she inclined her head toward me and we kissed again with those two ragged squares of plaster staring up at us like blind white eyes with Arnie's name written across them. We kissed for the simple animal comfort that comes with animal contact—sure, that, and something more, starting to be something more—and then we held each other without talking, and I don't think we were kidding ourselves about what was happening—at least not entirely. It was comfort, but it was also good old sex—full, ripe, and randy with teenage hormones. And maybe it had a chance to be something fuller and kinder than just sex.

But there was something else in those kisses—I knew it, she knew it, and probably you do too. That other thing was a shameful sort of betrayal. I could feel eighteen years of memories cry out—the ant farms, the chess games, the movies, the things he had taught me, the times I had kept him from getting killed. Except maybe in the end, I hadn't. Maybe I had seen the last of him—and a poor, rag-tag end at that—on Thanksgiving night, when he brought me the turkey sandwiches and beer.

I don't think it occurred to either of us that until then we had done nothing unforgivable to Arnie—nothing that might anger Christine. But now, of course, we had.

44 / Detective Work

Well, when the pipeline gets broken
And I'm lost on the river-bridge,
I'm all cracked up on the highway
And in the water's edge,
Medics come down the Thruway,
Ready to sew me up with the thread,
And if I fall down dyin
Y'know she's bound to put a blanket
*   on my bed.*

— Bob Dylan

What happened in the next three weeks or so was that Leigh and I played detective, and we fell in love.

She went down to the Municipal Offices the next day and paid fifty cents to have two papers Xeroxed—those papers go to Harrisburg, but Harrisburg sends a copy back to the town.

This time my family was home when Leigh arrived. Ellie peeked in on us whenever she got the chance. She was fascinated by Leigh, and I was quietly amused when, about a week into the new year, she started wearing her hair tied back as Leigh did. I was tempted to get on her case about it . . . and withstood the temptation. Maybe I was growing up a little bit (but not enough to keep from sneaking one of her Yodels when I saw one hidden behind the Tupperware bowls of leftovers in the refrigerator).

Except for Ellie's occasional peeks, we had the living room

mostly to ourselves that next afternoon, the twenty-seventh of December, after the social amenities had been observed. I introduced Leigh to my mother and father, my mom served coffee, and we talked. Elaine talked the most—chattering about her school and asking Leigh all sorts of questions about ours. At first I was annoyed, and then I was grateful. Both my parents are the soul of middle-class politeness (if my mom was being led to the electric chair and bumped into the chaplain, she would excuse herself), and I felt pretty clearly that they liked Leigh, but it was also obvious—to me, at least—that they were puzzled and a little uncomfortable, wondering where Arnie fit into all this.

Which was what Leigh and I were wondering ourselves, I guess. Finally they did what parents usually do when they're puzzled in such situations—they dismissed it as kid business and went about their own business. Dad excused himself first, saying that his workshop in the basement was in its usual post-Christmas shambles and he ought to start doing something about it. Mom said she wanted to do some writing.

Ellie looked at me solemnly and said, "Dennis, did Jesus have a dog?"

I cracked up and so did Ellie. Leigh sat watching us laugh, smiling politely the way outsiders do when it's a family joke.

"Split, Ellie," I said.

"What'll you do if I won't?" she asked, but it was only routine brattiness; she was already getting up.

"Make you wash my underwear," I said.

"The hell you *will!*" Ellie declared grandly, and left the room.

"My little sister," I said.

Leigh was smiling. "She's great."

"If you had to live with her full-time you might change your mind. Let's see what you've got."

Leigh put one of the Xerox copies on the glass coffee table where the pieces of my casts had been yesterday.

It was the re-registration of a used car, 1958 Plymouth sedan (4-door), red and white. It was dated November 1, 1978, and signed Arnold Cunningham. His father had co-signed for him:

SIGNATURE OF OWNER _Arnold Cunningham_

SIGNATURE OF PARENT OR GUARDIAN
(IF OWNER IS UNDER 18) _Michael Cunningham_

"What does that look like to you?" I asked.

"One of the signatures on one of the squares you showed me," she said. "Which one?"

"It's the way he signed just after I got crunched in Ridge Rock," I said. "It's the way his signature always looked. Now let's see the other one."

She put it down beside the first. This was a registration slip for a new car, 1958 Plymouth sedan (4-door), red and white. It was dated November 1, 1957—I felt a nasty jolt at that exact similarity, and one look at Leigh's face told me she had seen it too.

"Look at the signature," she said quietly.

I did.

SIGNATURE OF OWNER _Roland D. LeBay_

SIGNATURE OF PARENT OR GUARDIAN
(IF OWNER IS UNDER 18)_____

This was the handwriting Arnie had used on Thanksgiving evening; you didn't have to be a genius or a handwriting expert to see that. The names were different, but the writing was exactly the same.

Leigh reached for my hands, and I took hers.

What my father did in his basement workshop was make toys. I suppose that might sound a little weird to you, but it's his hobby. Or maybe something more than a hobby—I think there might have been a time in his life when he had to make a difficult choice between going to college and going out on his own to become a toymaker. If that's true, then I guess he chose the safe way. Sometimes I think I see it in his eyes, like an old ghost not quite laid to rest, but that is probably only my imagination, which used to be a lot less active than it is now.

Ellie and I were the chief beneficiaries, but Arnie had also found some of my father's toys under various Christmas trees and beside various birthday cakes, as had Ellie's closest childhood friend Aimee Carruthers (long since moved to Nevada and now referred to in the doleful tones reserved for those who have died young and senselessly) and many other chums.

Now my dad gave most of what he made to the Salvation Army 400 Fund, and before Christmas the basement always reminded me of Santa's workshop—until just before Christmas it would be filled with neat cardboard cartons containing wooden trains, little toolchests, Erector-set clocks that really kept time, stuffed animals, a small puppet theater or two. His main interest was in wooden toys (up until the Viet Nam war he had made battalions of toy soldiers, but in the last five years or so they had been quietly phased out—even now I'm not sure he was aware he was doing it), but like a good spray hitter, my dad went to all fields. During the week after Christmas there was a hiatus. The workshop would seem terribly empty, with only the sweet smell of sawdust to remind us that the toys had ever been there.

In that week he would sweep, clean, oil his machinery, and get ready for next year. Then, as the winter wore on through January and February, the toys and the seeming junk that would become parts of toys would begin appearing again—trains and jointed wooden ballerinas with red spots of color on their cheeks, a box of stuffing raked out of someone's old couch that would later end up in a bear's belly (my father called every one of his bears Owen or Olive—I had worn out six Owen Bears between infancy and second grade, and Ellie had worn out a like number of Olive Bears), little snips of wire, buttons, and flat, disembodied eyes scattered across the worktable like something out of a pulp hororr story. Last, the liquor-store boxes would appear, and the toys would again be packed into them.

In the last three years he had gotten three awards from the Salvation Army, but he kept them hidden away in a drawer, as if he was ashamed of them. I didn't understand it then and don't now—not completely—but at least I know it wasn't shame. My father had nothing to be ashamed of.

I worked my way down that evening after supper, clutching the bannister madly with one arm and using my other crutch like a ski-pole.

"Dennis," he said, pleased but slightly apprehensive. "You need any help?"

"No, I got it."

He put his broom aside by a small yellow drift of shavings and watched to see if I was really going to make it. "How about a push, then?"

"Ha-ha, very funny."

I got down, semi-hopped over to the big easy chair my father keeps in the corner beside our old Motorola black-and-white, and sat down. *Plonk.*

"How you doing?" he asked.

"Pretty good."

He brushed up a dustpanful of shavings, dumped them into his wastebarrel, sneezed, and brushed up some more. "No pain?"

"No. Well . . . some."

— "You want to be careful of stairs. If your mother had seen what you just did—"

I grinned. "She'd scream, yeah."

"Where *is* your mother?"

"She and Ellie went over to the Rennekes'. Dinah Renneke got a complete library of Shaun Cassidy albums for Christmas. Ellie is *green.*"

"I thought Shaun was out," my father said.

"I think she's afraid fashion might be doubling back on her."

Dad laughed. Then there was a companionable silence for a while, me sitting, him sweeping. I knew he'd get around to it, and presently he did.

"Leigh," he said, "used to go with Arnie, didn't she?"

"Yes," I said.

He glanced at me, then down at his work again. I thought he would ask me if I thought that was wise, or maybe mention that one fellow stealing another fellow's girl was not the best way to promote continued friendship and accord. But he said neither of those things.

"We don't see much of Arnie anymore. Do you suppose he's ashamed of the mess he's in?"

I had the feeling that my father didn't believe that at all; that he was simply testing the wind.

"I don't know," I said.

"I don't think he has much to worry about. With Darnell dead"—he tipped his dustpan into the barrel and the shavings slid in with a soft *flump*—"I doubt if they'll even bother to prosecute."

"No?"

"Not Arnie. Not on anything serious. He may be fined, and the judge will probably lecture him, but nobody wants to put an indelible black mark on the record of a nice young suburban white boy who is bound for college and a fruitful place in society."

He shot me a sharp questioning look, and I shifted in the chair, suddenly uncomfortable.

"Yeah, I suppose."

"Except he's not really like that anymore, is he, Dennis?"

"No. He's changed."

"When was the last time you actually saw him?"

"Thanksgiving."

"Was he okay then?"

I shook my head slowly, suddenly feeling like crying and blurting it all out. I had felt that way once before and hadn't; I didn't this time, either, but for a different reason. I remembered what Leigh had said, about being nervous for her parents on Christmas Eve. And it seemed to me now that the fewer the people who knew about our suspicions, the safer . . . for them.

"What's wrong with him?"

"I don't know."

"Does Leigh?"

"No. Not for sure. We have . . . some suspicions."

"Do you want to talk about them?"

"Yes. In a way I do. But I think it would be better if I didn't."

"All right," he said. "For now."

He swept the floor. The sound of the hard bristles on the concrete was almost hypnotic.

"And maybe you had better talk to Arnie before too much longer."

"Yeah. I was thinking about that." But it wasn't an interview I looked forward to.

There was another period of silence. Dad finished sweeping and then glanced around. "Looks pretty good, huh?"

"Great, Dad."

He smiled a little sadly and lit a Winston. Since his heart attack he had given the butts up almost completely, but he kept a pack around, and every now and then he'd have one—usually when he felt under stress. "Bullshit. It looks empty as hell."

"Well . . . yeah."

"You want a hand upstairs, Dennis?"

I got my crutches under me. "I wouldn't turn it down."

He looked at me and snickered. "Long John Silver. All you need is the parrot."

"Are you going to stand there giggling or give me a hand?"

"Give you a hand, I guess."

I slung an arm over his shoulder, feeling somehow like a little kid again—it brought back almost forgotten memories of him carrying me upstairs to bed on Sunday nights, after I started to doze off halfway through the *Ed Sullivan Show*. The smell of his aftershave was just the same.

At the top he said, "Step on me if I'm getting too personal, Denny, but Leigh's not going with Arnie anymore, is she."

"No, Dad."

"Is she going with you?"

"I . . . well, I don't really know. I guess not."

"Not *yet*, you mean."

"Well—yeah, I guess so." I was starting to feel uncomfortable, and it must have showed, but he pushed on anyway.

"Would it be fair to say that maybe she broke it off with Arnie because he wasn't the same person anymore?"

"Yes. I think that would be fair to say."

"Does he know about you and Leigh?"

"Dad, there's nothing to know . . . at least, not yet."

He cleared his throat, seemed to consider, and then said nothing. I let go of him and worked at getting my crutches under me. I worked a little harder at it than I had to, maybe.

"I'll give you a little gratuitous advice," my father said finally. "Don't let him know what's between you and her—and never mind the protestations that there isn't anything. You're trying to help him some way, aren't you?"

"I don't know if there's anything either Leigh or I can do for Arnie, Dad."

"I've seen him two or three times," my father said.

"You have?" I said, startled. "Where?"

My father shrugged. "On the street. Downtown. You know. Libertyville's not that big, Dennis. He . . ."

"He what?"

"Hardly seemed to recognize me. And he looks older. Now that his face has cleared, he looks much older. I used to think he took after his father, but now—" He broke off suddenly. "Dennis, has it occurred to you that Arnie may be having some sort of nervous breakdown?"

"Yes," I said, and only wished I could have told him that there were other possibilities. Worse ones. Possibilities that would have made my old man wonder if I was the one having a nervous breakdown.

"You be careful," he said, and although he didn't mention what had happened to Will Darnell, I suddenly felt strongly that he was thinking of it. "You be careful, Dennis."

Leigh called me on the telephone the next day and said her father was being called away to Los Angeles on year-end business and had proposed, on the spur of the moment, that they all go along with him and get away from the cold and the snow.

"My mother was crazy about the idea, and I just couldn't think of any plausible reason to say no," she said. "It's only ten days, and school doesn't start again until January eighth."

"It sounds great," I said. "Have fun out there."

"You think I should go?"

"If you don't, you ought to have your head examined."

"Dennis?"

"What?"

Her voice dropped a little. "You'll be careful, won't you? I . . . well, I've been thinking about you a lot lately."

She hung up then, leaving me feeling surprised and warm—but the guilt remained, fading a little now, maybe, but still there. My father had asked me if I was trying to help Arnie. Was I? Or was I maybe only snooping into a part of his life which he had expressly marked off-limits . . . and stealing his girl in the process? And what exactly *would* Arnie do or say if he found out?

My head ached with questions, and I thought that maybe it was just as well that Leigh was going away for a while.

As she herself had said about our folks, it seemed safer.

On Friday the twenty-ninth, the last business day of the old year, I called the Libertyville American Legion Post and asked for the secretary. I got his name, Richard McCandless, from the building's janitor, who also found a telephone number to go with it. The number turned out to be that of David Emerson's, Libertyville's "good" furniture store. I was told to wait a moment and then McCandless came on, a deep, gravelly voice that sounded a tough sixty—as if maybe Patton and the owner of this voice had fought their way across Germany to Berlin shoulder to shoulder, possibly biting enemy bullets out of the air with their teeth as they went.

"McCandless," he said.

"Mr. McCandless, my name is Dennis Guilder. Last August you put on a military-style funeral for a fellow named Roland LeBay—"

"Was he a friend of yours?"

"No, only a bare acquaintance, but—"

"Then I don't have to spare your feelings none," McCandless said, gravel rattling in his throat. He sounded like Andy Devine crossed with Broderick Crawford. "LeBay was nothing but a pure-d sandycraw sonofabitch, and if I'd had my way, the Legion wouldn't have had a thing to do with planting him. He quit the organization back in 1970. If he hadn't quit, we would have fired him. That man was the most contentious bastard that ever lived."

"Was he?"

"You bet he was. He'd pick an argument with you, then up it to a fight if he could. You couldn't play poker with the sonofabitch, and you sure couldn't drink with him. You couldn't keep up with him, for one thing, and he'd get mean for another. Not that he had to go far to get to mean. What a crazy bastard he was, you should pardon me fran-cayse. Who are you, boy?"

For an insane instant I thought of quoting Emily Dickinson at him: I'm nobody! Who are you?

"A friend of mine bought a car from LeBay just before he died—"

"Shit! Not that '57?"

"Well, actually it was a '58—"

"Yeah, yeah, '57 or '58, red and white. That was the only goddam thing he cared about. Treated it like it was a woman. It was over that car that he quit the Legion, did you know that?"

"No," I said. "What happened?"

"Ah, shit. Ancient history, kid. I'm bending your ear as it is. But every time I think of that sonofabitch LeBay, I see red. I've still got the scars on my hands. Uncle Sam had three years of my life during World War II and I never got so much as a Purple Heart out of it, although I was in combat almost all that time. I fought my way across half the little shitpot islands in the South Pacific. Me and about fifty other guys stood up to a banzai charge on Guadalcanal—two fucking million Japs coming at us hopped to the eyeballs and waving those swords they made out of Maxwell House coffee cans—and I never got a scar. I felt a couple of bullets go right by me, and just before we broke that charge the guy next to me got his guts rearranged courtesy of the Emperor of Japan, but the only times I saw the color of my own blood over there in the Pacific was when I cut myself shaving. Then . . ."

McCandless laughed.

"Shit on toast, there I go again. My wife says I'll open my mouth too wide someday and just fall right in. What'd you say your name was?"

"Dennis Guilder."

"Okay, Dennis, I bent your ear, now you bend mine. What did you want?"

"Well, my friend bought that car and fixed it up . . . for sort of a street-rod, I guess you'd say. A showpiece."

"Yeah, just like LeBay," McCandless said, and my mouth went dry. "He loved that fucking car, I'll say that for him. He didn't give a shit for his wife—you know what happened to her?"

"Yes," I said.

"He drove her to it," McCandless said grimly. "After their kid died, she didn't get any comfort from him at all. None. I don't think he gave much of a shit about the kid, either. Sorry, Dennis. I never could shut up. Talk all the time. Always have. My mother used to say, 'Dickie, your tongue's hung in the middle and runs on both ends.' What did you say you wanted?"

"My friend and I went to LeBay's funeral," I said, "and after it was over, I introduced myself to his brother—"

"He seemed like a right enough type," McCandless broke in. "Schoolteacher. Ohio."

"That's right. I had a talk with him, and he *did* seem like a nice enough guy. I told him I was going to do my senior English paper on Ezra Pound—"

"Ezra who?"

"Pound."

"Who the fuck's that? Was he at LeBay's funeral?"

"No, sir. Pound was a poet."

"A what?"

"Poet. He's dead too."

"Oh." McCandless sounded doubtful.

"Anyway, LeBay—this is George LeBay—he said he'd send me a bunch of magazines about Ezra Pound for my report, if I wanted them. Well, it turns out that I could use them, but I forgot to get his address. I thought you might have it."

"Sure, it'll be in the records; all that stuff is. I hate being fucking secretary, but my year's up this July, and never again. Know what I mean? Never-fucking-again."

"I hope I'm not being a real pain in the ass."

"No. Hell, no. I mean, that's what the American Legion's for, right? To help people. Gimme your address, Dennis, and I'll send you a card with the info on it."

I gave him my name and address and apologized again for bothering him at his job.

"Think nothing of it," he said. "I'm on my fucking coffee break, anyhow." I had a moment to wonder just what it was he did at David Emerson's, which really was where Libertyville's elite bought. Was he a salesman? I could see him showing some smart young lady around, saying, *Here's one fuck of a nice couch, ma'am, and look at this goddam settee, we sure didn't have nothing like that on Guadalcanal when those fucking stoned-out Japs came at us with their Maxwell House swords.*

I grinned a little, but what he said next sobered me quickly.

"I rode in that car of LeBay's a couple of times. I never liked it. I'll be damned if I know why, but I never did. And I never would ride in it after his wife . . . you know. Jesus, that gave me the spooks."

"I'll bet," I said, and my voice seemed to come from far away. "Listen, what *did* happen when he quit the Legion? You said it had something to do with the car?"

He laughed, sounding a little pleased. "You're not really interested in all that ancient history, are you?"

"Well, yeah. I am. My friend bought the car, remember."

"Well then I'll tell you. It was a pretty funny goddam thing, at that. A few of the guys mention it from time to time, when we've all had a few. I ain't the only one with scars on my hands. Get right down to the bottom of it, it was sort of spooky."

"What was?"

"Aw, it was a kid's trick. But nobody really liked the sonofabitch, you know. He was an outsider, a loner—"

Like Arnie, I thought.

"—and we'd all been drinking," McCandless finished. "It was after the meeting, and LeBay had been making an even worse prick of himself than usual. So a bunch of us are at the bar, you know, and we could tell LeBay was getting ready to go home. He was getting his jacket on and arguing with Poochie Anderson about some baseball question. When LeBay went, he always went the same way, kid. He'd jump into that Plymouth of his, back up, and then floor it. That thing'd go out of the parking lot like a rocket, spraying gravel everywhere. So—this was Sonny Bellerman's idea—about four of us go out the back door to the parking lot while Le-Bay's shouting at Poochie. We all get behind the far corner of the building, because we know that's where he'll finish backing the car up before he takes off. He always called it by a girl's name, I told you it was like he was married to the fucking thing.

" 'Keep your eyes open and your heads down or he'll see us,' Sonny says. 'And don't move until I give you a go.' We were all sort of tanked up, you know.

"So about ten minutes later out he comes, drunk as a skunk and feeling around in his chinos for his keys. Sonny says, 'Get ready, you guys, and keep low!'

"LeBay gets in the car and backs her up. It was perfect, because he stopped to light a cigarette. While he did that, we grabbed the back bumper of that Fury and we lifted the rear wheels right off the ground so that when he tries to pull out, spraying gravel all over the side of the building like usual, you know, he's only gonna spin his wheels and not go anywhere. You see what I mean?"

"Yeah," I said. It *was* a kid's trick; we had pulled the same thing from time to time at school dances, and once, for a joke, we had blocked up Coach Puffer's Dodge so that the driving wheels were off the ground.

"We got some kind of shock, though. He gets his cigarette lit, and then he turns on the radio. That's another thing that used to drive us all fucking bugshit, the way he always listened to that rock and roll music like he was some kid instead of old enough to qualify for Social-fucking-Security. Then he put the tranny into drive. We didn't see it, because we were all hunkered down so he wouldn't see us. I remember Sonny Bellerman was kind of laughing, and just before it happened, he whispers, 'They up, men?' and I whispers back, 'Your pecker's up, Bellerman.' He was the only one who really got hurt, you know. Because of his wedding ring. But I swear to God, those wheels *were* up. We had that Plymouth's rear end four inches off the ground."

"What happened?" I asked. From the way the story was going, I thought I could guess.

"What happened? He pulled out just like always, that's what happened! Just like all four wheels was on the ground.

He spun gravel and ripped that rear bumper out of our hands and pulled about a yard of skin off with it. Took most of Sonny Bellerman's third finger; his wedding ring got caught under the bumper, you know, and that finger popped off like a cork coming out of a bottle. And we heard LeBay laughing as he went out, like he knew all along we was there. He could of, you know; if he'd gone back to use the bathroom after he finished shouting at Poochie, he could have looked right out the window while he whizzed and seen us standing around behind the building waiting for him.

"Well, that was it for him and the Legion. We sent him a letter telling him we wanted him out, and he quit. And, just to show you how funny the world is, it was Sonny Bellerman who stood up at the meeting right after LeBay died and said we ought to do the right thing by him just the same. 'Sure,' Sonny says, he says, 'the guy was a dirty sonofabitch, but he fought the war with the rest of us. So why don't we send him off right?' So we did. I dunno. I guess Sonny Bellerman's a lot more of a Christian than I'll ever be."

"You must not have had the back wheels off the ground," I said, thinking of what had happened to the guys who had screwed around with Christine in November. They had lost a lot more than some skin off their fingers.

"We did, though," McCandless said. "When we got sprayed with gravel, it was from the *front* wheels. I've never to this day been able to figure how he pulled that trick off. It's kind of spooky, like I said. Gerry Barlow—he was one of us who did it—always claimed LeBay threw a four-wheel drive into her somehow, but I don't think there's a conversion kit for something like that, do you?"

"No," I said. "I don't think it could be done."

"Naw, never do it," McCandless agreed. "Never do it. Well, hey! I done jawed away most of my coffee break, kid. Want to get back and grab another half a cup before it all gets away from me. I'll send you that address if we got it. I think we do."

"Thank you, Mr. McCandless."

"My pleasure, Dennis. Take care of yourself."

"Sure. Use it, don't abuse it, right?"

He laughed. "That's what we used to say in the Fighting Fifth, anyway." He hung up.

I put the phone down slowly and thought about cars that still kept moving even when you lifted their driving wheels off the ground. *Sort of spooky.* It was spooky, all right, and McCandless still had the scars to prove it. That made me remember something George LeBay had told me. He had a scar to show from his association with Roland D. LeBay, as well. And as he grew older, *his* scar had spread.

45 / New Year's Eve

For this daring young star met his death
    while in his car,
No one knows the reason why—
Screaming tires, flashing fire, and gone
    was this young star,
O how could they let him die?
Still, a young man is gone, but his legend
    lingers on,
For he died without a cause . . .

                                        —Bobby Troup

I called Arnie on New Year's Eve. I'd had a couple of days to think about it, and I didn't really want to do it, but I had to see him. I had come to believe I wouldn't be able to decide anything until I actually saw him again for myself. And until I had seen Christine again. I had mentioned the car to my father at breakfast, casually, as if in passing, and he told me that he believed all the cars that had been impounded in Darnell's Garage had now been photographed and returned.

Regina Cunningham answered the phone, her voice stiff and formal. "Cunningham residence."

"Hi, Regina, it's Dennis."

"Dennis!" She sounded both pleased and surprised. For a moment it was the voice of the old Regina, the one who gave Arnie and me peanut butter sandwiches with bits of bacon crumbled into them (peanut butter and bacon on stone-ground rye, of course). "How are you? We heard that they sprung you from the hospital."

"I'm doing okay," I said. "How about you?"

There was a brief silence, and then she said, "Well, you know how things have been around here."

"Problems," I said. "Yeah."

"All the problems we missed in earlier years," Regina said. "I guess they just piled up in a corner and waited for us."

I cleared my throat a little and said nothing.

"Did you want to talk to Arnie?"

"If he's there."

After another slight pause, Regina said, "I remember that in the old days you and he used to swap back and forth on New Year's Eve, seeing the New Year in. Was that what you were calling about, Dennis?" She sounded almost timid, and that was not like the old full-steam-ahead Regina at all.

"Well, yeah," I said. "Kid stuff, I know, but—"

"No!" she said, sharply and quickly. "No, not at all! If Arnie ever needed you, Dennis—needed some friend—now is the time. He . . . he's upstairs now, sleeping. He sleeps much too much. And he's . . . he's not . . . he hasn't . . ."

"Hasn't what, Regina?"

"He hasn't made any of his college applications!" she burst out, and then immediately lowered her voice, as if Arnie might overhear. "Not a single one! Mr. Vickers, the guidance counsellor at school, called and told me! He scored 700s on his college boards, he could get into almost any college in the country—at least he could have before this . . . this trouble. . . ." Her voice wavered toward tears, and then she got hold of herself again. "Talk to him, Dennis. If you could spend the evening with him tonight . . . drink a few beers with him and just . . . just talk to him . . ."

She stopped, but I could tell there was something more. Something she needed to say and couldn't.

"Regina," I said. I hadn't liked the old Regina, the compulsive dominator who seemed to run the lives of her husband and son to fit her own timetable, but I liked this distracted, weepy woman even less. "Come on. Take it easy, okay?"

"I'm afraid to talk to him," she said finally. "And Michael's afraid to talk to him. He . . . he seems to explode if you cross him on some subjects. At first it was only his car; now it's college too. Talk to him, Dennis, please." There was another short pause, and then, almost casually, she brought out the heart of her dread: "I think we're losing him."

"No, Regina, hey—"

"I'll get him," she said abruptly, and the phone clunked down. The wait seemed to stretch out. I crooked the phone between my jaw and my shoulder and rapped my knuckles on the cast that still covered my upper left leg. I wrestled with a craven urge to just hang the telephone up and push this entire business away.

Then the phone was picked up again. "Hello?" a wary voice asked, and the thought that burned across my mind with complete assurance was: *That's not Arnie.*

"Arnie?"

"It sounds like Dennis Guilder, the mouth that walks like a man," the voice said, and *that* sounded like Arnie, all right—but at the same time, it didn't. His voice hadn't really deepened, but it seemed to have *roughened*, as if through overuse and shouting. It was eerie, as if I were talking to a stranger who was doing a pretty good imitation of my friend Arnie.

"Watch what you're saying, dork," I said. I was smiling but my hands were dead cold.

"You know," he said in a confidential voice, "your face and my ass bear a suspicious resemblance."

"I've noticed the resemblance, but last time I thought it was the other way around," I said, and then a little silence fell between us—we had gone through what passed for the amenities with us. "So what are you doing tonight?" I asked.

"Not much," he said. "No date or anything. You?"

"Sure, I'm in great shape," I said. "I'm going to go pick up Roseanne and take her to Studio 2000. You can come along and hold my crutches while we dance, if you want."

He laughed a little.

"I thought I'd come over," I said. "Maybe you and me could see the New Year in like we used to. You know?"

"Yeah!" Arnie said. He sounded pleased by the idea—but still not quite like himself. "Watch Guy Lombardo and all that happy crappy. That'd be all right."

I paused for a moment, not quite sure what to say. Finally I replied cautiously, "Well, maybe Dick Clark or someone. Guy Lombardo's dead, Arnie."

"Is he?" Arnie sounded puzzled, doubtful. "Oh. Oh yeah, I guess he is. But Dick Clark's hanging in there, right?"

"Right," I said.

"I got to give it an eighty-five, Dick, it's got a good beat and you can dance to it," Arnie said, but it wasn't Arnie's voice at all. My mind made a sudden and hideously unexpected cross-connection

(best smell in the world . . . except maybe for pussy)

and my hand tightened down convulsively on the telephone. I think I almost screamed. I wasn't talking to Arnie; I was talking to Roland LeBay. I was talking to a dead man.

"That's Dick, all right," I heard myself say, as if from a distance.

"How you getting over, Dennis? Can you drive?"

"No, not yet. I thought I'd get my dad to drive me over." I paused momentarily, then plunged. "I thought maybe you could drive me back, if you got your car. Would that be okay?"

"Sure!" He sounded honestly excited. "Yeah, that'd be good, Dennis! Real good! We'll have some laughs. Just like old times."

"Yes," I said. And then—I swear to God it just popped out—I added, "Just like in the motor pool."

"Yeah, that's right!" Arnie replied, laughing. "Too much! See you, Dennis."

"Right," I said automatically. "See you." I hung up, and I looked at the telephone, and presently I began to shudder all over. I had never been so frightened in my life as I was right then. Time passes: the mind rebuilds its defenses. I think one of the reasons there is so little convincing evidence of psychic phenomena is that the mind goes to work and restructures the evidence. A little stacking is better than a lot of insanity. Later I questioned what I heard, or led myself to believe that Arnie had misunderstood my comment, but in the few moments after I put the telephone down, I was sure: LeBay had gotten in him. Somehow, dead or not, LeBay was in him.

And LeBay was taking over.

New Year's Eve was cold and crystal clear. My dad dropped me off at the Cunninghams' at quarter past seven and helped me over to the back door—crutches were not made for winter or snow-packed paths.

The Cunninghams' station wagon was gone, but Christine stood in the driveway, her bright red-and-white finish sheened with a condensation of ice-crystals. She had been released with the rest of the impounded cars only this week. Just looking at her brought on a feeling of dull dread like a headache. I did not want to ride home in that car, not tonight, not ever. I wanted my own ordinary, mass-produced Duster with its vinyl seat covers and its dumb bumper-sticker reading MAFIA STAFF CAR.

The back porch light flicked on, and we saw Arnie cross toward the door in silhouette. He didn't even *look* like Arnie. His shoulders sloped; his movements seemed older. I told myself it was only imagination, my suspicions working on me, and of course I was full of bullshit . . . and I knew it.

He opened the door and leaned out in an old flannel shirt and a pair of jeans. "Dennis!" he said. "My man!"

"Hi, Arnie," I said.

"Hello, Mr. Guilder."

"Hi, Arnie," my dad said, raising one gloved hand. "How's it been going?"

"Well, you know, not that great. But that's all going to change. New year, new broom, out with the old shit, in with the new shit, right?"

"I guess so," my father said, sounding a little taken aback. "Dennis, are you sure you don't want me to come back and get you?"

I wanted that more than anything, but Arnie was looking at me and his mouth was still smiling but his eyes were flat and watchful. "No, Arnie'll bring me home . . . if that rustbucket will start, that is."

"Oh-oh, watch what you call my car," Arnie said. "She's very sensitive."

"Is she?" I asked.

"She is," Arnie said, smiling.

I turned my head and called, "Sorry, Christine."

"That's better."

For a moment all three of us stood there, my father and I at the bottom of the kitchen steps, Arnie in the doorway above us, none of us apparently knowing what to say next. I felt a kind of panic—somebody *had* to say something, or else the whole ridiculous fiction that nothing had changed would collapse of its own weight.

"Well, okay," my dad said at last. "You two kids stay sober. If you have more than a couple of beers, Arnie, call me."

"Don't worry, Mr. Guilder."

"We'll be all right," I said, grinning a grin that felt plastic and false. "You go on home and get your beauty sleep, Dad. You need it."

"Oh-ho," my father said. "Watch what you call my face. It's very sensitive."

He went back to the car. I stood and watched him, my

crutches propped in my armpits. I watched him while he crossed behind Christine. And when he backed out of the driveway and turned toward home, I felt a little bit better.

I banged the snow off the tip of each crutch carefully while standing in the doorway. The Cunninghams' kitchen was tile-floored. A couple of near-accidents had taught me that on smooth surfaces a pair of crutches with wet snow on them can turn into ice-skates.

"You really operate on those babies," Arnie said, watching me cross the floor. He took a pack of Tiparillos from the pocket of his flannel shirt, shook one out, bit down on the white plastic mouthpiece, and lit it with his head cocked to one side. The match flame played momentarily across his cheeks like yellow streaks of paint.

"It's a skill I'll be glad to lose," I said. "When did you start with the cigars?"

"Darnell's," he said. "I don't smoke em in front of my mother. The smell drives her bugshit."

He didn't smoke like a kid just learning the habit—he smoked like a man who has been doing it for twenty years.

"I thought I'd make popcorn," he said. "You up for that?"

"Sure. You got any beer?"

"That's affirmative. There's a six-pack in the fridge and two more downstairs."

"Great." I sat down carefully at the kitchen table, stretching out my left leg. "Where's your folks?"

"Went to a New Year's Eve party at the Fassenbachs'. When's that cast come off?"

"Maybe at the end of January, if I'm lucky." I waved my crutches in the air and cried dramatically, "Tiny Tim walks again! God bless us, every one!"

Arnie, on his way to the stove with a deep pan, a bag of popcorn, and a bottle of Wesson Oil, laughed and shook his head. "Same old Dennis. They didn't knock much of the stuffing out of you, you shitter."

"You didn't exactly overwhelm me with visits in the hospital, Arnie."

"I brought you Thanksgiving supper—what the hell do you want, blood?"

I shrugged.

Arnie sighed. "Sometimes I think you were my good-luck charm, Dennis."

"Off my case, hose-head."

"No, seriously. I've been in hot water ever since you broke your wishbones, and I'm still in hot water. It's a wonder I don't look like a lobster." He laughed heartily. It was not the sound you'd expect of a kid in trouble; it was the laugh of a man—yes, a man—who was enjoying himself tremendously. He put the pan on the stove and poured Wesson Oil over the bottom of it. His hair, shorter than it used to be and combed back in a style that was new to me, fell over his forehead. He flipped it back with a quick jerk of his head and added popcorn to the oil. He slammed a lid over the pan. Went to the fridge. Got a six-pack. Slammed it down in front of me, pulled off two cans, and opened them. Gave me one. Held up his. I held up mine.

"A toast," Arnie said. "Death to the shitters of the world in 1979."

I lowered my can slowly. "I can't drink to that, man."

I saw a spark of anger in those gray eyes. It seemed to twinkle there, like spurious good humor, and then go out. "Well, what *can* you drink to—*man?*"

"How about to college?" I asked quietly.

He looked at me sullenly, his earlier good humor gone like magic. "I should have known she'd fill you full of that garbage. My mother is one woman who never stuck at getting low to get what she wants. You know that, Dennis. She'd kiss the devil's ass if that's what it took."

I put my beer-can down, still full. "Well, she didn't kiss my ass. She just said you weren't making any applications and she was worried."

"It's my life," Arnie said. His lips twisted, changing his face, making it extraordinarily ugly. "I'll do what I want."

"And college isn't it?"

"Yeah, I'll go. But in my own time. You tell her that, if she asks. In my own time. Not this year. Definitely not. If she thinks I'm going to go off to Pitt or Horlicks or Rutgers and put on a freshman beanie and go boola-boola at the home football games, she's out of her mind. Not after the shitstorm I've been through this year. No way, man."

"What *are* you going to do?"

"I'm taking off," he said. "I'm going to get in Christine and we're going to motorvate right the Christ out of this one-timetable town. You understand?" His voice began to rise, to become shrill, and I felt horror sweep over me again. I was helpless against that unmanning fear and could only hope that it didn't show on my face. Because it wasn't just LeBay's voice now; now it was even LeBay's *face*, swimming under Arnie's like some dead thing preserved in Formalin. "It's been nothing but a shitstorm, and I think that goddam Junkins is still after me full steam ahead, and he better watch out or somebody just might junk *him*—"

"Who's Junkins?" I asked.

"Never mind," he said. "It's not important." Behind him, the Wesson Oil had begun to sizzle. A kernel of corn popped—*ponk!*—against the underside of the lid. "I've got to go shake that, Dennis. Do you want to make a toast or not? Makes no difference to me."

"All right," I said. "How about to us?"

He smiled, and the constriction in my chest eased a little. "Us, yeah, that's a good one, Dennis. To us. Gotta be that, huh?"

"Gotta be," I said, and my voice hoarsened a little. "Yeah, gotta be."

We clicked the Bud cans together and drank.

Arnie went over to the stove and began shaking the pan, where the corn was picking up speed. I let a couple of swallows of beer slide down my throat. Beer was still a fairly new thing to me then, and I had never been drunk on it because I liked the taste quite well, and friends—Lenny Barongg was the chief of them—had told me that if you got falling-down, standing-up, ralphing-down-your-shirt shitfaced, you couldn't even look at the stuff for weeks. Sadly, I have found out since that that isn't completely true.

But Arnie was drinking like they were going to reinstitute Prohibition on January first; he had finished his first can before the popcorn had finished popping. He crimped the empty, winked at me, and said, "Watch me put it up the little tramp's ass, Dennis." The allusion escaped me, so I just smiled noncommittally as he tossed the can toward the wastebasket. It banged the wall over it and dropped in.

"Two points," I said.

"That's right," he said. "Hand me another one, would you?"

I did, figuring what the hell—my folks were planning to see the New Year in at home, and if Arnie got really drunk and passed out, I could give my dad a call. Arnie might say things drunk that he wouldn't say sober, and I didn't want to ride home in Christine anyway.

But the beer didn't seem to affect him. He finished popping the corn, dumped it into a big plastic bowl, melted half a stick of margarine, poured it over the top, salted it, and said, "Let's go in the living room and watch some tube. What do you say?"

"Fine by me." I got my crutches, seated them in my armpits—which just lately felt as if they might be growing calluses—and then groped for the three beers still on the table.

"I'll come back for them," Arnie said. "Come on. Before you break everything all over again." He smiled at me, and for that moment he was nobody but Arnie Cunningham, so much so that it broke my heart a little bit to look at him.

There was some dorky New Year's Eve special on. Donny and Marie Osmond were singing, both of them showing their giant white teeth in friendly but somehow sharklike grins. We let the TV play and talked. I told Arnie about the physical therapy sessions, and how I was working out with weights, and after two beers I confessed that I was sometimes afraid that I would never walk right again. Not playing football in college didn't bother me, but that did. He nodded calmly and sympathetically through it all.

I may as well stop right here and tell you that I have never spent such a peculiar evening in my life. Worse things were waiting, but nothing that was so strange, so . . . so *disjointed*. It was like sitting through a movie where the picture is almost—but not quite—focused. Sometimes he seemed like Arnie, but at others he didn't seem like Arnie at all. He had picked up mannerisms I had never noticed before—twirling his car-keys nervously on the rectangle of leather to which they were attached, cracking his knuckles, occasionally biting at the ball of his thumb with his upper front teeth. There was that comment about putting it up the little tramp's ass when he tossed his beer-can. And although he had gotten through five beers by the time I had finished my second, just downing them one after the other, he still didn't seem drunk.

And there were mannerisms I had always associated with Arnie which seemed to have disappeared completely: the quick, nervous pull at his earlobe when he was talking, the sudden stretch of his long legs ending with the ankles briefly crossed, his habit of expressing amusement by hissing air through his pursed lips instead of laughing outright. He did do that last once or twice. But more often he would signal his amusement in a string of shrill chuckles that I associated with LeBay.

The special finished up at eleven, and Arnie switched around the dial until he found a dance-party in some New York hotel where they kept switching outside to Times Square, where a big crowd had already gathered. It wasn't Guy Lombardo, but it was close.

"You're really not going to college?" I asked.

"Not this year. Christine and I are going to head out for California right after graduation. That golden shore."

"Your folks know?"

He looked startled at the idea. "Hell, no! And don't you tell them, either! I need that like I need a rubber dick!"

"What are you going to do out there?"

He shrugged. "Look for a job fixing cars. I'm as good at that as I am at anything." And then he stunned me by saying casually, "I'm hoping I can persuade Leigh to come with me."

I swallowed beer the wrong way and began to cough, spraying my pants. Arnie slammed me on the back twice, hard. "You okay?"

"Sure," I managed. "Just went down the wrong pipe. Arnie . . . if you think she's going to come with you, you're living in a dream world. She's working on her college applications. She's got a whole file of them, man. She's really serious about it."

His eyes narrowed immediately, and I had a sinking feeling that the beer had betrayed me into saying more than I should have.

"How come you know so much about my girl?"

All of a sudden I felt as if I had been dropped into a long field that was full of loaded mines. "It's all she talks about, Arnie. Once she gets started on the subject, you can't shut her up."

"Chummy. You're not moving in, are you, Dennis?" He was watching me closely, his eyes slitted with suspicion. "You wouldn't do anything like that, would you?"

"No," I said, lying completely and fully. "That's a hell of a thing to say."

"Then how do you know so much about what she's doing?"

"I see her around," I said. "We talk about you."

"She talks about me?"

"Yeah, a little," I said casually. "She said that you and she had a fight over Christine."

It was the right thing. He relaxed. "It was just a little thing. Just a little spat. She'll come around. And there are good schools out in California, if she wants to go to school. We're going to be married, Dennis. Have kids and all that shit."

I struggled to keep my poker face. "Does she know that?"

He laughed. "No way! Not yet. But she will. Soon enough. I love her, and nothing's going to get in the way of that." The laughter died away. "What did she say about Christine?"

Another mine.

"She said she didn't like her. I think . . . that maybe she was a little jealous."

It was the right thing again. He relaxed even more. "Yeah, she sure was. But she'll come around, Dennis. The course of true love never runs smooth, but she'll come around, don't worry. If you see her again, tell her I'm going to call. Or talk to her when school starts again."

I considered telling him that Leigh was in California right now and decided not to. And I wondered what this new suspicious Arnie would do if he knew I had kissed the girl he thought he was going to marry, had held her . . . was falling in love with her.

"Look, Dennis!" Arnie cried, and pointed at the TV.

They had switched to Times Square again. The crowd was a huge—but still swelling—organism. It was just past eleven-thirty. The old year was guttering.

"Look at those shitters!" He cackled his shrill, excited laugh, finished his beer, and went downstairs for a fresh six-pack. I sat in my chair and thought about Welch and Repperton, Trelawney, Stanton, Vandenberg, Darnell. I thought about how Arnie—or whatever Arnie had become—thought that he and Leigh had just had an unimportant lovers' spat and how they would end the school year getting married, just like in those greasy love-ballads from the Nifty Fifties.

And oh God I had such a case of the creeps.

We saw the New Year in.

Arnie produced a couple of noisemakers and party favors—the kind that go bang and then release a cloud of tiny crepe streamers. We toasted 1979 and talked a little more on neutral subjects such as the Phillies' disappointing collapse in the playoffs and the Steelers' chances of going all the way to the Super Bowl.

The bowl of popcorn was down to the old maids and the burny-bottoms when I took myself in hand and asked one of the questions I had been avoiding. "Arnie? What do you think happened to Darnell?"

He glanced at me sharply, then glanced back at the TV, where couples with New Year's confetti in their hair were dancing. He drank some more beer. "The people he was doing business with shut him up before he could talk too much. That's what I think happened."

"The people he was working for?"

"Will used to say the Southern Mob was bad," Arnie said, "but that the Colombians were even worse."

"Who are the—"

"The Colombians?" Arnie laughed cynically. "Cocaine cowboys, that's who the Colombians are. Will used to claim they'd kill you if you even looked at one of their women the wrong way—and sometimes if you looked at her the right way. Maybe it was the Colombians. It was messy enough to be them."

"Were you running coke for Darnell?"

He shrugged. "I was running *stuff* for Will. I only moved coke for him once or twice, and I thank Christ that I didn't have anything worse than untaxed cigarettes when they picked me up. They caught me dead-bang. Bad shit. But if the situation was the same, I'd probably do it again. Will was a dirty, scuzzy old sonofabitch, but in some ways he was okay." His eyes grew veiled, strange. "Yeah, in some ways he was okay. But he knew too much. That's why he got wasted. He knew too much . . . and sooner or later he would have said something. Probably it was the Colombians. Crazy fuckers."

"I don't get you. And it's not my business, I suppose."

He looked at me, grinned, and winked. "It was the domino theory. At least, it was supposed to be. There was a guy named Henry Buck. He was supposed to rat on me. I was supposed to rat on Will. And then—the big casino—Will was supposed to rat on the people down South that were selling him the dope and the fireworks and cigarettes and booze. Those were the people Ju—the cops really wanted. Especially the Colombians."

"And you think they killed him?"

He looked at me flatly. "Them or the Southern Mob, sure. Who else?"

I shook my head.

"Well," he said, "let's have another beer and then I'll give you a lift home. I enjoyed this, Dennis. I really did." There was a ring of truth in that, but Arnie never would have made a dorky comment like, "I enjoyed this, I really did." Not the old Arnie.

"Yeah, me too, man."

I didn't want another beer, but I took one anyway. I wanted to put off the inevitable moment of getting into Christine. This afternoon it had seemed a necessary step—to sample the atmosphere of that car myself . . . if there was any atmosphere to sample. Now it seemed a frightening and crazy idea. I felt the secret of what Leigh and I were becoming to each other like a large, breakable egg in my head.

Tell me, Christine, can you read minds?

I felt a crazy laugh coming up my throat and dumped beer on it.

"Listen," I said, "I can call my dad to come and get me, if you want, Arnie. He'll still be up."

"No problem," Arnie said. "I could walk two miles of straight line, don't worry."

"I just thought—"

"Bet you're anxious to be able to drive yourself around again, huh?"

"Yeah, I am."

"There's nothing finer than being behind the wheel of your own car," Arnie said, and then his left eye slipped down in a bleary old roué's wink. "Except maybe pussy."

The time came. Arnie snapped off the TV and I crutched my way across the kitchen and worked into my old ski parka, hoping that Michael and Regina would come in from their party and delay things yet a while longer—maybe Michael would smell beer on Arnie's breath and offer me a ride. The memory of the afternoon I had slipped behind Christine's wheel, when Arnie was in LeBay's house, dickering with the old sonofabitch, was all too clear in my mind.

Arnie had gotten a couple of beers from the fridge—"for the road," he said. I considered telling him that if he got picked up DWI while he was out on bail, he'd probably go to jail before he could turn around. Then I decided I better keep my mouth shut. We went out.

The first early morning of 1979 was deeply, clearly cold,

the kind of cold that makes the moisture in your nose freeze in seconds. The snowbanks ringing the driveway glittered with billions of diamond crystals. And there sat Christine, her black windows cauled with frost. I stared at her. *The Mob,* Arnie had said. *The Southern Mob or the Colombians.* It sounded melodramatic but possible—no, more: it sounded plausible. But the Mob shot people, pushed them out of windows, strangled them. According to legend, Al Capone had disposed of one poor sucker with a lead-cored baseball bat. But to drive a car over some guy's snow-covered lawn and slam it through the side of his house and into his living room?

The Colombians, maybe. Arnie said the Colombians are crazy. But *that* crazy? I didn't think so.

She glittered in the light from the house and the stars, and what if it *was* her? And what if she found out that Leigh and I had our suspicions? Worse yet, what if she found out that we had been fooling around?

"You need help on the steps, Dennis?" Arnie asked, startling me.

"No, I can handle the steps," I said. "You might have to give me a hand on the path."

"No problem, man."

I got down the kitchen steps sidesaddle, clutching the railing in one hand and my crutches in the other. On the path, I set them under me, got out a couple of steps, and then slipped. A dull thud of pain rumbled up my left leg, the one that still wasn't worth doodly-squat. Arnie grabbed me.

"Thanks," I said, glad of a chance to sound shaky.

"No sweat."

We got over to the car, and Arnie asked if I could get in by myself. I said I could. He left me and crossed around the front of Christine's hood. I got hold of the doorhandle with one gloved hand, and a hopeless feeling of dread and revulsion swept over me. It wasn't until then that I really began to believe it, deep inside, where a person lives. Because that doorhandle felt alive under my hand. It felt like some living beast that was asleep. The doorhandle didn't feel like chromed steel; dear Christ, it felt like *skin.* It seemed as if I could squeeze it and wake the beast up, roaring.

Beast?

Okay, *what* beast?

What was it? Some sort of *afreet?* An ordinary car that

had somehow become the dangerous, stinking dwelling-place of a demon? A weird manifestation of LeBay's lingering personality, a hellish haunted house that rolled on Goodyear rubber? I didn't know. All I knew was that I was scared, terrified. I didn't think I could go through with this.

"Hey, you okay?" Arnie asked. "Can you make it?"

"I can make it," I said hoarsely, and jammed my thumb down on the button below the handle. I opened the door, turned my back on the seat, and let myself fall backward onto it, left leg extending stiffly. I got hold of my leg and swung it in. It was like moving a piece of furniture. My heart was triphammering in my chest. I pulled the door shut.

Arnie turned the key and the motor rumbled to life—as if the engine were hot instead of dead cold. And the smell assaulted me, seeming to come from everywhere, but most of all seeming to pour up from the upholstery: the sick, rich, rotten smell of death and decay.

I don't know how to tell you about that ride home, that three-mile ride that lasted no more than ten or twelve minutes, without sounding like an escapee from a lunatic asylum. There is no way to be objective about it; just sitting here and trying is enough to make me feel cold and hot at the same time, feverish and ill. There is no way to separate what was real and what my mind might have manufactured; no dividing line between objective and subjective, between the truth and horrified hallucination. But it wasn't drunkenness; if I can assure you of nothing else, I can assure you of that. Any mild high I retained from the beer evaporated immediately. What followed was a cold-sober tour of the country of the damned.

We went back in time, for one thing.

For a while Arnie wasn't driving at all; it was LeBay, rotting and stinking of the grave, half skeleton and half rotting, spongy flesh, greenly corroded buttons. Maggots squirmed their sluggish way up from his collar. I could hear a low buzzing sound and thought at first it was a short circuit in one of the dashboard lights. It was only later that I began to think it might have been the sound of flies hatching in his flesh. Of course it was wintertime, but—

At times, there seemed to be other people in the car with us. Once I glanced up into the rearview mirror and saw a wax dummy of a woman staring at me with the bright and sparkling eyes of a stuffed trophy. Her hair was done in a 50s pageboy style. Her cheeks appeared to have been wildly rouged, and I remembered that carbon monoxide poisoning was supposed to give the illusion of life and high color. Later, I glanced into the mirror again and seemed to see a little girl back there, her face blackened with strangulation, her eyes popping like those of some cruelly squeezed stuffed animal. I shut my eyes tight and when I opened them it was Buddy Repperton and Richie Trelawney in the rearview mirror. Crusted blood had dried on Buddy's mouth, chin, neck, and shirt. Richie was a roasted hulk—but his eyes were alive and aware.

Slowly, Buddy extended his arm. He was holding a bottle of Texas Driver in one blackened hand.

I closed my eyes once more. And after that, I didn't look into the rearview anymore.

I remember rock and roll on the radio: Dion and the Belmonts, Ernie K-Doe, the Royal Teens, Bobby Rydell ("Oh, Bobby, oh . . . everything's cool . . . we're glad you go to a swingin' school . . .").

I remember that for a while red Styrofoam dice seemed to be hanging from the rearview mirror, then for a while there were baby shoes, and then there was neither one.

Most of all I remember seizing the idea that these things, like the smell of rotting flesh and mouldy upholstery, were only in my mind—that they were no more than the mirages that haunt the consciousness of an opium-eater.

I was like someone who is badly stoned and trying to make some kind of rational conversation with a straight person. Because Arnie and I *did* talk; I remember that, but not what we talked about. I held up my end. I kept my voice normal. I responded. And that ten or twelve minutes seemed to last hours.

I have told you that it is impossible to be objective about that ride; if there was a logical progression of events, it is lost to me now, blocked out. That journey through the cold black night really was like a trip on a boulevard through hell. I can't remember everything that happened, but I can remember more than I want to. We backed out of the driveway and into a mad funhouse world where all the creeps were real.

We went back in time, I have said, but did we? The present-day streets of Libertyville were still there, but they were like a thin overlay of film—it was as if the Libertyville of the late 1970s had been drawn on Saran Wrap and laid over a time that was somehow more real, and I could feel that time reaching its dead hands out toward us, trying to catch us and draw us in forever. Arnie stopped at intersections where we should have had the right-of-way; at others, where traffic lights glowed red, he cruised Christine mildly through without even slowing. On Main Street I saw Shipstad's Jewelry Store and the Strand Theater, both of them torn down in 1972 to make way for the new Pennsylvania Merchants Bank. The cars parked along the street—gathered here and there in clumps where New Year's Eve parties were going on—all seemed to be pre-60s . . . or pre-1958. Long portholed Buicks. A DeSoto Firelite station wagon with a body-long blue inset that looked like a check-mark. A '57 Dodge Lancer four-door hardtop. Ford Fairlanes with their distinctive taillights, each like a big colon lying on its side. Pontiacs in which the grille had not yet been split. Ramblers, Packards, a few bullet-nosed Studebakers, and once, fantastical and new, an Edsel.

"Yeah, this year is going to be better," Arnie said. I glanced over at him. He raised his beer-can to his lips, and before it got there his face had turned to LeBay's, a rotting figure from a horror comic. The fingers that held the beer were only bones. I swear to you, they were only bones, and the pants lay nearly flat against the seat, as if there was nothing inside them except broomsticks.

"Is it?" I said, breathing the car's foul and choking miasma as shallowly as possible and trying not to choke,

"It is," LeBay said, only now he was Arnie again, and as we paused at a stop sign, I saw a '77 Camaro go ripping past. "All I ask is that you stand by me a little, Dennis. Don't let my mother drag you into this shit. Things are going to turn out." He was LeBay again, grinning fleshlessly and eternally at the idea of things turning out. I felt my brains beginning to totter. Surely I would scream soon.

I dropped my eyes from that terrible half-face and saw what Leigh had seen: dashboard instruments that weren't instruments at all, but luminescent green eyes bulging out at me.

At some point the nightmare ended. We pulled up at the curb in an area of town I didn't even recognize, an area I would have sworn I had never seen before. Tract houses stood dark everywhere, some of them three-quarters finished, some no more than frames. Halfway down the block, lit by Christine's hi-beams, was a sign which read:

MAPLEWAY ESTATES
LIBERTYVILLE REALTORS SOLE SELLING AGENTS
A Good Place to Raise YOUR Family
Think About It!

"Well, here you go," Arnie said. "Can you make it up the walk yourself, man?"

I looked doubtfully around at this deserted, snow-covered development and then nodded. Better here, on crutches, alone, than in that terrible car. I felt a large plastic smile on my face. "Sure. Thanks."

"Negative perspiration," Arnie said. He finished his beer and LeBay tossed it into a litter bag. "Another dead soldier."

"Yeah," I said. "Happy New Year, Arnie." I fumbled for the doorhandle and opened it. I wondered if I could get out, if my trembling arms would support the crutches.

LeBay was looking at me, grinning. "Just stay on my side, Dennis," he said. "You know what happens to shitters who don't."

"Yes," I whispered. I knew, all right.

I got my crutches out and heaved myself up onto them, careless of any ice that might be underneath. They held me. And once out, the world underwent a swimming, twisting change. Lights came on—but of course, they had been there all along. My family had moved into Mapleway Estates in June of 1959, the year before I was born. We still lived here, but the area had stopped being known as Mapleway Estates by 1963 or '64 at the latest.

Out of the car, I was looking at my own house on my own perfectly normal street—just another part of Libertyville, Pa. I looked back at Arnie, half-expecting to see LeBay again, taxi-driver from hell with his benighted cargo of the long-dead.

But it was only Arnie, wearing his high school jacket with his name sewn over the left breast, Arnie looking too pale and too alone, Arnie with a can of beer propped against his crotch.

"Good night, man."

"Good night," I said. "Be careful going home. You don't want to get picked up."

"I won't," he said. "You take care, Dennis."

"I will."

I shut the door. My horror had changed to a deep and terrible sorrow—it was as if he had been buried. Buried alive. I watched Christine pull away from the curb and head off down the street. I watched until she turned the corner and disappeared from sight. Then I started up the walk to the house. The walk was clear. My dad had scattered most of a ten-pound bag of Halite over it with me in mind.

I was three-quarters of the way to the door when a grayness seemed to drift over me like smoke and I had to stop and put my head down and try to hold onto myself. I could faint out here, I thought dimly, and then freeze to death on my own front walk where once Arnie and I had played hopscotch and jacks and statue-tag.

At last, little by little, the grayness started to clear. I felt an arm around my waist. It was Dad, in his bathrobe and slippers.

"Dennis, are you okay?"

Was I okay? I had been driven home by a corpse.

"Yea," I said. "Got a little dizzy. Let's get in. You'll freeze your butt off."

He walked up the steps with me, his arm still circling my waist. I was glad to have it.

"Is Mom still up?" I asked.

"No—she saw the New Year in, and then she and Ellie went to bed. Are you drunk, Dennis?"

"No."

"You don't look good," he said, slamming the door behind us.

I uttered a crazy little shriek of laughter, and things went gray again . . . but only briefly this time. When I came back, he was looking at me with tight concern.

"What happened over there?"

"Dad—"

"Dennis, you talk to me!"

"Dad, I can't."

"What *is* it with him? What's wrong with him, Dennis?"

I only shook my head, and it wasn't just the craziness of it, or fear for myself. Now I was afraid for all of them—my dad, my mom, Elaine, Leigh's folks. Coldly and sanely afraid.

Just stay on my side, Dennis. You know what happens to shitters who don't.

Had I really heard that?

Or had it been in my mind only?

My father was still looking at me.

"I *can't*."

"All right," he said. "For now. I guess. But I need to know one thing, Dennis, and I want you to tell me. Do you have any reason to believe that Arnie was involved some way with Darnell's death, and the deaths of those boys?"

I thought of LeBay's rotting, grinning face, the flat pants poked up by something that could only have been bones.

"No," I said, and that was almost the truth. "Not Arnie."

"All right," he said. "You want a hand up the stairs?"

"I can make it okay. You go to bed yourself, Dad."

"Yeah. I'm going to. Happy New Year, Dennis—and if you want to tell me, I'm still here."

"Nothing to tell," I said.

Nothing I *could* tell.

"Somehow," he said, "I doubt that."

I went up and got into bed and left the light on and didn't sleep at all. It was the longest night of my life, and several times I thought of getting up and going in with my mom and dad, the way I had done when I was small. Once I actually caught myself getting out of bed and groping for my crutches. I lay back down again. I was afraid for all of them, yes, right. But that wasn't the worst. Not anymore.

I was afraid of losing my mind. That was the worst.

The sun was just poking over the horizon when I finally dropped off and dozed uneasily for three or four hours. And when I woke up, my mind had already begun trying to heal itself with unreality. My problem was that I could simply no longer afford to listen to that lulling song. The line was blurred for good.

46 / George LeBay Again

That fateful night the car was stalled
Upon the railroad track,
I pulled you out and you were safe,
But you went running back . . .
                                        —Mark Dinning

On Friday the fifth of January I got a postcard from Richard McCandless, secretary of the Libertyville American Legion Post. Written on the back in smudgy pencil was George LeBay's home address in Paradise Falls, Ohio. I carried the card around in my hip pocket most of the day, taking it out occasionally and looking at it. I didn't want to call him; I didn't want to talk to him about his crazy brother Roland again; I didn't want this crazy business to go any further at all.

That evening my father and mother went out to the Monroeville Mall with Ellie, who wanted to spend some of her Christmas money on a new pair of downhill skis. Half an hour after they were gone, I picked up the telephone and propped McCandless's postcard up in front of me. A call to the operator placed Paradise Falls in area code 513—western Ohio. After a pause for thought I called 513 directory assistance and got LeBay's number. I jotted it on the card, paused for thought again—a longer pause, this time—and then picked up the phone a third time. I dialled half of LeBay's number and then hung up. *Fuck it,* I thought, full of nervous resentment I could not recall ever feeling before. *Enough is enough so fuck it. I'm not calling him. I'm done with it, I wash my hands of the whole crappy mess. Let him go to hell in his own handcar. Fuck it.*

"Fuck it," I whispered, and got out of there before my conscience could begin to bore into me again. I went upstairs, took a sponge bath, and then turned in. I was soundly asleep before Ellie and my folks came back in, and I slept long and well that night. A good thing, because it was a long time before I slept that well again. A very long time.

While I slept, someone—*something*—killed Rudolph Junkins of the Pennsylvania State Police. It was in the paper when I got up next morning. DARNELL INVESTIGATOR MURDERED NEAR BLAIRSVILLE, the headline shouted.

My father was upstairs taking a shower; Ellie and two of her friends out on the porch, giggling and cawing over a game of Monopoly; my mother working on one of her stories in the sewing room. I was at the table by myself, stunned and scared. It occurred to me that Leigh and her family were going to be back from California tomorrow, school would start again the day after, and unless Arnie (or LeBay) changed his mind, she would be actively pursued.

I slowly pushed away the eggs I had scrambled for myself. I no longer wanted them. Last night it had seemed possible to push away the whole ominous and inexplicable business of Christine as easily as I'd just pushed away my breakfast. Now I wondered how I could have been so naive.

Junkins was the man Arnie had mentioned New Year's Eve. I couldn't even kid myself that it hadn't been. The paper said he had been the man in charge of Pennsylvania's part of the Will Darnell investigation, and it hinted that some shadowy crime organization had been behind the murder. The Southern Mob, Arnie would have said. Or the crazy Colombians.

I thought differently.

Junkins's car had been driven off a lonely country road and battered to so much senseless wreckage

(*That goddam Junkins is still after me full steam ahead, he better watch out or somebody might just junk him. . . . Just stay on my side, Dennis. You know what happens to shitters who don't. . . .*)

with Junkins still inside it.

When Repperton and his friends were killed, Arnie had been in Philly with the chess club. When Darnell was killed, he was in Ligonier with his parents, visiting relatives. Cast-iron alibis. I thought he would have another for Junkins. Seven—seven deaths now, and they formed a deadly ring around Arnie Cunningham and Christine. The police could surely see that; not even a blind man could miss such an explicit chain of motivation. But the paper didn't say that anyone was "aiding the police in their inquiries," as the British so delicately put it.

Of course, the police are not in the habit of just handing everything they know over to the newspapers. I knew that, but every instinct I had told me that the state cops weren't seriously investigating Arnie in connection with this latest murder by automobile.

He was in the clear.

What had Junkins seen behind him on that country road outside of Blairsville? A red and white car, I thought. Maybe empty, maybe driven by a corpse.

A goose ran squawking over my grave and my arms broke out in cold bumps.

Seven people dead.

It had to end. If for no other reason than because maybe killing gets to be a habit. If Michael and Regina wouldn't go along with Arnie's crazy California plans, either of them or both of them might be next. Suppose he walked up to Leigh in study hall period three next Tuesday and asked her to marry him and Leigh simply said no? What might she see idling at the curb when she got home that afternoon?

Jesus Christ, I was scared

My mother poked in. "Dennis, you're not eating."

I looked up. "I got reading the paper. Guess I'm not that hungry, Mom."

"You have to eat right or you're not going to get well. Want me to make you oatmeal?"

My stomach churned at the thought, but I smiled as I shook my head. "No—but I'll eat a big lunch."

"Promise?"

"Promise."

"Denny, do you feel okay? You've looked so tired and peaked lately."

"I'm fine, Mom." I widened my smile to show her how fine I was, and then I thought of her getting out of her blue Reliant at the Monroeville Mall, and two rows back was a white-over-red car, idling. In my mind's eye I saw her walk in front of it, purse over her arm, saw Christine's transmission lever suddenly drop into DRIVE—

"Are you sure? It's not your leg bothering you, is it?"

"No."

"Have you taken your vitamins?"

"Yes."

"And your rosehips?"

I burst out laughing. She looked irritated for a moment,

then smiled. "Ye're a sassbox, Dennis Guilder," she said in her best Irish accent (which is pretty good, since her mom came from the auld sod), "and there's no kivver to ye." She went back to the sewing room, and in a moment the irregular bursts of her typewriter began again.

I picked up the newspaper and looked at the photo of Junkins's twisted auto. DEATH CAR, the caption beneath read.

Try this, I thought: *Junkins is interested in a lot more than finding out who sold illegal fireworks and cigarettes to Will Darnell. Junkins is a state detective, and state detectives work on more than one case at a time. He could have been trying to find out who killed Moochie Welch. Or he could have been—*

I crutched over to the sewing room and knocked.

"Yes?"

"Sorry to bother you, Mom—"

"Don't be silly, Dennis."

"Are you going downtown today?"

"I might be. Why?"

"I'd like to go to the library."

By three o'clock that Saturday afternoon it had begun to snow again. I had a slight headache from staring into the microfilm reader, but I had what I wanted. My hunch had been on the money—not that it had been any great intuitive leap.

Junkins had been in charge of the hit-and-run that had killed Moochie Welch, all right . . . and he had also been in charge of investigating what had happened to Repperton, Trelawney, and Bobby Stanton. He'd have to be one dumb cop not to read Arnie's name between the lines of what was happening.

I leaned back in the chair, snapped off the reader, and closed my eyes. I tried to make myself be Junkins for a minute. *He suspects Arnie of being involved with the murders. Not doing them, but involved somehow. Does he suspect Christine? Maybe he does. On the TV detective shows, they're always great at identifying guns, typewriters used to write ransom notes, and cars involved in hit-and-runs. Flakes and scrapes of paint, maybe . . .*

Then the Darnell bust looms up. For Junkins, that's nothing but great. The garage will be closed and everything in it impounded. Maybe Junkins suspects . . .

What?

I worked harder at imagining. I'm a cop. I believe in legitimate answers, sane answers, routine answers. So what do I suspect? After a moment, it came.

An accomplice, of course. I suspect an accomplice. It *has* to be an accomplice. Nobody in his right mind would suspect that the car was doing it herself. So. . . ?

So after the garage is closed, Junkins brings in the best technicians and lab men he can lay his hands on. They go over Christine from stem to stern, looking for evidence of what has happened. Reasoning as Junkins would reason—trying to, anyway—I think that there has to be some evidence. Hitting a human body is not like hitting a feather pillow. Hitting the crash barrier out at Squantic Hills is not like hitting a feather pillow, either

So what do they find, these experts in vehicular homicide? Nothing.

They find no dents, no touch-up repainting, no bloodstains. They find no embedded brown paint-flakes from the Squantic Hills road barrier that was broken off. In short, Junkins finds absolutely no evidence that Christine was used in either crime. Now jump ahead to Darnell's murder. Does Junkins hustle over to the garage the next day to check on Christine? I would, if it was me. The side of a house isn't a feather pillow either, and a car that has just crashed through one must have sustained major damage, damage that simply couldn't have been repaired overnight. And when he gets there, what does he find?

Only Christine, without so much as a ding in her fender.

That led to another deduction, one that explained why Junkins had never put a stakeout on the car. I hadn't been able to understand that, because he must have suspected that Christine was involved. But in the end, logic had ruled him—and perhaps it had killed him, as well. Junkins hadn't put a stakeout on her because Christine's alibi, while mute, was every bit as iron-clad as those of her owner. If he had inspected Christine immediately following the murder of Will Darnell, Junkins must have concluded that the car could not have been involved, no matter how persuasive the evidence to the contrary seemed.

Not a scratch on her. And why not? It was just that Junkins hadn't had all the facts. I thought about the odometer that ran backward, and Arnie saying, *Just a glitch.* I thought of the nest of cracks in the windshield that had seemed to grow smaller and draw inward—as if they were running backward too. I thought of the haphazard replacement of parts that seemed totally without rhyme or reason. Last of all, I thought of my nightmare ride home on Sunday night—old cars that looked new clumped up at the curb outside houses where parties were going on, the Strand Theater intact again in all of its yellow brick solidity, the half-built development that had been completed and occupied by Libertyville suburbanites twenty years ago.

Just a glitch.

I thought that not knowing about that glitch was what had *really* killed Rudolph Junkins.

Because, look: if you own a car long enough, things wear out no matter how well you take care of it, and they usually go randomly. A car comes off the assembly line like a new-born baby, and just like a newborn, it starts rolling down an Indian gauntlet of years. The slings and arrows of outrageous fortune crack a battery here, bust a tie-rod there, freeze a bearing somewhere else. The carburetor float sticks, a tire blows, there's an electrical short, the upholstery starts getting ratty.

It's like a movie. And if you could run the film backward—

"Will there be anything else, sir?" the Records Clerk asked from behind me, and I nearly screamed.

Mom was waiting for me in the main lobby, and she chattered most of the way home about her writing and her new class, which was disco dancing. I nodded and replied in most of the right places. And I thought that if Junkins *had* brought in his technicians, his high-powered auto specialists from Harrisburg, they had probably overlooked an elephant while looking for a needle. I couldn't blame them, either. Cars just don't run backward, like a movie in reverse. And there are no such things as ghosts or revenants or demons preserved in Quaker State motor-oil.

Believe in one, believe in all, I thought, and shuddered.

"Want to turn up the heater, Denny?" Mom asked brightly.

"Would you, Mom?"

I thought of Leigh, who was due back tomorrow. Leigh with her lovely face (enhanced by those slanting, almost cruel cheekbones), her young and sweetly luscious figure that had not yet been marred by the forces of time or gravity; like that long-ago Plymouth that had rolled out of Detroit on a carrier in 1957, she was, in a sense, still under warranty. Then I thought of LeBay, who was dead and yet undead, and I thought of his lust (but was it lust? or just a need to spoil things?). I thought of Arnie saying with calm assurance that they were going to be married. And then, with a helpless clarity, I saw their wedding night. I saw her looking up into the darkness of some motel room and seeing a rotting, grinning corpse poised over her. I heard her screams as Christine, a Christine still festooned with crepe streamers and soaped-on JUST MARRIED signs, waited faithfully outside the closed and locked door. Christine—or the terrible female force that animated her—would know Leigh wouldn't last long . . . and she, Christine, would be around when Leigh was gone.

I closed my eyes to block the images out, but that only intensified them.

It had begun with Leigh wanting Arnie and had progressed logically enough to Arnie wanting her back. But it hadn't stopped there, had it? Because now LeBay had Arnie . . . and *he* wanted Leigh.

But he wasn't going to have her. Not if I could help it.

That night I called George LeBay.

"Yes, Mr. Guilder," he said. He sounded older, tireder. "I remember you very well. I talked your ear off in front of my unit in what I believe may have been the most depressing motel in the universe. What can I do for you?" He sounded as though he hoped I wouldn't require too much.

I hesitated. Did I tell him that his brother had come back from the dead? That not even the grave had been able to end his hate of the shitters? Did I tell him he had possessed my friend, had picked him out as unerringly as Arnie had picked out Christine? Did we talk about mortality, and time, and rancid love?

"Mr. Guilder? Are you there?"

"I've got a problem, Mr. LeBay. And I don't know exactly how to tell you about it. It concerns your brother."

Something new came into his voice then, something tight and controlled. "I don't know what sort of a problem you could have that would concern him. Rollie's dead."

"That's just it." Now I was unable to control my own voice. It trembled up to a higher octave and then drifted back down again. "I don't think he is."

"What are you talking about?" His voice was taut, accusing . . . and fearful. "If this is your idea of a joke, I assure you it's in the poorest possible taste."

"No joke. Just let me tell you some of the stuff that's happened since your brother died."

"Mr. Guilder, I have several sets of papers to correct, and a novel I want to finish, and I really don't have time to indulge in—"

"*Please*," I said. "Please, Mr. LeBay, please help me, and help my friend."

There was a long, long pause, and then LeBay sighed. "Tell your tale," he said, and then, after a brief pause, he added, "Goddamn you."

I passed the story along to him by way of modern long-distance cable; I could imagine my voice going through computerized switching stations full of miniaturized circuits, under snow-blanketed wheat-fields, and finally into the ear of this man.

I told him about Arnie's trouble with Repperton, Buddy's expulsion and revenge; I told him about the death of Moochie Welch; what had happened at Squantic Hills; what had happened during the Christmas Eve storm. I told him about windshield cracks that seemed to run backward and an odometer that did for sure. I told him about the radio that seemed to receive only WDIL, the oldies station, no matter where you set it—that brought a soft grunt of surprise from George LeBay. I told him about the handwriting on my casts, and how the one Arnie had done on Thanksgiving night matched his brother's signature on Christine's original registration form. I told him about Arnie's constant use of the word "shitters." The way he had started combing his hair like Fabian, or one of those other fifties greaseballs. I told him everything, in fact, except what had happened to me on my ride home early on New Year's morning. I had intended to, but I simply could not do it. I never let that out of myself until I wrote all of this down four years later.

When I finished, there was a silence on the line.

"Mr. LeBay? Are you still there?"

"I'm here," he said finally. "Mr. Guilder—Dennis—I don't intend to offend you, but you must realize that what you are suggesting goes far beyond any possible psychic phenomena and extends into . . . ." He trailed off.

"Madness?"

"That isn't the word I would have used. From what you say, you were involved in a terrible football accident. You were in the hospital for two months, and in great pain for some of that time. Now isn't it possible that your imagination—"

"Mr. LeBay," I said, "did your brother ever have a saying about the little tramp?"

"What?"

"The little tramp. Like when you throw a ball of paper at the wastebasket and hit it, you say 'Two points.' Only instead of that, 'Watch me put it up the little tramp's ass.' Did your brother ever say that?"

"How did you know that?" And then, without giving me time to answer: "He used the phrase on one of the occasions when you met him, didn't he?"

"No."

"Mr. Guilder, you're a liar."

I said nothing. I was shaking, weak-kneed. No adult had ever said that to me in my whole life.

"Dennis, I'm sorry. But my brother is dead. He was an unpleasant, possibly even an evil human being, but he is dead and all of these morbid fancies and fantasies—"

"Who was the little tramp?" I managed.

Silence.

"Was it Charlie Chaplin?"

I didn't think he was going to reply at all. Then, at last, heavily, he said, "Only at second hand. He meant Hitler. There was a passing resemblance between Hitler and Chaplin's little tramp. Chaplin made a movie called *The Great Dictator*. You've probably never even seen it. It was a common enough name for him during the war years, at any rate. You would be much too young to remember. But it means nothing."

It was my turn to remain silent.

"It means nothing!" he shouted. "Nothing! It's vapors and suggestions, nothing more! You must see this!"

"There are seven people dead over here in western Pennsylvania," I said. "That's not just vapors. There are the signatures on my casts. They're not vapors, either. I saved them, Mr. LeBay. Let me send them to you. Look at them and tell me if one of them isn't your brother's handwriting."

"It could be a knowing or unknowing forgery."

"If you believe that, get a handwriting expert. I'll pay for it."

"You could do that yourself."

"Mr. LeBay," I said, "*I* don't need any more convincing."

"But what do you want from me? To share your fantasy? I won't do that. My brother is dead. His car is just a car." He was lying. I felt it. Even through the telephone I felt it.

"I want you to explain something you said to me that night we talked."

"What would that be?" He sounded wary.

I licked my lips. "You said he was obsessed and angry, but he wasn't a monster. At least, you said, you didn't think he was. Then it seemed like you changed the subject completely . . . but the more I think about it, the more I think you didn't change the subject at all. The next thing you said was that he never put a mark on either of them."

"Dennis, really. I—"

"Look, if you were going to say something, for Christ's sake, say it now!" I cried. My voice cracked. I wiped my forehead, and my hand came away slimy with sweat. "This is no easier for me than it is for you, Arnie's fixated on this girl, her name is Leigh Cabot, only I don't think it's Arnie who's fixated on her at all, I think it's your brother, your dead brother, *now talk to me, please!*"

He sighed.

"Talk to you?" he said. "*Talk* to you? To talk about these old events . . . no, these old suspicions . . . that would be almost the same as to shake a sleeping fiend, Dennis. Please, I know nothing."

I could have told him the fiend was already awake, but he knew that.

"Tell me what you suspect."

"I'll call you back."

"Mr. LeBay . . . please . . ."

"I'll call you back," he said. "I've got to call my sister Marcia in Colorado."

"If it will help, I'll call—"

"No, she would never talk to you. We've only talked of it to each other once or twice, if that. I hope your conscience is clear on this matter, Dennis. Because you are asking us to rip open old scars and make them bleed again. So I'll ask you once more: How sure are you?"

"Sure," I whispered.

"I'll call you back," he said, and hung up.

Fifteen minutes went past, then twenty. I went around the room on my crutches, unable to sit still. I looked out the window at the wintry street, a study in blacks and whites. Twice I went to the telephone and didn't pick it up, afraid he would be trying to get me at the same time, even more afraid that he wouldn't call back at all. The third time, just as I put my hand on it, it rang. I jerked back as if stung, and then scooped it up.

"Hi?" Ellie's breathless voice said from downstairs. "Donna?"

"Is Dennis Guilder—" LeBay's voice began, sounding older and more broken than ever.

"I've got it, Ellie," I said.

"Well, who cares?" Ellie said pertly, and hung up.

"Hello, Mr. LeBay," I said. My heart was thudding hard.

"I spoke to her," he said heavily. "She tells me only to use my own judgement But she is frightened, Together, you and I have conspired to frighten an old lady who has never hurt anyone and has nothing whatever to do with this."

"In a good cause," I said.

"Is it?"

"If I didn't think so, I wouldn't have called you," I said. "Are you going to talk to me or not, Mr. LeBay?"

"Yes," he said. "To you, but to no one else. If you should tell someone else, I would deny it. You understand?"

"Yes."

"Very well." He sighed. "In our conversation last summer, Dennis, I told you one lie about what happened and one lie about what I—what Marcy and I—felt about it. We lied to ourselves. If it hadn't been for you, I think we could have continued to lie to ourselves about that—that incident by the highway—for the rest of our lives."

"The little girl? LeBay's daughter?" I was holding the phone tightly, squeezing it.

"Yes," he said heavily. "Rita."

"What really happened when she choked?"

"My mother used to call Rollie her changeling," LeBay said. "Did I tell you that?"

"No."

"No, of course not. I told you I thought your friend would be happier if he got rid of the car, but there is only so much a person can say in defense of one's beliefs, because the irrational . . . it creeps in. . . ."

He paused. I didn't prompt him. He would tell, or he wouldn't. It was as simple as that.

"My mother said he was a perfectly good baby until he was six months old. And then . . . she said that was when Puck came. She said Puck took her good baby for one of his jokes and replaced him with a changeling. She laughed when she said it. But she never said it when Rollie was around to hear, and her *eyes* never laughed, Dennis. I think . . . it was her only explanation for what he was, for why he was so untouchable in his rage . . . so single-minded in his few simple purposes.

"There was a boy—I have forgotten his name—a bigger boy who thrashed Rollie three or four times. A bully. He would start on Rollie's clothes and ask him if he'd worn his underpants one month or two this time. And Rollie would fight him and curse him and threaten him and the bully would laugh at him and hold him off with his longer arms and punch him until he was tired or until Rollie's nose was bleeding. And then Rollie would sit there on the corner, smoking a cigarette and crying with blood and snot drying on his face. And if Drew or I came near him, he would beat us to within an inch of our lives.

"That bully's house burned down one night, Dennis. The bully and the bully's father and the bully's little brother were killed. The bully's sister was horribly burned. It was supposed to have been the stove in the kitchen, and maybe it was. But the fire sirens woke me up, and I was still awake when Rollie came up the ivy trellis and into the room I shared with him. There was soot on his forehead, and he smelled of gasoline. He saw me lying there with my eyes open and he said, 'If you tell, Georgie, I'll kill you.' And ever since that night, Dennis, I've tried to tell myself that he meant if I told he had been out, watching the fire. And maybe that was all it was."

My mouth was dry. There seemed to be a lead ball in my stomach. The hairs along the nape of my neck felt like dry quills. "How old was your brother then?" I asked hoarsely.

"Not quite thirteen," Lebay said with terrible false calm. "One winter day about a year later, there was a fight during a hockey game, and a fellow named Randy Throgmorton laid open Rollie's head with his stick. Knocked him senseless. We got him to old Dr. Farner—Rollie had come around by then, but he was still groggy—and Farner put a dozen stitches in his scalp. A week later, Randy Throgmorton fell through the ice on Palmer Pond and was drowned. He had been skating in an area clearly marked with THIN ICE signs. Apparently."

"Are you saying your brother killed these people? Are you leading up to telling me that LeBay killed his own daughter?"

"Not that he killed her, Dennis—never think that. She choked to death. What I am suggesting is that he may have let her die."

"You said he turned her over—punched her—tried to make her vomit—"

"That's what Rollie told me at the funeral," George said.

"Then what—"

"Marcia and I talked it over later. Only that once, you understand. Over dinner that night. Rollie told me, 'I picked her up by her Buster Browns and tried to whack that sonofabitch out of there, Georgie. But it was stuck down fast.' And what Veronica told Marcia was, 'Rollie picked her up by her shoes and tried to whack whatever was choking her out of there, but it was stuck down fast.' They told exactly the same story, in exactly the same words. And do you know what that made me think of?"

"No."

"It made me think of Rollie climbing in the bedroom window and whispering to me, 'If you tell, Georgie, I'll kill you.'"

"But . . . why? Why would he—?"

"Later, Veronica wrote Marcia a letter and hinted that Rollie had made no real effort to save their daughter. And that, at the very end, he put her back in the car. So she would be out of the sun, he said. But in her letter, Veronica said she thought Rollie wanted her to die in the car."

I didn't want to say it, but I had to.

"Are you suggesting that your brother offered his daughter up as some kind of a human sacrifice?"

There was a long, thinking, dreadful pause.

"Not in any conscious way, no," LeBay said. "Not any more than I am suggesting that he consciously murdered her. If you had known my brother, you would know how ridiculous it is to suspect him of witchcraft or sorcery or trafficking with demons. He believed in nothing beyond his own senses . . . except, I suppose, for his own will. I am suggesting that he might have had some . . . some intuition . . . or that he might have been directed to do what he did.

"My mother said he was a changeling."

"And Veronica?"

"I don't know," he said. "The police verdict was suicide, even though there was no note. It may well have been. But the poor woman had made some friends in town, and I have often wondered if perhaps she had hinted to some of them, as she had to Marcia, that Rita's death was not quite as she and Rollie had reported it. I have wondered if Rollie found out. *If you tell, Georgie, I'll kill you.* There's no proof one way or the other, of course. But I've wondered why she would do it the way she did—and I've wondered how a woman who didn't know the slightest thing about cars would know enough to get the hose and attach it to the exhaust pipe and put it in through the window. I try not to wonder about those things. They keep me awake at night."

I thought about what he had said, and about the things he hadn't said—the things he had left between the lines. *Intuitive*, he had said. *So single-minded in his few simple purposes,* he had said. Suppose Roland LeBay had understood in some way he wouldn't even admit to himself that he was investing his Plymouth with some supernatural power? And suppose he had only been waiting for the right inheritor to come along . . . and now . . .

"Does that answer your questions, Dennis?"

"I think it does," I said slowly.

"What are you going to do?"

"I think you know that."

"Destroy the car?"

"I'm going to try," I said, and then looked over at my crutches, leaning against the wall. My goddam crutches.

"You may destroy your friend, as well."

"I may save him," I said.

Quietly, George LeBay said, "I wonder if that is still possible."

47 / The Betrayal

There was blood and glass all over,
And there was nobody there but me.
As the rain tumbled down hard and cold,
I seen a young man lyin by the side
    of the road,
He cried, "Mister, won't you
    help me, please?"

—Bruce Springsteen

I kissed her.

Her arms slipped around my neck. One of her cool hands pressed lightly against the back of my head. There was no more question for me about what was going on; and when she pulled slightly away from me, her eyes half-closed, I could see there was no question for her, either.

"Dennis," she murmured, and I kissed her again. Our tongues touched gently. For a moment her kiss intensified; I could feel the passion those high cheekbones hinted at. Then she gasped a little and drew back. "That's enough," she said. "We'll be arrested for indecent exposure, or something."

It was January eighteenth. We were parked in the lot behind the local Kentucky Fried, the remains of a pretty decent chicken dinner spread around us. We were in my Duster, and that alone was something of an occasion for me—it was my first time behind the wheel since the accident. Just that morning, the doctor had removed the huge cast on my left leg and replaced it with a brace. His warning to stay off it was stern, but I could tell he was feeling good about the way things were going for me. My recovery was about a month ahead of schedule. He put it down to superior technique; my mother to positive thinking and chicken soup; Coach Puffer to rosehips.

Me, I thought Leigh Cabot had a lot to do with it.

"We have to talk," she said.

"No, let's make out some more," I said.

"Talk now. Make out later."

"Has he started again?"

She nodded.

In the almost two weeks since my telephone conversation with LeBay, the first two weeks of winter term, Arnie had been working at making a *rapprochement* with Leigh—working at it with an intensity that scared both of us. I had told her about my talk with George LeBay (but not, as I've said, about my terrible ride home on New Year's morning) and made it as clear as I could that on no account should she simply cut him off. That would drive him into a fury, and these days, when Arnie was furious with someone, unpleasant things happened to them.

"That makes it like cheating on him," she said.

"I know," I said, more sharply than I had intended. "I don't like it, but I don't want that car rolling again."

"So?"

And I shook my head.

In truth, I was starting to feel like Prince Hamlet, delaying and delaying. I knew what had to be done, of course: Christine had to be destroyed. Leigh and I had looked into ways of doing it.

The first idea had been Leigh's—Molotov cocktails. We would, she said, fill some wine-bottles with gasoline, take them to the Cunningham house in the early-morning hours, light the wicks ("Wicks? What wicks?" I asked. "Kotex ought to do just fine," she answered promptly, causing me to wonder again about her high-cheekboned forebears), and toss them in through Christine's windows.

"What if the windows are rolled up and the doors are locked?" I asked her. "That's the way it's apt to be, you know."

She looked at me as if I was a total drip. "Are you saying," she asked, "that the idea of firebombing Arnie's car is okay, but you've got moral scruples about breaking some glass?"

"No," I said. "But who's going to get close enough to her to break the glass with a hammer, Leigh? You?"

She looked at me, biting at her soft lower lip. She said nothing.

The next idea had been mine. Dynamite.

Leigh thought about it and shook her head.

"I could get it without too much sweat, I think," I said. I still saw Brad Jeffries from time to time, and Brad still worked for Penn-DOT, and Penn-DOT had enough dynamite to put Three Rivers Stadium on the moon. I thought that maybe I could borrow the right key without Brad knowing I had borrowed it—he had a way of getting tanked up when the Penguins were on the tube. Borrow the key to the explosives shed during the third period of one game, I thought, and return it to his ring in the third period of another. The chance that he would be wanting explosives in January, and thus realize his key was missing, was small indeed. It was a deception, another betrayal—but it was a way to end things.

"No," she said.

"Why not?" To me, dynamite seemed to offer the kind of utter finality the situation demanded.

"Because Arnie keeps it parked in his driveway now. Do you really want to send shrapnel flying all over a suburban neighborhood? Risking a piece of flying glass cutting off some little kid's head?"

I winced. I hadn't thought of that, but now that she mentioned it, the image seemed sharp and clear and hideous. And that got me thinking about other things. Lighting a bundle of dynamite with your cigarillo and then tossing it overhand at the object you wanted to destroy . . . that might look okay on the Saturday afternoon Westerns they showed on channel 2, but in real life there were blasting caps and contact points to deal with. Still, I held onto the idea as long as I could.

"If we did it at night?"

"Still pretty dangerous," she said. "And you know it, too. It's all over your face."

A long, long pause.

"What about the crusher at Darnell's?" she asked finally.

"Same basic objection as before," I said. "Who gets to drive her down there? You, me, or Arnie?"

And that was where matters still stood.

"What was it today?" I asked her.

"He wanted me to go out with him tonight," she said. "Bowling this time." In previous days it had been the movies, out for dinner, over to watch TV at his house, proposed study-dates. Christine figured in all of them as the mode of transport. "He's getting ugly about it, and I'm running out of excuses. If we're going to do something, we ought to do it soon."

I nodded. Failure to find a satisfactory method was one thing. The other thing holding us back had been my leg. Now the cast was off, and although I was on stern doctor's orders to use my crutches, I had tested the left leg without them. There was some pain, but not as much as I had feared.

Those things, yeah—but mostly there had been us. Discovering each other. And although it's going to sound stinking, I guess I ought to add something else, if this thing is going to stay straight (and I promised myself when I began to tell the tale that I'd stop if I found I couldn't get it straight or keep it straight). The spice of danger had added something to what I felt for her—and, I think, to what she felt for me. He was my best friend, but there was still a dirty, senseless attraction in the idea that we were seeing each other behind his back. I felt that each time I drew her into my arms, each time my hand slipped over the firm swelling of her breasts. The sneaking around. Can you tell me why that should have an attraction? But it did. For the first time in my life, I had fallen for a girl. I had slipped before, but this time I had taken the grand head-over-heels tumble. And I loved it. I loved *her*. That constant sense of betrayal, though . . . that was a snakelike thing, both a shame and a crazy sort of goad. We could tell each other (and we did) that we were keeping our mouths shut to protect our families and ourselves.

That was true.

But it wasn't all, Leigh, was it? No. It wasn't all.

In one way, nothing worse could have happened. Love slows down reaction time; it mutes the sense of danger. My conversation with George LeBay was twelve long days in the past, and thinking about the things he had said—and worse, the things he had suggested—no longer raised the hair on the back of my neck.

The same was true—or not true—of the few times I talked with Arnie or glimpsed him in the halls. In a strange way, we seemed to be back in September and October again, when we had grown apart simply because Arnie was so busy. When we did talk he seemed pleasant enough, although the gray eyes behind his specs were cool. I waited for a wailing Regina or a distraught Michael to call me on the phone with the news that Arnie had finally stopped toying with them and had given up the idea of college in the fall for certain.

That didn't happen, and it was from Motormouth himself—our guidance counsellor—that I heard Arnie had taken home a lot of literature on the University of Pennsylvania,

Drew University, and Penn State. Those were the schools Leigh was most interested in. I knew it, and Arnie knew it too.

Two nights earlier, I had happened to overhear my mother and my sister Ellie in the kitchen.

"Why doesn't Arnie ever come over anymore, Mom?" Ellie asked. "Did he and Dennis have a fight?"

"No, honey," my mother answered. "I don't think so. But when friends get older . . . sometimes they grow apart."

"That's never going to happen to me," Ellie said, with all the awesome conviction of the just-turned-fifteen.

I sat in the other room, wondering if maybe that was really all it was—hallucination brought on by my long stay in the hospital, as LeBay had suggested, and a simple growing-apart, a developing space between two childhood friends. I could see a certain logic to it, even down to my fixation on Christine, the wedge that had come between us.

It ignored the hard facts, but it was comfortable. To believe such a thing would allow Leigh and me to pursue our ordinary lives—to get involved in school activities, to do a little extra cramming for the Scholastic Achievement Tests in March, and, of course, to jump into each other's arms as soon as her parents or mine left the room. To neck like what we were, which was a couple of horny teenagers totally infatuated with each other.

Those things lulled me . . . lulled us both. We had been careful—as careful, in fact, as adulterers instead of a couple of kids—but today the cast had come off, today I had been able to use the keys to my Duster again instead of just looking at them, and on an impulse I had called Leigh up and asked her if she'd like to go out to the world-famous Colonel's with me for a little of his world-famous Crunchy Style. She had been delighted.

So maybe you see how our attention waned, how we became the smallest bit indiscreet. We sat in the parking lot, the Duster's engine running so we could have some heat, and we talked about putting an end to that old and infinitely clever she-monster like a couple of children playing cowboys.

Neither of us saw Christine when she pulled up behind us.

"He's buckling down for a long siege, if that's what it takes," I said.

"What?"

"The colleges he applied to. Hasn't it hit you yet?"

"I guess not," she said, mystified.

"They're the schools you're most interested in," I said patiently.

She looked at me. I looked back, trying to smile, not making it.

"All right," I said. "Let's go over it one more time. Molotov cocktails are out. Dynamite looks risky, but in a pinch—"

Leigh's harsh gasp stopped me right there—that, and the expression of startled horror on her face. She was staring out through the windshield, eyes wide, mouth open. I turned in that direction, and what I saw was so stunning that for a moment I was immobilized too.

Arnie was standing in front of my Duster.

He had parked directly behind us and gone in to get his chicken without realizing who it was, and why should he? It was nearly dark, and one splashed and muddy four-year-old Duster looks pretty much like another. He had gone in, had gotten his chow, had come out again . . . and stared right in through the windshield at Leigh and me, sitting close together, our arms around each other, looking deep into each other's eyes, as the poets say. Nothing but a coincidence—a grisly, hideous coincidence. Except that even now a part of my mind is coldly convinced that it was Christine . . . that even at that turn, Christine led him there.

There was a long, frozen moment. A little moan escaped Leigh's throat. Arnie stood not quite halfway across the small parking lot, dressed in his high school jacket, faded jeans, boots. A plaid scarf was tied around his throat. The collar of his jacket was turned up, and its black wings framed a face that was slowly twisting from an expression of sick incredulity into a pallid grimace of hate. The red-and-white-striped bag with the Colonel's smiling face on it slipped out of one of his gloved hands and thumped onto the packed snow of the parking lot.

"Dennis," Leigh whispered. "Dennis, oh my God."

He began to run. I thought he was coming to the car, probably to haul me out and work me over. I could see myself hopping feebly around on my not-so-good leg under the parking-lot lights that had just come on while Arnie, whose life I had saved all those years going back to kindergarten, beat the living Jesus out of me. He ran, his mouth twisted down in a snarl I had seen before—but not on his face. It was LeBay's face now.

He didn't stop at my car; instead he ran right past. I twisted around, and that was when I saw Christine.

I got my door open and began to struggle out, grabbing onto the roof gutter for support. The cold numbed my fingers almost at once.

"Dennis, no!" Leigh cried.

I got on my feet just as Arnie raked open Christine's door.

"Arnie!" I shouted. "Hey, man!"

His head jerked up. His eyes were wide and blank and glaring. A line of spittle was working its way down from one corner of his mouth. Christine's grille seemed to be snarling too.

He raised both fists and shook them at me. *"You shitter!"* His voice was high and cracked. *"Have her! You deserve her! She's shit! You're both shit! Have each other! You won't for long!"*

People had come to the plate-glass windows of the Kentucky Fried Chicken and the neighboring Kowloon Express to see what was going on.

"Arnie! Let's talk, man—"

He jumped in the car and slammed her door. Christine's engine screamed and her headlights came on, the glaring white eyes of my dream, pinning me like a bug on a card. And over them, behind the glass, was Arnie's terrible face, the face of a devil sick of sin. That face, both hateful and haunted, has lived in my dreams ever since. Then the face was gone. It was replaced by a skull, a grinning death's head.

Leigh uttered a high, piercing scream. She had turned around to look, so I knew that it wasn't just my imagination. She had seen it too.

Christine roared forward, her rear tires spinning snow back. She didn't come for the Duster, but for me. I think his intention was to grind me to jelly between his car and mine. It was only my bad left leg that saved me; it buckled and I fell back inside my Duster, bumping my right hip on the wheel and honking the horn.

A cold wave of wind buffeted my face. Christine's bright red flank passed within three feet of me. She roared down the take-out joint's IN drive and shot onto JFK Drive without slowing, rear end fishtailing. Then she was gone, still accelerating.

I looked at the snow and could see the fresh zig-zag treads of her tires. She had missed my open door by no more than three inches.

Leigh was crying. I pulled my left leg into the car with my hands, slammed the door, and held her. Her arms groped for me blindly and then grasped with panicky tightness. "It . . . it wasn't . . ."

"Shhh, Leigh. Never mind. Don't think about it."

"That wasn't Arnie driving that car! It was a dead person! It was a dead person!"

"It was LeBay," I said, and now that it had happened, I felt a kind of eerie calm instead of the trembly, close-call reaction I should have had—that and the guilt of finally being discovered with my best friend's girl. "It was him, Leigh. You just met Roland D. LeBay."

She wept, crying out her fear and shock and horror, holding onto me. I was glad to have her. My left leg throbbed dully. I looked up into the rearview mirror at the empty slot where Christine had been. Now that it had happened, it seemed to me that any other conclusion would have been impossible. The peace of the last two weeks, the simple joy of having Leigh on my side, all of that now seemed to be the unnatural thing, the false thing—as false as the phony war between Hitler's conquest of Poland and the Wehrmacht's rolling assault on France.

And I began to see the end of things, how it would be.

She looked up at me, her cheeks wet. "What now, Dennis? What do we do now?"

"Now we end it."

"How? What do you mean?"

Speaking more to myself than to her, I said, "He needs an alibi. We have to be ready when he goes away. The garage. Darnell's. I'm going to trap it in there. Try to kill it."

"Dennis, what are you talking about?"

"He'll leave town," I said. "Don't you see? All of the people Christine has killed—they make a ring around Arnie. *He'll* know that. *He'll* get Arnie out of town again."

"LeBay, you mean."

I nodded, and Leigh shuddered.

"We have to kill it. You know that."

"But how? Please, Dennis . . . how are we going to do it?"

And at last I had an idea.

48 / Preparations

There's a killer on the road,
His brain is squirming like a toad . . .
                    —The Doors

I dropped Leigh off at her house and told her to call me if she saw Christine cruising around.

"What are you going to do? Come over here with a flame-thrower?"

"A bazooka," I said, and we both started to laugh hysterically.

"Nuke the '58! Nuke the '58!" Leigh yelled, and we got laughing again—but all the time we were laughing we were scared half out of our minds . . . maybe more than half. And all the time we were laughing I was sick over Arnie, both over what he had seen and what I had done. And I think Leigh felt the same. It's just that sometimes you have to laugh. Sometimes you just do. And when it comes, nothing can keep that laugh away. It just walks in and does its stuff.

"So what do I tell my folks?" she asked me when we finally started to come down a little. "I've got to tell them *something*, Dennis! I can't just let them risk being run down in the street!"

"Nothing," I said. "Tell them nothing at all."

"But—"

"For one thing, they wouldn't believe you. For another, nothing's going to happen as long as Arnie's in Libertyville. I'd stake my life on that."

"You are, dummy," she whispered.

"I know. My life, my mother's, my father's, my sister's."

"How will we know if he leaves?"

"I'll take care of that. You're going to be sick tomorrow. You're not going to school."

"I'm sick right now," she said in a low voice. "Dennis, what's going to happen? What are you planning?"

"I'll call you later tonight," I said, and kissed her. Her lips were cold.

443

When I got home, Elaine was struggling into her parka and muttering black imprecations at people who sent other people down to Tom's for milk and bread just when *Dance Fever* was coming on TV. She was prepared to be grumpy at me as well, but she cheered up when I offered to give her a lift down to the market and back. She also gave me a suspicious look, as if this unexpected kindness to the little sister might be the onset of some disease. Herpes, maybe. She asked me if I felt all right. I only smiled blandly and told her to hop in before I changed my mind, although by now my right leg was aching and my left was throbbing fiercely. I could talk on and on to Leigh about how Christine wouldn't roll as long as Arnie was in Libertyville, and intellectually I knew that was right . . . but it didn't change the instinctive rolling in my guts when I thought of Ellie walking the two blocks to Tom's and crossing the dark suburban sidestreets in her bright yellow parka. I kept seeing Christine parked down one of those streets, crouched in the dark like an old bitch hunting dog.

When we got to Tom's, I gave her a buck. "Get us each a Yodel and a Coke," I said.

"Dennis, *are* you feeling all right?"

"Yes. And if you put my change in that Asteroids game, I'll break your arm."

That seemed to set her mind at rest. She went in, and I sat slumped behind the wheel of my Duster, thinking about what a terrible box we were in. We couldn't talk to anyone—that was the nightmare. That was where Christine was so strong. Was I going to grab my dad down in his toy-shop and tell him that what Ellie called "Arnie Cunningham's pukey old red car" was now driving itself? Was I going to call the cops and tell them that a dead guy wanted to kill my girlfriend and myself? No. The only thing on our side, other than the fact that the car couldn't move until Arnie had an alibi, was the fact that it would want no witnesses—Moochie Welch, Don Vandenberg, and Will Darnell had been killed alone, late at night; Buddy Repperton and his two friends had been killed out in the boonies.

Elaine came back with a bag clutched to her budding bosom, got in, gave me my Coke and my Yodel.

"Change," I said.

"You're a boogersnot," she said, but put some twenty-odd cents in my outstretched hand.

"I know, but I love you anyway," I said. I pushed her hood back, ruffled her hair, and then kissed her ear. She looked surprised and suspicious—and then she smiled. She wasn't such a bad sort, my sister Ellie. The thought of her being run down in the street simply because I fell in love with Leigh Cabot after Arnie went mad and left her . . . I simply wasn't going to let that happen.

At home, I worked my way upstairs after saying hi to my mom. She wanted to know how the leg was doing, and I told her it was in good shape. But when I got upstairs, I made the bathroom medicine cabinet my first stop. I swallowed a couple of aspirin for the sake of my legs, which were now singing *Ave Maria*. Then I went down to my folks' bedroom, where the upstairs phone is, and sat down in Mom's rocking chair with a sigh.

I picked up the phone and made the first of my calls.

"Dennis Guilder, scourge of the turnpike extension project!" Brad Jeffries said heartily. "Good to hear from you, kiddo. When you gonna come over and watch the Penguins with me again?"

"I dunno," I said. "I get tired of watching handicapped people play hockey after a while. Now if you got interested in a *good* team, like the Flyers—"

"Christ, have I got to listen to this from a kid that isn't even mine?" Brad asked. "The world really is going to hell, I guess."

We chatted for a while longer, just kicking things back and forth, and then I told him why I had called.

He laughed. "What the *fuck*, Denny? You goin into business for yourself?"

"You might say so." I thought of Christine. "For a limited time only."

"Don't want to talk about it?"

"Well, not just yet. Do you know someone who might have an item like that for rent?"

"I'll tell you, Dennis. There's only one guy I know who might do business with you on anything like that. Johnny Pomberton. Lives out on the Ridge Road. He's got more rolling stock than Carter's got liver pills."

"Okay," I said. "Thanks, Brad."

"How's Arnie?"

"All right, I guess. I don't see as much of him as I used to."

"Funny guy, Dennis. I never in my wildest dreams thought he'd last out the summer the first time I set eyes on him. But he had one hell of a lot of determination."

"Yeah," I said. "All of that and then some."

"Say hi to him when you see him."

"I'll do it, Brad. Stay loose."

"Can't live if you do anything else, Denny. Come on over some night and peel a few cans with me."

"I will. Good night."

" 'Night."

I hung up and then hesitated over the phone for a minute or two, not really wanting to make this next call. But it had to be done; it was central to the whole sorry, stupid business. I picked the telephone up and dialled the Cunninghams' number from memory. If Arnie answered, I would simply hang up without speaking. But my luck was in; it was Michael who answered.

"Hello?" His voice sounded tired and a bit slurred.

"Michael, this is Dennis."

"Hey, hi!" He sounded genuinely pleased.

"Is Arnie there?"

"Upstairs. He came home from somewhere and went right to his room. He looked pretty thundery, but that's far from unusual these days. Want me to call him?"

"No," I said. "That's okay. It was really you I wanted to talk to, anyhow. I need a favor."

"Well, sure. Name it." I realized what that slur in his voice was—Michael Cunningham was at least halfway snookered. "You did us a helluva favor, talking some sense to him about college."

"Michael, I don't think he listened to a thing I said."

"Well, something sure happened. He's applied to three schools just this month. Regina thinks you walk on water, Dennis. And just between me and thee, she's pretty ashamed of the way she treated you when Arnie first told us about his car. But you know Regina. She's never been able to say 'I'm sorry.' "

I knew that, all right. And what would Regina think, I wondered, if she knew that Arnie—or whatever controlled Arnie—didn't have any more interest in college than a hog has in mutual funds? That he was simply following Leigh's tracks, hounding her, fixated on her? It was perversion on perversion—LeBay, Leigh, and Christine in some hideous *ménage à trois*.

"Listen, Michael," I said. "I'd like you to call me if Arnie decides to go out of town for some reason. Especially in the next day or two, or over the weekend. Day or night. I have to know if Arnie's going to leave Libertyville. And I have to know before he leaves. It's very important."

"Why?"

"I'd just as soon not go into that. It's complicated, and it would . . . well, it would sound crazy."

There was a long, long silence, and when Arnie's dad spoke again, his voice was a near-whisper. "It's that goddam car of his, isn't it?"

How much did he suspect? How much did he know? If he was like most people I knew, he probably suspected a little more drunk than sober. How much? Even now I don't know for sure. But what I believe is that he *suspected* more than anyone—except maybe Will Darnell.

"Yeah," I said. "It's the car."

"I knew it," he said dully. "I knew. What's happening, Dennis? How is he doing it? Do you know?"

"Michael, I can't say any more. Will you tell me if he plans a trip tomorrow or the next day?"

"Yes," he said. "Yes, all right."

"Thanks."

"Dennis," he said. "Do you think I'll ever have my son back?"

He deserved the truth. That poor, devilled man deserved the truth. "I don't know," I said, and bit at my lower lip until it hurt. "I think . . . that it may have gone too far for that."

"Dennis," he almost wailed, "what is it? Drugs? Some kind of drugs?"

"I'll tell you when I can," I said. "That's all I can promise you. I'm sorry. I'll tell you when I can."

Johnny Pomberton was easier to talk to.

He was a lively, garrulous man, and any fears I'd had that he wouldn't do business with a kid soon went by the board. I got the feeling that Johnny Pomberton would have done business with Satan freshly risen from hell with the smell of brimstone still on him, if he had good old legal tender.

"Sure," he kept saying. "Sure, sure." You'd no more than started some proposition before Johnny Pomberton was agreeing with you. It was a little unnerving. I had a cover story, but I don't think he even listened to it. He simply quoted me a price—a very reasonable one, as it turned out.

"That sounds fine," I said.

"Sure," he agreed. "What time you coming by?"

"Well, how would nine-thirty tomorrow m—"

"Sure," he said. "See you then."

"One other question, Mr. Pomberton."

"Sure. And make it Johnny."

"Okay, Johnny, then. What about automatic transmission?"

Johnny Pomberton laughed heartily—so heartily that I held the phone away from my ear a bit, feeling glum. That laugh was answer enough.

"On one of these babies? You got to be kidding. Why? Can't you run a standard shift?"

"Yes, that's what I learned on," I said.

"Sure! So you got no problems, right?"

"I guess not," I said, thinking of my left leg, which would be running the clutch—or trying to. Simply shifting it around a little tonight had made it ache like hell. I hoped that Arnie would wait a few days before taking his trip out of town, but somehow I didn't think that was in the cards. It would be tomorrow, over the weekend at the latest, and my left leg would simply have to bear up as best it could. "Well, good night, Mr. Pomberton. I'll see you tomorrow."

"Sure. Thanks for calling, kid. I got one all picked out in my mind for you. You'll like her, see if you don't. And if you don't start calling me Johnny, I'm gonna double the price."

"Sure," I said, and hung up on his laughter.

You'll like her. See if you don't.

Her again—I was becoming morbidly aware of that casual form of referral . . . and getting damned sick of it.

Then I made my last preparatory call. There were four Sykeses in the phone book. I got the one I wanted on my second try; Jimmy himself answered the phone. I introduced myself as Arnie Cunningham's friend, and Jimmy's voice brightened. He liked Arnie, who hardly ever teased him and never "punched on him" as Buddy Repperton had done when Buddy worked for Will. He wanted to know how Arnie was, and, lying again, I told him Arnie was fine.

"Jeez, that's good," he said. "He really had his butt in a sling there for a while. I knew them fireworks and cigarettes was no good for him."

"It's Arnie I'm calling for," I said. "You remember when Will got arrested and they shut down the garage, Jimmy?"

"Sure do." Jimmy sighed. "Now poor old Will's dead and I'm out of a job. My ma keeps sayin I got to go to the vocational-technical school, but I wouldn't be no good at that. I guess I'll go for bein a janitor, or somethin like that. My Uncle Fred's a janitor up to the college, and he says there's an op'nin, because this other janitor, he disappeared, just took off or somethin, and—"

"Arnie says when they closed down the garage, he lost his whole socket-wrench kit," I broke in. "It was up behind some of those old tires, you know, on the overhead racks. He put them up there so no one would rip him off."

"Still there?" Jimmy asked.

"I guess so."

"What a bummer!"

"You know it. That set of boltfuckers was worth a hundred dollars."

"Holy crow! I bet they ain't there anymore anyway, though. I bet one of them cops got it."

"Arnie thinks they might still be there. But he's not supposed to go near the garage because of the trouble he's in." This was a lie, but I didn't think Jimmy would catch it and he didn't. Putting one over on a fellow who was borderline retarded didn't add a thing to my self-esteem, however.

"Aw, shit! Well, listen—I'll go down and look for em. Yessir! Tomorrow morning, first thing. I still got my keys."

I breathed a sigh of relief. It wasn't Arnie's mythical set of socket wrenches that I wanted; I wanted Jimmy's keys.

"I'd like to get them, Jimmy, that's the thing. As a surprise. And I know right where he put them. You might hunt around all day and still not find them."

"Oh, yeah, for sure. I was never no good at finding things, that's what Will said. He always said I couldn't find my own bee-hind with both hands and a flashlight."

"Aw, man, he was just putting you down. But really—I'd like to do it."

"Well, sure."

"I thought I'd come by tomorrow and borrow your keys. I could get that set of wrenches and have your keys back to you before dark."

"Gee, I dunno. Will said to never loan out my keys—"

"Sure, before, but the place is empty now except for Arnie's tools and a bunch of junk out back. The estate will be putting it up for sale pretty soon, contents complete, and if I take them after that, it would be like stealing."

"Oh! Well, I guess it'd be okay. If you bring my keys back." And then he said an absurdly touching thing: "See, they're all I got to remember Will by."

"It's a promise."

"Okay," he said. "If it's for Arnie, I guess it's okay."

Just before bed, now downstairs, I made one final call—to a very sleepy-sounding Leigh.

"One of these next few nights we're going to end it. You game?"

"Yes," she said. "I am. I *think* I am. What have you got planned, Dennis?"

So I told her, going through it step by step, half-expecting her to poke a dozen holes in my idea. But when I was done, she simply said, "What if it doesn't work?"

"You make the honor roll. I don't think you need me to draw you a picture."

"No," she said. "I guess not."

"I'd keep you out of it if I could," I said. "But LeBay is going to suspect a trap, so the bait has to be good."

"I wouldn't let you leave me out of it," she said. Her voice was steady. "This is my business too. I loved him. I really did. And once you start loving someone . . . I don't think you ever really get over it completely. Do you, Dennis?"

I thought of the years. The summers of reading and swimming and playing games: Monopoly, Scrabble, Chinese checkers. The ant farms. The times I had kept him from getting killed in all the ways kids like to kill the outsider, the one who's a little bit strange, a little bit off the beat. There had been times when I had gotten pretty fucking sick of keeping him from getting killed, times when I had wondered if my life wouldn't be easier, better, if I simply let Arnie go, let him drown. But it wouldn't have been better. I had needed Arnie to make me better, and he had. We had traded fair all the way down the line, and oh shit, this was very bitter, very fucking bitter indeed.

"No," I said, and I suddenly had to put my hand over my eyes. "I don't think you ever do. I loved him too. And maybe it isn't too late for him, even now." That's what I would have prayed: *Dear God, let me keep Arnie from getting killed just one more time. Just this one last time.*

"It's not him I hate," she said, her voice low. "It's that man LeBay . . . did we really see that thing this afternoon, Dennis? In the car?"

"Yes," I said. "I think we did."

"Him and that bitch Christine," she said. "Will it be soon?"

"Soon, yeah. I think so."

"All right. I love you, Dennis."

"I love you too."

As it turned out, it ended the next day—Friday the nineteenth of January.

49 / Arnie

I was cruising in my Stingray late one night
When an XKE pulled up on the right,
He rolled down the window of his shiny new Jag
And challenged me then and there to a drag.
I said "You're on, buddy, my mill's runnin fine,
Let's come off the line at Sunset and Vine,
But I'll go you one better (if you got the nerve):
Let's race all the way . . .
      to Deadman's Curve."

                    —Jan and Dean

I began that long, terrible day by driving over to Jimmy Sykes's house in my Duster. I had expected there might be some trouble from Jimmy's mother, but that turned out to be okay. She was, if anything, mentally slower than her son. She invited me in for bacon and eggs (I declined—my stomach was tied in miserable knots) and clucked over my crutches while Jimmy hunted around in his room for his keyring. I made small-talk with Mrs. Sykes, who was roughly the size of Mount Etna, while time passed and a dismal certainty rose inside me: Jimmy had lost his keys somewhere and the whole thing was off the rails before it could really begin.

He came back shaking his head. "Can't find em," he said. "Jeez, I guess I must have lost em somewhere. What a bummer."

And Mrs. Sykes, nearly three hundred pounds on the hoof in a faded housedress and her hair up in puffy pink rollers, said with blessed practicality, "Did you look in your pockets, Jim?"

A startled expression crossed Jimmy's face. He rammed a hand into the pocket of his green chino workpants. Then, with a shamefaced grin, he pulled out a bunch of keys. They were on one of the keyrings they sell at the novelty shop in the Monroeville Mall—a large rubber fried egg. The egg was dark with grease.

"There you are, you little suckers," he said.

"You watch your language, young man," Mrs. Sykes said. "Just show Dennis which key it is that opens the door and keep your dirty language in your head."

Jimmy ended up handing three Schlage keys over to me, because they weren't labelled and he couldn't tell which was which. One of them opened the main overhead door, one opened the back overhead door, the one which gave on the long lot of junked cars, and one opened the door to Will's office.

"Thanks," I said. "I'll have these back to you just as soon as I can, Jimmy."

"Great," Jimmy said. "Say hello to Arnie when you see him."

"You bet," I said.

"You sure you don't want some bacon and eggs, Dennis?" Mrs. Sykes asked. "There's plenty."

"Thanks," I said, "but I really ought to get going." It was quarter past eight; school started at nine. Arnie usually pulled in around eight-forty-five, Leigh had told me. I just had time. I got my crutches under me and got to my feet.

"Help him out, Jim," Mrs. Sykes commanded. "Don't just stand there."

I started to protest and she waved me away. "Wouldn't want you to fall on your can getting back to your car, Dennis. Might break your leg all over again." She laughed uproariously at this, and Jimmy, the soul of obedience, practically carried me back to my Duster.

The sky that day was a scummy, frowsy gray, and the radio was predicting more snow by late afternoon. I drove across town to Libertyville High, took the driveway which led to the student parking lot, and parked in the front row. I didn't need Leigh to tell me that Arnie usually parked in the back row. I had to see him, had to strew the bait in front of his nose, but I wanted him as far from Christine as possible when I did it. Away from the car, LeBay's hold seemed weaker.

I sat with the key turned over to ACCESSORY for the radio and looked at the football field. It seemed impossible that I had ever traded sandwiches with Arnie on those snow-covered bleachers. Impossible to believe that I had run and cavorted on that field myself, dressed up in padding, helmet, and tight pants, stupidly convinced of my own physical invulnerability . . . perhaps even of my own immortality.

I didn't feel that way anymore, if I ever had.

Students were coming in, parking their cars, and heading for the building, chattering and laughing and horsing around. I slouched lower in my seat, not wanting to be recognized. A bus pulled up at the doors in the main turnaround and disgorged a load of kids. A small cluster of shivering boys and girls gathered out in the smoking area where Buddy had taken Arnie on that day last fall. That day also seemed impossibly distant now.

My heart was thumping in my chest and I was miserably tense. A craven part of me hoped that Arnie simply wouldn't show up. And then I saw the familiar white-over-red shape of Christine turn in from School Street and cruise up the student drive, moving at a steady twenty, blowing a little plume of white exhaust from her tailpipe. Arnie was behind the wheel, wearing his school jacket. He didn't look at me; he simply drove to his accustomed place at the back of the lot and parked.

Just stay slouched down and he won't even see you, that craven, traitorous part of my mind whispered. *He'll walk right by you, like all the rest of them.*

Instead, I opened my door and fumbled my crutches outside. Leaning my weight on them, I yanked myself out and stood there on the packed snow of the parking lot, feeling a little bit like Fred MacMurray in that old picture *Double Indemnity*. From the school came the burring of the first bell, made faint and unimportant by distance—Arnie was later than he had been in the old days. My mother had said that Arnie was almost disgustingly punctual. Maybe LeBay hadn't been.

He came toward me, books under his arm, head down,

twisting in and out between the cars. He walked behind a van, passing out of my sight temporarily, and then came back into view. He looked up then, directly into my eyes.

His own eyes widened, and he made an automatic half-turn back toward Christine.

"Feel kind of naked when you're not behind the wheel?" I asked.

He looked back at me. His lips drew slightly downward, as if he had tasted something of unpleasant flavor.

"How's your cunt, Dennis?" he asked.

George LeBay hadn't said, but he had at least hinted that his brother was extraordinarily good at getting through to people, finding their soft spots.

I took two shuffling steps forward on my crutches while he stood there, smiling with the corners of his mouth down.

"How did you like it when Repperton called you Cunt-face?" I asked him. "Did you like it so well you want to turn it around and use it on somebody else?"

Part of him seemed to flinch at that—something that was maybe only in his eyes—but the contemptuous, watchful smile remained on his lips. It was cold out. I hadn't put on my gloves, and my hands, on the crossbars of the crutches, were getting numb. Our breath made little plumes.

"Or what about in the fifth grade, when Tommy Deckinger used to call you Fart-Breath?" I asked, my voice rising. Getting angry at him hadn't been part of the game-plan, but now it was here, shaking inside me. "Did you like that? And do you remember when Ladd Smythe was a patrol-boy and he pushed you down in the street and I pulled his hat off and stuffed it down his pants? Where you been, Arnie? This guy LeBay is a Johnny-come-lately. Me, I was here all along."

That flinch again. This time he half-turned away, the smile faltering, his eyes searching for Christine the way your eyes might search for a loved one in a crowded terminal or bus-station. Or the way a junkie might look for his pusher.

"You need her that bad?" I asked. "Man, you're hooked right through the fucking bag, aren't you?"

"I don't know what you're talking about," he said hoarsely. "You stole my girl. Nothing is going to change that. You went behind my back . . . you cheated . . . you're just a *shit-ter*, like all the rest of them." He was looking at me now, his eyes wide and hurt and blazing with anger. "I thought I could trust you, and you turned out to be worse than Repperton or *any* of them!" He took a step toward me and cried out in a perfect fury of loss, *"You stole her, you shitter!"*

I lurched forward another step on my crutches; one of them slid a little bit in the packed snow underfoot. We were like two reluctant gunslingers approaching each other.

"You can't steal what's been given away," I said.

"What are you talking about?"

"I'm talking about the night she choked in your car. The night Christine tried to kill her. You told her you didn't need her. You told her to fuck off."

"I never did! That's a lie! That's a goddam lie!"

"Who am I talking to?" I asked.

"Never mind!" His gray eyes were huge behind his spectacles. "Never mind who the fuck you're talking to! That's nothing but a dirty lie! No more than I'd expect from that stinking bitch!"

Another step closer. His pale face was marked with flaring red patches of color.

"When you write your name, it doesn't look like your signature anymore, Arnie."

"You shut up, Dennis."

"Your father says it's like having a stranger in the house."

"I'm warning you, man."

"Why bother?" I asked brutally. "I know what's going to happen. So does Leigh. The same thing that happened to Buddy Repperton and Will Darnell and all the others. Because you're not Arnie at all anymore. Are you in there, Le-Bay? Come on out and let me see you. I've seen you before. I saw you on New Year's Eve, I saw you yesterday at the chicken place. *I know you're in there; why don't you stop fucking around and come out?"*

And he did . . . but in Arnie's face this time, and that was more terrible than all the skulls and skeletons and comic-book horrors ever thought of. Arnie's face *changed.* A sneer bloomed on his lips like a rancid rose. And I saw him as he must have been back when the world was young and a car was all a young man needed to have; everything else would just automatically follow. I saw George LeBay's big brother.

I only remember one thing about him, but I remember that one thing very well. His anger. He was always angry.

He came toward me, closing the distance between where he had been and where I stood propped on my crutches. His eyes were filmy and beyond all reach. That sneer was stamped on his face like the mark of a branding-iron.

I had time to think of the scar on George LeBay's forearm, skidding from his elbow to his wrist. *He pushed me and then he came back and threw me.* I could hear that fourteen-year-old LeBay shouting, *You stay out of my way from now on, you goddam snotnose, stay out of my way, you hear?*

It was LeBay I was facing now, and he was not a man who took losing easily. Check that: he didn't take losing at all.

"Fight him, Arnie," I said. "He's had his own way too long. Fight him, kill him, make him stay d—"

He swung his foot and kicked my right crutch out from under me. I struggled to stay up, tottered, almost made it . . . and then he kicked the left crutch away. I fell down on the cold packed snow. He took another step and stood above me, his face hard and alien.

"You got it coming, and you're going to get it," he said remotely.

"Yeah, right," I gasped. "You remember the ant farms, Arnie? Are you in there someplace? This dirty sucker never had a fucking ant farm in his life. He never had a *friend* in his life."

And suddenly the calm hardness broke. His face—his face *roiled*. I don't know how else to describe it. LeBay was there, furious at having to put down a kind of internal mutiny. Then Arnie was there—drawn, tired, ashamed, but, most of all, desperately unhappy. Then LeBay again, and his foot drew back to kick me as I lay on the snow groping for my crutches and feeling helpless and useless and dumb. Then it was Arnie again, my friend Arnie, brushing his hair back off his forehead in that familiar, distracted gesture; it was Arnie saying, "Oh, Dennis . . . Dennis . . . I'm sorry. . . . I'm so sorry."

"It's too late for sorry, man," I said.

I got one crutch and then the other. I pulled myself up little by little, slipping twice before I could get the crutches under me again. Now my hands felt like pieces of furniture. Arnie made no move to help me; he stood with his back against the van, his eyes wide and shocked.

"Dennis, I can't help it," he whispered. "Sometimes I feel like I'm not even here anymore. Help me, Dennis. Help me."

"Is LeBay there?" I asked him.

"He's always here," Arnie groaned. "Oh God, always! Except—"

"The car?"

"When Christine . . . when she goes, then he's with her. That's the only time he's . . . he's . . ."

Arnie fell silent. His head slipped over to one side. His chin rolled on his chest in a boneless pivot. His hair dangled toward the snow. Spit ran out of his mouth and splattered on his boots. And then he began to scream thinly and beat his gloved fists on the van behind him:

"*Go away! Go away! Go awaaaaay!*"

Then nothing for maybe five seconds—nothing except the shuddering of his body, as if a basket of snakes had been dumped inside his clothes; nothing except that slow, horrible roll of his chin on his chest.

I thought maybe he was winning, that he was beating the dirty old sonofabitch. But when he looked up, Arnie was gone. LeBay was there.

"It's all going to happen just like he said," LeBay told me. "Let it go, boy. Maybe I won't drive over you."

"Come on over to Darnell's tonight," I said. My voice was harsh, my throat as dry as sand. "We'll play. I'll bring Leigh. You bring Christine."

"I'll pick my own time and place," LeBay said, and grinned with Arnie's mouth, showing Arnie's teeth, which were young and strong—a mouth still years from the indignity of dentures. "You won't know when or where. But you'll know . . . when the time comes."

"Think again," I said, almost casually. "Come to Darnell's tonight, or she and I start talking tomorrow."

He laughed, an ugly contemptuous sound. "And where will that get you? The asylum over at Reed City?"

"Oh, we won't be taken seriously at first," I said. "I give you that. But that stuff about how they put you in the loonybin as soon as you start talking about ghosts and demons . . . uh-uh, LeBay. Maybe in your day, before flying saucers and *The Exorcist* and that house in Amityville. These days a hell of a lot of people *believe* in that stuff."

He was still grinning, but his eyes looked at me with narrow suspicion. That, and something else. I thought that something else was the first sparkle of fear.

"And what you don't seem to realize is how many people know something is wrong."

His grin faltered. Of course he must have realized that, and been worried about it. But maybe killing gets to be a fever; maybe after a while you are simply unable to stop and count the cost.

"Whatever weird, filthy kind of life you still have is all wrapped up in that car," I said. "You knew it, and you planned to use Arnie from the very beginning—except that 'planned' is the wrong word, because you never really planned anything, did you? You just followed your intuitions."

He made a snarling sound and turned to go.

"You really want to think about it," I called after him. "Arnie's father knows something is rotten. So does mine. I think there must be some police somewhere who'd be willing to listen to *anything* about how their friend Junkins died. And it all comes back to Christine, Christine, Christine. Sooner or later someone's going to run her through the crusher in back of Darnell's just on general principles."

He had turned back and was looking at me with a bright mixture of hate and fear in his eyes.

"We'll keep talking, and a lot of people will laugh at us, I don't doubt it. But I've got two pieces of cast with Arnie's signature on them. Only one of them isn't his. It's yours. I'll take them to the state cops and keep pestering them until they have a handwriting specialist confirm that. People are going to start watching Arnie. People are going to start watching Christine too. You get the picture?"

"Sonny, you don't worry me one fucking bit."

But his eyes said something different. I was getting to him, all right.

"It's going to happen," I said. "People are only rational on the surface. They still toss salt over their left shoulder if they spill the shaker, they don't walk under ladders, they believe in survival after death. And sooner or later—probably sooner, with Leigh and me shooting off our mouths—someone is going to turn that car of yours into a sardine can. And I'm willing to bet that when it goes, you'll go with it."

"Don't you just wish!" he sneered.

"We'll be at Darnell's tonight," I said. "If you're good, you can get rid of both of us. That won't end it either, but it might give you some breathing space . . . time enough to get out of town. But I don't think you're good enough, chum. It's gone on too long. We're getting rid of you."

I crutched back to my Duster and got in. I used the crutches more clumsily than I had to, tried to make myself look more incapacitated than I really was. I had rocked him by mentioning the signatures; it was time to leave before I overplayed my hand. But there was one more thing. One thing guaranteed to drive LeBay into a frenzy.

I pulled my left leg in with my hands, slammed the door, and leaned out.

I looked into his eyes and smiled.

"She's great in bed," I said. "Too bad you'll never know."

With a furious roar, he charged at me. I rolled up the window and slapped down the door-lock. Then, leisurely, I started the engine while he slammed his gloved fists on the glass. His face was snarling, terrible. There was no Arnie in it now. No Arnie at all. My friend was gone. I felt a dark sorrow that was deeper than tears or fear, but I kept that slow, insulting, dirty grin on my face. Then, slowly, I raised my middle finger to the glass.

"Fuck you, LeBay," I said, and then pulled out, leaving him to stand there in the lot, shaking with that simple, unswerving fury his brother had told me of. It was that more than anything else that I was counting on to bring him tonight.

We'd see.

50 / Petunia

Something warm was running in my eyes
But I found my baby somehow that night,
I held her tight, I kissed her our last kiss . . .
　　　　　　　—J. Frank Wilson and the Cavaliers

I drove about four blocks before the reaction set in, and then I had to pull over. I had the shakes, bad. Not even the heater, turned up to full, could kill them. My breath came in harsh little gasps. I clutched myself to keep warm, but it seemed that I would never be warm again, never. That face, that horrible face, and Arnie buried somewhere inside, *he's always here,* Arnie had said, always except when—what? When Christine rolled by herself, of course. LeBay couldn't be both places at the same time. That was beyond even his powers.

At last I was able to drive on again, and I wasn't even aware that I had been crying until I looked in the rearview mirror and saw the wet circles under my eyes.

It was quarter of ten by the time I made it out to Johnny Pomberton's place. He was a tall, broad-shouldered man wearing green gum-rubber boots and a heavy red-and-black-checked hunting jacket. An old hat with a grease-darkened bill was tilted up on his balding head as he studied the gray sky.

"More snow comin, the radio says. Didn't know as you'd really be out, boy, but I brung her around forya just in case. What do you think of her?"

I got my crutches under me again and got out of my car. Road salt gritted under the crutches' rubber tips, but the going felt safe. Standing in front of Johnny Pomberton's woodpile was one of the strangest-looking vehicles I've ever seen in my life. A faint, pungent odor, not exactly pleasant, drifted over from it to where we stood.

At one time, far back in its career, it had been a GM product—or so the logo on its gigantic snout advertised. Now it was a little bit of everything. One thing it surely was, and that was big. The top of its grille would have been head-high on a tall man. Behind and over it, the cab loomed like a big square helmet. Behind that, supported by two sets of double wheels on each side, was a long, tubular body, like the body of a gasoline tanker truck,

Except that I never saw a tanker truck before this one that was painted bright pink. The word PETUNIA was written across the side in Gothic letters two feet high.

"I don't know *what* to think of her," I said. "What is she?"

Pomberton poked a Camel cigarette into his mouth and lit it with a quick flick of his horny thumbnail on the tip of a wooden match. "Kaka sucker," he said.

"What?"

He grinned. "Twenty-thousand-gallon capacity," he said. "She's a corker, is Petunia."

"I don't get you." But I was starting to. There was an absurd, grisly irony to it that Arnie—the old Arnie—would have appreciated.

I had asked Pomberton over the phone if he had a big, heavy truck to rent, and this was the biggest one currently in his yard. All four of his dump trucks were working, two in

Libertyville and two others in Philly Hill. He'd had a grader, he explained to me, but it had had a nervous bustdown just after Christmas. He said he was having a devilish job keeping his trucks rolling since Darnell's Garage shut down.

Petunia was essentially a tanker, no more and no less. Her job was pumping out septic systems.

"How much does she weigh?" I asked Pomberton.

He flicked away his cigarette. "Dry, or loaded with shit?"

I gulped. "Which is it now?"

He threw his head back and laughed. "Do you think I'd rentcher a loaded truck?" He pronounced it *ludded truck.* "Naw, naw—she's dry, dry as a bone and all hosed out. Sure she is. Still a little fragrant, though, ain't she?"

I sniffed. She was fragrant, all right.

"It could be a lot worse," I said. "I guess."

"Sure," Pomberton said. "You bet. Old Petunia's original pedigree was lost long ago, but what's on her current registration is eighteen thousand pounds, GVW."

"What's that?"

"Gross vehicle weight," he said. "If they pull you over on the Interstate and you weigh more than eighteen thousand, the ICC gets upset. Dry, she prob'ly goes around, I dunno, eight–nine thousand pounds. She's got a five-speed tranny with a two-speed differential, givin you ten forward speeds all told . . . if you can run a clutch."

He cast a dubious eye up and down my crutches and lit another cigarette.

"*Can* you run a clutch?"

"Sure," I said with a straight face. "If it isn't really stiff." But for how long? That was the question.

"Well, that's your business and I won't mess into it." He looked at me brightly. "I'll give you ten percent discount for cash, on account of I don't usually report cash transactions to my favorite uncle."

I checked my wallet and found four twenties and four tens. "How much did you say for one day?"

"How does ninety bucks sound?"

I gave it to him. I had been prepared to pay a hundred and twenty.

"What are you going to do with your Duster there?"

It hadn't even crossed my mind until just now. "Could I leave it here? Just for today?"

"Sure," Pomberton said, "you can leave it here all week, I

don't give a shit. Just put it around the back and leave the keys in it in case I have to move it."

I drove around back where there was a wilderness of cannibalized truck parts poking out of the deep snow like bones from white sand. It took me nearly ten minutes to work my way back around on my crutches. I could have done it faster if I'd used my left leg a bit, but I wouldn't do that. I was saving it for Petunia's clutch.

I approached Petunia, feeling dread gather in my stomach like a small black cloud. I had no doubt it would stop Christine—if she really showed up at Darnell's Garage tonight and if I could drive the damned truck. I had never driven anything that big in my life, although the summer before I'd gotten some hours in on a bulldozer and Brad Jeffries had let me try the payloader a couple of times after knocking off for the day.

Pomberton stood there in his checked jacket, hands stuffed deep into the pockets of his workpants, watching me with wise eyes. I got over to the driver's side, grabbed the doorhandle, and slipped a little. He took a step or two toward me.

"I can make it."

"Sure," he said.

I jammed the crutch into my armpit again, my breath frosting out in quick little gasps, and pulled the door open. Holding onto the door's inside handle with my left hand and balancing on my right leg like a stork, I threw my crutches into the cab and then followed them. The keys were in the ignition, the shift pattern printed on the stick. I slammed the door, pushed the clutch down with my left leg—not much pain, so far so good—and started Petunia up. Her engine sounded like a full field of stockers at Philly Plains.

Pomberton strolled over. "Little noisy, ain't she?" he yelled.

"Sure!" I screamed back.

"You know," he bellowed, "I doubt like hell if you got an *I* on your license, boy." An *I* on your license meant that the state had tested you on the big trucks. I had an *A* for motorcycles (much to my mother's horror) but no *I*.

I grinned down at him. "You never checked because I looked trustworthy."

He smiled back. "Sure."

I revved the engine a little. Petunia blew off two brisk backfires that were almost as loud as mortar blasts.

"You mind if I ask what you want that truck for? None of my business, I know."

"Just what it was meant for," I said.

"Beggin your pardon?"

"I want to get rid of some shit," I said.

I had something of a scare going downhill from Pomberton's place; even dry and empty, that baby really got rolling. I seemed incredibly high up—able to look down on the roofs of the cars I passed. Driving through downtown Libertyville, I felt as conspicuous as a baby whale in a goldfish pond. It didn't help any that Pomberton's septic pumper was painted that bright pink color. I got some amused glances.

My left leg had begun to ache a little, but running through Petunia's unfamiliar shift pattern in the stop-and-go downtown traffic kept my mind off it. A more surprising ache was developing in my shoulders and across my chest; it came from simply piloting Petunia through traffic. The truck was not equipped with power steering, and that wheel really turned hard.

I turned off Main, onto Walnut, and then into the parking lot behind the Western Auto. I got carefully down from Petunia's cab, slammed her door (my nose had already become used to the faint odor she gave off), set my crutches under me, and went in the back entrance.

I got the three garage keys off Jimmy's ring and took them over to the key-making department. For one-eighty, I got two copies of each. I put the new keys in one pocket, Jimmy's ring, with his original keys reattached, in the other. I went out the front door, onto Main Street, and down to the Libertyville Lunch, where there was a pay telephone. Overhead, the sky was grayer and more lowering than ever. Pomberton was right. There would be snow.

Inside, I ordered a coffee and Danish and got change for the telephone booth. I went inside, closed the door clumsily behind me, and called Leigh. She answered on the first ring.

"Dennis! Where are you?"

"The Libertyville Lunch. Are you alone?"

"Yes. Dad's at work and Mom went grocery shopping. Dennis, I . . . I almost told her everything. I started thinking about her parking at the A&P and crossing the parking lot, and . . . I don't know, what you said about Arnie leaving town didn't seem to matter. It still made sense, but it didn't seem to matter. Do you know what I'm talking about?"

"Yes," I said, thinking about giving Ellie a lift down to Tom's the night before, even though my leg was aching like hell by then. "I know exactly what you mean."

"Dennis, it can't go on like this. I'll go crazy. Are we still going to try your idea?"

"Yes," I said. "Leave your mom a note, Leigh. Tell her you have to be gone for a little while. Don't say any more than that. When you're not home for supper, your folks will probably call mine. Maybe they'll decide we ran off and eloped."

"Maybe that's not such a bad idea," she said, and laughed in a way that gave me prickles. "I'll see you."

"Hey, one other thing. Is there any pain-killer in your house? Darvon? Anything like that?"

"There's some Darvon from the time Dad threw his back out," she said. "Is it your leg, Dennis?"

"It hurts a little."

"How much is a little?"

"It's really okay."

"No B.S.?"

"No B.S. And after tonight I'll give it a nice long rest, okay?"

"Okay."

"Get here as quick as you can."

She came in as I was ordering a second cup of coffee, wearing a fur-fringed parka and a pair of faded jeans. The jeans were tucked into battered Frye boots. She managed to look both sexy and practical. Heads turned.

"Looking good," I said, and kissed her temple.

She passed me a bottle of gray and pink gel capsules. "You don't look so hot, though, Dennis. Here."

The waitress, a woman of about fifty with iron-gray hair, came over with my coffee. The cup sat placidly, an island in a small brown pond in the saucer. "Why aren't you kids in school?" she asked.

"Special dispensation," I said gravely. She stared at me.

"Coffee, please," Leigh said, pulling off her gloves. As the waitress went back behind the counter with an audible sniff, she leaned toward me and said, "It would be pretty funny if we got picked up by the truant officer, wouldn't it?"

"Hilarious," I said, thinking that, in spite of the radiance the cold had given her, Leigh really wasn't looking all that good. I didn't think either of us really would be until this thing was over. There were small strain-lines around her eyes, as if she had slept poorly the night before.

"So what do we do?"

"We get rid of it," I said. "Wait until you see your chariot, madam."

"My God!" Leigh said, staring at Petunia's hot-pink magnificence. It hulked silently in the Western Auto parking lot, dwarfing a Chevy van on one side and a Volkswagen on the other. "What is it?"

"Kaka sucker," I said with a straight face.

She looked at me, puzzled . . . and then she burst into hysterical gales of laughter. I wasn't sorry to see it happen. When I had told her about my confrontation with Arnie in the student parking lot that morning, those strain-lines on her face had grown deeper and deeper, her lips whitening as they pressed together.

"I know that it looks sort of ridiculous—" I said now.

"That's putting it *mildly*," she replied, still giggling and hiccuping.

"—but it'll do the job, if anything will."

"Yes. Yes, I suppose it should. And . . . it's not exactly unfitting, is it?"

I nodded. "I had that thought."

"Well, let's get in," she said. "I'm cold."

She climbed up into the cab ahead of me, her nose wrinkling. "Ag," she said.

I smiled. "You get used to it." I handed her my crutches and climbed laboriously up behind the wheel. The pain in my left leg had subsided from a series of sharp clawings to a dull throb again; I had taken two Darvon back in the restaurant.

"Dennis, is your leg going to be all right?"

"It'll have to be," I said, and slammed the door.

51 / Christine

'As I sd to my
friend, because I am
always talking,—John I

sd, which was not his
name, the darkness sur-
rounds us, what

can we do against
it, or else, shall we &
why not, buy a goddamn big car,

'drive, he sd, for
christ's sake, look
out where yr going.

—Robert Creeley

It was eleven-thirty or so when we pulled out of the
Western Auto parking lot. The first spats of snow were coming down. I drove across town to the Sykeses' house, shifting
more easily now as the Darvon took hold.

The house was dark and locked, Mrs. Sykes maybe at
work, Jimmy maybe off collecting his unemployment or
something. Leigh found a crumpled-up envelope in her handbag, scratched off her address and wrote *Jimmy Sykes* across
the front in her slanting, pretty hand. She put Jimmy's keyring into the envelope, folded in the flap, and slipped it
through the letter-slot in the front door. While she did that, I
let Petunia idle in neutral, resting my leg.

"What now?" she asked, climbing back into the cab.

"Another phone call," I said.

Out near the intersection of JFK Drive and Crescent Avenue, I found a telephone booth. I got carefully out of the
truck, holding on until Leigh handed down my crutches.

Then I made my way carefully through the thickening snow to the booth. Seen through the dirty phone-booth glass and the swirling snow, Petunia looked like some strange pink dinosaur.

I called Horlicks University and went through the switchboard to get Michael's office. Arnie had told me once that his dad was a real office drone, always brown-bagging it at lunch and staying in. Now, as the phone was picked up on the second ring, I blessed him for it.

"Dennis! I tried to reach you at home! Your mom said—"

"Where's he going?" My stomach was cold. It wasn't until then—at that exact moment—that all of it began to seem completely real to me, and I began to think that this crazy confrontation was going to come off.

"How did you know he was going? You've got to tell me—"

"I don't have time for questions, and I couldn't answer them anyway. Where is he going?"

Slowly, he said, "He and Regina are going to Penn State this afternoon right after school. Arnie called her this morning and asked her if she'd go with him. He said . . ." He paused, thinking. "He said he felt as if he'd suddenly come to his senses. He said it just sort of hit him as he was going to school this morning that if he didn't do something definite about college, it might slip away from him. He told her he'd decided Penn State was the best bet and asked her if she'd like to go up with him and talk to the dean of the College of Arts and Sciences, and to some of the people in the history and philosophy departments."

The booth was cold. My hands were starting to go numb. Leigh was high up in Petunia's wheelhouse, watching me anxiously. *How well you arranged things, Arnie,* I thought. *Still the chess-player.* He was manipulating his mother, putting her on strings and making her dance. I felt some pity for her, but not as much as I might have felt. How many times had Regina herself been the manipulator, dancing others across her stage like so many Punch and Judys? Now, while she was half-distracted with fear and shame, LeBay had dangled in front of her eyes the one thing absolutely guaranteed to make her come running: the possibility that things might just be returning to normal.

"And did all that ring true to you?" I asked Michael.

"Of course not!" he burst out. "It wouldn't have rung true

to her, if she was thinking straight! With college admissions what they are today, Penn State would enroll him in *July*, if he had the money for tuition and the College Board scores—and Arnie has both. He talked as if this were the fifties instead of the seventies!"

"When are they leaving?"

"She's going to meet him at the high school after period six; that's what she said when she called me. He's getting a dismissal slip."

That meant they would be leaving Libertyville in less than an hour and a half. So I asked the last question, even though I already knew the answer. "They're not taking Christine, are they?"

"No, they're going in the station wagon. She was delirious with joy, Dennis. *Delirious*. That business of getting her to go with him to Penn State . . . that was inspired. Wild horses wouldn't have kept Regina from a chance like that. Dennis, what's going on? *Please*."

"Tomorrow," I said. "That's a promise. Firm. Meantime, you've got to do something for me. It could be a matter of life and death for my family and for Leigh Cabot's family. You—"

"Oh my God," he said hoarsely. He spoke in the voice of a man for whom a great light has just dawned. "He's been gone every time—except when the Welch boy was killed, and that time he was . . . Regina saw him asleep, and I'm sure he wasn't lying about that. . . . Dennis, who's driving that car? *Who's using Christine to kill people when Arnie isn't here?*"

I almost told him, but it was cold in the telephone booth and my leg was starting to ache again, and that answer would have led to other questions, dozens of them. And even then the only final result might be a flat refusal to believe.

"Michael, listen," I said, speaking with all the deliberateness I could summon. For one weird moment I felt like Mister Rogers on TV. *A big car from the 1950s is coming to eat you up, boys and girls. . . . Can you say Christine? I knew you could!* "You've got to call my father and Leigh's father. Have both families get together at Leigh's house." I was thinking of brick, good solid brick. "I think maybe you ought to go too, Michael. All of you stay together until Leigh and I get there or until I call. But you tell them for Leigh and me: They're not to go outside after"—I calculated: If Arnie and Regina left the high school at two, how long before his alibi would be cast-iron-watertight?—"after four o'clock this afternoon. After four, none of you go out on the street. Any street. *Under no circumstances.*"

"Dennis, I can't just—"

"You *have* to," I said. "You'll be able to convince my old man, and between the two of you, you should be able to convince Mr. and Mrs. Cabot. And stay away from Christine yourself, Michael."

"They're leaving right from school," Michael said. "He said the car would be all right in the school parking lot."

I could hear it in his voice again—his knowledge of the lie. After what had happened last fall, Arnie would no more leave Christine in a public parking lot than he would show up in Calc class naked.

"Uh-huh," I said. "But if you should happen to look out the window and see her in the driveway anyhow, stay clear. Do you understand?"

"Yes, but—"

"Call my father first. Promise me."

"All right, I promise . . . but Dennis—"

"Thank you, Michael."

I hung up. My hands and feet were numb with the cold, but my forehead was slick with sweat. I pushed the door of the phone booth open with the tip of one crutch and worked my way back to Petunia.

"What did he say?" Leigh asked. "Did he promise?"

"Yes," I said. "He promised, and my dad will see that they get together. I'm pretty sure of that. If Christine goes for anyone tonight, it will have to be us."

"All right," she said. "Good."

I threw Petunia into gear, and we rumbled away. The stage was set—as well as I could set it, anyway—and now there was really nothing to do but wait and see what would come.

We drove across town to Darnell's Garage through steady light snow, and I pulled into the parking lot at just past one that afternoon. The long, rambling building with its corrugated-steel sides was totally deserted, and Petunia's belly-high wheels cut through deep, unplowed snow to stop in front of the main door. The signs bolted to that door were the same as they had been on that long-ago August evening when Arnie first drove Christine there—SAVE MONEY! YOUR KNOW-HOW, OUR TOOLS! *Garage Space Rented by the Week, Month, or Year,* and HONK FOR ENTRY—but the only one that really meant anything was the new one leaning in the darkened office window: CLOSED UNTIL FURTHER NOTICE. Sitting in one corner of the snowy front lot was an old crumpled Mustang, one of the real door-suckers from the '60s. Now it sat silent and broody under a shroud of snow.

"It's creepy," Leigh said in a low voice.

"Yeah. It sure is." I gave her the keys I'd made at the Western Auto that morning. "One of these will do it."

She took the keys, got out, and walked over to the door. I kept an eye in both rearview mirrors while she fumbled at the lock, but we didn't seem to be attracting any undue attention. I suppose there is a certain psychology involved in seeing such a big, conspicuous vehicle—it makes the idea of something clandestine or illegal harder to swallow.

Leigh suddenly tugged hard on the door, stood up, tugged again, and then came back to the truck. "I got the key to turn, but I can't get the door up," she said, "I think it's frozen to the ground or something."

Great, I thought. Wonderful. None of this was going to come easily.

"Dennis, I'm sorry," she said, seeing it on my face.

"No, it's all right," I said. I opened the driver's door and performed another of my comical sliding exits.

"Be careful," she said anxiously, walking beside me with her arm around my waist as I crutched carefully through the snow to the door. "Remember your leg."

"Yes, Mother," I said, grinning a little. I stood in profile to the door when I got there so I could bend down to the right and keep my weight off my bad leg. Bent over in the snow, left leg in the air, left hand holding onto my crutches, right hand grasping the roll-up door's handle, I must have looked like a circus contortionist. I pulled and felt the door give a little . . . but not quite enough. She was right; it had iced up pretty good along the bottom. You could hear it crackling.

"Grab on and help me," I said,

Leigh placed both of her hands over my right hand and we pulled together. That crackling sound became a little louder, but still the ice wouldn't quite give up its grip on the foot of the door.

"We've almost got it," I said. My right leg was throbbing unpleasantly, and sweat was running down my cheeks. "I'll count. On three, give it all you've got. Okay?"

"Yes," she said.

"One . . . two . . . *three!*"

What happened was the door came free of the ice all at once, with absurd, deadly ease. It flew upward on its tracks, and I stumbled backward, my crutches flying. My left leg folded underneath me and I landed on it. The deep snow cushioned the fall somewhat, but I still felt the pain in a kind of silver bolt that seemed to ram upward from my thigh all the way to my temples and back down again. I clenched my teeth over a scream, barely keeping it in, and then Leigh was on her knees in the snow beside me, her arm around my shoulders.

"Dennis! Are you all right?"

"Help me up."

She had to do most of the pulling, and both of us were gasping like winded runners by the time I was on my feet again with my crutches propped under me. Now I really needed them. My left leg was in agony.

"Dennis, you won't be able to work the clutch in that truck now—"

"Yeah, I will. Help me back, Leigh."

"You're as white as a ghost. I think we ought to get you to a doctor."

"No. Help me back."

"Dennis—"

"Leigh, help me back!"

We inched our way back to Petunia through the snow, leaving shuffling, troubled tracks in the snow behind us. I reached up, laid hold of the steering wheel, and did a chin-up to get in, scraping feebly at the running board with my right leg . . . and still, in the end, Leigh had to get behind me and put both hands on my kiester and shove. At last I was behind Petunia's wheel, hot and shivering with pain. My shirt was wet with snowmelt and sweat. Until that day in January of 1979, I don't think I knew how much pain can make you sweat.

I tried to jam down the clutch with my left foot and that silver bolt of pain came again, making me throw my head back and grind my teeth until it subsided a little.

"Dennis, I'm going down the street and find a phone and call a doctor." Her face was white and scared. "You broke it again, didn't you? When you fell?"

"I don't know," I said. "But you can't do that, Leigh. It'll be your folks or mine if we don't end it now. You know that. LeBay won't stop. He has a well-developed sense of vengeance. We can't stop."

"*But you can't drive it!*" she wailed. She looked up into the cab at me, crying now. The hood of her parka had fallen back in our mutual struggle to get me up into the driver's seat, where I now sat in magnificent uselessness. I could see a scatter of snowflakes in her dark blond hair.

"Go inside there," I said. "See if you can find a broom, or a long stick of wood."

"What good will that do?" she asked, crying harder.

"Just get it, and then we'll see."

She went into the dark maw of the open door and disappeared from view. I held onto my leg and sparred with terror. If I really had broken my leg again, there was a good chance I'd be wearing a built-up heel on my left foot for the rest of my life. But there might not even be that much of my life left if we couldn't put a stop to Christine. Now *there* was a cheery thought.

Leigh came back with a push broom. "Will this do?" she asked.

"To get us inside, yes. Then we'll have to see if we can find something better."

The handle was the type that unscrews. I got hold of it, unthreaded it, and tossed the bristle end aside. Holding it in my left hand along my side—just another goddam crutch—I pushed down the clutch with it. It held for a moment, then slipped off. The clutch sprang back up. The top of the handle almost bashed me in the mouth. Lookin good, Guilder. But it would have to do.

"Come on, get in," I said.

"Dennis, are you sure?"

"As sure as I can be," I said.

She looked at me for a moment, and then nodded. "Okay."

She went around to the passenger side and got in. I slammed my own door, depressed Petunia's clutch with the broom-handle, and geared into first. I had the clutch halfway out and Petunia was just starting to roll forward when the broom-handle slipped off the clutch again. The septic tanker ran inside Darnell's Garage with a series of neck-snapping jerks, and when I slammed my right foot down on the brake, the truck stalled. We were mostly inside.

"Leigh, I've got to have something with a wider foot," I said. "This broom-handle don't cut it."

"I'll see what there is."

She got out and began to walk around the edge of the garage floor, hunting. I stared around. *Creepy*, Leigh had said, and she was right. The only cars left were four or five old soldiers so gravely wounded that no one had cared enough to claim them. All the rest of the slant spaces with their numbers stencilled in white paint were empty. I glanced at stall twenty and then glanced away.

The overhead tire racks were likewise nearly empty. A few baldies remained, heeled over against one another like giant doughnuts blackened in a fire, but that was all. One of the two lifts was partially up, with a wheel-rim caught beneath it. The front-end alignment chart on the right-hand wall glimmered faintly red and white, the two headlight targets like bloodshot eyes. And shadows, shadows everywhere. Overhead, big box-shaped heaters pointed their louvers this way and that, roosting up there like weird bats.

It seemed very much like a death-place.

Leigh had used another of Jimmy's keys to open Will's office. I could see her moving back and forth in there through the window Will had used to look out at his customers . . . those working joes who had to keep their cars running so they could blah-blah-blah. She flipped some switches, and the overhead fluorescents came on in snow-cold ranks. So the electric company hadn't cut off the juice. I'd have to have her turn the lights off again—we couldn't afford to risk attracting attention—but at least we could have some heat.

She opened another door and disappeared temporarily from view. I glanced at my watch. One-thirty now.

She came back, and I saw that she was holding an O-Cedar mop, the kind with the wide yellow sponge along the foot.

"Would this be any good?"

"Only perfect," I said. "Get in, kiddo. We're in business."

She climbed up once more, and I pushed the clutch down with the mop. "Lots better," I said. "Where did you find it?"

"In the bathroom," she said, and wrinkled her nose.

"Bad in there?"

"Dirty, reeking of cigars, and there's a whole pile of mouldy books in the corner. The kind they sell at those little hole-in-the-wall stores."

So that was what Darnell left behind him, I thought: an empty garage, a pile of Beeline Books, and a phantom reek of Roi-Tan cigars. I felt cold again, and thought that if I had my way, I'd see this place bulldozed flat and pasted over with hottop. I could not shake the feeling that it was an unmarked grave of a sort—the place where LeBay and Christine had killed my friend's mind and taken over his life.

"I can't wait to get out of here," Leigh said, looking around nervously.

"Really? I kind of like it. I was thinking of moving in." I caressed her shoulder and looked deeply into her eyes. "We could start a family," I breathed.

She held up a fist. "Want me to start a nosebleed?"

"No, that's all right. For what it's worth, I can't wait to get out of here, either." I drove Petunia the rest of the way inside. I found that I could run the clutch pretty well using the O-Cedar mop . . . in first gear, at least. The handle had a tendency to bend, and I would have preferred something thicker, but it would have to do unless we could find something better in the meantime.

"We've got to turn off the lights again," I said, killing the engine. "The wrong people might see them."

She got out and turned them off while I swung Petunia in a wide circle and then carefully backed it up until the rear end almost touched the window between the garage and Darnell's office. Now the big truck's snout was pointing directly back at the open overhead door through which we had entered.

With the lights off, the shadows descended again. The light coming in through the open door was weak, muted by the snow, white and without strength. It spread on the oil-stained, cracked concrete like a pie-wedge and simply died halfway across the floor.

"I'm cold, Dennis," Leigh called from Darnell's office. "He's got the switches for the heat marked. Can I turn them on?"

"Go ahead," I called back.

A moment later the garage whispered with the sound of the blowers. I leaned back against the seat, gently running my hands over my left leg. The material of my jeans was stretched smoothly over the thigh, tight and without a wrinkle. The sonofabitch was swelling. And it hurt. Christ, did it hurt.

Leigh came back and climbed up beside me. She told me again how terrible I looked, and for some reason my mind cross-patched and I thought of the afternoon Arnie had brought Christine down here, of the be-bop queen's husband yelling for Arnie to get that hunk of junk out from in front of his house, and of Arnie telling me the guy was a regular Robert Deadford. How we had gotten the giggles. I closed my eyes against the sting of tears.

With nothing to do but wait, time slowed down. It was quarter of two, then two o'clock. Outside, the snow had thickened a little, but not much. Leigh got out of the truck and pushed the button that trundled the door back down. That made it even darker inside.

She came back, climbed up, and said, "There's a funny gadget on the side of the door—see it? It looks just like the electronic garage door-opener we used to have when we lived in Weston."

I sat up suddenly. Stared at it. "Oh," I said. "Oh, Jesus."

"What's the matter?"

"That's just what it is. A garage door-opener. And there's one of the transmitter gadgets on Christine. Arnie mentioned that to me Thanksgiving night. You've got to break it, Leigh. Use the handle of that push broom."

So she got down again, picked up the broom-handle, and stood below the electric eye gadget, looking up and bashing at it with the handle. She looked like a woman trying to kill a bug near the ceiling. At last she was rewarded with a crunch of plastic and tinkle of glass.

She came back slowly, tossing the broom-handle aside, and got up beside me. "Dennis, don't you think it's time you told me exactly what you've got in mind?"

"What do you mean?"

"You know what I mean," she said, and pointed at the closed overhead door. Five square windows in a line three-quarters of the way up its height let in minimal light through dirty glass. "When it gets dark you plan to open that door again, don't you?"

I nodded. The door itself was wood, but it was braced with hinged steel strips, like the inner gate of an old-time elevator. I'd let her in, but once the door was shut, Christine wouldn't be able to bash her way back out again. I hoped. It made me cold to think how close we'd come to overlooking the electronic door-opener.

Open the door at dusk, yes. Let Christine in, yes. Close the door again. Then I would use Petunia to batter her to death.

"Okay," she said, "that's the trap. But once she—it—comes in, how are you going to get that door shut again to keep her in? Maybe there's a button in Darnell's office that does it, but I didn't see it."

"So far as I know, there isn't one," I said. "So you're going to be standing over there by the button that shuts the door." I pointed. The manual button was located on the right side of the door, about two feet below the ruins of the electric door-opener box. "You'll be against the wall, out of sight. When Christine comes in—always assuming she does—you're going to push the button that starts the door coming down and then step outside in a hurry. The door comes down. And, bam! The trap's shut."

Her face set. "On you as well as her. In the words of the immortal Wordsworth, that sucks."

"That's Coleridge, not Wordsworth. There's no other way to do it, Leigh. If you're still inside when that door comes down, Christine is going to run you down. Even if there was a button in Darnell's office—well, you saw in the paper what happened to the side of his house."

Her face was stubborn. "Park over by the switch. And when she comes in, I'll reach out the window and hit the button and lower the door."

"If I park there, I'll be in sight. And if this tank is in sight, she won't come in."

"I don't like it!" she burst out. "I don't like leaving you alone! It's like you tricked me!"

In a way, that's just what I had done, and for whatever it's worth, I would not do it the same way now—but I was going on eighteen then, and there's no male chauvinist pig like an eighteen-year-old male chauvinist pig. I put an arm around her shoulders. She resisted stiffly for a moment and then came to me. "There's just no other way," I said. "If it wasn't for my leg, or if you could drive a standard shift—" I shrugged.

"I'm scared for you, Dennis. I want to help."

"You'll be helping plenty. You're the one that's really in danger, Leigh—you'll be outside, on the floor, when she comes in. I'm just going to sit up here in the cab and beat that bitch back into component parts."

"I only hope it works that way," she said, and put her head on my chest. I touched her hair.

So we waited.

In my mind's eye I could see Arnie coming out of the main building at LHS, books under his arm. I could see Regina waiting for him there in the Cunninghams' compact wagon, radiant with happiness. Arnie smiling remotely and submitting to her embrace. Arnie, you've made the right decision . . . you don't know how relieved, how *happy,* your father and I are. Yes, Mom. Do you want to drive, honey? No, you drive, Mom. That's okay.

The two of them setting off for Penn State through the light snow, Regina driving, Arnie sitting in the shotgun seat with his hands folded stiffly in his lap, his face pale and unsmiling and clear of acne.

And back in the student parking lot at LHS, Christine sitting silently in the driveway. Waiting for the snow to thicken. Waiting for dark.

At three-thirty or so, Leigh went back through Darnell's office to use the bathroom, and while she was gone I dryswallowed two more Darvon. My leg was a steady, leaden agony.

Shortly after that, I lost coherent track of time. The dope had me fuddled, I guess. The whole thing began to seem dreamlike: the deepening shadows, the white light coming in through the windows slowly changing to an ashy gray, the drone of the overhead heaters.

I think that Leigh and I made love . . . not in the ordinary way, not with my leg the way it was, but some kind of sweet substitute. I seem to remember her breath steepening in my ear until she was nearly panting; I seem to remember her whispering for me to be careful, to please be careful, that she had lost Arnie and could not bear to lose me too. I seem to remember an explosion of pleasure that made the pain disappear in a brief but total way that not all the Darvon in the world could manage . . . but brief was the right word. It was all too brief. And then I think I dozed.

The next thing I remember for sure was Leigh shaking me fully awake and whispering my name over and over in my ear.

"Huh? What?" I was spaced out and my leg was full of a glassy pain, simply waiting to explode. There was an ache in my temples, and my eyes felt too big for their sockets. I blinked around at Leigh like a large stupid owl.

"It's dark," she said. "I thought I heard something."

I blinked again and saw that she looked drawn and frightened. Then I glanced toward the door and saw that it was standing wide open.

"How the hell did that—"

"Me," she said. "I opened it."

"Cripes!" I said, strightening up a little and wincing at the pain in my leg. "That wasn't too smart, Leigh. If she had come—"

"She didn't," Leigh said. "It started to get dark, that's all, and to snow harder. So I got out and opened the door and then I came back here. I kept thinking you'd wake up in a minute . . . you were mumbling . . . and I kept thinking, 'I'll wait until it's really dark, I'll just wait until it's really dark,' and then I saw I was fooling myself, because it's been dark for almost half an hour now and I was only thinking I could still see some light. Because I wanted to see it, I guess. And . . . just now . . . I thought I heard something."

Her lips began to tremble and she pressed them tightly together.

I looked at my watch and saw that it was quarter to six. If everything had gone right, my parents and sister would be together with Michael and Leigh's folks now. I looked through Petunia's windshield at the square of snow-shot darkness where the garage entrance was. I could hear the wind shrieking. A thin creeper of snow had already blown in onto the cement.

"You just heard the wind," I said uneasily. "It's walking and talking out there."

"Maybe. But—"

I nodded reluctantly. I didn't want her to leave the safety of Petunia's high cab, but if she didn't go now, maybe she never would. I wouldn't let her, and she would let me not let her. And then, when and if Christine came, all she would have to do would be to reverse back out of Darnell's.

And wait for a more opportune time.

"Okay," I said. "But remember . . . stand back in that little niche to the right of the door. If she comes, she may just stand outside for a while." *Scenting the air like an animal*, I thought. "Don't get scared, don't move. Don't let her freak you into giving yourself away. Just be cool and wait until she comes in. Then push that button and get the hell out. Do you understand?"

"Yes," she whispered. "Dennis, will this work?"

"It should, if she comes at all."

"I won't see you until it's over."

"I guess that's so."

She leaned over, placed her left hand lightly on the side of my neck, and kissed my mouth. "Be careful, Dennis," she said. "But kill it. It's really not a she at all—just an it. Kill it."

"I will," I said.

She looked in my eyes and nodded. "Do it for Arnie," she said. "Set him free."

I hugged her hard and she hugged me back. Then she slid across the seat. She hit her little handbag with her knee and it fell to the floor of the cab. She paused, head cocked, a startled, thoughtful look in her eyes. Then she smiled, bent over, picked it up, and began to rummage quickly through it.

"Dennis," she said, "do you remember the *Morte d'Arthur?*"

"A little." One of the classes Leigh and Arnie and I had all shared before my football injury was Fudgy Bowen's Classics of English Literature, and one of the first things we had been faced with in there was Malory's *Morte d'Arthur.* Why Leigh asked me this now was a mystery to me.

She had found what she wanted. It was a filmy pink scarf, nylon, the sort of thing a girl wears over her head on a day when a misty sort of rain is falling. She tied it around the left forearm of my parka.

"What the hell?" I asked, smiling a little.

"Be my knight," she said, and smiled back—but her eyes were serious. "Be my knight, Dennis."

I picked up the squeegee mop she had found in Will's bathroom and made a clumsy salute with it. "Sure," I said. "Just call me Sir O-Cedar."

"Joke about it if you want," she said, "but don't *really* joke about it. Okay?"

"All right," I said. "If it's what you want, I'll be your parfit goddam gentil knight."

She laughed a little, and that was better.

"Remember about that button, kiddo. Push it hard. We don't want that door to just burp once and stop on its track. No escapes, right?"

"Right."

She got out of Petunia, and I can close my eyes now and see her as she was then, in that clean and silent moment just before everything went terribly wrong—a tall, pretty girl with long blond hair the color of raw honey, slim hips, long legs, and those striking, Nordic cheekbones, now wearing a ski parka and faded Lee Riders, moving with a dancer's grace. I can still see it and I still dream about it, because of course while we were busy setting up Christine, she was busy setting us up—that old and infinitely wise monster. Did we really think we could outsmart her so easily? I guess we did.

My dreams are in terrible slow motion. I can see the softly lovely motion of her hips as she walks; I can hear the hollow click of her Frye boots on the oil-stained cement floor; I can even hear the soft, dry *whish-whish* of her parka's quilted inner lining brushing against her blouse. She's walking slowly and her head is up—now *she* is the animal, but no predator; she walks with the cautious grace of a zebra approaching a waterhole at dusk. It is the walk of an animal that scents danger. I try to scream to her through Petunia's windshield. *Come back, Leigh, come back quick, you were right, you heard something, she's out there now, out there in the snow with her headlights off, crouched down, Leigh, come back!*

She stopped suddenly, her hands tensing into fists, and that was when sudden savage circles of light sprang to life in the snowy dark outside. They were like white eyes opening.

Leigh froze, hideously exposed on the open floor. She was thirty feet inside the door and slightly to the right of center. She turned toward the headlights, and I could see the dazed, uncertain expression on her face.

I was just as stunned, and that first vital moment passed unused. Then the headlights sprang forward and I could see the dark, low-slung shape of Christine behind them; I could hear the mounting, furious howl of her engine as she leaped toward us from across the street where she had been waiting all along—maybe even since before dark. Snow funnelled back from her roof and skirled across her windshield in filmy nets that were almost instantly melted by the defroster. She hit the tarmac leading up to the entrance, still gaining speed. Her engine was a V-8 scream of rage.

"*Leigh!*" I screamed, and clawed for Petunia's ignition switch.

Leigh broke to the right and ran for the wall-button. Christine roared inside as she reached it and pushed it. I heard the rattle-rumble of the overhead door descending on its track.

Christine came in angling to the right, going for Leigh. She dug a great clout of dry wood and splinters from the wall.

There was a metallic screech as part of her right bumper pulled loose—a sound like a drunk's scream of laughter. Sparks cascaded across the floor as she went into a long, slewing turn. She missed Leigh, but she wouldn't when she went back; Leigh was stuck in that right-hand corner with nowhere to hide. She might be able to make it outside, but I was terribly afraid that the door wasn't coming down fast enough to cut off Christine. The descending door might peel off her roof, but that wouldn't stop her, and I knew it.

Petunia's engine bellowed and I dragged out the headlight button. Her brights came on, splashing over the closing door, and over Leigh. She was backed up against the wall, her eyes wide. Her parka took on a weird, almost electric blue color in the headlights, and my mind informed me with sickening and clinical accuracy that her blood would look purple.

I saw her glance upward for a moment and then back down at Christine.

The Fury's tires screamed violently as she leaped at Leigh. Smoke rose from the new black marks on the concrete. I just had time to register the fact that there were *people* inside of Christine: a whole carload of them.

At the same instant that Christine roared toward her, Leigh leaped upward with a big ungainly Jack-in-the-box spring. My mind, seeming to run at a speed approaching light, wondered for a moment if she was intending to leap right over the Plymouth, as if, instead of Fryes, she wore boots of the seven-league variety.

Instead, she caught and gripped the rusted metal struts which supported an overhead shelf almost nine feet above the floor, over three feet above her head. This shelf skirted all four walls. On the night Arnie and I had first brought Christine in, that entire shelf had been crammed with recapped tires and old baldies waiting to be recapped—in some funny way it had reminded me of a well-stocked library shelf. Now it was mostly empty. Holding those angled struts, Leigh swung her jeaned legs up like a kid who means to throw his legs right over his own shoulders—what we used to call skinning the cat in grammar school. Christine's snout smashed into the wall directly below her. If she had been any slower getting her legs up, they would have been mashed off at the knees. A piece of chrome flew. Two of the remaining tires tumbled from the shelf and bounced crazily on the cement like giant rubber doughnuts.

Leigh's head smashed back against the wall with battering, dazing force as Christine reversed, *all four* of her tires laying rubber and squirting blue smoke.

And what was I doing all this time, you wonder? It wasn't "all that time," that is my answer. Even as I used the O-Cedar mop to depress Petunia's clutch and gear into first, the overhead door was just thumping down. All of it had happened in the space of seconds.

Leigh was still holding onto the struts supporting the tire shelf, but now she only hung there, head down, dazed.

I let the clutch out, and a cold part of my mind took over: *Easy, man—if you pop the clutch and stall this fucker, she's dead.*

Petunia rolled. I revved the engine up to a bellow and let the clutch out all the way. Christine roared at Leigh again, her hood crimped almost double from her first hit, bright metal showing through the broken paint at the sharpest points of bend. It looked as if her hood and grille had grown shark's teeth.

I hit Christine three-quarters of the way toward the front and she slid around, one of her tires pulling off the rim. The '58 slammed into a litter of old bumper jacks and junk parts in one corner; there was a booming crash as she struck the wall, and then the hot sound of her engine, revving and falling off, revving and falling off. The entire left front end was bashed in—but she was still running.

I slammed on Petunia's brake with my right foot and barely managed to avoid crushing Leigh myself. Petunia's engine stalled. Now the only sound in the garage was Christine's screaming engine.

"*Leigh!*" I screamed over it. "*Leigh, run!*"

She looked over at me groggily, and now I could see sticky braids of blood in her hair—it was as purple as I had expected. She let go of the struts, landed on her feet, staggered, and went to one knee.

Christine came for her. Leigh got up, took two wobbling steps, and got on her blind side, behind Petunia. Christine swerved and struck the truck's front end. I was thrown roughly to the right. Pain roared through my left leg.

"Get up!" I screamed at Leigh, trying to lean even farther over and open the door. "*Get up!*"

Christine backed off, and when she came again she cut hard to the right and went out of my line of vision, around the back of Petunia. I caught just a glimpse of her in the rearview mirror bolted outside the driver's side window. Then I could only hear the scream of her tires.

Barely conscious, Leigh simply wandered off, holding both hands laced to the back of her head. Blood trickled through her fingers. She walked in front of Petunia's grille toward me and then just stopped.

I didn't have to see in order to know what was going to happen next. Christine would reverse again, back to my side, and then crush her against the wall.

Desperately, I shoved the clutch in with the mop and keyed the engine again. It turned over, coughed, stalled. I could smell gasoline in the air, heavy and rich. I had flooded the engine.

Christine reappeared in the rearview mirror. She came at Leigh, who managed to stumble backward just out of reach. Christine slammed nose-on into the wall with crunching force. The passenger door popped open and the horror was complete; the hand not clutching the mop-handle went to my mouth and I screamed through it.

Sitting on the passenger side like a grotesque, life-sized doll was Michael Cunningham. His head, lolling limply on the stalk of his neck, snapped over to one side as Christine reversed to make another try at Leigh, and I saw his face had the high, rosy color of carbon monoxide poisoning. He hadn't taken my advice. Christine had gone to the Cunninghams' house first, as I had vaguely suspected she might. Michael came home from school and there she was, standing in the driveway, his son's restored 1958 Plymouth. He had gone to it, and somehow Christine had . . . had gotten him. Had he maybe gotten in just to sit behind the wheel for a moment, as I had that day in LeBay's garage? He might have. Just to see what vibrations he could pick up. If so, he must have picked up some terrible vibes indeed during his last few minutes on earth. Had Christine started herself up? Driven herself into the garage? Maybe. Maybe. And had Michael discovered that he could neither turn off the madly revving engine nor get out of the car? Had he maybe turned his head and perhaps seen the true guiding spirit of Arnie's '58 Fury, lounging in the shotgun seat, and fainted in terror?

It didn't matter now. Leigh was all that mattered.

She had seen, too. Her screams, high, despairing, and shrill, floated in the exhaust-stinking air like hysterically bright balloons. But it had, at least, cut through her daze.

She turned and ran for Will Darnell's office, blood splattering behind her in dime-sized drops as she went. Blood was soaking into the collar of her parka—too much blood.

Christine backed up, laying rubber and leaving a scatter of glass behind. As she pulled around in a tight circle to go after Leigh, centrifugal force pulled the passenger door shut again—but not before I saw Michael's head loll back the other way.

Christine held still for a moment, her nose pointed toward Leigh, her engine revving. Perhaps LeBay was savoring the instant before the kill. If so, I'm glad, because if Christine had gone for her right away, she would have been killed then. But as it was, I had an instant of time. I turned the key again, babbling something aloud—a prayer, I guess—and this time Petunia's engine coughed into life. I let the clutch out and stepped down on the accelerator as Christine leaped forward again. This time I struck her right side. There was a shrill scream of tearing metal as Petunia's bumper punched through her mudguard. Christine heeled over and smashed against the wall. Glass broke. Her engine raced and raved. Behind the wheel, LeBay turned toward me, grinning with hate.

Petunia stalled again.

I rattled off a string of every curse I knew as I grabbed for the key again. If not for my goddam leg, if not for the fall I'd taken in the snow, this would be over now; it would just be a matter of cornering her and smashing her to pieces against the cinderblock.

But even as I cranked Petunia's engine, keeping my foot off the gas to keep from stalling her again, Christine began to reverse with an ear-splitting squeal of metal. She backed out from between Petunia's grille and the wall, leaving a twisted chunk of her red body behind, baring her right front tire.

I got Petunia going and found reverse. Christine had backed all the way down to the far end of the garage. All her headlights were out. Her windshield was smashed into a galaxy of cracks. The bent hood seemed to sneer.

Her radio was blasting. I could hear Ricky Nelson singing "Waitin in School."

I stared around for Leigh and saw her in Will's office, looking out into the garage. Her blond hair was matted with blood. More blood ran down the left side of her face and soaked into her jacket. *Bleeding too damn much*, I thought incoherently. *Bleeding too damn much, even for a head wound.*

Her eyes widened and she pointed past me, her lips moving soundlessly behind the glass.

Christine came roaring straight up the empty floor, gaining speed.

And the hood was uncrimping, straightening out and down to cover the motor cavity again. Two of the headlights flickered, then came back strong. The mudguard and the right-hand side of her body—I only caught a glimpse, but I swear it's true—they were . . . *reknitting* themselves, red metal appearing from nowhere and slipping down in smooth automotive curves to cover the right front tire and the right side of the engine compartment again. The cracks in the windshield were running inward and disappearing. And the tire that had been pulled off its rim looked as good as new.

It all *looks as good as new,* I thought. *God help us.*

She was going directly for the wall between the garage and the office. I let the mop-handle off the clutch fast, hoping to interpose the tanker's body, but Christine got past me. Petunia backed into nothing but thin air. Oh, I was doing great. I backed all the way across the floor and crashed into the dented tool-lockers ranged there. They crashed to the floor with dull metallic janglings. Through the windshield I saw Christine hit the wall between the garage and Will's office. She never slowed; she went full speed ahead.

I'll never forget those next few moments—they remain hypnotically clear in my memory, as if seen through a magnifying crystal. Leigh saw Christine coming and stumbled backward. Her bloody hair was matted to her head. She fell over Will's swivel chair. She hit the floor, out of sight behind his desk. An instant later—and I mean the barest *instant*—Christine slammed into the wall. The big window Will had used to keep track of the comings and goings out in his garage exploded inward. Glass flew like a cluster of deadly spears. Christine's front end bulged with the impact. The hood popped up and then tore off, flying back over the roof to land on the concrete with a metallic sound that was much like the sound the falling tool-lockers had made.

Her windshield shattered, and Michael Cunningham's body flew through the jagged opening, legs trailing, his head a grotesque flattened football. He was catapulted through Will's window; he struck Will's desk with a heavy grainsack thud and skidded over onto the floor. His shoes stuck up.

Leigh began to scream.

Her fall had probably saved her from being badly lacerated or killed by the flying glass, but when she rose from behind the desk her face was contorted with horror, and utter hysteria had its hold on her. Michael had skidded from the desk and his arms had looped themselves over her shoulders and as Leigh struggled to her feet she appeared to be waltzing with the corpse. Her screams were like firebells. Her blood, still flowing, sparkled deadly bright. She dumped Michael and ran for the door.

"Leigh, no!" I screamed, and slammed down the clutch with the mop again. The handle snapped cleanly in two, leaving me with a stump five inches long. *"Ohhhh—SHIT!"*

Christine reversed away from the broken window, leaving water, antifreeze, and oil puddled on the floor.

I stamped down on the clutch with my left foot, barely feeling the pain now, bracing my left knee with my left hand as I worked the gearshift.

Leigh tore the office door open and ran out.

Christine turned toward her, its smashed, snarling snout sighting down on her.

I revved Petunia's engine and roared at her, and as that damned car from hell grew in the windshield, I saw the purple, swollen face of a child pressed to the rear window, watching me, seeming to beg me to stop.

I struck her hard. The trunk-lid popped up and gaped like a mouth. The rear end heeled around and Christine went skidding sideways past Leigh, who fled with her eyes seeming to swallow her face. I remember the spray of blood along the fur fringe of her parka's hood, tiny droplets like an evil fall of dew.

I was in it now. I was in the peak seat. Even if they had to take my leg off at the groin when this was done, I was going to drive.

Christine hit the wall and bounced back. I stamped the clutch, rammed the gearshift into reverse, backed up ten feet, stamped the clutch again, rammed it back into first. Engine revving, Christine tried to pull away along the wall. I cut to the left and hit her again, crushing her almost wasp-waisted in the middle. The doors popped out of their frames at the top and the bottom. LeBay was behind the wheel, now a skull, now a decayed and stinking cameo of humanity, now a hale and hearty man in his fifties with a crew-cut turning white. He stared out at me with his devil's grin, one hand on the wheel, one balled into a fist that he shook at me.

And still her engine would not die.

I got into reverse again, and now my leg was white iron and the pain was all the way up to my left armpit. The hell it was. The pain was *everywhere*. I could feel it

(*Michael Jesus why didn't you stay in the house*)

in my neck, in my jaw in my

(*Arnie? Man, I am so sorry I wish I wish*)

temples. The Plymouth—what remained of her—lunged drunkenly down the side of the garage, spraying tools and junk metal, pulling out struts and dumping the overhead shelves. The shelves hit the concrete with flat, clapping sounds that echoed like demon applause.

I stamped the clutch again and floored the gas. Petunia's engine bellowed, and I hung onto the wheel like a man trying to stay aboard a bucking mustang. I hit her on the right side and smashed the body clear off the rear axle, driving it into the door, which shivered and rattled. I went up over the wheel, which slammed into my belly and drove the breath out of me and dumped me back into my seat, gasping.

Now I saw Leigh, cowering in the far corner, her hands clapped to her face, dragging it down into a witch's mask.

Christine's engine was still running.

She dragged herself slowly down toward Leigh, like an animal whose rear legs have been broken in a trap. And even as she went I could see her regenerating, coming back: a tire that suddenly popped up full and plump, the radio antenna that unjointed itself with a silvery *twingggg!* sound, the accretion of metal around the ruined rear end.

"*Stay dead!*" I screamed at it. I was crying, my chest heaving. My leg wouldn't work anymore. I braced it with both hands and *jammed* it onto the clutch. My vision went hazy and gray with the white-metal agony. I could almost feel the bones grating.

I raced the engine, got first gear again, and charged it; and as I did I heard LeBay's voice for the first and only time, high and cheated and full of a terrible, unquenchable fury:

"*You SHITTER! Fuck off, you miserable SHITTER! LEAVE ME ALONE!*"

"You should have left my friend alone," I tried to yell—but all that would come out was a tearing, wounded gasp.

I hit it squarely in the rear end, and the gas tank ruptured as the back of the car accordioned inward and upward in a kind of metal mushroom. There was a yellow lick of fire. I shielded my face with my hands—but then it was gone. Christine sat there, a refugee from a demolition derby. Her engine ran choppily, missed, fired again, and then died.

The place was silent except for the bass rumble of Petunia's engine,

Then Leigh was running across the floor, screaming my name over and over, crying. I was suddenly, stupidly aware that I was wearing her pink nylon scarf around the arm of my jacket.

I looked down at it, and then the world grayed out again.

I could feel her hands on me, and then there was nothing but darkness as I fainted.

I came to about fifteen minutes later, my face wet and blessedly cool. Leigh was standing on Petunia's driver's-side running board, mopping my face with a wet rag. I caught it in one hand, tried to suck it, and then spat. The rag tasted strongly of oil.

"Dennis, don't worry," she said. "I ran out into the street . . . stopped a snowplow . . . scared the poor man out of ten years of his life, I think . . . all this blood . . . he said . . . an ambulance . . . he said he'd, you know . . . Dennis, are you all right?"

"Do I *look* all right?" I whispered.

"No," she said, and burst into tears.

"Then don't"—I swallowed past a painful dry lump in my throat—"don't ask stupid questions. I love you."

She hugged me clumsily.

"He said he'd call the police, too," she said.

I barely heard her. My eyes had found the twisted, silent hulk that was Christine's remains. And hulk was the right word; she hardly looked like a car at all anymore. But why hadn't she burned? A hubcap lay off to one side like a dented silver tiddlywink.

"How long since you stopped the plow?" I asked hoarsely.

"Maybe five minutes. Then I got the rag and dipped it in that bucket over there. Dennis . . . thank God it's over."

Punk! Punk! Punk!

I was still looking at the hubcap.

The dents were popping out of it.

Abruptly it flicked up on its rim and rolled toward the car like a huge coin.

Leigh saw it too. Her face froze. Her eyes widened and began to bulge. Her lips mouthed the word *No* but no sound came out.

"Get in here with me," I said in a low voice, as if it could hear us. How do I know?—perhaps it could. "Get in on the passenger side. You're going to run the gas while I run the clutch with my right foot."

"No . . ." This time it was a hissing whisper. Her breath came in whining little gasps. "No . . . no . . ."

The wreckage was quivering all over. It was the most eerie, most terrible thing I have ever seen in my life. It was quivering all over, quivering like an animal that is not . . . quite . . . dead. Metal tapped nervously against metal. Tie rods clicked jittery jazz rhythms against their connectors. As I watched, a bent cotter-pin lying on the floor straightened itself and did half a dozen cartwheels to land in the wreckage.

"Get in," I said.

"Dennis, I can't." Her lips quivered helplessly. "I can't . . . no more . . . that body . . . that was Arnie's *father*. I can't, no more, please—"

"You have to," I said.

She looked at me, glanced affrightedly back at the obscenely quivering remains of that old whore LeBay and Arnie had shared, and then came around Petunia's front end. A piece of chrome tumbled and scratched her leg deeply. She screamed and ran. She clambered up into the cab and pushed over beside me. "Wh-what do I do?"

I hung halfway out of the cab, holding onto the roof, and pushed the clutch down with my right foot. Petunia's engine was still running. "Just gun the gas and keep it gunned," I said. "No matter what."

Steering with my right hand, holding on with my left, I let the clutch out and we rolled forward and smashed into the wreckage, smashing it, scattering it. And in my head I seemed to hear another scream of fury.

Leigh clapped her hands to her head. "I can't, Dennis! I can't do it! It—it's *screaming!*"

"You've got to do it," I said. Her foot had come off the gas and now I could hear sirens in the night, rising and falling. I grabbed her shoulder and a sickening blast of pain ripped up my leg. "Leigh, nothing has changed. You've got to."

"It *screamed* at me!"

"We're running out of time and it still isn't done. Just a little more."

"I'll try," she whispered, and stepped on the gas again.

I shifted into reverse. Petunia rolled back twenty feet. I clutched again, got first . . . and Leigh suddenly cried out. "Dennis, no! Don't! Look!"

The mother and the little girl, Veronica and Rita, were standing in front of the smashed and dented hulk of Christine, hand in hand, their faces solemn and sorrowing.

"They're not there," I said. "And if they are, it's time they went back"—more pain in my leg and the world went gray—"back to where they belong. Keep your foot on it."

I let out the clutch and Petunia rolled forward again, gaining speed. The two figures did not disappear as TV and movie ghosts do; they seemed to stream out in every direction, bright colors fading to wash pinks and blues . . . and then they were totally gone.

We slammed into Christine again, spinning what was left of her around. Metal shrieked and tore.

"Not there," Leigh whispered. "Not really there. Okay. Okay, Dennis."

Her voice was coming from far down a dark hallway. I fetched up reverse and back we went. Then forward. We hit it; we hit it again. How many times? I don't know. We just kept slamming into it, and every time we did, another jolt of pain would go up my leg and things would get a little bit darker.

At last I looked up blearily, and saw that the air outside the door seemed full of blood. But it wasn't blood; it was a pulsing red light reflecting off the falling snow. People were rattling at the door out there.

"Is it good enough?" Leigh asked me.

I looked at Christine—only it wasn't Christine anymore. It was a spread-out pile of twisted, gored metal, puffs of upholstery, and glittering broken glass.

"Have to be," I said. "Let them in, Leigh."

And while she went, I fainted again.

Then there were a series of confused images; things that came into focus for a while and then faded or disappeared completely. I can remember a stretcher being rolled out of the back of an ambulance; I can remember its sides being folded up, and how the overhead fluorescents put cold highlights on i s chrome; I can remember someone saying, "Cut it, you have to cut it off so we can at least *look* at it"; I can remember someone else—Leigh, I think—saying, "Don't hurt him, please, don't hurt him if you can help it"; I can remember the roof of an ambulance . . . it had to be an ambulance because at the periphery of my vision were two suspended IV bottles; I can remember a cool swab of antiseptic and then the sting of a needle.

After that, things became exceedingly weird. I knew, somewhere deep inside, that I was not dreaming—the pain proved that, if it proved nothing else—but all of it *seemed* like a dream. I was pretty well doped, and that was part of it . . . but shock was part of it too. No fake, Jake. My mother was there, crying, in a room that looked sickeningly like the hospital room in which I had spent the entire autumn. Then my father was there, and Leigh's dad was with him, and their faces were both so tight and grim they looked like Tweedledum and Tweedledee as Franz Kafka might have written them. My father bent over me and said in a voice like thunder reverberating through cotton batting: "How did Michael get there, Dennis?" That's what they really wanted to know: how Michael got there. *Oh*, I thought, *oh my friends, I could tell you stories. . . .*

Then Mr. Cabot was saying, "What did you get my daughter into, boy?" I seem to remember replying, "It's not what I got her into, it's what she got you out of," which I still think was pretty witty under the circumstances, doped up the way I was and all.

Elaine was there briefly, and she seemed to be holding a Yodel or a Twinkie or something mockingly out of my reach. Leigh was there, holding her filmy nylon scarf out and asking me to raise my arm so she could tie it on. But I couldn't; my arm was like a lead bar.

Then Arnie was there, and of course that *had* to be a dream.

Thanks, man, he said, and I noticed with something like terror that the left lens of his glasses was shattered. His face was okay, but that broken lens . . . it scared me. *Thanks. You did okay. I feel better now. I think things are going to be okay now.*

No sweat, Arnie, I said—or tried to say—but he was gone.

It was the next day—not the twentieth, but Sunday, January twenty-first—that I started to come back a little. My left leg was in a cast up in its old familiar position again amid all the pulleys and weights. There was a man I had never seen before sitting to the left of my bed, reading a paperback John D. MacDonald story. He saw me looking at him and lowered his book.

"Welcome back to the land of the living, Dennis," he said mildly, and deliberately marked his place in the book with a matchbook cover. He put the book in his lap and folded his hands over it.

"Are you a doctor?" I asked. He sure wasn't Dr. Arroway, who had taken care of me last time; this guy was twenty years younger and at least fifty pounds leaner. He looked tough.

"State Police Inspector," he said. "Richard Mercer is my name. Rick, if you like." He held out his hand, and stretching awkwardly and carefully, I touched it. I couldn't really shake it. My head ached and I was thirsty.

"Look," I said. "I don't really mind talking to you, and I'll answer all of your questions, but I'd like to see a doctor." I swallowed. He looked at me, concerned, and I blurted out, "I need to know if I'm ever going to walk again."

"If what that fellow Arroway says is the truth," Mercer said, "you'll be able to get around in four to six weeks. You didn't break it again, Dennis. You severely strained it; that was what he said. It swelled up like a sausage. He also said you were lucky to get off so cheap."

"What about Arnie?" I asked. "Arnie Cunningham? Do you know—"

His eyes flickered.

"What is it?" I asked. "What is it about Arnie?"

"Dennis," he said, and then hesitated. "I don't know if this is the time."

"*Please.* Is Arnie . . . is he dead?"

Mercer sighed. "Yes, he's dead. He and his mother had an accident on the Pennsylvania Turnpike, in the snow. If it *was* an accident."

I tried to talk and couldn't. I motioned for the pitcher of water on the bedtable, thinking how dismal it was to be in a hospital room and know exactly where everything was. Mercer poured me a glass and put the straw with the elbow-bend in it. I drank, and it got a little bit better. My throat, that is. Nothing else seemed better at all.

"What do you mean, *if* it was an accident?"

Mercer said, "It was Friday evening, and the snow just wasn't that heavy. The turnpike classification was two—bare and wet, reduced visibility, use appropriate caution. We guess, from the force of impact, that they weren't doing much more than forty-five. The car veered across the median and struck a semi. It was Mrs. Cunningham's Volvo wagon. It exploded."

I closed my eyes. "Regina?"

"Also DOA. For whatever it's worth, they probably didn't—"

"—suffer," I finished. "Bullshit. They suffered *plenty*." I felt tears and choked them back. Mercer said nothing. "All three of them," I muttered. "Oh Jesus Christ, all three."

"The driver of the truck broke his arm. That was the worst of it for him. He said that there were three people in the car, Dennis."

"Three!"

"Yes. And he said they appeared to be struggling." Mercer looked at me frankly. "We're going on the theory that they picked up a bad-news hitchhiker who escaped after the accident and before the troopers arrived."

But that was ridiculous, if you knew Regina Cunningham, I thought. She would no more pick up a hitchhiker than she would wear slacks to a faculty tea. The things you did and those you never did were firmly set in Regina Cunningham's mind. As if in cement, you could say.

It had been LeBay. He couldn't be both places at once, that was the thing. And at the end, when he saw how things were going in Darnell's Garage, he had abandoned Christine and had tried to go back to Arnie. What had happened then was anyone's guess. But I thought then—and do now—that Arnie fought him—and earned at least a draw.

"Dead," I said, and now the tears did come. I was too weak and low to stop them. I hadn't been able to keep him from getting killed, after all. Not the last time, not when it really mattered. Others, maybe, but not Arnie.

"Tell me what happened," Mercer said. He put his book on the bedtable and leaned forward. "Tell me everything you know, Dennis, from first to last."

"What has Leigh said?" I asked. "And how is she?"

"She spent Friday night here under observation," Mercer told me. "She had a concussion and a scalp laceration that took a dozen stitches to close. No marks on her face. Lucky. She's a very pretty girl."

"She's more than that," I said. "She's beautiful."

"She won't say anything," Mercer said, and a reluctant grin—of admiration, I think—slanted his face to the left. "Not to me, not to her father. He is, shall we say, in a state of high pissoff about the whole thing. She says it's your business what to tell and when to tell." He looked at me thoughtfully. "Because, she says, you're the one who ended it."

"I didn't do such a great job," I muttered. I was still trying to cope with the idea that Arnie could possibly be dead. It was impossible, wasn't it? We had gone to Camp Winnesko in Vermont together when we were twelve, and I got homesick and told him I was going to call and tell my parents they had to come get me. Arnie said if I did, he'd tell everybody at school that the reason I came home early was that they caught me eating boogers in my bunk after lights out and expelled me. We climbed the tree in my back yard to the very top fork and carved our initials there. He used to sleep over at my house and we'd stay up late watching *Shock Theater*, crouched together on the sofa under an old quilt. We ate all those clandestine Wonder Bread sandwiches. When he was fourteen Arnie came to me, scared and ashamed because he was having these sexy dreams and he thought they were making him wet the bed. But it was the ant farms my mind kept coming back to. How could he be dead when we had made those ant farms together? Dear Christ, it seemed like only a week or two ago, those ant farms. So how could he be dead? I opened my mouth to tell Mercer that Arnie couldn't be dead—those ant farms made the very idea absurd. Then I closed my mouth again. I couldn't tell him that. He was just a guy.

Arnie, I thought. *Hey, man—it's not true, is it? Jesus Christ, we still got too much to do. We never even double-dated at the drive-in yet.*

"What happened?" Mercer asked again. "Tell me, Dennis."

"You'd never believe it," I said thickly.

"You might be surprised what I'd believe," he said. "And you might be surprised what we know. A fellow named Junkins was the chief investigator on this case. He was killed not so very far from here. He was a friend of mine. A good friend. A week before he died he told me that he thought something was going on in Libertyville that nobody would believe. Then he was killed. With me that makes it personal."

I shifted positions cautiously. "He didn't tell you any more?"

"He told me that he believed he had uncovered an old murder," Mercer said, still not taking his eyes from mine. "But it didn't much matter, he said, because the perpetrator was dead."

"LeBay," I muttered, and thought that if Junkins had known about that, it was no wonder Christine had killed him. Because if Junkins had known that, he had been much too close to the whole truth.

Mercer said, "LeBay was the name he mentioned." He leaned closer. "And I'll tell you something else, Dennis—Junkins was one hell of a driver. When he was younger, before he got married, he used to run stockers at Philly Plains, and he won his share of checkered flags. He went off the road doing better than a hundred and twenty in a Dodge cruiser with a hemi engine. Whoever was chasing him—and we know someone was—had to be one hell of a driver."

"Yeah," I said. "He was."

"I came by myself. I've been here for two hours, waiting for you to wake up. I was here until they kicked me out last night. I don't have a stenographer with me, I don't have a tape recorder, and I assure you that I'm not wearing a wire. When you make a statement—if you ever have to—that'll be a different ballgame. But for now, it's you and me. I have to know. Because I see Rudy Junkins's wife and Rudy Junkins's kids from time to time. You dig?"

I thought it over. For a long time I thought it over—nearly five minutes. He sat there and let me do it. At last I nodded. "Okay. But you're still not going to believe it."

"We'll see," he said.

I opened my mouth with no idea of what was going to come out. "He was a loser, you know," I said. "Every high school has to have at least two, it's like a national law. Everyone's dumping ground. Only sometimes . . . sometimes they find something to hold onto and they survive. Arnie had me. And then he had Christine."

I looked at him, and if I had seen the slightest wrong flicker in those gray eyes that were so unsettlingly like Arnie's . . . well, if I had seen that, I think I would have clammed up right there and told him to put it on his books in whatever way seemed the most plausible and to tell Rudy Junkins's kids whatever the hell he pleased.

But he only nodded, watching me closely.

"I just wanted you to understand that," I said, and then a lump rose in my throat and I couldn't say what I maybe should have said next: *Leigh Cabot came later.*

I drank some more water and swallowed hard. I talked for the next two hours.

At last I finished. There was no big climax; I simply dried up, my throat sore from so much talking. I didn't ask if he believed me; I didn't ask him if he was going to have me locked up in a loonybin or give me a liars' medal. I knew that he believed a great deal of it, because what I knew dovetailed too well with what he knew. What he thought about the rest of it—Christine and LeBay and the past reaching out its hands toward the present—that I didn't know. And don't to this day. Not really.

A little silence fell between us. At last he slapped his hands down on his thighs with a brisk sound and got to his feet. "Well!" he said. "Your folks will be waiting to visit you, no doubt."

"Probably, yeah."

He took out his wallet and produced a small white business card with his name and number on it. "I can usually be reached here, or someone will throw me a relay. When you speak to Leigh Cabot again, would you tell her what you've told me and ask her to get in touch?"

"Yes, if you want. I'll do that."

"Will she corroborate your story?"

"Yes."

He looked at me fixedly. "I'll tell you this much, Dennis," he said. "If you're lying, you don't know you are."

He left. I only saw him once more, and that was at the triple funeral for Arnie and his parents. The papers reported a tragic and bizarre fairy tale—father killed in driveway car accident while mother and son are killed on Pennsylvania Turnpike. Paul Harvey used it on his program.

No mention was made of Christine being at Darnell's Garage.

My family came to visit that night, and by then I was feeling much easier in my mind—part of it was baring my bosom to Mercer, I think (he was what one of my psych profs in college called "an interested outsider," the sort it's often easiest to talk to), but a great lot of the way I felt was due to a flying late-afternoon visit by Dr. Arroway. He was out of temper and irascible with me, suggesting that next time I just take a chainsaw to the goddam leg and save us all a lot of time and trouble . . . but he also informed me (grudgingly, I think) that no lasting damage had been done. He thought. He warned me that I had not improved my chances of ever running in the Boston Marathon and left.

So the family visit was a gay one—due mostly to Ellie, who prattled on and on about that upcoming cataclysm, her First Date. A pimply, bullet-headed nerd named Brandon Hurling had invited her to go roller skating with him. My dad was going to drive them. Pretty cool.

My mother and father joined in, but my mother kept throwing anxious don't-forget glances at Dad, and he lingered after Mom had taken Elaine out.

"What happened?" he asked me. "Leigh told her father some crazy story about cars driving themselves and little girls who were dead and I don't know whatall. He's damn near wild."

I nodded. I was tired, but I didn't want Leigh catching hell from her folks—or have them thinking she was either lying or nuts. If she was going to cover me with Mercer, I would have to cover her with her mother and father.

"All right," I said. "It's a bit of a story. You want to send Mom and Ellie around for a malt, or something? Or maybe you better tell them to go to a movie."

"That long?"

"Yeah. That long."

He looked at me, his gaze troubled. "Okay," he said.

Shortly after, I told my story a second time. Now I've told it a third; and third time, so they say, pays for all.

Rest in peace, Arnie.

I love you, man.

Epilogue

I guess if this was a made-up story I would end it by telling you how the broken-legged knight of Darnell's Garage wooed and won the lady fair . . . she of the pink nylon scarf and the arrogant Nordic cheekbones. But that never happened. Leigh Cabot is Leigh Ackerman now; she's in Taos, New Mexico, married to an IBM customer service rep. She sells Amway in her spare time. She has two little girls, identical twins, so I guess she probably doesn't have all that much spare time. I keep up on her doings after a fashion; my affection for the lady never really faded. We trade cards at Christmas, and I also send her a card on her birthday because she never forgets mine. That sort of thing. There are times when it seems a lot longer than four years.

What happened to us? I don't really know. We went together for two years, slept together (very satisfactorily), went to school together (Drew), and were friends with each other. Her father shut up about our crazy story after my father talked with him, although he always regarded me after that as something of a dubious person. I think that both he and Mrs. Cabot were relieved when Leigh and I went our separate ways.

I could feel it when we started to drift apart, and it hurt me—it hurt a lot. I craved her in a way you continue to crave some substance on which you have no more physical dependency . . . candy, tobacco, Coca-Cola. I carried a torch for her, but I'm afraid I carried it self-consciously and dropped it with an almost unseemly haste.

And maybe I do know what happened. What happened that night in Darnell's Garage was a secret between us, and of course lovers need their secrets . . . but this wasn't a good one to have. It was something cold and unnatural, something that smacked of madness and worse than madness; it smacked of the grave. There were nights after love when we would lie together in bed, naked, belly to belly, and that thing would be between us: Roland D. LeBay's face. I would be kissing her mouth or her breasts or her belly, warm with rising passion, and I would suddenly hear his voice: *That's about the finest smell in the world . . . except for pussy.* And I would freeze, my passion all steam and ashes.

There were times, God knows, when I could see it in her face as well. The lovers don't always live happily ever after, even when they've done what seemed right as well as they could do it. That's something else it took four years to learn.

So we drifted apart. A secret needs two faces to bounce between; a secret needs to see itself in another pair of eyes. And although I did love her, all the kisses, all the endearments, all the walks arm-in-arm through blowing October leaves . . . none of those things could quite measure up to that magnificently simple act of tying her scarf around my arm.

Leigh left college to be married, and then it was goodbye Drew and hello Taos. I went to her wedding with hardly a qualm. Nice fellow. Drove a Honda Civic. No problems there.

I never had to worry about making the football squad. Drew doesn't even *have* a football squad. Instead, I took an extra class each semester and went to summer school for two years, in the time when I would have been sweating under the August sun, hitting the tackling dummies, if things had happened differently. As a result, I graduated early—three semesters early, in fact.

If you met me on the street, you wouldn't notice a limp, but if you walked with me four or five miles (I do at least three miles every day as a matter of course; that physical therapy stuff sticks), you'd notice me starting to pull to the right a little bit.

My left leg aches on rainy days. And on snowy nights.

And sometimes, when I have my nightmares—they are not so frequent now—I wake up, sweating and clutching at that leg, where there is still a hard bulge of flesh above the knee. But all my worries about wheelchairs, braces, and built-up heels proved thankfully hollow. And I never liked football that well anyway.

Michael, Regina, and Arnie Cunningham were buried in a family plot in the Libertyville Heights cemetery—no one went out to the gravesite but members of the family, Regina's people from Ligonier, some of Michael's people from New Hampshire and New York, a few others.

The funeral was five days after that final hellish scene in

the garage. The coffins were closed. The very fact of those three wooden boxes, lined up on a triple bier like soldiers, struck my heart like a shovelful of cold earth. The memory of the ant farms couldn't stand against the mute testimony of those boxes. I cried a little.

Afterward, I rolled myself down the aisle toward them and put my hand tentatively on the one in the center, not knowing if it was Arnie's or not, not caring. I stayed that way for quite a while, head down, and then a voice said behind me, "Want a push back out to the vestry, Dennis?"

I craned my neck around. It was Mercer, looking neat and lawyerly in a dark wool suit.

"Sure," I said. "Just gimme a couple of seconds, okay?"

"Fine."

I hesitated and then said, "The papers say Michael was killed at home. That the car rolled over him after he slipped on the ice, or something."

"Yes," he said.

"Your doing?"

Mercer hesitated. "It makes things simpler." His gaze shifted to where Leigh was standing with my folks. She was talking with my mother but looking anxiously toward me. "Pretty girl," he said. He had said it before, in the hospital.

"I'm going to marry her someday," I said.

"I wouldn't be surprised if you did," Mercer replied. "Did anyone ever tell you that you've got the balls of a tiger?"

"I think Coach Puffer did," I said. "Once."

He laughed. "You ready for that push, Dennis? You've been down here long enough. Let it go."

"Easier said than done."

He nodded. "Yeah. I guess so."

"Will you tell me one thing?" I asked. "I have to know."

"I will if I can."

"What did—" I had to stop and clear my throat. "What did you do with the . . . the pieces?"

"Why, I saw to that myself," Mercer said. His voice was light, almost joking, but his face was very, very serious. "I had two fellows from the local police run all those pieces through the crusher out back of Darnell's Garage. Made a little cube about so big." He held his hands about two feet apart. "One of those guys got a hell of a bad cut. Took stitches."

Mercer suddenly smiled—it was the bitterest, coldest smile I've ever seen.

"He said it bit him."

Then he pushed me up the aisle to where my family and my girl stood waiting for me.

So that's my story. Except for the dreams.

I'm four years older, and Arnie's face has grown hazy to me, a browning photograph from an old yearbook. I never would have believed that could happen, but it has. I made it through, made the transition from adolescence to manhood—whatever that is—somehow; I've got a college degree on which the ink is almost dry, and I've been teaching junior high history. I started last year, and two of my original students—Buddy Repperton types, both of them—were older than I was. I'm single, but there are a few interesting ladies in my life, and I hardly think of Arnie at all.

Except in the dreams.

The dreams aren't the only reason I've set all this down—there's another, which I'll tell you in a moment—but I would be lying if I said the dreams weren't a big part of the reason. Maybe it's an effort to lance the wound and clean it out. Or maybe it's just that I'm not rich enough to afford a shrink.

In one of the dreams I am back where the funeral service was held. The three coffins are on their triple bier, but the church is empty except for me. In the dream I am on crutches again, standing at the foot of the central aisle, back by the door. I don't want to go down there, but my crutches are pulling me along, moving by themselves. I touch the middle coffin. It springs open at my touch, and lying inside in the satin interior is not Arnie but Roland D. LeBay, a putrescent corpse in an Army uniform. As the bloated smell of gassy decay rushes out at me, the corpse opens its eyes; its rotting hands, black and slimy with some fungoid growth, grope upward and find my shirt before I can back away, and it pulls itself up until its glaring, reeking face is only inches from mine. And it begins to croak over and over again, *Can't beat that smell, can you? Nothing smells this good . . . except for pussy . . . except for pussy . . . except for pussy. . . .* I try to scream but I can't scream, because LeBay's hands have settled in a noxious, tightening ring around my throat.

In the other dream—and this one is somehow worse—I've finished with a class or proctoring a study hall at Norton Junior High, where I teach. I pack my books back into my briefcase, stuff in my papers, and leave the room for my next class. And there in the hall, packed in between the industrial-gray lockers lining it, is Christine—brand new and sparkling, sitting on four new whitewall tires, a chrome Winged Victory hood ornament tilting toward me. She is empty, but her engine guns and falls off . . . guns and falls off . . . guns and falls off. In some of the dreams the voice from the radio is the voice of Richie Valens, killed long ago in a plane crash with Buddy Holly and J. P. Richardson, The Big Bopper. Richie is screaming "La Bamba" to a Latin beat, and as Christine suddenly lunges toward me, laying rubber on the hall floor and tearing open locker doors on either side with her doorhandles, I see that there is a vanity plate on the front—a grinning white skull on a dead black field. Imprinted over the skull are the words ROCK AND ROLL WILL NEVER DIE.

Then I wake up—sometimes screaming, always clutching my leg.

But the dreams are fewer now. Something I read in one of my psych classes—I took a lot of them, maybe hoping to understand things that can't be understood—is that people dream less as they grow older. I think I am going to be all right now. Last Christmas season, when I sent Leigh her annual card, I added a line to my usual note on the back. Below my signature, on impulse, I scribbled: *How are you dealing with it?* Then I sealed the card up and mailed it before I could change my mind. I got a postcard back a month later. It showed the new Taos Center for the Performing Arts on the front. On the back was my address and a single flat line: *Dealing with what? L.*

One way or another I guess we find out things we have to know.

Around the same time—it seems as though it's around Christmas that my thoughts turn to it the most often—I dropped Rick Mercer a note, because the question had been on my mind more and more, gnawing at me. I wrote and asked him what had become of the block of scrap metal that had once been Christine.

I got no answer.

But time is teaching me how to deal with that too. I think about it less. I really do.

So here I am, at the tag end of everything, old memories and old nightmares all bundled into a neat sheaf of pages.

Soon I will put them in a folder and put the folder in my file cabinet and lock that drawer and that will be the end.

But I told you there was something else, didn't I? Some other reason for writing it all down.

His single-minded purpose. His unending fury.

I read it in the paper a few weeks ago—just an item that got put on the AP wire because it was bizarre, I suppose. *Be honest, Guilder,* I can hear Arnie saying, so I will. It was that item that got me going, more than all the dreams and old memories.

The news item was about a guy named Sander Galton, whose nickname, one would logically assume, must have been Sandy.

This Sander Galton was killed out in California, where he was working at a drive-in movie theater in L.A. He was apparently alone, closing up shop for the night after the movie had ended. He was in the snack-bar. A car ripped right through one of the walls, plowed through the counter, smashed the popcorn machine, and got him as he was trying to unlock the door to the projection booth. The cops knew that was what he was doing when the car ran him down because they found the key in his hand. I read that item, headed BIZARRE MURDER BY CAR IN LOS ANGELES—and I thought of what Mercer had told me, that last thing: *He said it bit him.*

Of course it's impossible, but it was all impossible to start with.

I keep thinking of George LeBay in Ohio.

His sister in Colorado.

Leigh in New Mexico.

What if it's started again?

What if it's working its way east, finishing the job?

Saving me for last?

His single-minded purpose.
His unending fury.

About the Author

Stephen King grew up in Maine and has lived most of his adult life there, both in Bangor and in the Portland area. He and his wife, Tabitha, have three children, Naomi, Joe, and Owen Philip.

He is the author of the best-selling books CARRIE, 'SALEM'S LOT, THE SHINING, NIGHT SHIFT, THE STAND, THE DEAD ZONE, FIRESTARTER, CUJO, and DIFFERENT SEASONS, also published by The New American Library.

STEPHEN KING
CONJURES UP FIVE JOLTING TALES OF HORROR:
FATHER'S DAY
LONESOME DEATH OF JORDY VERRILL
CRATE
SOMETHING TO TIDE YOU OVER
THEY'RE CREEPING UP ON YOU

ART BY BERNI WRIGHTSON · COVER ART BY JACK KAMEN

A LAUREL ® PRODUCTION
"CREEPSHOW"™ · A GEORGE A. ROMERO FILM
Starring HAL HOLBROOK · ADRIENNE BARBEAU · FRITZ WEAVER
LESLIE NIELSEN · CARRIE NYE · E. G. MARSHALL and VIVECA LINDFORS as Aunt Bedelia
Production Design: CLETUS ANDERSON · Makeup Special Effects: TOM SAVINI
Director of Photography: MICHAEL GORNICK · Associate Producer: DAVID E. VOGEL
Executive Producer: SALAH M. HASSANEIN · Original Screenplay STEPHEN KING
Produced by: RICHARD P. RUBINSTEIN · Directed by: GEORGE A. ROMERO

DISTRIBUTED BY WARNER BROS. Ⓦ
A WARNER COMMUNICATIONS COMPANY

Buy it at your local bookstore or use this convenient coupon for ordering.
THE NEW AMERICAN LIBRARY, INC.
P.O. Box 999, Bergenfield, New Jersey 07621

Please send me_____paperback copies of CREEPSHOW (0452-253802
—$6.95)* I am enclosing $_____(please add $1.50 to this order
to cover postage and handling. Send check or money order—no cash
or C.O.D.s. Prices and numbers are subject to change without notice.

Name_____

Address_____

City_____State_____Zip Code_____

*In Canada, $7.95
Allow 4-6 weeks for delivery.
This offer is subject to withdrawal without notice.

Sensational Fiction from SIGNET

(0451)

☐ **THE OMEN by David Seltzer.** (111478—$2.50)

☐ **DAMIEN: OMEN II by Joseph Howard.** (119908—$2.95)*

☐ **THE FINAL CONFLICT: OMEN III by Gordon McGill.**
(110420—$2.95)

☐ **ARMAGEDDON 2000: OMEN IV by Gordon McGill.**
(118189—$3.50)*

☐ **SMALL WORLD by Tabitha King.** (114086—$3.50)

☐ **JUDGMENT DAY by Nick Sharman.** (114507—$2.95)

☐ **HARRIET SAID by Beryl Bainbridge.** (119576—$2.95)

☐ **LAST RITES by Paul Spike.** (116127—$3.50)

☐ **THIS HOUSE IS BURNING by Mona Williams.**
(116224—$2.50)*

☐ **NEW BLOOD by Richard Salem.** (116151—$2.50)†

☐ **BLOOD CHILD by Joyce Christmas.** (114124—$2.75)*

☐ **THE SWARM by Arthur Herzog.** (080793—$2.25)†

☐ **THE POLTERGEIST by William Roll.** (121104—$2.95)

*Prices slightly higher in Canada
†Not available in Canada

**Buy them at your local
bookstore or use coupon
on next page for ordering.**

Great Fiction From SIGNET

(0451)

☐ THE SHRINE by James Herbert.   (127242—$3.95)*
☐ THE JONAH by James Herbert.   (110668—$2.95)*
☐ THE DARK by James Herbert.   (094034—$2.95)
☐ THE FLUKE by James Herbert.   (083946—$1.95)
☐ THE FOG by James Herbert.   (129377—$3.50)*
☐ THE LAIR by James Herbert.   (086503—$2.25)*
☐ THE RATS by James Herbert.   (113942—$2.50)
☐ THE SPEAR by James Herbert.   (090608—$2.50)*
☐ THE SURVIVOR by James Herbert.   (113950—$2.50)
☐ CHILD OF HELL by William Dobson.   (117689—$2.95)*
☐ THE RIPPER by William Dobson.   (112059—$2.25)

*Prices slightly higher in Canada

Buy them at your local bookstore or use this convenient coupon for ordering.

THE NEW AMERICAN LIBRARY, INC.,
P.O. Box 999, Bergenfield, New Jersey 07621

Please send me the books I have checked above. I am enclosing $_____
(please add $1.00 to this order to cover postage and handling). Send check
or money order—no cash or C.O.D.'s. Prices and numbers are subject to change
without notice.

Name_____

Address_____

City _____ State _____ Zip Code _____
Allow 4-6 weeks for delivery.
This offer is subject to withdrawal without notice.

Exciting Fiction from SIGNET

(0451)

☐ **HOUR OF THE CLOWN by Amos Aricha.** (097173—$2.95)*
☐ **PHOENIX by Amos Aricha.** (098455—$2.95)
☐ **EYE OF THE MIND by Lynn Biederstadt.** (117360—$3.50)*
☐ **GAMES OF CHANCE by Peter Delacorte.** (115104—$2.95)*
☐ **DOUBLE CROSS by Michael Barak.** (115473—$2.95)*
☐ **POSITION OF ULTIMATE TRUST by William Beechcroft.**
(115511—$2.50)*
☐ **SAVANNAH BLUE by William Harrison.** (114558—$2.75)*
☐ **THE SEA GUERILLAS by Dean W. Ballenger.**
(114132—$1.95)*
☐ **THE DELTA DECISION by Wilbur Smith.** (113357—$3.50)
☐ **HUNGRY AS THE SEA by Wilbur Smith.** (122186—$3.95)
☐ **THE LONG WALK by Richard Bachman.** (087542—$1.95)
☐ **THE RUNNING MAN by Richard Bachman.** (115082—$2.50)*
☐ **NIGHT AND FOG (Resistance #1) by Gregory St. Germain.**
(118278—$2.50)*
☐ **MAGYAR MASSACRE (Resistance #2) by Gregory St. Germain.**
(118286—$2.50)*
☐ **SHADOWS OF DEATH (Resistance #3) by Gregory St. Germain.**
(119991—$2.50)*
☐ **ROAD OF IRON (Resistance #4) by Gregory St. Germain.**
(122313—$2.50)*

*Prices slightly higher in Canada

Buy them at your local
bookstore or use coupon
on next page for ordering.

Super SIGNET Reading

(0451)

- ☐ **THE DHARMA BUMS by Jack Kerouac.** (123131—$2.50)
- ☐ **ON THE ROAD by Jack Kerouac.** (122909—$2.95)
- ☐ **THE LONELINESS OF THE LONG DISTANCE RUNNER by Alan Sillitoe.** (114361—$1.95)
- ☐ **SATURDAY NIGHT AND SUNDAY MORNING by Alan Sillitoe.** (121627—$2.50)
- ☐ **NOT AS A STRANGER by Morton Thompson.** (110501—$3.50)
- ☐ **INSIDE MOVES by Todd Walton.** (096614—$2.50)*
- ☐ **MY SWEET CHARLIE by David Westheimer.** (098196—$1.95)*
- ☐ **VON RYAN'S EXPRESS by David Westheimer.** (078152—$1.75)
- ☐ **MINOTAUR by Benjamin Tammuz.** (115821—$1.50)*
- ☐ **SOME KIND OF HERO by James Kirkwood.** (115767—$2.95)*
- ☐ **ANDERSONVILLE by MacKinlay Kantor.** (113241—$3.95)
- ☐ **THE GRADUATE by Charles Webb.** (086333—$1.50)

*Prices slightly higher in Canada

Buy them at your local bookstore or use this convenient coupon for ordering.

THE NEW AMERICAN LIBRARY, INC.,
P.O. Box 999, Bergenfield, New Jersey 07621

Please send me the books I have checked above. I am enclosing $_____
(please add $1.00 to this order to cover postage and handling). Send check
or money order—no cash or C.O.D.'s. Prices and numbers are subject to change
without notice.

Name_____

Address_____

City _____ State _____ Zip Code _____
Allow 4-6 weeks for delivery.
This offer is subject to withdrawal without notice.